The Collapse

by
Jeff Stanfield

Bloomington, IN

authorHOUSE™

Milton Keynes, UK

AuthorHouse™
1663 Liberty Drive, Suite 200
Bloomington, IN 47403
www.authorhouse.com
Phone: 1-800-839-8640

AuthorHouse™ UK Ltd.
500 Avebury Boulevard
Central Milton Keynes, MK9 2BE
www.authorhouse.co.uk
Phone: 08001974150

First published by AuthorHouse 01/17/06

ISBN: 1-4259-1455-1 (sc)

Library of Congress Control Number: 2006900282

Printed in the United States of America
Bloomington, Indiana

This book is printed on acid-free paper.

Chapter 1

Steve Roberts and his fiancée Diane Beck sat on the couch in Diane's apartment watching the National News Service. Things were not looking good at all. The North Koreans and the Chinese were in an uproar. The President had deployed two Navy battle groups off the coast of Korea and was demanding that the Koreans cancel their missile and nuclear program. The Koreans had finally managed to successfully explode two nuclear bombs. The Chinese had sold them their newest inter-continental ballistic missile. This missile could reach the heartland of America. Also to top matters off, Panama had allowed the Chinese to build two naval bases on each coast of Panama.

The Chinese had quickly fortified the bases with ground troops, anti-aircraft batteries, radar stations, and small, but deadly naval fleets on both sides of the canal. They were threatening to start charging hefty fees for the use of commercial shipping to pass through the canal. This force could effectively close off the canal, which would cause economic repercussions in the United States. It would also play havoc with America's ability to deploy troops around the globe and hamper its war on terrorism.

The commentator then began discussing the internal security of the United States. Ten Chinese nationals had been caught by the Border Patrol coming across the Mexican border into Arizona. They had large packs containing unassembled AK-47's, ammunition, semtex plastic explosives, satellite phones, night vision equipment, GPS's, radios with scanners with radio frequencies of all federal law enforcement agencies programmed in, and laptop computers. The laptops had thousands of files containing information on all the major infrastructure of the United States, rail lines, nuclear plants, oil refineries, harbors, and agriculture centers also. The Chinese government denied any knowledge of the men. The captured men also refused to talk to FBI investigators. All the electronic equipment was French military issue. France denied any knowledge of the sale of equipment to China, or any other parties. China and Korea threatened dire consequences for the United States if any more pressure was placed on them. They also demanded all sanctions levied by the U.S. against the two countries be lifted.

The commentator then began to discuss all the latest terrorist attacks in America. Trains had been derailed; police officers ambushed and killed, several propane and gas companies had been sabotaged, and blown up, killing hundreds, and damaging blocks of city streets in a dozen cities. Damage in financial terms was estimated to be in the tens of millions.

In Dallas a gas truck and propane truck had been laden with plastic explosives and detonated on Interstate 20. Police investigators determined two fake accidents were staged in both east and west bound lanes, backing up afternoon traffic for miles in both directions before the two rigs which were in the middle of the traffic jam, were detonated. The explosions killed over seven hundred twenty three people and injured another fifteen hundred.

The FBI and the Office of Homeland Security were still unsure if all the attacks were from Muslims, Koreans, or Chinese, but told the citizens not to worry, that those responsible would be caught and put in prison." The commentator then stated it was time for a commercial break.

As the commercials began to play Diane turned down the volume and looked at Steve. "What do you think will happen?"

Steve looked into his fiancées green eyes. He could see the fear lurking behind them. He gave her a reassuring squeeze of the hand. "It will be all right Diane, we are ready for anything. My house is stocked and ready to go. If things get bad we'll pack you up and get you there ASAP."

Steve hoped that the uncertainty and fear he felt would not register with Diane. He had only recently gotten into this preparedness thing as the attacks in America began to increase. He regretted not having taken the threat to the nation, Diane's and his own personal safety in the event of a major terrorist event seriously. He had recently purchased a Glock 17 for himself and a Glock 19 for Diane. He also had purchased one thousand rounds for each pistol. He already had an AK-47, with two seventy five round drums, and ten thirty round magazines, and five thousand rounds for the weapon. He had chosen the AK not only for its reliability, but the ammo could be bought for around seventy five dollars per thousand rounds.

He also had a Ruger MKII .22 caliber target pistol with twenty thousand rounds of ammo. The MKII was also extremely reliable and very accurate. .22 caliber ammunition could be purchased at Wal-Mart for nine dollars per five hundred and fifty round boxes. Steve felt this pistol could be used to forage for small game in the area around his cabin should he need to supplement his food stock in the event of food rationing or shortages if an attack occurred. Also if he had nothing else at hand the pistol was accurate enough that he could make head shots at twenty yards consistently at the range. Of course he did not know how well he would do if the shit hit the fan for real, and bullets were flying around.

A Remington 870 was his choice for a shotgun. The local police carried the weapon and all spoke favorably about it. He had chosen the riot shotgun version with an eighteen inch barrel, butt stock with pistol grip, and a six round side saddle. The weapon had a three point sling so he could carry it at the ready and quickly let it drop in front of him if he had to transition to his pistol. He felt this weapon would be his best choice for home defense. Ammunition wise for the shotgun he had purchase five hundred rounds of #4, 00 buck, and 100 rounds with slugs, and over eight hundred rounds of number four shot. This round could be used to hunt small game if need be, and still packed enough punch at twenty yards to put a man down.

Steve had purchased a Mosin Nagant for a bolt gun. Though the rifle was not the most accurate rifle on the market, it had only cost him $49.00 at the local gun store. The rifle was like all Russian made battle rifles, made to last forever. The Mosin Nagant had been used by the Russians during World War II. They had produced hundreds of thousands of the rifles and they could be had cheaply at just about any gun store around. Since he was on a limited budget he had picked it.

Like his other weapon choices, the ammunition could be bought at an inexpensive price. He had over two thousand rounds for the rifle which had the relative same knock down power as a 30-06.

He had gone to a local discount grocery store in Florence last week and spent four hundred and fifty dollars. He had purchased cases of canned goods, rice, wheat, sugar, corn meal, flour, ramin noodles, dried beans, powdered milk, canned meats, and a ton of those just add water, pancake mixes, and blue berry muffin mixes, syrup, peanut butter, honey, grits, oatmeal, and dried noodles. Steve had figured it out and it was enough to last him and Diane about five and a half months if things got really bad in Florence like it had in some of the major cities. He doubted there would be riots in Florence though. Heck he doubted he would need half the things he had purchased. Surely the terrorist had better targets to blow up then something in Florence, Alabama. He had also purchased bulk supplies of hydrogen peroxide, rubbing alcohol, aspirins, flu medicine, bandages, splints, ace bandages, gauze pads, burn salve, bandages, generic Motrin, and numerous other medicines and medical supplies at Wal-Mart

He hoped it would be enough, he just didn't know enough about this stuff. Not only that, his budget was limited since he had just been laid off from the textile company where he had worked at as a forklift driver. Good thing Diane was an RN and had a lot more available cash on hand. She had been the one who had purchased the generator for his place in the country. She had also bought several white fifty-gallon barrels for water. And to his surprise, four fifty-gallon barrels of gasoline, and one filled with kerosene. Steve had placed fuel stabilizer in them to help with the life span of the fuel while it was stored.

Steve got up so Diane would not see the uncertainty that he was sure was written all over his face. "I am going to get some coke do you want some?"

"Sure get me a glass too." Diane replied.

Steve went into the little kitchen and got out two glasses and filled them with ice. He reached over into the fridge and pulled out a bottle of Coke. As he was filling the second glass Diane called to him. "Steve! Get in here quick. You have got to see this. I can't believe what is happening."

Steve grabbed the two glasses and headed back into the living room. Diane sat on the edge of the couch leaned forward with a look of shocked horror on her face. "What's happening?" He said as he took his seat beside her.

"Hush and watch. I can't believe this." Diane said in a muted voice, her eyes glued to the TV.

Steve focused on the TV. The TV had pictures from a live feed in Boston. EMT personnel, firemen, and police in biohazard suits were dragging bodies onto a side walk, laying them out in a long row. The shot was from a bridge overpass. The camera then panned back to the newsman, as he began his live report.

"Approximately a quarter of a mile away from my current position emergency personnel have responded to what we have been told by our sources inside the fire department as a nerve agent attack. Information on just how the attack was carried out and by whom is sketchy at this time.

From my count here on the overpass, using binoculars, I was able to identify approximately ninety bodies. There are more I am sure that we cannot see. This is a tragic day for the city of Boston. Bostonians lay in misshapen, twisted heaps at the hands of faceless cowards. I will continue to keep you informed from my position here. We should be safe here since the wind is blowing toward the scene."

Just as he said this a voice from off screen could be heard. "Blake I think the wind has changed. Man, we should get out of here!"

Suddenly the image on the screen shook as the camera fell or was dropped. The sound of people vomiting and moaning could be heard. Then Blake Spire's body came into view as he fell face first to the pavement in front of the camera. His normally tan face was pale, he was puking and convulsing. His face was racked with pain, eyes bulging as he began choking on his own vomit. The scene quickly disappeared and the National News Service studios replaced the gruesome images. The anchor woman's usual perky face had a look of trepidation, and fear on it.

She arranged herself as best she could and began her expert commentating. "Ladies and gentlemen, St. Louis, Kansas City, Boston, Phoenix, Ft. Worth, Seattle, Tampa, Charlotte, Nashville, Birmingham, Las Vegas, Jersey City, Dover, Little Rock, and New Orleans according to Federal agencies have sustained some type of biological or chemical attack.

Also two dams in Kentucky and Tennessee have been attacked. The power stations at those dams have been destroyed with explosives. It is unknown at this time whether the dams themselves or just the power stations were attacked. Power for hundreds of thousands of people is out. We are taking you now to the White House for a press conference with the President."

The President's face came into view. Fury and gloom were two emotions that could clearly be seen on his face. "My fellow Americans today is day which will be considered one of the saddest days in our great history. Once again, innocent men, women and children have been murdered by cowardly agents of death and terror. Fifteen cities were simultaneously attacked with either biological or chemical agents. I can not discuss the method of deployment of these agents at this time due to national security concerns, but they were sophisticated to say the least. From the information I have received from both intelligence and military sources, only a few nation states had the equipment and technology to carry this act of spinelessness out. At this time I will not say who we believe is behind this until certain elements of this investigation are concluded, and assets are in place to deal out the deserved retribution for this attack. The death toll for these fifteen cities is not yet available but I will bring you that information as soon as I am informed of it.

Also two dams operated by TVA have been attacked. Their power stations were destroyed by the use of explosives. At this time agents of the FBI, ATF and other intelligence agencies are combing through the debris, and rubble for evidence. We will soon know what types of explosives were used. The death toll at these two dams is estimated at approximately one hundred and thirty two people.

The dams though are still structurally sound. We do not know who is responsible at this time. Let me assure you that those that have participated in this act of terror will be hunted down and brought to justice. We have crushed two oppressive regimes since 9/11 and if more must be toppled we will do it.

To the family members of those murdered and injured you have the sympathy of your fellow countrymen, and government. We will pray for you and your loved ones in this hour of your greatest need." Without taking any questions from the assembled White House Press Corps, the President turned and walked from the room.

Steve reached for the channel changer. His hand shook as he picked it up and turned off the TV. He looked over at Diane who was sobbing. "Diane listen to me." Steve said as he placed his hand on her shoulder.

"Steve I am so scared, what are we going to do?" Diane said between sobs before Steve could say anything.

"We are going to be okay Diane. We have supplies to make it through if things get bad here. I don't think Florence will be hit but Birmingham isn't that far away. If some of those minor attacks that happened this past fall caused entire cities and states to go into panic there is no telling what these attacks may bring. We could have food rationing like they did after the California attacks last year. Tell you what, lets head to the store and pick up some additional supplies then we will head to my place, sit back and wait for this to blow over."

"Are you sure we should head over there? Won't everyone be jammed in there buying stuff?"

"Well I think if we can get there before the news spreads we should be all right."

Diane composed herself. "Ok, let's go." She said as she picked up her purse.

"Have you got your pistol Diane?" Steve asked. Since he had purchased the pistol for her he made a point of reminding her to carry it at almost every opportunity. One could never be too careful these days.

Diane reached into her purse and pulled out the Glock 19, showed Steve she had her pistol and put it back.

"That's my girl." Steve said with an approving smile.

"Have you got your pistol Steve?"

"Sure do!" He said as he patted his right hip. "It's not there." He exclaimed looking around with a look of perplexity on his face. Then he saw it sitting on the end table beside him. He sheepishly looked at Diane giving her an uncomfortable smile and picked up the pistol holstering it.

"That's my man!" Diane said with a loving smirk on her face. "Let's go. "

The two went outside and got in Steve's 1997 Jeep Wrangler, and headed to Wal-Mart.

Chapter 2

Steve pulled out of the apartment complex onto Chisholm Rd. and drove south. Slowing as he came to the turn lane, the arrow had just turned green for him to make the turn onto Cox Creek Pkwy. As he was halfway through the west bound lane he heard the squall of tires coming from the right. He looked over just in time to see a green Buick locking up its brakes swerving to miss him. Diane screamed as Steve jammed the break pedal to the floor. The Buick's driver swerved just in time and gunned the engine flying off into the distance. "You freaking idiot!" Steve screamed rising up his fist and giving the finger to the disappearing car.

"Dang that was close." Diane said. Diane tried some humor to ease the tension. "I think I wet myself, put new panties for me on the list."

Steve chuckled," We'll have to add toilet paper too, because I think I just shit my pants."

Steve eased off the break and clutch and continued his turn. The closer he got to the retail district, the more erratic and crazy the traffic became. Steve maintained a steady 50 mph in the right hand lane giving other drivers a wide berth.

"Do you want me to turn on the radio to the news station?" Diane asked."

"No I think we have heard enough news for now, let's just get some of the extra stuff we need and get to my place."

As Steve pulled into the Wal-Mart parking lot the parking was already close to capacity. Steve found a parking space at the outer limits of the parking lot and the two exited the Jeep and walked into the entrance. Steve nodded to the police officer standing at the door as they entered.

"Is everything ok inside officer?" Diane asked a bit worried since there was never an officer stationed at the entrance to the store.

"So far it is mam. Everyone is just spooked with the attacks and all. Yall have a good one if you can."

"You too, officer." she replied.

Both of them grabbed one of the few remaining shopping carts as the made their way into the store. "Steve, I am going to the pharmacy and grab all the medicine and other things I can. You make a run through the food aisles, and then to the camping section and we will meet back here in 30 minutes ok."

"Sure thing sweetheart, and remember, you packed up plenty of makeup and nail polishes in your kit so just get the important stuff." He said jokingly.

Diane playfully punched him on the arm. "Well you stay out of the tool section and no toys just important stuff." Diane laughed, turned and walked to the pharmacy.

Steve made his rounds through the food aisles. Steve could feel the tension and panic in the air. In Steve's opinion it wouldn't take much to set these people off. People were just grabbing things and shoving them in their carts. There was no more bread, milk, frozen foods, or meats. Steve knew that it would be a big mistake to purchase perishable items. If there was an attack and the power was out, all of the perishable foods would ruin. It was best to stick with canned goods, and dried goods such as pasta, beans, and macaroni and cheese. His first stop was to pick up several cases of assorted canned fruits. Then he got a couple of cases of soups, rice, beans, powder milk, sugar, salt, pepper, and spices. He also got the last two big bags of potatoes. His cart was almost full so he threaded his way through the mass of people for the sporting good section. As he passed the tool aisle he smiled and picked up an axe and hammer. Steve grinned to himself and thought "That will show that little lady who wears the pants in this future family."

Once in the sporting good section Steve walked up to the ammo counter. "May I help you?" A plump gray haired woman asked from behind the counter. Her hair was frazzled, her face fatigued, and the day was just beginning.

"I would like ten boxes of 9mm, ten boxes of 7.62x39 and five bricks of Federal .22 caliber." The lady unlocked the case and pulled out nine boxes of 9mm, five boxes of 7.62x39 and three fifty round boxes of Federal, Remington, and Winchester .22 cal.

"This is all I have left. Can I get you anything else?"

"Any boxes of 12 gauge slug, 00, and #4, and 7.62x54R?"

"We're out of 12 gauge in every shot size." She did produce eleven boxes of 7.62x54R.

Steve took a quick scan around. Almost no ammo was in the display cases, and no guns were left in the display on either side of the counter. "Do you have any of the calibers I mentioned in the back?"

"Sir, everyone in Florence has been in here buying up everything in the past hour. We don't have anything in the back, this is it."

Steve thanked her and walked to the camping section. There were no Coleman stoves, or lanterns. All of but two cans of Coleman fuel gone. Steve picked these up, since he had a stove and lantern that could use them. He also had 10 one gallon cans of Coleman fuel back at the house. He managed to find two small kerosene lamps on the back of the shelf. He picked up four emergency blankets, the last three packets of emergency candles, the last camp saw, the last four bottles of water purification tablets, three packs of four boxes of water proof matches, and the last Maglight.

Steve stood there for a moment thinking about some of the topics he had read on a survival bulletin board on the internet his buddy had turned him onto. He scanned the near bare shelves. Man, why hadn't he listen to his buddy Phil after 9/11 he could have been so far ahead of the curve. Well he hadn't, but at least he had a better start than most people, or should he say as they called them on the bulletin board, Sheeple. Heck what was he thinking he wasn't too far out of the flock himself. Well back to shopping for stuff I can't afford.

Steve next picked up a 12 quart Dutch oven when he remembered the thread about things you could bake in a Dutch oven. Winter was coming on so he grabbed four of the fleece light weight sleeping bags, and two zero degree double sleeping bags. He had plenty of surplus wool army blankets that he had got from a military surplus supply magazine, but if the power went this winter, his generator ran out of gas and his wood stove went tits up they would be a welcome addition.

He then turned the corner onto the automotive section of the store. He picked up a couple of gas siphons, oil filters, tire patches, extra belts and hoses for the Jeep, and an air freshener. "I've got to keep the Jeep smelling good when the shit hits the fan." He thought with a smile.

Steve could barely maneuver the cart and it was near over flowing so he decided to meet back with Diane.

It did not take long for Diane to pick up the items she thought they would need. Of course there was not a whole lot left. She had gotten lucky when she got five large bottles of generic aspirin. She also picked up the remaining bandages, joint supports, feminine products, cold and flu medicine, aloe Vera, burn cream, lice shampoo, calamine lotion, and a big bottle of Aleve.

Diane then decided to head over to the fabric section. As she rounded the corner two large black women were being stopped by a loss prevention officer. Voices began to rise then tempers flared. The fatter of the two with dreadlocks in her hair struck out, and slapped the loss prevention officer with a meaty open handed slap. Caught off guard the loss prevention officer was knocked into a display. The display buckled, and then collapsed under the loss prevention officer's weight sending him to floor. The other woman joined in by administrating well placed kicks to his head and ribs. A near by customer seeing the attack charged into the fray and tackled the woman with dreadlocks. Her accomplice came to the rescue and dove into the heap. The fight was on. Diane quickly vacated the area, as other shoppers either looked on or grabbed items out of the ladies' shopping carts.

Once in the fabric section, Diane picked up a dozen different spools of heavy duty thread, Sewing needles, and safety pins. She got several bundles of denim, and cotton fabric in different colors. "Never know when the next time we will be able to buy clothes" she thought.

Diane then made her way through the throng of people to the spot she and Steve were supposed to meet. She spotted Steve and made her way to him.

"Steve let's get out of here now. I just saw a hell of a fight going on in the pharmacy."

"I'm with you. Folks are starting to get panicky." Just then the lights went out in the store.

Nearby several people let out panic stricken screams. "Make your way to the doors folks!" A voice said from the front of the store. Steve looked towards the front of the store and could make out the police officer with his flashlight on starting to direct people towards the exits. "Leave your carts people, the cash register's are down, make your way calmly to the front."

Then a woman's voice full of fright came from somewhere nearby, "My God they must have blown up Wilson Dam! The terrorist are here!"

People began to panic and started to make a run for the doors. Shopping buggies crashed and people ran into one another in the darkness. People were tripping and falling. Some trampled in the stampede for the front doors.

Steve quickly decided it wouldn't be wise to make a blind dash for the exits. It was quite likely he and Diane could be separated or injured in the almost pitch black store filled with hundreds of panic stricken people.

"Diane back up over here between these cutting tables," Steve said as he shined his small blue LED light to the spot. Diane and Steve backed the carts into the nook between the cutting tables. People rushed blindly by the couple. They couldn't see all that went on around them, but it didn't take much of an imagination to realize people were getting seriously hurt.

"Leave your carts people, you haven't paid for those items." The officer was trying to stop people as they made a dash for the door with their goods. He reached out and grabbed a young man wearing gang clothes pushing a cart." Get off me you cracker Mother Fucker." Then out of the darkness came a second banger who tackled the officer from behind. The officer was hit below the knees and jack knifed backwards. The officer put up a good fight even though he had hit his head hard on the concrete floor. He struck one of the gang bangers twice across the head with his Maglight. The three struggled for several seconds more then two gunshots echoed threw the store.

Steve just barely made out the muzzle flashes from the pistol. Steve could just barely make out the two thugs running and pushing a cart full of stereo equipment through the doors to freedom. Steve cursed himself for not being able to assist the officer.

13

Once the gun went off the pandemonium got worse. "Steve, should we make a break for the door now?" Diane said, her voice trembling a bit.

"Let's just sit tight till folks clear out, ok. We need to let as many people get out of here as possible. I want to see if we can help that officer, and I don't want to get trampled doing it."

"Alright, how long should we wait?"

"I don't know. Let's just play this by ear for now." Steve said as he tried to make out what was going on in the darkness. He didn't want to use his LED light for fear of someone possibly targeting him.

After about fifteen minutes, the crowd had mostly fled the store. During this time screams, crashing cars, squealing tires, and even several gunshots could be heard in the parking lot. The volume of car noises had dropped but screams and shouts could still be heard but even those seemed to just come from a few people. "I think now is the time Diane."

"What about the carts Steve?"

"We take them." Steve said standing up taking Diane's hand.

"Shouldn't we pay for the stuff? It would be stealing if we don't?"

"Yeah we should pay Diane, but the world has gone mad and we need this stuff. Besides that all the cashiers are gone." They made there way to the front of the store. They had to stop several times to avoid running the carts over bloodied, battered bodies. They also had to walk carefully. The soles of their shoes were soaked with the blood of the dead and injured that littered the floors of the store.

Steve and Diane stopped where the police officer lay in the floor. Steve shined his LED light on the officer as Diane knelt down to check him out. Diane felt for a pulse, though she knew there was no need. The officer had been shot in the neck; most of the back side of the neck was gone. Blood pooled around his body. Steve shined the light on the officer's holster, the gun was gone. Steve checked the magazine pouches and found that the officer carried two high capacity Glock 17 magazines. Steve felt guilty but pocketed the two magazines which contained eighteen rounds each. One of the reasons he had chosen the Glock was because so many officers carried the weapon.

"Let's go Diane; there is nothing we can do for this poor guy."

Diane sighed and got up. "He was so polite and nice Steve, I hope his family will be all right with out him."

"They will Diane, police look after their own when something like this happens."

The two walked outside into the dimming sunlight of late afternoon. The parking lot was a mad house. Cars rested in groups of crushed metal, one was even on fire. People still ran back and forth in the parking lot as if they did not know were to go. Some sat in their cars in a daze staring off to no where. Steve and Diane had parked on the North West side of the store, near the back of the side lot. This is where most of the employees parked. They made it to Steve's Jeep with out incident.

They began piling their goods into the jeep. Steve had removed the back seat a few days ago when he had gone to the lumber yard for some wood. It was a good thing too because the back cargo area filled up quickly. They put the remaining items onto the safari rack on the top of the Jeep. Just as the two had finished packing the Jeep up a black teen in red gang bangers clothing, and a white kid, who thought he was black stepped around a crashed car.

"What's up homey? Glad you packed my ride up." The black youth said as he pimp walked his way towards Steve and Diane. Steve turned to look at the approaching punks. Diane instinctively went around to the passenger side of the Jeep to gain some distance from the two young thugs.

"Yeah, you and yo bitch need to walk on away from my man's ride," the white boy said in his best ghetto slang.

"No man, the ho gonna ride with us, bring me some pleasure." The black kept walking forward reaching into his waist band.

"Diane get down!" Steve yelled as he reached under his own shirt and began running to the back of the Jeep for cover. The black youth produced a cheap 9mm handgun and fired three shots off at Steve. Steve rolled on his shoulder, a round striking just in front of his face as he rolled behind the back of the Jeep. The white boy had pulled out a small Jennings .25 caliber, holding the pistol sideways just as he had seen it done in his favorite movies and popped off two rounds at Steve. Both rounds struck the rear brush guard with a metallic clang, ricocheting down to the asphalt parking lot.

Steve came up with his Glock fired three panicky rounds at the two assailants. He completely missed with all three shots, but the two dove to the ground to take cover. Diane pulled out her Glock and fired twice at the black male who was more exposed than the other teen. She was in a kneeling position shooting through the space where the doors had been. Steve had taken them off yesterday.

White boy seeing that his homey was in troubled fired another round, this time at Diane. The round struck the hood of the Jeep digging a small gash across the hood. The teen rolled twice to his left and prepared to fire again.

As the teen came up on a knee, Steve snapped off six rounds at him. This time he had taken the time to get a good sight picture and took a deep breath and released half of it before squeezing the trigger. The first two rounds struck the gang banger in the stomach, as the gun began to recoil three rounds worked their way up into his chest, the last round striking the banger in the top of the head as he collapsed forward, already dead.

At the same time Diane fired a round at the white teen. He returned fire, one round striking the roll bar, the second the passenger seat, his third hitting home. Diane felt a burning sensation just to the lower right of her left breast. She knew she had been hit, but she stayed calm. Just like Steve had taught her, she aimed center mass and fired three rounds in quick succession. All three rounds struck white boy in the heart and lungs ripping the vital organs to shreds as the Federal Hydra Shock rounds mushroomed open as they penetrated his flesh.

He dropped straight to his knees and then fell forward on his face. One round had exited through his back leaving a silver dollar size hole. His white t-shirt immediately began to soak through with blood.

"Diane are you ok?!" Steve shouted over his shoulder as he covered the two thugs.

"No, I've been shot." Diane said as she collapsed down on her butt, the Glock sliding from her weakening grip.

Steve holstered his pistol and ran to Diane's side. "Where are you hit Diane?" Steve's hands trembled has they searched her body for the entrance wound. Diane pulled her hand away from hear chest, there was little blood coming from the wound. A tiny hole was in her shirt.

Judging from how pale her face had become Steve guessed that she must be bleeding internally.

Steve gently undid the top buttons on her blouse. Just to the right of her breast was a small almost invisible bullet hole. "I've got to get you to the hospital Diane."

"I don't think I will make it Steve." Diane closed her eyes; her breathing had become shallow and ragged. Steve felt for her pulse. It was there, but just barely. Steve fumbled for his cellular phone and dialed 911 and received a busy tone. He tried two more times with the same results. In frustration he threw the phone to the ground.

Steve took Diane's pistol and shoved it into his waist band. Then crouching down he reached down and lifted Diane's limp form up. He placed her into the seat and buckled her in. Running around the Jeep he jumped into the driver's seat and started the Jeep up. He backed the Jeep, then shifted into first and started forward. He stopped when he realized that he would never make it out of the parking lot through all the wrecked vehicles, and people who still ran around in confusion.

Steve threw the Jeep into reverse cutting the wheel, and turning the Jeep towards the curb. The Jeep swayed a bit as the big off road tires crushed over the body of the white thug who had shot Diane.

He floored the Jeep over the curb and down the embankment. Diane groaned as the Jeep slammed onto the roadway. Steve cut the wheel hard to the right and accelerated down the back road that led towards the county. Steve wanted to avoid driving in the city. He would try to make it to Doc Morrison's who had a home just down the road from his cabin. If Wal-Mart's parking lot was a small example of what the rest of the city was like, the hospital would be a mad house and he would have to drive all the way downtown to get there.

He raced the six miles to Doc Morrison's home. Several times Steve had to throw the Jeep into four wheel drive and cut across open fields when he saw that there was traffic starting to back up ahead of him. He didn't think he would have ever made it to Doc's if he and Diane had taken her small sedan.

When he pulled up to Doc's home he was out front unloading supplies from his truck. Steve gunned the Jeep down the dirt drive coming to a sliding halt beside Doc's truck.

"Doc Diane has been shot." Steve screamed as he bailed out of the Jeep running around it to Diane's side.

Doc dropped a feed bag he was unloading and ran to Diane's side. The old man pushed a panic stricken Steve to the side as he came around to see her injuries for himself. He calmly felt for her pulse, it was weak and fading. "Get her inside Steve, and take her straight down to my old office in the basement."

Steve pulled Diane from the Jeep and rushed her into Doc's house. He went straight to the basement were Doc had his old office and examination room. Doc had started his medical practice in the office in the early sixties.

"Hang on Diane, Docs gonna save you." He whispered to her as he gently laid her on the examining table.

Chapter 3

Maude Morrison stood at the kitchen sink washing dishes. As she stared out the window into the back yard she wondered why the power had gone out. Herb had become fanatical about the events unfolding during the past couple of years. He swore to her that the America they knew growing up was going to end. He believed that the events would spiral out of control. He started buying supplies, ammunition, medical items, and a few new guns. The only good thing he bought was the generator. It had come in handy several times when the power had gone out.

"Now if that old coot of a husband would quit running around stashing his supplies like a squirrel in fall, and start the dang thing I could get the dishwasher going." Maude said talking to herself.

Suddenly Maude heard the front door being opened, and then slammed against the wall. The sound of the door hitting the wall had made the big woman yelp in surprise. She had also dropped the iron skillet into the dishwater. She heard Herb run down the hall towards the stairs to the basement. When his feet hit the floor it sound as if he was carrying something. That mischievous scoundrel had bought something else he didn't want her to know about and was trying to race down to the basement and lock it up in one of the lockers so she would not find out.

"Herb Morrison, whatever it is you bought you can't hide it from me!" Maude looked around for something to knock some sense into her husband. First she looked at the skillet. No she couldn't hit him with that, he was getting to old. The last time she had hit him with it was in

1954 when he came home with lipstick and the smell of perfume on him. He had claimed it was from widow Simpach, who had given him a kiss and hug for helping her with a flat tire. The smell of liquor he said was just a toddy he had shared with that old scoundrel friend of his, Amos Brown. She had laid him out good for that. Of course it was unfortunate that she later found out he had been telling the truth. But the duty of a good wife was to keep sneaky husbands in line. So if he did not deserve it that time she was sure he had gotten away with something else she had not caught him for.

"Well I guess I will settle for the wooden spoon." Maude reached down with a meaty hand and picked up the spoon from the sink. She straightened her fiery red hair and started marching toward the kitchen door. As she reached the door to the hallway she collided with Herb who was coming down the hall from the front door. Herb was knocked to the floor. Herb weighed in at around 160 lbs. He was 5'11 and of willowy build. Maude on the other hand at 6', 250 lbs., looked the part of a Norwegian serving wench from the dark ages.

"Just what on earth is going on Herbert?" Maude's ice blue eyes peered into Herb's cow brown eyes. Herb looked up into Maude's blazing icy eyes. "Maude, calm down! Steve and Diane are here."

"Well what in the blazes are they running to the basement for, and why did they slam my door open?" She stated in an even tone. The wooden spoon was pointing out at Herb like a Viking's sword.

"Maude, Diane has been shot and I......." Herb didn't get a chance to finish the sentence. Maude reached down and grabbed Herb by the scruff of the neck, and pulled him to his feet in one quick motion.

"Well, what are you sitting in the floor for? Get down there and work your magic! I will be down in a second." Maude said. She gave Herb a nudge down the hall. If anyone could save that lovely girl, it was her man. He might be a sneaky little rogue, but he was a superb physician. Herb dashed down the stairs as fast as his old bones could carry him.

--- ⋇— ⋇---

The white Chevrolet panel van descended the slope of the bridge leading to the dam. As they drove across the dam they could see the huge concrete structure built at the end of the dam. This was where the entrance to the powerhouse and the inside of the dam itself was.

The captain of the six-man assault team, Kim Dong, pointed to the door located on the north wall. "That is were we will make our entry. We will most likely have to blow the door. Corporal do you have the plastic explosive and detonators prepared?"

"Yes sir." The slight built man sitting behind the front passenger seat said. The six Koreans were dressed identically. All wore Level IIIA Point Blank bullet resistant vest, under their black BDU clothing. Each had a nomex balaclava pulled down over his face. Each also wore matching TAC-V1 tactical vest, black Kevlar helmets sat on their heads, and Bolle goggles were worn over their eyes. The Helmets had police painted across the front, and the vest had police on the front and back. Most of their gear had been purchased through a police supply catalog. The only thing they had to have smuggled into the United States were their fully automatic AK-47 rifles, grenades, and plastic explosives. These items were smuggled up via the porous Mexican border. They were one of fifteen teams operating in northern Alabama, southern Tennessee, and eastern Mississippi. All had entered the U.S. legally on student visas. Other sleeper teams were activated across the U.S. weekly. Members made up of soldiers posing as students and businessmen. Other teams came across the Mexican, and Canadian borders. Once across the borders they melted into the population awaiting orders.

The van finally crossed the dam. The driver turned right into a parking area that led to the west side of the power house. The captain was the first to spot the TVA Police Ford Explorer sitting in the tree line. "Pvt. Wei, you will pull up twenty feet from that police vehicle turn the van to the left, and then stop." He looked back at the two-team members sitting next to the sliding door. You two will exit and set down covering fire. The rest of the team will exit and charge the vehicle. Hopefully the officer will be dead before we exit the van."

"Yes sir!" The team answered in unison.

⌐═══⌐

Don Savage, and Carl Atkins, sat with the seats leaned tilted halfway back; windows rolled down in their TVA police SUV. It had been a long day sitting and watching the approach to Wilson Dam, and the powerhouse. This was their last day in a string of twelve-hour shifts. Since the onslaught of terrorist attacks TVA had kept officers on guard around all of the agencies dams and property. Both officers sat in a stupor when the radio crackled to life. "Baker 7, to unit 21."

"Shit, what does he want now?" Don said with a sigh as he leaned forward to grab the mike.

"Go ahead, Baker 7."

"What's your 10-20?"

"Is he smoking crack or what? He knows exactly where we are, he made up the damn schedule." Carl said.

"Well sergeant, the power-house, where you assigned us." Don said with as much contempt as he could possibly muster for the overweight sergeant. He looked over at Carl with a smirk on his face. "What a dumb ass!"

"That's right, stand by there I need to 10-22 (meet you) with you about next week's schedule." The sergeant replied.

"Crap! Don pop the back lid and break out those M-16's. You know how pissed Jaba the Hutt gets if we don't have those things up front with us." Carl said raising his seat up.

"Yeah, yeah, I know." Don said as he opened the door to the SUV to walk around back to grab the rifles. Don mumbled and cussed his sergeant on his way back to the rear of the vehicle. Carl sat up and smiled at some of the choice expletives his partner used to describe the sergeant.

As Don was breaking out the two rifles from the cases Carl noticed a white Chevrolet van pulling in at a high rate of speed. He could not make out the faces since the setting sun reflected off the front glass. The van made straight for them. Carl opened his door and started to step out.

"Don, you know who these yahoo's are?"

"Nope, can't say that I do. Maybe Domino's has a van load of pizza for Jaba." Don snickered as he shut the lid to the Ford, and started walking to the passenger side; pocketing three extra thirty round magazines in his cargo pocket. As the van continued towards them at an increasing speed the hair on the back of Carl's neck felt like it was standing up. He broke the snap on his holster that held his issue Sig Sauer 226 9mm. Don had stopped by the rear passenger wheel as the van slid sideways not fifteen feet from the Ford. Suddenly the side doors flew open. Carl watched as two black clad men dressed out in police tactical gear stormed out rifles coming to the ready. He saw the words police written on the helmets and tactical vest.

In that brief moment before his life was snuffed out Carl was trying to remember if he had been advised about some sort of drill the tactical guys were holding. That was what the sergeant was probably coming to tell them about so they would be prepared and not get caught unaware causing the sergeant embarrassment. His pistol was just clearing leather his draw slowing at this false realization. That is until he noticed the AK-47's not the standard M-4's the tactical response team carried.

Both soldiers started firing full auto as soon as their feet hit the ground. The shots were not well aimed since they were firing full auto. Steel core rounds began to shred the Ford, shattering windows, and ripping through metal in their wake. Two seconds into the fusillade the rounds started to tear into Carl Atkins. As the two opened up Carl dove to the left, simultaneously bringing his insignificant pistol to bear. As he dove a round shattered through his shin exiting through the calf taking most of his lower calf muscle with it. A second and third round entered his lower abdomen laying his stomach open. Carl's intestines poured out of his stomach to the gravel parking lot. Carl started to squeeze the trigger. Hours of training coming into play, his brain ordering him to squeeze the trigger over and over again. Pain racked his body from the wounds inflicted upon him by the two men. He felt as if someone had dropped him into molten lava when his body struck the ground his knees crushing down on his intestines that now piled up on the ground.

"Die, damn you, and die!" He screamed his finger pumping as fast as it could. Despite his desire to destroy the scum before him he could not put metal into flesh. His rounds impacted in the pavement in front of the two, some rounds striking the side of the van. Then it was over. The passenger in the front seat kicked open his door leveling his pistol at Carl. Carl saw it all clearly and in slow motion. His mind affected by what is known as sensory distortion.

Rounds from the two AK's still tore into the Ford and around his body on the ground. Then his eyes locked with the black clad man in the front seat. Those eyes looked at him over the barrel of the pistol and then all was black after the split second flash from the muzzle. His last thought was one of confusion. He just couldn't understand why the tactical team would kill him. Then the bullet entered his brain.

Don was just as confused as Carl at first until the bullets started flying. He dropped the M-16 in his left hand, and dove into a bough of a downed pine tree. Once there he low crawled five more feet taking up position behind a tree trunk. As the firing stopped he placed his sights on the black clad figure on the right. The one in the front passenger seat had exited already and was out of sight. He slowly squeezed the trigger as the sights rested on his target.

The driver turned the van into the parking and punched the accelerator as he straightened the big van out. "I only can make out one in the vehicle captain." The driver was almost shouting. Adrenaline coursed through his body, this would be his first combat operation. As he accelerated forward he saw the officer exit the driver side of the police vehicle.

"Get ready!" Dong shouted to the two in the back.

Wei leaned over unlatching the van's side sliding door. The van broke hard, the rear end swinging around as the driver cut the wheel. Pvt. Wei and Pvt. Hoe crouching and ready to spring forward like lions getting ready to pounce on their prey. The van stopped and they were out in seconds. As their feet came to a rest on the ground and they were able to achieve a stable shooting platform both men opened fire. Both rifles set on full auto, rounds spewed out like a river of steel. Wei could see the rounds tearing into the police vehicle. As the police officer started to dive he walked his rounds towards him. He was rewarded with a spray of blood and bones as part of the officer's lower leg disappeared in a shower of red blood, and flesh.

The man was screaming something, he could not tell what. Then as the officer's body hit the ground the officer began to fire. He could hear the rounds whipping past his head. He continued to fire at the prone officer but with no effect. In his pumped up state he forgot to release his finger from the trigger. The big rifle continued to pump out bullets from the seventy-five round drum and down the barrel, the rifle recoiling up and to the right. His rounds began tearing into the back quarter panel of the police vehicle.

Pvt. Hoe immediately lost sight of the officer as he dove for cover. He continued to lay down fire as the Captain had ordered. He worked his rifle in a figure eight pattern blowing the police vehicle to pieces.

Captain Dong pushed the door open with his leg as he turned his body to exit the van. Dong saw the officer dive left. Dong could still make out his head and upper body. Wei's rounds dug gouts out of the earth all around him and in the vehicle itself. Dong stopped his exit and raised his pistol, the sights resting on the forehead of the downed officer. He pulled the trigger once. He felt the recoil ride up his arm as he fired the Glock 17. The back of the officers head exploded as the 115-grain hydra-shock round exited his brain.

The two privates continued to fire. "Cease fire! Cease fire!" Dong shouted. The order was in vain though until the two AK's clicked dry, the magazine drums depleted.

"Reload you worthless son's of whores! You were not trained to shoot like that." Dong was almost in a state of rage about the terrible shooting his men had demonstrated. He exited the van and moved towards the downed officer. He scanned the area as he moved; the two privates began to place new drums into their weapons. Wei moved forward with Captain Dong.

Don lined up his sights, and tried to calm his rapid breathing. The shooting had stopped, and the one with the pistol was shouting in some oriental language he could not place. Don got his breathing under control, and flipped the selector lever on the M-16 A1 to full auto. He aimed at the lower abdomen of the man who was reloading his weapon. He pulled the weapon in tight to his shoulder preparing himself for the light recoil and rise of the weapon as it fired. Just as the man had the drum seated into the magazine well, and had charged the weapon he pulled the trigger. Six rounds spat out at the man. Two tearing into his groin and lower intestines, one blowing off three fingers curled around the pistol grip of the AK. The next round hit him in the shoulder spinning him. The next round struck him in the throat. The last one slammed into the soft metal of the interior of the van as he let off the trigger.

Dong could tell the officer was dead; he was just turning to tell Wei and Hoe to clear the truck when the distinct sound made by the American M-16 rang out. Dong ran to the rear of the Ford placing himself in front of the rear tire. Wei ran to the front of the vehicle beside the front tire, concealing him behind it and the engine block. Dong and Wei watched as Hoe staggered forward and then pitched face first into the gravel, blood immediately pooling around his neck and head area. The driver and last two team members exited the van firing at a clump of trees on the other side of Dong, and Wei. Controlled burst rang out as the three laid down a constant steady stream of fire. Return fire came back at them and three rounds struck the right front quarter panel and two rounds hit the windshield of the van.

The three by the van dove for cover. Wei took this opportunity to peer over the hood of the SUV into the wood line. He saw the dirt and leaves being kicked up from the unseen assailant's rifle fire in the trees. Taking careful aim Wei let off a three round burst just to the right of the large pine were he believed the hidden man to be. Dong peered around the back of the SUV into the woods. Wei had just fired off three rounds into the woods, and the other team members were replying in kind as well.

Dong noticed that the back hatch of the Ford was slightly ajar. He lifted it up a little bit to see the butt stock of a long gun that sticking out. It had blocked the hatch from being closed. Dong reached up and pulled the long gun to him. It was a Remington 870 shotgun with black synthetic fore-grip and butt stock. The stock was a Choate speed feed and it had a six round sidesaddle. He pumped a round into the chamber, released the safety, pulled the trigger and sent a load of 00 aught buck into the area of the unseen shooter.

Dan buried his face into the pine needles as rounds kicked up all around him. "Bad move dumb ass." He said to himself. He heard shots ringing out from the Explorer and simultaneously felt a round tug at his vest. The round went through his vest like a knife through hot butter, and then dug a shallow gouge out of his left side. Then the pine tree shuttered as he heard the tell tale sound of a shotgun going off, the pellets shaving off bark and wood, cascading the debris on and around his head.

"You've got to move out of here Danny Boy, or your dead meat!" He told himself. Dan rolled left and came up on one knee, leveled the M-16 and sent a four round burst at the van. As he rose up onto his feet he and emptied the rest of the magazine into the area around the Explorer. As he turned to run he dumped the empty magazine, and reached into his cargo pocket for a fresh one. He was going to make a break for the ravine that was not more than thirty feet away. If he could get down hill and follow the creek, he may have a chance. Dan made his break for it.

"Daddy didn't raise a coward, and momma didn't raise any fool." He thought to himself in gallows humor most cops have.

The rounds from the M-16 slammed into the Explorer. Both side windows exploded in a shower glass. Neither Wei, nor Dong took cover as they attempted to gain a shot at the police officer that was now rising and firing at them and their comrades. Both took careful aim at the retreating figure. Wei fired two controlled three round burst at the officer. He was pleased to see the man flinch then stumble, but was disheartened when he kept running. Then Wei heard three loud booms from the Captains weapon. He did not know where he got the shotgun, but was pleased with the results. The man fell out of sight into the brush. Surely Captain Dong's rounds had shred the man into small pieces.

Dan was halfway to the ravine when he heard the report of the AK. He felt a round strike his portable radio on his left hip. He stumbled, knocked off balance by the shot, but continued to run. Then he heard three shots coming from what he knew to be a shotgun. Pellets whizzed past his head like angry hornets. The third shot though was the one that got him. He felt the pellets slam into his back and the left side of his rib cage. Dan went down face first into the steep ravine. His body tumbled end over end till he had fallen the entire thirty feet to the bottom. He landed at the bank of the creek, and rolled into the water letting the current carry him along away from the nightmare. Then darkness engulfed him.

Dong and Wei ran forward intent on locating their ambusher. They halted when Corporal Mau called out. "Captain Dong! A second police vehicle is coming into the lot. The six predators turned as one at the new threat.

-+=-+=-+-

"Well sergeant, the power-house, where you assigned us." Sergeant Ortega's fat face bunched up in what he considered a scowl.

"Who does that worthless piece of trash think he is using that tone of voice with me?" Sergeant Ortega said out loud. "Keep being a smart ass Savage I can't wait to tell you and Atkins I have you starting the mid-night watch tomorrow."

Ortega pushed the gas pedal down on his Crown Victoria. Ortega could not stand Atkins or Savage. Both men stood over six feet tall and weighed in around two hundred pounds. Both were avid weight lifters and loved to shoot at the departments range. They always showed him up at training events when firearms and hand-to-hand courses were being taught. Well he knew paper work, and that was just as important. The thing that bugged him the most was that they called him Jaba the Hutt behind his back, hell sometimes to his face. He could not help he had a thyroid problem. He had to eat all those sweets to keep him going.

He pushed the gas pedal to the floor; he was going to relish giving out their new assignment. As he approached the parking area he scanned it for Savage's Explorer. Ortega slowed his cruiser as he turned into the parking lot of the powerhouse. That's when he noticed the smoking ruin of the Explorer. Smoke rose from the front end and windows were busted out. A white van was parked in front of it sideways. Several men dressed in what looked to be SWAT gear stood around the van.

"If those dunderheads have crashed into a SWAT van I'll have their badges." His fat bulldog face puckered up even more as anger swelled over him. Captain Smith would surely fire his little darlings, this time he would have to.

"Don't fire yet, let him get closer." Dong ordered his men. He and Wei had taken up positions in the wood line. Wei scanning the area behind them for the missing officer, he would also provide cover fire if necessary on the new threat.

As Ortega slowed the cruiser he undid his seat belt preparing to get out of the car. "Why do they make these cars so small?" He said to himself while thinking about having to exit in what he considered a small car. He brought the car to a stop about eight feet from the SWAT officer standing by the driver door.

"I am Sergeant Ortega, what's happened here? Did those two idiots run into you?" There was no reply from the SWAT officer.

"What strange looking machine guns." Ortega thought. He would never get his answer about the wreck, or why SWAT was carrying those nasty assault rifles he hated so much.

"Take him now Mau!" Dong cried from the trees. Mau did not hesitate for an instant. The AK came to his hip and he depressed the trigger. Fifteen rounds spat out of the barrel at almost point blank range. All fifteen rounds chewed into Ortega's fleshy mass. His head exploded like a pumpkin, his level IIIA vest torn to shreds. His right arm was shot off at the elbow. Ortega's now dead body stood for a few seconds then collapsed down coming to rest against his cruiser. A mass of brains, blood and bone sat where once a three hundred pound man had been.

"Back to the van and let's grab the packs. We have work to complete, and things have already gone badly. More officers may arrive." Dong ordered, and the team moved to the rear of the van.

"What of the other officer Captain? Should we not go look for him and finish him?" Wei said.

"It is paramount that we destroy the power supply for this area. Even if it will only be a temporary thing, it will sew fear into these lazy capitalist dogs. Besides I know my shots hit the man, he is finished." Dong replied in confidence. With a nod Wei ran to retrieve his pack that was laden with explosives. "Mau, take one of the men and plant charges around those two towers." Dong pointed to two of the massive steel power poles that helped carry tens of thousands of kilowatts to the surrounding area known as the Shoals. "Then make entry to that relay station and plant explosives around those large transformers."

"Yes sir!" Mau tapped one of his men and they went to carry out the captain's orders.

"The rest of you let's go!" The group fell into a wedge formation with Dong in its center. They made their way to the steel door on the north side of the powerhouse. Surprisingly the door was unlocked. The team made entry into the powerhouse. As they made there way to the massive hydroelectric generators, employees were shot on sight. Grenades were thrown into offices and workshops. Not many survived the attack. Once the charges were set the team made its way back to the surface. They met up with Mau and his partner who had finished planting their explosives. Ten minutes after they pulled off in the van heading north towards highway 157 the explosives went off. Across

Lauderdale and Colbert Counties power lines and substations were simultaneously destroyed by other teams similar to Captain Dong's, and the lights in the Shoals went out.

Steve laid Diane gently on the examining table. "Are you still with me Diane?" He said softly as he placed his lips next to her ear. All Diane could muster was a slight nod of her head. "Doc's going to take care of you, I know he will. So hang on, I am going to be right here with you, ok."

Doc Morrison scrambled down the stairs to the basement. As he entered the room he saw Steve bent over Diane. As he approached the table he reached out and gently touched Steve's shoulder. Steve's body jolted as if someone had shocked him with a live electrical wire. "Sit down over there on the couch Steve and let me take a look." Doc said in a well-practiced bedside voice.

Steve slowly let go of Diane's hand and made his way haltingly to the couch five feet away. "How are you Diane?" Doc asked.

Diane shook her head, and managed to get out a few feeble words. "Not good...not going to make it Doc."

"You let me be the judge of that little lady." Doc stroked her sweat soaked face. Her skin was pasty white and she had already gone into shock. "I am going to undo your blouse and take a look at your wound, ok?"

"Ok Doc." She smiled and then whispered, "No peaking or Maude will get you."

Doc grinned. "That's a girl, still plenty of spirit left in you. You will be fine." His grin faded as he undid the buttons on her blouse. The bullet had struck her below the breast, most likely in her heart. After a quick look he knew she was bleeding internally. How she had made it this long he did not know.

"Doc...need to talk to Steve." She said in a raspy low voice.

Doc looked over to Steve who was sitting on the edge of the couch staring at his fiancé. "Steve she wants to talk to you."

Steve got up and made his way quickly to Diane's side. "I'm here Diane."

Diane swallowed trying to get her voice back. "I'm sorry I told you I wanted to wait to get married until we saved enough for a house. I should have married you right away." Diane coughed, blood oozed down from the corner of her mouth.

"It's ok Diane. You were just thinking about making things work out right. You're the smart one not me." Steve said. His eyes were starting to tear. He could see the life slipping from the woman he loved.

"You were always such a sweet man. Did whatever I asked of you." She reached up stroked a tear away from his cheek. Then her hand slowly dropped back down on her chest, and she breathed her last breath and died. Steve leaned over and hugged her body, to him and began to cry. Doc Morrison bowed his head, crushed at the loss of such a wonderful woman. He knew when he saw the wound there was nothing he could do here in his basement. Maybe not even if he was in a fully equipped OR. Maude Morrison stood at the base of the stairs looking in on the scene.

After several minutes she slowly walked over to Steve. "Steve let her go." She said in an uncharacteristically gentle voice. Steve laid Diane's body back to the table. Doc covered her up with a wool blanket that had been at the foot of the table. Maude guided Steve back to the couch and sat with her arms around him. Steve's body was racked with sobs. "I'll be lost with out her Maude, lost. I'll just be lost here with out her." Steve began to cry again burying his head into Maude's chest. Maude rocked him and gently stroked his back.

Chapter 4

Team 4 cleared the table of their lunch. It was around noon and the team leader knew they had much to accomplish before night fell. The team had come to Alabama on student visa's two years earlier. Since then they had attended the University of North Alabama. The forged papers had stated that each was the son of U.S. serviceman or U.S. citizens who had been to South Korea. This helped with the visa process, and got them into the country much quicker than was expected. All had chosen American first names to make their assimilation into American life easier. People were more likely to feel at ease with someone named Charlie Yuan than Lu Toc Yuan. Americans were funny in that sense. All four had arrived at UNA within months of each other. The school was very helpful in putting the four Koreans together and helped pay for their housing, and getting them assimilated into living life in the south.

Charlie was nervous; he knew their job would not be as difficult as the assault teams hitting the area's dams and other hard targets. They did not have the hard contact training as some of the other teams had received. They had just received training in setting demolition explosives. Captain Dong from team one had met him two days ago and given him the plastic C-4, timers and detonators. His superiors had advised him that it was up to him to secure their own weapons for protection when they first entered the country.

At first all the members had chosen fighting knives as their weapons of choice. All were well trained in the use of knives, staffs, and various other hand weapons; also each was a martial arts expert. But after several weeks in Alabama he saw how and heard how almost everyone owned a firearm. Why blood did not flow in the streets from shootouts was beyond him. If the citizens of North Korea owned as many weapons he knew there would have been much blood shed as many different factions attempted to seize power He did however hear a line in an action movie that made acquiring firearms a must. "Never bring a knife to a gunfight." Bells and whistles sounded in Charlie's head at that line.

The next day he made contact with a black youth who lived in west Florence. This is where the majority of the housing projects were located in the city. It would also be the best place for him to gather undocumented weapons. He paid the teen up front for weapons. The teen had him meet the following night at the parking area at Cypress Creek Bridge on U.S. Highway 20 just outside the city. He had arrived early and placed his men in hiding.

The youth arrived alone and opened the trunk of the rusted out Cutlass Supreme he drove. He produced two semi-rusted single barrel 12 gauges, a Jennings .25 caliber pistol, and a Rossie .32 caliber revolver. Charlie was offended that the youth would try to give him weapons such as the ones in the trunk. He had paid the youth three thousand dollars to find weapons. Charlie had visited several gun shops and knew he had given the teen enough cash to buy decent rifles, shotguns, and pistols.

Charlie had quickly pulled the hidden knife from its scabbard and placed the tip of the knife to the boy's neck. He had also put him in an arm lock and broke two fingers. He took his money back, kept the guns and told the teen that next time he asked for weapons they had better be of a higher quality. The teen had pissed his pants and Charlie released him and let him leave in his car.

Charlie had to come up with a new plan to obtain weapons. John suggested befriending some of the college students that they knew hunted or shot skeet at one of the local gun ranges. It seemed every American male in the south owned at a minimum some type of hunting shotgun.

This new task was taken on. All four befriended students that hunted and shot recreationally. They each had convinced their knew friends to purchase weapons for them. Charlie decided not to go with assault type weapons; he wanted to be low profile keep things simple. There would be less of a chance that someone would question them possessing weapons used for hunting and target shooting than if they were to obtain the semi-automatic versions of AK-47's.

Each had friends purchase Mossberg 500 sawed off riot shotguns. Each had synthetic pistol grips, with pistol grips attached to the pump, and a six round magazine tube extension, tactical sling, and heat shield. Their side arms consisted of four Ruger GP100 .357 magnums. He also purchased over 2000 rounds per weapon from an ammunition dealer online. He purchased more ammunition at a local gun store in down town Florence. Charlie was elated to find out that anyone could purchase ammunition from a variety of places. Much of the ammunition would be used for training, and familiarization firing.

Next they had their new friends teach them to use the weapons. Their American friends were eager to teach the Koreans the fundamentals of firearms, and proved to be excellent instructors. This bothered Charlie somewhat. If college age students were this knowledgeable in the use of firearms, how good would U.S. military and police forces be? If America came unglued at the seams like it was hoped, how could their forces be able to fight in an environment where he knew there were over eighty million gun owners? Charlie decided to quit worrying about that. Those were matters better left to the leaders of the party. He was sure they had plans in place for such things.

The four became quite proficient in the use of their new weapons. Using the cash they had been given Charlie purchased assault vests, drop leg holsters, combat boots, and Kevlar lined leather gloves. For their clothing he picked up surplus German battle fatigues with a flectar camouflage pattern. The flectar pattern would work well here in North Alabama. He had also purchased rappelling rope, grappling hooks, GPS's, speed loaders for the revolvers, bandoleers to hold extra shotgun shells bolt cutters, hand held blow torches, surplus police surplus smoke, and CS/CN canisters, two stun guns, and numerous other items that would assist them in their mission.

Well it was time to quit reminiscing about the past and get ready for the future ahead of them. Charlie rose from the table picking up his plate and glass and walked over to the kitchen sink. "John! Thomas!" Charlie called to the two who had walked into the living room.

"Yes, what is it Charlie?" Thomas answered.

"Break out the weapons. I want them field stripped and cleaned for our operation tonight. Paul meet me in the garage we must arrange the explosives."

Paul exited the kitchen as Charlie had ordered and went to the garage to begin preparations. Charlie looked in on John and Thomas to make sure they had begun their tasks. He then went to the garage to assist Paul. After several hours Charlie and Paul had completed setting up the delayed fuses and timers. The explosives and charges were placed in satchels. The workbench was cleared of scraps and debris and tools were put away.

John and Thomas had the weapons cleaned and laid out. Ammo pouches filled, bandoleers filled with shells, tools and equipment placed on the LBV's. They had showered eaten, and had dressed in their flectar camouflage clothing, and boots. Charlie and Paul grabbed a bite to eat. Once they had eaten both headed off to separate bathrooms to shower. Once that was done, they too dressed in their camouflage clothing.

It was four o'clock and the sun was starting to go down behind the trees. Charlie called his teammates to the kitchen for their brief. Once each had taken a seat at the kitchen table Charlie laid out a map of the city of Florence. "Comrades we have waited over two years for this mission. I have spoken with the cell leader from team one. This evening just before sunset an attack will be carried out on Wilson Dam. The objective of this attack is to cut power to Florence, Muscle Shoals, Sheffield, Tuscumbia, and the surrounding smaller cities. Team two shall hit Wheeler Dam to the east so that the city of Athens and surrounding area will be without power. Other attacks will be carried out by other cells against substations, power lines, cell towers, and phone junction boxes."

"Will these attacks permanently destroy the dams?" Paul asked.

Charlie stood and began to pace back and forth. "No. These attacks are designed to temporarily disrupt power for one to two months. Also by disrupting the phone system and cellular towers communication via cell phone, telephone, and internet will be hampered. This will slow the ability for the government to communicate and coordinate recovery operations."

John raised his hand like a small child in school. Charlie nodded for him to ask his question. "Then why even do it? I know it will show

36

the imperialist dogs they are not safe in their own backyard, but what does our nation gain?"

"By striking the dams in combination with our attacks Americans in every city will fear attacks may be conducted on them. No longer will citizens of small towns and cities think that they are safe, and only their cousins in the big cities are vulnerable to attack. Our part in this phase of the Chairman's plan is quite simple. We are to hit two propane and natural gas distributors. The first is located on Court St. three blocks from the Florence Police Dept. This blast will devastate at least a two-block area. The blast will be visible to the citizens across the river in Sheffield, Tuscumbia, and Muscle Shoals. Our second target is located three miles outside of Florence on Hwy 17 in Lauderdale County. The area of this propane company is mostly rural. Casualties will most likely be limited to a few residents who live nearby. Though human casualties will be light, the psychological damage done to the area and nation as a whole will be tremendous.

Remember, we will not be the only ones attacking. Other small to mid size cities across the nation are going to be hit as well"

"Then why bother with attacking it?" Thomas asked.

Charlie took a deep breath to calm him. He had just explained the reasons for the attacks. Though he liked Thomas and he followed orders well, he was not very bright. When he was composed he tried to explain some of the reasoning behind the attacks to help Thomas fully understand. "This will let everyone know that the explosions in Florence were not some type of industrial accident. The dogs in Washington will not be able to convince the people that both explosions were not the act of sabotage. If we only hit one of the targets it could be spun by the government as an accident. This way there is no denying the truth. With the dams attacked, power outages, no communication and city streets on fire, how can the President convince his people that he is still in control? The hope is to cause political turmoil as well. The U.S. has troops around the globe, fighting their so called War on Terror. We know it is just a move the U.S. is making to further dominate the world. With their homeland under attack, the citizens will demand an end to their imperialist actions, thus taking the U.S. out of certain countries that should be controlled by our nation, or our Communist brothers in China. Do you understand now Thomas?

Thomas nodded his head "Yes, comrade." He said. Charlie was still somewhat skeptical, but at least he had, with any luck, satisfied Thomas.

The sun was fading as the four continued to pour over the map, making sure they knew the areas they would be operating in. It was not necessary, as the four had made a habit of attempting to drive all the county roads, walk as many city streets as possible to learn about the area where they would fight in the shadows. They also went over who would place what charges where as Charlie produced photos of the targets to study. Then suddenly the lights went out. The four looked up from the maps, and photos at one another. "Our time is coming close comrades. It seems Team 1 and the others have begun. As soon as the sun sets we will begin our mission."

Charlie rose from the table and walked into the living room to collect his thoughts. As darkness fell over the city the four terrorist donned their gear. LBV's tightened or loosened, pistols and shotguns were checked for function and ammunition. They picked up their backpacks, which contained tools and explosives and walked to the Kia four-wheel drive SUV in the garage.

Once they loaded up in the SUV the garage door was opened and they backed out onto Cedar St. and began their drive to Smith's Propane and Natural Gas on Hwy 17. None of them noticed a black male standing in the shadows across the street. The drive through the city though uneventful was a maze of accidents and delays. It took them almost two and a half hours for the six-mile drive. Charlie smiled to himself. It seemed the attacks had already started to cause chaos and confusion. He wondered what was happening in other cities across this country. By tomorrow America would be a different place he was sure.

Once they were within a mile of the propane company they took a dirt farm road for a quarter of a mile and parked the SUV in a wooded area. They exited the vehicle and put on their packs. They trudge the mile and half on foot with relative ease. They moon was full and the expected cloud cover had not appeared yet. Once they arrived at the 10' chain link fence, topped with razor wire Paul pulled out his wire snips. He cut a four-foot by four-foot hole in the fence. The four entered the area where the storage tanks were located.

Each separated to his assigned area to plant the charges on the large natural gas and propane tanks. Thomas had been assigned the storage bin area where the 30lbs. Propane tanks were stacked. The bin containing these tanks was situated by the office building. As he placed the last charge on one of the tanks the back door to the building suddenly opened. A heavyset man wearing a red flannel shirt with cut off sleeves stepped outside. He turned and looked directly at Thomas. A cigarette dangled from the corner of his mouth.

"Hey, what the hell are you doing there?" The man said in a gruff voice with a southern drawl. The big man pulled what appeared to be a blackjack from his back pocket, and he made his way towards Thomas.

Thomas did not say a word he just bladed his body to the man his right hand easing to the fighting knife on his back right hip, his left hand coming up in a defensive position.

"I'm talking to you, you little dink fuck stick!" The man turned towards him his right fist raising the black jack. Suddenly the man sprang at Thomas.

Web Hornsby sat at the desk checking over the delivery route for the next day. Mr. Smith had him set up for a propane run up to Savannah, Tn., then over to Iron City, Tn. Then he had to drive to Athens, Al. and after that he could begin his regular route across the river in Colbert Co. Smith just pissed Hornsby off to no end. "You would figure after driving a truck for a man for ten years he might get a descent route." Hornsby said to the four walls.

He reached up under the shoulder of his cut off sleeve flannel shirt and pulled out a pack of Camel filter less cigarettes. He pulled out a smoke and his Zippo lighter. Lighting the cigarette he took a long drag from the cancer stick. From outside he heard something like metal against metal banging together.

"Wonder what the hell that was?" Hornsby said as he got up from the desk and walked to the back door. Taking another drag from his smoke he opened the back door and stepped out into the night. As he stepped out he caught movement out of the corner of his left eye. He turned to look and saw a small slender Asian man with a back pack and wearing some weird camouflage. He stood next to the propane tanks that were sold to folks for their grills.

"Hey what the hell are you doing there?" Hornsby said. Hornsby turned to face the little man. The little man said nothing to him just stared with cold dead eyes. "I guess he needs a good old fashion redneck ass whipping." Hornsby thought to himself as he reached in his pocket for his blackjack. "I'm talking to you, you little dink fuck stick!" Hornsby raised his fist and charged the little man. This shouldn't take long. As his fist came down to hammer the man, the little man bladed his body to Hornsby. He sidestepped as the blackjack approached his head and struck out with his left hand hitting Hornsby on the top of the forearm. The blow struck the nerve that is located in the middle of the top forearm numbing his forearm and hand.

Then the little Asian kicked him across the back of the knees as his body's momentum carried him forward. Hornsby dropped to his knees from the kick. The Asian dexterously moved in behind him. Hornsby saw the glint of steel as the man's arm came down in front of his face. Suddenly a fiery burning sensation was felt across his throat. He felt the blood poor down into his windpipe, as he began to choke. Hornsby's last thoughts played across his brain as he collapsed face first to the ground. "Damn that little bugger is fast." Web Hornsby wouldn't have to worry about getting shafted on a delivery route ever again. His world faded to black.

Thomas stood there stunned as he looked down at the body of the American. Blood pooled around his head and shoulders his convulsions had ceased, the American no longer a threat. A voice from behind him startled him.

"Well done comrade. You are the first member of our team to strike a blow against the imperialist Americans. I will make sure your family knows of your valor here tonight." Charlie walked forward and put his hand on Thomas shoulder. "Come comrade it is time to go, we are finished here."

Thomas numbly turned and followed Charlie and the others back to the SUV. As they drove back to Florence the traffic had cleared and was light, the streets dark except for an occasional passing car or truck. There was not much moving, fear had began to take its hold on the Shoals. They drove slowly through the downtown area and noticed a lot more foot traffic than normal. They could see that many of the areas blacks, from the projects in West Florence had walked the six blocks to the downtown area and were beginning to test the police response to the area by breaking out windows. No alarms were going off. No phones worked so there was no one to call 911. A riot was brewing.

Driving down Court St. they passed the police department. Looking up the hill they could see Florence's Special Operations Team loading up their gear into the SWAT van, a large Snap On type diesel truck. The parking lot was also filled with dozens of officers armed with rifles and shotguns. It seemed the police department was about to give the roaming bands of thieves' downtown a big surprise.

"Let's make this quick. The riots will begin soon, and we must make it back to our home before that starts." Charlie said.

Paul killed the headlights as he drove the SUV within fifty yards of Downtown Propane Company. As he pulled into the lot the other three quickly exited with their gear. Paul turned the vehicle around and used the emergency brake to stop the SUV so as not to light up the area with his break lights. The three that exited the vehicle quickly placed their charges. The large storage tanks had no fencing around them and were easily accessible.

Once John had placed his charges he walked over to the area that contained the gas grill propane tanks. He cut the bolt on the gate that surrounded the storage area. He quickly walked through opening the valves to the canisters. Once he had about twenty or so open he dashed out to the others now waiting in the SUV.

The SUV sped into the night towards home less than two miles away. "What were you doing?" Charlie asked.

"Hopefully when the charges go off, the tanks with the open valves will be propelled up and out. Not only from the blast but with the valves opened maybe the escaping gas will act like a rocket and rain death on those fools running around downtown." John smiled at the thought of the canisters raining down on the mobs of project dwellers roaming the downtown district.

Charlie nodded his head. "We shall see, we shall see."

Soon they made it back to the house and pulled into the garage. They were in a jovial mood. Congratulating one another on how brave they had been on their mission. They all especially congratulated Thomas who had struck the first blow by killing the worker. Grabbing up their gear they moved into the house making their way from the kitchen to the living room.

The house was pitch black due to the power outage. John who was in the lead bumped into the coffee table. "Where is the flashlight Charlie?" John asked bending down to place his LBV and pack on the floor and to rub his shin.

"Right here mother fucker" Suddenly a bright light blinded the four. But they all knew whom the voice belonged to. It was the voice of "Dapper" Donte. It was the young black gang banger who had purchased the shoddy weapons for them.

"Keep them hands were I can see them china boys." Light played down towards their hands. They could make out Donte sitting in the recliner, his left leg draped over the arm of the chair. His left hand held the flashlight, his right with a blue steel handgun. He was holding it sideways, gangster style. Five other gangsters stood spread out on either side of the chair. Two armed with sawed off pump shotguns, the other three with handguns.

"Yawl monkey faced freaks thinks I forgot how you done disc'd me down at da creek? I thinks I'm gonna strip you down naked and drag your yellow asses down the skreet." He said in his best Ebonics.

Donte paused long enough to chuckle and look at his homeys. "Nope, don't tink so." Donte pulled the trigger on the Lorcin 9mm. The other bangers opened up with their weapons also. The darkened room was lit up with the muzzle flashes. In seconds Sleeper Team 4 died in a hail of bullets and blood. The six members of "West Side Posse" did not know it, but they had actually made history. They were the first people in Lauderdale County to strike a blow against the onslaught of this new wave of terrorism.

Donte got up from the recliner and panned the light on the four bloody bodies in the floor. His homeboys circled around also. They gazed down at the bullet riddled corpses, all smiling proudly of their handy work.

"Man, I never killed me no china man before. Look at all that blood man. I figured them yella fuckers would at least try some of dat kung fu chit on us. Hell I thought they was all supposed to be bad ass like Jackie Chan." Donte said.

"Brightlight", an albino black reached down and drew Charlie's GP100 from his holster. "Check out da gats boys! We goin to be da shit out on da skreet tonight."

Hi fives were exchanged along with a long procession of gangster handshakes. The six bangers collected all the guns and ammunition in the house and began to walk to the garage to check out their new ride when the house shuddered and a loud explosion was heard. The six ran back to the front door and then out onto the front porch. A large orange mushroom cloud came from the downtown area bathing the night in an eerie orange glare.

"Man looks like the party has started downtown! Brightlight, Tater, and Shady go get the caddie. Da rest o us is gonna take the china man's ride. Let's go kill some crackers and rape some ho's!"

The "West Side Posse" loaded up and headed north to some of the finer sections of Florence, where the pickings were good and white women were plenty.

Chapter 5

Bob Novacheck and his wife Caroline had arrived home from their screen-printing business. It had been a hectic day but now it was coming to and end. The two sat on their large black leather couch, Bob swigging down a Sam Adams, Caroline sipping white wine. They stared transfixed at the 52" big screen TV that sat against the north wall of their plush and lavish home. Lauren Green, the news commentator, gave a running narrative about events unfolding around the nation. Lauren looked into the camera her voice almost breaking and eyes watered up with tears. "Ladies and gentlemen FEMA has released the updated death toll from what is now being confirmed as a nerve gas attack on the following cities."

The screen faded Lauren out and a list rolled down the screen in three columns: City/ Injured/ Dead/: Boston 411 264, St. Louis 216 91, Kansas City 111 47, Phoenix 201 143, Ft. Worth 321 65, Seattle 198 78, Tampa 402 365, Birmingham 96 23, Jersey City, 134 41, Dover 81 53, New Orleans 319 302, Little Rock 182 165, Nashville 187 191.Then Lauren's face appeared back on the screen. Her makeup was smeared from where she had tried to wipe the tears off her face while the list had been scrolled.

"The total number of injured from the attacks stands at 2,457, the dead number 1,828. Not since the 9/11 attacks have so many Americans been killed at one time in what is obviously a coordinated terrorist attack. The death toll from the two dams attacked in Tennessee is 76, wounded and the injured are listed at 56. State officials in Tennessee are trying to reroute power to the stricken area. Hundreds of thousands are without power this afternoon. It is unknown when power will be cut back on. We now take you to the White house for a press conference with the President."

Caroline and Bob listened to the President's speech. When it ended Caroline picked up the remote and muted the talking heads. "Bob are we safe? Do you think they will attack Wilson Dam or Wheeler Dam?" Caroline stared almost blankly at her husband.

"Honey, this is Florence, Alabama. We have the lowest crime rate in the state, and are considered the fifth safest city in America. Who would attack us? We don't have a thing to worry about. Besides we have a great police department. Remember that article about the police department's SWAT team; they are rated as one of the best in the South East. If anything goes wrong I am sure those men will take care of it."

Caroline noticeably swallowed. "But what if they do? Are we ready?" "Ready! Heck yeah we're ready. Remember when the Office of Homeland Security first brought up that everyone should have the seventy two hour kit?"

"Yes." She said in a meek voice.

"Well you do remember I went to Sam's and bought up all those canned goods, rice and stuff?"

Caroline nodded her head slightly trying to figure out in her fear filled mind what good food stored had to do with anything.

"Baby it's all right down in the basement in those pantry cabinets I picked up at the hardware store. We've got enough food to last at least at least six months. We also have three guns. I bought that Benelli M-1 for turkey hunting last year. Jack Wilson loaded me up about four hundred rounds of turkey loads. Then we've got my old S&W .357 and I picked up five hundred rounds for it last year. And to top it off you've got that little Sig .380 in the dresser drawer. After the attacks in California last year I bought you four more magazines for it and three hundred rounds. If anyone comes barging in here we have enough firepower to blast them into next week." Bob looked at his wife seeing the fear recede somewhat.

In the back of his mind though he was running a mental checklist of things on hand they would need in case everything went to hell in a hand basket.

"Do you think we should load the guns up, and see what we have in case things do go bad? She asked.

"Sure sweetheart let's get cracking on it." Dang I married one smart lady Bob thought to himself. Now at least she won't think I am worried to death and this will give her something to think about instead of doomsday. They both rose from the couch and began their task. Bob walked to the bedroom and opened the door to his large walk in closet. The closet was large, about fifteen by ten feet. He opened a mahogany box that contained his Benelli and an extra barrel. Bob took off the 26" barrel and replaced it with the 18' one that laid in the red satin lined box. Once the barrel was attached he leaned the shotgun against the dresser. On a shelf just below the shotgun case was a sliding shelf that contained two large surplus .50 caliber ammo cans. He opened the one on the right.

This one contained five hundred rounds of assorted slugs and double aught buck. Jack Wilson had loaded him up about four hundred rounds of 3 ½" turkey rounds. But Bob, though hating to keep things from his wife felt if had purchased the five hundred rounds of 00 and slugs would worry her to death. He then took down a bandolier type sling for the shotgun; it had twenty-five loops for the shells. He attached the sling to the shotgun and then filled the loops up with alternating slugs and 00 buck. He then got down a belt bandolier that could hold thirty shot shells. He filled these loops up also.

Then he opened a smaller mahogany case that contained his stainless S&W Model 10 with pachmyer grips. He loaded six Gold Dot rounds that were fitted into individual holes in the box. He put the pistol in a leather holster that was draped over a hanger. Next he removed the six speed loaders from the case one at a time, each containing six .357 Gold Dot rounds. Each was placed in the speed loader holder that was on the same belt as the holster.

He had felt stupid when Jack had convinced him to buy all of this stuff, but now it did not seem like such a bad idea. As he walked back out of the closet Caroline was sitting on the bed, her Sig 230 in her hand. Four loaded magazines lay on the bed beside her. She did a quick function check of the weapon, and then quickly loaded a magazine and racked a round in the chamber.

"Hey have you been taking shooting lessons behind my back or what. You looked like Steven Segal or something."

"Unlike you my dear husband those two weeks we spent at the range after the California attacks, I retained what we learned. Would you like me to teach you about sight picture, and sight alignment, and trigger squeeze?" Caroline finished with her ribbing, her large smile and straight white teeth accented her amusement.

Bob held up his hands in defeat. "Ok, ok, let's head down to the basement and checkout what we have there, Ms. Segal." Bob beamed back with his own smile.

The two made their way to the large finished basement. Once down stairs Caroline opened all the pantry doors. "Well I guess you were right about food for a while. Now what about have you done about water?"

"What do we need to worry about water for?" Bob asked somewhat confused.

"No power, no water dufus. Just like when we don't have power after ice storms once the water pressure runs out our water pump needs electricity to pump water into the house."

"Well we have the generator." Bob said.

"Do you have fuel?" Caroline retorted.

Bob smiled "That my dear we do have. I have eight five-gallon containers in the shed. I was going to take them down to the lake house and put them there so we would not have to run to town for extra fuel like we did last year after we bought the jet skis. What are we going to do about our water problem?"

Caroline crossed her arms and thought for a moment. "Are those four big white barrels in the shed still?"

"If you mean the ones we got from Dillon, we have two of them left. I gave Jack two of them. He acted as if I gave him fifty bucks or something. Do you want to put water in them or something?"

"Yeah I think it would be a good idea. If you will clean them out and bring them down here we can have water in the house if water becomes a problem."

"I'll get on it now." Bob turned to leave. His relief about his wife's demeanor from scared to death, to an eager participant in self-preservation was evident in the bounce in his step as he left the basement. She was a good woman, and had a brilliant mind when it came to business and logistics. She had proven that a million times at their business. She was the main reason they were so wealthy.

However he had concerns that if things got really bad she may not handle it. She was pampered growing up in a wealthy family, and had met him well after he had started his successful screen-printing business. Of course without her help, input, and ability to network, his business would not have grown to half of the size it was now. Who would have ever thought he would have six hundred employees.

Caroline searched the basement for useful items. She found four oil lamps that she had bought at the Dollar Store, right before the last ice storm. She also located two one-gallon jugs of lamp oil. Sitting beside the lamp oil on the floor was a gallon jug of oil used for the teke torches outside in the summer. She took these items upstairs. Digging around the kitchen she found two four packs of emergency candles purchased last winter.

She inventoried the food and determined they had enough in the upstairs pantry to eat on for about two weeks. It was a good thing she went to the grocery store yesterday. Bob came upstairs a short time later. Caroline was in the hallway sorting through the medicine, bandages and other medical supplies.

"Well we now have 110 gallons of water on hand. I also found our old camp stove and a couple of cans of fuel for it. I don't know if it will still be good or not, but we will see if worse comes to worse."

Caroline stacked the medical items back in the closet. "Let's grab a sandwich and see what else is going on. It's almost six and I want to take a shower and go to bed. I have got to do payroll in the morning."

The two fixed some sandwiches and chips got a couple of glasses of tea and sat down in front of the TV. After finishing their sandwiches Caroline picked up the remote to turn the TV back on. Just as the picture came back on, the lights went out and the picture on the TV went off. It was 5:42 pm. The sun sat low behind the trees.

The couple looked at one another Caroline was the first to speak. "I pray someone just shot out a transformer and the power will be back on soon. Hopefully we are worried about nothing. I am going to take a shower; do you care to join me?"

Bob didn't know what to think. He did know it was unlikely someone in the neighborhood shot out a transformer, or a car crashed into a power pole. The reason was that all the electrical for this neighborhood was underground. His stomach did flip-flops. Caroline was worried he could tell, but she had decided to play it cool so he would too.

"Sure let's go." He said.

Caroline gave him a wink and mischievous grin. She hoped up and ran to the bathroom stripping, and laughing as she went. Bob wasn't far behind, and a thought crossed his mind, "If this was how Caroline dealt with doomsday it sure was going to be a fun ride.

—⊷⊶—

"Dapper" Donte cruised in his new Kia heading north. The first subdivision he wanted to hit was Heathrow. The homes were large, just like their owners' wallets. Rap music blared from the speakers. As he pulled into the subdivision he stopped by a phone junction box. He got out of the little SUV and walked back to the Caddie that followed them. "Brightlight, yews and Tater break out the tools in the back and smash that phone box. We don't need no 5-0 rolling down ruin'n our fun now do we?" Though a usually smart move to make it was unknown to them that it wouldn't be necessary. No ones phone worked in Florence now.

Brightlight and Tater went to the trunk of the Caddie while Shady rolled a joint with Donte. Brightlight and Tater walked back around the car with a crowbar, sledge hammer and wire cutters. Once at the box Tater pried open the box. The doors groaned open under the assault of the crowbar. Brightlight took the wire cutters and systematically cut every visible wire he could see. Once he finished Tater began beating the circuit boards to pieces with the sledgehammer. They completed their work walked back to the truck and threw the tools in. Walking back to the front of the car with Donte and Shady they were soon joined by Fat Cat, and High Yella.

Fat Cat was rolling a hefty joint as he walked up to the rest of the group. He lit up the doobie coughed and held out the joint. "Which one of you nigga's is up for some of this shit?"

"Man gimme some of that shit!" Brightlight reached out and took the joint and then sucked down a large hit. He exhaled, passed the joint off to Tater and wiped the sweat from his brow. "Man" he thought to himself "Dat was some hard work beating down that phone box."

Once the group finished with the two joints Donte filled them in on his plan. "Ok, dis is what we's going to do. Do yall member that big house they builts in da back of da subdivision?" the others nodded "Well, we hit'n it first. Brightlight can yews still do that talk like one of dem uppity crackers?"

Brightlight giggled a bit, the weed taking hold of his brain. Donte slapped him across the face. "Cut dat shit out man dis is business time not no play time you fucking shit bucket."

"Sho can Dapper. Yew wants to hear?"

Donte shook his head. "Yeah I do's. Cause yew gonna knock on that door and tell them folks yew is lost and you car broke down. We gonna be hidin on the side and when they lets you in to use the phone yew goings to pull out that new .357 of yours and make um get down. Then we gonna come up inside that house and have us a little party. Da momma looks fine and so do her daughters." Brightlight was give them his best-educated white boy accent, which was pretty good. Brightlight had been taking acting classes in high school and had shown a great talent for it. That is until he stabbed his drama teacher for not giving him the part of Romeo in "Romeo and Juliet"

"Ok, let's roll on these crackers." The six got into their vehicles and headed to the back of the subdivision. The back street where this house was located was ideal for a home invasion. There were few houses and large wooded lots stood between the homes. They turned the headlamps off as they approached the house. They exited the cars Brightlight handed his shotgun to Tater. He checked the load on his .357, felt his right pocket to make sure the ammo he had dumped in his pocket was all there. The rest checked the loads on their pistols and shotguns. They stuffed extra ammo into pockets, readjusted their new .357's in their waistbands after they checked to make sure they were all loaded.

"Do your shit Brightlight." Donte ordered.

Brightlight ran up the front door of the house and waited till the others were ducked down below the hedges near the front door. Once all were in position he knocked on the large oak door. He peeked in the window on the side of the door. He saw a figure carrying what appeared to be a candle. Then the door opened. "Can I help you?" The good-looking brunette said.

Brightlight gave her a quick once over. Long tan muscled legs stuck out beneath her shorts, and what pretty damn eyes. "Yes, my name is Daryl Smith my 4 Runner broke down, just up the street. I tried to get assistance at the neighboring homes but no one answered and you are the people to answer the door. May I come in and use your phone?"

The woman felt a little suspicious but she didn't want anyone thinking she was a racist for not helping a black man so she stepped back and said, "Sure, come on in."

◈━◈

The Donovan's sat in the living room floor playing Uno, candles burned on the mantel and the coffee table where the four had been trying to keep occupied since the lights went out. Celina Donovan thought about how boring life was without a computer, CD players, and TV. The seventeen year old stared at her cards and pretended to enjoy the game. She could tell her father was nervous but was not sure why, heck all it was, was a power failure. Then she heard the knock at the door.

"I'll get it!" She said as she stood to go answer the door.

Her 15-year-old sister also stood. "I'm going with you." Daphne told her sister.

Nancy Donovan stood also. "Sit down you two. Who knows who it might be?" The two girls sat, and Nancy stretched her arms out over her beautiful body, and then walked to the door.

"If it is Martin, tell him whatever he ask to borrow we don't have. That man borrows everything in the world." Her husband Carl Donovan said.

Nancy took a candle with her and opened the door. A light skinned young black man stood there. Hey explained how he had come there and asked to use the phone. She was a bit confused since she knew everyone on the street, and everyone was home, which also made her a bit suspicious. Well let him use the phone and send him on his way. "Sure come on in." Nancy stepped to the side and as he entered she turned and began to close the door.

"Who is it, Nancy?" Carl asked from the living room. "This man needs to…" she didn't finish the sentence. The man spun and struck her across the jaw with a powerful right fist. Nancy fell to the ground on her hands and knees. Carl heard his wife's gasp of pain and stood to investigate. Then the man came around the corner holding a gun in his hand.

"Sit yur ass down boy, fore I shoot your uppity white ass." Brightlight said. The rest of the crew barged in the front door as soon as Brightlight knocked the woman to the ground. As he entered Tater grabbed the woman by the hair and drug her into the living room. The rest of the crew followed in behind him shotguns at the ready.

"Now see here you can't just barge in here…" Carl began, but Fat Cat, despite his size was on him before he could finish his sentence. A quick butt stroke to Carl's mouth ended his protest. The two girls screamed as there father fell back onto an end table crushing it under his weight. Fat Cat spun to face the girls.

"Damn, Dapper yews was right about these ho's. I am looking forward to get'n some of dat."

"Ain't any one get'n nut'n till we check this place out then we can have some fun." Dapper said. "Shady get your rope and tie dese fine white honkey bitches up, with their momma."

About that time the family dog, Princess; an old toy poodle entered the room disturbed from her nap by all the commotion. She didn't know these strangers so it was time for her to go to work. She began yapping at the intruders. "Shut dat mutt up!" Dapper ordered.

High Yella being the closest to the dog spun, and leveled the Mossberg 500. He pulled the trigger and the dog not ten feet away dissipated into a fine red mist. The women screamed, and began to cry, the father cowered on the floor. The homies all grabbed for their ears.

"What the fuck you think you doing!" Shady screamed.

"Tell a nigga when you gonna shoot next time!" Fat Cat yelled.

"Enough of dis messing around, Fat Cat yew and Shady watch these folks, the rest of you find start looking for some da loot."

Dapper then walked over to the father still laying in the floor, almost in a fetal position. Dapper kicked him in the face. The man's head snapped back as the boot connected to his nose. Blood gushed from the cavities of the broken nose. "Where's the loot rich boy?" Dapper kicked him again this time in the stomach. The man went to the fetal position. "Now talk up fore I whip yo ass some more."

"Okay!" Carl began to sob. The safe is in the closet in my bedroom. There is a key to it in my wife's jewelry box.

"Carl! All of my expensive jewelry is in there!" Nancy said in a disgusted voice. She was going to say more until Fat Cat slapped her hard across the face turning the cheek red almost immediately.

"Shut yo mouth bitch!" Fat Cat screamed. The daughters screamed in fright. Fat Cat and Shady began to punch the girls screaming at them to shut up. Dapper turned to the two. "Now yall don't be mess'n up them pretty things to bad. We got us a booty call coming soon."

The two quit the beating and smiled at their leader. Dapper called out to the rest of the crew about the safe. They said they had already found it. Twenty minutes later they all returned to the living room carrying jewelry, TV's, CD players, and money. After going through the loot Dapper decided it was time for some fun.

"Shady you and Tater get the young one. It's time for her to feel what a man can do to her."

The two smiled at one another Shady stood up and grabbed Daphne by the arm and jerked her to her feet. She began to sob as they untied her.

"It's alright baby you goin to like it. Pretty soon you goin start hav'n jungle fever all the time." Tater said with an evil smile.

"Brightlight you and High Yella take mommy and give her a little brown sugar." Dapper ordered.

When High Yella grabbed Nancy she began to kick and scream. Brightlight punched her in the stomach. "Calm down woman, you gonna like get'n some Mississippi Black Snake." Brightlight said.

"Just do as they say girls, don't fight it will only make it worse." Carl said.

He was still laying in the fetal position in the floor. Blood still flowed from his nose, and his eyes had started to swell and blacken.

"Man yew ain't anything but a worm. Yews ain't even gonna fight for you women." Dapper walked up to the man and kicked him three times in the ribs. "Now shut your mouth while my boys show these women what a booty call is all about.

"Shady and Tater had taken Daphne to one of the bedrooms by this time, her screams could be heard in the living room as the two slapped her and began to rip her clothes off. Their laughs could also be heard.

"What about me!" Fat Cat asked. He was bouncing from foot to foot. "You done good tonight Cat, take that one by yerself, you earned it."

Fat Cat grabbed Celina up off the couch and began to drag her to her parent's bedroom. Tears streamed down her cheeks. Once in the bedroom Fat Cat threw her to the bed. Celina lay on her back with her hands tied behind her. Fat Cat stripped off his clothes in record time. "I'm gonna give you some sweet loving pretty thing."

Celina's mind raced. She could hear her mother and sister screaming in the other rooms. Through the French doors the moonlight streamed into the room. Celina looked to her left and saw a chance. Sitting on the nightstand was the 6" long needle that her mother stuck phone messages on. She looked back to her would be rapist. He was naked and staring at her. She heard more screams. She made up her mind; she wasn't going to be raped.

"Could you untie me please?" Celina asked in a soft voice.

"What the hell for bitch?"

"My father told me not to fight. If you untie me I will take my clothes off and let you do what you want."

This was a fantasy come true for Fat Cat, a willing young white girl. He leaped on the bed and rolled the fine little hussy over. His fat hands shook as he untied her. He rolled off the bed and stood up. "Now get up and strip little whore." He tried to sound as mean as he could, but his voice was a few octaves higher and quivered with excitement. Celina stood up. She began to undress slowly. First she took off her t-shirt, and then she undid the buttons on her shorts. As she slid them down she scanned the fat man's clothing. "There!" In the moonlight she could just make out the shotgun and pistol laying by the heap of clothing.

"Now the Bra and panties bitch!" Fat Cat ordered. His fat body quivered with excitement.

Celina undid her bra and took off her panties. As she rose up the man slapped her across the face knocking her onto the bed. Her head spun, and stars danced before her eyes. Fat Cat quickly got on the bed and maneuvered the girl's head onto the pillow. He sat up on his knees looking down at the brunette beauty. He was one lucky brother. Dapper was one cool dude. He had her all to himself and wouldn't have to listen to his homies tease him about how fat he was. "Spread your legs bitch." He ordered.

Celina did as she was told. The obese man lowered himself onto her. She could barely breathe when he put his whole three hundred pounds down on her. As he struggled to enter her Celina began to reach out for the message needle. She could feel the pain between her legs as he began to penetrate her. Finally she had it.

"No! No! No!" She screamed each time driving the six inch needle into his shoulders and neck. Fat Cat was just starting to enter her when he felt the first stab in between his shoulder blades. He let out a scream and reared up. Then the next one struck him in the neck. The third struck the fleshy part of his jaw at an angle coming through the left side of his neck. The needle stuck there and Celina was unable to pull it free. Fat Cat rolled off of her screaming in pain. Blood covered his neck and shoulders.

In the other room Dapper sat in the recliner next to where Carl lay. Occasionally he would grab his shotgun by the barrel and strike Carl with the pistol grip end across the head or back. He lay there crying and sobbing, "Please don't hurt me." He would say till the beating stopped, and sometimes for a little while after.

Dapper sucked down on his joint, and took a look at his new Rolex watch, and began counting out the money. The screams from the trios in the other rooms had continued unabated. Then he heard the girl in the master bedroom with Fat Cat. "NO! NO! NO!" she screamed. Then Cat's screams joined hers. Dapper giggled "What was that fat piece of lard in there doing?" Dapper shook his head and he reached down and lifted up his shotgun pointing the barrel at the man's head. He was seriously considering shooting him so he would quit his crying.

Fat Cat's continued screaming came back to the forefront of his drug induced mind. Dapper stood, it was time to go find out what was going on in Fat Cat's room, and maybe have a turn with the girl himself.

Celina rolled off the bed, and looked back over her shoulder. The fat man was rolling on the bed screaming and holding onto the needle in his neck. The fat man's clothes were right in front of her. She quickly found the pistol and picked it up. It was a revolver similar to the one her Uncle Joe had let her shoot at his farm. She had to save her family. Quickly she stood and quietly walked out of the room towards the living room.

Just as Dapper stood up High Yella walked in. "What is that fat lard screaming for." Yella was butt naked and had his shotgun in his hands.

"Hell if I know, but I'm goin to finds out." Dapper replied. Then the loud crack from a pistol and the flash of fire from a gun interrupted their conversation. Yella dove back into the other hallway, and Dapper dove towards the couch.

Celina peeked around the corner into the living room. She could hear the two men talking. She raised the pistol and pointed it at the man who was standing by her father who was still lying on the ground. She could hear his sobs. She raised the pistol and fired. The round shattered the Mirror behind the man's head. He dove towards the couch, and she spun to fire at the second man. He had just cleared the doorway when she fired at him missing.

Dapper saw the second muzzle blast. He stood up and fired towards the doorway without aiming. The pellets tore apart the right side of the doorframe missing the girl. Yella turned and put his shotgun around the door, the rest of his body stayed behind the wall. He pulled the trigger on the shotgun. A large hole appeared in the wall five feet to the left of the door. Then more gunfire came from the door way and the two gangsters had to take cover.

"Get out here and bring yo damn guns!" Dapper screamed to his posse, as bullets whizzed around his head.

Celina felt splinters pierce her arm as the blast from the shotgun tore into the doorframe to her left. Then the second thug fired from the hallway. Sheet rock blew out at knee level just two feet from her legs. She stepped back around the doorway and fired at the man in the hall. Turning she fired three more rounds at the leader. Then she heard the revolver click. She knew she was out of bullets and probably out of time. She turned and rushed back to the bedroom.

As she entered the bedroom she could see the fat man sitting on the edge of the bed swaying back and forth holding the needle that was stuck through his neck. He looked up as she entered and began to stand. Celina didn't slow down a bit. With all her might she reared back and threw the now empty pistol straight at the fat slug. He never even had a chance to duck. The revolver struck him between the eyes, the hammer digging into his skin over his left eye, and the barrel coming down across his nose breaking it. He fell backwards screaming. When his head hit the bed the needle was partly ripped out of his neck. His screaming rose in volume, his fat little legs kicking at the air.

Celina reached down grabbed her clothes and the shotgun. She saw two boxes of shot shells sticking out of the thug's pants pocket. She grabbed them too and stuffed them in her bundle. She was startled when the thugs in the living room opened up with shotguns and pistols at her former position. It was time to run; she would have to come back for her family. She spun and ran to the French doors opening them she ran out into the backyard and the woods beyond. Behind her she could hear the fat man screaming and the fusillade of gunfire the gang still poured on.

The others came into the living room in various forms of dress, guns in hand. They could hear Cat screaming. Dapper turned to his crew "let's take that bitch!" They all opened up on the door that led to the other hall. After they sent a hail of bullets into the door they charged forward and ran through the shattered door and down the hall to the master bedroom. The French doors were open and the moonlight lit up the room. Cat was on the bed bleeding like a stuck pig and screaming.

"Cat, where the hell is she at?" Dapper demanded.

"She stabbed me man, she stabbed me!" Fat Cat cried.

"Shut up fool I can see that!" Dapper said in disgust and slapped Fat Cat across the face. This of course only caused Fat Cat to let out more screams of pain.

Shady was looking out the French doors into the backyard. The moon reflected off of the dew in the grass. He could see the girl's foot prints leading into the woods. "She's gone man." He said as he pointed towards the footprints and wood line.

"Get yall's crap together it's time to blow dis crib." They all went back in the living room. Shady and Brightlight helped Cat gather his stuff. Yella drug Nancy back into the living room and had also located a first aid kit. "Fix that fat boy up sweetie." Yella slapped her on her naked buttocks as she moved forward. Shady and Tater held him down while Nancy treated his wounds. Occasionally she would look over at her husband still lying in the floor.

Once she fixed up the fat thug they pushed her to the couch, were she sat down hard. Daphne had been brought in and put on the couch also. She reached for her mother and laid her head in her lap. Both sat silently while the thugs collected their things. Their bodies were bloody and bruised.

Dapper looked around him everything had been gathered up. He looked at the woman. "What kind of rides yew got?"

"We have a Land Rover and Expedition in the garage." Nancy said in an exhausted voice.

"Where da keys at ho?" Dapper asked.

"My husband's pants pockets."

Dapper looked over at Brightlight and motioned towards the man on the floor. Brightlight kicked the man in the kidneys before he began to search his pockets for the keys. A few seconds later he came up with two sets of keys.

"Yall load up while I take care of business." Dapper told his crew. The posse gathered their things and the loot and went to the garage to look over their new rides. Dapper walked up and placed the barrel of his pistol next to Nancy's head. "Ya know I aint never killed no woman before. Ya think I ought to start now?" An evil grin crossed his face as he looked into her weeping eyes. "Nah, not today!"

With that said he raised his other hand that held the shotgun. With the pistol to her head he pointed the shotgun at her husband and pulled the trigger and stopped his crying and wailing forever. Nancy Donovan peed herself. Dapper looked down at the growing wet stain under Nancy and laughed. "See ya around pretty lady." He turned and walked out to the garage.

Nancy heard the engines crank up and the garage door open. "Let's ride West Side Posse!" She heard the leader yell. The trucks backed out of the garage and down out into the street headed off for more terror. Nancy began to cry harder pulling Daphne to her while staring at her husband's lifeless form.

Celina Donovan had gotten her clothes on and made her way through the woods and came out on the street thirty or so yards from her house. She slipped across the street and hid directly across from her house. She lay in a clump of bushes watching and waiting for what she did not know. Then the garage opened up and she could make out figures moving in and around their family's two vehicles. Then she heard the report from a shotgun in the house and saw the front window light up from muzzle flash. Tears welled up in the young girl's eyes and spilled over onto her cheeks. Another figure came into the garage. She could tell it was the leader when the headlamps from the Sequoia came on. "Let's ride West Side Posse!" he yelled as he got into the Land Rover. Both vehicles backed down the drive and then drove down the street. It would be morning by the time Celina would make her way back across the street and into her house. By that time America, as she knew it would cease to exist.

Chapter 6

Elbert Little sat in his bass boat, fishing pole in one hand a beer in the other. His friend David Miller sat at the front almost in the same position. The only difference in the two was the brand of beer they were drinking. They had gone to boot camp together, Advance Infantry Training, jump school, Ranger school, and then on together to fight in Panama before leaving the Army and coming home. Both worked at Browns Ferry Nuclear Plant in Limestone County, but remained residents of Lauderdale County. Every week the two friends would come to the river, go out in the boat, drink beer, and tell each other lies. For them it was a good life.

Their boat bobbed up and down near the Colbert County side of the Tennessee River. Wilson Dam loomed over them. As the two drank and dozed, the quite afternoon was disturbed by the sounds of gunfire.

Both men were instantly alert, long dormant combat experience kicked in as they both began reaching for M-16's that used to be their constant companions in battle. The rifles weren't there but the tell tale sound of AK-47 fire that came from the bluff above them was. They both new it was AK-47 fire, hell they had, had enough fired at them in Panama.

"What the hell is going on up there?" Elbert said, as he scanned the bluff. "Don't know friend, but maybe we should raise the police." David replied.

Elbert picked up the marine radio that was beside him. He raised the Marine police and advised them of the situation. "Calling Alabama Marine Police do you copy? I have a possible emergency to report."

"This is the Alabama Marine Police. What is the nature of your emergency?"

"You aren't going to believe this, but it sounds like there is AK-47 gunfire coming from the powerhouse area Wilson Dam. We can't see anything above us, but we can sure hear it."

"Stand by at your present location. We have two boats in route to your location."

"10-4, we aren't going anywhere."

Now mixing with the sounds of the AK fire was the sounds of pistol and shotgun, and M-16 fire. "Hell of a firefight going on up there. Think we should vamoose, Elbert?"

"Not just yet, let's ease up to that cove where the stream comes in and sit it out. Don't think we need to make any unnecessary noise by starting the motor. That is unless you think we can take them boys on with my flare gun." Elbert smiled at his friend and took a sip of his beer. He started the trawling motor and eased into the cove.

Once in the cove Elbert cut the motor. They heard a long rip of M-16 fire, and then two three round burst from an AK, followed by three booms from a shotgun. Then the sounds of something crashing down the ravine and a splash in the creek about thirty yards around the bend from where they sat.

David took a swallow of his beer. "Reckon that was one of the good guys or bad guys?"

"Don't know David." Elbert reached down and picked up the flare gun. It was better then nothing. A few minutes later a body came floating around the bend. Both recognized the TVA Police uniform. The officer's body floated face up his arms was spread wide.

"Guess it was one of the good guys." Elbert eased himself over the side of the boat and into the chilly water trying to be as quite as possible. His life vest keeping him afloat, he kicked away from the boat and swam to the approaching officer. Once he had hold of him, he pulled him back to the boat.

David took hold of the officer's shirt in both hands and began to pull him aboard. Elbert lifted the officer's body from underneath. The two half drunk fishermen struggled to get Don's large frame in the boat, and finally succeeded.

Don opened his eyes. His vision was slightly blurred and pain racked his body. Through his hazy vision he saw two hands reaching down towards his body. He felt as if his body were, weightless, and floating.

"Well I guess this is were I find out if I'm going up or down, hope them are the good Lord's hands." Don said in an inaudible voice.

As his body was lifted over the side of the boat, the officer let out a groan of pain. David knelt over the officer and began probing him for wounds. He found a tear in the officer's vest. Blood came away on his hand when he pulled it out. "It'll be alright big man. We're gonna get you out of here."

Elbert got back in the boat and got in the driver's seat. He lifted the radio and called the Marine Police again. "Mayday, Mayday. We've got a TVA officer who has been shot up." The Marine Police responded to his call for help, and asked for his exact location. "We're on the Colbert County side of the Tennessee near the power house right where we were last time I called you." As Elbert was about to continue the sounds of multiple AK-47s firing filled the air above them.

David looked back at Elbert "Get us the hell out of here, now!"

Elbert started the engine of the boat, swung it around, and as soon as he was in open water he threw the throttle open on the big Mercury 250 hp motor. He screamed in the radio mike so that he could be heard. "There is more gunfire coming from the Powerhouse above us. Meet us across the river at Florence Harbor."

"10-4." Replied the Marine Police dispatcher. The boat rocketed across the river towards the Lauderdale County side of the river. As they approached Florence Harbor, they could make out the red and blue lights of waiting Florence Police and rescue vehicles. They eased the boat to the dock, rescue personnel ran up pushing a gurney. Three police officers stood by, one catching the tie down rope David threw to him.

David turned back to the downed officer, "You're safe now man. You got some rescue guys and Florence Police who are going to take care of you."

Don stared at the man; a pained smile crossed his lips. "Thanks, what is you and your buddy's name?"

"Don't worry about our names just get better so you can hunt them thugs down and kill them later." David pulled a cold Budweiser from the cooler and held it up in front of the officer's face. "This is for the trip to the hospital." He grinned and put the beer in the cargo pocket of the officer's Uniform pants.

Don gripped David's shoulder. "Not thugs, Asian, paramilitary."

Then the rescue personnel had Don snatched up and soon loaded into the ambulance. As it drove away to ECM Hospital the uniformed cops began their questioning. David and Elbert sipped on their beer and, followed the officers to their cars and answered their questions as they walked to the patrol cars.

Within minutes they were at the Police station being taken in to the Detective Bureau for a more thorough question and answer session. It didn't last long. The two men knew nothing about what actually happened at the dam. The only useful information was the description Don had given of his assailants. When the detectives were through the two men were carried back to the harbor. David and Elbert might have been good old boys, but they were not stupid. They left the boat tied up where it was and made their way to the parking lot. The two were headed for their adjoining farms to batten down the hatches. They knew that all hell was about to break loose, they could feel it in their bones.

Chapter 7

Doc Morrison watched as Maude helped Steve stand, walking him towards the stairs to take him back up stairs to one of the extra bedrooms. Steve's face was flushed, his eyes red and swollen. He had given Steve a sedative shot to calm him and help him sleep. After twenty minutes of crying the sedative had taken effect and Maude had convinced him to go upstairs. Steve looked over his shoulder at Diane's body as he mounted the stairs. He just shook his head and then bowed it and walked up the stairs with Maude's help. Doc buttoned Diane's blouse back up, and bent over and opened a drawer on the examination table. He took out a clean white sheet and covered Diane's body leaving her face uncovered.

He stared down into the face of a friend who he had no chance of saving. This was the worst part of being a doctor, loosing someone. He did not know how long he had stood there when Maude came to his side. Maude turned Herb to face her; he could not meet her steady gaze.

She folded him into her arms. "Don't beat yourself up Herbert, I saw the wound and there was nothing you could do to save her."

"I didn't even get a chance to try Maude. It was too late."

"Don't blame yourself, if it is anyone's fault it would be mind. I stood there chiding you in the hall when you should have been down here with her."

"Now Maude don't go blaming yourself, you didn't know. Did Steve tell you what happened?"

"Yes. It appears things have begun to unravel. Steve and Diane were leaving Wal-Mart and got in some sort of shoot out with some common

65

thugs. I guess you were right when you said things were going to get worse and we must prepare. I am sorry for berating you about it. Now go get the generator started and any other preparations that are needed. I will take care of Diane." She pushed Herb back and leaned over and kissed his forehead.

Herb smiled weakly and turned away to go get things ready. "Oh, I called the Sheriff's Office and told them. They said it maybe a day or two before anyone can come out. It seems there have been a number of shootings, robberies and the like. The Sheriff's Office is being overwhelmed with calls."

Maude gathered a bowl, washcloth and soap from the shelves. Filling the bowl with soap and water she set it on the instrument tray next to Diane's body. Uncovering Diane she gently took her clothes off and began to wash her body. When she was done she walked over to a shelf and pulled down a cardboard box that contained her sister's clothing that had been left at the house the summer before. She and Diane were about the same size. She opened the box and dug through it. Finding the knee length flower pattern summer dress she pulled it out.

She remembered Diane commenting to her sister how much she loved the dress. Maude dressed Diane in the dress. When she was finished she went back up stairs and fetched her make up case. She came back down stairs and put fresh makeup on Diane. When she was finished she looked down at her work. Diane looked beautiful and peaceful, this is the way she would have Steve should remember her. She covered Diane's body back up and went upstairs.

Herb fueled and primed the diesel generator. With a couple of tugs on the pull start the generator kicked to life. He turned and pulled the main from the circuit breaker box. After ten minutes he plugged the power cable into the secondary circuit breaker box. The lights came on around the property. It was now completely dark outside. Herb walked back to the front of the house and went to his truck. He started unloading food from the back. Maude stepped out onto the front covered porch.

"Could you use some help?" She inquired.

"Sure could. Once we finish unloading the truck I would like to get Steve's jeep around back and into the barn." The two worked for the next hour unloading and storing the food, ammunition, medical supplies, and bottled water. When they finished with their work Maude suggested dinner.

"That would be great Maude, I could eat a horse."

Maude rolled her eyes knowing that her husband wouldn't eat half of what she put before him. She walked to the kitchen and began preparing supper. Herb came in poured himself a glass of water.

"I'm going to find out what is going on in the news." Maude just nodded her head, Herb walked to the den. Once seated in his favorite chair Herb unlaced his work boots and kicked back in the recliner. He picked up the remote and turned on the TV. The channel was already set to his favorite news station. Herb lowered the footrest of his recliner and sat up. The picture was unclear a lot of snow played across the screen, with an occasional glitch in the picture. Herb did not recognize the news anchor, or the studio behind him. The network logo was there, but it did not look like the regular studio. There had not been any storms so why was the reception on his picture so bad?

He turned up the volume. "I'm Mike Sunderland, Dallas, Ft. Worth bureau. We again would like to remind everyone to stay calm and stay indoors. For those of you just tuning in here is the latest update. Thirty-five minutes ago we lost contact with our bureaus in several major cities. New York, Washington, and Los Angeles were the first one's we lost contact with...." The news anchor turned his head to someone off screen. "We are taking you know to a news conference with the new Speaker of the House, John Engle, who is coming to us from our affiliate in Denver."

The screen went blank for a moment and then the face of John Engle came into view. Herb took a quick glance at his watch and was amazed to see that it was 9:40 pm. He had not realized that he and Maude had been working so long.

"My fellow country men, I come here tonight to bring you grave news concerning the state of our fine Republic. I will get straight to the point and when I am finished I will not answer any questions. However you shall all soon receive all the information we have and what precautions you need to take.

As most of you know earlier this afternoon many major U.S. cities were hit with nerve agents from an unknown terrorist group or country. Two hours ago military labs came up with the origins of the nerve agents used in those cities. Those origins are from the communist countries of China and North Korea." A murmur came from the group of reporters before him. Engle continued.

"At 10:05 pm eastern time tonight, nuclear explosions were detected by NORAD in the following American cities: Washington D.C., New York, Miami, Los Angeles, Seattle, Portland Oregon, Portland Maine, San Diego, San Francisco, Houston, New Orleans, Galveston, Mobile, Tampa, Jacksonville Fl., Charleston, and Jacksonville NC. Philadelphia, and New Port News VA." Engle paused to pick up a glass of water from the podium. "Also further attacks have been carried out in the interior of the U.S. Twenty Seven hydroelectric dams across the U.S. have been attacked. There capacity to produce electricity has been obstructed. It is not know at this time how long repairs will take.

Many casualties have been taken in these attacks. At one of the dams the body of one of the terrorist was found. A local deputy had shot the terrorist. The nationality of this individual is Korean. Ordinance that was found on his body was of modern Chinese production."

Engle took another sip of water and set the glass down. He looked straight into the camera; anger filled the eyes of the onetime Stealth Bomber pilot. "There is more tragic news tonight ladies and gentlemen. On top of the deaths of millions of Americans, most of the Congress, Supreme Court, and the Vice President, and President are presumed dead." Engle let those words settle in. "Not ten minutes ago I was sworn in as President by Justice Delaney. If the President or Vice President is found alive I shall step down. Once I was sworn in as President I ordered an all out nuclear attack on Korea and China. A total 75 nuclear missiles were launched from submarines near those countries. Another 100 land based missiles were launched. I assure you nothing remains of any major city in those two countries.

Russia and other nuclear powers were notified before the launch. There have been confirmed nuclear explosions in many major European nations. The method of delivery for all of these nuclear attacks is believed to be back pack nukes. There have been no identified bomber, or missile launches detected by NORAD.

As we speak the Chairman of the Joint Chiefs of Staff is ordering all American troops home to assist in the rebuilding of our country. That is all I have for now. Thank you and God Bless each of you tonight." Engle stepped away from the podium and left the room.

Herb pushed the power button to the TV. He lowered his head all the energy seemed to have left his body. What had his nation done to deserve this he thought to himself?

Maude stood in the door to the den. When the new President finished his speech and Herb turned off the TV she watched her husband a moment. Then she spoke. "Herb, there is nothing you can do about what has happened. Come and eat, then we will get to bed. We will have a lot to do in the morning, and Steve will need help also. So you must not show weakness in front of him. It will only feed his own weaknesses that he is feeling right now."

Herb looked up at his wife. "You're right dear. I am coming." Herb got up and followed his wife to the dining room. They ate a satisfying meal despite the grave news that both had just learned about. Then they cleaned up the dishes. When they were done Maude got out two oil lamps she lit one and took it with her to the bedroom and prepared for a well-deserved rest. Herb went outside and cut the generator off. He then went and joined his wife in bed for a fitful night's rest.

The two woke early the next morning ate a cold breakfast and each went separate ways. Herb went out to the field got on his tractor and began picking up bales of hay out in the field. Maude organized their food supplies, and checked in on Steve from time to time.

Around 11:00 Steve woke. He was confused at first as he woke up in the strange bedroom. Then the memories of yesterday came to him like a slap across the face. Steve fell back to the pillows. He stared blankly at the ceiling above him. Finally after twenty minutes of reflection on the previous day's events, and happier times he and Diane had shared Steve rose from the bed and dressed.

He stared at the Glock 17 that lay on the nightstand staring at the pistol he had not used well enough or fast enough to save Diane. He heard the sound of dishes rattling coming from the kitchen. He walked towards the noise, leaving the Glock behind.

Maude turned as Steve walked into the kitchen. "You okay Steve?"

"Yes Maude, okay as I can be."

"Let me fix you a sandwich, alright."

"Sure I could use one." He said in a lifeless voice.

Maude turned and began making a couple of roast beef sandwiches, and poured a couple of glasses of lukewarm tea. Herb walked in the kitchen from his work out in the fields. He squeezed Steve's shoulder and sat at the table with him. Maude turned and noticed that her husband had walked in and began to fix another sandwich and poured another glass of tea. She brought the food and drinks over and sat with the two men.

They ate in silence for a while until Steve broke the gloomy silence. "Have you heard any further news Doc?"

Doc sat his sandwich down and filled Steve in on the events that had occurred after he went to bed. Steve sat dumbfounded.

"What about Diane?"

Maude looked at Steve. "Steve I called the Sheriff last night and they said it might be a couple of days before they can get here. That was before the attacks though. I tried to call this morning, but it seems all the phone lines are not working. I think we will have to bury Diane here if that is alright with you."

Steve nodded. "Where is she now?"

"She is still downstairs Steve." Maude answered.

Steve rose from his chair and walked to the basement. Maude and Doc followed him, Maude carrying an oil lamp. She lit it before they went down. Once downstairs Steve went to Diane's body, uncovered the sheet from her body. In the oil lamplight she looked beautiful, as if she were still alive. He looked at Maude when he took in the dress and makeup.

"I felt it was the least I could do for you two Steve."

"She looks beautiful Maude, thank you."

Doc and Maude stayed behind Steve and gave him time alone with his fiancé. "I guess you are right about having to bury her here. Steve said.

Doc stepped forward. "I already have picked out a site and dug out her resting place." Doc had used his small backhoe to complete the job after he had finished bailing the hay.

"Doc can we do it now? I don't think I can stand to have her here like this anymore."

"Sure Steve. Go on outside to the duck pond, her resting place is there beneath the big oak." Steve took one last look at his fiancé, and walked upstairs and then outside.

Doc followed and then brought his truck around to the garage door in the basement. Maude had Diane rapped in a homemade quilt. The two loaded her into the truck and took her to the pond. Once there Steve and Doc lowered her into the grave. Tears streaked down Steve's cheeks as he helped lower her.

When they were finished Doc asked them to bow their heads and he led them in prayer. Then Maude sung Amazing Grace in a beautiful voice that did not match her physical features. When they were done Steve and Maude walked back to the house and into the den. There Maude and Steve talked about the good memories each had of Diane. Doc got the backhoe out and buried the dirt over Diane's body. Then he too joined his wife and friend to remember.

The next several days Steve kept himself busy around Doc's farm. The TV quit receiving signals after the second day. The three had watched news reports from around the country and some from around the world. Russia took the opportunity of China being down on her knees to launch a full-scale attack. Both sides in the fierce engagements had used some tactical nukes. Pakistan and Indian had not launched nukes yet but they were engulfed in war.

Like Russia, South Korea took the opportunity to devastate what remained of North Korea's army. Civil unrest broiled throughout eastern and western Europe. The nations of Europe were headed down the slippery slope and the chances of them stopping were slim to none. Nothing had been heard out of the Dark Continent. It seemed as if Africa ceased to exist.

Economies in South and Central America, the Middle East and Asia went in the toilet. Military coupes were occurring around the world. Evil began to gain a firm toehold in the world as the good were stomped into oppression. There was no radio traffic on any of the radio stations in the area. Occasionally they would catch snippets of news at night from distant cities as the radio waves bounced around the atmosphere. Doc did not have a short wave radio. Steve had one back at his place but he had not even been there yet.

After a week and a half of hard manual labor, soul searching and coming to terms with the death of his fiancé. Steve had made a few decisions. Number one was that he would hold a special place in his heart for Diane and always remember her. The time for mourning was over and his life must go on. Number two was that he needed to get back to his place. Number three was that he would kill every gangbanging thug he came across no questions asked. If that made him just as evil as they were then so is it.

As Steve and the Morrison's sat at the kitchen table finishing up some fresh apple pie made by Maude Steve cleared his throat. Doc and Maude turned to look at him. "I just want to say that I am going to be going home in the morning. It is about time I quit imposing on you."

"Steve we've really enjoyed you being here and I don't feel as if you are imposing. Under the current circumstances don't you think we should stick together?" Doc asked.

"I just need to have some time alone for awhile. I am only a mile down the road and I will check in with you about every other day. Plus I have a couple of CB's back at my place we can use to communicate with each other

I thought about discussing with you the possibility of me moving in and bringing my stuff, but I decided for a short time I need to have some space. In a few weeks I think we should seriously discuss me hauling my stuff over here and setting up. It would mean we could help defend against anyone with ill will a lot better."

Just before Doc opened his mouth to argue that he should stay Maude placed her hand on his thigh and squeezed. The iron like grip closed around Doc's leg making him jump in his seat. Steve hid a smile that played across his face by looking down at the remnants of his pie.

Then Maude spoke up. "Steve that sounds just like what you need to do. Do you want to leave the stuff you purchased from Wal-Mart here with us or are you going to take it with you? We have plenty of room in the pantry and it only makes sense that if you are coming back you won't have to unload and load it all twice."

"Yeah I had planned on leaving most of it. I was just going to take a few cases of canned food with me."

They then discussed a few other matters that would need to be taken care of for Steve's return. They also agreed that Doc would ride to Steve's when he left and pick up one of the CB's. Communication in his absence could mean life or death to either Steve or Maude and Doc. Then each took an oil lantern and went to bed.

The next morning Steve followed by Doc in his truck went to his place. They checked the area and nothing seemed to be disturbed. They went inside and Doc picked up the CB. After some idle chit chat Doc left. Once Doc left Steve went to the kitchen and pulled out a dusty bottle of Jack Daniels. He poured himself a stiff drink, picked up a map of the city of Florence and sat at the kitchen table. Steve studied the areas where the cities housing projects and the more seedy side of town. After finishing his drink, Steve went and sat in his large leather chair. Diane had called it his throne. The thought of Diane made his heart ache but he pushed the feeling aside. It was time to plot vengeance, not reminisce about the past. There would be time for that later, after the fire of hate had been quenched.

Chapter 8

Dan "Spider" Rostenkowskie tightened the oil filter on big 440 Hemi. Once he was sure it was on good and tight he rolled out from underneath the big black Road Runner. He stood back and gazed at the car. It shimmered in the shop lights. On the hood he had painted a huge black widow spider. He had got the car after getting out of prison in 1999. He had done five years for robbery. The police had screwed up on the case and he had got off on the kidnapping and rape charges. It was the first time he had ever been caught for his numerous rapes and robberies.

His parole officer had allowed him to move to Molten, Alabama to work at his uncle's garage. It was a shame that his aunt and uncle had died when the brakes on their truck had failed. He was the only living relative so he inherited the business. He smiled to himself, after all their death's were only business.

Spider was a hell of a mechanic and could make anything run, and run well. The bonus to running the business was that he could laundry his drug sale money through his all cash business. There was also an additional advantage of getting names and addresses of his clients when they filled out their work request forms. He just loved it when farmer Smith or whoever would come in and ask for a tune-up before they left town on a vacation.

He had a small crew that would clean up on burglary and theft. Strip down farm equipment and part the pieces out. He had not been able to commit his favorite crime though. Rape was something that was hard to get away with in a hick town. "Man Me Miss Chicago." He said to himself, as a flood of memories flowed through his mind. He missed all those trashy women who had just begged for man like him to slap them around, and show them a glimpse into his carnal fantasies.

"Yep, hard to get away with rape when everyone is always noticing what a stud you are." Spyder spun around in a 180 and stopped with his feet shoulder width apart. He stared into the eight foot by eight-foot mirror on the shop wall. He had installed it not only to look at himself, but his car also. He liked to look at himself with his car sitting behind him. Every time he looked at himself in the mirror he felt he resembled one of those posters for the movies, the tough guy and his car.

He stared at himself now. He started at his feet on which he wore a pair of black engineer boots. Faded blue jeans came next, followed by a white t-shirt, and out of his shirt were his diminutive milk white arms with prison tattoos. His hands were small and feminine. In his own sick mind he felt his arms were like steel cables, his hands dexterous the word love was printed across one set of fingers, and hate on the other.

Then his favorite part, his face and hair, a teardrop was tattooed by the corner of his right eye. Squiggy, from the 1970's "Lavern and Shirley" show flashed through his mind. That's what the kids in high school had called him, especially the girls.

Of course revenge was sweet. He had shown two cheerleaders the time of their life on graduation night. They would carry the scars for the rest of their miserable lives, both mental and physical. His mind flashed to the vision of the two tied spread eagle, nude, in a burnt out building. After he had finished he had caught two wolf spiders and tormented the spiders till they began to bight the girls.

He shook the pleasant thoughts from his mind; it was time to find out what was going on in the rest of the world. Plus the Carmichaels had left for Mobile and he had to check the list of items that his fencer wanted from the home. Spider went to the office turned on the TV to CNN, and hit the mute button. He then opened the left hand drawer and pulled out his fixings. He gingerly poured the white powder on the mirror in four neat rows. Taking a dollar bill from his pocket he rolled it into a straw and placed it by the mirror. Snorting the coke into his nose he felt an immediate rush flush over his body followed by a wonderful high. He then picked up the phone and called the crew. While he dialed the phone numbers he set himself up four more lines to snort.

Once he got hold of his right hand man he advised him of the score that was to go down tonight and gave out instructions. That done he picked up the dollar bill and snorted all four lines of coke. The wave of euphoria washed through him again. After a few minutes the initial rush left his body. He reached into his shirt pocket and pulled out a joint. He lit up the weed and leaned back in his chair, and turned up the volume. Things were getting bad according to the anchor. When the anchor started talking about all the biological attacks and dams that had been hit he jerked up out of the chair. He stared at the scenes of riots that flooded through the streets of the major cities. He thought back to the events of the past two days. He realized that everyone was buying up supplies and where in a restrained panic here in Moulton. Then he thought about all the conversations with his customers talking about needing their rigs fixed up "just in case." He wondered how busy the ten-man police force was.

Spider reached over to his telephone, picked it up and called the police dispatch. "Molten Police how may I help you?" A female voice answered.

"Yeah, this is Spider Rostenkowskie, down at Spider's Speed Shop. I just wanted to report that I saw a couple of suspicious guys over behind the feed store. Could you send an officer to check it out?"

"Sir it will be awhile before we can send a unit over. We are swamped and half the force has called in sick."

"Okay thanks, I will keep an eye on the guys till the cop gets here." Spider hung up the phone. Could this be it? Law enforcement was swamped all over the nation, even here in little old Molten. Could he chance it?

"By God, I will give it a shot. It's been to long and I need it." Spider got out of the chair and walked to his car and got in. Once in he pushed a button on the dashboard and the garage door began to open. Spider cranked up the big Hemi. He slowly backed the car once the door opened. Once out of the garage he pushed the button again and the door began to close. He eased onto the street; it was time to find him a woman and a good time.

Spider looked at himself in the rearview mirror and ran his fingers through his greased up hair. He leaned over and opened the glove box. He slid out the nickel-plated Colt .357 and placed it on the seat beside him. Then he picked up his cell phone. "Pete, this is Spider." He said into the phone.

"I got everyone together Spider just waiting on you." Pete said his country drawl grating on Spider's nerves.

"Look, I won't be coming tonight. I have something to take care of. Just do the job and get the stuff over to Mike's place in Colbert County."

"No problem man. What have you got going?" Pete asked.

"That's none of your damned business you stupid fucking hey seed. Now get loaded up and get to work." Spider punched the end call button and tossed the phone into the passenger seat. He headed towards the McDonalds where the teens liked to cruise around and hang out.

Charlotte Hanna cussed as she hit the steering wheel of her pickup truck. Steam boiled out from under the hood. She got out and walked around to the front of the truck. She popped the hood on the old Ford and stepped back as the steam rolled out. "Crap, Terry is going to kill me. Well I guess I better call him and let him know his truck is dead." Charlotte was a beautiful red head with green eyes.

She had just graduated and had started attending the University of North Alabama in Florence. Terry, her 24 year old brother had graduated from Auburn and returned home to help work the farm. He had let her use his old 1971 F100 to go back and forth to school. The deal was that she was to maintain the truck if she was going to use it. Well she had not. And he was probably going to beat her to a pulp like he did when they were kids. He loved this piece of crap truck. He had bought it when he was sixteen and taken it to Auburn with him when he graduated from High School. Charlotte dialed her brother's cell phone. The phone rang several times then his voice mail picked up. She left a message and told him where she was and what had happened to his truck.

She then called the house. No answer there either. Everyone must still be out in the fields or in the barn. She left a message hoping her dad would get it before Terry, and come to her rescue. Charlotte walked around to the rear of the truck and dropped the tailgate down. She hopped up and sat down. "Well nothing to do but wait." She said.

As Spider came to the intersection he looked over to the big parking lot by McDonalds. A green Ford truck sat in the middle of the lot with steam rolling out from under the hood. A sexy looking red head stood with a cell phone to one ear and her left hand on her hip. The girl then walked to the rear of the truck in a noticeable amount of disgust as she slapped the cell phone closed. She dropped the tailgate and grabbed a seat.

He smiled, his crooked teeth bared like fangs. "Well, well, well it looks like it is time for the Spider to feast." He turned the car into the lot and made a slow beeline for the stranded girl, running his fingers through his greased hair, and checking himself out in the mirror.

Charlotte looked up as she heard the rumble of a car approaching. It was that Beetle or Bug, guy. She could never remember his name. Her dad took his trucks to this guy to work on. The car slowed to a stop. Bug guy got and ran his fingers through his greased hair. "What a freak." She thought.

"Hey pretty lady. Got engine problems?" Spyder said. He cocked his head to the side and raised an eyebrow. He had also hooked his thumbs through his belt loops. He knew he had to look damn cool standing there like a stud next to his car.

"Ya think?" What a dork. Why does her dad take his trucks to this guy? He looked like a 16 year old trying to be 30.

Spider ambled over to the truck. He spotted the leak in the radiator. "She is finished for the day darling. You going to need a ride home, or is someone coming for you?"

Charlotte sighed. "I can't get hold of anyone at the house. I'm sure someone will return my call and come get me."

"You might not want to wait; it's starting to get dark. Of course I'm sure you can take care of yourself though. Probably got nothing to worry about none of them rioters will mess with you." Spider said as he walked up closer to the girl.

"What rioters? She asked, truly confused.

"Haven't you been listening to the news?" Spider asked as he put an incredulous look on his face.

"Well yeah I heard about them but those are all in the big cities."

Spider thought quickly, and spun his lie. "Naw, have you seen a Moulton Cop all day? They're all over in Florence helping with the riots there. The thugs around here know this and are starting to get frisky." It was a lie, but a pretty good one. He did not even know if there were riots in Florence, but it was a reasonable assumption.

"Well now that you mention it, I haven't seen one all day." Charlotte sat down on the tailgate of the old Ford.

Spider sat down beside her. He leaned his ferret like face close to hers. She looked around at the growing darkness. Bug man had just got her imagination stirring. What if they rioted here? Could she make it home in a riot?

Spider could sense and see the indecisiveness play across her face. "Come on girl. I do work for your daddy. You think your daddy would bring his trucks to someone who is untrustworthy? Heck you know who I am, and where my shop is. I would be crazy to do something to you now wouldn't I?"

Charlotte thought for a second and took a second look around. Heck all it will be is a ten-minute ride. Surely her father wouldn't deal with some kind of psycho. "Okay, I will take the lift." Maybe she could get home before Terry listened to his voice mail or checked the answering machine. Then daddy could come get the truck and take care of the problem.

They got up off the tailgate and got into the Road Runner. Spider drove from the lot and headed west on U.S. Hwy 157. Spider had a look of satisfaction on his face as he drove down the highway. He couldn't wait to show this uppity girl what a man was like; he had seen the look of disgust briefly cross her face when he first got out of the car. It had been just like the look the cheerleaders gave him everyday back in high school.

Charlotte looked back over her left shoulder as they drove past the road that led to her family farm. "Hey you just missed the turn."

Spider looked over at her "I know a short cut to your place."

After another ten minutes of driving Charlotte started getting a little worried. "I think you need to turn around and go back the other way." She looked at him; his face had an eerie green tint to it from the glow of the instrument panel. A shiver went up her spin.

"I told you, I know a short cut to your place." Spider turned his head back to the road to look for the turn off to the old abandoned barn. Charlotte knew something was not right now.

"Take me home right now! And how did you know where I lived. I never told you?" An edge of panic crept into her voice.

Spider reached down beside the door panel and driver seat with his left hand and grabbed the Colt. He pulled it up and pointed it at her in one fluid motion. "Shut up, you're ruining my train of thought." If it had not been nighttime Spider could have seen her face turn white. He did however see the fear come over her face. "Now that I have your attention go ahead and strip."

Charlotte hesitated for only a fraction of a second and Spider suddenly lashed out and backhanded her with the pistol across the forehead. The blow knocked her head back into the glass of the window and doorframe.

He put the gun to her head. "Do it! Don't make this harder than it has to be. You might find that you like it."

Charlotte did as she was ordered and took off her clothes and piled them in her lap. She sat there meekly with her head bowed as her body trembled in fear. Tears rolled down her face as she tried to comprehend what was happening to her.

Spider found the turn off for the barn. He cut the wheel left and traveled down the bumpy dirt road. Several minutes later he came to a clearing that had an old dilapidated barn sitting in the middle of it. The doors were open and Spider pulled the Hemi inside. He kept the gun pointed at her as he came to a stop. With his left hand he turned the ignition off, and then put the car in park. He then opened the door and started to back out, the pistol still pointed at her. "Now slide across to me, and no funny business bitch."

Charlotte complied, tears raced down her cheeks and her bottom lip quivered. She kept telling herself to stay calm, quit crying and figure a way out of this. She had to be strong, and smart like her daddy taught her to. Once out of the car he tied her to a workbench with some rope he pulled out of the trunk of the car. He laid his pistol on the bench and took off his clothes. Then the nightmare began. It started with a quick, unexpected punch to her stomach. The night wore on for what seemed like hours. The beatings and the violations of her body seemed to go on for ever. She ended up laying on the dirt floor, the hideous man laid atop her pumping himself into her. Finally his body shuddered and he was through. He rolled off and retrieved his clothes.

He put his clothes back on and picked up the pistol. "You liked what the Spider did to you didn't you?" he said, his face inches from her ear.

He grabbed her by the hair and shook her head up and down. "That's what I thought."

Charlotte stared at the pistol in his hand. She had to think fast she knew her time was almost over. The man would never let her live, she knew who he was, and where he worked. "Thanks for teaching me about what a man can do Spider." She was trying to play on his inferiority complex she was sure he had. Spider was about to cock the pistol and shoot the girl but stopped at her words.

"What did you say?"

"I said thank you. You're so, so…tough. I never had a man like you. I think I liked the way you took control of me." When Charlotte looked at his face she knew she was gaining ground.

"You want to meet up again sometime." He asked he was a bit confused by the girl's words. Usually they would scream and cry and tell him how sick he was or would beg him to let them live and he would shoot them.

"Sure, anytime you want to Spider." Please God let this work she prayed. Because if it does I swear I'm going to get this creep back so he can't do it again.

Spider's confusion grew, but so did his desire to have a woman submissive to his every pleasure. This had never happened before. This girl liked what he did to her. Maybe he had found a soul mate. "When?" Is all he said, almost in desperation and hope. He knew he was taking a chance, but this might be for real. Hell what were the chances of him going out hunting for a woman and finding one so beautiful and possibly now so willing. It had to be destiny.

Charlotte could see that the sick freak actually was buying it. "How about tomorrow some time, I could come by the shop about lunchtime."

Spider was elated; he tucked the pistol into his waistband, then reached into his pocket and pulled out his pocketknife. He flipped the blade open and cut the ropes that bound her hands, and stepped back. He motioned with the knife "Get in the car and I will take you home."

Charlotte walked unsteadily to the car and opened the door. She took out her clothes and dressed, then sat down. Her body ached all over.

Spider hopped in almost like a teenage kid happy about the events of his first date. To Spider's sick and twisted mind this had become his first date. He couldn't wait for more. No more worrying about cops, and hunting for prey. The prey would just come to him now. He backed the car out of the barn and drove towards Charlotte's house.

Just before reaching the road that lead to Charlotte's house, Charlotte spoke up. "Let me out here Spider."

Spider looked over at her, wariness replaced his elated expression. He stopped the car. "Why do you want out here? Shouldn't I meet your parents if we are going to be an item?" He said his right hand dropping to the butt of the pistol in his waist band.

Charlotte had thought about this the whole way home. "It's kind of late Spider. How will I explain that my truck broke down and it took me two hours to get home, and I suddenly have a new boyfriend. Besides I have this mark across my forehead." She pointed to the welt left by Spider's pistol. "I'm going to tell them I walked home and cut through the woods and hit my head on a branch or something."

Spider's face and mood immediately returned to being euphoric. "You're one smart girl." He reached over and grabbed her by the throat and pulled her to him. He planted a slobbery kiss on her lips then released his grasp and shoved her back. "See ya tomorrow."

Charlotte rubbed her throat as she backed out of the car. "Yeah, I will see you tomorrow at lunch." She got out of the car and began to walk home. Spider pulled the car back onto the road and drove off.

"Tomorrow you freak, you're going to pay for what you did." A tear spilled down her cheek.

Chapter 9

Ted Hanna, his wife Sheryl, and son Terry listened to news in stunned silence. They were all sitting in the living room eating supper. With the world rapidly changing around them they had took to eating in front of the TV. They did not have much time for TV or radio while working on the farm. So dinnertime was a time to catch up on events across the nation, and world. Ted looked at his watch and then his son. "What time did Charlotte say she was leaving Florence?"

Terry took a bite of the roast beef, chewed for a second and with a mouth half full of food he answered, "She should be here anytime now dad." He went back to devour more food. Terry like his father was a tall rangy man. He wasn't overly muscled but years of hard work on the farm made his arms and legs look like steel cables.

These new incidents that the news spoke of worried Ted. Things were getting rough quick. "Terry how much ammo do we have?"

"I don't know a few hundred for each gun, I guess. Why do you ask?"

"Son things aren't looking so hot. I think we are about to be knee deep in shit. How are we set for reloading supplies?"

"Well I guess I can set you at ease dad. We have a total of 90 pounds of powder total for rifle, shotgun, and pistol. Probably about 300 pounds of #2 shot, tons of shells and wads. We got a couple of thousand rounds, primers, and shells for every caliber we got. So if you're worried about ammo you shouldn't." Terry said continuing to eat as he gave his father a run down on the shooting supplies.

The two Hanna men were avid shooters, hunters, and down right gun enthusiast. They had a large collection of bolt-action rifles, lever actions, revolvers, semi-auto pistols, and shotguns. A week did not go by that they did not shoot at least 100 rounds out of one type of weapon or another.

"Maybe you should run into town tomorrow and get some more ammo, and reloading supplies. We may not have enough. Get some new cleaning kits too."

"If things go bad it won't be all about guns and bullets you two logger heads." Sheryl cut in. "Without food, water, and medicine you're sunk."

"So how are we set on food and stuff mom?" Ted asked.

Sheryl rolled her eyes and replied good-naturedly. "Boy you're as dense as your daddy sometimes. You not only got his good looks, you unfortunately got his brains." Sheryl loved to tease the two men about how dense they were. Of course they weren't. Both Ted and Terry had graduated with honors at Auburn getting Agriculture degrees. Sheryl continued. "We do live on a farm so food is not a problem." She then grew more serious. "However, we could stand to use a good deal more in the medical field, so I would suggest a trip to the drug store instead of your second home down at the gun shop."

"Can you take care of that tomorrow Sheryl?" Ted asked.

"Yeah, I guess so. I will take Charlotte with me; I would like to spend some time with her. We have hardly got a chance to talk since she headed to UNA. Speaking of Charlotte I sure wish she would get home. Ted have you checked the answering machine in the office to see if she called?"

"No. I will in a little while. She probably stopped by a friend's on the way home."

Charlotte walked the mile down the county road to her family farm. When she reached it she walked around the back of the house to the barn. Once inside she turned on the bare light bulb that hung over the deep sink. She turned on the cold water and let it run into her cupped hands. She cleaned off the dried blood on her face and fixed her hair. She wanted to be as presentable as possible. There was no way she wanted to let her family know what had happened. The cold water had helped reduce the puffiness of her eyes. When she felt she was ready she walked to the house. She went through the kitchen and heard the TV going in the living room. She headed that way. As she entered her parents and brother looked away from the TV.

"Where have you been, I was getting worried her mother asked?"

Ted peered closely at her face. "What the heck happened to your forehead?"

"Sorry folks, the truck overheated and I had to walk home. I left a message on Terry's voice mail, and one on the answering machine, but no one returned my calls." Terry glanced down at the cell phone clipped to his belt. The cell phone was turned off.

Sheryl cast a menacing look over her shoulder at Ted. Ted held up his hands, "Sorry Sheryl I forgot to check the messages." The look Sheryl gave Ted told him he was definitely going to be sorry later.

Sheryl reached out and touched her daughter's injured forehead. "What happened? Did you have a wreck or something too?"

Charlotte pulled from her mother's reach, "No I cut through the woods and fell down an old creek bed and hit my head on a branch." Charlotte hated to deceive her family. The old saying came to her mind "What a wicked web we weave when we practice to deceive." She had to deceive them though, because she had her own web she was going to weave for Spider.

"I'm going to soak in the tub for awhile and then get some sleep." Charlotte put her best fake smile on her face and left the room. Once in the bathroom she stripped off her clothes and filled the tub with steaming hot water. She looked at herself in the full-length mirror that hung behind the door. Bruises had already started to appear where Spider had punched, and kicked her. Other parts she could not see hurt worse. She did not want to think about those. She just wanted to wash away Spider's touch, get some sleep and then teach him a lesson in the morning.

Once the tub was full she got in and scrubbed her body until her skin was pink and close to raw from the scrubbing she gave herself. Then she pulled the plug and got out and toweled off. Charlotte wrapped the towel around herself. She reached up and opened the medicine cabinet. She pulled out the bottle of Lorecet's the doctor had prescribed her after a car accident six months ago. She popped two of the 750 mg tablets, filled a glass of water and drank them down. She bent over and picked up her clothes and went to her room where she collapsed on the bed. Charlotte pulled the comforter over her body and fell asleep.

Charlotte woke the next morning around 10:00. Her body still ached but she put those thoughts to the side, she had to pay someone back today. Charlotte dressed in a pair of tight fitting jeans, a tank top, and a pair of flip-flops. She walked over to her window and saw her father and brother at work in the fields. Charlotte walked into the kitchen where her mother stood at the sink canning fruit. "Mom where is the picnic basket?" Charlotte inquired.

"What do you need that for sweetheart?"

"I told Kathy I would come by and we would have a picnic." Charlotte lied.

"It's up in the pantry dear." Sheryl said without turning to look at her daughter. Charlotte retrieved the basket and set it on the counter. She then began to make sandwiches and poured fresh lemonade into mason jars and capped them. She threw in some chips and cloth red and white-checkered napkins into the picnic basket. Charlotte heard her father and brother talking outside and then the doors to her dad's truck opening and closing, then the truck starting up. She glanced out the window and saw them pulling onto the gravel drive and then out onto the road and head towards town. "Where are they headed mom?"

"They're going to get your truck." Sheryl answered.

Charlotte closed the lid on the basket. "Can I borrow your car to go to Kathy's mom?"

Sheryl looked at her daughter "Sure the keys are in my bedroom. How is your head sweetheart?"

Charlotte unconsciously touched her forehead. It still throbbed. "Oh, it feels fine. I almost forgot about it." Charlotte lied again. Charlotte took the basket and went to her mother's room. Once in the room she glanced out the door to make sure her mother wasn't going to walk in on her. Once satisfied she would be safe from interruption she placed the basket on the bed. She walked over to her father's gun cabinet and opened the two doors. Hanging on pegs above the long guns were approximately fourteen pistols. She found the one she was looking for, her father's S&W .44 caliber Mountain Gun.

She checked the cylinder to see if it was loaded, she knew it wouldn't be, but one must be careful. Charlotte liked the pistol, and she shot it quite regularly. Her father and Terry weren't the only Hanna's who liked to shoot. She went back to the cabinet and opened the bottom drawer. It was filled with various boxes of ammunition. She picked up a box of .44 hollow points and dumped out six rounds. She replaced the box and closed the drawer. Turning back to the bed she loaded the pistol. Charlotte opened the lid of the picnic basket and took out a napkin. She rapped the pistol in it and placed it back inside. She picked up the basket and her mother's keys.

She shouted to her mom, "I'm leaving mom, I will see you in a bit."

"Have fun sweetheart, and tell Kathy hello for me." Sheryl called from the kitchen.

Charlotte got into the car and drove to town. Spider was sitting at the front desk when he saw the Buick pull in the parking lot. Despite being worried that Charlotte had lied and would call the cops, the world had turned upside down. Several cities had been nuked. He was going to have to steal a dump load of supplies if things got worse. Maybe he would just take over the Carmichael's they had been in Mobile and it was supposed to have been nuked.

Spider glanced up again as he heard the car door shut. A smile played across his face when he saw the red haired beauty coming to the front door carrying a picnic basket. His smile broadened when she came into the room. "It hadn't been a fantasy she wanted me last night and still does." He said to himself.

Charlotte placed the basket on the chair by the door. She had to make this look good and seem like it was for real if she was to pull it off. She put on her best smile. "Hey handsome, remember me?" Charlotte quickly walked up to him wrapped her arms around him and kissed him full on the mouth.

Spider held her by the waist and pushed her back a bit. "You're damn right I remember you baby."

Charlotte still had her hands on his shoulders, arms stretched straight out extended. Suddenly Spider snapped a punch into her stomach.

Charlotte dropped to her knees clutching her stomach, and trying to gain her breath. After a few seconds Spider stepped back, smiled and put his hands on his hips. "You like that didn't you?"

Charlotte composed herself. At first she thought he had seen through her deception. Now she realized this was Spider's sick way of saying "I love you." She looked up and put a smile on her face. "You know I like it baby."

Spider started to step around her "What's in the basket?"

Charlotte grabbed his leg and stopped him. "I'll show you." Charlotte stood and Spider stepped back. She walked over to the picnic basket and opened it. "I brought sandwiches, lemonade, some chips and a special toy for you."

"What kind of toy?" Spider raised his head a bit as if to look over her and into the basket.

Charlotte turned around. "I'll show you, but first I got to get you warmed up baby." Charlotte almost puked looking into his pasty white face, with a weasel grin plastered across it. "You got to do what I say though and when I start I want you to slap me around."

The weasel grin broadened, as she knew it would. Spider almost danced in place in anticipation. This was greater than his wildest dreams. "What do I do, what do I do!" He was close to groveling.

"Drop your pants and underwear and get ready for me to go down on my knees." Charlotte said this as seductively as possible. What she really wanted to do was puke. She watched as Spider dropped his pants and stained underwear.

"Now put your hands behind your back so I can see it all." Spider complied; she was in complete control of this piece of trash now. "Now let me get your toy."

Spider watched as Charlotte turned and reached into the basket. She came out with something that was wrapped by a napkin. "Oh baby, you got me so hyped up! I'm glad I didn't dust your ass last night. "If she didn't hurry he would bust right then and there he thought to himself.

Charlotte turned to him with a smile on her face. The pistol was still under the napkin as she turned back to him. "Are you ready baby?" Charlotte said. Charlotte's web was now almost complete, and the spider was going to be trapped in it.

"You know it, now come on over here and show me how you like it."

Charlotte pulled the napkin from the big pistol and let the napkin fall to the floor. She raised the pistol and pointed it right between his eyes, which were now the size of saucers. "This is what I like." The old quote crossed her mind again. "Oh, what a wicked web we weave when we practice to deceive."

Spider raised his hands. "Come on now baby let's be careful with that thing." Spider started to bend over to pull up his pants.

"Spider stand back up and put your hands behind your back." Spider hesitated for a moment. Charlotte cocked back the hammer and the cylinder rotated. Spider quickly complied. He started to sob.

"You're going to die today Spider baby." Piss drained from his small, shrunken member. Charlotte smiled and shook her head as she took a step closer.

Spider started to shake. When Spider closed his eyes to push more tears from them Charlotte struck. She planted her foot right into his groin. The power of the blow dropped Spider into the fetal position. He landed on his face with a wet smack. Spider puked several times and began to dry heave.

"You like that didn't you?" She mocked. When she didn't receive an answer she struck out again. This time she landed a kick to his face. "Get up!" She screamed.

Spider pushed his body into the kneeling position. Tears streaked his dirty face; puke caked his shirt and thighs. Spider looked up at her, "Please don't hurt me Charlotte."

"You know things are different today. On the way over here I heard on the news that several cities got nuked. There is chaos in the streets, looting, killing, and RAPING!" Charlotte lashed out with her pistol striking Spider across the bridge of the nose. Blood cascaded from his nose. His hands left his groin and went to his face. Blood oozed through his fingers. Though in pain his fear filled eyes were still locked with Charlotte's.

"Our President is gone, our Congress, and maybe our nation. When something like that happens predators come out to find their prey. That's what you did to me. And the way you did it convinced me I wasn't the first was I?" Her voice had lowered now to a low hoarse pitch.

Spider still holding his face with one had his groin with the other shook his head back and forth.

"Please don't hurt me Charlotte, please." Spider started to raise, his buttocks coming off of his calf muscles.

Charlotte lashed out with the pistol again. A gash appeared on the side of Spider's head just above the left ear. "Stay down freak, cause that's were you going to stay!" Charlotte took a deep breath and pointed the pistol at his head. Images of the previous night's brutality danced in her mind. "You'll never hurt me again, or anyone else for that matter. Since the Supreme Court is gone I will pass your judgment." Spider's eyes grew wider if that was at all possible.

"Your sentence is going to be death. To bad it has to be quick." Charlotte pulled the trigger. The big gun boomed, .44 slug ripped into Spider's groin.

Spider's hands grasped what was left of his groin, a high pitched scream emitted from his lips. "Oops look like I am not so good at aiming. Maybe this next one will hit you in the right spot and put you down for good." Charlotte said, a sadistic smile playing across her lips.

Charlotte took her time and aimed at Spider's head as he rolled back and forth on the garage floor. Spider looked up at her, his eyes beseeching her for mercy.

"See ya around shit bag." Charlotte pulled the trigger and the big gun spat out another piece of lead, and Spider Rostenkowskie was no more. Charlotte turned from the scene of carnage, and went over to the basket. She put the pistol in the basket and picked it up. She had never killed before, had never thought about doing it. But she felt she could live with it. The man deserved what he got, and no one else would get what he gave. Charlotte walked out to her mom's car and got in. Maybe she would have that lunch with Kathy after all. Charlotte drove off into a future that was now filled with uncertainty.

Chapter 10

Amos Brown slowed his new tractor; and he gazed out over his farm. It was a small farm of only forty acres, but it was his. Amos took off his straw hat and ran his black craggy hand through his close cut graying hair, and then situated the old worn straw hat back on is head. He hopped down off his tractor. It wasn't exactly new, only around twenty years old but it ran well. He smiled as he pulled a shovel and tin pin off the back of the tractor.

He turned to look at the fence line near the barn. There stood Festus, his mule, companion, and four-legged tractor of eighteen years. "I told you if you bit my butt again I would buy me one of these here tractors you dumb old mule."

Festus stared at him, his only response was to lift his tale and deposit some natural fertilizer.

"You're one nasty old bastard Festus." Amos turned and dropped the metal tin on the ground. He dug out a 12"by12" piece of earth and threw it in the pan. He then started sifting through it with his fingers. He was looking for earthworms. It was an old trick his granddaddy had taught him. It was used to find out how fertile and organic the soil was. It was also a good way to get fishing bait. One or two earthworms meant that the soil needed organic help. Five to nine worms meant you were getting there but you needed more organic matter. Ten or more and you had healthy, biological soil.

Amos dug out about sixteen earthworms. Looking back over his shoulder he shouted to Festus. "Well at least you're good for something you mangy old jackass." Amos used Festus's manure and that of his little burrow Midget as fertilizer. Picking up the shovel and pan he dumped the dirt and worms and placed the shovel and pan on the back of the tractor. Then he hopped up into the seat. Well not exactly hopped, his knees popped and back creaked. He was 63 after all.

Pushing the ignition switch, the tractor coughed a couple of times and then started. He exited the field and drove over to the barn. Once there he maneuvered to the new side stall he had built for it.

He grinned at the memory of seeing old Festus standing in the new stall when he pulled up in his truck with the tractor in tow. That old fool of a mule thought he had done and got him a new stall. It only took him twenty minutes to get Festus out the stall when he realized it was for his replacement.

Amos shook his head a smile creased his face and he got down. He walked into the barn and there stood Midget near the canvas bag filled with old apples. "I see you're waiting on a treat Midget." Amos walked over and scratched Midget behind the ears. He reached in and got out three apples. The first he fed Midget by hand, the other two he dropped off at his feet. Scratching him behind the ears he walked towards the back of the barn, and out the back doors.

Festus stood beside the doors near the water hose and spigot. For the past fifteen years he would give Festus a wash down after a day in the field, followed up by a good brushing. Festus loved the ritual.

Amos stopped and pushed his straw hat back on his head. "Festus, you ain't done a lick of work in two weeks, and you still expecting me to wash you down? I done told you, you are heading for the glue factory. Now leave me alone."

Festus stamped a foot and nudge Amos with his nose. Amos grinned, "Well alright I guess that they like to have the mules clean down at the glue factory fore they buy them."

Festus gave Amos an indignant look and turned sideways and got ready for his favorite part of the day. Amos filled the bucket with water and soap and cursed the mule for all he was worth. Despite his words he loved his mule and treated it like a king. The bucket full, he sprayed Festus down and then began to scrub him. Once done with the washing he took out a wire brush and brushed the beast down. He soon finished, and coiled up the hose and hung the bucket on a nail that stuck out of the wall. Amos walked to the house tired but satisfied with the day.

Once inside he took off his work boots and straw hat. He then walked over to the deep sink that sat on the left wall of the mudroom. He turned the water on and picked up his homemade bar of soap and began to wash his hands. When he finished he walked into the kitchen and began to prepare his supper. He filled his plate with pork chops, collards, corn, and mash potatoes, and then poured himself a tall glass of sweet tea. He carried his supper to the den and sat down in his chair and placed his meal and drink on the TV tray.

Picking up the remote he turned on the TV for the evening news. The news was not good. He watched as news reporter pointed out bodies being laid out in the street, the victim of some kind of gas attack. He didn't like what he was seeing. America was coming apart at the seams, riots in the streets, troops and police at checkpoints almost like the old Soviet Union.

After the national broadcast a man from FEMA came on the air and explained what one needed in case of a gas attack, civil disorder, and brought up the fact that everyone should have a 72-hour kit in his possession. Amos guffawed at that. Them fools at the federal government telling folks that if things got bad all they would need was an extra 72 hours worth of supplies. Anyone with any sense knew that if it got bad enough for a 72-hour kit the government wouldn't be there for probably seventy-two days.

Amos's larder had enough food to last him a year, more if he rationed it. Amos muted the TV and took a long pull on his glass of tea. He put down the glass and reached in the front of his overalls and pulled out his pipe and tobacco. Fixing the bowl and lighting it he leaned back to think about what, if anything he needed. As far as food was concerned he was well stocked. Water was not a problem; he had several hand pump wells around the farm, and all of them with potable water. If the wells went dry there was the creek at the back of the property, plus his catfish pond. He had plenty of herbs in his green house that could take care of a lot of minor medical things.

Now what about defense? Amos only had a sawed off double barrel shotgun. He had about 300 rounds #4 shot, 100 rounds of 00, and another 40 rounds of slugs. He would have to be careful about how he used the rounds. Not only would he need them for hunting if things got bad, he might have to use it on a few two legged creatures too.

His house sat off the old county road up on a hill. It was hidden from the road by a thick stand of trees that encircled his entire property. Inside the tree line was all-open except for the small orchard of apple, peach, and pear trees on the south side of his property. Though hidden from view he was vulnerable to folks with rifles. The shotgun was great close in, but wasn't worth spit if someone was taking pot shots at him from the trees. Maybe he would go to town tomorrow and buy a bolt gun, or that Ruger Mini 14 he saw at Wal-Mart. Of course it might be quicker to drive down the road and see Steve Roberts; it was possible he would have a rifle for sale.

Amos thought about how he and Steve Roberts had met. It had been what, two years ago? His old Chevy C-10 pickup had broken down not a quarter of a mile from his house. He had been under the hood of the truck putting on the new belts when the big blue Ford had pulled up in front of his truck. Three cornbread fed white boys had got out of the cab. "Got engine problems boy?" the driver said. Amos had turned with a large open-ended wrench taken out of the toolbox when the boy had spoken the words.

The driver let out a snicker and looked to his companions. "It looks like we got us a frisky one fellas." The two passengers just smiled and advanced on him. The tall blonde was the first to take a swing. Amos had ducked under the punch and driven his fist into his stomach, and followed it up by striking him across the jaw with the wrench. The big man fell to the ground and Amos turned on the second who was just starting to throw a right hand round house punch.

Amos was able to block the blow, but was suddenly hit in the left kidney by the driver who had moved up on his blind side. The blow stunned him, and the second passenger grabbed him by the head and shoved it into his knee. Amos was down for the count after that. If he had been just ten years younger he probably would have made mince meat of the three young rednecks.

The passenger rose to his feet and Amos began to receive a good old fashion ass stomping. That is until Steve showed up. A gunshot sounded in the air stopping the trio. "I think you boys need to move on." Steve had said.

One of the passengers spoke up. "What, you want this here nigger for yourself?"

"No. But I know what's going to happen to three punks if they don't haul ass." Then there was a second gunshot and the sound of glass shattering.

"Hey! You son of a bitch, you shot out my back window."

"Your next if you don't leave now." Steve said.

Amos heard the sound of the three run to the truck, doors open and close and the squeal of the tires as they left. One of the passengers shouted out the window. "We know were you two live and we will be back!" They had never come back though.

Then he felt a firm hand grasp his shoulder and roll him over. "Hey there fella, looks like you could use a hand up."

Amos reached up to grab the hand that was offered and was lifted from the ground. The man had kept his hand and introduced himself. "My name is Steve Roberts. I'm your neighbor. I've seen you around but have not had a chance to say hi." The man smiled and released his hand. "Amos Brown, I appreciate the help." Amos had just stood there and rubbed his blooded and bruised body. The man placed a hand on his shoulder and said "Come on up to the house and we'll get you cleaned up."

"Best I get that belt on and drive on home son."

"Tell you what. I will fix your belt, but let me take a look at you inside first, okay."

Steve pulled out a tow rope from his Jeep and towed Amos to his house that looked to be still under construction. After cleaning up his wounds and bandaging him up Steve had gone back outside to fix the truck. He left Amos inside to sip on a glass of some of the best sweet tea he had ever had. Then he came back in washed his hands picked up his own glass of tea and sat down at the small kitchen table with him.

"What kind of gun were you shooting there Steve. Sounded like a cannon?" Amos asked.

Steve got up and walked to the corner and picked up the rifle. He unloaded it and left the bolt to the rear and handed it to Amos. "That is a Mosin Nagant M-44. It fires a 7.62x54R round. You can pick them up for around $50-$60."

"Are they any good? I have always stuck to my stage coach sawed off 12 gauge, don't know much about rifles." Amos had said.

"Don't let the price fool you. They are fine rifles, well built and fairly accurate out to 300 yards. The bonus is that you can buy 1,000 rounds for around $75.00." Steve had smiled at the last part.

Amos examined the rifle. He liked the feel of it. Maybe he would buy one someday. He handed the rifle back and he and his new friend talked for a bit. Then Amos bid him farewell. The two had become good neighbors after that. Steve helped him on the farm. Naturally that worthless mule of his took an instant liking to him. Did whatever Steve tried to get him to do. Just like that worthless mule turning traitor on me Amos thought with a smile.

Amos also helped Steve out at his place. He helped Steve finish construction on his cinder block two story home. He let Steve use his cousin's bulldozer to cut a slot through the hillside in front of his house for the driveway. Steve was so thankful he bought Amos a three hundred dollar Rattray's Tan pipe. Amos refused the gift but Steve kept leaving it at his home. Finally he accepted the gift and it was the best smoking pipe he had ever had.

Amos quit reminiscing, "Think I will head over to Steve's and see if he has an extra one of those rifles he could let me buy." Amos knew Steve had several guns he had shot a few of them with him from time to time. Amos got up and took his dishes to the kitchen. After cleaning up he put his boots and hat back on and walked to the barn. He was going to take the truck but decided to saddle Festus up instead. "Lazy heathen needed some exercise."

Festus had put himself in his stall and stood staring at Amos. Amos saddled him up, "Festus we're going to go see your sweetheart." Amos reached over to a straw hat that hung on the wall. It was identical to his except it had a pink ribbon with a flower wrapped around it. Two pink strips hung down so he could tie it onto his head. Amos had used the pink ribbon and flower to embarrass Festus.

"Maybe it would shame him into submission once all the other buck mules saw him with it on. Make them think he was light in the loafers." He grinned. Of course it didn't work Festus loved to wear his hat. Amos fit the hat over Festus's head and put his ears through the two slots he had cut out for the ears. When he was done tying the bow he scratched both sides of Festus's jaws.

"Don't you look sweet you nasty old fart?" Festus answered by tossing his head back and knocked Amos's straw cap to the ground behind him.

"You lily livered piece of trash, don't think I was joking about the glue factory." Amos growled. Amos turned and retrieved his hat. Once in the saddle he nudge Festus's sides. Festus just stood there. "Come on you old goat let's get out of here". Still Festus stood there. "Come on, dang it, I thought you might want to go see Steve." With the mention of Steve's name Festus walked out the barn and without direction from Amos headed to Steve's through the woods. Amos just grinned. "Who said mules were stupid?"

Once at Steve's Amos got down from the saddle. He knew Steve probably wasn't home because the Jeep was not in the drive. "Probably at that pretty little Diane's apartment getting sweet sugars." He said to no one in particular. Amos knocked on the door and after several minutes gave up. He got back in the saddle and told Festus to take them home. "Yep, Festus, your boyfriend is out running around with that Diane again. Guess you're out of luck."

In reply Festus turned and nipped his left thigh. "Owe, you God awful bag of bones!" Amos took the reins and swung at Festus's head only to hit Festus's straw hat. Amos would have to settle with giving the mule a good cursing.

Once back at the house, he unsaddled Festus and went inside. He headed for the bathroom to take a shower. He got the water steaming hot and stepped in. After a quick shower Amos dried off and dressed in his pajamas. He thought about the news reports for the day and picked up his shotgun and took it to the bedroom with him. He loaded it with two rounds of #4, and leaned it in the corner by the bed. Amos crawled in the bed and reached to turn out the lamp. Before his hand reached it the lights went out and his clock radio blinked off. Amos shook his head in frustration, "Dang, lights probably come back on at midnight and wake me up." Amos closed his eyes and asked the Lord to tell his wife hello. He soon was in a deep dreamless sleep.

+=—=+

The three men stood there shocked at what they had done. Well not really shocked, mad was more like it. After the power went out they had loaded up into the truck and headed out to correct a wrong that had been committed two years ago. They had broken into the house and snuck into the main bedroom. Once there they pulled out their pistols and shot into the sleeping form in the bed. Then turned on their flashlights, and jerked the covers back. Lying in the bed were two bloody bodies. In the beams of the lights lay the bullet riddled bodies of a white man and woman who would never wake from their slumber.

"Is it him?" The driver asked. His buddy walked over and rolled the man over.

"Damn! It ain't him." He threw the cover back down on the body in disgust.

"Well shit. I was sure this was the house."

"I told you the coon lived in the next house and the white guy in the cinder block one next to his farm."

"Shut the hell up! Let's get out of here and visit that worthless black piece of shit."

The three turned and left the house and got into the truck and drove down the road to Amos Brown's farm. Unknown to them the two murdered people had a ten year old son who watched the hole affair from a the crack in his bedroom door. Little Benny Carlyle tried to call 911 only to find the phones were not working.

The truck pulled to a stop about fifty yards from Amos's house. The three got out of the truck and reloaded their pistols. Two carried Ruger Red Hawk .44's the third carried a Ruger Black Hawk in .357. The one loading the .357 spoke up. "Think we should to take the rifles?" He motioned to the three rifles in that hung from the trucks gun rack.

One was a semi-auto Remington 2700 in 30-06, it had a ten round magazine loaded with hollow points. The second was an old M-1 Garand also in .30-06. The third was a Remington 700 in .308 with iron sights.

"Naw let's leave them. I want this to be up close and personal." The driver said.

"You want to make this personal I say we kill that damn mule of his. I saw him last year at Mule Day loving all over that thing."

"Sounds like a plan. We kill his mule then him. Let's go."

Once there one of three pushed the sliding barn door open about three feet. They walked as quietly as they could. None had remembered to bring a flashlight and the moon was covered by a heavy overcast.

"I can't see a thing; one of you got a flashlight?" The driver asked.

"No, I can't find my lighter either. I must have left it in the truck too." He said as he dug into his pockets.

The third one in the door stepped in and went to the right. He immediately tripped over a metal five-gallon bucket that rested in his path. He flailed his arms looking for something to catch his fall. The only thing that broke his fall was the boards of the corner stall. The old wood snapped and the man let out a howl of pain as some of the larger wood splinters entered his arms.

"What the hell are you doing, you damn fool." His friend called out in a loud voice.

"Shut up you dumb freak! You want to wake that black fool up?"

Amos had just got up and used the bathroom when he heard the loud crash and yelling come from the barn. He picked up the flashlight that he had sat on the back of the toilet tank and ran to the bedroom. He quickly slipped on a pair of fresh overalls, then his boots that rested by his shotgun.

He opened the dresser drawer and pulled out a two boxes of 00 buck and put them in the front pouch of his overalls. Amos reached over and picked up his shotgun and headed for the back door. Once outside he stepped to the side of the door and crouched down. He could still hear the a commotion coming from the barn. He leveled the shotgun from the hip holding it with his right hand. He held out the flashlight in his left hand and shined it at the barn. The sliding door was open. He clicked off the flashlight and headed for the barn.

The driver saw the light sweep by the front of the barn. "Someone's out there, let's hide."

The three found hiding places as best they could. The driver stepped into one of the stalls. Amos reached the barn door and laid his back against the wood next to the opening. He took a deep breath and cocked back both ears of the hammer. Then he quickly stepped into the barn and moved to the left side of the door so he would not be silhouetted. The driver saw the movement and started to squeeze the trigger of his pistol. Suddenly pain flared through his shoulder and part of his neck as something powerful clamped down on him. He let out a scream of pain and his pistol fired bucking in his hand, his shot going wide. He turned to face whatever the hell had just gotten hold of him.

As the man turned Festus butted him in the face causing him to see stars, and knocking him backwards out of the stall and into the open area of the barn. The full moon came out from behind the clouds just as the driver stumbled out of Festus's stall.

Light filtered into the barn and Amos saw a shadowy figure reeling backward. Amos leveled the shotgun and squeezed the trigger. The blast of #4 shot caught the figure full in the upper body folding him like a knife. "You bastards shouldn't be messing with my mule!" shouted. They were almost his last words as rounds filled the air around him. Amos dove behind some bags of quick Crete. One of the bullets tugged at the calf of his left leg cleaving a gash into it. Amos ignored the blaze of pain, and without aiming Amos lifted the barrel of the shotgun over the small pile of concrete bags in front of him and pulled the trigger.

He thumbed the release ejecting the two spent shells. More rounds pounded into the bags. Amos pulled two rounds from his front pocket and loaded up. The shooting stopped and he chanced a quick peek. He could see nothing.

With his left hand he took the flashlight turned it on and threw it to the other side of the barn. It was a risk but he had to have some light. His old eyes couldn't make out things like they used to. Just as the light came to a rest on the dirt floor Amos caught sight of a second man with a pistol pointed to the ground and it looked as if he was loading it. The man had his head turned looking at the flashlight that was pointed at him. He was in the stall that had been broken by one of his friends.

Amos brought the 12 gauge to bare and let loose a volley at the unsuspecting man. The nine thirty two caliber pellets tore into his body driving him backwards. He lay on the ground with his knees pointed upward, his feet up under his butt, his arms laid out as if he was preparing to embrace someone.

The third man finished reloading and took a shot at Amos. Amos stood and came around the pile of quick Crete. His left calf burned with pain. As he ran he brought the shotgun to his shoulder. The third man began firing at him. Rounds blazed by only inches from Amos.

When he was halfway to the man he fired. The shotgun roared, the pellets striking the man full in the face. His head exploded, a chunk of his brain and skull striking the wall behind him.

Amos ejected the rounds and fished out two more as he entered the stall where the now headless man lay. He loaded the shotgun again, and stood behind a large wooden beam. His chest heaved as he tried to breath. There were no more stalls left in the barn the rest of the barn was a large open area. Only the empty hayloft remained. Backing out of the stall Amos pointed the shotgun up at the loft. When he had backed far enough to pick up the flashlight he squatted down and picked it up.

He had the shotgun to his shoulder and the fore end rested in the crook of his left arm. His left hand held the flashlight. He played it back and forth across the loft and could see it was empty. Amos then turned and checked the bodies of the three men. He collected the pistols and put them in the large pockets of his overalls.

Festus stepped out of his stall and took a gander around the barn. He didn't seem impressed at all and walked back into the stall. Amos just shook head, "You know I saved your hide you worthless mule. You don't even appreciate it. Next time I will let them take you." Amos turned and walked to the house, he had to call the Sheriff.

Once inside he laid the guns on the kitchen table. He picked up the phone and dialed 911. The line was dead. Amos had not heard the news about the limited nuclear war. Feeling the men may have cut his phone lines he picked up the shotgun and flashlight, and limped back outside to check the phone lines. The line appeared to be intact. "Maybe someone hit a telephone pole." Amos said to himself.

He staggered as he turned to go back inside. The loss of blood, though not great, was making him feel weak and light headed. He steadied himself leaning against the wall. Once his mind quit spinning he went back inside. Once inside Amos grabbed the first aid kit on top of the refrigerator and sat at the kitchen table. He rolled up his pants leg and poured hydrogen peroxide over the wound. Then he put first aid crème ointment on it followed by a large gauze and wrapped it with tape. The wound was not bleeding much, but it had torn out a chunk of his leg. Amos got up and put the kit back on top of the fridge. He hobbled over to the cabinet and pulled down a large glass, and the bottle of unsealed Jack Daniels Steve had brought him. He wasn't a big drinker but he wanted something to dull his senses. He poured the glass and then picked up the shotgun. He took the glass and shotgun to the unlit living room.

He sat in his recliner shotgun across his lap. He finished off the whiskey in a few gulps. "I have got to go see Steve about getting one of those big rifles in the morning." He mumbled to himself. The adrenaline high wearing off, Amos felt as if his entire body was void of energy. His eyes fluttered as he struggled to keep them open but exhaustion won, and he was fast asleep.

Chapter 11

Ten-year-old Benny Carlyle woke with the sun shining on his face through his bedroom window. He laid in the fetal position, a pillow wrapped in his arms. The Sheriff Department never came last night after he called 911. He couldn't understand, his mother always told him to dial 911 if help was needed. Well it was needed last night and they never even answered the phone.

The urge to pee was becoming overwhelming, but he was still too scared to get up and leave his room. He knew that his mother and father were dead, and that the men had left, but he was still scared. He was not sure if the men who came into their home last night were the terrorists his father and mother had talked about so much. They must be, because who would want to come in and kill his mom and dad.

After ten more minutes of laying there he could not stand it anymore. He got up out of the bed and ran to the bathroom. Once he relieved himself, he turned to turn on the light switch. Nothing happened. He flipped the switch up and down a few more times, still nothing.

Benny peeped his head out into the hallway. He looked at the open door of his parent's bedroom. He could make out his mother's hand hanging off the bed. He then looked to the right trying to see as much of the living room as possible. He stood quietly for about a minute. He heard nothing, just the morning birds outside chirping. Benny could see the telephone sitting on the end table by his father's recliner.

Benny tip toed to the living room and picked up the phone. He dialed 911 again. The phone didn't have a dial tone, but he dialed 911 again.

He sat rocking in the recliner for about an hour. His mind raced, what was he supposed to do?

His stomach rumbled so Benny got up and walked to the kitchen. He poured a glass of milk and made a bowl of Lucky Charms. The milk was lukewarm but hunger over road his desire to pour it out.

After finishing his breakfast Benny made his way back to his bedroom. He made it a point to stare at the floor so he would not see his mother's bloody hand again. Once in the room Benny dressed himself in a pair of jeans and a t-shirt. He put on his brown leather boots. He then walked to the door of his room again. Peeking to the left he saw that his mother's hand was still there. He had to shut the door he could not stand to see his mother's hand. Tears filled his eyes.

Walking to his parent's bedroom he kept his head down staring at the hardwood floor. Once at their door he reached out for the doorknob, eyes still cast down. He finally found it with his hand and pulled it to him. The door bounced into his foot and out of his grasp, because he had tried to shut it so quickly. Out of reflex he raised his head and looked up to find the door. He did not see the doorknob only the bodies of his parents. Benny stood horrified at the condition of their bodies, and of the blood the soaked the sheets. Twenty minutes he stood there in silence staring until he slid down the wall to his butt, where he began to weep.

Amos woke when he heard the rooster crow. He sat in the chair confused for a moment. What was he doing sitting here and why did he have his shotgun across his lap? He picked up the remote to the TV and tried to turn it on. When nothing happened, the realization of the night before hit him like a ton of bricks. Laying the shotgun on the couch Amos got up and limped as he walked to the telephone. He was surprised to hear a dial tone. He quickly dialed 911 hoping to get hold of the Sheriff's Office. He sat on the arm of the couch as he waited for someone to answer the phone. Ten minutes later there was still no answer. Surely they couldn't be so busy that the 911 operator would not answer the phone.

Amos hung up the phone, and parted the blinds to look outside. The sun was shining and not a cloud was in the sky. He could have sworn he heard thunder in the distance last night. As he closed the blinds and realized the thunder he thought he had heard may have been gun shots. If these thugs came for him maybe they had come for one of his neighbors. He would check on the Carlyle's and Steve. Amos stood quickly and his left leg almost gave out as he put weight on the leg. "First things first, I've got to take care of my leg then I will go take a look down at the Carlyle home."

Amos hobbled to the kitchen and got out his first aid kit. He sat down in the chair and peeled back the gauze bandage. The wound did not look too bad. He tossed the old bandage into the trashcan. He then poured some more hydrogen peroxide on the wound and watched it fizz. He dried it with a clean gauze then took out some Neosporin. He applied the cream followed up by gauze and secured it with tape.

Amos walked back into the living room and picked up his shotgun. As he came back to the kitchen he stared at the three pistols. He thought about taking one, but since the Sheriff had not arrived he felt it best to leave them for the law to take. Once out the back door he walked to his truck. He started the old Chevy up and laid the shotgun in the passenger seat within easy reach.

Amos pulled to the end of the driveway. He looked both ways; the only thing he saw was the rednecks pickup. Amos put the truck in park got out and walked up to the Ford. Opening the driver door he saw the three rifles in the gun rack. The keys still dangled from the ignition switch. Amos reached in and pocketed the keys. Then he locked up the truck and went back to his own.

Amos pulled into the Carlyle's driveway. He shut down the engine and got out of the truck. He was about to shut the door when he stopped and reached back and got the shotgun. Walking to the carport door he saw that it was slightly ajar. The lock looked as if someone had used a screwdriver to pry it open, small flecks of paint, and wood lay on the ground under the doorknob.

Amos eased the door open. Stepping into the small mudroom Amos kept the shotgun at waist level pointing it out before him. "Hello in the house! Mr. Carlyle it's Amos Brown from next door. Kelly or Benny is you in here?" There was no answer.

Amos had known the Carlyle's for about six months. They had moved in from up north somewhere to get away from big city life. They had no family and few friends here in Alabama.

Amos stepped into the kitchen and then made his way towards the living room and hallway. As he turned the corner he saw little Benny sitting in the floor by his parent's bedroom door. His knees were pulled up to his chest and he rocked back and forth staring into the room. "Benny, it's me Amos where is your mom and dad?" Benny did not register his call, he continued to rock back and forth.

As he moved closer he saw a bloody arm outstretched from the bed. His stomach began to tighten. He knew what he would find. As he came up to Benny he looked into the room that the child had transfixed with his gaze. Both Benny Sr. and Kelly lay in a pool of their own blood. Amos leaned the shotgun against the doorframe and knelt beside Benny.

"Benny it's me Amos." He said soothingly as he placed his hand on the boy's shoulder.

Benny turned and looked up at Amos, "Why did they do it Mr. Amos? Why?"

"I don't know son, but they came to my house last night and I took care of them." Amos wasn't sure he had killed the right men, but it was a good assumption. "Get up now and come on into the living room Benny." Benny got up and followed Amos to the living room like a automaton.

Benny looked at Amos, "I tried to call the Sheriff last night and this morning but no one would come, my phone doesn't even work. Mom always told me to call 911 if bad things happened, why didn't they come Mr. Amos?"

"Benny the world is turning upside down. I imagine something terrible has happened and the police went home to take care of their own. If they did that they must all feel things are getting out of control and they want to make sure their own families are safe." With that said Amos realized something bad had to have taken place last night while he slept.

"Come with me Benny. We're going to my place." Amos stood and reached out his hand. He looked down at Benny and thought of his own son who had been killed during Operation Iraqi Freedom some years before. Benny rose and took his hand and they turned to walk out the door.

"Are we going to just leave mom and dad Amos?"

"No I'll be back for them later. I will take care of them and you if the local authorities don't show." Benny just shook his head.

Once back at the house Amos took Benny to his son's old bedroom. The boy looked exhausted. As they stepped into the room Benny stood and looked in wonder at the room.

"You never let me in here before Mr. Amos. Whose room is this?

"It was my boy Andy's room Benny. He died fighting in Operation Iraqi Freedom. He was always proud to serve his country and the Corps."

The two gazed around the room. It was filled with Marine posters, models of Harrier Jump Jets, and several different models of helicopters hung from fishing line attached to the ceiling. Along one wall was a bookshelf that contained dozens of pictures of Marines and many were of a tall well-muscled black one holding a FN 240 heavy machinegun.

Amos picked up an 8x10 picture of his son; the one with the machinegun and bullets draped over one shoulder. "This is Andy." Amos handed the picture to Benny.

"He was a machinegun man?" Benny asked and handed back the picture.

"Yes that was what he did." Amos answered

Benny pointed to a picture frame on the wall. "What are those?" He asked.

Amos took down the picture frame that contained all of his son's medals. "These are his medals."

"What do they mean?" Benny asked

Amos pointed to the Silver Star. "He got this one when he was killed. Some of his fellow Marines were pinned down by rocket and machine gun fire. Andy jumped up and charged the enemy and took out three enemy machine gun nests. This second one is the Bronze Star. He got that in the first Gulf War. He had some friends stuck out in the open and were wounded and he rushed out and rescued them. This purple one with the gold cluster is called the Purple Heart. They give that to men who are wounded or killed in combat. Andy got his first one when he won the Bronze Star; the second one was for..." Amos's voice trailed off when he thought back to the Marines in Dress Blues who came to his door that morning long ago. Amos hung the medal box back on the wall.

"Benny lie down and get a rest I think you need it." Benny complied and lay down on the bed. With in minutes he was asleep.

Amos walked out to the barn. He dragged the three rednecks into the central area of the barn. He then searched their pockets. He came up with twenty-four rounds of .357, and sixty rounds of .44 between the three. Amos walked over to the phone on the wall of the barn and picked up the phone on the wall, this time his phone had no dial tone.

"Well I guess if the law ain't coming I sure aint letting these three stink up my barn."

He went out and brought his tractor into the barn. He then tied a rope to the ankle of each man. Once that was done he drug their bodies out into his field. He took the tractor back and got in his cousins backhoe. Taking the backhoe to the field he dug a six-foot deep hole by about eight feet, then used the backhoe to drag the bodies into the hole. Finally he buried the dirt on top of them. "Dang, Sheriff's office can dig them up if they want to see them." Amos said.

Amos then went to the small rise near the catfish pond. Under three large Cypress trees he dug two separate graves for the Carlyle's bodies. Then he drove back to the barn and parked the backhoe. The whole process had taken about five hours and his stomach was grumbling.

Walking into the kitchen he fixed a peanut butter sandwich for himself and one for Benny. Benny came walking into the room rubbing his eyes. "Are you hungry Benny?"

"Yes sir." Benny said as he sat down at the kitchen table. Amos poured him a glass of warm milk from the refrigerator and one for himself.

Amos picked up the phone while he chewed on his sandwich. There was still no dial tone.

"Well Benny it looks like we're on our own for a awhile."

"Amos what are we going to do about mom and dad?"

"Benny I got them a resting place up on the hill over looking the pond. Do think they would like to lay there and rest?"

"Yes sir, I think they would."

"Well this is what I am going to do. I am going to go to your house and pick up your folks and take them up there. When I get them there I will blow the horn when I am ready for you to come on up. Then we will say a prayer. Is that okay with you?"

Benny thought for a moment and then shook his head. Tears started to well up in the boy's eyes as the realization hit him again that his parents were dead. He went to Amos and wrapped his arms around Amos's waist. Amos held him for a moment then stepped back.

"Alright I am going to leave now you just sit back and rest okay" Benny gave him another shake of the head.

Amos arrived at the Carlyle's house. He could now smell the death in the air. He rapped both bodies in clean sheets and took them out to the bed of his truck. He went back inside and got to large white comforters and took them with him to the truck.

Once back at the farm Amos backed the trucks up to the gravesite. First he wrapped Benny Sr. up in one of the comforters then Kelly. He dragged the two bodies as gently as possible and placed them into their graves. Once that was done he walked to the cab of the truck and tooted the horn.

Shortly Benny was there beside him standing over his parent's grave. Amos said a prayer over the two. Then Benny prayed to God to take his mother and father into heaven. Tears rolled down his cheeks. When they were done Amos told Benny to go on back to the house and that he would take care of the burial.

Benny reached into the back of the truck and took out one of the shovels that lay in the bed. "No Mr. Amos, you have done enough. I will do this. It's time for you to take a rest."

Amos eyed the young boy for a moment. "Okay son go ahead."

Benny began burying his parents. Amos stood by and watched for the next three hours as the ten-year-old boy worked none stop tears running down his cheeks the whole time. When Benny was done his hands were bloody and his face swollen from crying. Amos picked up the courageous boy, hugged him and then took him back down to the house.

Chapter 12

After Amos cleaned and wrapped little Benny's hands he carried the youth to Andy's room and laid him in the bed. Amos looked down at the young boy in the fading light. "Don't look a thing like my boy Andy, but you sure do have his heart and guts." Amos said to the sleeping boy. He took a look around the room looking at the artifacts that chronicled his son's life. Amos walked to the display that held his son's medals. Opening the display he pulled the Silver Star from the case. Thinking of the courage it took for the ten year old boy to bury his own parents he pinned the medal to Benny's chest. "I think Andy would want you to have that Benny." Amos said in a whispered voice. He then turned and walked from the room. Amos had things to do. He had already missed a whole day in the fields.

Amos walked to the kitchen and opened the pantry door. Opening the circuit breaker box he pulled the main. He then walked down stairs to the basement, flashlight in hand. At the bottom of the steps he scanned the far wall and pinpointed the generator. Above the generator was an oil lamp and some strike anywhere matches. Amos lit the lamp and turned off the flashlight.

After priming the generator and checking the oil and fuel levels he grabbed hold of the pull start. With a couple of yanks the old diesel generator coughed to life. The generator was purchased last year. He had been over at Steve's when he set up his home to run off a generator for power outages.

"Where did you get this idea" he had asked.

Steve had answered, and told him about the set up that Doc Morrison had. With all the ice storms and wind storms that frequented the Tennessee Valley area it seemed prudent to Amos that he too should set his home up. Though he had seen it done in many homes over the years it never really dawned on him to do it for himself. So Amos had gone out and purchased a 30 hp diesel generator that was capable of running everything in his house and barn. Steve and Doc Morrison had helped him get the old diesel engine running and in perfect condition. He had only had to use it one time during the last ice storm.

Once the power was flowing to the secondary circuit breaker box Amos limped up stairs. He was going to have to give Doc a call about his wound, and Benny's hands. Once up stairs he clicked on the TV, he had to have some news about what was going on in the outside world.

The reception he received was a bit snowy but it would have to do. He had picked up a Fox TV station out of Birmingham. The news was not good. Nuclear strikes at a dozen or so major ports, fighting around the globe, and police forces across the nation overwhelmed with calls for service, riots, and protecting bridges, dams, water treatment plants, and the list went on and on. U.S. troops were on their way home from several different countries, and they probably would not land in time to help restore any semblance of order. That was all Amos needed to see and hear; he limped over to the telephone and picked up the receiver.

"Hot damn I've got a dial tone!"

He tried 911 again with no answer, and then he dialed Steve's. No answer there either. He would try Doc Morrison's next. It startled him when Doc answered the phone for a second he did not respond.

"Hello. Is anyone there, hello?" Doc said in an somewhat impatient voice.

"Doc this is Amos."

Doc's voice took on a cheerier tone. "Oh, hello there Amos, the phone call surprised me. The phones have been down, and I didn't realize they were back up. Is all well with you?"

"Best as can be expected Doc, I need some help." Amos said in a tired voice.

"Are you hurt Amos?" Doc questioned.

"Got a little bullet wound to the left calf and Benny Carlyle's hands could use a looking at."

"What happened Amos?" Doc said with a little hint of shock in his voice.

"Tell you about it when you get here Doc. I have some things to take care of before I hit the rack."

"Ok I will see you in about thirty minutes Amos. Bye." With that Doc hung up the phone and so did Amos.

Amos walked outside the house and to the road. He pulled the keys to the Ford pickup out of his pocket and opened the truck door. He got it cranked up and drove it up to the barn. Once in the barn he got out. He walked over to the North wall and got the wheel barrel, and took it to the side of the truck. He reached in and took the three rifles out and placed them in the wheel barrel.

He then checked the glove box and found three boxes of Winchester .30-.06 rounds. He tossed these in the wheel barrel also. Amos checked under the seats and found four loaded ten round magazines that apparently went with the Remington semi-auto. He also found a three D cell Maglight; he slipped it into the hammer loop on his overalls. Behind the seat he found a toolbox that he took out and put on the workbench. There was nothing else of value in the cab of the truck.

Amos walked around to the tailgate and opened it up. He groaned with pain as he climbed into the bed of the truck to get a good look in the toolbox.

Amos felt something watching him and turned to see Festus staring with interest. "What are you looking at you ingrate? Look at me. I have been all shot up had to clean out the dead bodies from the barn and all for you. All you can do is stare at me and crap in the floor." Festus looked on munching on some hay. Amos shook his head and opened the toolbox.

Inside the toolbox Amos found around 400 rounds of 30-06 in a large clear plastic bag. 200 rounds of .357 in boxes and an additional 250 rounds of .44 were also located. He leaned over the side of the truck and gently dropped each item into the wheel barrel. He found a Coleman camp stove, lantern and two gallons of Coleman fuel; a four-man tent was crammed in its storage bag. He also found a variety of camping gear, which he left in the toolbox for now.

Amos climbed down from the truck and pushed the wheel barrel back to the house. At about the same time Doc Morrison was pulling up in the drive in his pickup. Doc slowed to a stop and climbed out of the truck.

When Amos heard the truck door close he called out to Doc. "I'm in here you sorry excuse for a physician!"

"Evening Amos, looks like you got that generator going. Getting that generator started is a pretty amazing feat for a half ass dirt farmer. "

"Yeah, Doc sure did, of course I didn't need any help. I am sure your weak ass had to get your wife to start yours." Amos snickered. "Come on inside with me. Hold the door for me when we get to the house so I can get this loot inside."

"Where on earth did you get all that Amos?" Doc said as he held the mudroom door open for Amos.

"Tell you about it shortly Doc. I want you to take a look at Benny's hands if he is up."

The phone rang and startled Doc. He looked over at Maude "Hey the phone is working. I wonder who's calling?"

"Well pick the thing up before it wakes up Steve." Maude said in a sharp tone.

Doc reached for the phone and picked it up. "Hello."

"Hello is anyone there, hello?" Doc was about to hang up the phone when Amos answered.

Doc talked to Amos and then hung up the phone and looked at Maude. "Looks like Amos has had some problems. He has been shot in the calf, and apparently little Benny Carlyle is with him. He has some type of hand injuries."

"Well get your bag and get over there. Amos is a good man, and Benny is a sweet boy. Did Amos say anything about Benny's parents?" Maude asked.

"No not a thing. Let me get my stuff and head on over there." Doc turned to leave the room to get his black medical bag.

Once down stairs Doc loaded up his bag. He stared for a second at the examining table where he had been unable to save Diane. He shook his head and started for the stairs. He stopped and went back to one of the cabinet drawers. Opening it he pulled out a Colt 1911A1 Gold Cup 70 series. He thumbed the safety down and eased the slide back to make sure it was loaded. Once he confirmed it was he thumbed the safety back up, and tucked the pistol in the small of his back. He went up the stairs and out the door to his truck.

As Doc pulled up Amos was pushing a wheel barrel and what appeared to be ammo and three long guns in it. "Evening Amos, looks like you got that generator going. Getting that generator started is a pretty amazing feat for a half ass dirt farmer. "

"Yeah, Doc sure did, of course I didn't need any help. I am sure your weak ass had to get your wife to start yours." Amos snickered. "Come on inside with me. Hold the door for me when we get to the house so I can get this loot inside."

"Where on earth did you get all that Amos?" Doc said as he held the mudroom door open for Amos.

"Tell you about it shortly Doc. I want you to take a look at Benny's hands if he is up."

Amos parked the wheel barrel in the kitchen. Doc was just behind him. He looked on the table and saw the three Ruger pistols lying there. "I imagine this is going to be an interesting story."

Amos pulled out a chair and sat at the table to get the load off his feet. "Yeah it is Doc. Reads like a western shootout novel."

"Where is Benny?"

"He's in Andy's room sleeping; at least I think he is still asleep."

Doc picked up his bag and started to walk to Andy's room. "Let me check in on him and I will be right back."

Doc walked to Andy's room. As quietly as possible he opened the bedroom door. He walked to the bedside and turned on the lamp.

Andy was still asleep. Doc pulled a syringe from his bag and then filled it with antibiotics. Clearing it of air bubbles Doc poked it into Benny's shoulder. The boy never moved when the needle entered his arm, he slept on. Doc took a look at the bandages and it appeared that Amos did a good job of wrapping them. No blood seeped through them. It was obvious the wounds were not life threatening so he decided to check out Amos's more serious gunshot wound.

Back in the kitchen Doc had Amos put his foot up on the chair, and between his thighs. Doc twisted the leg a bit to get a better look. Amos winced in pain. The wound seemed to be fairly clean but Doc decided to scrub it up a bit anyway. Amos almost reached out and grabbed hold of Doc when he poured the alcohol on the wound. "Quit squirming like a sissy Amos." Doc said with a bit of humor in his voice.

"What happened to that great bedside manor you're always bragging about?" Amos said with a slight grimace on his face.

Doc smiled. "It died with your good looks years ago you old crybaby."

Amos just frowned, Doc, like his worthless mule loved to goad him at every possible chance.

"Tell me what happened here Amos." Doc said as he continued to work on the wound.

Amos related to Doc what had happened over at the Carlyle's and then here at his own home.

"Those boys had been waiting two years to get me. Bet they would have gone to get Steve next if they had finished me off."

"Well they would have missed out on Steve because he hasn't been home."

"Where is he? Is he holed up in Florence with Diane?" Amos asked in obvious concern for his friends.

Doc looked up from his work and then back down at the wound. He started to work again and told Steve's tale. Amos was distressed when he reached the part about Diane dying at the farm.

"Whish I could have been there to help them out." Is all Amos could say. His face told of the sadness he felt for the loss of Diane.

"Steve will be staying with us for a few more days. Then he will probably head back over to his place. Maude and I discussed him staying with us but I don't know if he will agree to it. You're welcome also Amos."

"Thanks for the offer Doc, but I have plenty here that needs to be taken care of. I guess we can all look after one another though. Recon I ought to come by and see Steve?"

Doc put Amos's leg down as he finished up with his work. He gave Amos an antibiotic shot like Benny's. He then fished in his medicine bag and pulled out two large pain pills. "Take one now and one in the morning it should knock out most of the pain"

Amos took the pills and put them on the table. "As far as coming to see Steve I would give the boy some time. Once his head is cleared

I think we should all sit down and talk about what we need to do. Have you seen the news?"

"Yeah and it doesn't look good. I think we are in this for the long haul."

"I agree Amos. We need to organize though and soon. Well I have to get back to the house before Maude comes down here and drags me back. Be sure to clean Benny's hands when he wakes. Let me know of any change in your or Benny's condition."

Doc shook hands with Amos. "I will see you in a day or so Amos."

"Have a good night Doc. Glad you, Maude and Steve are okay."

Doc waved to Amos and left the house for home. Amos sat back in the chair and started making mental notes of what needed to be done.

Chapter 13

After the attack on Wilson Dam, Capt. Dong and his men drove to the small town of Leighton, AL. in Colbert Co. Once there they had pulled into a small mini-storage facility just outside of the town. They had chosen a storage garage at the south end of the facility that faced the woods. They had chosen it because it was located on the corner and because there was no view of it from the road.

Once there they had exited the van and opened the storage bay. Inside Ford Excursion was parked, also other supplies such as food, medical supplies, ammunition, and weapons. They quickly loaded the Ford with all of the supplies. The vehicle was pulled out and the van parked inside. They then changed into civilian attire. On the way to Florence every two to three miles they would wrap power poles with detonation cord and set them off by time delayed detonators. This effectively cut power to many sections of the county even if they got the power station at the dam back on line.

They then drove back to Florence to a small house on Reeder St. It was there that they waited for their next attack. This attack would almost ensure no power was returned to this particular area.

⌗═══⌗

Pvt. Nah stood in the living room of the small house peering out the window through a small open space in the drapes. He was watching for potential threats and also the Florence Utilities Departments main warehouse. This huge warehouse and supply yard took up a whole block. It contained extra telephone poles; transformers, trucks, tools, wire and a hundred other things needed to support a county of 90,000 citizens with proper power. It was also where in emergency situations such as ice storms, tornados, and windstorms all the work crews would meet to receive their instructions. So far not many of the utility crews had showed up to assist TVA in restoring power, but the parking lot was filling. There were only four Florence Police Officers present to provide security.

The one hundred-man force was already overwhelmed and could not even contain the riots that were occurring since the power had gone out two days ago. This suited Pvt. Nah just fine. He was amazed that one of his comrades had been killed by simple police officers. The one who had laid up in ambush with the machine gun that killed Pvt. Hoe was very good with his weapon. They had not been told that the police would set up ambushes, and for one of their own to sit and wait in the truck as bait...such discipline.

He had not spotted any other officers except the four. Where would the hidden officers be? Surely these officers had set up snipers for a facility such as this. Nah turned to look over his shoulder as the back door opened. It was Pvt. Hengyang coming in from the outside observation and guard post.

Pvt. Mau walked out past Hengyang to go and take his place for the two-hour watch. He was dressed almost identical to Hengyang. He wore black BDU pants, black light weight turtleneck, black gloves, and a black balaclava. A radio headset was on his head. He was armed with a U.S. Marine K-Bar fighting knife; silenced Ruger MK II suppressed .22 cal. Pistol, and a folding stock AK-47 with a 75 round drum. Though the drum was a bit unwieldy and heavy, being out numbered, as they were the extra firepower could be beneficial to the team.

<hr />

Pvt. Mau thread his way carefully to the clump of bushes that sat twenty feet from the front corner of the house. From this vantage point both front and most of the back yard could be seen. He and Cpl. Wei had strewn trash such as beer bottles and coke cans through out the yard. This debris field was dense enough that anyone walking through the yard would step on or kick one of the items. Tangle wire had also been put up at ankle level. The trash around the yard did not appear out of place in the run down neighborhood.

One and a half hours into his watch Mau heard the sound of someone trying to kick in the back door of the vacant house next door.

"It must be looters." Mau thought. So far they had been lucky to not have any in their immediate area. If they were forced to defend their position it could throw the plan into jeopardy.

He finally heard the door give and the voices of at least two looters. He could not make out what they said though. Mau lifted his night vision monocular to his eye and scanned the officers across the street. They had not heard the door being kicked in. They were approximately three hundred feet away. Maybe they had become jaded to the sounds of the collapse of their city and were biding their time before they slipped away from their duties to their own homes and families.

Mau then shifted his position to face the house next door and wait what he was sure to be the inevitable. The looters would come to their position. He un-holstered the Ruger from its holster and kept it at the ready.

Mau then advise the team by radio of the situation. "Watch to command." He said in a whispered voice.

"Cpl. Wei to Watch, go ahead."

"I have possibly two or more individuals in the house next door. I believe they may be looters. The police are unaware at this time. Stay alert, I will notify if there is a change in the situation."

"Roger that Watch, command out."

⊹⊱━⊰⊹

Serif kicked at the door several times before it gave way to the blows from his boot. He stepped to the side once it opened breathing heavily.

"Cedric, you're kick'n the next one in home slice." He said to his partner.

"Man you just like a girl. Bent over and breath'n all heavy like you was get'n some. If we's find a dress an a wig in here I'm go'n to make sho you look sweet." Cedric replied.

The two made a sweep of the empty house finding nothing. "Aint noth'n in here bro" Cedric said to Serif as they met back in the empty living room.

"You want to flame up a rock?" Serif held up a broken antenna with wire mesh tucked in one end, and a rock of crack cocaine.

"How much we go left? We can't smoke it all up in a couple o' days, the supply going to be cum'n up short here soon."

"Don't sweat it Ced. I still got's an eight ball left, and a hundred dollar sack of powder blow." Serif smiled and lit up the crack pipe. He inhaled deeply letting the euphoria wash over him.

"Gimme that chit for you smokes it all up." Ced took the pipe from Serif and took his turn. After a couple of hits apiece the crack rock was gone. "Serif you buy good chit man."

"True, true my brother" Serif said with a stoned grin on his face.

Serif put his pipe away in his pocket. "Let's hit the next house."

The two went out of the house and into the yard next door. Serif suddenly fell on his face tripping on one of the hidden tangle wires. He hit the ground like a sack of potatoes.

"Damn man, what I trip on? "He said as he began to rise up.

Cedric giggled. "Don't know but you sho look stupid crawl'n all round on da ground like a bug." Cedric stepped towards his friend with his hand outstretched to help him up. He crushed two beer cans stepping over to him.

⊹⊨⊨⊹

Mau watched as the two young black men walked towards his position. The one on the left suddenly tripped and fell, possibly on the tangle wire. His friend laughed and turned his back to Mau extending a hand to his friend.

Mau rose to his feet advancing like a jungle cat, silently and quickly, on his unsuspecting victims. He pointed his pistol at the head of the man on the ground. At the same time he drew his K-Bar knife.

When he was three feet from the man with his back to him he shot the man on the ground twice in the head. The standing man turned towards the clacking sound the slide made. He had not registered the fact that two small bullet holes appeared in his friend's head.

⊹⊨⊨⊹

As Cedric reached for Serif's hand he heard two barely audible pops and the sound of something metallic clacking. He started to turn to see what was up. What was up horrified him.

"Who da hell..." Cedric never finished the sentence.

Mau lashed out with a sweeping high kick that caught the man in the right shoulder spinning him so that he faced Mau. The man went to one knee Mau using a backhanded slash with his left hand sliced into the man's throat. The razor sharp blade of the Marine fighting knife glided through Cedric's throat as if the blade had been cutting through paper. Cedric's eyes went wide; his hands went to his throat to try to stop the bleeding and pain. Blood rapidly poured through his hands unable to stop the flow. He collapsed on the ground on his right side. Mau casually pumped two rounds into the man's temple.

Mau wiped the blood off the knife on the man's trousers, and then sheaved the knife. Just to be certain he pumped one more round in each dead man's head. He ejected the almost empty magazine and pocketed it, then took out a fresh magazine, reloaded and holstered.

Mau keyed up the radio. "Watch to Command."

Wei replied. "Command to Watch, go ahead."

"Two subjects eliminated. It appears there were only the two."

"Mau what is the status on the officer's across the street?"

"Stand by Command." Mau lifted the night vision monocular to his eye. The police were still unaware. "Watch to Command"

Wei replied in an irritated voice. Mau knew Wei preferred to keep things simple and just use their names instead of acronyms and codes for each soldier. "Go ahead Mau."

"They have not been alerted. You may stand down."

Wei may not care if Capt. Dong chewed him out for inappropriate radio use, but he sure did.

Mau then removed the bodies to a small pile of brush behind the house. He then returned to his observation post. Mau tucked his body and bent below the bushes and pushed the light on his watch. Fifteen minutes till he was off watch.

Five minutes before his watch ended four yellow buses pulled into the lot of the warehouse. Men began to file out of the bus. Mau raised the NVG to his eye. The men were dressed in work clothes and some wore hard hats. "Watch to Command."

Capt. Dong's voice spoke in his ear. "Command to Watch. We see them come back into the house, Command out"

Mau keyed the radio. "Watch copies. Watch out." Mau rose and threaded his way silently back the house.

Once inside the house he went to a back windowless bedroom. A kerosene lamp illuminated the small room. The rest of the team stood around a small card table that had the blue prints to the warehouse resting on it. He joined the team at the table.

Capt. Dong began to review the plan that they had formulated and discussed for the past two days. "Cpl. Wei will climb the ladder to the sniper post on the roof. Once he is in an over watch position and engages the police officers we shall make our way to these doors. From our surveillance we have not observed this door being locked at all. The room behind this door is large and has many seats in it and maps are located on boards at the front of the room. This appears to be the briefing room and is where the bus loads of men entered. Once we arrive at the door." he pointed to Hengyang, "you will toss in three hand grenades. After the third detonation we shall enter and eliminate those left alive inside. Then we shall sweep the building for survivors. Are there any questions?" There where none. "Then let us begin."

The team exited the rear of the house. Wei climbed the ladder and got on the roof. The rest of the team stacked up in a tactical file along the side of the house. Each man was armed with four grenades, fighting knife, and six extra magazines, AK-47 loaded with a seventy-five round drum. Two, Mau, and Hengyang carried the suppressed Rugers. The rest carried Glock 17 9mm handguns with three extra high capacity magazines.

<hr>

Wei brought the rifle, a Dragonauve with suppressor, and night vision scope, into his shoulder and scanned the parking lot. He found the four officers one at a time. He had clear shots on all but one who kept walking from position of cover and concealment to similar positions. He was never moving in the same pattern or in the open for long. He would try for the nearest officer since he had the best chance to see the team moving.

Wei settled the cross hairs on the man's head. He kept his breathing steady and then slowly exhaled halfway and gently squeezed the trigger. The officer died halfway through a tired stretch.

He picked up the second officer who had just unprofessionally lit up a cigarette. Wei allowed the man to take a good drag and exhale the smoke. He was a smoker also and felt he should at least give the man a last puff before dying. As the officer let smoke exhale from his mouth he died.

+=====+

Officer Joel Crumpton moved to the dumpster walking in a zigzag pattern. Once there he scanned the area using peripheral vision knowing from experience that at night you picked up movement better with the peripheral vision rather than looking straight at what you thought moved. He squeezed the pistol grip on his AR-15. It was a civilian version of the M-4 he had carried in Somalia. Though it lacked the knock down power of a good .308 a rifle similar to the one he carried tonight saved his butt many years ago.

Joel heard a thwacking sound but was unsure what it was. He scanned the lot and saw Andy Turner light up a smoke. "That dumb ass. He knows better than that." Then Andy collapsed to the ground and at the same moment Joel heard the thwacking sound.

It wasn't loud but Joel recognized the sound of the suppressed rifle. He had watched Delta operators use them from time to time and learned the sound. He raised the rifle and scanned the outer perimeter.

"There!" He saw a faint orange flash and heard the thwack again. Joel started to pump rounds at the general area of the muzzle flash. After six rounds Joel ducked and moved to a new position.

+=====+

Wei lined up the third officer in his cross hairs. This one was leaning against the trunk of his patrol car. "Fish in a barrel" the thought of the American phrase made him smile. Americans had so many funny little phrases. He squeezed the trigger, and the third officer died.

He adjusted to where he saw the last officer, the only tactical one of the bunch. Then he heard the report of what had to be an M-16. Rounds zipped by his head two struck in front of him on the roof. Wei rolled twice to the right.

"Where do these American Police keep getting these M-16's?" Then he remembered the briefing officer telling him that many American citizens owed assault type weapons, though most were semi-auto.

He scanned again and caught movement in the scope. The officer was running in a crouched down position. His rifle pointed in his general direction. Wei snapped off a quick shot at the transitory target.

+>==+==+-

Joel moved to the next car over, his rifle pointing towards the area of the threat. He knew which roof the sniper was on and general vicinity. He was using a suppressed weapon so that meant he most likely had military training and that meant he would have fled the area or rolled left or right.

Then a jolt of pain emanated through his left leg dropping him to the pavement. He saw the minute muzzle flash as he was falling to the ground, pinpointing his assailant. When he hit the ground his rifle was already in the pocket of his shoulder. He rolled to the prone position and fired four rounds and then began to crawl for the car.

+>==+==+-

Wei watched the man drop and smiled. Then suddenly to his surprise the man began to fire. He felt one round crease his left ear. His body gave an involuntary spasm and he rolled again. Three more rounds crashed into the roof where his former position had been.

Wei brought the rifle back up to his shoulder. Then put his eye to the scope. He had to finish the officer quickly or he would be dead. He was amazed at the skill this officer was showing. He both admired and hated him in the same instant as his cross hairs rested on the officer's chest. Pvt. Nah had been correct when he said they must be wary of the police. It appeared some had some type of military training. Wei pulled the trigger.

Joel was crawling on his side now attempting to make it to cover behind the car. Then he felt the round pierce the left side of his chest. The round spun him onto his back. His breathing immediately became labored. He knew he had just lost a lung.

Joel refused to give up though, his Army Ranger training kicking in. Pushing with his legs he made it behind the car. He pushed himself up into a sitting position behind the car's tire. Then he heard three explosions and felt the ground vibrate, and then a sounded that he grew to hate in Somalia, full auto AK fire. "Shit another terrorist attack." He said to himself. "I've got to finish this sniper off."

Pushing the pain from his mind he rose up from behind the car. With the help of the moon he saw the black outline of a man standing up on the roof. His vision was blurred and breathing ragged as tried for a good sight picture. When he thought he had it he unleashed the final twenty rounds of his magazine coming up to a full standing position as he fired.

Wei took a deep breath as he stood. The team had entered the building and the staccato of machinegun fire could be heard across the street. Then suddenly rifle fire came from the parking lot. Wei brought his rifle to his shoulder. Then felt pain on his left side. It dropped him to one knee but he maintained his hold on the rifle still held to his shoulder. Rounds snapped all around him.

Wei brought the scope to his eye. There he saw the officer standing and firing for all he was worth. Wei laid the cross hairs on the man's head. He fired the rifle this time keeping it in his shoulder and his eye to the scope. He watched as the officer dropped the rifle, as his body was flung backwards onto the hood of the car. Slowly the officer's body slid to the pavement, a swath of blood painted on the hood from the gaping hole in the back of the officer's head. When his body finally came to a rest on the ground more blood pooled around his head. He was dead.

Wei did not feel satisfaction in this kill. The American had fought like a true warrior. He did not give up even though it probably would have saved his life if he had managed to crawl away and find help. Wei saluted his fallen enemy and turned and climbed down off the roof.

When he got to the ground he could only hear the occasional gunshot coming from the warehouse across the street. The team was mopping up. He went inside to tend to the flesh wound in his side. He hopped all Americans would not put up a fight like this officer and the one who fought so well at the dam.

Chapter 14

Chief Byron Hopkins sat at his large mahogany desk. He felt vanquished and disheartened about the performance he had been given in this time of great need. In the past two days he had lost twelve officers in shootouts. Four last night at the massacre at the Electricity Department's warehouse. The chief took a long pull from the glass of whiskey in his hand.

Only twenty-seven of his one hundred officers had shown up to work, only 25% of his force on duty. I guess he couldn't blame a lot of the men and women for not showing up, twelve dead, fifteen wounded in two days of riots. The only thing that had kept the city from totally burning to the ground was his Special Operations Team. He had used them on all officer need's assistance calls. Crowds seemed to melt away when they arrived. Those that chose to shoot at the team died in a withering hail of bullets. They had also gone in and rescued over thirty people, mostly women, who had been kidnapped and raped. Those thirty had been rescued in seven different raids just yesterday.

The team was already worn out. They could not keep up this tempo for much longer. Today would be the team's last mission, also the last call to duty for the other fifteen officers that had shown up this morning. Then he would relieve the officers of their duties and send them home. He had received no help from the state, or any of the alphabet soup federal agencies. Communications with other departments throughout the state had confirmed that they were all on their own for the near future. All available resources were being sent to the metropolitan areas.

Lt. Brian Holsted knocked on the open door. "Chief the officers are assembled down stairs in roll call."

Hopkins looked up at the Lieutenant, "Brian give me five minutes and I will be downstairs."

Holsted nodded his head, "Okay, boss I will let the men know." Holsted turned and left back down the hall.

Hopkins leaned back in the plush leather seat, and took another swallow of his whiskey. He hated to abandon his post, but he saw no other option. He would not allow more of his officers to lose their lives in vain. They had families that they needed to look after, and with no one coming in to help, to stay would be a waste of lives. How could things go so bad so fast? Only the historians would be able to sort that out, if there were any historians left.

Hopkins drained the last of his whiskey. He stood from his chair and straightened his uniform. It was time to face the troops. He walked from the office and downstairs to the briefing room.

The briefing room was in total disarray. Coffee cups lay about the floor along with other debris. Part of the back wall has scorched black by flames. Yesterday someone had fired an arrow that had a stick of dynamite attached to it at the building. The blast had taken out part of the outside wall above roll call. Luckily a fire truck had been close by and doused the flames before the building was engulfed. Two officers had been wounded in the blast.

No one except the bomber had come close to the police department since the first day of the riots. The police had brutally repulsed hundreds of rioters during the first hours of the riot. Their bodies still littered parts of the parking lots and the surrounding streets.

The officers sat in the roll call room's chairs, many with their heads laid on the desk in front of them, some lay sleeping on the floor. Exhaustion filled the being of every officer in the room.

The patrolman wore blue cotton uniforms; the pants had cargo pockets similar to BDU pants. Each officer was armed with a Glock 22 .40 caliber pistol, a Remington 870 shotgun, and several had personally owned AR-15's and AK-47's. Many officers wore bandoliers filled with shot shells. Instead of the usual two extra magazines for their pistols many carried nine or ten extra high capacity magazines. They all wore blue Kevlar helmets and level IIIA bullet resistant vest, Surplus military gas mask road on their thighs.

The Special Operations Team members were clad differently. They wore black Kevlar helmets, green nomex pilot flight suits and gloves. Underneath their flights suits they too wore the level IIIA bullet resistant vest. The assault vests were black and had ceramic inserts in them that had been purchased through the state. These ceramic shells could withstand shots from a .308 rifle round. Each wore a drop leg tactical holster that contained a Glock 22 .40 caliber with a tactical light attached. Each carried ten high capacity magazines for the pistol plus the one in the weapon. Each team member also had a Camelback Mother Load backpack filled with extra gear. Attached to one of the sides of the pack was a Remington 870 shotgun with a 14" barrel with a bandolier type sling that held twenty-five rounds. They were also armed with H&K UMP .40 caliber submachine guns. They had eight magazines for this weapon.

Chief Hopkins entered the roll call room. He looked around at his exhausted officers. This would defiantly be their last call; he would ask no more from these officers. He walked to the podium as officers sat up, some being awaken by those sitting next to them.

Hopkins cleared his throat and began. "Men earlier this morning I received a phone call from my cousin. He lives in Wildwood Terrace subdivision on Cypress Creek. He advised me that he and approximately sixty of his neighbors have been taken hostage by a large number of gang members. He was able to hide his cell phone when everyone was being rounded up and stripped of valuables." Hopkins paused for a moment to let that sink in.

He turned and gave a nod to Lt. Holsted. Holsted pulled a large map down that was rolled up on the back wall. "The gang members have placed everyone in two houses in the back of the subdivision that are on this bend of the creek." Hopkins pointed to the location on the map.

"The gang members have a roadblock set up here at Waterloo Rd. and Hwy 20. They have another heavily manned roadblock set up on the Cypress Creek Bridge on Waterloo Rd. As you all know Waterloo Rd. is the only road that leads to this subdivision. We are going to attack the bridge roadblock and send in the Special Ops guys to take down the two houses. The houses have about ten to fifteen gang members at any given time in each one." Hopkins paused for a moment to catch his breath and sort out in his mind what he wished to discuss next.

Officers who wanted to ask questions raised hands. Hopkins held up his left hand to stop any outburst or questions. "I want each of you to know now that this is strictly a voluntary operation. I don't want you to think I am doing this just for my cousin either. If you chose to go on this assignment or if you do not, after it is over I am relieving each of you from duty. We have no help from the outside coming in, and each of you has family to take care of. Does anyone wish to opt out and go ahead and head home?"

Hopkins was pleased with what he saw. No one raised a hand or said they wished to leave. What he saw now on their faces wasn't exhaustion, but a determined look on each face. These guys were tired of the lawless element taking their town and destroying it. They were ready to exact some punishment to those that had caused the destruction of this once fine city. A smile spread out across his face.

"Good! This is how we are going to conduct this operation. Lt. Erickson will now give the operation briefing." Hopkins stepped away from the podium and Lt. Erickson took his place.

"As the chief just stated there is only two ways in which to get into the subdivision by road. We don't have the manpower to hit both roadblocks at the same time. So what we are going to do is pin the gang members at the bridge down with suppression fire. We are going to caravan to within a quarter of a mile of the bridge near Wildwood Park. Patrol officers led by the chief will go by foot into the wood line and follow the bike trails to this hill that over looks the bridge."

Erickson pointed to a hill on the map. "The Special Operations Team will cross the creek at the jump off point and cross this ridge."

He pointed to the ridgeline. "We will then cross the creek again at this bend, then up and over this ridge. Our snipers will then take out any guards on the backside of the two target houses. Hopefully many of the thugs will go to the bridge to investigate and reduce the number of gang members in the houses. Once the snipers take out any sentries we will cross the creek for a third time in two six-man teams and simultaneously hit both houses. We will then send any hostage that is able across the creek to safety."

"Now once the hostages are free we will radio you and let you know. We will then begin clearing houses from the rear of the subdivision. Hopefully you will have taken out enough gang members to rush the roadblock and hold it. I am sure you will have gang members attempt to counter attack and take the bridge back from you. Are there any questions?"

There were few questions and the meeting quickly wrapped up. Hopkins took the podium again for the last time. "Okay men let's load up and kick some ass! Officers started to clear the room and head for squad cars. The Special Ops team headed for their large SWAT van.

The caravan of squad cars and the SWAT van left the police department parking lot. It was pitifully small, the van and six patrol cars led by the chief. They drove at high speed, no lights, and no sirens through the debris-choked street. Buildings still burned, bodies littered the streets. An occasional looter would fire a shot at the speeding police vehicles.

There was only one casualty on the way to the jump off point, Officer James Fulmer, who was sitting in the front passenger seat of the second patrol car. A looter had stepped from a doorway and raised his stolen .45 pistol and fired. The lucky shot struck Fulmer just in the right side of the face, just under the lip of his helmet. Officer Fulmer had pulled his last watch.

The looter had pulled the trigger for the last time. Officer Jerry Gant riding shotgun in the third squad car, his Remington 870 pointed out the window took care of the looter. A blast of 00 buck caught the man in the abdomen. It would take the man several excruciatingly painful hours to die.

⊹╼━╾⊹

The officers arrived at the jump off point five minutes later. Everyone checked his or her gear and weapons. The patrolmen circling around the chief, the Special Ops guys around Lt. Erickson.

Chief Hopkins looked at his assembled officers. "Let's do this right folks, and then let's get home" The chief turned and walked up the embankment, followed by the patrolmen. He located the bike trail and headed towards his objective.

The Special Ops team went down hill into the creek, across its twenty-yard span, and up the next ridge. The Florence Police would soon exact a stiff revenge against those that stood against law, and order.

—————

After slowly walking the quarter of a mile the patrol unit had reached its objective. The chief and his fourteen patrolmen spread out on line and took cover. Below, approximately thirty-five yards away was the roadblock. The roadblock consisted of two cars parked across both lanes of travel. There were several cars behind and in front of the cars that blocked the lanes.

Chief Hopkins swept the roadblock with his binoculars. He counted approximately forty-two gang members. Only a few were fully alert. They were armed with an assortment of weapons, shotguns, bolt rifles, lever actions, pistols, and quite a few military looking rifles. He then panned the surrounding area. Several bodies lay at both ends of the bridge. Flies swarmed around the dead decaying bodies. Down in the creek six more bodies lay half in half out of the water, the corpses bloated beyond recognition.

Of the fourteen officers under his command, five had AR-15's, three had AK-47's, and all were armed with shotguns. Before leaving everyone had loaded up with slugs. He had ordered the men with rifles to make up both his right and left flanks. They would start the ambush by taking out those with any military style weapons followed up by attempting to take out anyone with a bolt or lever rifle. The rest of the officers would use the shotguns on targets of opportunity.

The chief keyed up his radio. "Adam 1 to Lincoln 17. We are in position and are waiting for you to give the signal." Erickson keyed the mike twice to acknowledge.

—————

The Special Operations Team fanned out just below the military crest of the last ridge. The two snipers set up their rifles. Erickson took in the two houses across the creek.

What he saw encouraged him somewhat. There were only two sentries posted at the rear of each house. He could not tell about the front, but his snipers could make quick work of the four men, giving the rest of the team time to cross the creek and stack up on their points of entry.

A commotion caught his attention at the house on the left. A man was shoved out the door followed by two gang bangers. The two bangers were pointing their pistols at the man and telling him to walk out in the creek. The man backed into the creek till the water was knee deep. He held his hands out before him in a submissive manner. Erickson heard the thug holding a Mac 10 speak.

"Watch this shit man!" He turned from his companion lifted the Mac and fired off about a ten round burst. The man in the creek collapsed backwards as five rounds exploded into his chest, and stomach. Red stains of blood grew on his white polo shirt. The two laughed and turned to go back inside as their victim floated down stream.

Rage filled Erickson. He looked at his two snipers. "You boys ready?" He received minute nods from the two snipers. "Take them out."

The two snipers fired almost instantly. Two heads forty yards across the creek exploded. A fine pink and red mist floated on the morning air. Then the second set of sentries collapsed to the ground dead seconds later, a third eye had grown between their two eyes.

Erickson keyed the mike on his radio. "GO! GO! GO!" The chief heard the command given to the Special Ops Team. He and his men opened fire. The Tactical team rose from its position and swarmed across the creek.

Jack Bowman ran, his UMP held up a little higher than chest level as he crossed the shallow creek. He watched as a gang banger stepped around the corner of the house firing a handgun. The gang banger's chest exploded as one of the snipers took him out.

Jack stepped up onto the shore and began to approach the house. He had the UMP shouldered, and scanning for targets as he quickly walked in a crouched position to the back of his target house.

Suddenly gunfire came from above him. Rounds made a thwacking sound as they passed by his head and into the ground at his feet. He scanned up and spotted the gang banger who was firing from a large open window on the second floor. He was shooting what appeared to be an M-1 Carbine. Jack fired two three round burst. The forty caliber rounds stitched up the man's body shredding the man's groin, stomach and chest area. The rifle dropped from the bangers hands and hit the ground. The banger collapsed, half of his upper torso hanging from the window frame. Then Jack was in the stack and ready to enter the home.

The rear team member came up with a sledge hammer in his hands. Swinging the big sledge hammer he hit the door knob and knocked the door in, and then stepped to the side. Gunfire erupted, and rounds began to shred through the open door and the wall. The second man in the stack stepped out of the stack and deployed a flash bang through the open door.

BOOM! The flash bang exploded. The team exploded into the room. Jack entered and buttoned hooked to the right. A subject, gun in hand began to fire. Jack fired three rounds from his UMP as soon as the dot from his target laser rested on the man's head. His head popped like a balloon sending brain matter and pieces of skull against the wall behind him. Other team members were firing at multiple targets. They went room-to-room shooting armed suspects and handcuffing those that surrendered. When the team finally reached the large living room they found approximately twenty-five citizens cowering on the floor.

One gang banger was left. He held a gun to the head of a fifty-year-old woman. "GET BACK! GET BACK! I Will DO HER MAN!" He shouted.

Jack stepped towards the man and in a calm voice he said, "its cool man I am going to put my gun down. We'll let you go." Jack watched the man's eyes. They shifted between him and the other team members.

Jack lifted his right hand away from the pistol; his left still held the fore grip to the UMP. "Look man I'm dropping it."

Jack watched the man's eyes follow the UMP as he brought it down. Then fast as a snake Jack cleared his Glock 22 from his thigh holster with his right hand. Bringing it up he fired one shot striking the thug just below the right eye. The white curtains behind the thug were showered in blood and gray brain matter. The man dropped. The woman stood screaming.

Both teams had cleared the houses. Sporadic gunfire came from surrounding houses, blowing out windows and hitting the brick walls. The team was able to evacuate the fifty-three hostages to safety across the creek.

⊢•━•⊣

Chief Hopkins heard the report of the sniper rifles echo through the hills. Gang members below began to sit up. He took aim at a female gang member who had raised a lever action rifle to her shoulder. He fired the shotgun, the slug striking her below the right shoulder, severing the arm just below the shoulder, blood spouting from the stump. Her high wailing scream also reached his ears, but was immediately drowned out by the eruption of gunfire from his officers.

Ten gang bangers fell in the first volley. As the officers continued to fire the volume of return fire rose as the gang bangers located the officer's position. Tree limbs and branches fell from the surrounding trees. Chunks of bark were blow out of the trees that the chief was standing next to.

Chief Hopkins reloaded the shotgun and began to fire again. He spotted three of the gang members start to run down the bridge embankment attempting to flank them. He fired at them, BOOM! BOOM! BOOM! BOOM! The forth round took one of the bangers square in the back. One of the officers with an AK had also begun to fire at them. He had bump fired the AK making it fire as if it were full auto sending thirty rounds down at the two remaining thugs. AK rounds ate into the dirt around them several hitting the creek sending up geysers of water. Then two rounds found the lead banger striking him once in the back of the right thigh, the other in the back of the neck. The officer walked the rounds into the last banger shredding him from his left shoulder to his right foot. His body fell in the creek where he laid still, his body bobbing like a cork.

The return fire was still coming in hot and heavy as the chief took a knee behind a small tree to reload. Officer Kevin Maloney looked over just in time to see a round hit the tree in front of the chief. The round pierced the six -inch diameter tree then continued into Chief Hopkins head. The shotgun fell from the chief's hands as his body fell forward, his body supported by the tree. A second round fired by the same thug, shooting an 8mm rifle, struck the chief in the shoulder knocking his body to the ground.

Maloney spotted the deadly shooter. He raised his AR-15 and sent five rounds down range. Three rounds struck the banger in the chest sending up plums of blood.

Within ten minutes the firefight at the bridge was over. The ten remaining officers advanced and took control of the roadblock. But there they were pinned down by small arms fire from a house that sat atop a hill at the front of the subdivision. Lt. Holsted contacted the Tactical Team and advised them of their predicament.

―――――

The two snipers made their way across the creek and set up inside the captured houses. Their presence became immediately know to at least seven, now dead gang members.

Lt. Erickson ordered the two elements of his team to rush in pairs of twos to the house across the street. Cover fire would come from the rest of the team. As the first two pairs rushed across the street and onto the lawn across the street a pipe bomb landed just in front of Officers Clunk and Davis.

Davis dove left just before the bomb went off. Clunk was not so lucky. The bomb exploded as his right foot landed right beside it. The explosion sent him flying six feet back the way he had just come. When he hit the ground on his back his hands were already clasping his right knee. That was all of the leg he could grab, the stump where his leg once was pumped blood. Clunk rolled left and right holding the leg screaming. His screams increased when he saw the other part of his leg by the simmering hole in front of him.

The thug stepped out to throw a second bomb at the injured officer, the smoke from its fuse flowing behind him. Davis had just come up on his knees and saw the bomb thrower. He unleashed half a magazine from his UMP on full auto. Rounds peppered the thug's torso some going straight through him into the wall behind him. He collapsed three feet from the door. Then the second bomb exploded. Taking most of the wall behind the thug and ripping the dead man's body apart. The only thing left of him was his lower torso.

―――――

The team had made it almost to the front of the subdivision. It appeared they only had the one house left to go. This was the house that was keeping the patrolmen on the bridge penned down. It was also keeping the team pretty well pinned down.

Tim Buchanan checked his load. He was down to one magazine for his UMP, and one for his Glock. He advised the LT. The entire team was down to almost nothing for ammo. The patrolmen below had also radioed and advised they were almost out. No one had thought to bring extra ammo from the ammo room where over 200,000 rounds of various calibers sat.

Erickson looked around the garage of the house they were in. He found a gas can with about one quart of gas left in it. Then and there he decided they would burn out these thugs. There was no more law to stand in his way to get those gang members out. They seemed to have plenty of ammo where as they were almost out. He filled a mason jar full of the gas and made a gas bomb. He then went back the rest of the team. "Guys we're gonna burn these fuckers out."

Buchanan spoke up. "Sir, I believe the FBI did that once or twice and I don't think the citizens approved of it to much, especially the militias and patriots."

Erickson looked at Buchanan. "Tim there aint no laws right now, no courts, no TV. And if these guys across the street were Patriots, or Militia they would be fighting with us not against us. Plus those thugs already used bombs. They just upped the ante. Also the law says we can use greater force than is used against us to affect an arrest. I say a fire bomb is equal to not greater than a pipe bomb."

Tim just shrugged his shoulders. "Okay, good enough for me boss. I'll do it."

Erickson handed him the firebomb. Tim took it out the back door and lit it. "Cover Me!" he shouted as he ran towards the gang-infested house. The team opened up.

Tim ran in a zigzag pattern across the street. Rounds ricochet off the pavement around him. One round grazed his right thigh but he kept running. He was halfway into the yard when he stopped to through the firebomb through a busted out window. A thug fired a 30-30 rifle at him; the round striking Tim in the left shoulder exiting his arm into his armpit and then finally into his spine.

Tim dropped straight down on his butt, legs out in front of him. Rounds bounced off or flattened against his ceramic entry vest, one round striking his helmet knocking it from his head.

Tim knew he was done for. He stared at the firebomb in his left hand. His last act as a crime fighter was to toss the firebomb through the window. It exploded with a whooshing sound. Soon the house was flaming up.

The gang bangers jumped from windows and out of doors and were gunned down like dogs. None survived the attack. In fact none survived at all. Those that had been captured where later turned over to the residents of the neighborhood where they stood a quick trial and were killed by a variety of methods. One was burned to death at the stake for raping a small child. The captured weapons were also turned over to the residents along with the ammunition.

The officers collected their dead, and returned to the Police Department were each member was given a share of the ammo in the storage room and equipment around the department.

Of the twenty-seven officers that participated in the "Battle At Cypress Creek", as historians would later call it, only fifteen lived. A historical marker would later be placed at the site of Chief Hopkins death. The Florence Police had answered their last cry for help for a very long time.

Chapter 15

It had been three days since Don's shootout at Wilson Dam. Beside several FPD cops taking a few statements from him in the emergency room, Don had not seen any other police official. Not even anyone from his department.

He had watched TV in his private room that his insurance covered. He was shocked, but not surprised at the events that had unfolded. He was just so surprised it had taken this long for someone in the world to step to the plate and take a swing at his hated country. Of course in his opinion the hate was not justified. America had done a lot for the world.

The TV reception was gone at 8:30 am. Five minutes later two nurses wheeled in a man on a gurney and parked him beside his bed. "Hey what's going on nurse? This is a private room."

The tired nurse looked at him blankly for a moment. Her hair was a mess, bloodstains on her white scrubs. She looked like she could use some sleep.

"Officer Savage the hospital is about out of room. We are overflowing with patients. I know your ribs are cracked but it would probably be best if you left and went home." She and the other nurse turned and walked out of the room.

Don looked over to the man in the gurney. "What's going on out there?"

The man turned his head and looked at Don. He was around fifty with graying black hair. His left leg was wrapped in a layer of white bandages.

Blood and seeped and spread on the gauze. "It's bad all over. I run a hardware store over by the post office on Seminary St. I held off the looters for the past three days. The sons of bitches finally got me though. Shot me up real good. I took down a whole bunch of them though. Luckily for me that ambulance drove by while I was crawling down the sidewalk." He let out a short quiet laugh to himself and shook his head.

Don was surprised at what he had just heard. "What about the police? How bad is the looting and rioting? No one has told me much."

The man smirked and shook his head. "What police? They're getting torn up out there. I think they have had ten or fifteen killed, it just depends on who you talk to"

"I think it's time for me to get home" Don swung his feet to the floor. He let out a groan as a acute pain went through him as he shifted his weight around. His ribs were killing him.

Don walked over to the tall wall locker and opened it up. His uniform and vest had been cleaned and put in the locker. There were holes from the shotgun blast in his shirt and some of the pellets were still embedded in the back of his vest.

Don dressed himself and winced when he tightened the Velcro straps on the vest. His boots and leather gear had dried out. Don had cleaned his pistol, magazines and bullets as best he could yesterday. They had been returned to him since there was no place for them in the hospital. Don pressed checked the Sig to make sure a round was in the chamber. There was, and he holstered the pistol.

The man behind Don spoke. "Are you one of the TVA officers that got shot up three days ago?"

"Yeah I am." Don said as he tightened the laces on his boots.

"Did you kill any of those bastards?"

"Yeah, I got one but the rest got me."

"Well all a man can do is try as best he can." The man dozed off as the pain medication took hold of him.

Don walked from the room and headed for the elevator. The hallway was clogged with people in different states of injury, and misery. "Damn!" He said to himself.

"If it's this bad on the fourth floor, I wonder what the lower levels look like." Don walked through the throng of wailing and moaning people, and got into the elevator.

Don pushed the button that would take him to the ER exit. Maybe he could hitch a ride from an ambulance crew member or police officer down stairs. He would soon find out.

The elevator went non-stop to the ER. It was quiet in the elevator on the way down, but that all changed when the doors opened and he stepped out into the ER. People were screaming in pain, the floor, chairs, and beds were full of people with an assortment of injuries, and stages of medical treatment. Nurses and doctors ran in every direction. Don made a beeline for the exit where the ambulances dropped off patients.

He stood out under the canopy of the loading bay. Two ambulances sat idling the back doors open. A tired looking security guard of around sixty stood by scanning the area smoking a cigarette. Don noticed that the guard had a .38 revolver hanging from his belt. "Since when do they let yall carry guns?"

The old man looked at Don, "Ever since some crack head went bonkers in the ER and shot two doctors and a nurse who refused to give him drugs."

"What happened to the crack head?" Don asked

"Well I shot him. I had my .38 chief special in my pocket. No one said a thing to me about it except to keep bringing it to work."

Don nodded his head, "Well at least they didn't raise a stink about it, and made the decision to keep you coming back armed."

"I wouldn't be here without it. Want a smoke."

The old man held out a cigarette.

Don took the Marlboro and a light from the old man. He inhaled deeply on the cigarette; the nicotine seemed to calm him almost immediately. Then two EMTs came out of the double doors of the ER.

Don turned to look at the two. "Mind if I hitch a ride fellas?"

"Where are you headed to?" Replied one of the EMTs as he threw his medical bag in the back of the ambulance.

I live about two miles north of the city limits just off of HWY 17" Don said.

The two EMTs looked at each other for a second. The blonde EMT nodded his head to the other EMT.

"We'll give you a lift to the city limits. Really shouldn't you know? We don't have much diesel left. Hop in the back." Don boarded into the back of the ambulance tossed his smoke and gave a wave to the security guard who just nodded and turned to scan the area again.

The driver kicked on the lights and sirens and tore out of the parking lot. "What're you running code for? "Don asked.

The passenger looked back and answered. "For some reason they don't shoot at us or try to stop us if we run code."

The passenger pointed over at the sidewall of the ambulance where three bullet holes had come through. Don just shook his head in disbelief.

Through the front window Don observed the devastation that was now the city of Florence. Don was dumbfounded by the devastation and wreckage. There were dead bodies, dead animals, burned out cars and homes everywhere one looked. Some people walked the streets boldly brandishing rifles and pistols. Others scurried for the nearest cover or concealment at the approach of the ambulance.

"Why are some of the folks running when they see the ambulance?"

The EMT looked back again. "Well one of our trucks had stopped to help some folks that were injured. A crowed of folks started throwing crap at them and even a few took some potshots. Hank, he's a former Marine, ran back to the truck and pulled out his M-14 and started dusting folks. He did it again two hours later when he watched a few looters robbing some dying folks. Killed six of the rioters, the rest hauled ass. So I guess word spread to leave the injured alone, especially when an ambulance rolls in to help out. We all carry now." The man un-holstered a Berretta 92 F that for some reason Don had missed while talking to the two EMTs.

Don smiled, "What are the mailmen carrying?"

The man looked at him seriously. "Well the ones I have seen still on the job are carrying all kinds of main battle rifles, plus pistols and shotguns. Folks stay the hail away from them. I guess they don't want those boys going postal on them." He laughed.

Don just sat there in silence, had it really only been three days? How in the heck had things gone to hell in a hand basket so fast?

Ten minutes later the ambulance slowed to a stop at the city limits. "Here we are partner! Hurry up we don't want to sit here to long."

Don opened the back door and hopped out. He shut the door, slapped the door twice with his palm to let him know he was out. The ambulance did 180, tires squealing siren and lights going and headed back to town. Don started to walk home.

He really wanted to get off the road but felt it would be a bad idea. Houses lined this portion of HWY 117 and steep ditches on both sides. Hopefully he would make it home without incident. The walk was killing his ribs; his breathing came in labored gasps.

Finally he came to the dirt county road that led to his house. His home lay another half mile down the road. Don's step quickened at the thought of getting home. Within fifteen minutes he could see his home. He was sweating profusely in the uniform and vest. He was dying for a drink. His mouth and throat were dry and parched; he had to try hard to work up some saliva in his mouth just to spit.

The house sat one hundred yards off the road. A few shade trees surrounded the house. The rest of his six-acre property was open field. He had a small shooting range just out back of the house. Don walked into the tree line that surrounded the open fields around his home. He squatted and looked at the house.

He saw that an unfamiliar car sat in the driveway. The front glass door swung back and forth, the front door open. Don pulled out his pistol and made his way stealthily as a man with three cracked ribs could towards the house.

Within a few minutes he was even with the house. The engine of the red Pontiac idled. He saw a bunch of items in the car. Many of them were not his. Then tall thin man walked out with Don's stereo in his hands. A short squat man with a beard followed him; Don could not make out what was in his hands.

Don was about twelve yards from the car, and as the two men drew near it he made his move. "Police, don't move or I am going to blow your shit away!"

Don advanced and got behind the front of the car, the engine block between him and the two burglars. The first man froze in mid stride. The second stepped out around his friend. Don's eyes went wide, as he saw the man bring up the sawed off double barrel shotgun. The twin holes on the twelve inch barrels looked colossal. He ducked behind the car, just as one of the barrels belched fire.

Don heard the pellets striking the car. His ribs screamed at him as he bent over. Don came back up with his pistol the pain now forgotten in the heat of the shootout. The man was adjusting his grip and grabbing the front of the stock with his left hand Don fired two shots and ducked back down again. He moved towards the truck of the car. The second man had disappeared. He had to find him before he got caught in crossfire. The back passenger window blew out in a shower of glass as he moved under it.

Don popped back up and caught the man flat footed. The shotgun was broke open and draped across his left arm, his right hand held two shotgun shells. Don didn't hesitate. He fired two more rounds. One striking the burglar in the right shoulder the second struck the man in the right cheek. The man dropped to the ground as his legs collapsed under him. Don also noticed that there was blood on his left thigh. One of his first two rounds must have hit him, the 9mm round failing to drop the man or hinder him in the fight.

Don moved again a back towards the front of the car. His pistol was extended out in front of him. He moved his upper torso like a tank turret, left and right scanning the area for threats. As he looked towards his carport two rounds careened into the hood of the car just in front of him. Don turned back to the front door a fired a shot at the man. The burglar had his head just out far enough to look down the sights of the small caliber pistol in his hand.

Don's round struck the bricks just below and in front of the man's face. The burglar let out a yelp of pain and fired off a wild round before ducking back in the house.

Don made a break for the carport. He had noticed that the carport door wasn't open. Don didn't stop as he hit the door with his shoulder. It buckled inward as his 6'3" 220 lbs. body hammered into it.

As he made his way quickly but cautiously through the kitchen the second burglar did a quick peek around the corner. As soon as he saw Don he ducked back. Don did not wait for him to stick his head or gun back out. Don fired five rounds into the sheetrock wall where the man had vanished.

Don heard the groan of pain and a split second later the burglar fell out into the open. Don approached cautiously his gun trained on the man. As Don walked up he placed his foot on the man's wrist that held the small pistol. Don took the gun from his hand and placed it on the counter.

"Is there anyone else in the house?" Don said to the man.

The man rolled his head to look up at Don. His eyes were vacant his breathing coming in labored short wheezes. Don looked at the man's chest. Blood pumped from a small hole near the man's heart. Then the man gave a sigh as if frustrated and died. Don did a quick search of his house and found it empty. The house had obviously been ransacked before these two had arrived. His guns and ammo were gone from his gun cabinet. The kitchen cabinets were strewn open most of the food gone.

Don walked into the walk-in closet in the spare bedroom. The back wall of the closet appeared to the uninitiated as just a plain paneling. Don pushed the left hand side near the corner. The panel popped open. Don stepped back as he pulled it the rest of the way open. A large cabinet and shelf stood behind the panel, above the shelves hung an FN-FAL, and a Kimber 1911A1 pistol. The shelf directly below these two weapons contained ten magazines for the rifle and ten for the pistol. There were two cases of ammo for each on the next shelf. Don then opened the large drawer below the ammo. The drawer contained a LBV and a tactical assault pack with assorted gear, two sets of OD green BDU's socks and a pair of Danner boots. He opened the cabinet below the drawer. Twelve cases of MREs rested there. Don closed the panel back up and decided to check to see if the Scout II was still in the shop.

Dan walked to the shop. The door was up and the Scout was visible inside. He entered the shop and saw most of his tools were gone. The hood on the Scout was up and he walked over to it. He smiled nothing was missing. He had the battery, plug wires and distributor cap in a hidden box. He then walked around outside to the back of the shop. His fuel was still in place. He wrapped his knuckles on the two metal 55-gallon drums that sat up on supports. Both were full, the looters had missed them.

"Well" he said to himself, "I'm down but not out." Don walked back to the house to remove the bodies.

Chapter 16

After two days of the power being out Bob and Caroline Novacheck realized that the thirty gallons of fuel they had on hand would not carry them very far running the generator five to six hours a day. The evening of the second day they decided only to run the generator for thirty minutes to an hour so they would be able to wash clothes or heat the hot water heater for a quick warm shower.

They had also taken all of the cold food and put it in the deep freezer. They made as much ice as possible the first and second day. They had turned on the generator and used the refrigerator's ice machine. Also they took over 150 Styrofoam cups that had been destined for work, and filled them full of water and froze them making huge ice cubes for the deep freeze.

It had now been three days since the power was out. Bob and Caroline were on their huge deck in the back of the house. Bob sat back in a lawn chair drinking a cup of coffee, his S&W Model 10 in a holster on his hip. He was wearing flip- flops and jogging pants. They were already rationing the coffee. Though they had three large tins of coffee they knew that it would be a precious commodity for barter if things stayed bad. They allowed themselves one cup of coffee in the morning.

Bob also cut his smoking down to four cigarettes a day. That would make a pack last five days. He had four cartons of cigarettes in his closet, and he knew that smoking a half a pack a day would eat through them. Caroline also told him how valuable they would be to barter. He said he would have no part in bartering away his one vice. He had countered her recommendation with how the prospect of how lucrative prostitution was during times like these. That of course had earned him a quick jab to the solar plexus from Caroline.

Caroline stood in her bathrobe cooking the last of their eggs over the propane grill. Her Sig .380 was in the large right hand pocket. They had decided to use the propane grill instead of the Coleman camp stove. The two bottles were full and would last quite awhile. They only had a couple of one-gallon cans of Coleman fuel.

The two now remained armed at all times. The morning of the second day Bob saw both of his neighbors packing up their vehicles. Dan Bullion had told him about a group of gang members that had murdered and raped several people on two different blocks in the neighborhood. As Dan had told the story more neighbors had come out to hear the story and discuss what was going on. Panic swept through his street and word spread throughout the neighborhood. By noon everyone on his street had packed and left.

Each one of them he and Caroline had talked to did not have a real destination in mind, most heading to family members in other cities and states. Bob took a walk around the neighborhood and it was the same story on each street. He could feel the fear in the air. There were now very few people left one or two families on each street, some with none at all.

Caroline pushed a loose hair away from her face. "What are we going to do today Bob?"

Bob took a sip of hot coffee and a slow drag from his cigarette before answering. Caroline did not mind the wait; she knew how he liked his morning coffee and cigarettes. "Cigarette" she corrected herself with a smile, if this last much longer than a few weeks he will have to quit.

"I thought about breaking out the chainsaw and cutting a few trees down for some firewood." He motioned to the heavily wooded one-acre back yard with his cigarette.

Caroline looked back at him over her left shoulder with a questioning expression on her face. "Don't you think the noise might attract unwanted visitors?"

"I thought about that. But from what most of the folks at the front of the neighborhood said the gang left early on the morning of the second day. They said the gang was driving in the Donavan's Land Rover and Expedition. Do you know the Donavan's? I can't place them."

"I think they lived two blocks over I am not sure. You still haven't answered me yet. Get back on the subject of using the chainsaw." Caroline said as she turned and pointed the spatula at him.

"Okay. Okay. Be careful with that thing you can put an eye out." He said with a smile.

"I think while folks are still in the area and folks are still moving around it would not seem to out of place yet. The longer this goes, the less fuel will be around. So the use of cars, trucks, tractors, chainsaws and whatever else uses fuels will diminish as time goes on. So if it is used now people will not think it out of place. If this thing is a prolonged event, and we wait, folks who are scavenging will hear it and come to investigate. Plus it will give the wood time to age a little before winter hits."

"So the short of it is that people have not yet adapted to the possible loss of modern conveniences, and won't find the sound out of place?" Caroline said.

Bob took another drag on his cigarette. "Yes."

"Sweetheart next time I ask you a question remind me to pull up a chair. You are the longest winded person I know." She turned to finish up the eggs. Bob timed his smoking and coffee drinking perfectly, as he finished both at about the same time and he got up to go inside to get plates and forks for breakfast.

The two finished their meager meal and took their dishes to the sink inside. They put the dishes in a Tupperware try filled with soapy water. Bob scrubbed them and then handed them to Caroline to rinse and dry. Caroline poured the water from a small pitcher. They were washing dishes this way to conserve water in the hot water heater in case the water plant quit pumping water. They felt this would happen any day now. As she stood drying the dishes she turned to look at her husband. "Bob, this is a terrible waste of water, especially our drinking water. I don't know how long the water pressure will remain but we need to start to think about where else to get water from."

Bob leaned back against the counter. "Well do you have any ideas because I sure don't?"

"As a matter of a fact I do. We need to take some of those new trashcans that we were going to take to work and use them to catch rain water."

"Caroline, I am glad you thought of that but it would take weeks of rain to fill those things up."

"Well there boy genius, I did not mean leave them out in the open to fill up with rain water. I meant take part of the down spouts off the gutters and fill them like that." Caroline said with an expression on her face that said "You Dumb ass." Of course he knew the look, because she gave it to him quite regularly.

"Oh. Do you intend to drink this water?" Bob noticed the expression grow bigger on her face. It was time to put the thinking cap on before she had him sent to some sanitarium for the completely stupid.

"We could if we had to. We would have to either make charcoal filters of some sort or boil it. What I meant though was to use it to flush the toilets, and bathe in. That would save us a lot of drinking water." Caroline crossed her arms and gave him that look that mothers have for children who have trouble comprehending what they were just told.

"Oh I get it. Hey, sounds like you have been talking to Jack Wilson."

"Yes I have. We discussed what could possibly happen. I had him load me up some nifty little rounds for my pistol. I would imagine that was about the time you bought all those 00 buck and slug rounds for your shotgun." Bob's mouth hung open a little and he had the proverbial deer caught in the headlights look.

"Don't worry I am not mad at you. After Jack and his wife opened my eyes a little bit I thought it was sweet." She smiled to let him know she was not truly mad because he hid the purchase from him. "Besides it was sweet thinking about my man buying all those bullets to protect little old me." She said in her best southern bell accent.

Bob finally regained the power of speech. "I am sorry I did not tell you about all the ammo and food I was buying. I just didn't want you to get all worried."

Caroline walked to her husband and put her arms around him and kissed him on the cheek. "It's all right Bob. I am the one who should be apologizing not you."

"You didn't do anything Caroline. There is no need for you to apologize." Bob said a little confused.

"Bob I did not believe everything Jack and his wife told me. But, I did realize things were going bad and some preparations were necessary. Instead of coming to you about it, and the two of us discussing what we might need I let you purchase things piecemeal. Now things have hit the fan, and what you have purchased may help us for a little while, it still is not enough. So accept my apology."

Bob kissed his wife and smiled. "I'm not mad at you Caroline. I should have told you about some of my fears. You're the better planner and organizer. If you and I had talked this out we would be sitting pretty right now."

Caroline gave him a peck on the lips and pushed away. "Well we're not so quit kissing on me and go get your chainsaw. You have work to do while I sit inside on the couch and eat chocolate covered cherries." Caroline laughed as she walked away to go change clothes for the days work ahead. Bob also followed to change into his work clothes.

Once outside Bob went out back and cut down two thirty-foot tall elm trees. They were both about two feet in diameter. After he cut them down he trimmed away the branches. He cut the logs into about two-foot lengths. He used the chainsaw to cut them in half.

When he was finished he went to the shop to get the dolly. He loaded up the wood and stacked it on the wood rack on the back deck. Bob knew he would need more wood if this incident was going to last into the winter. It was a good thing he had purchased the soapstone wood burning stove for his office last year. It wouldn't heat the whole house but they could close off most of the house and use a couple of rooms. Tomorrow he would cut down three or four larger trees. For now though he wanted to talk to Caroline about the plan he wanted to implement, and get some lunch.

Caroline's job had been to keep watch while Bob cut wood. When he was finished and washed up the two fixed a couple of peanut butter and honey sandwiches and drank water.

Bob wiped his mouth with his napkin and set it on the crumb filled plate. "Caroline I have been thinking about what to do about supplies." He said.

"Well let's hear it boy genius." She smiled at her husband. She teased him a lot about being dimwitted, but he was one of the smartest and best businessmen she had ever met. She took another bite of her sandwich while her husband explained what he wanted to do to increase their chances of survival.

"Well, yesterday when I was walking around the neighborhood I watched a lot of people load up their cars. They were mostly taking clothes and keepsakes. I did not see anyone packing up food, extra gas, or that many guns. You see..."

Caroline did not let him finish detailing his plan. She had already figured out what he wanted to do. "You want to break into peoples houses and steal their things. Well I don't agree with you."

Bob looked frustrated. Because number one she did not let him finish, and number two it sometimes bugged him that she could figure out what was going on in his brain before he finished talking. "I'm not going to steal Caroline. I will leave a note at each house telling them who was there and what I took. We'll keep the stuff we take in reserve in case ours run out. If they come back we return it. If they come back and we have used it I will pay them for it when things get back to normal."

The expression on Caroline's face told Bob that she was considering what he had planned. He pushed more. "Caroline, our lives are in jeopardy. Well, maybe not this instant, but if things get worse or last more than a couple of months we will starve or freeze to death when the winter comes. We need fuel for the generator, medicine, and food."

Caroline sat back in her chair and folded her hands in her lap. Her head slightly tilted down her brow wrinkled as she pondered the moral dilemma that they faced. Finally she raised her head and looked into her husband's eyes. "I will go along with it. You will not however take jewelry, furs, cars, money, or furniture. Food, medicine, gas, ammunition, matches, and guns should be about the only thing you need to take. I'm sure there will be a few other things but just the basic necessities."

Bob exhaled in relief. He sat back in his chair. "I figured you would agree. The first house I want to go into is Dan's. I doubt he will be back, said he was going to his family farm in Mississippi. I don't think he would be to upset either, I think he would understand. I want you to keep watch while I go over though okay?"

"Alright Bob. I will hurry up and finish eating so you can get started." Caroline took a sip of water and then finished off her sandwich.

Bob walked out to the shop and got his wheel barrel and head next door to Dan's place. He went into the back yard and pushed the wheel barrel next to the back door. Bob reached down into the flower bed and picked up the fake rock that held the back door key. He took the key out and unlocked the door and then replaced the key to its hiding place.

Bob lifted up on the handles and went into the kitchen and set the wheel barrel down. He then opened all of the cabinet doors. He found were Dan kept his can goods and began loading the cans into the wheel barrel. He netted thirty cans of food. Beans, beef stew, chicken noodle soup, and an assortment of fruits, and types of vegetable cans.

Dan then moved to the next cabinet. He found two five pound bags of sugar, a ten pound bag of rice, a five pound bag of flour, several smaller bags of dried pinto beans, black eye peas, kidney beans, and two large boxes of powdered milk.

As he rose up he noticed the spice rack. He took it and added it to his growing pile of groceries. He also noticed a Hostess Cup Cake sitting there. He opened up the package and ate the treat.

In the next cabinet he got a box of instant oatmeal and another of instant grits. In this cabinet he also located numerous boxes of Jiffy instant cornbread, blueberry muffins and pancake mix.

He found nothing else in the cabinets so he opened the freezer. Two loaves of thawed out bread were located and added to the pile. He then opened the refrigerator door. The food had not gone bad yet, but he really was not interested in left over dishes. He opened one of the drawers and found about twenty eight ounce juices that Dan's seven year old son loved so much. Pulling the drawer out he dumped them on the pile. The wheel barrel was close to over flowing so Dan headed back to the house. Before leaving he made a list of the food he had taken.

Caroline and Dan spent the next thirty minutes adding the food to their own cabinets. Dan turned to walk out the door and continue his search. Caroline noticed he had not taken the wheel barrel. "You forgot your shopping cart Bob."

Bob turned, "I will be right back. I'm going to get Dan's propane tank from his grill." He turned and went next door.

The propane tank's fuel gage read half full. Dan was hoping that it would be full since it was the beginning of spring and most folks did not use their gas grills for cooking in the winter. "Guess Dan forgot to fill it up." He said to himself. He unhooked the tank and took it back to the house.

Once back in the kitchen Bob got a glass from the cupboard. He turned on the facet and when the glass was half full the water quit flowing. Bob tried the other faucet, nothing. "I think we just lost our water Caroline."

"Well I was hoping for a few more days. Let's hope it rains soon so we can get some fresh water from the trash cans." Caroline replied.

Bob downed his water, picked up the wheel barrel and headed back. He had to hurry it was getting on towards late afternoon and soon he would not have any light to search by. Once inside Dan's house he first checked the bathrooms.

In the first bathroom he opened the medicine cabinet and found a bottle of prescription pain pills, aspirin, Tums, Aleve, first aid cream, a small box of bandages, Vaseline, dental floss, and two new tubes of toothpaste.

He then took the half roll of toilet paper off of the holder and threw it in the barrel. "Now that's bartering material." Bob thought. He had not even thought about what a luxury toilet paper really was.

On the way to Dan's bedroom Bob paused at the hallway closet. He stopped and opened up. He scanned the shelves and found nothing useful. That is until he looked on the floor. There set two packages of twelve, rolls of toilet paper. "Gold mine!" Bob added the rolls to the barrel.

In Dan's room he located a box of number eight shot twelve gauge shells. He did not locate anything else of use. He did however get two more rolls of toilet paper and some feminine products out of the master bedroom. He then ran these items back to his house and returned.

Searching Dan's son's room he found a drawer full of new batteries. There were C's, D's, nine volt, and AA. Shannon was a gadget freak and needed tons of batteries for all of his gadgets. The only other useful item that he located was a Buck sheath knife.

He searched the rest of the house and found nothing that he thought would be useful. His next stop was Dan's garage. In the garage Bob found a half empty can of Coleman fuel, a Coleman lantern, a kerosene heater two gallons of kerosene, and one five gallon can full of fuel sitting by the lawn mower and hot water heater.

As he moved the mower to get at the gasoline the front wheel of the mower hit the hot water heater scraping the paint. Bob stopped and stared at the water heater. Next to the scratch was the drain valve. Then he let out a whoop and grabbed the gas can and wheel barrel and headed back to his house.

After putting the gas, kerosene and heater in the shop he burst into the house with the wheel barrel. Caroline was not in the kitchen. "Caroline where are you!" he shouted.

Caroline's voice came from the den. "In here looking out the front window."

Dan ran into the den. "Caroline our drinking water problem may be solved. I have had an inspiration."

Caroline turned with a look of surprise on her face. "What did you find a well?"

"No nothing that great, but it will get us by for a while." He said excitedly.

Caroline gave him the make it quick and to the point look. "Tell me what it is Bob, I don't need a drawn out story."

"Water heaters!" he said. "We hook up a hose to all the water heaters and drain them into containers. Almost everyone has left the neighborhood. There will be at least a hundred to tap. The average water heater holds fifty gallons so that is roughly five thousand gallons of water!"

Caroline's face broke into a big grin. "Well boy genius I guess you finally have earned that nickname Jack gave you."

"I am going down to the basement and get a couple of those trash cans you were talking about. I will fill them up and that will give us a fair amount of drinking water to add to our supplies. We can leave the water in the white barrels. The water will store better in them. We can go ahead and use what we get in the trash cans." Bob turned and ran downstairs. Caroline just smiled and shook her head. She turned to watch the street.

On his way over to Dan's, Bob grabbed the dolly and a garden hose. Once back in Dan's garage he hooked up the hose and filled the first trash can about three quarters of the way full. He took it back to the house and put it in the kitchen. The trip to the house was slow and tedious. Bob did not dare to spill his precious cargo. He returned and filled the second one. Once that was filled Bob grabbed one of Dan's five gallon buckets. He filled this also. He would use it to flush the toilet tonight.

Once back in the kitchen of his own house Caroline directed him to where she wanted the second garbage can. Once it was in place his wife gave him a full kiss on the mouth. "I believe your idea could save our bacon." Caroline turned to walk over to kitchen table and sat down and bumped into the wheel barrel.

As she looked down she saw all of the toilet paper and feminine products. She turned to her husband. "Baby, you sure do know how to treat a doomsday girl. First trashcans full of water, and now a wheel barrel full of toilet paper and Maxi pads."

"You ain't seen anything yet! Wait till the food runs out and I forage out couple of cases of dog food. It will be a feast Mad Max and his dog would be proud of." Bob said jokingly. Of course, in the back of his mind he realized that they could wind up in the same boat as one of his all time favorite movie heroes.

Dan pulled out his list and added all the items that he had forgot to list. He then signed and dated it. "Be right back, I am going to put this on Dan's kitchen table." Bob went next door.

Caroline looked around her kitchen. A lot of the food Bob brought home would not fit in their cabinets. Since she had just gone grocery shopping the day before everything went to hell. Just this one house had probably added another two to three weeks worth of food and fuel to their supplies. She felt extremely guilty about what she had agreed to let Bob do. What if the people returned and they had eaten all of the food that they had took from their homes. It was not right, but starving to death while food sat all around you in empty houses would be obtuse.

Chapter 17

Celina Donovan woke from her fitful slumber. The early morning sun cascaded through the gap in her bedroom curtains across her tired face. She was wrapped snuggly in her sheets and dozed for a bit in the early morning silence. She rolled over to look at her digital clock to see what time it was. She had school this morning.

As she rolled over and looked at the blank clock she realized she did not have school. What she realized was that she was living in a nightmare. The events of the night after the lights went out flashed through her mind. She could still hear the fat gang member's screams of pain from the vicious stabbing she had given him. The sight of her father's body laying lifeless in the living room floor, and screams of her mother and sister being raped also flooded her mind.

⟡⟡⟡

The events that took place at the Donovan's residence on the second day:

The morning following the gang member's assault on her home Celina entered her house. She had found her mother and sister still nude and asleep in each other's arms. She had gotten her sister awake, covered her mother with a blanket. She then covered her father's body with another blanket that had draped the recliner. She then took her sister, who walked in a zombie like state, to the bathroom. She ran a hot bath for her and put her in. Then she bathed her sister, scrubbing away the blood that had stained her thighs and buttocks.

After bathing Daphne, Celina dried her off and walked her to her bedroom. There she dressed her sister in some jogging pants and a t-shirt and lay her back down. She went to the medicine cabinet in their bathroom and found the bottle of pain pills Celina had been prescribed when she broke her arm several months ago. She poured a glass of water from the bathroom sink and took the pill into her sister.

Daphne took the pill and looked into her sister's eyes. Daphne spoke in a whisper "Thanks sis." Shame filled her face and she turned her head from her older sister and lay down.

Celina then went to the den and woke her mother. Nancy had awaked with horror still in her eyes. She too was in an almost automaton like state. Celina sat down beside her mother and hugged her. Nancy's arms sat limply in her lap, tears rolled down her face.

"Mom we need to get you cleaned up. I have already got Daphne cleaned up and she is sleeping in her room." Celina's mother had not answered. So Celina stood up and took her mother's hands and led her to the bath just as she had done with her sister. They went into the master bath instead of hers. When Celina walked her mother into the bedroom she saw all of the blood on her parent's bed. Instead of putting her mom in the bath Celina had turned on the shower, helped her mother scrub her body.

She had left her mom standing under the spray of hot water and returned to her parent's bedroom. She stripped the bed of the bloody sheets and took them to the laundry room. She returned and put fresh sheets on the bed. She wished she had thought of doing it for Daphne, but it had not crossed her mind.

After cleaning up the room a bit she went back to get her mother. She turned the water off and then toweled her mother off. She gave her mother some fresh clothes to put on. "Here mom, get dressed." Nancy just did as she was told, she moved in unthinking motions. Celina gave her mother a glass of water and two of the pain pills and took her mother to her bed.

Celina's mother spoke hoarsely, "Where is your sister?"

"I took care of her mom. She is cleaned up and asleep." Celina covered her mother with the fresh sheets.

"Did they hurt you too Celina?"

"No mother I stabbed the one who tried to hurt me and ran out back after I shot at those fuckers." Celina's voice quivered with anger.

"What about your father, is he okay?" Tears welled up in her mother's eyes.

Celina had fought back tears when she answered her mother. "No mother, he did not make it. You just go to sleep and I will take care of dad." Her mother just lay back on the pillow staring at the wall. Her eyes seemed dead to Celina.

Celina then went to the kitchen and dialed 911. The phone rang and rang until an exhausted sounding dispatcher answered, "911 what is your emergency?"

Celina took a deep breath, "My name is Celina Donovan. My father was shot and killed last night and my mother and sister were raped. We need help."

The dispatcher's tone of voice turned from frustrated and tired to caring. "Listen Celina, it may be a day or two till we can get to you if we can get to you. I don't want to frighten you but you need to know what is going on. There have been riots all over, hundreds of killings, arsons, and everything else you can think of. We just can't get everywhere. FEMA and the state and federal government are nowhere to be found. So get with some neighbors and have them help you okay?"

Celina took the phone from her ear and looked down at the receiver dumbfounded. Then she just hung up the phone. She decided she would go next door and ask for Martin's help. Celina walked out the door.

After knocking repeatedly on the door for several minutes Martin Laurel finally answered. He had opened it just a crack and then fully when he saw it was Celina. A small .22 caliber revolver was in his right hand. "Celina is everything all right at your house. We heard the shooting and screaming. I was going to come help but felt it might be too dangerous. I did call 911 but the police never came."

Celina had stood for several seconds staring at Martin and his wife, who had just walked up behind him. "They killed dad and raped mom and Daphne. The 911 operators said it could be days before the police or any help get here. They said to get help from the neighbors. Will you help us?"

Martin's face was filled with fear his eyes darted from Celina to the surrounding area as if more gang members were coming at any moment. He stepped back and started to close the door. "Celina I would like to, but we have to pack. We're heading for my brother's place in Tennessee." With that he shut the door in her face.

Celina had gone from house to house asking for help. Each time everyone had said not to worry the police would soon arrive. All said they were leaving. Celina had gone back to her house and sat in a rocker on the front porch and cried for almost two hours. In those two hours several of her neighbors had packed cars, trucks, and SUV's and left the neighborhood.

Celina had gotten up after some time and went back into the garage. She knew she had to take care of her father's body before her sister and mother woke up. In the garage she gathered up two large painting plastic drop cloths, and an old military poncho. She then went back into the den.

With trembling hands she removed the blanket that covered her father. His chest was covered in blood, his eyes open and lifeless. Using her fingers she closed his eyes, the tears came streaming down her face. She sobbed several times then stood up and retrieved one of the drop cloths.

She laid the cloth beside her father's body and then got on her knees and grasped his shoulders and hip. She pulled him onto the cloth. She then got on the other side of his body and began to roll him in the drop cloth. This gruesome task had taken her fifteen minutes. She continually had to stop and wipe the tears from her eyes. Once that was done she laid the other cloth down beside his body and repeated the process. Finally she used the military poncho.

When she finished this ghastly chore, Celina leaned back against the recliner exhausted. She still had to take her father's body outside. She had decided to bury him in the larger hole her father had dug out for a goldfish pond. It was roughly seven feet long, four feet wide and about four feet deep. The large black hard plastic liner was already in place. There were also six eighty-pound bags of quick Crete. She would cover the body with the quick Crete and then use the dirt that had been piled beside the hole to cover the body. She felt that after the first good rain the quick Crete would soon harden and entomb her father so that animals did not try to dig him up.

Celina got up from the floor and checked on her mother and sister. Both were still deep asleep. She had gone into the kitchen washed her hands, dried them and then used some antibacterial gel. Celina then made a banana sandwich and a tall glass of water.

She sat for a few moments after finishing her sandwich, and water. Celina was gathering up the courage to bury her father. She had contemplated waking up her mother and sister, but felt that the added trauma of burying her father would only deepen their catatonic state. Best to bury him and then let them grieve over the grave. Celina took a deep breath and pushed away from the kitchen table and walked to the spacious den.

She opened the back door and then walked to the body of her father. She reached down and grabbed hold of his legs and began to pull him through the den. Her father was not a big man and weighed no more than 160 pounds. Dragging him like this made Celina think she was dragging twice that.

As she pulled the body through the back door her father's head had made an audible almost hollow sound when it hit the concrete on the patio. Celina dropped his legs as more tears welled up. "I am sorry daddy. I didn't mean to bump your head." Celina cried for five more minutes while she stood there looking at the plastic wrapped corpse of her father.

She finally recomposed herself and began her dreaded chore. It took her almost five minutes of dragging and stopping to rest to reach the dug out form of the goldfish pond. Celina was exhausted, both mentally and physically. She knew however that she had to continue with her task before her sister and mother woke. There was no telling how they would react, and if she did not finish it now she did not know if she could come back and finish it later.

She stared at the four-foot deep hole wondering how to get the body in. She did not want to just roll the body in and let it drop. Somehow it seemed to disrespectful to her father. She finally decided to get in the hole and drag him in by the shoulders and help lower the body to the ground.

Celina lined the body up with the head at the foot of the hole. She got in the hole and grasped the poncho liner near her father's shoulders.

She placed her foot along the wall and pulled with all of her might. The body only moved about six inches.

Slowly Celina worked the body towards her till most of the upper torso was over the grave. As she gave one final pull the body shot into the grave and knocked her to the ground. The body landed on her stomach and legs. Celina had scrambled backwards on her butt kicking with her legs and pulling her self with her arms. Celina whimpered loudly and gasped for air as she struggled to free herself from her father's dead body.

Finally she freed herself, and jumped to her feet and leaped from the hole. She turned and gazed down at the body, her chest heaving as she struggled to regain her breath and control of herself. Her legs trembled a bit and finally with a final tremble she calmed herself.

Now she had to bury him. Celina pulled the first bag of quick Crete to her and opened it up. She dumped the mixture on top of her father's body. Each time she lifted one of the heavy bags her arms and back screamed in pain and exhaustion. She had continued though until the quick Crete was covering her father's body. She then turned the water hose on and put the nozzles setting on shower. She soaked the concrete down. Once she completed that she began to shovel the dirt into the grave. The job had taken a little over two hours. Celina had gone back inside exhausted. She felt bad because she had not even offered up a prayer for her father, but her body demanded rest.

Once inside she took off her clothes, and showered. She changed and went to the kitchen to find something to eat. Her mother and sister both had woken up and said little or nothing. There was almost nothing to eat; her mother had not been shopping this week. She finally boiled some water on the outside grill and made the three of them Ramen Noodles. After eating, her mother and sister both went to their rooms and slept.

Nightfall was coming on fast so Celina lit one of the oil lamps. She then went to her bedroom and picked up the sawed off shotgun she had taken from the thug that tried to rape her. She was so glad her uncle was an avid shooter and had taught her to shoot revolvers and shotguns. Her father and mother hated guns, and it drove them nuts when she went shooting with her uncle, maybe that is why she enjoyed it so much. She usually used a twenty gauge when she shot skeet, but knew she could handle a twelve if she had too. She checked the load of the shotgun.

She pumped out six rounds from the breach, insured the magazine tube and chamber were empty then pulled the trigger. She then placed the shotgun back on safety, and reloaded it. Celina was not sure if she would like the fact that the shotgun just had a pistol grip, but assumed maybe the strange sling, a tactical sling Uncle Joe had called it, might help with recoil when she fired it.

Celina then laid the twelve gauge down and reached over to her dresser. She picked up the two five round boxes she had taken. One said tactical slugs, the other 00 buck. Well she had six in the shotgun, six on the sidesaddle, and ten loose rounds. She felt she needed to put the rounds from the boxes in something she could retrieve easier if she had to.

She chose a small black nylon handbag that had a zipper on the top. She dumped the ten rounds in. The bag could easily hold another twenty or so rounds she guessed. She tossed the bag on the bed by the shotgun, and left the room to check on her family.

Daphne was crying and talking in her sleep, probably reliving the nightmare of her rape. Celina sat down on the bed and gently soothed her sister until she quieted down. Then she went to check on her mother. Her mother was sitting upright in bed. She was sleeping soundly. Then Celina had noticed the bottle of her pain killers on the night stand. Celina ran and dumped the pills in her hand and counted them. Only two more of the 800mg pills were missing. She listened to her mother's breathing. She sounded okay, and Celina had hoped she would be. She knew she had to keep an eye on her sister and mother, suicide was a real possibility.

The house was dark when she finally went to the den and picked up the oil lamp. She took it with her to the bedroom and sat it on the dresser. She then put the sling of the shotgun around her neck, and then the bag of shells. She then took a flashlight out of her drawer and walked back to the den. She prepared herself to take a walk around the house to check things out.

Once outside Celina stood still on her front porch and listened for any strange noises. The only strange thing was that there was no noise. She scanned the horizon and noticed faint orange glows in the distant. Either something was on fire or someone had lights on. Celina then cautiously circled her yard; she subconsciously avoided her father's grave.

After the quick and frightening walk around the house she went back inside. She then checked all of the doors and locked them Celina then went to the kitchen and opened the recycle bin. She pulled out the box that contained all of the aluminum cans. She then went back to the front door. She placed several cans in front of it and then went to the back and side doors and did the same. It wasn't the best alarm system in the world but it would at least wake her if someone picked the lock and opened the door. Of course if they kicked it in she would definitely know someone was trying to break in. If the gang came back she wouldn't be caught by surprise again and would have one for them in the form of a 12-gauge shotgun.

Celina had then went to the garage and got a five-gallon bucket and cleaning material. Once she filled the bucket with water she went to the den and cleaned up the blood as best she could. Once she had finished she poured the water out in the toilet and then scrubbed her hands.

When she finished she went to her room. She lay down on the bed and reached over and turned off the oil lamp. Her body ached all over. Her hands felt numb, and she had a severe headache coming on. Celina fell asleep almost instantly.

⊶━⊷

Celina tossed the sheets from her body and got up. Her body still ached, but she knew she had to take care of her mother and sister. Celina stretched her body to try and work some of the kinks out. Then she heard the sounds of cans being knocked around and one of the doors opening.

Celina grabbed the shotgun from the bed, and eased the safety off. As stealthily as she could she made her way down the hall. As she reached the doorway that led to the den she stopped and raised the shotgun. She stood silently for a moment and heard nothing.

Then Celina sprang as fast and quietly as she could into the den the shotgun extended in front of her. She panned the room and only saw her mother and sister in the den. Daphne sat staring blankly at the empty TV screen. Her mother stood by the wide-open back door staring into the back door. Celina lowered the shotgun.

"Is everyone okay?" She asked.

Daphne just turned her head and stared at her. Her mother turned and looked at her. "What are you doing with that gun Celina?"

Celina looked down at the shotgun, and then back at her mother. "It's the one I took from those men."

Her mother seemed not to even register her answer. "Where is your father Celina?"

Celina swallowed hard and met her mother's gaze. "I buried him yesterday mom."

A perplexed look crossed her mother's face. "Why? Where are the police? Why did you bury your father Celina?"

In an obstinate voice she answered her mother. "I called 911. The lady said they may take several days to get here or they may not show up at all. They told me to get help from the neighbors but no one would help me. Most everyone has packed up and left." Celina made her way to her mother's side as she spoke.

"But where did you bury him?" Tears started to pervade in her mother's eyes again.

Celina wrapped an arm around her mother's waist and turned her to face the back yard. She pointed to the fresh mound of dirt. "I buried him over there mother."

Her mother walked from her side and sat down beside Daphne. Daphne had listened to the entire conversation. It had not only overwhelmed the fourteen-year-old girl, it had overwhelmed her mother. The two sat sobbing in unison.

Celina needed help and she needed it now. They were not going to make it long if her mother and sister did not get some type of help. She did not know how or where to get food or medical help, both physical and mental for her family.

Celina walked from the den to her mother's room and sat on the edge of the bed. She picked up the phone and got a dial tone. She dialed 911 and got no response. She then dialed the direct number to the police station and again got no response. She dialed the fire departments number with the same result. Then she called Uncle Joe's and got no answer. Frustration washed over her.

She reached in the nightstand and pulled out the phone book. She looked up the National Guard's phone number and dialed it.

After about four rings a voice answered the phone. "This is the National Guard Armory, Sgt. Spitz, how may I help you?"

Celina breathed a sigh of relief. The Guard would help. "My name is Celina Donovan. My family needs help. My father was murdered two nights ago and the police have not shown up, and everyone in the neighborhood has left."

"Well Ms. Donovan, I would like to help you." Then the sergeant's voice became lower and filled with obvious regret and concern. "I'm sorry but we can't help. We are pulling out for Birmingham in thirty minutes. The whole unit is going; I will tell the police if I see one. Where do you live?"

Anger swelled up inside Celina. "What the HELL difference does it make? None of you care! You're all to worried about the big cities and won't help out your own town. SCREW YOU!" Celina slammed the phone down.

Celina looked up and closed her eyes and prayed to God for some help. When she lowered her head and opened her eyes she was looking at the pill bottle she had left last night. She picked it up and looked at the label. In large bold print was the doctor's name, her doctor's name was printed! "Thank you God!"

Celina new Dr. Morrison's number by heart. Her father and the doctor had played golf together for years, and he had been her doctor since she was a baby. She dialed the number.

―――•――•――

Doc kicked off his boots and sat in his chair. He was worried about Steve. Steve was taking Diane's death hard. Hopefully the boy would pull out of his sorrow. He too grieved for Diane but years of being in the medical field had somewhat hardened him towards death.

He sat in silence for another fifteen minutes. Then he was startled out of his contemplation of current events by the telephone. The phone rang several times, and then Maude's voice came from the kitchen. "Are you going to answer that or let it ring all day?"

Doc picked up the telephone. "Uh, hello."

A voice he recognized immediately came from the receiver. "Thank God! Doctor Morrison this is Celina Donovan. I need help. Please don't hang up on me. No one, the police, the Guard, or our neighbors will help." Her voice was pleading, crying out for help.

"What's wrong Celina?" Doc said as he sat up in his chair.

"Some men came into the house and they, they..." Her voice paused, and silence filled the line.

Doc spoke and probed for an answer. "Tell me what they did Celina." Doc knew with almost certainty what they did. The Donovan women were all beautiful. Dread filled his stomach while he waited for the girl to answer.

Celina spoke, her voice wavering. "They killed dad. Mom and Daphne got raped. Please help us."

"What about you Celina are you all right?" The doctor asked.

"The fat one tried to rape me but I stabbed him. I took his gun and shot at his friends then I ran from the house. No one came to help us Doctor Morrison. Please help us."

Doc wasn't surprised to hear about what actions Celina took. She had been a fighter since she was a baby. She never quit until she achieved what she wanted. "Celina, can I talk to your mother?"

In a helpless, pleading voice Celina answered. "That's what I am trying to tell you Doctor Morrison. Mom and Daphne are walking around like zombies. Mom talked a little while ago until I showed her where I buried dad. Now she is on the couch with Daphne crying. We're almost out of food. The only thing in the house that works is the water. Please Doctor Morrison help us."

"Okay Celina calm down. You know I will help you. I am going to have to get help. It's to dangerous for me to come alone."

Celina interrupted Doc. "THANK YOU! THANK YOU! When will you come?" The relief was evident in her voice.

"I am going to have to get hold of two men I know. Can you hold on a minute?"

"Yes sir." Celina replied.

Doc covered the receiver with the palm of his hand as Maude walked into the room. "It's Celina Donovan. Mr. Donovan has been killed, Daphne and Nancy raped. Celina is okay. They're almost out of food and Daphne and Nancy are in a state of depression and shock."

Maude rubbed her chin with her hand thinking. "You will need help to get them. Tell her they can stay here. You will need to get Steve and maybe Amos."

"I had planned on that, I will let her know we will be there in an hour or so." Doc was about to talk again when Maude raised her hand to stop him.

"Ask her if she can hold out one more day. Steve needs to have a little time before he goes running around trying to save people. Let him rest today then get hold of him in the morning, if he can't go call Amos."

Doc put the phone back to his ear. "Celina, can you hold out for one more day? The man I am going to get to help me lost someone a couple of days ago too. I think he needs a little time alone."

Celina's voice sounded deflated as she replied. "Yes sir, we can. You will be here tomorrow though, right?"

"Count on it Celina. If my friends can't help Maude and I will come get you."

Celina said her thanks and hung up the phone.

Maude turned and headed for the bedrooms. "I better get things straightened up in the bedrooms. I can't wait till they get here. Finally some intelligent conversation may take place in this house again."

Chapter 18

Doc watched Maude head to the bedrooms to clean up. He walked down the hall towards the basement in his socked feet. He started running a mental checklist of the things he would need for the trip into to town to get the Donovan women.

Once down in the basement he went to the cabinets on the back wall. Opening one of the doors he pulled out a surplus military company size first-aid kit. He put the heavy bag on the counter next to him and opened the medicine cabinet.

He chose several different types of sedatives, and some antibiotics. He placed these items in the bag. He then did a quick inventory of the medical bag. Seeing everything was in order he carried the bag to the foot of the stairs.

After setting the bag down Doc walked over to the weapons and ammo side of the basement. Reaching up to a bare looking wood panel he flipped a release switch that unlocked the hidden weapons. He then eased the hidden panel door open.

The panel door opened up quietly on well-greased hidden hinges. Doc looked over his small arsenal. Doc had set up pegs and clamps to hold the pistols, rifles, and shotguns in place. The guns rested between each stud.

Doc knew he would probably not need one of the main battle rifles that hung in the hidden safe. His job was going to be looking after, and treating the Donovan women. Doc reached in and grabbed a Remington 870 Magnum Express. The shotgun had an 18" barrel, and a six round magazine extension tube. Next he grabbed a black leather fifty round bandolier.

After setting the Remington on the counter top Doc reached in the safe and grabbed a Ruger Stainless .357 revolver, three sets of two black basket weave speed loader holders and a black leather basket weave holster. Doc scanned over the assembled weapons and decided to take an old U.S. Air Force survival knife that sat in its sheath hanging on a peg. He then closed and locked the hidden weapons.

Doc bent over and opened the cabinet below the safe and pulled out two boxes of .357 rounds. The rounds were Federal Hydra Shock hollow points. He then pulled out a cardboard box that was marked Federal 00 Buck Low Recoil Tactical rounds.

First Doc loaded the Ruger and placed it in its leather holster. He then loaded each speed loader and replaced them in their holders. Doc loaded up the bandolier first with the deadly 3" 00 rounds. Then he loaded the shotgun making sure a round was not in the chamber and the weapon was on safe.

Doc looked around the basement to find something to help him carry the supplies up stairs. He spotted an old duffle bag sitting in the corner went over and retrieved it. Surely he was forgetting something. Then it dawned on him he would need water and some food.

Doc picked up the duffel and then walked to the closet. Opening the closet he took down a Camelback "Mother Load" backpack that contained a 100 oz. Water bladder, two MREs, first-aid kit, matches, fishing material, fire starters, Zippo lighter, signal mirror, sewing kit, three emergency blankets, poncho, poncho liner, three hundred feet of 550 cord, handsaw, and a hatchet attached to the side. He dropped the pack into the duffle and shuffled over to the guns and put them in and the first-aid pack.

Doc groaned as he picked up the heavy load, and began ascending the stairs. His old knees popped as he climbed the steep staircase. "Well at least we will be driving, I hope." He said to himself. He was tempted to leave it all but the medical bag and the revolver, however it was better to be over prepared than be caught needing something and not have it. There would be no help from the authorities; they would be on their own.

Once in the den Doc set his load down and then he set himself in his recliner. Bending over he grabbed his old work boots and laced them up. Doc rose from them chair and walked to the bedrooms where Maude was cleaning.

He peeked in the bedroom to see Maude putting some fresh sheets on the bed. "Maude I am going down to see Amos."

Maude looked over her shoulder as she tightened up the bedspread. "If you think you are going down there to drink some of that homemade brew Amos has you've got another thing coming. I'm about tired of you two old coots liquoring yourselves up all the time."

Doc's brow knotted a bit. "How did she know about the shine?" He thought.

"No Maude I am going to ask him to keep an eye on things while Steve and I go get the Donovan's. Or I will ask him to go in Steve's place if Steve won't go. See ya in a bit." Doc turned to leave.

"Herb Morrison, I better not smell or taste one drop of shine from your lips when you get back!" Maude shouted to him as he walked out of the house.

Doc cranked up the old truck and leaned over and pulled the Ruger SP101 .38 revolver from the glove box and tucked it in his pocket. He slipped the truck into drive and headed for Amos's place.

⊱————⊰

Doc pulled up in Amos's driveway and came to a halt. He stepped out of the truck keeping one hand on the center of the steering wheel. He blew the horn twice. "Amos it's me!" He shouted.

The front door opened and Amos waved to Doc. His twelve gauge carried in his left hand. "Come on in Doc."

Doc entered the house. "Sorry to bother you I know it is getting late. I need to ask a favor or two from you." Doc turned as little Benny walked into the room. It shocked him at first. With everything going on he almost forgot about the boy.

Amos spoke up as Benny stared at Doc. "Benny this is Doc Morrison."

"Hi. Hey Amos my hands hurt." Benny said.

"Come here and let me look at them Benny. I am a doctor after all." Doc said as he gestured with his hand for the boy to come to him.

Benny looked surprised. "You're a real doctor?" He said as he walked to Doc.

"Well they don't call me Doc for nothing."

"Well Bugs Bunny calls Elmer Fudd doc, and he isn't one." Benny said a little defensively.

Doc let out a chuckle. Oh how he loved the logic of young children. "You've got a point Benny, but I really am a doctor." Doc took Benny's hands and unwrapped the gauze.

"Amos, get me my bag out of the truck if you don't mind." Doc said to Amos as he probed the boy's hands. Amos returned a few minutes later with the bag in hand.

Doc opened the bag and got out some hydrogen peroxide. He doused the boy's hands and watched them fizz. He then dabbed them dry with a sterile gauze pad. He put some antibacterial salve on the hands and then rewrapped them. Doc then took his temperature, 100 degrees. You must have a little infection setting in. I wish I had some antibiotics with me. Amos do you have any?"

"Now Doc you know I don't use that store bought stuff. I do have some Echinacea herbs, and Feverfew I could brew up." Echinacea is a herb that is widely used to stimulate or support the body's immune system. Feverfew, as the name implies is a hardy medicinal herb that is credited with many beneficial properties.

"That would be fine Amos." Doc said. Doc and Benny talked some more as Amos brewed up his natural medicine. Doc had used some of Amos's medicines himself from time to time. They were all natural and they worked.

Amos finished up and brought over a glass of the medicine. "Hear you go Benny." Amos handed the boy the glass. Benny drank down the concoction and looked a bit surprised that at the taste.

Doc took the glass from Benny. "Go rest up now Benny, Amos and I have to talk."

Benny did not argue at all. His body still ached with pain from digging his parent's grave. "Goodnight Amos. Good to meet you Doc." Benny headed back to bed.

As soon as Benny left the room Amos spoke up. "What's up Doc?" He said in his best Bugs Bunny voice, his hand at his mouth miming eating a carrot.

Doc grinned. "Well Bugs I need to get Steve in the morning and go and get some friends of mine. There are two girls and a woman. The husband was murdered and the one of the girls and the mother were raped by a gang."

A look of anger flashed across his face. "Who are they?"

"The Donovan's, they live about ten miles from here in Heathrow Subdivision. Celina, one of the girls is a real tough cookie by the way. Stabbed one of the gang and shot it out with them before running off to the woods. She says they have almost no food in the house. Maude and I are going to put them up. I was hoping you could look after Steve's place and Maude while we are gone. Hopefully it will only take a few hours."

Amos's face now looked concerned. "Things sure are getting rough out there Doc. Are you sure you don't want me to go too?"

"That is alright Amos. They may need medical attention and Steve is a lot better than either one of us with a gun. If he can't or won't go I guess I would need you for a back up. Benny can stay at our place if you have to go."

Amos nodded his head. "Yeah Steve is damn good with a gun. I will look after his place and Maude while you are gone. Of course I doubt Maude needs looking after. Hey, would you like a drink."

"Sure. What have you got?" Doc said.

Amos grinned as he turned and pulled down the jug of homemade whiskey. He held it out in front of him, smiled and wiggled his eyebrows.

"Just something an old fart needs before hopping on his white horse and rescuing a few pretty young ladies."

Doc's head tilted just a bit his lips pursed together. "Maude said I better not come home smelling like shine."

Amos poured two stiff ones, and turned holding one to Doc. "Now who the hell wears the pants in your family Doc? Besides this batch is peppermint flavored, she'll never know. You can just tell her I gave you some peppermint tea."

Doc's eyebrows raised his eyes wide. "Why you know who wears the pants. Same as in your house when your dear Eleanor was alive. So don't pull any macho crap with me you old spineless snake. I recall stitching up, and bandaging you several times when Mrs. Eleanor decided you had transgressed into sin." Doc and Amos smiled as Doc took the glass.

The two tipped the glasses together and Amos toasted. "Here is to sin, and mean God fearing women." They gulped the whiskey down.

Sweat immediately beaded on Doc and Amos's forehead. Doc exhaled loudly. "For an ignorant dirt farmer you make some fine brew."

"I will take that as a compliment even though it came from a man who handles his liquor like a twelve year old girl. Look at your face all beat read and sweaty. All you had was a tiny sip" Amos said as he wiped the sweat from his grinning face.

Doc stood. "I've got to get back to my palatial spread. No more time to slum with the unwashed. Could you get me a little bottle of that stuff? It's for medical uses only of course."

Amos stood and walked back to the cabinet and pulled down a metal flask. With black marker the word "Doc's" was written across it. "Well look what I found, and it's full too. You must have left it here last time you came over." He handed it over to Doc who put it in his medical bag.

Doc shook Amos's hand and turned for the door. "We'll leave around 8:00. I will come by and let you know if I will need you to go with me. If Steve will go with me I can let you know to look after things.

Amos opened the door. "Goodnight Doc. Be safe. If you're gone to long me and Festus will come and get you."

Doc was stepping off the porch and looked back. "That's just what I need for a rescue party, two jackasses." Doc giggled a bit, the alcohol starting to take effect. Amos was right about how well Doc handled his liquor, he couldn't He waved, got into his truck and drove away.

Amos went back inside and took another hit of the "good stuff". He lit an oil lantern and then went and shut the generator off. He was soon in bed and sleeping soundly.

Doc staggered a bit when he got out of the truck. "I shouldn't have had so much. It's a good thing I only live a mile downs the road, and the cops aren't around to hook me up. Now I just hope Maude don't hook me up." He walked to the house and into the living room. The generator was off and an oil lamp lit the living room. Hopefully Maude was in bed asleep. He tiptoed towards his chair.

Doc about pissed himself as Maude's voice came from the darkened kitchen doorway. "Have we been drinking Herbert? Or are you tiptoeing cause you worry about my beauty rest?" Maude stepped into the dimly lit room, arms folded across her ample breast.

"Why dear, I was worried about your beauty rest of course." Doc's voice stammered his words sounding a bit mushy.

Maude walked up to him and looked down. "How sweet, how about a good night kiss?"

Doc audibly swallowed. He tilted his head up and kissed his wife. "See no whiskey."

Suspicion filled Maude's eyes. "Why does your breath smell like peppermint?"

"Amos gave me a couple of pieces while we talked. I need to go rest for the morning dear. Goodnight." Doc set his medical bag on the coffee table and staggered off to bed.

After a few minutes Maude went to the bedroom door and peeked in. Moonlight flooded in through the curtains. Her husband lay in bed fully dressed and already snoring. She went back to the living room and opened the medical bag. There was his metal whiskey flask hidden in a side pocket where he always put it.

Maude picked up and unscrewed the cap and took a sniff. "Yep, peppermint, just what I thought." Then Maude looked over her shoulder at the doorway that led to the bedrooms, took a quick glance around to make sure no one was looking and took a stiff swing of the concoction. A smile crossed her face as the shine worked it's way down to her stomach. "Damn good stuff." Maude capped the flask and put it back in the bag. She then went off for a good night's sleep.

⊹⊱⊰⊹

Steve heard the pounding at his front door. At first he thought was just the pounding of his head. He had too much Jack Daniels the night before as he studied the maps plotting his revenge. He opened his heavy eyelids and looked at his wristwatch. It took a few seconds for his eyes come into focus. The sound of someone pounding the door came again. "Six-thirty, who in the hell could that be?" Memories of Diane started to flood forward. He pushed the thoughts back and rolled over and picked up his Glock 17 off the nightstand.

Rolling out of bed he put on a pair of jeans and made his way downstairs and went to the front door. Standing to one side his pistol pointed at the door he spoke. "Who is it, and what do you want?" His voice boomed out making his brain think someone was sticking an ice pick in it.

A somewhat muffled voice replied. "Steve it's me, Doc open up." Steve unlocked the door and opened it. There stood Doc wearing a blue cotton long sleeve shirt, a fedora and khaki pants. A bandolier of shot shells across his chest, and a revolver strapped to his waste. Doc tilted the fedora back on his head.

Steve gave him a confused once over. "Is something wrong Doc? What are you all dressed up like Indiana Jones for?"

Doc stepped into the house and made for the living room where he took a seat on the couch. Steve followed and sat in his chair. "Well Steve, I need your help. I should have came by yesterday, but got tied up at Amos's." Doc filled Steve in on what had happened to the Donovan's, and what he was going to do.

"Are you out of your mind? I don't think you realize what the city is like. I am sure it is a hell of a lot worse than three days ago." Steve said. He stared at Doc as if he actually was crazy, while Doc paused to collect his thoughts.

Doc cleared his throat. "Steve, these women are good people. Their father was a good friend of mine. They will starve to death without our help. You are the only one I can think of that could help me get there and back in one piece."

"I'm sure they are good folks Doc, but you can't go running around trying to save everyone." Steve said.

"I'm not trying to save everyone, just these three women. If you won't go I will get Amos. If he can't Maude and I will go." Doc said with a defiant tone that said he wasn't here to talk but was here for action.

Steve let out a sigh. "Ok Doc let me get my things together." Steve got up shaking his head. "I can't believe I'm going back into that hell hole."

Steve went back upstairs and got dressed. He went to the bathroom and took a couple of BC Powders for his headache. He then went back down stairs and into his gunroom.

He picked up a thigh holster and strapped it on. He holstered the Glock in place. Then Steve checked the four magazine pouches on his belt and made sure each high capacity magazine was loaded. Then he cinched up the strap on the three pouch magazine holder on his left thigh. The magazines in these pouches were also high capacity.

Steve opened his metal gun safe that he had purchased not long ago. The gun safe could hold fourteen rifles or shotguns. It looked bare with Steve's three weapons, his Remington 870, Mosin-Nagant M-44, and his AK-47. Steve reached in and pulled out the AK and closed the safe back up.

Walking to the closet he opened it up. He took down an LBV that held six magazines for the AK, a 100-ounce camel back bladder, compass, knife, twenty foot of rappelling rope attached to the side of the camel back, a Gerber multi tool, and fire starting materials. He then picked up a case of ammo and set it on the desk with the LBV. He went back to the closet and took out two seventy-five round drums. Doc walked in and started helping Steve load up the drums and magazines for the AK.

When they were done Steve donned the LBV and picked up his back pack which contained extra clothing, three days worth of food and assorted camping items. "Well let's get this over with Doc."

The two walked outside to their vehicles. Steve started the Jeep up and drove to the gate followed by Doc. The entrance/exit to Steve's place was unique. The drive was cut through the hillside. He had placed two metal gates that opened by a counter balance. The area between the two gates could only accommodate one vehicle at a time. You had to open the first gate and latch it in the upright position and pull your vehicle in. Close the first gate then walk to the front of your vehicle and do the same with the second. The entire area was a kill zone if someone was stupid enough to try and come in that way with bad intentions. Steve had planted holly bushes, and rose bushes down the length of the road frontage to discourage people on foot.

Once they cleared the gates Doc took the lead heading towards Florence, it was 7:15. After several miles the landscape changed from woods to farms, and eventually they began to enter the city limits. No one stopped or challenged them. Occasionally they would catch a glimpse of someone running in the shadows. They were being watched though and could feel the eyes on them.

As they entered the city limits the amount of trash and debris seemed to increase. The smell of fire and smoke filled the air. Now on almost every street they turned onto they saw dead bodies that had been left where they fell. Some had started to bloat as gases built up inside them. Crows, buzzards and packs of dogs seemed to have taken over the town. Also the occasional gunshot or scream could be heard in the distance.

After almost two hours of slow and cautious driving they turned into Heathrow Subdivision. It seemed to Doc and Steve as if everyone in the subdivision was gone. There were no children playing in the yards no neighbors out talking to one another, nothing. Several homes had been burned out, the owners laying dead in their driveways, in open garages, or in their front yards.

They wound their way through the debris littered streets and finally pulled into the Donovan's driveway. Doc blew the horn three times and got out of the truck. The front door opened, the barrel of a shotgun pointed out towards them.

Steve saw the barrel pointing out of the door and in his general direction. He grabbed the AK that was laying on the front passenger seat and rolled out of the Jeep. Making his way towards the front of the Jeep he racked a round into the chamber. The AK had one of his seventy-five round drums attached and its weight felt reassuring in his hands.

Doc looked back at Steve. "Steve, Don't shoot! Celina Don't shoot it's me Herb Morrison."

Celina heard the vehicles pull in the drive. She took a quick glance out the window and saw a young man with some kind of vest on. She did not know who he was and snatched up the shotgun.

Walking quickly to the front door prepared to engage and kill the man and whoever was with him. Her family would not be violated again. Then she heard a familiar voice reach her ears. "Steve, Don't shoot! Celina, Don't shoot it's me Herb Morrison."

Relief filled her body. She opened the door all the way and lowered the shotgun. She stepped out onto the porch and looked over to see Dr. Morrison standing by his truck. "I'm so glad you came doctor." Celina kept a wary eye on the other man who had just stood up. A machinegun held at port arms in his hands.

Doc and Steve walked around and met Celina on the front porch. Celina hugged Doc and squeezed him tightly to her. "Thank you." Was all she said.

Doc had to almost pry the young girl off of him. "Celina, this is Steve. Steve, meet Celina."

Steve slung his rifle. "It's nice to meet you Celina."

Celina gave Steve a half-hearted smile, still not fully trusting the man. "Mom and Daphne are inside Doc. Let's go tell them we're getting out of here." Celina turned to lead them inside.

Once inside Doc stopped Celina. "Listen we need to get out of here quick. I want you and Steve to gather clothing and anything useful you three will need. I'm going to go in here and give your mom and sister a quick checkup."

Celina apprehensively eyed Steve for a moment. "Come on, follow me. Doc they're sitting on the couch in the living room." Celina turned and went to the garage to grab some suitcases. Steve followed silently along.

Once they had the suitcases they went to each room packing up clothes and shoes. Steve was impressed with the young lady. Though she obviously came from a well to do family she did not pack needless items. She packed toiletries, sensible pants, shoes and shirts. She did however pack a few family albums, and took down and packed up family pictures.

Doc had told him how she had reacted with the gang members. He was definitely right about her, she was a smart cookie, and appeared as tough as Doc's story made her out to be. Doc had said she was seventeen going on eighteen but she certainly looked like a twenty-year-old model to him. Her brain had obviously matured along with her body.

Within about twenty minutes they had packed the suitcases and loaded them into the back of Doc's truck. They went back inside to see how Doc was doing. "Doc we're finished packing how are things going in here?" Steve said.

Doc had just stood up; Daphne in front of him seated on the couch, her mother sitting beside her. Both obviously traumatized. "They seem physically fine. However they are both are suffering from a form of Post Traumatic Stress Syndrome. The events of the other night were just to harsh for the two of them. They have never in their lives had to deal with something so life threatening. Time will heal them though. Celina help me take your sister and mom to my truck. I want you to ride in the Jeep with Steve."

Celina glanced over dubiously again at Steve. Her fingers tightened a bit on the pistol grip and pump of the shotgun. "Yes sir." Celina helped Doc to get her family into the truck. Then she got in Steve's Jeep and stared straight ahead.

Steve started the Jeep and backed out of the driveway. Steve and Celina road in silence for half an hour neither saying a word, finally Steve broke the silence. "Celina, I am not going to hurt you or your family. I am here to help. I am not saying trust me, but I want you to know any friend of Doc is a friend of mine, and I take care of my friends."

Celina looked at Steve, even if he was a friend of Dr. Morrison's she still didn't know him. It was now her job to take care of her mother and sister. The barrel of the shotgun pointing towards the firewall shifted a bit towards Steve, but not pointing at him. "I know you won't hurt me." Her voice was almost deadpan.

Steve just shook his head and turned back to the front scanning for threats. Man this little lady was the ice queen herself. Came all the way to town to help her out and she lets me know she will blow my shit away at the least bit of provocation, he thought cutting his eyes down at the shotgun that she had shifted in his general direction.

⊹━━⊹

The drive towards home had, so far, been just as uneventful as the drive to the Donovan's. They had taken the same route back believing once they had drove through an area and not been attacked there were no threats. To their thinking it was better than driving into the unknown.

They had gone five miles and were about at the city limits as Steve's Jeep rounded the curve. Just as Steve slammed on the brakes as he realized two trucks sat blocking the roadway a bullet crashed through the front window. The round missed Steve's head by inches.

Snatching up his AK Steve shouted to Celina. "Get out of the Jeep! Find cover!"

Celina leaped out of the Jeep and lunged into the ditch beside the roadway. A driveway crossed the ditch and provided cover for her as she hugged up to the dirt embankment. Rounds struck the concrete drive ricocheting over her head. Clouds of white powder concrete shot into the air.

Steve jumped from the Jeep. His AK was in his left hand; with his right he drew the Glock 17. Steve too was making for the ditch and the embankment of another driveway on the opposite side of the road. Rounds snapped past his head, some tearing huge gouges out of the asphalt around his feet. Steve snapped off eight rounds with out aiming as he ran, most completely off target hitting nothing but air. One slammed into the front end of one of the trucks, the other blew out the passenger side window of the other.

Finally after several heart stopping seconds he made it to the ditch and took cover. Rounds peppered the drive as Steve lifted the pistol over the embankment. As fast as he could he emptied the remaining nine rounds. He then reloaded and holstered the pistol. He put the sling for the AK around his neck and hunkered down.

-+|=—=|+-

Doc locked the breaks up on the truck as Steve slammed on his breaks. Smoke billowed from the tires of Doc's truck as the truck skidded to a stop. Doc saw the front windshield of Steve's Jeep spider webbed. Then a bullet slammed into the hood of his truck tearing a deep gouge in the hood.

As Doc bailed out of the truck he screamed to the two women. "GET DOWN!"

Doc ran to the back of Steve's Jeep kneeling down as he drew his .357. Peeking around the side Doc saw four scruffy looking men firing their weapons. They were intent on shooting Celina and Steve, who were pinned down on both sides of the road.

Doc raised the pistol and sighted in on one of the men who was starting to reload what appeared to be an SKS. He gently squeezed the trigger. The recoil and loud boom of the pistol surprised him as it went off.

The round from Doc's pistol struck the would be highwayman in the shoulder. The magnum round exiting out of the man's back in a spray of blood and taking pieces of his shoulder blade with it. Doc crouched there stunned for a moment. His hands had always been used to save life not take it. The man's partner spun, searching for the new threat, he was holding a Mini-14. Then he spotted Doc and raised the rifle to his shoulder.

Doc jerked back behind the Jeep as rounds peppered the pavement beside him. He looked at the cab of his truck. Daphne and Nancy still sat motionless in the front seat.

Then the unthinkable happened. A round struck the headlight of the truck. The man started walking his rounds up the truck. The bullets hammered holes into the hood then holes started appearing in the windshield. Finally they found their way into Nancy, one, two, three, four, five times. Each time bullets struck her body and head her body was sent into an involuntary spasm. Then she slumped forward dead. The windows and interior of the truck bathed in blood. Daphne suddenly scrambled for the drivers door and was off running towards the houses that lined the road, her long legs carrying her as if her life depended on it and they did. No bullets found her has she ran between the houses.

Doc swung himself up, pistol in hand. He began to fire, screaming as he pulled the trigger each time, several rounds striking the murderer. Out of the corner of his eye he saw Celina raise up shotgun in hand a flame shooting out of the end of the barrel. She too was screaming, though Doc could hear none of it. Sound had ceased for the moment for Doc. Then his pistol clicked on an empty cylinder, he continued to pull the trigger. Then the murderer's head exploded.

⊹⊱──⊰⊹

Celina watched in horror as the bullets tore into her mother's body. Rage filled her young body as she watched the death of her mother. Raising up she ran up the embankment, she fired a round from the hip missing the man who had just killed her mother. As she ran forward she lifted the shotgun out in front of her. She fired the second and a third round. This time the pellets found their mark. The man's body danced as if he was a puppet on a string. As she completely rounded the back of the truck she fired her fourth round. The man's head exploded. His body dropped as if someone had kicked his legs out from underneath him. As his body hit the ground she fired her last round into the twitching corpse.

She stared for a second at what she and Doc had done then she looked up. The other two men seeing the death of their friend rose from kneeling positions and turned their rifles on her. She knew then that she was dead. At least she had killed the man that had murdered her mother. Her only wish was that Daphne would make it through these dreadful times. She closed her eyes and waited to meet God, the shotgun slipped from her fingers.

⎯⎯◆⎯⎯

Steve saw Doc fire his pistol and then take cover as rounds came in on him. Then he too witnessed the death of Nancy Donovan. He turned back to see Doc stand and fire towards the trucks. He could hear the boom from a shotgun just on the other side of the truck. It sounded if Celina had gotten into the fight.

Suddenly there was just a moment of silence as several loud booms from a shotgun rang out. The rounds had ceased to impact around his position. "It's now or never Steve." He said to himself as he rose up.

Steve let the AK hang from the sling around his neck. He gripped tightly to the front stock of the rifle. His left hand was just barely on the pistol grip his middle finger lightly touching the trigger. The two thugs he spotted were turning from him and raising their rifles at someone on the other side of Doc's truck.

Steve pulled the rifle forward with his left hand causing the trigger to strike his finger. The AK bucked as he bump fired the rifle. By holding it with a loose grip and the way the rifle hung from the sling the recoil caused the rifle to go back and forth causing the rifle to fire fully automatic even though it was semi automatic. Steve had practiced this and learned to shoot quite well and accurately on area targets.

Flames spit out of the barrel as the AK rocked on full auto. Shell casings showered the asphalt like rain in a summer thunderstorm. The steel core rounds tore into the trucks side. They cut through the thin outer sheet metal like it was paper. Then Steve walked the rounds in a figure eight pattern. Within seconds the rounds not only punched through the truck's thin metal, but they punched through the even thinner skin of human flesh. Both men were cut to pieces like a rabbit sliced up by a bush hog. Then the seventy-five round drum emptied and both men fell dead.

Steve dumped the drum and fed in a magazine. He walked out of the ditch and glanced at Doc who was running to the truck to check Nancy. Smoke and the smell of cordite filled the air. Steve stepped around the end of the truck and looked at what he had wrought. Then he gazed up at Celina standing there transfixed at the death in front of her.

Steve walked slowly to Celina, slinging the AK behind his back. Putting his arms around her he looked down at her. She looked up at him tears still spilling down her cheeks. "Celina, I told you I was here to help you. I always will." Steve bent down and picked up her shotgun and walked her away from the carnage and set her back down in the passenger seat of the Jeep.

Chapter 19

Steve walked Celina back to his Jeep. She was crying now, the events of the past four days had bubbled to the surface of her emotions and burst through her. "Go, ahead and cry it out Celina. I'm going to go talk to Doc and then find Daphne." Steve turned and walked to Doc's truck. Doc was sitting in the driver seat his legs hanging out the door. The old man's thinning gray hair blew wantonly about his head. He looked up as Steve approached. "Steve I can't believe I just killed a man. I don't feel guilty about it, yet I feel I failed since I did not kill the other in time to save Nancy. I thought only of protecting myself when he shot at me." He stared at Steve; the happy go lucky gleam in his eyes had changed to a forlorn stare.

Steve reached out and placed a gentle hand on his friend's shoulder. "Doc, you did what you had to do to survive. No one can judge you. You acted in a valiant manner. Now I want you to take a deep breath and compose yourself. I want you to go and help Celina out."

Doc started to rise. A look of anxiety affixed his face now. "Is she hurt?"

Steve shook his head. "Her body is fine Doc. It's her soul that is hurting now. She needs someone who knows how to heal it. That someone would be you. Go on and help her, I'm going to find Daphne." Doc walked hastily to Celina. Steve gazed in on the dead woman that he had only met hours ago. Her head rested on the dashboard, the back of her head was a cavity of hideous human wreckage. Steve turned from the woman, checking the load on his AK as he did.

He walked towards the houses that Daphne had fled towards, his rifle at the ready. Steve scanned left and right as he headed for the first house directly in front of him. As he walked up on the porch he could see that the front door had been kicked in. Steve stood at the side of the door, took a deep breath. He was in a half crouch position the rifle at the low ready.

With a burst of speed Steve button hooked into the first room. He stayed about twelve inches off the wall and went into the room about six feet to the right. He continually scanned seeking danger. His rifle pointing where ever his head turned. His chest started to hurt a bit as he realized that he had held his breath when he entered. He sucked in a lung full of air and a putrid smell assailed his senses. His stomach rolled and he puked on the dirty floor. Steve knew the smell, and the smell was death. After wiping his mouth off on his shirt sleeve Steve started to breath through his mouth. It wasn't much help; he could almost taste the death in the air. Slowly he cleared the house until he was at the last bedroom.

Like a flash he entered the room and came up short when he saw what was in the floor. Two bodies lay in the room, the clothing almost bursting at the seams. Dried blood was pooled around both. Maggots and flies swarmed the room. As fast as he could Steve fled to the back door of the house and walked out into the back yard. The back yard had no fence so Steve continued his search in the direction of the next block.

He came upon a half dry mud puddle and a small, fresh footprint was in the middle. Daphne had gone this way he was sure of it. As Steve approached the back of the next house he saw a muddy footprint on the steps that led to the open back door. Steve could hear a male voice coming from inside the house but could not make out what was being said. Steve quietly entered into the kitchen of the small house.

The kitchen had been ransacked and was clear of any threats. He moved into an equally looted living room. A hallway was to his left. There were two doors on the right, one on the left and another at the end of the hallway. Steve pulled the rifle in tight to his shoulder walking forward, his feet stepping one in front of the other as if he was walking a tight rope. He still could not make out the voices, but knew it was two different voices, both male.

Glancing in on the first room he could see the room was devoid of people. The next room was a small bathroom that only contained a sink, toilet, and shower stall. Now that he was halfway down the hall he could make out the voices.

"Come on baby give it up." The first male voice said.

"Yeah, don't make us cut you to get what we want" said the second.

Then Daphne appeared in the room. She had backed herself into the corner and had not seen Steve. Neither had the squalid looking man who was holding a rusty butcher knife. Steve took two more steps toward the room lining up the man in his sights. His finger took up the slack as he gained a good sight picture on the man's upper torso. Steve pumped the trigger twice hitting the man under the right armpit, the second round catching him at the base of the skull as the rifle raised from its powerful recoil.

The man collapsed to the floor in a disheveled heap. With a burst of speed Steve bound forward. Daphne began to scream, her fists in tight balls down at her sides. As he hooked left into the bedroom he had lowered his rifle so no one would grab the barrel as he entered the room. Immediately turning left into the room Steve slid to a halt on the bare wood floors. The second man began to raise his fist, a Bowie knife clutched in his hand. Steve started pulling the trigger as he raised the rifle.

The first two rounds smashed into the floor in front of the man sending up large wooden splinters as the rounds tore into the floor. The third round found flesh and bone as it burst through the shin and exited out of his calf. The man fell forward as his leg was flung back. The fourth and fifth round sliced through the man's loose fitting shirt. The sixth and final round crashed into the back side of his shoulder plowing through the flesh. The man's screams joined in with Daphne's as he held onto his shin with one hand, the wounded arm dangled useless, the now forgotten knife lying on the floor.

"OH GOD! OH GOD! YOU SHOT ME YOU SON OF A BITCH." Steve ignored the man as he tried to calm Daphne. He gripped her shoulders and shook her.

"Daphne it's me Steve, Doc's friend. You've got to come with me."

Daphne's screams were now just a low guttural wail. Steve shook her one more time and then the ruffian on the floor screamed at him.

"Damn you! You got to get me a doctor. You can't just leave me here like this, I will die!"

Anger surged through Steve's body as he turned on the man. Steve took the rifle from the shoulder he had slung it on. "You're right you probably will die!" Steve took three purposeful strides towards the man. The man's eyes went wide in fear. Steve raised the rifle over his head and came down with a crushing blow with the butt stock of the rifle The butt struck the man in the forehead. His head snapped back and struck the wood floor below him. He lay there unconscious blood oozing down his face from a large gash in his forehead.

Steve turned as he slung the rifle back over his shoulder. He walked up to Daphne who was still moaning. "Daphne, come with me. Let's go see your sister." After several more tries to get through to the girl Steve became frustrated. He did not have the luxury to piddle around with this girl; they had to get back home before dark. Suddenly Steve's fist crashed into the back of the girl's jaw knocking her unconscious. Steve caught her before she hit the floor. He then threw her over his shoulder and walked back towards the Jeep and the truck.

⊹—⊷⊶—⊹

After several minutes of talking to Celina, Doc had convinced her to take the mild sedative he had offered her. "Celina you and Daphne can stay with Maude and me as long as you want. Do you want to do that?"

Celina looked at the old man who had cared for her when she was sick as long as she could remember. He always made things better no matter how sick or how bad she had hurt herself. She knew he would keep her safe.

She nodded her head. "Yes, Doctor Morrison. I would like that very much. I'm glad you and your friend Steve came for me. Where are Daphne and Steve?"

"Celina, Daphne ran off during the shootout. Steve went to go get her." Doc could see the immediate fear, and concern on her face. He placed a caring, gentle hand on her shoulder. "Don't worry sweetie, Steve will bring her back safe and sound."

Celina searched his face for any type of deception about Daphne's fate. She knew what she would find though. Doc had always been an upright and straightforward man. "I believe you…" Celina's reply was cut short by the loud snap of two shots being fired close by.

Doc grabbed Celina by the arm and pulled her out of the Jeep and down beside it. Celina was surprised at the strength in the old man's grip. With his right hand Doc drew his pistol. They heard six more rounds fired, and then silence. Doc was unsure of the distance of the shots, they seemed somewhat muffled. Doc scanned the area. Then he felt someone tugging his pants leg. He looked down at Celina.

"Doc hand me my shotgun. I think Steve put it in the back of the Jeep." Celina's hand remained outstretched waiting for him to comply.

Doc grabbed the shotgun and handed it down to her. "Stay down Celina. If someone comes you will be the my little surprise." What a surprise she would be Doc thought as he watched her eyes transform when the shotgun touched her hands. He had seen the same eyes on the faces of his friends when he served as medic on the battlefields of Viet Nam. Doc saw a flash of movement coming from behind the house that Steve had gone into. Doc raised the magnum and pointed it towards the back corner of the house.

Then he recognized Steve and he was carrying Daphne over his shoulder coming into view. "Oh, shit." Doc said as he holstered the pistol and ran around the Jeep towards Steve and Daphne.

Celina scrambled to her feet and looked at Steve and Daphne. "No!" The word rasped across her lips in despair. She threw the shotgun in the front seat as her feet grasped for purchase on the asphalt as she ran to her sister. This was almost too much for her. She could not loose her entire family could she?

⊹⊱──⊰⊹

Steve stopped in the front yard as Doc and Celina ran up to him. Doc helped him ease her to the grass, asking about her injuries in rapid fire secession. "Was she shot? Did she receive a head injury? Is she bleeding?"

Celina just stood transfixed looking at her prone sister. Steve took a knee beside Daphne and reached across and put a hand on Doc's shoulder as he searched for her injuries. He looked up into Celina's despondent eyes. "She is okay. I had to knock her out she was hysterical. I'm sorry Celina. I had to. There just did not seem any other way of getting her to come with me."

Relief inundated Celina. "It's okay Steve. I understand." Celina knelt beside her sister her hand stroking her forehead.

Doc reached under Daphne's shoulders. "Come on Steve we need to get out of here. Celina pull the tailgate down on my truck so we can lay her down there while we get ready to leave." Steve grabbed her feet and Celina ran to the truck careful to avoid looking into the cab.

Once Daphne was laid out on the tailgate Doc took out some smelling salts and placed them under her nose. Daphne's head jerked to the side, her eyes springing open. She started to panic until her eyes met Celina's. Celina soothed her sister while Doc went to Steve who was standing in front of his Jeep. Looking at Steve's face Doc knew there was a problem.

"Steve how bad off is the Jeep?"

"Not good." Steve said as he raised the hood on his Jeep.

As Doc walked around to the front of the Jeep and looked at the engine compartment he knew it was not good. The radiator was leaking in several places the coolant pooled on the street below.

Steve pointed to the alternator "Well they destroyed the alternator, and it looks like they hit the master break cylinder too. It's toast."

Doc pointed to the carburetor. "They hit the carburetor too Steve. It looks like your Jeep is not going anywhere. We'll have to pile in my truck. I think it would be best if you drive and I will sit in the back with the girls. We need to get Nancy wrapped up in something so the girls don't have to see their mother that way."

"Crap!" Steve turned and leaned against the front of his Jeep. His gazed moved to the two trucks blocking the roadway. One was a blue 1975 Ford F100. The other was a black 1984 Dodge ¾ ton 4x4, diesel crew cab.

"Maybe not Doc, I might have an alternate ride." Steve walked to the Dodge. Beside a couple of bullet holes it looked in excellent shape. He walked up to the truck and looked into the cab. The keys dangled from the ignition switch. Steve opened the door to the truck and hoped in. He clicked the key forward one notch to wait for the glow plugs to warm. Once the glow plug light went out he cranked the big diesel.

It fired up on the first try. Steve backed the truck and pulled it up to his Jeep, and got out after shutting it down. "I think I have a new ride Doc. You wonder if the DMV will require the former owner's signature on the transfer title." Steve said with a smile.

Doc smiled back and looked into the bed of the truck. Several five gallon gas cans and all kinds of items filled the back. "You might have to call the police and file a found property report. Look at all this stuff."

Steve glanced in the back. "We'll go through that later. Get the girls in the back seat; I want you to drive this rig. I'm going to check the other truck out."

Doc nodded and trotted over to the girls. Steve walked back to prostrate forms of the two men he had killed. He pried the SKS from one man's hands and laid it beside him. He then pulled the surplus ammo vest off the man. It contained six thirty round SKS detachable magazines. On the man's hip was a Ruger MKII .22 caliber pistol. Steve relieved the man of this and took two extra magazines for it out of the man's back pocket and laid them beside the SKS.

He then went to the next man and picked up the Mini-14, and laid it with the SKS. He then retrieved the web belt the man wore. Attached to it was a USMC K-Bar knife, and two M-16 magazine pouches. Each pouch contained three thirty round magazines for the Mini-14. There was a parachute cord around the man's neck and Steve jerked it off from around the man's neck. Attached to the cord was a pouch. Inside Steve found gold rings, diamond earrings, and gold chains. They were all high dollar items.

One of the chains had a two karat diamond pendant. These guys must have been doing some serious looting. Steve pocketed the pouch. The jewelry could be useful for bartering if things stayed in the crapper. Steve looked back as the diesel truck started and the girls climbed in to the back. Steve went back to the task at hand. He knew they had to leave but many of these items could come in handy if the crisis continued.

He walked to the two men that Doc and Celina had killed. The first held a Stainless Ruger Mini-14 with a synthetic top folding Ruger factory stock. Steve knew this was a rare find. He took it from the man's hands and laid it on the ground. He removed the man's web belt which contained only four smaller M-16 magazine pouches that were used to hold twenty round M-16 magazines. Each pouch contained three twenty round Mini-14 magazines. One of the pouches had a hole in the front of it. Steve detached this one and threw it to the ground. One of his rounds had smashed into it destroying two of the magazines before entering his intended victim. Blood had soaked it through the entire thing.

Steve went to the next man who lay face down in a crumpled ball resting on his shins and knees. Steve kicked the man with the flat of his foot knocking the corpse onto its back. This man also wore a surplus AK ammo vest. His vest however contained six AK magazines. Steve took this from the man's body. He removed one of the magazines that had been pierced by his bullets and threw it aside. Tucked in the man's waste band was a Sigma 9mm pistol.

Though Steve thought the gun was a piece of crap he decided the growing group could use it. He tucked it in his own waste band after dropping the magazine and clearing the chamber. He put the spent round in the magazine and reinserted the magazine. He looked around and in the shot up Ford and found nothing of real value. They must have just stolen this thing because there was nothing in it.

Then Steve noticed that each man wore almost new military combat boots. "You guys had to have hit a gun store or surplus store." Steve said to the lifeless forms around him. He decided that the boots could be used for barter or they might even fit him, Doc, or Amos. Good boots could save one's life in times like these. Steve pulled out his knife and went to each man cutting the shoelaces and removing the boots.

About that time Doc walked up. "Doing a little Christmas shopping Steve?" Doc said in gallows humor.

Steve looked up at Doc. "We may need all this stuff Doc swing the Dodge around here and help me load up the stuff."

Doc walked back to the truck and swung it around. Celina and Daphne sat in the back seats of the cab. Daphne had her head on Celina's shoulder while Celina stroked her sister's head.

Doc and Steve loaded the gear up into the bed of the truck. "What do we do about Nancy?" Doc asked.

Steve pondered for a moment and grabbed a plastic ground cloth from the bed of the truck. "Doc on the way home I want you to drive the Dodge. I'll be driving your truck. We're going to wrap Nancy up in this tarp and we will put her in the bed of your truck."

Doc nodded. "Let's get this done." The two men worked in silence as they removed Nancy's mangled body from the truck. They lay her gently on the tarp and wrapped her. They then lifted her up and placed her in the bed of the truck. Steve wiped some of the blood from his hands with a dirty shop rag that he had pulled out of the bed of the truck.

"Okay Doc let's get home. We'll take it slow again. We don't need anymore incidents like this one."

The two walked to their respective trucks. Doc turned to Steve, "I have to stop by Amos's and let him know we are home."

Steve shook his head no. "I'll do it Doc. You get them girls to Maude. She will take care of them like no one else can."

⊱──⊰

The rest of the trip home had been uneventful. As they passed Amos's place Doc blew his horn and waved to Steve as he drove on to his house. Steve waved back and turned on to Amos's drive. Pulling up to the front of the house Steve saw Amos come around from behind a blue Ford 4x4 that he had not seen before.

Amos walked up to Steve and shook his hand. "Where is Doc?" Amos said as he looked over the bullet riddled truck. Then his eyes settled on the tarp in the back shaped like a human cocoon. "Tell me he aint dead Steve." He said as he walked to the back of the truck

Steve gently stopped Amos with his hand. "He's okay Amos. That is Nancy Donovan. We ran into a roadblock a few miles back. She never got out of the truck before they killed her."

Amos nodded his head and let out an exhale of breath in relief that his friend was not dead. "What about the girls are they okay?"

Steve put his hands in his pockets. "Well enough for two girls who lost both of their parents in the past four days. The youngest, Daphne is having a lot of trouble dealing with it. The older girl is holding up better. She even shot and killed one of the bandits."

Amos looked surprised. "How many were there?"

"There were four. Doc got one, Celina took one and I took out the other two. Had to go hunt Daphne down after it was over. She was probably the only smart one in the group; she got the hell out of Dodge when the bullets started flying. I had to shoot two other guys in a house that she ran to. They had her at knife point."

197

Amos shook his head in disbelief. "Things have gotten bad haven't they?"

Steve took his hands from his pockets and pointed over his shoulder with his thumb. "Where did you get the truck?"

"I had a few problems of my own. Remember those three guys that beat the living hail out of me?"

Steve nodded as a smile played across his face at the memory of shooting up the racist thug's truck. "Yeah I do."

"Well they came back for seconds. They're fertilizing the back field now. Got some nice guns off of them I would like to show you." Amos said

."Maybe tomorrow Amos, I need to get the girls mom back to Doc's, and start digging her grave." Steve said walking over to the cab of the truck.

Amos started to walk towards his own truck. "I'll follow you over and help you out."

╼╾

When Steve and Amos arrived Doc and Maude met them out front. Amos took off his hat when Maude approached. "Good evening Mrs. Morrison."

Maude's face was grim. She was ready to get back in the house quickly and tend to the girls after she talked about what the plan was. Good evening to you Amos." She turned to Steve. "Are you okay Steve?"

Steve nodded. "Yes I'm alright." Steve turned his body so that Doc could be included in the conversation. "Amos and I are going to dig a grave for Nancy. I think it will be best to bury her as soon as possible. The girls need to put this behind them."

Maude spoke up. "If yall will bring her around to the basement I will clean her up and get her ready."

Doc turned to his wife. "Maude, there isn't much left of Nancy. She took a round to the head and several to the chest. She literally looks like a torn up rag doll. As much as I would like to, it would be a wasted effort. Besides I don't think the girls need to see their mother's body. Let's get her buried and then we will have a service for her." Maude just nodded her head.

Doc looked back at Steve. "Steve, would you mind if we buried Nancy next to Diane?"

"That would be fine Doc. Diane would like the company." Steve walked off headed for the tool shed for shovels. Amos and Doc followed behind. Maude went back into the house to look after the girls.

After several hours of digging the grave was complete. Doc drove his truck down to the grave site. The three men gently lowered the woman's body into the grave. After they finished replacing the dirt the three went to the house to clean up and have supper.

The following afternoon a cool breeze blew in the spring air. All of them had gathered and a small service was held. Doc said a few prayers, Maude sang as she had for Diane's funeral. Then Doc, Amos, Steve, and Maude left the girls to have some time alone with their mother. The two knelt by the grave talking of happier times with their mother and father. Then they rose and walked back hand in hand to the house

Chapter 20

Don Savage stood in front of his sink drinking a tall glass of water. He was pondering what to do about the two men he had killed in the front yard. Setting the glass down he walked over and picked up the telephone. Hearing the dial tone he dialed 911. Five minutes later Don hung the phone up after the line went dead. "Well guess I will take care of the trash myself." Don took off his uniform shirt and vest before walking outside. He did however keep his gun belt on.

Walking to the first body Don leaned over and grabbed the already stiffening body by the ankles. He dragged the corpse over by the second which lay near the thugs cars. Straitening up after dropping the legs Don put his hands at the base of his back and stretched his back He almost doubled over as a sharp pain raced through his rib area.

The sound of an approaching car caught his attention. Coming around the curve heading towards his driveway was an old 1980's model Toyota Corolla. It was gold in color and the fenders on the passenger side were rusted out. It was occupied by four scruffy looking, white trash rednecks. The car slowed as it approached his driveway. It turned in driving slowly, the occupants clearly checking Don out. The car slowed and came to a stop about thirty yards from Don. The occupants did not attempt to get out just looked Don and the area over.

"Well, well, what do we have here?" Don said as he drew the Sig from his SS3 duty holster. Don took two steps back and one over placing himself behind the front end of his recent attacker's car, his feet crunching on in the gravel as he backed. Suddenly the driver threw the Toyota into reverse, the front tires churning in the gravel spewing up rocks and a cloud of gray and white dust. The front seat passenger leaned out of the window, a pistol in his hands. He opened fire, rounds, whipping in the air around Don. Sparks flew from the front passenger door of the car Don was behind as two underpowered small caliber rounds ricochet off the door and slammed into the ground beside the car.

"Shit!" Don went to one knee, ducking his head down below the front end of the car.

The firing quickly stopped as the shooter ran out of ammo. Don popped up leveling his pistol across the hood of the car. The car was almost fifty yards away now and the distance was widening. As soon as Don had a good sight picture he squeezed off a round; the round smashed six inches below his point of aim which had been about halfway up the window. Don saw the passenger jump, and then slump forward, and over onto the drivers arm. The little car swerved in an uncontrollable manner going off the driveway and out into his field. The driver locked up the brakes and spun the wheel.

The front seat passenger's body slung sideways into the passenger door, the head thrown back between the seat, and door jamb. Don adjusted his aim as the back seat passenger fired a revolver of some sort out of his window. The driver put the car in drive and floored the gas pedal, the cheap balding tires grasping for traction in the grassy field. The car was now almost seventy-five yards away, close to the end of his driveway. Don knew it was a long shot, but wanted these thugs to know to stay the hell away from him, and his property.

Don squeezed the trigger again just as the car had straightened out and was heading to the roadway. Don was rewarded for his patient marksmanship. The back glass shattered in a shower of glass. Don sprang to his feet and let a whoop, just like a kid who makes his first basketball goal in a game. He did not know if his round found its mark. He really did not care; it was a heck of a shot, a moving car at over seventy-five yards. He couldn't wait till he got to tell the guys back at the station house. That is if things were ever going to get back to normal.

Don had recognized one of the thugs in the car, as a guy who lived in the seedy trailer court a mile down the road. That's were they came from, and he was sure that's where they were headed now. When the trailer court first had opened Don had not minded one bit. The folks that had moved in were all descent hard working young folks just starting out in life. Then over the past two years the trash had moved in. The blue lights of the Lauderdale County Sheriff's Office cars streaking by his house at all hours of the day heading to the trailer court had become a regular occurrence.

Don had talked to several of his buddies at the S.O. about the park. They said now the only people left in the trailer park were drug addicts, thieves, meth, and crack dealers.

Don turned holding his aching ribs as he walked back in the house to call the S.O. "Hell what am I thinking? There probably aint no Sheriff's Office left." Don stopped and turned back to the car, he had a plan. Popping the trunk, Don took all of the loot in the trunk out and stacked it on his front porch.

Walking to the shop in the back yard Don retrieved a thirty foot length of hemp rope. When he got back to the front he struggled with the two bodies and stuffed them in the trunk of the car. He hopped in and adjusted the seat. Turning the key in the ignition the car coughed a couple of times and started up. A white blue-gray cloud of smoke poured from the tail pipe.

Don put the car in drive and cut through the front yard and back onto the driveway. At the end of the drive Don crossed the road and parked on the shoulder. Getting out with the hemp rope in hand Don fashioned a noose. He took the noose and put it around the neck of the man that lay on top of the other thug.

Don dragged the body to a sturdy oak tree that had several sets of low limbs. Don tossed the rope over a sturdy looking limb that was about eight feet off the ground, and began to hoist the body up, his large arms bulging with strain. Once the man was about two feet off the ground he tied the rope off on another limb. Cutting the extra rope off with his knife he repeated the process with the man's accomplice. The second took a little longer since he weighed about forty pounds more than the other. Finally he had the second man hanging. "I don't know how long I've wanted to do that to a few thugs. Of course I would have preferred them alive." He said to himself.

Hopping back into the car Don drove back across the road to his house a cloud of smoke billowing behind him. Don had something else he had wanted to do for the past couple of years. Once at the house he took a little time storing the loot inside. He finished emptying out the car and decided he would inventory it all later, after he completed a more important task.

Don went back to the kitchen and drank another two glasses of water. He took a zip lock bag out of the cabinet and put his pistol in it. He then went to the bathroom and stripped off his now dirty clothes. Getting in the shower he scrubbed down his body getting the dirt and blood scrubbed off. His pistol sat on the soap dish encased in the plastic baggy. He finished bathing, turned the water off and began toweling off.

Once dry Don strode nude down the hall to his bedroom, Don went into his closet and popped the hidden panel. He retrieved his BDU's, a pair of socks and boots. He picked up his dirty patrol pants and took out the bottle of pain pills he had been given at the hospital. He took two out of the bottle and swallowed them dry. He pulled a first aid kit from under the bed and took out several ace bandages. Don wrapped his ribs tightly hoping he did a good enough job.

Once he finished up with he ribs he quickly dressed. Heading back into the closet he took down his FN-FAL and leaned it against the wall. Next he put on the LBV buckling it up and adjusting the straps. Taking out the magazines for his 1911 Kimber Warrior he loaded all of the magazines up. Then he secured them in their proper places on his vest, slapping the last one in the pistol and chambering a round. He holstered the pistol and began to load the FN magazines, taking the last and loading it into his battle rifle.

"Now it's time for a little pest control." Don said with a smile as he walked out of the closet.

He filled his canteens in the kitchen before beginning his trip to the small trailer court. Walking through the front door he contemplated the action he was about to take. Granted the trash in the trailer court had not been found guilty in the eyes of the law for any crimes against him, but if he did not take care of them now they would surely come for him later.

He felt sure they would. He had already killed at least three that he knew for sure lived in the trailer court, and the other three in the car most likely came from there also.

After walking as quietly as possible for thirty minutes he arrived within one hundred yards of the trailer court. Don took a knee in a small depression and applied his "war paint" as he had called it in the Army. Once he finished up he began to stalk closer to the trailer court. He stopped at the military crest of a small hill that over looked the park and lay in the prone position. He pulled out a small pair of Bushnell binoculars and scanned the park. In the center of the park sat the gold Corolla that had come to his house.

About twelve people stood about smoking and drinking booze. The body of the man he had shot still sat in the passenger seat. One of the men in the center of the group was miming as if he was shooting a gun, his arm straight out, fingers pointing like a gun. Don observed the group for another hour. There were only seven trailers in the court now, and he had not seen anyone else come or go into the surrounding trailers. It was time to act, he was sure everyone that lived in the court was present.

Don tucked the binoculars back into their pouch in his vest. He pulled out a canteen and drained the quart of water in several gulps quenching his parched throat. He then lifted the rifle to his shoulder and scanned for his first target. Don found who he was looking for. It was the man who had been in the rear passenger seat and had shot at him. He was smoking a joint and drinking a beer while talking to scraggly looking woman who looked as if she had just walked out of a concentration camp. Centering the front sight post on the man's chest he slowed his breathing. Just as he was about to squeeze the trigger the woman stepped into his sight picture. "Well if I'm going to take them all out I might as well get two birds with one stone." He thought.

Don squeezed the trigger on the big rifle. It bucked against his shoulder making him lose sight of his prey for a second. As he came back down on target he watched the pair collapse into each other and then fall to the ground. Don changed his point of aim and fired at a man dressed in a dirty green trench coat. The round caught him low in the stomach jackknifing his body as he fell. Don took aim on another man who had crouched down to one knee. He held a sawed off shotgun in his hands. Don rested the front sight post just below his chin and squeezed off another round. The round hit him in the left cheek, the back, and top of his head exploding outward.

The drunken and drugged out group finally realized what was happening and began to scatter for the trailers like cockroaches running for cover when someone turns on the kitchen light. Don fired catching a woman in the hip as she sprinted for a trailer. The pistol in her hand clattered to the concrete as her body slammed into the side of a trailer. Her body slid down the side of the trailer leaving a crimson streak as she fell.

A bullet kicked up dirt to Don's left as he was about to shoot another man. He rolled twice to the right, his military and police training kicking in. Another shot barked from the trailer court and the round hit were he had just been. Don located the man kneeling down beside a gas grill. Don took aim. Not on the man but the propane tank. Not only would it kill the man if it exploded but it would add to the confusion and possibly take out a few more people.

Don fired twice, both rounds striking the metal tank. Suddenly flames engulfed the area around the gunman as the tank exploded. Don watched as the explosion lifted a man that had been running close by. His body flaming as he flew threw the air. When the human torch hit the ground he began to roll and scream in pain. Though Don was wantonly killing these sorry excuses for human beings he was not cruel. Two rounds through the chest ended the man's mortal misery. Of course Don felt the man was leaving one fire and probably headed for another one that waited for him in hell.

Don did a quick mental count in his head. He had killed seven people and that left approximately five to go. He watched two women run into a trailer at the end of the park. Don lay scanning the park for a second and then shots erupted from the second trailer near the entrance. Don counted the muzzle flashes as they came from the darkened windows. Three different windows, three different muzzle flashes.

Don waited for the individual at the front window to fire again. As soon as he did Don shifted his point of aim and emptied the remaining rounds in the magazine into the area were the shots had come from. Don quickly reloaded and rolled down the back side of the hill.

Don stayed in the small valley that ran along the hills that surrounded the park. He made his way to the front of the park and darted across the open area to the first trailer. He then worked his way down the back side of the trailer. He peeked around the corner at the second trailer.

He could hear gunshots coming from inside it. They were still shooting into the tree line.

Don went to the small deck that led to the back door of the trailer. He was about to kick it in when the words of his old field training officer came to mind, "Always check to see if the door is unlocked before you go kicking it in. You may be able to catch the bad guy by surprise." Don slung his FN and drew the Kimber.

He tried the door knob and turned it slowly. It was unlocked! Opening it just a crack when the gunfire started up again he took a peek. He saw two men standing at the living room windows firing out the windows at an angle towards the tree line. Don jerked the door open and rushed inside. He raised the pistol and as soon as the front sight post lay on the man's torso he fired three quick rounds.

The three 230 grain bullets tore into the man, his body flung against the wall. The rifle fell from his hands as he followed it to the floor. Don moved left towards the kitchen panning his pistol to the right to shoot the next man. The man was dressed in a biker jacket and wore grease stained jeans. A look of astonishment was on his blonde bearded face.

The man turned trying to bring a semi-auto deer rifle that had been sawed off to about fourteen inches to bear. The man began firing as the rifle swung towards Don.

Don dove towards the floor, the big .45 bucking in his hands as he emptied the pistol. As he hit the floor Don ejected the spent magazine pulling out a fresh magazine and slamming it home. As Don rolled up on one knee the thug's gun went dry. Don took aim and fired a round into the man's face.

The now faceless man fell backwards smashing an end table as his body fell over the arm of the couch where he came to rest. Don got to his feet and slowly made his way to the bedroom where the other man was. He stepped into the room and found the man in a pool of blood. His shirt had several blood soaked holes in it. "I guess I got him."

Don left the trailer and searched the remaining trailers. He finally came to the one were the two women had run into. Stepping into the open door Don found the two women huddled in the living room floor. Don raised the pistol and paused as he was about to pull the trigger. "Is there anyone else in the trailer?"

"No, no we are the only ones left. Please don't kill us." One of the dirty meth fiends on the floor said.

Don motioned with his pistol for the two to get up. "Stand up and come outside." Don slowly backed out as the two complied with his order. Once outside Don followed them to the litter filled street. "Get walking and when you get to the road turn left and don't ever come back. Do you understand?"

The two nodded and walked at a quick pace constantly looking back over their shoulders. Don watched them walk through the smoke their bodies blurred a bit as the heat of the flames from the fire cast a mirage over their bodies. Once they turned down the road Don sat down on the stoop exhausted. Taking out his second canteen he began to sip from it. He wasn't sure how he felt about what he had just done. In a civilized world he was a mass murderer.

In the world that he now found himself in he was a survivor. He knew he had to do what he did. Eventually, as a man alone in this now strange land the group of thugs would have caught him off guard and killed him. Don rose from the stoop and began to check the bodies for weapons and other useful items. He would later check the trailers and find large amounts of food, liquor, drugs, and ammo. All stolen of course but he would use it and hopefully survive till civilization rose again

Chapter 21

The day after Nancy Donovan's funeral Steve had told Doc to come by his place and they would sort through the items that they had found in the Dodge 4x4 taken from the thugs. He was so tired that night at Doc's place he immediately crashed after digging the grave. What really perturbed him was that Amos had forgot all about his cousin's back hoe at his place, that is until the three had finished digging Nancy's grave. Even worse was that Doc had forgotten his own. They figured the memory lapse was due to the stress and fatigue they had all been through.

Amos helped with chores around Doc's till the funeral the next afternoon. Amos had told Steve he would come by and bring the items taken from the three men he had killed. He really wanted Steve to go over the weapons that he had procured, and find the best ones that would suit him. Amos had headed straight home to check on Benny and tend to his animals that he had neglected. He hopped in the big Ford 4x4 and drove home. He had always been a Chevrolet man but the Ford sure rode nice, and had AC to boot!

—⊷⊷—

Steve rolled out of bed and checked his watch, 6:00 am. He stretched and let out a yawn, then slipped on his flip-flops and went downstairs. He put water and coffee in the coffee maker then headed outside to the generator shack. He could actually get to it from an access panel in the house but it was easier to start out in the shack itself. Walking through the morning dew, the wet grass sent a chill through him. He opened the shack door and went in. Once inside he primed up the generator checked the fluid levels. With a couple of pulls the generator roared to life. After a ten minute wait he hooked up the generator to the fuse box. Walking back inside he realized he had just made a serious blunder. He had walked outside in flip-flops and his underwear as if nothing was wrong with the world.

He stared at his AK-47, and Glock 17 lying on the kitchen table where he had left them when he went to bed exhausted last night. "I have got to be a freaking idiot!" Steve said as he stood there shaking his head in disbelief at what he had done.

Steve picked up the AK and the Glock and walked into the gun room while the coffee perked. Sitting at the bench he field stripped the two weapons. Steve stopped what he was doing. "Okay idiot no more stupid moves." Steve opened the gun safe. He pulled out Diane's Glock 19 unloaded it and emptied the extra rounds into a little bullet box he kept for extra bullets. He laid it on the table.

Turning back to the gun safe he looked over his remaining weapons. He would have to keep one with him at all times for now on. He decided he would take the Ruger MKII out while he cleaned the dirty weapons on the table. His hand stopped as he reached to take it off its pegs. "Oh, Shit! Those damn guns we took off those guys yesterday are in the truck."

Steve grabbed the Remington 870 from the rack. He rammed seven rounds into the magazine tube and chambered a round. He locked the front door as he ran by heading up stairs to his room. Once upstairs he threw on a pair of pants and some tennis shoes.

He picked the shotgun back up and walked to the bedroom window. Standing to the side of the window he peered down at the black truck. He did not see any foot prints in the wet dew around the truck just his leading to the back of the house. The back end of the truck was still full of all the gear that they had not even bothered to remove since capturing the truck. He continued scanning the front of the house and the area around the gate.

Once satisfied he headed to the back room. Peering out the back window, and the two side windows in the room he scanned the woods surrounding the back side of his house. After a ten minute vigil Steve turned to head back downstairs. He went into the gun room and grabbed an empty duffle bag that lay in the corner. Picking it up he headed for the front door. He stopped himself from opening the front door. "Nope someone could be watching it there brain child. Quit acting like things are normal."

Walking through the kitchen dining area he made his way to the back room next to his gun room. Steve had made this room his electronics room. A short wave radio, computer, stereo system, TV, DVD player, and CB were in this room. Also the small access panel to the generator shack. Though Steve had sound proofed the generator shack and put a bigger muffler on the exhaust pipe he could still hear the steady drone of his generator. Steve knelt down and opened the three foot by three foot door.

Ducking down he entered the shack. Steve reached for the door knob, which he had failed to lock when leaving. Turning it he opened the door just a crack and peered out into the woods. Nothing, it appeared to be safe. Steve exited the shack and walked to the corner of the house nearest the truck. Getting down on one knee he peered cautiously around the corner. Pulling his head back he realized another mistake. In his back pack, was a small mirror attached to a collapsible antenna. One of the ones you can pick up at any auto store. He had bought it to use to look around corners. Steve quietly talked to himself again, "You got a lot to learn if you're gonna live. If you keep making stupid mistakes you're going to wind up dead."

Steve rose up and trotted to the truck. He opened the back door to the crew cab, which of course he had naturally left unlocked. All the weapons and most of the ammo pouches lay in the back bench seat. Steve leaned the 870 against the truck and unfurled the duffle bag. He reached in and grabbed the rifles and pistols one at a time and put them in the duffle. Next he grabbed the ammo pouches and threw them in.

He gave the back and front seat a once over, he did not think he had missed anything that someone else could use against him. Steve walked to the front door, his eyes examining every feature of the surrounding terrain. As Steve stepped onto the front porch he realized the front door was locked, and that he had left the door to the shack unlocked.

Steve's heart skipped a beat realizing that simple mistakes like the one's he was making this morning could get him killed. Not being aware of his surroundings, and little things like leaving a door unlocked, or locked were things he had to think about, plan for, and remember. Survival was the name of the game in today's world. Steve made his way around back and entered the generator shack. Placing the duffle bag full of guns in the corner he opened the panel. He climbed through the door reached back and dragged the bag in into the room.

"Damn I'm exhausted." Steve thought as he wiped the perspiration from his forehead. Steve dropped the duffel by the gun safe when he went back into the gun room. He walked over to the work bench and reassembled Diane's Glock. He put in the loaded magazine from his Glock 17 in the magazine well, and walked to the bathroom.

Stripping down Steve kicked his shoes and pants in the corner. Pistol in hand he turned on the hot water. He figured the generator had heated up the water in the hot water tank by now. Reaching in the shower he turned on the water. After a short wait steam rose from the shower. Steve adjusted the water temperature and got in. He placed the pistol on the shampoo rack above the shower head.

Steve quickly bathed and turned the precious hot water off. After toweling off he picked up the jeans out of the floor and put them back on. He tucked the pistol in the back of his waist band. He went up stairs finished dressing and put on a pair of boots. Back down in the kitchen Steve poured a large cup of coffee and picked up his smokes and headed back into the gun room. He dis-assembled the Glock 19 again after ensuring the 870 was close at hand. Smoking his first cigarette of the day and sipping his coffee he cleaned each of his weapons as he waited for Doc, and Amos to show up.

⊹—◆—⊹

Amos had been up since 4:00 am. He had fed the chickens, slopped the hogs, and checked his goats, fed Midget and his worthless jackass Festus. He walked from the barn rubbing his left triceps still tender from two nips Festus had given him while he had got out some oats for the mule. "Guess I had it coming, leaving him in the barn like that." He said to himself.

Amos was walking with a limp. The bullet wound on the back of his leg was aching and tender this morning. He would make himself a glass of Valerian root tea. Valerian root was a natural herb. It is a type of sedative and has mild pain relieving properties. It was also good for stress, insomnia, and anxiety. It has also been used for menstrual cramps, migraine headaches, and rheumatic pains. It was one of his grandmother's favorite herbs.

Though it worked well Amos thought she gave it to the grandkids to keep them from faking illness. The dang tea made from the root smelled like dirty socks, and tasted about the same. Amos stepped up on the back porch and picked the basket of eggs up that he had got from his laying hens earlier. Walking inside to the kitchen he picked up the already greased iron skillet and put it on the gas stove. He was glad he had made the decision to fill the natural gas tank up a few weeks ago while gas prices where down.

He mixed up a batch of biscuits and put them in the stove. Within about twenty minutes he had breakfast ready. Benny walked in the kitchen just as Amos finished putting out the plates and forks. A pang of guilt tugged at Amos because he had left the boy by himself while he was at Doc's. It had not even occurred to him that he would be gone so long when he left for Doc's. After Amos had apologized profusely the boy had just laughed and told him not to worry about it. He knew he had to grow up quick and would be left alone at times. "One tough kid." Was all Amos could think.

"Good morning Amos." Benny said as he shuffled in to the kitchen rubbing the sleep from his eyes. The boy wore one of his son's Marine Corps t-shirts. Amos did not mind though, the boy had already proved to him he had the guts in him that it took to become a Marine. Besides, Andy would really have liked the boy.

"Hey there munchkin man, are you hungry?" Amos said as he put a couple of biscuits and some eggs on the plates.

"Sure am. Smells like my granny's kitchen in here." The boy said as he pulled up a chair to the table. The two quickly ate their meal. "You interested in heading over to Steve's with me today?" Amos said pointing a half eaten biscuit at Benny.

The boy's face brightened. "Sure are we going to take that new truck of yours?"

Amos shook his head and smiled. "Nope, I reckon we'll take Festus and Midget. We need to save as much fuel as possible."

Benny smiled right back at him. "Do I get to ride Festus or Midget?"

Amos finished off his biscuit. "Can't let you ride that crazy old Festus. He is liable jerk you out of the saddle and start gnawing on you like a half crazed coyote. You'll ride Midget."

"Okay! When do we leave?" The boy asked excitedly.

"Well if you will wash the dishes, I need to go out and finish plowing up the last five acres of my field. I got to get the corn in real soon if it's gonna grow right. I think that will take me until around 8:30. How does that sound?" Amos said his head tilting to the right a bit as he asked the question.

Benny about leapt out of his chair. "Well what are you sitting around for get out there and plow?" Benny started to clean up the kitchen while Amos went out to start up the tractor. He stuck out his tongue at Festus as he drove by heading for the field. Festus just turned his back and went inside the barn and snuck a few apples out of the sack that hung inside the barn.

By 8:15 Amos was done with the plowing. He had put all the guns and ammunition for them in two old five-foot long canvas sacks and saddled both Festus and Midget. He tied off the ends of the two bags with some ¼" rope, and hung them over the saddle. Then they headed down the road for Steve's place. His coach gun lay across the saddle horn.

As they rounded the bend of the road Amos pulled up sharply as he saw a man and woman not twenty yards ahead of them. Amos cautiously brought the shotgun up so that it rested at the ready in both of his hands.

The man and woman stopped dead in their tracks. They had both had their heads down wearily putting one foot in front of the other. They were oblivious to their surroundings.

"Hello there! Where are you headed?" Amos asked in friendly tone that held more friendliness than he felt.

"We're coming down from Iron City. Heard tell there might be some government help in Florence. Say do you got any food, and water you can spare?"

Amos slowly shook his head from side to side. "From what I understand there isn't anything but a lot of death in Florence." Amos gave the pair a thorough once over.

He noticed that the two appeared to carry no weapons. The man wore a dirty white Coors Light t-shirt, dirt covered jeans, and a pair of sneakers with a hole around the left big toe area. He had skinny arms and legs, but a huge beer belly. The woman wore a pair of spandex pants, a dirty pink t-shirt and sandals. Her feet looked as if she had walked through mud. The sweat pouring down her legs onto her feet cutting small rivers in the road dust that caked her feet. She was a bit shorter than the man, though she probably outweighed him by thirty pounds.

The woman ran her fingers through her sweaty blonde hair that hung limply about her head. It appeared as if she had not washed it in several days. "Mister, we sure could use some water."

Amos cut his eyes over his right shoulder, keeping the pair in his peripheral vision. "Benny ride up here and open my saddle bag. Grab two of those MREs and a couple of water bottles for me." Amos had put four one liter bottles and four MREs in the saddle bags. Steve had given Amos a case of the MREs last year. Amos did not think he would ever need them since he canned about everything he grew. But glass jars had a tendency to break when traveling by mule.

Benny pulled Midget to a halt and dismounted. The little burrow pawed the ground and then leaned his head and nibbled at the grass on the side of the road. Benny opened the side flap of the saddle bag and pulled out the requested items.

"What do you want me to do with them?"

Amos motioned with his head back behind them, his eyes never leaving the two refugees. "Put them back there about twenty yards." Benny ambled to the rear and placed the food and water on the shoulder of the road. He walked back and mounted Midget. Amos pushed his straw hat back on his head.

"How do things look in Iron City?"

The man wiped the sweat from his face with the palm of his hand. "Well most folks got food since about everyone farms, gardens, or has family that does. We don't have any at all though."

Amos looked a bit confused. "Why don't you have food? Bugs or weather get your crops?"

This time the woman spoke up. "No nothing like that. Me and Earl here, well we got disabilities. The grocery store in town refused to take our food stamps. Said we had to have cash, gold, silver, or something to trade. We live in the Section 8 housing and were not supposed to have to worry about stuff like that. The government gives us food stamps and everyone should take them, the government's good for it."

Amos looked at the two in disgust. "Well mam there aint no hand outs in Florence or around here. Best thing you two can do is head back home."

The man shuffled a bit his face held down. "No. I'm sure Florence will have something or some kind of government aid."

"Well if you intend to head on in to Florence you need to watch out. Especially around here." Amos said.

"What do we need to watch out for?" The fat dirty woman asked. Her sudden fear was evident on her face.

Amos wrinkled his nose as the wind blew up from behind the two. He could smell their unwashed bodies. "Well the next two houses are full of Black Panthers, and they hate white folks." He lied. "Only reason they don't bother me is because I'm black. Yall got guns to protect you don't you?"

The man nervously rubbed his nose. "Well no we aint got no guns. Could you give us some?"

Amos shook his head. "Don't have any to spare son. Your best bet if you head on to Florence is to stick to the left side of the road in the trees so they don't see you. Have you heard anything about Memphis, or Nashville?"

"They had a whole mess of Army and National Guard show up. Lot's of riots over food and water. There's talk that a bunch of groups of china men are running around shooting folks, and blowing things up. Can we have our food and water now?"

"Sure go ahead." Amos said.

The man reached under his shirt. Amos brought the shotgun to his shoulder in a flash. "You interested in dying today son?"

The man froze. "Just gonna take my belt off." He slowly raised his shirt. A huge belt buckle with the Confederate Battle flag emblazed on it came in to view. "I don't reckon them Black Panther folks would take kindly to this."

"Alright go ahead take it off." Amos motioned with the shotgun. The man threw the belt buckle in the ditch at the side of the road. "Get your food and water and get on out of here." Amos said. The two sprinted for the water and food and began to tear into the food packets, and drinking in gulps from the water bottles.

Amos swung Festus around. "I would eat and walk if I were you. You never know when those Panthers will show up. The two refugees moved to the left side of the road and began walking up into the tree line, Amos and Benny road on to Steve's.

⊷⊶

Steve was on his second cup of coffee and just finished cleaning and reloading his two pistols and the AK. Placing the AK back into the gun safe he turned to get the Diane's pistol when he heard a horn blow out front. Making his way to the living room window he peered out. Maude's truck was sitting outside the gate.

Steve walked outside the 870 in his hands, his Glock tucked in the back of his waist band. Doc got out of the truck and raised the first gate. Steve was just reaching the second gate to lift it as Doc closed the first gate. Then he noticed the passenger in truck. Steve mentally admonished himself for failing to notice. He raised his hand and waved. "Hey Doc, hello Celina, how are yall today?"

"Good morning Steve!" Doc said as he hopped back in the cab of the truck to drive through the now open second gate. Celina meekly waved to Steve as if she was embarrassed to be noticed. Steve followed the truck up to the house.

Doc and Celina got out, Doc stretching his arms out wide getting the kinks out of his old frame. "Got any coffee Steve?"

"Got a fresh pot brewed. Yall come on in." The three went into the house, Steve was last. He stood on the porch for a few extra seconds looking about for anything out of the ordinary. Once inside Steve turned the dead bolt.

"Expecting trouble Steve?" Doc asked as he walked into the living room.

Steve walked toward the kitchen area to grab some coffee for his guest. "Doc I just think we need to start taking a lot of extra precautions."

Doc and Celina sat on the couch. Doc crossed his legs and placed his hands behind his head. "Steve I really doubt we will run into anything bad around here. We're in the middle of nowhere, and we have nothing of value that anyone would know about."

"Celina would you like some coffee?" Steve called from the kitchen.

"Yes please." She replied. Her voice was barely audible to Steve in the kitchen.

"How do you take it Celina?"

"I like cream and sugar if you have any." She said.

A few moments later Steve walked in and gave Doc and Celina their coffee. He walked to the kitchen table and picked his up. He returned and sat in his leather recliner. "Doc you are absolutely wrong about having nothing of value. We have homes with power and well water. We have food. You and Amos have animals, and crops. Plus now you have two pretty young girls to protect."

Celina said something to Steve he could not quite catch. Her face was downcast looking at the floor.

"What's that Celina?" Steve asked.

Celina looked up and stared into Steve's eyes. "I'm not a girl. I will be eighteen very soon. Doc doesn't have to take care of me. I can take care of myself and Daphne if need be. I'm not some fragile little porcelain doll. You sound just like my father. Well If my Uncle Joe was around he would tell you I can take care of myself." Her voice had risen from a whisper to a forceful tenor.

Steve sat his coffee down and held up his hands in defense. "What a minute there Celina, I did not mean it like that. I know you can take care of yourself. I meant…"

Celina leaned forward on the couch, "I know what you meant, and you better learn a little bit about someone before you make any judgments about them."

Doc placed his hand over his face to hide the smile that had appeared there as the little brown haired beauty told Steve what for. Steve had a lot to learn about Celina Donovan that was for sure.

Steve stood up and grabbed his coffee. "I got it Celina. I'm getting some more coffee." Steve turned and retreated for the kitchen, not particularly interested in tangling with the young "woman". Mostly because he was not sure he could win the argument. "Women were so touchy".

Doc reached over a laugh escaping from his mouth, and placed a hand on Celina's knee. "Don't be so rough on the man Celina. He's a good guy. Steve is just concerned about us, that's all."

Celina sat back on the couch. "Sorry about that Dr. Morrison. You know I just can't stand when a guy tries to treat me like a pretty and dumb little girl."

A knock came at the door. Doc peered out the window as Steve walked in from the kitchen, his pistol in his hand. "It's Amos and little Benny." Doc said as he stood up and went and unlocked the door and opened it for Amos.

Steve put the pistol away. "Come on in Amos. We were just drinking up all of Steve's good coffee."

Amos pushed Benny forward into the room and followed him in dragging the two large canvas bags behind him. "Steve I don't think you ever met little Benny here. You knew his dad though. Steve put a hand out and shook the boy's bandaged hands. "How are you big guy?" Steve looked at Amos as he gestured questioningly with his eyes at the bandaged hands. Amos just mouthed "Later". Steve shook his head in understanding. What ever had caused the injury must been traumatic.

Celina walked out of the kitchen with a fresh cup of coffee in her hands. "Good morning Mr. Amos." She said as she offered him a cup of coffee. Amos leaned the bags against the wall and gratefully took the steaming brew. "Thanks Celina. You sure look pretty this morning." He took a sip of the coffee. "There just isn't anything like being served good cup of coffee in the morning by a pretty woman."

Celina blushed and turned to hide her embarrassment from Amos. Then she glanced over her shoulder and gave Steve a look that said, "See I told you I'm a woman. The old man knows why you don't?"

Steve flinched from the stare and turned spilling the hot coffee over his hand. "Crap! Oh, that burned." Steve walked, or more like withdrew from the dining area to the gun room. "Amos bring those guns in here and let's have a look." He shouted. Amos, Celina, Benny and Doc came into the room. Steve had the weapons he had taken on the large table in the middle of the room. Amos reached in the bag and took out the weapons he had taken.

Steve looked down at the small arsenal. "Well let's see what we got here." Steve paused looking over the weapons absent mindedly he rubbed his chin. "Well as far as rifle's are concerned we have an SKS, Mini-14, stainless Mini-14, SAR-1 AK-47, Remington 2700 semi-auto 30-06, M-1 Garand, and a Remington 700. Pistols we have two Ruger Red Hawks .44 magnums, a Ruger Black Hawk .357, Ruger MK II .22 target, and an S&W Sigma 9mm. Not a bad haul guys.

Amos put his hands in his pockets "How do you want to divvy them up Steve?"

Steve thought for a moment. "Well, I would say we give the MK II to Benny so he will have something to carry, and..."

Benny stepped around from behind Amos his eyes full of excitement. "Which one is that Steve?"

Steve reached down and picked up the Ruger MK II. "This one is the one you will learn to shoot with. You can't have it till you prove you can handle it safely and shoot it well okay?"

Benny seemed a little disappointed. "Okay. Can I go watch TV?"

Doc looked down at the boy. "The TV stations aren't on anymore Benny."

Steve broke in, "Benny if you know how to operate a DVD player there is one in the next room. I have some Dragon Ball Z, and Pokemon DVDs that belong to my nephew. Since the generator is running I don't see a problem with you watching them."

"THANKS!" Benny said over his shoulder as he ran at top speed for the back room. The adults in the room all smiled at seeing the boy so excited at something that just a few days ago was just something kids did to kill time.

Steve turned back and looked at the table. "Okay back to business. I think Celina and Daphne should take the Mini-14's. Though they aren't supper accurate they are tough durable rifles with low recoil." The men nodded in agreement.

"Which one is the Mini-14?" Celina asked, Steve reached over and picked up the stainless Mini with the folding stock. He checked the chamber to ensure it was unloaded, and handed it to Celina. Celina mimicked Steve's actions of checking the chamber to see if it was loaded.

Steve looked a little surprised that she would know to do that. Celina caught his surprised look. "Don't look so surprised Steve. My Uncle Joe taught me all about guns. My parents hated it but I love to shoot, mostly shotguns though." She had a smug look on her face. "I like it. Could one of you teach Daphne how to shoot the other one when she comes around?" Celina said as she placed the rifle back on the table.

Steve nodded his head. "I would be glad to Celina."

Celina actually smiled at Steve. "Thanks."

Amos picked up the Remington 2700. "I like this rifle. Not to long, it has several ten round magazines. I will take it." Steve and Doc nodded in approval.

Steve reached down and picked up the Garand. He handed it over to Doc. "I believe you spent quite a lot of time with one of these in the Army Doc. Besides it's so ancient you're probably the only one old enough to know how to use it."

"I didn't use it as much as my Marine buddies. Of course that was right before we got M14's and the M16 in Viet Nam. I did use one enough to know it's the finest battle rifle ever." Doc leaned the rifle on the shelves behind him.

"Well what do we do with the Remington, the AK, and the SKS?" Steve said.

Doc spoke up. "You already have an AK so I think you should take this one as a spare, and the SKS shoots the same ammo so you keep it too. Amos can take the Remington 700. I don't need anymore guns, I have plenty. What do you think Amos?"

"Sounds like a plan to me." Amos picked both Remington's up and leaned them over in the corner. "What about the pistols?"

"Well I think you should keep the three Rugers Amos. That way you have a good reliable sidearm. You can keep the other two positioned in the house so they are easy to get to if something happens."

Amos nodded his head in agreement. Doc pulled a chair out from under Steve's desk and took a seat. "Steve I know times are bad but do we really need to preposition weapons around our homes? I know we have prepared for the worst and all but I just don't think we need to worry much about being attacked way out here. The chances of people wondering around out here are slim to none."

Amos looked down at his friend. "Well Mr. Intellectual, Benny and I ran into two folks on the road over here. They were two pieces of white trash heading to Florence looking for handouts. They said they hailed from Iron City."

Doc sat up surprised. "What's going on in Iron City?"

"According to the two, folks didn't accept their food stamps. They're only taking gold, silver, cash, or barter. So that means we may have a slew of government dependents wondering this way looking for help in Florence or even from Florence."

"Why didn't they head for Lawrenceburg, or Waynesboro?" Steve asked.

"Apparently the military has moved into Memphis and Nashville because of rioting and terrorist attacks. So maybe those cities have been inundated with refugees and the two knew there was nothing left in those towns for them."

"Let's get out to the Dodge get it unloaded and sort through the gear. I don't like what I am hearing. When we get done we need to sit down and go over what we need to do."

The four got up and headed for the truck. Before they walked out Amos picked up one of the .44's and walked over to the bag with the ammo and pulled out a box of shells. Doc came up to next to him.

"Could you hand me some 30-06 ammo and a couple of clips for the Garand. The two old men loaded up their weapons and went outside to help Steve and Celina unload the truck.

Celina walked to Doc's truck and pulled out the sawed off Mossberg and ensured the weapon was on safe and loaded. Steve pulled the Dodge up to the front porch. Once everyone was outside they worked for an hour unloading and sorting through the truck's contents. Celina came back out on the front porch with a pen, and pad of paper. They were ready to take inventory.

Amos had brought the canvas bag full of ammo out to add to the ammo found in the truck. Steve's porch was large, fifteen by twelve foot, and it was covered with gear. The four painstakingly went through everything they had found in the truck and written it down.

Before they finished Doc had gone inside and brewed some sweet tea. He came out with four large glasses on a tray. Each glass had ice floating in the warm brew. The ice machine had made enough for everyone while they had been working. Doc passed the glasses out and everyone took a grateful drink.

Steve wiped his mouth with his sleeve and pointed his glass in Celina's direction. "Well let's hear what have Celina."

Celina walked over and sat beside Amos on the front porch swing, glass in one hand and her list in the other. "Okay, here we go." Celina began reading off the list.Ammunition:4,000 rounds of 5.56mm 3,000 rounds of 7.62x39 800 rounds of .308 1,740 rounds of .30-06 3,250 rounds of .22 caliber 400 rounds of .44 magnum 250 rounds of .357 310 rounds of 9mm.

Food: 2 cases of beef stew 1 case of chicken noodle soup 3 cases of MREs 4 cases of mixed vegetables 10 cans of tomato soup11 cans of peaches 2 cans of pears 2 five pound bags of sugar 2 bags of flour 8 cans of vegetable soup 3 cans of black eye peas 4 ten pound bags of rice 4 five pound cans of coffee 3 boxes of powdered milk 1 box of powdered eggs.

Camping equipment:1 five man tent 2 tarps 3 1 gallon cans of Coleman fuel1 Coleman stove 1 Coleman lantern1 Dutch oven 1 Skillet 4 Sterno cans 3 camp stools 1 camp hatchet 1 camp saw 2 back packs 6 emergency blankets 3 surplus wool blankets 4 sleeping bags 4 sleeping mats 1 camp cook set 1 solar shower.

Clothing:1 combat boots size 9 (Doc's size) 2 combat boots size 10 ½ (Steve's size)1 combat boots size 8 (No ones size keep for Benny when he grows into them)6 sets of BDU tops and Bottoms size med regular (Steve's size) 2 sets of BDU tops and bottoms size small regular (Celina and Daphne can wear) 1 set of BDU top and bottom size small regular urban camo (for Benny) 12 pair of socks military 2 pair of blue jeans size 32w 32l (Steve) 5 pair of jeans 28w 30l (keep for Benny to grow into) 9 t-shirts assorted colors 3 military field coats 1 medium regular (Steve) 2 small regular (Daphne and Celina)

Assorted items:4 holsters 5 web belts 2 LBV's 2 LBV's (AK and SKS pouches) tool bag with assorted tools 4 tubes of tooth paste 24 rolls of toilet paper11 large boxes of strike anywhere matches 5 five gallon cans of diesel 1 five gallon can of gas 2 fishing poles 1 tackle box 200' of ½" nylon rope blue hand wench for truck 11 D cell batteries 10 AA batteries 9 nine volt 6 AAA batteries 14 C batteries 2 Maglight 1 rechargeable Maglight with recharge adapter in truck 4 towels 5 wash cloths 8 extra shoe strings 3 folding knives 11 bottles of water purification tablets 3 army platoon size first aid kits 2 bottles of aspirin "That's it." Celina took a sip of her tea.

Amos spoke up. "Well I say we split the ammo, and toilet paper. Steve you can have most of the rest of the stuff. I think Doc and I are pretty well set as far as food and tools are concerned. What do you think Doc?"

Doc stood from where he was sitting on the front steps. "That sounds good to me. I think you and Steve should keep one of the first aid kits though Amos. I would like to keep one also. Let's get this stuff separated and packed up. Eat some lunch and make some plans about what to do in case of an emergency." The four got to work.

The five sat around the kitchen table eating peanut butter and jelly sandwiches, drinking the last of the iced sweat tea. Steve had cut the generator off much to Benny's chagrin; he had been on his third Dragon Ball Z DVD.

Doc leaned back in his chair. "I think you two," He pointed at Steve and Amos. "should pack up and move down to my place. I think it would be safer if everyone was in one place."

Amos shook his head. "Now hold on one minute there Mr. High and mighty, I'm not moving from my place Doc. I understand what you mean and all but I'm not leaving. Maybe Benny would like to move up there with you, though I could sure use his help around my place." Amos looked across the table to Benny.

Benny held up his chin proud that Amos was obviously giving him a chance to make a decision like one of the adults at the table. "I'll stay with you Amos. Besides we got to look after my house too."

Doc shook his head. "What about you Steve? You said you were probably going to move up to my place soon."

"Well Doc you have two more people at your place. I know you have a large house but it may get little cramped over time. Why don't we wait and see how things go. We each have a CB. I say every morning we check in around 8:00 am, then at noon, and then about 8:00 pm. Then if a lot of folks start showing up we need to get together and think things over. We've all gone through a lot and I think each of us needs to get mentally squared away before we go through the upheaval of clearing out our places."

Doc didn't look so sure. The news about the two refugees on the road from Iron City had got him worried. "The biggest problem is that

I live a ¾ of a mile down the road from you Steve, and about a mile from Amos."

Amos spoke up rubbing his chin. "Maybe you should move in with me Doc. I got plenty of room too you know."

"I know Amos, but I have my little medical office downstairs and that means a lot. There aren't any hospitals anymore." Doc said as he leaned forward towards the table.

The discussion lasted another thirty minutes. It was decided things would stay as they were for now. If the flow of refugees increased then they would have to change a few things. Until then however or before if they decided it was right the moves would be made. Each got up and cleaned up their mess. They helped Steve load the gear in his house, and then loaded up the things they had wanted. With a wave each of the friends went back to there homes.

Steve stood on the front porch as he watched Doc and Celina drive to the road. Celina looked over her shoulder and waved. Steve waved back.

Amos smiled. "Pretty little lady isn't she Steve?"

Steve took a drag off of his cigarette. "Yeah she is Amos."

Amos waved and he and Benny rode away. Steve had a pang of guilt touch his heart when he mentally compared the young woman to Diane. He pushed the guilt, and thoughts of Celina to the back of his mind. Once in the house he sat in his chair drinking the last of the tea. In his left hand he held a picture of Diane. He leaned his head back and fell asleep thinking of better times.

Chapter 22

Don Savage walked up to one of the bodies lying on the ground shortly after the two crack whores had left the park. Sticking out of the man's blood stained front shirt pocket was a pack of Winston's. Though they weren't his brand he reached down and retrieved the half full pack. Lighting the cigarette up, Don began to walk through the trailer park.

He went in to one of the trailers to take a look around. Inside the trash littered trailer Don found several cases of food and bottled water. Picking up one of the water bottles Don cracked the top and downed the eight ounce bottle. In the back bedroom Don found a large bag of marijuana, and some scales. Smaller zip lock bags littered the bed. Walking into the bathroom he saw two pill bottles. Picking up both he read the prescription labels. One was Darvocet, the other Lorecet. Don's cracked ribs were throbbing he pocketed the Darvocet and popped the lid on the Lorecet. He put two 500 mg tablets in his hand and replaced the lid and then pocketed the other pill bottle.

He walked into the living room and picked up another bottle of water. Tossing the two pills to the back of his throat Don chased them with another eight ounces of water. Don stepped back outside of the trailer and looked at the carnage around him. Two of the trailers were on fire, but the flames were quickly dying. He could still feel the heat from the flames however. Maybe shooting the propane tank was not such a good idea. The smoke may bring others to this location.

"Well I guess I better sort through this crap and salvage anything useful." He said to himself as he stepped off the front porch of the trailer. Don began at the front of the park going through the bodies, picking up weapons, ammunition, jewelry, knives and whatever else of value he could find on each body. Then he headed for the trailers. Each trailer was a roach infested jumble of trash, clothes, rotting food, and empty beer cans. The group had done well for themselves however when it came to food, water, and prescription drugs, and clothes. They must have done some serious looting in town, and the surrounding homes.

There were four vehicles in the park. An old red beat up Mazda B2000 pickup, the gold Toyota, a Ford Fiesta, and a 1979 Cutlass with flat tires. Don found a wheel barrel leaning against one of the trailers. He used it to load up items that he salvaged from the trailers. He stacked all of the items near the Toyota. After two hours of hard work he had accumulated quite a pile. Don grabbed another bottle of water and took another pain pill. His ribs were killing him but he knew he had to get these items to the house.

He took a manual can opener that he had found and opened a can of peaches. He washed his hands as best he could. He drank the peach juice then ate the peaches. Tossing the can to the ground he walked over to the Mazda truck. Hopping in the driver's seat he saw that the steering column had already been busted out two loose wires hanging out. Touching the two wires together he got the truck started. The gas tank read full. He shifted the truck into reverse and backed it to the pile. The first thing he loaded was the cases of food and water. These would be a definite necessity since his pantry had been looted.

He grabbed a large brown paper bag that he had found and put all of the prescription medication and antibiotics in it. He tossed the bag into the front seat. Next he grabbed up all the ammo he could and loaded them into the cab. There was still a lot left but he would get them on the return trip. Getting back into the truck he cut the wheels and drove the short distance to his house. It took him thirty minutes to unload and stack all of the items in his living room. Don walked over into the kitchen and poured himself a couple of more glasses of water. His body was drenched in sweat, his side ached and still he had to get the rest of the stuff at the park before anyone came to investigate the gunshots and smoke from the fire.

Taking a deep breath Don walked back out to the truck. He drove to the trailer park cigarette in hand and sipping bottled water. His FN laid across the passenger seat, the Kimber .45 tucked under his right thigh the butt sticking out for easy access. About sixty yards before he reached the trailer park Don pulled the truck to the shoulder of the road. He took one last drag off the cigarette and thumped it out of the window. He raised the bottle of water and finished it off and threw the bottle to the passenger side floor board. He cut the truck off and eased the door open. As he stood he holstered the pistol and reached in and grabbed the FN. "No sense in getting ambushed." He thought to himself.

Don crossed the road and headed into the tree line. His ribs throbbing as he walked. He had to get this stuff loaded and get some rest. His ribs had not really hurt so badly when he had snuck up to the trailer court the first time. "Guess I was hyped up." He thought. "They sure hurt like hell now though."

Don made his way quietly through the trees as only a trained combat veteran can. Twenty yards short of the end of the tree line Don stopped and took a knee in a clump of bushes. He pulled out the binos and scanned the park. He could hear several people talking and the rumble of a motor idling. He could not make anything out. He was going to have to move closer to get a better view of the center of the trailer park.

Don surreptitiously moved through the forest. The birds, animals and insects sensed the lethal predator dressed in green walking the forest floor and an unnatural silence filled the air. The people in the park however did not sense or even bother to hear the eerie afternoon silence.

Don had moved ten yards closer in to the tree line, and down another fifteen yards. He did not need to use his binoculars now; he could clearly see the primer black Chevrolet 4x4 idling next to the gold Toyota. Don took a knee behind a deadfall. The trunk of the tree was about chest level when he kneeled and would make a perfect firing position, giving him both concealment and cover.

Then he heard the voices coming closer from the other side of the truck. "Look at this shit, Blade. Some fucker has killed everyone, and then stole a lot of stuff. It looks like he is coming back for the rest."

One of the crack whores he had spared came around the front of the truck her arms gesticulating around in the air. She was followed by her friend. Then two men clad in black followed behind them. "What are you two going to do about this guy? It's that cop that lives down the road." The second woman said as she stopped and hopped up sitting on the trunk of the Toyota, a cigarette hanging from her lips.

The first man wore a black vest, and jeans. An FN almost identical to Don's was in his left hand, a scope road in mounts above the receiver. Two black nylon magazine pouches hung from a web belt on his left hip. On his right hip was a World War II 1911 holster, two OD green magazine pouches road beside the holster. "Shut up bitch!" He said. His muscular right arm striking out, his large open hand collided with the side of her face.

Don could hear the audible smack from where he kneeled. The woman was knocked to her right the cigarette ejected from her lips to the ground. She slid off the truck to her butt holding her face. "Sorry, sorry." Was all she could say.

The second man dressed in blue jeans, combat boots, and a white t-shirt with cut off sleeves barked out a laugh. He held what appeared to be a Cetme rifle. This man also wore a web belt, but only had one magazine pouch for his MBR. He wore a brown leather shoulder holster with what appeared to be a revolver sitting in the holster. He turned to the second woman. "You mean to tell me one guy did all this?" The man rested the butt stock of the rifle on his right hip.

"You guys must be smoking some bad shit if you think we're going to believe that crap?"

Don lined the sights up with the man clad in black. He was the obvious leader and therefore the most dangerous since gangs usually followed the toughest man. "You better believe it." Don whispered as he squeezed the trigger.

The recoil surprised him when the rifle fired. The .308 round plowed into the big man's heart like a run away locomotive. As Don regained the sight picture attempting to acquire the second man the girl that had been talking stood screaming in his way. Don pulled the trigger again. The bullet penetrated through her body. The round buried itself into the front quarter panel of the truck. The woman's body followed close behind the bullet, her lifeless body sliding down the quarter panel leaving rivulets of blood. Her body came to rest, with her hands still at her sides, her body arched, her face, and part of her stomach resting on part of the big 31" tire.

The second man had dove behind the Toyota. He popped up with only part of his upper torso exposed and fired off six blind shots into the tree line and then went back down for cover. Don noticed the first girl had gone into the fetal position and had hugged her knees to her chest. He could clearly make out the wet stain on the crotch area of the back of her jeans.

Don held his fire waiting, his sights rested on the side of the car. He was not concerned yet. The man had fired twenty-five yards to his right. His patient was rewarded as the man popped up, this time with his pistol. Just part of the man's head and the arm holding the pistol exposed. The man fired two rounds as he dropped back for cover.

Don fired five rounds into the side of the car about even with where the man hid on the opposite side. He knew the heavy .308 slugs would rend through the thin metal and hopefully find the flesh of the man on the other side. He shifted aim and put three rounds just to the left side of the back tire ricocheting the rounds off the pavement through to the other side. Shifting his aim again he repeated the process on the other side. Then Don dumped the magazine and put in a fresh one. He fired three more rounds through the quarter panel.

As he fired the last round, the bullet found its mark. The man fell into view, a patch of blood forming under his right shoulder blade. The man rolled to his back and struggled to prop himself up with his left arm. Don fired two quick rounds, both finding their mark in his upper torso. The man collapsed back, his right arm stretched out to his side, his left buried underneath his lifeless form. His left knee was bent up and Don noticed that the left leg twitched a couple of times, then the man lay still.

Don stood from his hidden firing position. He cautiously walked into the park. He kept the big rifle pointed at the sobbing form of the woman on the ground. Her body position had not changed since the shooting had started. Then Don loomed over her prostrate form.

She looked over her shoulder when she sensed him standing there. After seeing the green wraith standing over her, she jerked her head back and covered it with her hands. "Please don't kill me, I told them not to come back. He made me, he made me." Her body was shaking uncontrollably, she gasped for air between her fear filled sobs.

Don slung the FN, and pulled out the Kimber. He pointed the pistol at her head. As he started to squeeze the trigger he stopped and lowered the pistol. Though every one of these people he killed probably deserved the death that he had given them he knew he had to stop killing just to kill what he hated most. The woman was no longer a threat, and if he stood here and put a bullet in her brain he was no better than the ones he had killed.

Don holstered the pistol. Reaching down he grabbed her by the right wrist and jerked her arm behind her. He bent her hand backward with his fingers and pulled the arm straight causing the woman to turn to her stomach. He reached back and pulled out a set of hinge cuffs and slapped them on her wrist. Then he grabbed the other wrist and cuffed that one. "Sit up, and shut up. I'm not going to kill you."

When she did not comply Don nudged her with his boot. "Do it or I will change my mind and slit your throat." The woman expertly twisted her body and came to the sitting position. It was quite apparent she had been in this position before, no doubt dozens of times during her life dealing with the local police.

"What are you going to do with me?" She said as she looked up at him.

"I haven't decided yet. How many more friends do you have that are not here at the trailer park?" He asked. His eyes glared into hers. She quickly looked away avoiding the hate she saw in his eyes.

"None, you killed everyone I know." She began to sob again.

"I said quit the crying or I will kill you." His hand rested on the pistol. She quickly swallowed the sobs and wiped the tears from her face on her knees that were pulled up to her chest.

Don reached down and pulled her to her feet. "Come with me." Don said as he shoved her forward.

"Where are we going?" Don didn't answer just prodded her in the back with the barrel of his rifle. They walked past the smoldering remains of the two burned out trailers. The smoke from the fires hung lazily in the air. They walked to the end of the road and Don pointed to the right. "Walk to the truck." The woman complied without answering. When they reached the truck Don lowered the tailgate. "Get in." The girl sat on the tailgate and swung her legs up. She stood and made her way to the upraised wheel well and sat.

Don got in and touched the two wires together and started the old truck. He pulled to a stop beside the Chevrolet that still sat idling. He opened the door and groaned as he got out. His ribs felt like someone had just thrown bricks at them. He walked to the pile and grabbed another bottle of water. Reaching into his pocket he took out the pain pills. He opened the lid and popped one into his mouth chasing it with water. Don gestured with the water bottle to the woman in the back of the truck to sit back down as she started to get up, she complied.

Don walked over to the Chevrolet and reached in and killed the ignition switch. Turning back he looked at the squalid woman. "Come here I'm going to take the cuffs off." She walked up to him and turned around. Don removed the cuffs putting them back in their case on his web belt. He pocketed the key and pulled out his pistol.

The woman, who now leaned against the truck stood upright, her eyes bulged in fear. "But…But, you said you wouldn't kill me."

Don rolled his eyes. "Just shut the hell up. I'm not going to kill you. You however are going to do the first honest days work of your life. Drop the tailgate on the Chevy." The woman slowly walked to the back of the truck staring over her shoulder at the big pistol in his hand, as she dropped the tailgate.

"Now get your nasty ass over here to this stuff and start loading it up." Don reached into the pile of goods and pulled out a camp stool. He popped it open and took a seat pistol in hand, and another water bottle in the other. The girl worked slowly at first.

That is until Don cocked the hammer on the .45. "You sure are working pitifully slow for someone who said she doesn't want to die." The girl quickly switched gears to over drive. Thirty minutes later the sweating, panting woman sat exhausted, leaned up against the truck. "What now? Can I have some of those?" She pointed to the pack of smokes in Don's pocket.

Don pitched the pack of cigarettes and the lighter. "Keep them." The girl lit up the cigarette and inhaled the poisonous nectar she craved. She tilted her head back and exhaled.

"You can go now. I'll tell you one more time though. If I ever see you again I will kill you." Don opened a fresh pack of cigarettes that had come from one of the cartons in the pile of loot. He lit a cigarette and put the pack and his new Zippo lighter in his front pocket.

"Can't I have something to eat and drink?" She asked her feet shuffling like a little girl.

"Grab that knapsack out of the front seat of the Toyota. You can fill it with as much food, water and cigarettes as you can carry." Don took a drag off the smoke, and exhaled.

The woman opened the door to the car and carefully avoided looking at her dead friend who still sat in the passenger seat. The stench of his dead body, and loosened bowls gagged her. She pulled the blue knapsack out from underneath his feet and hastily got out of the car. She went to the back of the truck and grabbed two cartoons of Newport cigarettes, four, one liter bottles of water, and about nine cans of soup, and two cans of fruit. The bag was full. "How will I open the cans?" She said.

Don stared at her for a moment. Reaching into his left pocket he pulled out one, of the two Swiss Army knives he had found. "There is a can opener on that knife. Now get the hell gone." He tossed the woman the knife.

She caught it and pocketed the knife in one swift motion and put it in her pocket. Shouldering the pack she turned and walked without a word towards the road. He watched the woman walk away, pistol still in his hand. He sat smoking waiting for her to get out of sight. The woman stopped at the end of the trailer park and turned. Raising a hand to her mouth she shouted. "If I ever see you again I'll kill you motherfucker! FUCK YOU!" She raised her hand above her head, her arm outstretched in front of her. Her middle finger prominently rose to the sky.

Don lazily and without aiming fired a round from the .45. The woman let out a yelp and ran as fast as her bony legs could carry her. The round Don fired went no where near her. He stood laughing at the sight of the woman as she ran as hard as she could. Shaggy, from ScoobyDoo, running from ghost flickered across his mind. Don reached down and picked up the camp stool. He folded it up and tossed it in the back of the Chevy. He eased himself up into the jacked up truck and turned the ignition key. The engine roared to life. He put the truck into drive and headed home. The truck was obviously well maintained; it drove smoothly and handled well for a big truck. He pulled into the drive of his house a short time later.

Don made it home and backed the big truck into the carport. He was too tired, and in too much pain to unload the truck. His cracked ribs may very well have broken. Hopefully they had not. He didn't regret clearing the area of looters, as soon as possible or he reasoned they would have eventually killed him, but the job sure killed his ribs. Opening the carport door he went inside.

He went to the faucet in the kitchen and picked up the glass as he turned the faucet handle. The faucet spat out a little water then started to vibrate, nothing. "Well there goes the water. At least I have the hand pump well in the work shop." Don walked to the living room and picked up one of the large bottles of water in from the pile in the living room floor. Cracking the top he took a long pull of water from the bottle. He replaced the lid and walked to his bedroom. He stripped off the LBV and rested the FN against his empty dresser. Sitting on the edge of the bed he leaned over to untie his boots. A groan escaped his lips. Once his boots were untied he kicked them off and lay back and drifted off into a deep sleep.

The next morning Don opened his eyes. He listened to the silence around him. He started to sit up but gasped in pain, and fell back to the mattress. "Damn, forgot about the ribs." This time he eased his body up. He picked up his LBV off the end of the bed, and then his FN. He groggily went to the back door and opened it up. He walked out to his shop and rested the FN against the door. He opened the door and retrieved his FN. He stepped into the shop and walked over to the work bench. He laid the LBV and FN on the bench. He took off his web belt and holster next, and rested it on the bench.

The shop had originally been an old barn when Don had bought the place. He had fixed it up and added on to it. The barn had an old hand pump connected to the well head, and the farmer had put an old cast iron bathtub beneath the spout. Don had used the tub to wash in after working on his truck, instead of getting his bathroom all smeared with grease. Don put the stopper in the drain and slowly pumped the handle till the water flowed. After about ten aching minutes of pumping the tub was full. Don stripped his sweat stained clothes off. He took out the pill bottle and dry swallowed two pills. He pumped the handle a few more times and got the water flowing again and leaned over to drink.

Then he climbed into the tub reaching over grabbing a bar of soap, he washed the grime from his body. When he finished bathing he laid back letting the cool water soak his ribs. With his right hand he reached over and pulled up his BDU shirt and reached in the front pocket for his smokes. He lit one up and lay back. The tub was almost large enough for him to completely stretch out.

Soon he was asleep the cigarette dangled between two fingers a length of ash protruded from the slow burning tobacco. After sleeping for almost an hour Don woke up. He felt a lot better, though his ribs still hurt. He hoisted himself slowly to his feet. He reached for an old towel that hung by the tub and toweled off. Then he reached down and emptied the pockets of his BDU's. He tossed them in the tub and knelt on the concrete floor. With the bar of soap he scrubbed the clothes clean. Then he unstopped the drain plug, and watched as the water quickly drained away.

Then he pumped in fresh water and rinsed and twist dried the clothes. He hung them on a nearby drying rack. Don picked up his weapons and walked naked back to the house. Once inside he went to his room and donned on a fresh pair of BDU's, t-shirt, and socks. Instead of putting on his boots he slipped his feet into a pair of running shoes that had not been stolen when his house had been looted.

Don thought about eating breakfast but was not too hungry. Best get to work sorting through all this gear. Don went outside and began to unload the truck. He had to work slow and carefully due to his ribs. Within the hour though he had the truck's contents unloaded, and in the living room. Don spent the next several hours sorting and placing items in piles by similarity. By two o'clock he had finished sorting things up. The only thing he did not need to put away was the food and water. He had taken it all to the kitchen first and filled his once empty cabinets. His countertops were stacked with canned goods, and his cabinets completely full.

He had lucked out on clothing taking anything in the trailer park that looked like it would fit him. Many of the clothes had price tags still on them, the names of the stores printed on the tag let Don know were they were looted from. It was apparent they had been to the mall. There were clothes from J.C. Penny, Dillard's, and North West Outdoors. He had obtained several new pair of hiking boots and tennis shoes. He had new underwear still in plastic. One of the thugs had, had the foresight to get a couple of pair of long johns.

There had been all kinds of camping equipment. They must have gone from isle to isle in the sporting good section of Wal-Mart. "I think I've got two of everything Wally World sold in the camping section." He chuckled to himself. Don took half of the camping gear and loaded it into one of the front bedrooms to be sorted and packed properly later. The other half he took out to the shop and placed in most of it in large plastic bins. The rest he just put where he had room for it in the shop.

He put the six gallons of Coleman fuel out on the back porch. He was going to have to use it to cook with. The Coleman stove was put on top of his now useless electric stove. Don sorted through the weapons weeding out the junk guns from the good ones. The junk pile was bigger. He unloaded them and put the ammo aside. He could use both the ammo in calibers he did not have good guns for, and the junk guns for possible trade. He looked over the good gun pile. Don had acquired two AK-47's, one SKS, one scoped Enfield .303, one Springfield 03-A3 .30-06, and the Cetme, and scoped FN from the last two men he had killed.

As far as pistols went, he obtained the Colt Silver Cup from the leader of the gang, a S&W model 64 .38 special, two Kel-Tec .32's, a blued S&W model 639 9mm with three eight round magazines, and a Colt Woodsman .22 caliber. Don placed these guns in his gun cabinet. The junk guns went in a drawer in the same room as he had put the camping equipment. He faired very well on ammo however. He had six thousand rounds for the .22. That was more than he could shoot in years. It would be very useful for foraging for small game this fall. Being one of the most popular rounds in the world, the .22 ammo would be great for bartering. Don had seven hundred rounds of .32, five hundred 9mm, three hundred rounds of .38, two thousand rounds of .308, eleven hundred rounds of .30-06, four hundred rounds of .303, and seventeen hundred rounds of 7.62x39. All the ammunition boxes had stickers that belonged to a gun shop downtown. He wondered if they had been the first in the store, or had just got seconds when they looted it.

He had also gotten tools, motor oil, transmission oil, filters, belts, hoses, and four five gallon plastic cans of gas, Medicine, band aids, foot, arm, hand, and leg braces. He also had about fifteen rolls of Ace bandages. Apparently the leader of the gang was no slouch when it came to looting. He knew what you needed to survive.

Don went to the kitchen and fired up the Coleman stove. He opened a couple of cans of chili and dumped them into one of his new pots. After he was done cooking he sat at his kitchen table and pondered on what he had to do next. He was tired and sore and knew he must rest to heal properly. He thought about the abandoned cars at the trailer park. He would go over tomorrow and if they were still there he would drop the gas tanks and bring them home.

Don finished his chili, sat back and lit a smoke. Cigarettes weren't going to be a problem for awhile either. He had over sixty cartons of assorted brands. He was good to go on the liquor side of the house too. He was not much of a drinker but knew that the liquor could be used to trade, and sterilize wounds. Don sipped on a Capri Sun juice packet.

He was pretty well stocked now, but was at a distinct disadvantage. If he went out in the future to locate people to trade with, or just patrol the area he had no one to help guard his place while he was gone. He needed to link up with others that had some skills, like farming, medical, dental, wood working, and a dozen other things. Don rose from the table and went to the medical pile. He picked up four rolls of Ace bandages and headed to his room. After he wrapped his ribs he would take another pain pill. "Got to be careful about the intake of those, I would hate to become a pill head." Then he would lie down for some much need rest. Tomorrow he would finish putting the stuff away. Then he would head out the day after and retrieve the gas tanks, right now though he needed to get as much rest as possible.

Chapter 23

Bob gave Caroline a kiss on the cheek as he headed out the door. "I'll be back in about two hour's tops. I'm going to work the west side of Shadow Brooke Lane. I'll start at the corner house on Heathrow. So if I don't show in three hours that's were you can start looking for me."

Caroline nodded her head. "Well I think the number one priority right now Bob should be some type of communications. A Walkie talkie, CB's something we can communicate with. We're going to need some gas too, so see if you can find any old lawn mower gas cans. I think the way I have it figured we have enough gas for two more weeks on the generator, then we're screwed as far as power goes."

Bob opened the front door, "Okay, no problem. I'll see you in a little while." Bob turned and walked into the still dark morning. Even though the power was off the street lights still burned. Caroline watched her husband walk into the shadows. It had been a good idea to scavenge for food, and water. They had enough now to last an additional two months on top of the food they already had in the pantry.

Bob had lucked out and found four gallons of gasoline the day before. Gas was a big concern for Caroline. They had to use it sparingly, because she knew this winter it would be useful, if not down right essential for life. He had also found an old semi-auto Winchester .22 rifle, and four fifty round boxes in the Everett's house down the street. Bob said it would very useful to take small game with. The rabbits and squirrels in the neighborhood had become brazen now that almost everyone had fled the neighborhood. Bob suggested leaving them alone till the winter when food would be scarcer.

It was time to get back to work. Bob had gone down to one of the new houses under construction and taken a trailer full of 2x4's, 4x4's, and dozens of sheets of plywood in varying thickness, from ¼" to ¾". While the generator was running Bob had cut the plywood down to fit over the windows. Then he cut view ports in each. Caroline was busy now fitting the ¾" plywood to the downstairs windows. She, and Bob, when he returned, would then reinforce them with 2x4's. She and Bob had already finished the front side of the house, now she would start the back while he was gone. As she picked up the hammer she realized how much she was ready to get out of the house. She had been no farther than across the street in four days. Cabin fever was setting in. When Bob returned she would tell him, she was going to go with him on his next outing.

She felt uneasy about Bob out there all alone with no communications. She also knew that soon looters and refugees would soon run out of food and other necessities in different parts of the city and start doing the same thing Bob was doing but it would probably be in her neighborhood. For some reason people always thought the rich were always the best prepared in any type of calamity. How false that belief was. Most of the rich always had the money for whatever they needed and unlike the poor did not see it necessary to stock up on everything when money was available. For the rich, money was always available, and so was everything they needed.

She was blessed that her husband had the foresight to stock up with at least three months worth of supplies. He had not thought of some things, such as feminine products. He was however rectifying that. He had found several months worth of feminine products on the block, thank goodness. Caroline got back to work and started hammering, the Sig 230 swinging in its holster on her hip as she hammered in another nail.

Bob walked slowly in the early morning darkness. He kept to the shadows as much as possible. What he could not figure out was that if the power was out why did the street lights still work? He cradled the Benelli M-1 in his hands, keeping it at the low ready. Armed with the shotgun and his S&W Model 10 .357, he felt he could handle just about anything that came his way. So far they had been lucky as far as looters and rioters were concerned.

Bob adjusted the straps on the empty High Sierra tan back pack he had found. He took a knee and peered around the corner. Scanning the darkness he saw nothing moving, only the hanging fog that was suspended low over the ground. So far in his outings he had not run into anyone else. Everyone on his block had headed for the hills. He was pretty sure the same was true for most of the neighborhood. He was sure that others were still here in small numbers.

He rose up off the ground and walked towards the dark house before him. He would cut though the backyard since there was no fence. As quietly as possible he stepped up on the back deck. Taking several steps forward a sharp pain ran up his shin followed by a metallic crash. Bob grimaced, "SHIT!" looking down he had ran into what appeared to be a wrought iron coffee table. Bob made his way to the brick wall and put his back flat up against it. He waited in silence for what seemed an eternity, but in actuality were only five or six minutes. When he was confident no one was coming he eased himself to the back door.

Holding the shotgun in his right hand, barrel pointed skyward, he reached out with his left hand. The door knob turned, but the door held fast. He could bust out one of the many window panes in the door but decided to check around first. At half of the houses he had been to most have the good old American "Key Rock". Spotting a flower pot by the back door he pulled it to him. The dirt under the flowers was covered with white rocks. These people had been much wiser than their fellow neighbors. He smiled as he picked up the frog that sat amongst the white rocks. Flipping it over to him he opened the small compartment and pulled out the back door key.

Turning on his knee he placed the key in the deadbolt and unlocked the door. Rising up he flicked the safety switch off of the shotgun. This was the part he hated the most. His heart hammered in his chest. "What if someone was home?" In his mind he knew they would be justified in shooting him. "Hell he would if positions were switched." Stepping out of what his friend Jack had called the "Fatal Funnel" he took a knee again.

He closed his eyes and tried with failure to slow his breathing, and pounding heart. He listened intently to the darkness around him. Hearing nothing he stood. He slung the shotgun behind his back, it was one the features that convinced him to buy the tactical sling. He pulled the pistol from its holster and the Surefire 6P rechargeable flashlight from its holder. First he had to clear the house before he started to salvage anything useful. Pushing the button on the back of the flashlight he quickly scanned the kitchen and dining room, nothing. He was glad this was a single story home, he hated going through homes with two stories. One of his biggest fears in homes with two stories was someone sneaking down into one of the downstairs rooms he had cleared and ambushing him once he thought it was safe. The house was a typical split room floor plan. The master bedroom to the right of the kitchen and dining area, and two to three bedrooms on the other side of the house.

Bob cleared the master bedroom first. It was empty. He made his way through the living room, having to use the flashlight less now that the morning sun had started to rise. As he came to the "T" intersection of the hallway he paused. Swallowing hard, he adjusted the grip on the pistol. "One, two, three!" he mentally counted in his head. Then he burst around the corner to the left. Seeing no threat he spun to the right to make sure no one was behind him. He breathed in deeply thankful no one was there. He searched the left side bedroom and bath first, then made his way to the other side of the hall, flicking the light in short one, or two second burst. The bedrooms and other bathroom were clear. Bob wiped the sweat away from his forehead as he sat down on the small single bed. Reaching behind him he pulled out an old military surplus canteen he had found. He drank deeply from the canteen and put it away.

Bob stood up and turned the stem on the Phoenician blinds letting the morning light spill in the room. He did not open it all the way but just enough to let some light in. He took off the pack and tossed it on the bed. Looking around the room it appeared to be a young boy's room, probably early teens. He found that the kid's rooms were the best place to find batteries. Looking over to his right he spotted a remote control sitting on top of a 19" TV. Bob pulled a medium size plastic bag from the pack's front pouch. Walking back to the TV he picked up to the remote and pushed one of the buttons. The small red light on the top corner came on. Bob flipped the remote over and pulled out two AA batteries and put them in the bag.

Scouring the room for anything useful he located several more batteries of varying size. He placed each into the plastic bag. The next item he found was a folding Boy Scout Knife sitting atop a Boy Scout Field book. He put the book in the pack, slipped the knife into his pocket. Bob found nothing else of value in the room. His next stop was the bathroom. He got two rolls of toilet paper from under the sink. In the medicine cabinet Bob found bottles of aspirin, Tylenol, and some cold and flu medicine. Also four new bars of soap were in the medicine cabinet.

Bob searched the other children's bedrooms and found nothing of interest. In the second bathroom, Bob got another roll of toilet paper, and a small bottle of bleach. Nothing else was found except a half full bottle of shampoo, which he took also. Going back into the kitchen Bob only found four cans of soup, a small bag of sugar, and half a tin of coffee. Other than that the kitchen had been cleaned out. Bob walked disappointed to the master bedroom. "Well." Bob thought, "We may starve, but at least we will be able to wipe our asses a little while longer."

Going through the drawers he found a Rossi .22 revolver and a box of shells. He unloaded the pistol and pulled the double action trigger. It had a crisp pull to it and the sights lined up nicely when he pointed it. Bob was happy to have the pistol. A .22 caliber pistol or rifle had not crossed his mind when he began to prepare for the worst. The round had no knock down power whatsoever. But like Jack had told him one day shooting one of his .22's. "It's all about shot placement. Most folks can shoot a .22 well. A shot to the head at twenty five yards, or the heart for that matter and the person will die. Plus you can carry a thousand rounds of .22 in a daypack."

Bob had not listened to his knowledgeable friend and passed on buying a .22 rifle or pistol. Now he had both! Bob turned to head for the big walk in closet. He bypassed the bathroom knowing he would probably only find toilet paper. He had become a toilet paper finding master. For some reason everyone seemed to leave it behind. If he went into a house and found nothing else of value he would find toilet paper. Maybe some folks just didn't wipe thoroughly and therefore had no use for large quantities of the paper gold, or Bob had some serious problems with his bowels and he need to have a check up.

Bob pulled his flashlight out and scanned the closet. On the woman's side of the closet Bob saw a new looking pair of hiking boots. Bending over he flipped the tongue of the boot back, size 7. Caroline could wear these; he tossed them out of the closet towards his pack that leaned on the bed. Under the clothes rack was a small dresser. Bob sorted through each drawer finding nothing in the first four. In the fifth and last drawer Bob found a house hold first aid kit like you would find at Wal-Mart. He tossed it out the door also.

Next he scanned the man's side of the closet. None of the clothes that hung there interested him. Unless he decided to face the end of time wearing Armani suits. Bob went to the matching dresser on the man's side of the closet and started to rummage through the drawers.

This time he found more useful items than he had in the woman's drawers. He found a pair of high quality brown leather driving gloves, a Swiss Army knife, and a compass, a Zippo lighter still in the box, lighter fluid, and two packs of Marlboro Lights. Then he found a brick of five hundred fifty .22 shells, he wasn't sure which was the better find, the cigarettes or the shells.

Bob took the items to the pack and stuffed them in. He opened one of the packs of cigarettes and put them in his front shirt pocket. He smiled to himself, "Eight more days of extra smoking. Caroline will just love it. Hoisting his pack he put it on his back. Before he left he shined the flashlight into the bathroom. The cabinet drawers were all open and empty. Sitting on the counter top though was one roll of toilet paper. Bob smiled and shook his head, "I hope this is God's way of telling me, that I'll not starve through all this turmoil.." When he picked up the roll of toilet paper he half expected to see a not on top that read "Bob, we know we didn't leave you much but please enjoy this fine roll of paper." He walked in the bathroom picked up the roll and tossed in the air and caught it with one hand and walked to the kitchen.

Taking out a small note book and pen Bob made a list of what he had taken. He made sure to put the words TOILET PAPER in bold print. He signed his name, tore the sheet of paper off the pad and laid it on the table. Reaching in his front pocket and pulled out a cigarette. He lit it with his old Bic lighter and inhaled. Blowing the smoke out he reached back and grabbed the canteen. He walked to the living room and up to the front window.

Cracking the blinds he scanned the area. Looking across the street and at the light pole he saw a bird sitting atop one of the solar panels that operated the lights. "SOLAR PANELS!" He shouted. Dropping the cigarette on the tile floor Bob sprinted for the back door.

Thoughts of stealth and security left his mind as he ran for home. The weight of the pack on his back was all but forgotten. Bob sprinted up the driveway and leapt onto the front porch. "Caroline! Caroline!" He shouted as he banged on the front door which was locked.

The door sprung inward and Bob had to keep himself from hitting Caroline in the face as he was about to bang on the door again. "Solar panels!" He shouted at her as she pulled him inside, the small Sig in her hand down by her side.

She did a quick scan for danger and shut the door. "Caroline, solar panels, and street lights!" He shouted to her face as he grabbed her shoulders.

Caroline took a step back. "Bob, quit yelling I'm right here. What the hell are you talking about?"

Bob took a deep breath to calm himself down. Caroline reached up and helped remove the pack from his shoulders as he began to talk. "Remember when we moved in the realtor told us all the street lights operated off of solar powered batteries?"

"Yes, I remember but why are you so..." Caroline didn't finish the sentence as the realization dawned on her.

"Honey the light post is only about fifteen feet tall. I've got a twenty foot ladder in the shop. I can climb up and get the solar panels, take out the battery packs, and then take down the lights. I know how to do it. One of the guys down the street worked for the Electricity Department, he took me up in one of the bucket trucks when they were replacing the bulbs and showed me how they worked." Bob looked at his wife and waited for her approval to get some of the lights.

Caroline took his face in her hands and kissed him full on the lips. "What are we waiting for? Let's go get some lights."

The two went to the shop and grabbed Bob's tool belt, some rope and the ladder. They walked two doors down and set up the ladder. Bob climbed up while Caroline held the ladder in place. Once Bob unscrewed the solar panel and disconnected it he lowered it down by rope. Next took the battery and control box. Finally he was able to take the light fixture down. He almost dropped it twice but got it safely to the ground.

They walked further down the street and repeated the process. Three hours later Bob and Caroline were back at the house. It took Bob another four hours to get one of the lights to work. After that he managed to finish the second one up in two hours. He took one upstairs and the left the other in the living room.

When he was done Caroline had dinner ready. The two sat and ate a quiet meal together. The course for the evening's dinner was rice, beef stew, and red wine. As the sun began to fade they headed for the bathroom with an oil lamp in hand. Stripping down each took a turn in the bathtub, where they used a five gallon bucket of water to wash the days grime away.

Caroline had bathed first then Bob had his turn. Slipping on a pair of shorts he walked into the bedroom. Caroline looked up at him as he walked in. "Well, are you going to turn it on?"

"You bet!" Bob walked over to the street light. It lay on its back, the light pointing up. Bob connected the circuit and the light hummed to life. "Hot damn baby, it works!" Bob shouted.

Caroline lay back on the bed fluffing a pillow behind her back. "Bob you're such a smart man. And smart men get whatever they want." She smiled seductively.

Bob made his way to the bed and crawled over to his wife. "I love being smart. I think you know what I want. Should I turn out the light?" He said looking over to the bright light.

Caroline wrapped her arms around his neck as he lay on top of her. "Nope, that's why you're getting lucky."

Chapter 24

Craig Wolfe was twenty-five years old. He had been with the Florence Police Department for four years when the world fell apart. He had been on the Special Operations Team for one year and had come to love that part of the job. The battle at Cypress Creek had been a harrowing experience under fire for Craig; the team had lost two members. Even with all that had happened during the past few days Craig had never been present when another officer had been killed. He had performed well according to the others on the team, but the experience had shaken him to the core, but he had come out of it alive, and came to grip with the death of his friends.

Once back at the station the surviving members of the Team and other officers buried the fallen, including the Chief. After they had finished everyone went to the weapons room. Ammunition, weapons, and equipment were passed out between the Team and other officers. Then each person went his own way. Many of the team members banded together and headed for Johnson's place up near the state line, their family members waited for them there. Craig had opted out of going. He was going to go back to his grandmother's home in the historical district on Wood Ave.

The house had been in the family for over one hundred years. It was one of the last standing after all of the riots. The team had helped him defend it and his grandmother against numerous rioters and gang members during the first two days.

Unfortunately Craig's grandmother had died of a heart attack. They had buried her, and then scrounged around at one of the salvage yards down by the river finding numerous metal plates. They had spent several hours fortifying the house. The windows now had sheets of metal bolted over them with firing ports. Inside, all of the exit doors had sheets of metal placed on either side of the frame. The interior walls by the windows also had metal plates around them.

The house was a large two story brick colonial, with a tile roof. An eight-foot tall brick wall surrounded the one-acre lot. On top of the walls Craig had placed broken glass, and thin strips of triangle pieces of sheet metal with sharp ends. It now had the appearance of a fortress, and the people in the area stayed away from the home once the bodies of those who had attempted to storm the place started to line the street.

There was water well in the back yard with a hand pump by what at one time had been a brick stable. The stable was now a three-car garage and work shop. The house was over five thousand square feet and Craig had tried to convince some of the others to stay at his grandmother's with him. None had wanted to stay in the ravaged city.

After a few handshakes, and hugs Craig got into his black Chevrolet K-5 Blazer and drove to his grandmother's. The trip was short; his grandmother only lived about ten blocks from the Police Department. Craig drove slowly and took in everything. The entire downtown area had been looted. Buildings, cars and homes had been burned to the ground. Bodies lay on the ground everywhere in crumpled heaps. To Craig they appeared almost like rag dolls that had been thrown around by an angry child. The occasional gunshot still echoed through the air. In the distance he heard the wail of a siren, probably an ambulance. He wondered how long they would keep running.

When Craig had crossed Tennessee Street he took a look at his favorite gun store. It was still standing. The windows were shot out, but the wrought iron bars over the doors and windows were still in place. The brick walls were blackened by fire; bullet holes pocked the walls like craters on the moon. Dozens of bodies littered the sidewalks and streets surrounding the building.

"Guess old Howard is still alive and kicking." He said to himself. He would have to go by and check on the gun shop owner. They were good friends and had known each other since childhood.

When he arrived on his grandmother's block he slowed the big 4x4 to a crawl. He surveyed the block. Nothing moved, except the birds that picked at the bodies of the dead. Every house but his and two others had been burned. He was going to have to get rid of the bodies soon. The flies and bugs that enveloped the bodies would carry all type of germs. He could not afford to get sick in times like these.

He pulled into the drive of his house, and left the engine running as he got out of the truck to unlock the Iron Gate across the driveway. He scanned the area one more time before reaching for the padlock. Suddenly a blur of brown fur leaped in front of him slamming into the gate. Craig fell backward into the grill of the truck as the immense animal before him barked several times.

Craig looked up as he reached for the Glock 22 that rested in a thigh holster on his right hip. He relaxed as he realized it was Meat. Meat was Craig's two hundred and ten pound Mastiff. Meat stood waiting for his master to open the gate. His tail wagged as he let out an occasional bark at his master.

"You dumb dog. What were you trying to do, make me piss my pants?" Craig said as he stood up.

He reached his hand through the gate and ruffled the big dog's ears. That was when he noticed the blood that covered the dog's muzzle. "What the heck happened to you Meat?" Craig said as he quickly unlocked the gate.

When the gate opened the big dog leaped up placing his front paws on Craig's shoulders. "Get down dog, and let me see how bad you're hurt." Meat sat down on his haunches and lovingly stared at his master. Craig gave the dog a good once over and found no injuries. "Must have got hold of a rabbit, come on boy get in the truck." The two walked to the truck. Meat hopped in and went to the passenger seat when Craig opened the door. He pulled the truck up the drive and once clear got out and secured the gate.

As Craig walked back to the truck something in the front yard caught his eye. Turning he saw a body lying on the front lawn. Craig drew his pistol and approached the body. Meat jumped out of the driver's side window and walked to Craig's side. Craig looked down at the dog noting that the fur on the back of the dog was hiked up, his tail straight out.

The body lay face down with the arms spread out wide. Chunks of flesh were torn from the man's back and arms. A pool of congealed blood was under the face of the man. Craig leaned forward and grabbed the man's wrist and flipped him over. Meat let out a low guttural growl as the man was flipped over.

There was no need for Craig to see if he was alive. The throat had been torn out, and huge chunks of flesh were missing from the face and chest area of the man. Craig patted down the man and found a small Beretta .22 caliber pistol in the front pocket. In the other pocket he found a box of .22 shells, and two loaded magazines for the pistol.

Craig slipped the items into the front pocket of his green nomex flight suit as he stood up. "Meat you better hope Animal Control has shut down." Craig scanned the area for any other signs of entry into the yard. Over by the front wall Craig saw a tennis shoe. He walked over and picked it up.

The shoe lay at the base of the wall and was covered in blood. The wall had drying blood smeared on it up to the top. Craig stood on his tiptoes and saw a large amount of blood covering the bricks, and broken glass, most of the glass was missing though. Probably in someone's body or brushed to the ground when they scaled the fence.

Craig looked back at the body and noticed that the dead man had two shoes on. "Got two of them boy?" He said to Meat as he scratched the big dog behind the ears. Craig tossed the shoe over the fence and went to unlock the front gate. He then dragged the man out of the yard and across the street. When he was done he secured the gate and pulled the truck up to the front doors.

Craig went around to the garage and threw some wood into the old wood burning kitchen stove that was there. He started a fire and then gathered four large metal buckets. He filled them with the hand pump and placed them atop the stove. Then he got two of the plastic buckets he had hanging on the wall filled them and walked to the house. Setting the buckets down Craig unlocked the door and opened it.

The room he walked into was just behind the kitchen. It had been added on eighty years earlier as a mudroom and bathroom. The bathroom was small, and consisted of a claw foot tub, sink and toilet. Craig put the rubber stopper in the tub and dumped the two six gallon buckets in. He went out and refilled them and dumped them in the tub also. Once that was done he walked through the house to the front doors and unlocked them. Craig was not worried that someone had gotten into the house or was still on the grounds. If they were, Meat would still be going crazy trying to get at them, or he would be dead from trying.

Meat was all business when it came to protection. Craig had bought Meat two years ago as a puppy for his grandmother. He purchased him not only for his grandmother to have a companion, but for her protection as well. The mastiff was a very protective and loyal breed of dog. For the last year one of the K-9 officers at the department had helped Craig train the dog, on bite work, and tracking. Meat had proved to be exceptionally smart and an eager learner.

Craig began to unload all of the gear from the truck and placed it in the parlor. He went ahead and organized it in separate piles, ammunition, equipment, food, and weapons. When he was done he locked the front door and pulled the truck around back.

In the garage Craig took a long round metal pole from the corner. He then got an old towel and picked up the buckets of boiling water. He ran the pole through the handles, and carefully lifted the load to a shoulder. He walked slowly so he would not spill the scalding water on him. Once in the bathroom Craig put his load down and filled the tub up with the steaming water.

Craig stripped down and placed his pistol on the toilet lid within easy reach of the tub. Then he got in the tub, the hot water almost unbearable as he slowly lowered his grimy foul smelling body into the water. He then spent the next ten minutes, scrubbing and rescrubbing his body and hair. When he was done he reached over to his flight suit and pulled it to him. Taking out a small metal tin he opened it and pulled out a cigar. He lit it with his Zippo lighter and leaned back and enjoyed the smoke. His muscles relaxed and the tension of the last few days was soaked away.

After he dried off Craig emptied all of the pockets of his flight suit and threw it in the still hot water of the bathtub. He pulled the ballistic panels of his bullet resist out of the shell and threw it along with the rest of his clothes into the water. He spent the next few minutes scrubbing the clothes clean. When he was finished he put on a pair of shorts that were in a laundry basket in the mudroom. Taking the clothes outside to the hand pump he rinsed them and then twisted as much water as possible out of them. He then hung them to dry out on the clothesline.

Then he grabbed a dolly from the garage and headed back into the house and went to the parlor.

Craig spent the next thirty minutes taking all of the items from the parlor to one of the downstairs bedrooms. The day everything went to hell Craig had loaded everything of value into his truck, left his apartment and brought it all to his grandmother's. He had not wanted her staying alone when the trouble started. He had not been at the house much in the past few days. The second day he was glad he had asked the Lieutenant to swing the team by his grandmother's to check on her, and eat some lunch.

It was a good thing they had. When they turned on to Wood Ave. hundreds of people were running from house to house looting, fighting, and burning. The team had poured out of the SWAT van and had commenced to clearing the street. The gun battle had raged for nearly an hour. The unorganized and undisciplined mob hastily retreated from the volley of submachine gun, and sniper fire the team had lain down. Once the general area was secure the team went to his grandmother's. Craig had to call out to his grandmother to unlock the gate. The old woman came out on the front porch, with her double barrel shotgun and Meat. When they had got inside the smell of cordite and smoke hung in the air. The empty hulls of shotgun shells littered the floors beside the windows in the parlor and library. The old woman had not killed anyone but she had definitely got a few. Large droplets of blood were found all over the front porch, and driveway. After eating Craig and several of the guys drove to the city barn and picked up one of the dump trucks and took it to the metal salvage yard and collected the large metal plates that now protected the windows and doors.

After several hours of hard work the home was fortified, and Grandma Wolfe's home stood a better chance against attack. The team stayed for supper and decided to sleep there for the night.

That night the mob came back. Again the battle raged, and lasted until dawn. The responding police had torn the mob to shreds when the team had called for assistance and the mob was hit from behind and on its flanks. Word had spread about the blood bath and few dared to travel near the block, fearing that they too would join the other rioters laying dead on the street and yards in the 700 block of Wood Ave. His grandmother had a heart attack during the battle in the early morning hours.

Craig cleared his mind of the recent past and got to work taking inventory. On the bed he had laid out all of the firearms he had brought home. Some were his personal weapons; others, the departments, and some had come from the evidence vault. He had quite a collection of weapons. He decided he would function check each, load them, and then place them around the interior of the house at strategic locations. "Man what an arsenal. It would have taken me years on my salary to buy all this stuff." That was not necessarily true though. Craig's family was wealthy and his parents had left him a large sum of money in a trust fund when they died in a plane crash ten years earlier. His grandmother was extremely wealthy and had offered numerous times to help her only grandson financially. Craig had always declined, and never touched the money in the trust. He always made his own way in life never asking for handouts.

Craig had two Law Enforcement only M-16's with fourteen inch barrels, and collapsible stocks, two Glock 22's, Glock 19 and 17, three Remington 870's, SAR-1, FN-FAL, S&W 639 9mm, Beretta 92F, Colt 1991 A1, Colt Gold Cup 70 series, Ruger MKII, S&W Model 19, Ruger Security Six, Mini 14, and a 98 Mauser in 30-06 with a 3x9 power Nikon scope and synthetic Monte Carlo stock, and his H&K UMP .40 caliber submachine gun.

Stacked against a wall were cases of ammo. He had at least three thousand rounds for each caliber of weapon except he only had about one hundred rounds apiece for the FN, and Mauser. Craig also lucked out and got one hundred rounds of 12 gauge TKO entry rounds that were capable of blowing off doorknobs and hinges. He wasn't in bad shape as far as ammo was concerned but at the rate he had gone through it lately he would definitely run out quickly. He was going to have to come into contact with as few people as possible, run when he did not have to fight, and fight only when his life depended on it.

Craig had an assortment of equipment and gear. He had taken some of the stuff others felt would be useless. He had thirty smoke grenades, thirty CN-CS canisters, forty-eight flash bangs. A 37mm teargas gun with eight round drum that came with about sixty rounds, two hundred feet of repelling rope, two collapsible grappling hooks, twenty-foot rope ladder, a ballistic entry shield, hooligan tool, bolt cutters, two extra gas masks. He also got hundreds of D, C, AA, AAA, and nine-volt batteries, several rechargeable batteries for his Maglight and Surefire 6P flashlight from the evidence tech locker. He also had taken camping gear, camping clothes, and boots, which had been recovered from a hijacked semi truck. The best thing he kept from his SWAT gear was a pair of 3rd generation night vision goggles.

He broke out his cleaning kit and spread a towel down over a large steamer trunk with flattop. He spent about two hours breaking down the different weapons giving each a quick cleaning and function check. Once the cleaning was done he fixed himself a sandwich and drank some juice.

Going back outside he pulled his now dry clothes off of the line. He took the clothes inside and dressed back in them. His shirt hung around his waist as he put on a t-shirt, and his ballistic vest. He then strapped on his thigh holster, and holstered his pistol. As the sun set Craig spent the remaining time he had light left placing the extra weapons in strategic locations around the house.

When he finished placing the weapons he boiled a pot of water. Once the water was boiling he threw in a couple of packages of Ramin Noodles. Once the noodles were done he turned off the Coleman stove and poured the noodles into a large bowl and ate. It had not been long since his late lunch but he felt his body would need all the fuel it could get for tonight. Cleaning up his dishes he prepared to leave and recon the area.

Craig went towards the back wall and walked into a small gap in the hedgerow that stood about eight feet tall and four feet wide. Hidden behind the hedgerow was a small wrought iron gate. The gate was concealed by another set of bushes on the other side of the wall.

He scratched Meat behind the ears. "Look after things Meat. I will be back in an hour or so."

Craig took a knee at the edge the bushes and closed his eyes. He listened to the sounds of the night straining to hear anything out of the ordinary. Hearing nothing he rose and moved forward, his UMP out in front of him moving left to right.

After circling the block he found no evidence of people so he moved south. His destination was Tennessee St. He wanted to recon the area around Howard's gun store. He had decided while bathing that he would pay the gun dealer a visit the next day. Maybe he could trade some things for more ammo and MREs. He really wanted to convince Howard to pack up his stuff and stay at his place. Craig could use a partner; he needed someone to help watch his back.

Craig moved slowly as he came towards Mobile St. He was only about a block from the gun store and had not seen anyone. He lowered the night vision goggles down over his eyes and turned them on. The dark night turned green, and he checked his surroundings. He saw nothing that appeared to be a threat. A house was just ahead of him, he moved to it slowly. Once on the porch he could tell that the front door had been kicked in.

He quickly entered the front room of the house. He was in what appeared to be a living room. The furniture lay in broken piles. Craig cleared the entire house in a matter of minutes. Once he had made sure the house was secure he went to a back bedroom and kneeled by the window.

There was no one in the general vicinity of the gun store. He could barely make out some figures moving in the distance off to the west. Organized groups were one of his biggest concerns. The gangs had ranged out into the city but always made their way back to the "West Side" late at night or in the early morning hours.

Craig climbed out of the broken window and into the yard. He went from bush to tree, and sometimes crawled in the high grass. He was going to make his way to the large Baptist Church that loomed across the street from the gun store.

The first couple of days after everything started, several of the larger churches downtown opened their doors to feed the hungry and house those that had lost their homes to the looting. It wasn't long before the gangs, and those who didn't think the churches were giving out enough began to attack the clergy and church members who had opened their doors to the masses. Some churches were able to hold out a couple of days, their members were armed and fought back viciously. The numbers against them were too great though, and they were soon vanquished.

Once the church members were defeated they were killed, raped, or kept in bondage. Those that escaped scattered in different directions.

Most headed south across the Tennessee River towards the refugee camps north of Birmingham. The roads south to Birmingham looked like a river of people. No one headed towards the camps in Huntsville. Everyone knew the camps there were filled beyond capacity. Refugees from the cities surrounding Huntsville, and tens of thousands of refugees had flooded south from Nashville and other Tennessee cities near the border.

Craig entered the dark church and climbed to the second floor. He entered a Sunday school room and walked to a broken out window. The window was six feet tall and about two feet across. Craig lay on his stomach his UMP held to his shoulder as he peered into the darkness surrounding him. Seeing nothing in the gun store across the street and surrounding area he turned off the Night vision goggles and pushed them on top of his head. He wiped the sweat away from his face, the cool breeze felt refreshing on his face.

The moon came out from behind the clouds and Craig rolled up into a sitting position against the wall. He didn't want anyone to spot him and a put a bullet between his eyes. It was then that he noticed the hundreds of shell casings that littered the floor. Then he noticed two bodies that lay against the wall across from him. He could make out a trail of dried blood that led to one of the bodies. The dried blood appeared black in the moonlight against the white tile floor.

Craig got up and checked the first body. He found a Gerber Mark I boot knife attached to the man's belt. He took the knife and slid it into his pocket. He found a magazine that appeared to be for a Beretta 9mm. He took this also. Craig found nothing else on the body.

He searched the second body and found a box of .38 Special rounds, and one shotgun shell. The only other thing he found was a set of Peerless hinge cuffs. He found nothing else of value and he pocketed the cuffs and shells. As he stood he heard the roar of car engines in the distance. The engine noise grew louder as Craig made his way back to the window and took a knee.

Looking to the west Craig spotted five older model cars traveling at a high rate of speed east on Tennessee St. coming his way. As the cars approached the intersection of Wood Ave., and Tennessee St, two turned south on Wood Ave. and stopped at the corner of the building that was next store to the gun store. He counted about eight subjects jump from the cars and head around the back of the building, all appeared to be armed.

The next two stopped in front of the building next door to the gun store. Eight more men climbed out and took cover behind the car. Then the eight began to open fire towards the interior of the gun store. The last car jumped the curb of the parking lot in front of the church. Four men jumped out and ran towards the church. Then from the second floor of the gun shop Howard opened up with what Craig knew had to be Howard's favorite weapon, the FN-FAL.

Craig lowered the night vision goggles over his eyes and rose to his feet. He thumbed off the safety to the UMP and headed to the door. He could hear the four men as they ran up the concrete stairs, their feet echoing in the empty building. Craig positioned himself in the door, the UMP pointed towards the stairwell.

Craig held his fire as the first figure came into view. He would wait until all four were out of the stairwell before opening up on them. As the last man came around the banister; the first was just twenty feet in front of him. With his left hand Craig flipped the goggles up on his head and started to squeeze the trigger at the same time.

He pumped four rounds into the first man as he brought his left hand back to the broom handle grip attached to the fore grip. The first man crumpled to the floor, crashing face and chest first his body sliding a few feet on the tile floor before stopping.

The other three men slid to a stop attempting to bring their weapons to bear. They were not quite sure where the shots had come from. The hallway in front of them was dark; Craig could see their silhouettes perfectly. A large stained glass window over the stairwell gave Craig all of the light he needed to see by.

Craig pumped one round each into the next two men, and then three into the third who fell backwards and flipped over the banister. He transitioned his point of aim back to the other two men. One was down on a knee, his pistol boomed, and a huge flame stretched out in front of the man. The round struck against the wall ten feet down from Craig's position.

The second man was still standing flames licked out of the barrel of his carbine, and the rounds peppered the wall and doorframe above Craig. Craig fired low into the standing man's abdomen. The man grunted and his body folded, he continued to fire as he doubled over. His rounds kicked up chips of tile and concrete around his friend. The man on one knee twisted his body trying his best to get out of the other man's line of fire. He failed to move in time as a round caught him in the back of the head. His head exploded as it was snapped forward pulling his body to the floor.

Craig stood and pumped a round into the upper torso of each man. The only movement the three made was when the .40 caliber slug from the UMP burrowed into them. Craig lowered his night vision goggles again and made his way to the stairwell. He kept his back to the wall as he made his way down the stairwell. The man who had flipped over the banister lay twisted on the first landing. The man's left leg was twisted up at an abnormal angle his left foot rested near his armpit. Craig lifted the goggles and raised the UMP to his shoulder, and fired a round into the man's chest. The man did not move. He was dead.

Craig heard the gunfire still going on outside. He expeditiously climbed the stairs and returned to his position by the window. There were six men firing behind the cars now. One lay dying on the street, and another had made his way to the front door of the shop. Craig heard the several loud booms coming from the rear of the gun shop. Howard had moved to fire on the men at the rear of the shop. It was time to lend a hand to his friend.

The man at the front door was approximately seventy-five yards away. It would be a long shot, and he would be pushing the maximum effective range of his UMP. Craig aimed about six inches above the man, as he attempted to pry the front door open with a large crow bar. Craig squeezed the trigger his sub-gun bucked and he came back on target. The man staggered back as the round struck just left of him and into the door. He looked back at his friends and shouted something. One of the men yelled back and pointed towards the door. The thug went back to work.

Craig took aim again. This time he put the sights between the man's shoulder blades. As the thug tugged on the bar, his arms locking out Craig squeezed the trigger. The thug released the crow bar and it fell to the ground. The man dropped to his knees his back arched inward, hands groping for the wound in his lower back.

Craig shifted his aim to the six behind the cars. Their backs were exposed to him. He sighted in on a man who was kneeling behind the front of the first car. He was reloading his weapon. Just as he slapped the magazine home, Craig fired. The round caught the man in the right knee. He pitched forward screaming pulling his wounded leg to him.

Craig shifted his aim to one of the men who were firing from the second car. He fired hitting the man as he stood up and began to fire at the gun shop. This round hit low too. It struck the man in the side perforating his flesh and into his kidney. He fell backwards, his head bouncing off the asphalt. He rolled from side to side struggling for breath.

Craig was about to acquire another target when he caught motion in one of the upper windows of the gun shop. "It must be Howard." He thought. He raised a hand and waved. In response Howard opened fire on him. Craig dove for cover as rounds slammed into the churches brick walls, some passing through the open window and on threw the sheetrock walls of the room.

"Crap! What was I thinking? Howard doesn't know I'm here." Howard then shifted fire back to the thugs on the street.

Craig crawled on his stomach and out of the room and headed down stairs. He made his way out of the back door, and headed west. He quickly made his way down the street and then crossed over Tennessee St. Cutting into a small alley he made his way back east towards the rear of the gun shop.

Hiding behind a dumpster in the alley Craig pulled down the night vision goggles again. At the back of the gun shop Craig spotted his unsuspecting quarry. Four men beat on the iron bars that covered a roll up delivery door. A fifth man hid behind a dumpster his rifle pointing up at the second floor. Three bodies lay motionless in the back parking lot.

Craig lifted the goggles and looked up to the moon. It lit the thugs up well, which meant it would illuminate him as well. Craig waited for the dark clouds to cover the brightness of the moon again. It only took a few minutes. Once the blackness enveloped the area again Craig made his move.

As quietly as possible he made it to the corner of a building that was on South Wood Ave. just behind the gun shop's rear parking lot. When the clouds floated past the moon Craig took in what he was looking at. The four men still beat and pried at the gate, the fifth man panned his rifle left and right waiting for Howard to reappear. Craig sighted in on the man and waited. He knew the man would get jittery soon enough and fire again. The gunfire out front was still raging.

Just as he knew he would the man fired four rounds into the second floor. Before the man fired his fifth round Craig fired from his position twenty-five yards away. The round hit the man in the bicep traveling through his skinny arm and into the armpit, and finally coming to rest lodging in his heart. He crumpled to the ground with out a word, his rifle clutched in his hands.

The four men paid no attention to Craig's shot. They thought it was their friend shooting. Craig shot two before the last two became aware of the danger they were in. Both scrambled for their rifles that were propped against the wall five feet away. Neither man made it as Craig peppered each man with the remaining rounds left in his magazine.

Craig brought the sub-gun down and dropped the spent magazine placing it in a small pouch he carried. Just as he locked the fresh magazine into the weapon the loud booms from Howard's FN reverberated down towards him. The brick wall beside him exploded in a spray of cement splinters. Craig rolled back out of the shower of lead death that reached out for him, and cascaded down into the sidewalk and brick wall.

"Howard! Howard! Quit shooting at me you dumb son of a..." Two more rounds crashed into the wall as Howard kept shooting at Craig. "Howard stop shooting!"

The gunfire stopped. "Who is that?" Howard yelled down into the darkness.

"Craig Wolfe you dumb ass. Who do you think has been shooting these thugs out here, Peter Pan?" Craig rolled back up on his knees he pointed his weapon towards Tennessee St. waiting for the other thugs to come around the corner at any moment.

"Come on around front and I will let you in." Howard answered.

"How many are left in front?" Craig called back

"Zero my friend. There just isn't anything like armor piercing rounds to make Swiss cheese out of a car and the folks dumb enough to hide behind it. Come on hurry up before the reinforcements show up."

Craig stood and trotted over to the four dead men and picked up their rifles by the slings and went around front. As he rounded the corner he took in the two cars. Howard had not lied about cars turning into Swiss cheese. Smoke rose from the engines of the cars gasoline mixed with the blood that flowed from underneath the cars and to the street curb, the grisly mixture making its way towards the storm drain.

Craig walked around the one of the cars, his UMP at the ready. He let the weapon drop and hang from its tactical sling, all the men were dead He turned to retrieve the rifles that he had leaned against the wall. His head turned as the front door opened. Howard stepped into view, his Glock 10mm in his right hand. He jumped when Howard fired a round at the man who lay in front of the door. "Dang it Howard, let a guy know before you shoot someone next time."

"Sorry buddy. I just don't need someone shooting me in the back. That one was still kicking."

Craig walked over and shook his FRIEND'S hand. "Man this part of town has gone down the tubes. Have you ever thought about relocating your store?" The two turned and walked back into the store. Howard secured the front door.

"As a matter of fact I was planning on leaving this afternoon but hadn't planned on packing so much crap. Now I will have to wait till morning."

"Where were you headed to?" Craig asked as the two walked to the back of the store. The back room was lit by two oil lanterns that sat on a large wooden worktable in the center of the room. He laid the four rifles, two Mini 14's and two SKSs on the worktable.

"I was going to head out to the Wild Life Refuge out in Waterloo." Howard said as he pointed over his shoulder. Behind him was a 4x4 Suburban with a ten-foot trailer attached to it. Both were loaded down with gear and supplies.

"Well you're welcome to come over to my place and stay. I could use some help."

"How is your grandma Craig?" Howard said as he took a drink from his canteen. He wiped his mouth with his sleeve as he took the canteen from his lips and offered it to Craig.

Craig took the canteen and a long drink. "She died the other day, had a heart attack during a shoot out with some looters.

Howard walked up and put his arm around Craig's shoulder. "Jeez man, I'm sorry."

Craig just shook his head in acknowledgement. "Listen Howard, I'm going to head back to my place. If you want, come by in the morning and we will get you moved in."

Howard slapped Craig on the back and smiled. "It's a deal my friend. I was running low on water. I can't believe I thought about just about everything someone could need in times like these except water. Does that old well of your grandma's still pump out water?"

Craig shook his head yes and began to walk to the front of the store. "How are you doing on food, and ammo?"

"I have about twenty cases of MREs. I have thousands of rounds of ammo though. I've got enough .308, 5.56, .30-06, and 7.62x39 to start a war with."

Craig laughed. "Well from the looks of things out front you have started a war."

Howard smiled. "Hey I didn't start a thing. I was just minding my own business and all these folks just started shooting at me." Howard stopped at the front counter. "Hold up Craig let's get you reloaded." Howard turned to the near empty rack behind him and picked up several boxes of .40-caliber ammo. Craig took out the empty magazines and they began to load them up.

When they finished Craig put them back in the ammo pouches on his LBV. "You just were going to leave that .40 ammo here?" Craig pointed to the seven boxes behind Howard.

"Actually I was. I don't have much room left in the truck, and I don't carry a .40 caliber. Here take these." He turned and retrieved the boxes of ammo and put them on the counter. "Consider it my first months rent. I will pack up as many cases of .40 caliber for you as I can."

Craig picked up an old butt pack that lay on the surplus gear table. He stuffed the seven boxes in the butt pack. "I need to get moving. I'll see you in the morning okay?"

Howard unlocked the front door for Craig. "See you in the morning and be careful, it's a jungle out there." Craig chuckled at his friends little joke.

The door locked behind him and Craig lowered the goggles once again and scanned the area. He didn't pick up anything so he moved out. It took him forty long minutes to traverse the five blocks to his house. At the back gate he heard a low growl as he began to unlock the padlock. "It's me Meat." The growling stopped and Meat stepped out of the shadows and greeted his master.

The two walked to the house and Craig unlocked the back door and went inside. Using the tactical light on the UMP he made his way to the parlor. He lit an oil lamp in the parlor, and made his way upstairs and made his rounds. He insured everything was in place, and then looking through the firing ports in the metal window covers he looked for trouble in the area outside of his yard. Nothing, it was time to hit the sack.

He went back downstairs and retrieved the oil lamp. He walked into one of the downstairs bedrooms and stripped. Once in bed he turned out the light and slept through the night.

Craig woke up early the next morning. Not because he had gotten enough sleep, but because of the putrid stench that hung in the air. It had gotten worse over the past two days. He swung his legs off of the bed and sat up. "I've got to do something about the bodies."

Craig had just slipped on a pair of jeans and a t-shirt when he heard Meat outside barking. He snatched up his UMP and headed to the front of the house. Peering out of the slit in the front window Craig could see Meat wagging his tail standing at the driveway gate. Then he saw Howard's face stick through the gaps in the iron. "Craig!" He could just barely make out Howard calling his name. He went outside to let his friend in.

Howard pulled in the drive and Craig locked the gate back in place. He shook hands with Howard as he exited the Suburban. "Everything going good, no troubles on the way over her was there?"

"Not one. Craig I hate to sound like an ingrate but it stinks worse here than it does at the shop." Howard said as he unconsciously put his hand up to his nose.

"Yeah I've already thought about that. I think I have a plan that will help us out."

"Really, what have you got in mind?" The two turned and walked towards the house as Craig told Howard about his plan.

Once inside the kitchen he fixed coffee, then Craig poured the two of them a cup of coffee. Howard took a sip, "So where are we going to get this bulldozer again?"

Craig swung his leg over one of the chairs and sat down. "The city barn down on Railroad Ave., I drove by there two days ago. The thing is sitting on the back of a flatbed, and the trailer is attached to a big diesel. All we have to do is make our way over there, crank it up and we're home free. We move the bodies into a big pile torch them and no more stink."

Howard stared at his life long friend, and sipped his coffee. "Craig you are out of your mind. What about all those fine folks that would like to kill us along the way? What about fuel? What if the thing is gone?"

"Number one I am completely sane. Number two; I don't think we will have to worry about folks shooting at us if we leave early enough. Number three; there is still plenty of fuel left in the underground tanks. Number four, who would be crazy enough to want a diesel and bulldozer?"

Howard rolled his eyes "Number one you are crazy. Number two folks will shoot at us no matter what time it is. Number three; you may be right about the fuel. Number four, who would want a diesel truck, and bulldozer?" Howard paused as he took a sip of coffee. "Well dork, I see one crazy son of a bitch sitting in front of me, so I am sure there are at least a hundred more running around this mad house that would just love to have a bulldozer. I'm going to go along with you on this though. Not so much for the bulldozer idea, but the fuel. I brought a diesel and gas-burning generator. Whether we get the dozer or not, we get as much fuel as possible.

Craig downed his mug of coffee. "So what are we waiting for? Let's roll!"

"How about we unload my trailer first? We can unload the Suburban later. We hook up my trailer to your K-5. That way if the diesel and dozer are gone we will still have something to load the fuel onto."

"Alright let's get to work." Craig and Howard walked back outside to the trailer, and began to unload Howard's gear.

Two hours later the pair turned onto Railroad Ave. The trip over had been slow but uneventful. They saw a few people wondering around, some armed some not. No one bothered them though.

As they neared the fenced in area of the "City Barn" Craig observed that the main gate had been torn loose. He turned into the parking area and spotted the rig and bulldozer. "Just like I said, see she is sitting right there just waiting on us."

Howard rolled his eyes. "Well before we see if that rig runs let's siphon out some fuel and get the fuel cans filled up. Then I say we look for some other containers to fill up, we only have eight five gallon cans."

Craig parked the Blazer near the fuel pumps. He got out and popped the metal lids that were used to pump fuel into the underground tanks. Howard dragged a long hose with a siphon pump attached to it over to the first tank. "Is it diesel or gas?"

Craig kneeled down and took a sniff over the hole. "I do believe we have gas in this one." He got up and started lining up the fuel cans. Howard lowered the hose down into the hole.

"While you pump out the gas I will look for more containers." Craig pulled his UMP out of the Blazer and began to search the compound.

He checked around the building first and found nothing. He decided he would check the garage area next. He shouldered the UMP in tight and turned on his tactical light and button hooked into the open door that led into the garage.

The place was a wreck. Tool chest had been overturned, the walls that once held belts, and hoses were now bare. It took him several minutes to clear the large garage area. As he checked the last stall he found what they would need.

Howard was filling up the last of the gas cans. He continually scanned the area around him, looking and listening for danger. He had not been to keen on Craig's idea at first. Now though the more he thought about it the better he liked it. The fuel they were getting would be a lifesaver later this winter.

The more he thought about using the bulldozer the better he liked the idea. It would be nice to be able to move the bodies without having to touch them. What he really liked about the bulldozer though, was the fact that they could use it to possibly tear down the burned up houses surrounding Craig's place. The way he pictured it, over time they could form a large debris type wall around the area. He knew it would not be perfect, but if constructed properly they could leave openings that would funnel people into kill zones

Howard was shaken out of his thoughts by a loud metallic sound of metal screeching. He let go of the hose as he spun, drawing his 10mm Glock. He just shook his head as one of the garage bay doors opened up. Craig stood there with a big smile on his face.

"What're you so jumpy for buddy." Craig said as he walked from the bay towards Howard.

Howard holstered his pistol and turned to cut off the siphon. The gas can was flowing over with fuel. "You scared the crap out of me you turd."

Craig walked up to his friend and stopped. "I believe I found what we need. Come on and have a look." He turned and walked back towards the garage.

"Let me load this last can into the trailer." Howard lugged the heavy can onto the trailer. Setting it with the others he turned and jogged to catch up with his friend.

Craig stood at the door of the open bay. He pointed as Howard came to a stop beside him. "Well, what do you think?"

Howard looked to where Craig was pointing. In the corner stall were eleven blue thirty gallon barrels. "What's in them?" He asked.

"Not a thing. There is no label on them and I opened one and could not smell anything. So who knows what they were going to be used for. They were probably going to use them to put old motor oil in them." Craig walked forward and hefted one over his shoulders. "Well don't just stand there and think I'm going to do all the work. Get hopping." He smiled as he walked past Howard.

Howard grabbed one and followed Craig out to the fuel pumps. Craig sat his in the trailer. "Let's load them on the trailer so we don't have to lug them on when they are filled up. Plus if we have to get gone in a hurry, we will at least get away with some fuel."

It took the two another four hours to load the barrels and get them filled with fuel. They filled six with gasoline and five with diesel. When they were done they stopped to eat an MRE for lunch.

Craig took a spoonful of his Chicken Ala King. "Am I the man or what?" He said with a mouthful of food.

Howard took a spoonful of peaches and shoved them in his mouth and swallowed. "You know you remind me of some of the guys I knew in the Navy. The Senior Chief would send them out to locate things we did not have, procure them and bring them back. The lucky little turds could come across anything the Senior Chief needed. The Senior Chief called them his little scavengers. I always thought of them as little roaches scampering across the base. Yep. That's what you are, a lucky little cock roach." He smiled and spooned in another mouthful of peaches.

"Hurry up and finish, you little whine bag. I'm ready to get back home." Craig's eyes roved the perimeter. He stopped when looking when he noticed that the fence was topped with razor wire. "Howard, after we see if the dozer and rig run, I think I have another idea."

"What kind of ludicrous plan have you got now?"

"Well I was just thinking about the razor wire on top of the fence. Do you think we could get it loose, coil it back up and take it to the house? I figure we can get enough to surround most of the area around the brick wall with it."

Howard put his empty peach container into the MRE bag, tilting his head he looked at Craig for a moment. "You know for a mentally ill S.O.B. you have come up with a good idea. Let's finish up and check the dozer out, then we will take a look at the razor wire." The two hurriedly ate the remainder of their meal in silence. When they finished they walked over to the big diesel rig and dozer.

Howard climbed up on the trailer and got into the driver seat of the bulldozer. The key hung in the ignition slot. "Well, we are in luck." He turned the key and let the glow plugs warm, then cranked the metal beast. Smoke billowed from the stack, as Howard let out a whoop of joy.

Craig got into the cab of the diesel, their luck was still holding out. Craig found the key in the ashtray of the truck. He put the key in the ignition and turned the key. The diesel's engine fired up after it turned over twice. He left the engine to idle as he climbed out of the cab.

Howard walked up to him and slapped him on the shoulder. "Look's like the big man upstairs is smiling on us today!"

"Yeah it does. There is only one problem." He said grinning with embarrassment.

"What's that?" The expression on Howard's face turned from joy, to concern.

"I don't know how to drive an eighteen wheeler."

"What do you mean you don't know how to drive an eighteen wheeler? What the hell are we doing here then?" Howard's hands went to his hips, and he looked upward searching for help from the man upstairs.

"Don't sweat it. You're a fast learner, and I'm sure you will figure it out." Craig said as he grinned and walked by. "Let's get some of that razor wire down."

Howard just stood there as Craig walked to his truck for a pair of leather gloves. "What do you mean me? This was your idea Craig Wolfe!"

Craig pulled on his gloves and turned to smile at his friend. "Now Howard you wouldn't want a mentally incompetent man like me behind the wheel of that monster would you? You will remember you said I was crazy. Heck I might snap and just decided to run you over or something." Craig turned and walked towards the garage area where he had spotted a stepladder.

An hour and a half later they were headed home. Craig turned up the air conditioner and smiled as he looked in the rearview mirror. Howard was in the driver seat of the eighteen-wheeler. He was covered in sweat. To Craig's amusement Howard had signaled for him to pull up along side him when they had first started out. "The air conditioner doesn't work on this thing." Howard had shouted. Craig had let out a laugh, "I'll notify the City Council about it when we get home." He had replied with a shit eating grin, and sped off to check things out ahead.

They turned onto Tennessee St. and Craig slowed to a stop. He put the Blazer in park and pulled out his binoculars. He opened the door and stood up leaning his body against the door. There was nothing up ahead that looked out of the ordinary. He could see a few people picking through piles of debris, or carrying items out of storefronts. Howard pulled up beside him and stopped.

Craig looked up at his friend. His face was covered in sweat, his hair was matted down and it looked like he had not washed it in a month. "Hey there buddy! Are you ready to go get a job with a trucking company? You drive that thing so well. Are you sure you never drove one of those things before?"

Howard glared down at Craig. "Just shut the hell up. Do you see anything up there?"

"No, it looks clear, just a few folks picking through some stuff, no weapons. I say we take it nice and slow; we have plenty of sunlight left to make it home. What do you think?" Craig smiled mischievously up at his friend.

"Craig Wolfe, I suggest you get back in that truck and get home as fast as you can. If you get in my way I'm going to run your stinking butt over. I don't know how I let you convince me to drive this thing."

"Well friend, some of us are leaders, and some followers. I lead in the air conditioned vehicle, while you loyally follow me in the big sweat box." Craig hopped back in the Blazer before he had to listen to the stream of curse words that Howard shot at him. He slipped the truck into drive and headed out. He looked in his rearview mirror and hung his hand out the open window and waved Howard on. He grinned when he saw Howard give him the finger with both hands. Then the big truck lurched forward, the cab bouncing as Howard played with the clutch and gears. Finally the truck quit its lurching as Howard gave the rig enough gas for the engine to smooth out.

Fifteen minutes later they were home. Craig had the gate open and his Blazer pulled up into the drive by the time Howard had the big rig stopped down on the street. Craig was sipping water from his canteen and leaning against the wall as Howard came around the front of the rig. "Man it sure is hot out today." He said with a grin.

"I'll show you hot when you feel the burning sensation of my boot up your ass." Howard replied as he walked up and snatched the canteen out of Craig's hand. He took several large gulps almost emptying the canteen and poured the rest out over his head. "I think you need to get up there and back that dozer off the back of the trailer and get to work."

"Why me? You're the one with all of the experience driving diesels."

Howard just gave Craig a look. Craig backed off knowing his friend though not truly angry was probably worn out from the all the heat. "Okay, I'll get to it, would you mind running me a bath?" Craig smiled and walked up to the flat bed trailer hopped up and began to unhook the chains. Howard pulled the ramp slats down so Craig could back the dozer off. Craig got in the driver's seat and un-slung the UMP. He folded the butt stock and placed the weapon at his side.

Starting it up Craig backed the bulldozer off the trailer. Craig knew how to operate the bulldozer. When he had first got on the team he worked on surveillance detail and posed as a city worker. He was taught how to operate the big bulldozer, by one of the men in the Street Department.

While Craig backed the dozer Howard went back to the cab of the rig and got his FN out and slung the weapon over his shoulder. He walked over to one of the large oak trees that lined the sidewalks, and enjoyed the shade. He would watch for danger while Craig did some hot dirty work himself.

Craig worked slowly at first; the main reason was that one of the bodies he had scooped up had burst open when the metal blade pushed into it. Now each time he scooped up a body he prayed it would not burst. In the first twenty minutes Craig had vomited two times from the smell. Howard just walked along at a distance, managing to stay in the shade of the tall oaks. A smile spread across his face each time Craig vomited or started to dry heave.

Within another hour and a half Craig had piled up more than seventy bodies, which had littered the streets. When it appeared he was finished he drove the dozer to a corner lot south of his house. He used the big dozer to dig a large trench. When he was finished with that he began the gruesome task of moving the piled up bodies into the trench. This took almost another hour.

He then drove the dozer across the street to Mr. Thompson's burned out home. In the backyard was three cords of firewood. He managed to scoop up the wood and took it and dumped it over the bodies. After that was completed he tore down a neighbor's privacy fence, and pushed that wood into the trench. When he was done he drove the dozer back to his place.

Howard leaned against an oak tree sipping on his third canteen of water since Craig had started working. "Sure is hot today." He said smiling.

"Quit with the joking you lazy dog, and help me get one of the barrels of diesel from the trailer." Craig said as he hopped down from the dozer.

The two of them rolled one of the barrels of diesel off the trailer. Craig ran inside and got the dolly. The two then manhandled the barrel onto the dolly. Craig rolled it down to the bulldozer and put it in the bucket of the blade. He climbed back up in the driver's seat and started it up. Once at the trench Craig tilted the bucket forward a little and eased forward until the blade was out over the trench.

Craig got out of his seat and climbed up one of the arms to the blade. He hoped into the bucket and with a bit of struggling got the top of the barrel halfway out over the edge of the blade. Then he held onto the lip of the barrel with his right hand. Using his left he unscrewed the cap. The diesel fuel flowed from the hole dowsing the wood and bodies below. When the barrel was empty Craig made his way back to the driver's seat and backed it away from the trench.

Howard walked up to Craig as he climbed down from the bulldozer. He held out a road flare. "Would you like the honor or should I?"

Craig was wiping the diesel off of his forearm and hands with a dirty towel. "You do it Howard I've got diesel all over me."

Howard made his way to the base of the pile of dirt and took a knee. He lit the flare and threw it over hand towards the center of the trench. Howard pushed off the dirt and ran with all his might as the flare tumbled down into the center of the trench. When he was about forty feet away he stopped and turned, wondering if he had missed the center of the trench where the diesel fuel was. He turned to Craig. "You think I missed?"

Before Craig could answer a ball of flame mushroomed towards the sky. The flash of heat caused the two to cringe back. "Nope, I think you got it." Craig said sarcastically.

The two headed towards the garage to wash up. When they had cleaned up they went inside for a couple of MREs and ate supper. The two were worried that the black smoke that billowed from the trench would attract someone. They lucked out and no one showed up to investigate. When they were done eating they pulled the bulldozer into the yard. Then Howard asked Craig if he knew how to disconnect the trailer from the rig so they could pull it in the yard.

"You're the one who knows about eighteen wheelers not me."

Howard shook his head in disgust. "Just grab your gun and come cover me while I try to figure it out." The two headed back outside.

An hour later Howard had the trailer removed and the big rig pulled into the yard. "I think tomorrow we need to get busy putting out the razor wire. I also have some plans for that dozer of yours. Have you got any ideas about what we need to do next" He asked Craig as they walked back to the house.

"Well I figure first thing I will do is cover up the bodies. After that I think my calendar is open. What kind of plans do you have for the dozer?"

"I think we should demolish as many of the houses as possible that have been burnt. We create a wall of debris that people will have to move around to areas we want them to enter. We just try to make sure we have a good field of fire for the gaps. Also I think we should use the dozer to dig a trench along the inside of the wall."

Craig scratched his head and thought for a moment. "You know that's not a bad idea. We can also build a trench on both sides of the yard and the back. If you want after we dig them out we can head down to one of the salvage yards and get hold of some metal poles and scrap metal with sharp edges. Then we line the floor of the trench with the stuff. You know make the poles into something like pungi sticks, that way no one can use it as a firing position."

"Sounds good to me, let's go inside I'll set up one of the generators. Then we can hook up my short wave radio and find out what's going on out there. I never hooked it up at the shop. Have you heard anything about what's going on out there?"

"Just caught bits and pieces, I know we are at war with China, and North Korea. We used tactical nukes on both. Apparently they nuked a few of our cities. I think all of them were port cities. The new President, I forgot his name, is trying to bring most of our troops home from Europe. I don't know how that's going either. FEMA has set up relocation camps, mostly around major metropolitan areas. Smaller cities have been left on their own for now."

"Let's go find out." The two walked into the house eager to hear some news.

Chapter 25

Joe Donovan closed the lid on the small pistol cleaning kit. It consisted of a cleaning rod, .22 caliber bore brush, patches, medium size CLP bottle, and a few Q-tips. He placed it in his Camelback "Mother Load" pack as he glanced over at the small stainless coffee pot that sat on the Sterno stove. He could smell the strong brew simmering in the pot and was ready for his first cup of the morning.

Glancing at his watch, which read 5:30, he ran his fingers through his matted black hair and let out a yawn. He picked up the stainless Ruger MK I with a four and a half inch barrel from the kitchen table. He then picked up the ten round magazine that had lain next to the pistol. Joe inserted it and racked a round into the chamber and holstered the pistol. Joe picked up the four remaining loaded magazines and placed them in a small black nylon pouch that hung on his belt.

Joe stood up and stretched. It seemed every muscle in his five foot nine inch frame ached. Joe had always considered himself in great shape for a thirty five year old man. He ran two miles, three times a week, and lifted weights three days a week. Thinking back on the past five days he should have trained to run biathlons wearing his thirty pound Camelback. He picked up the stainless coffee cup and walked over to the coffee pot and poured himself a cup.

Joe blew the steam from coffee as the cup rested on his lips, and then took a welcome drink of the scalding drink. Walking over to the back door he insured that the kitchen door was still locked and the chair he had placed under the door knob was secure. He reached up and parted the blinds a bit and took a look at the back yard. Nothing moved in area of the back yard except a few birds hopping on the ground hunting worms. Letting the blinds fall back in place he walked through the spacious kitchen to the hallway. He stopped at the edge of the tile where the plush white carpet of the hallway began and looked down at his boots. The brown leather work boots were caked in mud. His khaki pants appeared no better, muddy with a small tear in the left knee.

"Sorry folks." He said to the family that was no longer home as he stepped on the carpet and walked towards the front door. He felt bad about messing up the beautiful carpet with his boots. Of course the people who owned the house may be dead. Most likely though, they were never coming home. No cars had been in the garage, and the drawers in the bedroom were empty.

In the foyer he tried to turn the locked door knob and shook the door. Joe knew he had just checked the door twenty minutes ago, but it was better to be safe than sorry. He decided to be even safer and pulled a large chest that rested beside the door in front of it. It wouldn't stop a determined person, but it could buy him some valuable time. Joe finished off the coffee that remained in his cup and walked back to the kitchen for a refill.

Joe drained the last of the coffee into his cup, and extinguished the flame on the little Sterno by placing the cap over the flame and screwing it on. He picked the coffee pot up and took it to the sink where he rinsed it out. He had been surprised to find the house still had water pressure. He had filled the water bladder for the Camelback up as soon as he had discovered the water still worked.

Joe had then found a large thirty two ounce cup in a cabinet and drank four overflowing cups of water. He had been near dehydration because he had found no drinkable water source for the past two days. After securing the house Joe had waited several hours before he chanced a quick cold shower. He was sure he had lost his pursuers but didn't want to chance washing his clothes. It would have really sucked he thought to try and evade them again wearing nothing but a backpack. He probably shouldn't have had a shower last night, but after four days of running, fighting and hiding he took the chance to wash the sweat and grime from his body.

He took a power bar from the pack before putting the coffee pot, stove, and Sterno container in the pack. Joe picked up the pack and his coffee cup and walked to the living room. Setting the pack down Joe chose a plush leather chair to sit in. He let out a groan of relief, and satisfaction as he sat down. He kicked his feet up on a large leather ataman that matched the chair, while he ripped open the rapper of the power bar with his teeth.

He took a bite off of the bar and slowly chewed, then took a sip of his coffee. Eating the power bar made Joe think of his food situation, he had six power bars left, and two MREs. He had a can of soup; one can of peaches, chili, and green beans that he had found in an abandoned house in Memphis. The only thing edible he had found in the house he was in now was a small two and a half pound bag of rice. Joe had enough coffee for two cups a day for the next seven days. Not bad but did he have enough food to make it across the state line into Alabama, and then on to Florence?

"Probably not." He said to himself. Joe had found that over the past couple of days he had started talking to himself out loud, usually in a soft whisper. He found that by doing so, it helped him to come up with answers to some of the problems he faced. He cleared his mind of the problems at hand and drank his coffee. Then he finished the power bar.

When Joe was done with his meager breakfast he closed his eyes and started thinking about the problem at hand. That problem was a gang. He had crossed paths with the gang in north Memphis, and several times since then. Joe closed his eyes to rest them for a moment and thought about what he had done in the past few days, and how he had got into situation he was now in.

Just five days ago Joe had been just north of Memphis, TN. Joe was a farm equipment salesman, probably one of the best in the Southeast. For a week he had been working on the sale of fifteen tractors to a local farm equipment wholesaler. It was a$650,000.00 deal, and he needed the sale to go through. He had been in a slump for the past two months, and the $62,250.00 commission check would help pay for the new farm he had been looking at just north of Florence.

The day of the first big attacks Joe had been in a meeting in his hotel room with the owner of the supply company till almost 9:00 pm. He had finally convinced the man that the deal that he had been offered was a good one. They decided to meet for a late breakfast the next morning and sign the sales contracts. After his client had left Joe had taken a hot shower and gone to bed, oblivious of a world gone mad.

The next morning he had woke up and showered again. He dressed himself in a pair of Khaki pants with cargo pockets, and a green short sleeve cotton button down shirt and his boots. Joe found that people didn't like the spit and polish look of a business suit that most of his competitors wore. They seemed to prefer the casual everyday average guy look that Joe preferred himself.

He flipped the news on and sat back in the sofa of his hotel room drinking a large cup of coffee. When he saw the news about what was going on he had to flip to several different news channels before he could make himself believe what he was seeing.

Picking up the phone he had called his brother's house in Florence to check on how things were going there. Knowing his brother would be unprepared for any kind of possible hardship he needed to convince him to go stock up on a few things. The only one of his brother's family that had any sense, in his mind, was Celina. The girl was one tough cookie. Unlike her younger sister Daphne who dreamed of being a model, Celina chose a different path, a tougher path.

Celina had shown an interest in martial arts and shooting at a young age. His brother had allowed her to take martial arts as long as Joe had been willing to take her. He did not approve of it, but as Joe knew, it was hard to tell the beautiful strong willed girl no. So at age seven Celina started taking martial arts and had attained a black belt by the time she was fourteen.

Celina had begged to learn to shoot but her father had been adamant about not letting her do it. Even Joe had tried to convince him it was a great sport. But her father had said proper young ladies did not participate in such events.

Celina eventually got her way after the family joined the local country club. They had a skeet range there and two skeet teams. One was a boys team the other a girls team. Celina had convinced her father to let her tryout for the team. He approved after she had pointed out that obviously, according to the country club administrators, young girls from affluent families should be able to shoot skeet. Her father was all about keeping up with the Jones'. So if girls from other rich families were shooting skeet then his daughter had to learn also.

His brother had insisted that Joe should teach the girl the fundamentals of shooting before she began to shoot skeet. Celina had taken to shooting like a fish does to water, first with .22 caliber pistols, and rifles, then on to shotguns. She could shoot a 12 gauge well, but preferred the 20 gauge. Within a few months she was on the country clubs skeet team and winning matches. Shooting cemented a tight bond between Joe and his lovely niece.

After getting no answer at his brother's he called the owner of the farm supply company. He finally got an answer after several attempts. The woman said the meeting was canceled for the foreseeable future because the boss had headed to his farm. She was unsure when he would return or when the business would open back up, she was in the process of locking up when he called.

Joe had hung up the phone and turned back to the TV. He watched news reports concerning National Guard call ups, rioting on the east and west coast, and video clips of nuclear and chemical horror. They had no real news about the southeast except for Birmingham, Al. and Atlanta. Those two cities had exploded with violence. The Memphis news reported that some unrest was starting to occur but had not been wide spread.

He had flicked off the TV and went to pack his bags, he was heading home. After packing his clothes bag, Joe pulled out a medium size military OD green tool bag. Inside the tool kit was his emergency kit. It consisted of his Ruger MK I, two bricks of .22 caliber shells, five magazines, leather gloves, K-Bar, emergency first aid kit, ten chocolate power bars, lighter, emergency blanket, water purification tablets and a Leather man. He loaded the magazines and inserted one into the pistol.

He picked up his Camelback and placed it on the table. The Camelback contained a poncho, poncho liner, first aid kit, fire starting materials, and cooking kit. Taking out the 100 oz, water bladder Joe filled it up from the faucet in the bathtub. He walked back into the sleeping area and placed it in his Camelback. He completed a search of the room making sure he had everything. Then he slung the Camelback onto his shoulders, placed the pistol and magazines back in the bag where he had gotten them, picked his things up and headed out to his truck.

Joe hadn't bothered to check out; he would just call later and let them know the key was on the TV. When Joe had arrived in the parking lot he took a quick look around. Most people walked with heads down, few made eye contact. They all seemed to walk in a nervous, agitated manner. The vehicle traffic was heavy, drivers seemed impatient, horns blew, and curse words filled the air at the smallest infraction of other drivers. Joe could feel the restless uncertainty in the air. He shook off a chill that ran through his body. "Damn. I haven't even left the parking lot and I already have the jitters." He walked to his truck.

Joe's truck was a couple of years old. It was an F-350 4x4, diesel. Though diesel was a bit more expensive than regular gas, Joe liked the diesel for its dependability and because he put so many miles on his vehicles each year.

Joe threw his suitcase in the back of the extended cab truck and his Camelback in the passenger seat. Taking a brown leather gun belt from behind the seat he laid it on the seat. Then he took out the pistol and magazines and placed them on his belt and strapped it on. He hopped in the truck and cranked it up, and pulled the truck to the parking lot exit.

Just as Joe found a break in traffic he eased forward but had to jam on his brakes when he spotted four police cruisers flying his way. Their blue lights flashing, and sirens wailing the four cruisers screamed past him. They were followed by a military convoy, that consisted of six five tons packed with troops, and four Hummers. Two of the Hummers had M-60's mounted on the top, one a .50 caliber machine gun, and the last a MK-19 automatic grenade launcher.

As soon as the convoy went by him Joe had accelerated into the roadway and paced the convoy. Soon the convoy hit US 51 and headed south into Memphis. Joe was pleased with this because if the convoy continued heading down US 51 they would run into US 72. US 72 would lead him straight into Florence. The only downside to this was that he would have to head through Memphis and then into Mississippi through Corinth. Once out of Mississippi and in Alabama he would have to go through Tuscumbia, Muscle Shoals, and Sheffield before he could cross the river into Florence.

Joe had heard no news of the conditions of Mississippi, or north Alabama. He knew that Birmingham had been hit with biological agents, and that Mobile was nuclear ash, but nothing about the rest of the state. The more Joe thought the more he realized his four hour drive to Florence could turn into two or three days. Luckily the truck was topped off with fuel, and he had two five gallon cans of diesel chained up in the back.

He scanned the Memphis skyline ahead of him. He had spotted several huge pillars of smoke reaching into the sky. There were dozens of smaller plumes of black smoke scattered across the skyline. "The unrest isn't widespread my ass." Joe said to himself as he leaned forward and turned on the radio to a local news station. His stomach started doing flip flops as the news announcer reported the current conditions in Memphis.

"...National Guard troops are being deployed throughout the city. According to sources inside the Guard all off and on ramps on the interstates and major highways will be blocked. Residents of the city are asked to remain in their homes, visitors and travelers through the city will be detained and sent to various parks around the city. The purpose according to our sources is to attempt to identify any terrorist, and citizens who may be contaminated from any biological agents.

So far the terrorists have only deployed nerve agents, but government agencies are unsure if some victims were not killed by biological agents. The CDC in Atlanta will begin testing victims when they arrive at their facility. Until then all travelers will be detained.

FEMA and the National Guard have set up refugee camps at the following city parks, Memphis Memorial, Marquette Park, Halle Park, and May Park. Travelers hearing this broadcast should consult maps and head for these areas to help facilitate the process of identifying people who could be contaminated, and finding the perpetrators of these acts."

Joe flipped off the radio. "Crap!" he said as he slammed his hand on the steering wheel. He looked to his right and saw a road sign that said US 72 was a quarter of a mile away.

Joe let his foot off the gas as he saw the red break lights come on the vehicles from the convoy. He pulled to the shoulder and stopped as the troops deployed from the back of one of the five ton trucks. One of the hummers turned sideways, the soldier in the turret swung his

M-60 machinegun back towards his direction. The rest of the convoy continued. They were sixty yards away.

One of the soldiers, possibly a sergeant or an officer, stepped to the front of the newly formed road block. Most of the motorist had come to a stop at about the same place Joe had. The soldier started to motion with his left hand for the vehicles to start forward. Joe sat on the side of the road and watched the cars start to inch forward.

"You're not putting my butt in some freaking refugee camp. I've got a home!" Joe floored the gas pedal. Rocks and gravel churned under the tires as he cut the wheel to the right heading for the grassy area beside the road.

As he had got the truck turned around Joe heard the distinctive staccato of the M-60 machinegun. Dirt kicked up in front of the truck, and then he heard metallic clanks as several rounds impacted on the back of his tailgate. The firing stopped as he drove father along the line slow moving cars. Looking into his review mirror he saw other cars begin to peel out of line, some coming to an abrupt stop or continuing to roll forward into the chain link fence as the machine gunner sprayed the fleeing cars.

Eventually Joe had made his way back north, and then east. Soon he approached the area near an area known as White Station. Joe intended to drive the back streets and parallel US 72 hoping for little trouble. Looking around he thought for a fleeting moment it might have been better to go to the refugee camp.

Several buildings burned, cars were overturned and people were breaking out store windows. Joe locked his door and unsnapped the strap on his holster. No one paid much attention to him probably suspecting he too was a looter. Cars and trucks drove down the streets with looted goods packed in the vehicles. Joe had not seen anything like this since he had watched the scenes of the "Rodney King" riots in L.A.

Joe came to an abrupt stop as he turned onto North Quail Hollow Rd. A small white Honda Civic sat in the road in front of him, the doors open. In front of the car were at least nine older model cars blocking the road. The impromptu road block is not what caught his eyes, it was what was going on in front of the Civic that had.

Joe jerked his door open and pulled the Ruger from its holster as he stepped from the truck. He walked quickly to the left and forward, pistol pointed out in front of him. As he approached the rear of the Civic he called out.

"What the hell do you think you're doing?" He yelled at the four young black males, clad in blue shirts and bandanas.

The four were beating a young black man who lay curled up in a ball at their feet. The four looked up from the young man. "You better carry your ass whitey, or your next!" One of the men said as he raised the crowbar in his hands to strike the prone man.

Joe squeezed the trigger on the Ruger. His sights aimed squarely at the man's face. The crowbar dropped from his upraised arm and clattered to the ground. His hands went to a spot just under his right eye. He looked over at Joe, a look of astonishment on his face, and then fell forward dead. The other three raced for their cars.

Joe moved forward to the front end of the car shifting the point of his aim towards five more gang members who were in the process of attempting to rape a young black woman. She lay screaming for help from her now unconscious, disfigured husband.

The five had abruptly stopped with their immoral act when they heard the gunshot. Two sat crouched holding the woman's arms their heads turned looking over their shoulders at Joe. Two more held each ankle, the fifth looked up at him, his body in a push up position over the woman.

Impulsively Joe's finger squeezed the trigger again. His round caught the man that was on top of the woman in forehead. The man's head snapped back, as his arms collapsed beneath him. His body fell lifeless on top of the flailing woman.

Years on the streets had steeled the survival instinct in the four youths that held the woman to the ground. They bolted from their positions and ran towards their cars. Two produced guns and began firing wildly at Joe as they ran.

Rounds snapped past Joe and into the Civic. Joe began to fire as he moved to a kneeling position behind the car. Two of his last eight rounds caught one of the running gang members between the shoulder blades. His legs failed to support him as his spinal cord was pierced and severed. He fell to the hard asphalt his now useless arms unable break his fall as his face ground into the roadway.

Joe pulled the empty magazine from the grip and slid it into his back pocket. Reaching into the small pouch on his belt he pulled out a fresh one and slapped it into the gun. As he racked the slide forward more rounds from the other gang bangers peppered the area around him.

He got up off his knee and began to back up towards his truck. He fired his pistol slowly from right to the left. The slide locked back as he emptied the second magazine. Joe quickly reloaded the pistol again and jumped into the driver's seat and slammed the door. He threw the big truck in reverse and pressed the accelerator to the floor.

He leaned over the arm rest peering over the dashboard at the area around him searching for an escape route. Suddenly he was thrown to the floorboard as his truck slammed into a light pole behind him. The truck sat motionless as he crawled back into the driver's seat. Two fresh bullet holes had spider webbed the front windshield when he was thrown to the floorboard.

Joe scanned the roadblock. He saw more gang members running up to assist the ones already trying to kill him. Rounds began to hit the front of the truck as he sat there unsure what to do.

After several seconds Joe decided on a course of action that he would soon regret. He started the truck. "Well I can't go over them, can't go around them. So I guess I will go through them." Joe angrily jerked the gear shift into drive and punched the accelerator. The big truck lumbered forward like a wounded rhino. Bullet holes appeared in the windows, and quarter panels as it surged forward.

Joe aimed the nose of the truck for a three foot gap that lay between two of the cars. He braced himself as he rocketed forward. Then the truck struck the two cars spinning them out of the way like tops. Joe heard the sound of metal crumpling and men screaming as the big cars were forced out of his way. More rounds impacted the back and sides of his truck as he fled for safety. One of the gang members lay dead, crushed by one of the cars. Two others lay on the ground screaming in pain with multiple broken bones.

Gang members piled into the undamaged cars cranked the engines and gave chase to the fleeing truck. Like the cold hearts they were, they left the two injured members of their gang lying screaming on the ground.

Joe looked in the review mirror and was shocked to see the gang members coming after him. He pushed the accelerator to the floor. He was already going fifty miles per hour doing his best to avoid other cars and people on the streets carrying their stolen items. Joe knew he was in trouble as he watched the much faster gas powered cars gain on him. Joe began taking side streets. Even though he had been to Memphis numerous times he was quickly lost.

The cars were now right up behind Joe, gang members firing wildly out of the car windows trying their best to kill him. Just ahead Joe saw a large street sign that read Poplar Estates Pkwy. Joe racked his brain trying to visualize where in the city he was.

He flew through the intersection, barely missing several cars that had come screeching to a halt avoiding the huge truck. Joe glanced in the mirror to see four of the cars fly through the gap in traffic. Then he saw a tremendous crash as one of the gang's car, a 70's model Buick Electra, crash into a Suzuki Samaria laden with stolen goods. Two gang members were ejected from the car, their bodies tumbling like rag dolls as they hit the street. The Suzuki looked like it had exploded as stolen goods ripped through the rag top as it went spinning towards the sidewalk.

Joe looked back at the road just in time to avoid hitting several people who were running across the street with arms full of clothing. He jerked hard left and then straightened out the big truck.

"Crap!" Joe exclaimed as he noticed an extensive amount of steam start to whirl over the hood of the truck. Joe checked the mirrors to see if he had pulled away from the pursuing gang members. He was having no such luck. In the driver side mirror Joe watched as a primer colored Galaxy 500 started to pull along side of him. One of the passengers started to lean out the window, pistol in hand.

Joe checked the mirror again to see the car pulling up along side of him. The gang banger with the pistol now set on the edge of the window, his pistol pointed towards Joe. The other cars were about forty yards behind. Then the side back window exploded as a round crashed through it. Joe looked ahead and saw that a car was parked in his lane of travel. A second car was parked on the left hand shoulder of the opposite lane.

He floored the gas pedal again, and jerked the wheel hard to the left. The truck and smaller Galaxy collided in a shower of sparks. Joe's eyes shot to the side view mirror in time to see the gunman fall through the open window. The driver of the Galaxy locking the brakes up and cutting the wheel to the right as smoke billowed up from the tires as the car began to fishtail. Joe's truck shot through the two parked cars missing the one on the right by inches.

He smiled with satisfaction as he watched the Galaxy sliding sideways; it hit the car that was parked on the shoulder of the road. The parked car lurched backwards, and father up on the sidewalk. The Galaxy was propelled into the air rolling upside down as it descended down onto the trunk of the parked car. The top of the Galaxy crushed in as it hit the concrete surely killing everyone inside. The other gang member's cars came to a screeching halt as the Galaxy slid to a halt just past the two parked cars effectively blocking the road.

As Joe turned to look back at the road the satisfied look on his face changed to a look of fear at what lay just ahead. He never had time to hit the brakes as his truck crashed through a huge metal sign that read Forgey Park. On the other side of the sign was a steep grassy embankment.

The heavy truck was airborne for only a second before it crashed back to the ground as it went over the edge of the embankment. Joe came up out of his seat, his head slamming into the roof of the car. His hands fought for control of the steering wheel as he rocketed towards a cluster of trees.

As soon as he landed back in the seat Joe had slammed on the breaks. The knobby tires dug for purchase in the slick soft grass. The truck slid almost one hundred feet before crashing into one of the small trees that halted his travel down the hill side.

Joe sat in silence for a moment his knuckles white as he still gripped the steering wheel. Finally he loosened his death grip and began to breathe again. "I hope I didn't shit myself." He said as he reached for the door handle.

Getting out of the truck Joe's legs wobbled a bit. He turned and looked back up the hill in time to see a black man in a blue shirt turn and run the other direction shouting something he could not make out.

Adrenaline surged through him as he turned back to the cab of the truck reaching for his green bag and Camelback.

Joe unzipped the green bag and took out the contents and added them to his pack. Slinging the pack Joe ran deeper into the small park. After running forty yards Joe took cover behind a large oak, and checked the area behind him. Two hundred yards or so behind him Joe counted approximately twenty of the gang members clad in blue shirts and bandanas running down the hill. They all appeared to be armed with handguns, some carried sawed off shotguns.

He ducked back behind the tree, his back resting against it and searched the park for an escape route. He could hear the sounds of a few car engines on the perimeter of the park. They were trying to flank him. The ones on the ground would herd him towards whatever kind of ambush the ones in the cars were going to set up. The park was not empty of people; in fact he was surprised to see dozens of what appeared to be transients milling about.

Joe pushed off the tree with his foot and began to jog through the trees. As he ran he spotted an area of woods where a thick layer of smoke flowed through the trees. He didn't know what was burning, and he didn't care. The smoke would mask his movements increasing his chances of survival.

He started to sprint faster as he approached the smoke filled woods. Safety of concealment was not the only reason he sprinted. The gang had spotted him and several let loose sporadic shots. The shots struck no where near him, but they spurred him on nonetheless.

Then he was in the thick of the smoke. He had to slow himself down, not only because the smoke made it hard to see, but it choked him as well. Joe tried his best to slow his breathing. His chest was heaving from the sprint as he tried to fill his lungs with air.

Joe walked for another ten minutes threw the hazy smoke. Soon he came out of the smoke. Scanning an open area he spotted the end of the park. Across the street he could see several looted buildings. He sprinted for the buildings as fast as he could. Jumping a chain link fence he crossed the road to the buildings.

The streets were littered with debris, and few people milled about. Weaving his way through the people and trash Joe made it to an open doorway and entered. He took a quick glance around the small food mart and found it to be almost completely looted. Walking towards the back he looked for any occupants.

No one was in the building. He made his way back to the front of the store picking up a small eight ounce bottle of water that lay on the floor. He twisted the cap and turned the bottle up over his open mouth. In several gulps he finished off the bottle and threw it back down among the other trash. He made his way to the broken out window and took a knee.

He peered out into the smoke filled park looking for his pursuers. Then he saw two of them break through the wall of smoke. Joe eased his way back in the store and made his way behind the counter and took a knee again.

He watched as several more of the gang members came out of the park. Then two of the cars pulled up on the street just down from the store. Two of the thugs walked up to the passenger window. He could not make out what they were saying but they all seemed to be very animated.

Then one of the men who had been leaning in the car window stood up and walked around the car. Joe had to move down the counter so that he could see where he went. The thug was saying something to an older man dressed in a dirty brown overcoat and a grungy looking red knap sack on his back. The man shrugged his shoulders. The thug reared back and slapped the old man across the face. He stumbled back, and the thug reached forward and grabbed him by the coat lapels. Joe's hand subconsciously went to the butt of his pistol.

More of the gang showed up on the street. They milled about the cars looking around, searching for Joe. Suddenly the old man doubled over and dropped to his knees as the thug drove his fist into the old man's stomach. The old man struggled for breath, his arms clasped tightly to his stomach. The thug reached down and grabbed the old man by his shaggy gray hair and yelled at him again. Joe just barely caught some of his words, "Where is he…?" The old man lifted his arm and pointed to the right, away from Joe.

The thug brought his knee up to the old man's face as he pulled his head down. The old man's body recoiled back after the cruel blow; he then slumped sideways and fell to the ground. The gang member ran back to the waiting cars. Again Joe could not hear him, but the man pointed down the street. The four cars made U-turns and the other gang members jogged down the center of the street, shoving, and punching people out of the way.

Joe was about to stand when he noticed one of the gang members standing in the middle of the street. The thug had a look of suspicion on his swarthy face. He slowly began to walk towards the store that Joe was hiding in. He held a sawed off pump shotgun in his hands, and Joe could make out a bandolier of shot shells wrapped around his waist.

Joe ducked down behind the counter and began making his way to the end of the counter so that he could head out the back door. He stopped and picked up what appeared to be a cut off shovel handle about sixteen inches long. The center was hollowed out and filled with lead. He then made his way to the back of the store. He had to dodge into a small alcove as he heard the thug's feet crunch on the broken glass in the front door of the store.

Joe tried to calm his breathing and slow his heart rate down. He just knew the thug could hear his heart hammering in his chest. Joe thought his heart would explode when the thug racked a round into the chamber of the shotgun. The man had to be at the doorway that leads into the back room. Joe slowly eased the shovel handle over his head.

Joe tried to melt into the wall behind him as the barrel of the shotgun came into view. Then it stopped. Joe heard the thug twist the bathroom doorknob. As the thug jerked the door open he moved forward turning his back to Joe as he peered into the dark bathroom. The man let the door handle go and began to turn. As he turned his body Joe leaped into action. His right arm came down and he delivered a furious blow to the thug's temple.

The thug's knees buckled as he dropped to the ground. Joe kicked out with his left foot striking the shotgun, and effectively knocking it from the thug's hands. As his foot came back to the floor Joe swung the handle directly into the man's face. Joe aimed for the nerve ending that lies just below the nose and top of a person's lips. That's exactly where Joe hit. The thug fell forward as teeth and blood gushed from his mouth. As the thug hit the floor Joe came down with his last blow hitting the man at the base of the skull. The man's skull broke and fractured. Small splinters of bone shot into the thug's brain killing him. His body shook in a shuttering spasm twice and was still.

Joe's body shook with adrenaline as he watched a pool of blood form under the man's head. Sliding the handle in his cargo pocket he looked around him. Several canned goods lay in the floor by the cooler door. He pulled off his pack and unzipped it. He shoved the cans in the bulging pack. He then rolled the man over and stripped him of his shotgun and bandolier. He wrapped the bandolier around his waist. Then he patted the man down for anything else of value. In the front right pocket he found two boxes of .22 magnum shells. In the other pocket he found a small six shot derringer revolver. He slipped it and the shells into his front pockets and stood.

He picked up two more small bottles of water as he walked out the front of the store. He looked to his right and saw the old man sitting in the middle of the street. His legs were spread out in front of him and he was holding his face.

Joe walked up to the old man and knelt beside him. "I appreciate what you did for me old timer."

"I can't stand those fuckers, always messing with people, the names Taylor Williams." The old man held out his hand.

Joe took the old man's hand and shook it. "Joe Donovan is my name, are you hungry Taylor?"

The old man stood up with Joe's help. "You bet I am."

The two walked back to the store and stood at the counter. The old man regarded the dead thug in the back room. "Nice work. Wish I was still young enough to do that to some of them scum."

Joe opened his pack and pulled out two cans of chili, a can of soup, and a can of black eye peas, a can of pears and one of the water bottles on the counter top. "These are for helping me."

A tear welled up in the old man's eyes. "In normal times I would have refused your offer. I haven't eaten a thing in two days. The gang bangers steal my food every time they find me. I appreciate it." Taylor wiped the tears from his eyes struggling to regain his pride.

Joe walked over to a rack that was still standing. He had spotted a manual can opener hanging from the rack. Taking it off, he pitched it to Taylor. "You'll probably need that."

Taylor caught the can opener and gave Joe a salute with it. He then began to open the can of pears. Joe walked back to the front window and examined the surrounding area. "Besides the gang should I worry about anyone else around here?"

Taylor answered his mouth full of pears. "Naw, there is mostly old homeless folks like myself wandering around here. Most everyone else has cleared out." Joe turned to watch Taylor turn the can of pears up gulping down the juice left inside. "Man that was great!" Taylor pulled the red knapsack from his shoulders and unzipped it. He stuffed the remaining cans in the pack.

Joe walked back up to the old man. "Is there any good route that leads out of the city?"

Taylor swung the pack back on his shoulders. "Sure a couple of blocks south of here are a railroad track. It heads southeast. The trains are still running, but not regularly though. Where are you headed Joe?"

"I'm going to try to make my way back south to Florence, Alabama."

Taylor whistled. "That's a long way on foot. Now if you can hop a train you could be there in a day. You know I worked in Florence back in the early sixties. Nice town then, don't know about now though."

Joe glanced out the front window and noticed the waning daylight. Taylor any place around here I can hole up for the night?"

Taylor turned and headed for the back door, stepping over the dead gang banger. "Sure is. If you follow me I will put you up at my place."

Joe followed the old man out the back and into the back alley. They made there way along several alley ways. Joe was surprised to see how many homeless people wandered through the alleys. "Taylor I didn't realize there were so many homeless folks in Memphis."

The old man trudged on ahead of Joe, looking back over his shoulder as he answered. "Well the numbers have swelled since the economy went into the crapper. Most stay out of sight of the general public. If we don't folks call the police on us and we wind up in the pokey. Of course the pokey is where you want to be during the winter. I usually go in a store and blatantly steal some gum when winter hits. The police show up, and then it's a cot, and three hot meals a day.

Now that the crap has knocked the fan off the table though, no one needs to keep out of sight. Hell, everyone is dang near homeless now."

"How did you wind up on the streets Taylor?" Joe asked.

"It's a long story Joe."

"I've got plenty of time." Joe said as he stepped over a dead dog.

"Well in '67 I went and joined the Marines. I was twenty two at the time, and jobs weren't paying much around here. My two best friends joined up with me. Before you would know it we were in the 'Nam. We were two weeks shy of heading home on the Freedom bird and were out on a patrol. We run into two companies of NVA regulars. They damned near wiped out the entire platoon. There were just six of us left when the Lieutenant called in arty on our position. That broke the NVA and they booked for the hills. I came away without a scratch from that, but my two childhood friends Dale and Ryan never made it home.

I did three more tours after that. I was kind of a lost soul. I wanted to kill every gook I could find. I never got hit the entire time until my last month in country." Taylor turned and began walking backwards. He lifted the front of his shirt as he walked. Joe took in a hideous scar almost eight inches wide covering his stomach from left to right. Taylor lowered his shirt and turned walking on. "We were charging this fortified enemy hill when one of the little yellow bastards threw a grenade in front of me. I dove sideways, but it was too late. The dang thing went off and ripped me wide open.

Anyway I made it back to the states, and when I recovered I wandered from job to job for awhile. I got married and had a son. His name is Taylor Jr. I got divorced after a few years, lost my job and kind of lost it mentally for awhile and ended up on the street."

"Where is your son now?" Joe asked.

"Well that boy done went and made me proud. He finished high school and got a full scholarship to West Point. He's a Major now, went into the infantry. Sure did make me proud even though he's an Army dog now." The two were quiet for awhile as they walked.

"When is the last time you heard from him Taylor?"

I talked to him two weeks ago. He shipped out for Korea. I don't know if he's alive or dead. I may never know."

Joe wiped the sweat from his brow and continued to prod the man. He was genuinely interested in Taylor's life. "You have a telephone at your place? Is that how he called you?"

Taylor let out a long baritone laugh. "There ain't a phone at my place Joe." He reached into his jacket pocket. "This is the 21st century man, get with the times." Taylor held up a cell phone. "Jr. bought me this phone so we could keep in touch. Before he shipped out, I talked to him two or three times a week. Sure do hope he's alright."

"How come you never got back up on your feet? Did you get strung out on drugs or alcohol?"

"Naw, I saw what drugs can do to a man when I was in 'Nam. That's some evil stuff. I never got the taste for liquor. I guess after living for years on the street it became normal to me. I get a VA disability check every month direct deposit, keeps food in my belly. About twice a year I would get some new clothes, get cleaned up and would go see Jr. wherever he was stationed. He tried to get me to move in with him, but I don't want to put that kind of burden on his wife and family.

He has a knock out wife and two beautiful girls. They headed up to Minnesota where her folks live when things went bad. I'm sure they're okay. Well this is it Joe." Taylor stopped in front of a vacant building and held his arms out wide.

The two went in and climbed up to the top floor. Joe unlocked a padlock and they went inside. The room was large and had old weather beaten furniture in it. A small wood burning stove sat beside the window, the metal chimney tube stuck out of the bottom window pane. The place was neat and well organized. "It ain't much Joe but there ain't any rent. This building has been abandoned for four years. Two other vets live on the first two floors. We keep the riff raff out, and the cops leave us alone. Grab a seat." Taylor waved his hand towards the couch.

The room was getting dark as the sun set so Taylor got up and lit a small oil lamp. Joe pilfered through his pack and came out with two cans of chili. "Are you ready for some supper Taylor?"

"Shoot yeah! You're buying so I'm cooking." Taylor caught the two cans as Joe flipped them over to him one at a time. Taylor then rustled the coals in the bottom of the stove and put some wood on the glowing red embers.

An hour later the two had finished eating and were engaged in some small talk. Joe stretched and let out a yawn. Leaning over he unzipped his pack. Digging past the can goods he pulled out a poncho liner. He stood and spread it over the couch, and sat back down. He pulled his boots off and lay down. "I've got to get some sleep Taylor. Goodnight."

"Good night Joe." Taylor eased the big bright orange recliner back and kicked off his boots. He too pulled out a poncho liner and rapped it around him.

Joe woke to the smell of cooking meat. He opened his eyes and took in Taylor sitting in front of the wood stove. He held a cloth in his hand that was rapped around a thin metal pole. On the pole was some kind of carcass. "What are you cooking Taylor?"

Taylor looked over his shoulder. "Brian, the guy who lives below me, snared four rabbits this morning. He brought me one. It's about done you in the mood for some rabbit?"

Joe sat up. "You bet I am."

Taylor cut the rabbit up into equal shares and handed Joe a plate. The meat burned Joe's mouth when he bit into it, but it was the best rabbit he had ever tasted. The two ate in silence enjoying the morning quiet. When they were done Joe pulled out his small coffee pot, and coffee.

"How would you like some coffee Taylor?" Joe said as he held up the coffee pot and bag of coffee.

"I haven't had any coffee in four days. I would love a cup." Taylor got up and went over to a plastic water jug. He filled the pot with water, and then Joe added the coffee. Fifteen minutes later the two enjoyed one cup apiece.

When they were done Joe cleaned out the coffee pot and put it back in his pack. He took out a small toilet kit and brushed his teeth. When he was done he pulled out his empty water bladder. "Taylor can you spare some water?"

"Sure. Bring it over here and we will fill it up." Joe walked over and held the bladder while Taylor poured the water.

Once it was filled Joe walked back to the pack and inserted the bladder back in place. "Thanks Taylor. I didn't know where I was going to find some clean water to drink. I have water purification tablets, but it still makes me nervous using them. You never know if some type of chemical or something will be in water that you find."

Taylor sipped the last bit of his coffee as he watched Joe shrug the pack onto his shoulders. "Are you heading out now Joe?"

"Yeah I've got to get going. The sooner I make it home the better. I've got a brother who is a financial genius, but when it comes to things like what's happening now he'll be lost. He's got a wife and two girls and only one of them could probably handle herself in this situation."

Taylor nodded his head in understanding as he stood to shake Joe's hand goodbye. "Good luck Joe." The two men shook hands and walked to the door. They walked down stairs to a fire exit door. Taylor reached out to open it for Joe.

Joe reached out and stopped Taylor from opening the door. "Before I go Taylor I just wanted to say thanks for not telling those punks where I was at." Taylor began to respond, but Joe held up his hand to silence him. "Most folks would not have done that. So I want to give you a couple of things."

"You don't have to do that Joe. You already shared your food with me. That's enough."

Joe reached down in his cargo pocket and pulled out the lead filled shovel handle. "This will help knock some sense into them boys if they bother you again."

Taylor hefted the heavy handle in his hands. "Thanks, I'm sure it will do a number on them."

"And if that doesn't make them see the light maybe this will." Joe pulled out the small derringer, then the two boxes of ammo. He placed them in Taylor's other hand.

"Dang Joe you might need that."

"I've already got two guns. This shotgun and pistol should get me where I need to go. So take the club and pistol and stay safe. I wouldn't have either if you hadn't sent those thugs in the wrong direction." He patted Taylor on the shoulder and walked out the door. "See you around friend. Look me up if you ever get to Florence again."

Three hours later Joe was headed southeast along the railroad tracks that Taylor had told him about. He traveled slowly not making much distance. Anytime he saw people or something suspicious he would find the nearest cover and hide. He did not relish getting in anymore shootouts, or fights.

As Joe rounded the bend he saw a car leaning over sideways just off the railroad crossing ahead. Joe made his way up into the tree line, he took a knee and took the shotgun, and pack from his shoulders. Out of the front pouch of his pack he pulled out a monocular. Lifting it to his eye he gazed at the scene before him.

A blonde haired woman was dangling through the open driver side window. Her left arm outstretched as if she was reaching for something on the ground. The front window had bullet holes perforating through it. The rear passenger side door was open and the body of a man lay crumpled on the ground, one leg still inside the car.

Joe worked the eyeglass farther out and panned the area around the car. No buildings were close by, and he saw no people. He put the monocular back in his pack and then hefted the pack back onto his shoulders. Picking up the shotgun, he pushed the slide release and eased the bolt back and ensured a round was chambered. There was a round in the chamber so he snapped off the safety, and began moving through the trees.

When he reached the end of the wooded area he moved up behind a tree. He searched for any signs of a trap, and when he was satisfied it was safe he moved cautiously forward. As he approached the car he could tell both people were dead. He moved around to the passenger side of the car and found the body of a teenage boy. He lay face up with both arms outstretched, his face was swollen and bloody, and his throat had been slashed. Joe just shook his head as he looked into the young boy's dull blue, dead eyes. Two suitcases lay torn open nearby, clothes and other personal belongings were strewn about.

Joe looked around and found nothing that he could use. When he looked in the car he saw that the keys were still in the ignition. Opening the passenger door he reached in and took out the keys. He made his way to the trunk of the car and pooped it open.

Inside he found family photo albums, and other personal effects. Crammed into the right hand corner near the taillight Joe found a brown grocery bag with the top folded over. He lifted it up and found it to be half full of something. Joe took the bag and headed for the tree line again to check out the contents. He already felt he had been out in the open to long.

Once out of the sun and in the shade Joe sat with his back against a tree. He was overjoyed when he saw the contents of the bag. There were several cans of food, three bottles of water, and four Snicker bars. Well it looked like lunch time.

Joe set up his Sterno stove and opened two cans of chicken noodle soup. He cooked the soup in the cans not wanting to dirty up his dishes.

After the first can was steaming hot he pulled it off and started heating the second while he ate.

He finished both cans of soup quickly. Though nothing had occurred in the past few hours he was on pins and needles, and his body needed fuel. Unwrapping a Snickers bar and devoured it in three large bites. He finished his lunch with two bottles of water. His hunger and thirst satisfied Joe packed up and headed out again.

Joe walked slowly on for another three hours and was nearing a residential area. He felt like he was being watched. He left the tracks and headed down into the ditch. He walked another fifty yards or so and stopped, he kneaded the pump of the shotgun. He sensed something was wrong. Joe moved slowly up the embankment away from the tracks hoping to catch a glimpse of the danger he sensed.

As he neared the top he spotted a young black man dressed in blue with a blue bandanna on his head. Joe immediately knew the man was part of the gang that had chased him yesterday. The man raised a pistol and fired a round off and turned to run.

Joe dropped to the ground his shotgun coming to his shoulder. The man was now about thirty yards away, really too far for the range of the sawed off shotgun. Joe squeezed the trigger anyway. The man stumbled, but continued around the corner of a house.

"Crap!" Using the butt of the shotgun to help him stand Joe turned and ran down the hill and across to the other side of the tracks. As he neared the top of the other side he looked over his shoulder to see about eleven gang members sixty yards away running his direction.

Joe hoped over a chain link fence and ran for the maze of houses and streets ahead of him. As he neared one of the houses he turned and fired at the pursuing group. He knew he would not hit any but it had the desired effect he was looking for. The gang scattered in several directions returning wild shots as Joe turned to run.

He ran for several blocks his chest heaving; he caught an occasional glimpse of the pursuing gang. He was going to have to find a place to hide and soon. He was tiring to fast. The men in the gang were at least fifteen years his junior and were still fresh.

The neighborhood he had run into was a run down area. He stuck out like rice in a pot of black eye peas, it was a black neighborhood. He noticed blue graffiti spray painted on the sides of businesses and homes. Joe knew he was deep in the heart of the pursuing gang's territory.

As he crossed a yard he saw two men in blue shirts talking beside their cars. One of the cars had the engine running, and loud rap music blared from a set of speakers that took up the entire back seat. The two gang members didn't see Joe until he was right up on them. One reached into his waistband while the other walked towards him, swaggering as he came forward. "What you doing in my hood whitey?"

Joe answered his question with a blast from the shotgun as he ran forward firing from the hip. The pellets shredded into the man's chest causing him to stumble backwards and then fall to the ground. The second man had just got his pistol out of his waist when Joe fired the second round.

Joe's aim was off and the barrel bounced as he ran. The pellets from the shotgun blast caught the thug in both thighs, and the groin area. The man discharged the pistol as his fingers gripped in reflex from the pain. The barrel was pointed down when the gun went off. The round drove into the man's kneecap bursting it like an exploding watermelon. He fell forward screaming in pain.

Joe charged forward still running at top speed and slammed the butt of the shotgun into his face before he hit the ground. The force of the butt stroke was tremendous smashing out the man's front teeth and knocking him unconscious.

Joe slid to a halt and jumped into the idling car. He slammed the door and threw the car into reverse. Ice-T's song "Cop Killer" blared from the speakers. Charging towards him Joe saw the gang members who had been chasing him come running around the corner. Joe slammed on the emergency brake and cut the wheel hard right. The car slung around in a perfect "J" turn. Once he straightened out he released the emergency brake and threw the car in drive. The tires squealed as the tore into the pavement.

Looking in the rearview mirror Joe saw several of the gang jumping into the other car. "When will these guys quit." Joe said as he reached forward and shut the stereo off. Joe began evasive maneuvers, taking side roads, and alleys. Black faces stared at him as he flew threw the city streets.

"I've got to get out of here. I sure don't want to die here, and not in this car." The car was a canary yellow 1971 Cadillac. It had a white vinyl roof; the windows were tinted bright yellow. The dashboard and steering wheel were covered in fake white fur. A set of big fuzzy dice hung from the rearview mirror. Joe was cruising in the ultimate pimp mobile.

Joe eventually made it back to the railroad tracks and crossed over them to the other side. He had not seen the other car for twenty minutes. He slowed the car down to about ten miles an hour. He drove for five more blocks and turned right. He jammed on the brakes when he saw what was ahead. Two blocks up was a military road block. Army soldiers were hustling two car loads of people out of their cars. The soldiers searched the trunks and cars and then allowed the people to grab a few suitcases. They were then lead like sheep to a waiting five ton truck.

One of the soldiers noticed Joe and waved for him to come forward. "Last time one of your guys did that they shot my truck up." Joe stomped the gas and cut the wheel right and turned down the street. Joe looked over his shoulder as he turned seeing the soldier unlimber his rifle. Then he was out of sight as he passed by the first house. "I was to fast for you this time, soldier boy."

Joe sped down the street blowing through stop signs. As he crossed one intersection he looked left and saw two Humvees heading down the road towards him. "You're not putting me in some camp." Joe pulled his seat belt on and floored the gas. He rocketed through several intersections the low slung car shooting up sparks with every bump in the road.

Joe turned right then back left and held the gas wide open. As he approached the intersection two older model cars came into the intersection. The occupants were clad in blue. Joe slammed on the brakes and cut the wheel left. The other cars had locked their brakes down too. Everything happened to fast for Joe to take in.

The front right bumper of his car slammed into the left front edge of the lead car. Joe's car spun wildly. It hit the curb sideways and rolled twice before coming to rest in someone's front yard. The gang members in the lead car were knocked sideways, and then crushed from behind as the second car plowed into it.

Joe sat stunned shaking his head to clear it. Looking back over his shoulder he saw the other two cars. He saw movement in both and then one of the doors to the rear car opened up a gang-banger stumbled out.

Joe unsnapped his seatbelt and retrieved the shotgun and his pack that lay in the passenger floorboard. He got out dragging the pack and shotgun. He took a knee behind the car and put the pack on, he then filled up the magazine tube of the shotgun. He made his way to the front of the car and peered over the hood. Seven gang members had piled out and still seemed disoriented. An eighth was leaned forward on the steering wheel. His chin caught on the top of the steering wheel, his neck broken.

Joe shouldered the shotgun and took aim. He knew he was going to lose this fight. He didn't think he could run much farther. His body ached all over, he was going to stand and fight. The front bead sight centered on the nearest gang member who had just reached in his pocket and pulled out a gun, the man started forward towards Joe.

Joe fired the shotgun, catching the man full in the chest. The thug just simply collapsed where he stood. As Joe pumped another round into the chamber, other gang-bangers came to their senses and began to open fire. Joe fired again and then ducked down for cover. Rounds tore into the shielding car.

Suddenly Joe tensed as the sound of heavy continuous booming hit his ears. Joe looked up over the hood to see several gang members' bodies twisting like marionettes on a string. Others fired at something to Joe's right. Joe looked right to see two hummers with M-60 gunners mounted in the turret. Not one to look a gift horse in the mouth, Joe turned and fled behind the house.

He jumped several fences and ran on, the sounds of the heavy machine guns, and the occasional pop form one of the gang member's pistols echoed behind him. Joe crossed over several blocks and slowed to a walk. He pulled the drinking tube from his Camelback to his lips. Once his thirst was quenched he walked into some large bushes and sat. Looking at his watch it was 4:55pm. He was going to have to find someplace soon to get some much needed rest.

After a ten minute rest he stood and surveyed the area. The homes were no longer shabby looking. It appeared he was in a lower middle class neighborhood. It also appeared that most had been abandoned and looted, nothing stirred before him. Joe spotted a two story house just ahead. He would head for it and sleep there for the night.

It was nine o'clock at night and Joe hadn't hurt this bad in years. Every muscle in his body cried out for relief. Joe had eaten some canned soup and a Snickers bar for supper. He paced the house going from window to window, watching for danger. Once he had seen an Army patrol walk by, twice two cars loaded down with gang members had crept by.

He decided it was time to get some sleep. He popped two Aleve tablets in his mouth and washed them down with a mouthful of water. Pulling out his poncho liner Joe crawled onto the bed and fell asleep.

He woke around four in the morning and ate a cold breakfast of Spaghetti O's. Taking two more Aleve tablets he finished the last bottle of water. He looked out the window and saw nothing moving in the still dark streets. It was time to leave.

Joe stayed in the shadows as much as possible until the rising sun stole that bit of security from him. Eventually he found the railroad tracks, and made his way to them. The morning was cool and quiet.

After several hours of slow walking the cityscape around him began to change. The businesses and homes became larger and fancier. He wondered how close to Germantown he was. Joe stopped suddenly as the sound of several engines reached his ears.

Running from the tracks he made his way to a strip mall and climbed through the broken windows. Hiding behind a turned over shelf Joe watched as a Army patrol drove by, the machine gunner's swiveling the barrels of their weapons left to right. A five ton truck followed with several civilians sitting in back. As they drove out of sight Joe let out a sigh of relief. The government wasn't assisting anyone. They were rounding them up like cattle and taking over the city streets. No wonder he had not seen many people this morning.

Once the sound of the patrol faded Joe climbed out of the storefront window and began to walk, hopefully in the right direction to reach Germantown. An hour later he saw the Germantown city limit sign several blocks ahead. He stopped to wipe the sweat from his forehead. "Thank God." Joe asked for thanks just a little to soon as a bullet zipped past his ear.

Joe didn't look back he just ran. Several more shots were fired from different weapons. Joe rounded the corner of a building and stopped. He slung the shotgun on his shoulder and drew his pistol. Peeking around the corner he saw several gang members dressed in blue walking his way. They were about sixty yards away. "Who said today's youth weren't driven."

Joe took aim at the lead man. His front sight post rested just below the man's chin and Joe squeezed the trigger. The group of thugs froze for a second then scattered in several different directions returning fire as they ran. They were not sure exactly where the shot came from. The man Joe shot just stood there for several more seconds holding his chest. Then he slowly sat down in the middle of the street. One of his buddies ran up and kneeled beside him, trying to pull his hand away to see the damage.

Joe aimed carefully and fired. His round struck the kneeling man in the right kidney. The man threw his head back, and fell to the ground. He gritted his teeth and grunted in pain.

Joe turned and ran up a lightly wooded slope to the next strip mall. Running around the back of the businesses Joe spotted a dumpster next to one of the buildings. Running hard he made it to the dumpster and climbed on top of it, and then to the roof of the building.

Spotting a service access Joe ran for it. He could hear the gang members coming up the hill. The service door was unlocked and Joe went in and sat down on the stairs listening for pursuit.

Thirty minutes went by when Joe heard someone pull on the door at the bottom of the stairs. Luckily the door was locked and whoever it was didn't try to force their way through the door. Joe could now hear the gang members going through the already looted store below him, searching for him. Within an hour they were gone from the area.

Joe went back to the roof top and surveyed the surrounding area. He saw nothing. Going back to the service door he made his way downstairs and into the store. He left through the front doors and headed towards Germantown.

Three hours later Joe ran across HWY 72 and towards one of the gated communities. He climbed over the brick wall and into a backyard. Joe made his way towards the front yard.

The neighborhood appeared deserted some of the houses were burnt to the ground. Other's had doors kicked in, furniture and clothing strewn across the yards. Even the wealthy had been affected by this calamity.

Joe made his way to one of the large homes and went to the front steps. The door was ajar. As quietly as possible he entered the home. Few things were disturbed, but it had obviously been gone through. Joe stepped forward and stopped before he stepped on the plush white carpet. He looked down and at himself. He was filthy, and covered in grime, and mud.

Joe made himself realize that this home was most likely abandoned and moved into the living room. He searched the house and found no one. The only thing that had not been stolen was a bag of rice. He put this in his pack. He discovered that the house still had water pressure and he immediately filled his water bladder up. Joe walked around the interior of the house and secured all of the doors and windows as best as possible. He ate supper shortly before night fall. When he could not stand it any longer he stripped down and bathed in a cold shower. When he was done he dressed again and climbed into bed exhausted.

Joe jerked awake, and looked around the living room confused for a moment. He must have fallen back asleep. Joe set up and stood and stretched. He reached down for the pack and shotgun. His heart hammered in his chest when he saw the shotgun was gone. After a few seconds he sorted out his mind and realized he had left it on the kitchen counter. He walked quickly back to the kitchen and was relieved to see the shotgun still lying where he had left it while he was cleaning his pistol.

Joe looked out the window in the kitchen again just to make sure nothing had changed while he had dozed off. "I've got to get back home." He said to himself. He realized that the past few days had not only been physically demanding, but mentally exhausting. Leaving the shotgun in the kitchen had been a serious mistake. A mistake that could have gotten him killed. He needed to get home as soon as possible and be with his family. Though they may not be prepared for what had happened, he could teach them, and they would be there to watch his back.

Going back to the living room, shotgun in hand this time, Joe reached over and picked up the pack and put it on. He was leaving and leaving now. He decided he would head back to the train tracks; he would follow them out of Germantown. Once he was past the city limits he would hunker down and wait for a south bound train. According to Taylor the tracks led south through Mississippi to Corinth. From Corinth they went straight to Colbert County in Alabama. Joe headed out the front door still concentrating on his route as he walked.

Once across the state line he had two options. He could hop off the train in Cherokee, and make his way on foot up to the Natchez Trace. Once on the Trace he could follow it and cross the Tennessee River into Lauderdale County. It would be a long walk, and the Trace Bridge might have a roadblock set up by Army troops or thugs.

His second and best option was to stay on the train and wait until it crossed the river. Once across the river he knew the train would travel near Florence Industrial Park. He could jump off the train there and make his way to Chisholm Rd. Follow it south until he reached Wright Dr. Once on Wright Dr. it would take him to Cloverdale Rd. Then all he would have to do is cross Cloverdale Rd. and he would be in his brother's neighborhood.

Within twenty minutes of leaving the house Joe found the tracks and followed them south. He managed to make it out of town without incident. "I guess my little shadows in blue decided to give up on me."

Joe approached a sharp curve in the tracks and decided he would wait in the woods beside the curve. The train would have to slow and he would have a better shot at boarding a moving train. He just hoped a train would show today. He did not have the supplies for an extended wait.

Once in the tree line Joe checked his surroundings for any hostiles. He found none so he dropped his pack, and rested the shotgun on it. He began doing some stretches hoping to loosen up his aching muscles. After fifteen minutes of stretching his body felt a little better, but not much. Glancing at his watch he was stunned to see it was only a little after ten. He felt like he had been waiting an eternity.

"Well I might as well take a nap." He said as he kneeled down to get his camouflage poncho. He decided to use it to cover up with. It might make him hot but it would definitely help conceal his position. Just as he unzipped his pack he heard the rumble of a southbound train.

Joe snatched his pack up and put it on and then slung his shotgun over his shoulder and ran to the edge of the woods. He gazed to the right and sure enough a train was headed his way. He could hear the breaks squeal and the big diesel motors powering down as the train approached the sharp curve.

As the engines passed Joe stepped behind a tree, and he watched several empty flat cars go by then stepped out into the clearing by the tracks. Even though the train was going slow, being so close to colossal train cars was enough to make anyone a little apprehensive about jumping up on one.

To his right Joe saw what he was looking for. Several open freight cars were approaching. Joe began to trot away from them, the faster moving cars passing him by. He let the first car pass and as the second approached he reached out and grabbed hold of the side.

Joe placed both hands on the open doorway and simultaneously twisted his body and pushed up with all he had. Once his chest was halfway into the car he swung a leg up and rolled into the empty car. He sat up with a huge grin on his face. "I'm the man!" He was heading home.

Joe took off the pack and shotgun and rested them near the door. He felt the train start to pick up speed. It must have cleared the curve. Soon the train was traveling at over fifty miles per hour. Joe did some quick math in his head. He should be in Florence in less than two hours. Joe rewarded his good fortune by eating the last Snickers bar.

Forty minutes later Joe was sitting in the open door, his legs dangled over the side. He watched the passing country side. He looked to his left at HWY 72. He noticed that the closer to Corinth he got the more cars he saw on the road. The cars weren't moving though. They were abandoned. Two miles outside of Corinth the cars were stacked bumper to bumper in both lanes. Clothing, suitcases, backpacks, and an occasional body lay among the silent cars.

As the train rolled through Corinth he saw virtually no people. Those that he did see seemed to walk as if in a trance. Their clothes appeared squalid and soiled. Like the skyline in Memphis, Joe saw large black pillars of smoke rising skyward. Joe wondered to himself how such a great nation could topple so easily. With all of its technology, military might, and wealth the nation's leaders had failed to set up a system to counter, and maintain itself in the event of a catastrophic event. The result would probably be the same if the country had been racked with some type of natural disaster, or medical event such as the plague. Everyone's attitude it seemed in America was "It will never happen here." Well it had happened and Americans were paying the toll for their attitude, and so was the rest of the world.

Soon the train came to the eastern city limits of Corinth. The scene here was almost identical to the scene on the other side of the city. The line of cars stretched for almost four miles though. There were more bodies on this side also. Joe noticed many of the westbound cars had Alabama tags. The eastbound cars had mostly Mississippi tags. Obviously no one in either state's government advised people what was going on. The folks from 'Bama were probably fleeing to Corinth feeling it was safe, and the Mississippians were headed to Alabama for safety. Joe wondered how many thousands across the country had died just outside of cities thinking they were fleeing from danger or heading to safety.

Soon all Joe saw was country homes, and farms again. Some of the farms actually had tractors out in the fields working. "Well at least someone was prepared and ready to keep on living life." Joe thought.

Thirty minutes later Joe spotted the "Welcome To Alabama" sign. As he crossed the line he stood up and let out a Rebel yell that probably made Confederate soldiers in their graves smile with pride, and Yankee ones cringe in fear. It wouldn't be long now and he would be home.

Joe decided to stay on the train just before it reached Cherokee. He needed to go as far and as fast as he could. Soon the train crossed over into Lauderdale County. On the outskirts of Florence the train began to slow as it twisted its way through the woods. The train was at a crawl now as it went through the industrial park. Joe had his pack on and shotgun in hand as he stood in the door. Up ahead he spotted what he knew was Rose Dr.

Joe knew that just past Rose Dr. was a grassy field to the left. He would jump there before the train began to pick up speed again once it was outside of the industrial park. Joe readied himself as the train crossed the intersection. As soon as he saw the first patch of green grass Joe jumped. He landed on his feet and let his body roll when he hit. His roll ended almost picture perfect.

Joe sat on his knees and checked the barrel of his shotgun to make sure he had no obstructions. He got up and watched as the train went by. Several minutes later the train disappeared down the tracks. Joe moved forward at a quick pace.

It took Joe almost three hours to get to Cloverdale Rd. Florence it seemed had a lot more of its people around than even Memphis. "Guess the Army hasn't got around to rounding up folks in the smaller cities yet." No one bothered Joe as he walked. It seemed they were more intent on finding the essentials to live another day, than to fight for them. That was fine with Joe because that is all he intended to do. Most of the houses in the upper middle class neighborhood Joe had traveled through appeared to have been looted. Some had been burned to the ground. Some looked as if people were still living there.

Joe scanned the road in both directions as he prepared to sprint across the big six lane road. Seeing nothing he ran hard. Once on the other side he ran into a burned out shell of a home. He picked his way through the burned timbers and looked out back through a huge burned out hole. He saw no one.

It took Joe another fifteen minutes to reach his brother's house in the back of the neighborhood. It seemed the entire street was devoid of life. The front door of his brother's house stood open. Joe eased himself inside and stood motionless for a couple of minutes listening. Hearing nothing he stepped farther into the house.

Joe looked left and right and saw all of the bullet holes in both walls. He looked in the living room and saw a dark stain near his brother's recliner. He walked stiff legged knowing what the dark stain most likely was. Joe tried his hardest to maintain control but a tear still ran down the left side of his cheek.

Joe walked back towards the girl's bedrooms. Both were empty. Turning from Daphne's room he walked back to the hallways that lead to the master bedroom. The door frame that led to the hall where his brother's room was located had been shot out. Bullets had also punctured through on both walls. His brother's room was empty. He checked the garage next. Both cars were gone.

Joe walked into the kitchen and took his pack off. He went to the table to set it down. On the table was a note. Joe picked it up and began to read it.

Uncle Joe,

I hope you are okay. Things didn't go so well for us. Dad is dead, killed by a group of guys called the West Side Posse. They did some bad things to Daphne, and mom. I buried dad in the backyard. Dr. Morrison and some guy named Steve are coming to get us today. If you find this and I hope you do we will be at Dr. Morrison's place. I hope you remember where that is. I don't want to right it down in case someone else finds this note. I hope you are safe. Please come and find us I am sure Dr. Morrison will not mind if you stay with him too.

I Love You

C.

Joe sat in one of the chairs the note clutched in his hands. Though his brother had always been a bit uppity, he had been a good man, and a great husband and father. He always looked out for those in the family that were less fortunate, and never expected anything in return. Joe let the tears come. He knew he had to get them; his brother's family was now his responsibility.

An hour later Joe stood up and walked to the back door, as he looked down confused as he stepped on several coke cans. Shaking his head he walked out back. He spotted the wood cross that sat above a pad of cement. In the cement his brother's name, date of birth and death were inscribed. He stood there for awhile and thought back on some of the good times he had with his brother. He said a prayer for his soul and then made him a promise he would find his family and care for them.

As the sun set Joe found that he was not hungry. What he wanted to do was sleep but before he went to sleep though he needed to secure the house. He placed furniture in front of the back door. He moved the washer in front of the door that led into the garage. He picked up the coke cans and laid them in front of the front door. He then went into his brother's closet and took the shoestrings from several pairs of shoes. He tied them into a long thin chain. Then went to the kitchen and opened a drawer where he knew his brother kept a hammer, nails, and a few other tools for household needs.

He took two nails and put them into the studs on each side of the foyer entrance. He then took the shoestrings and tied them across the opening about ankle height. Then he bent the nails back so if someone tripped over the shoestrings they wouldn't pull it loose. He also placed some cans around the foyer area.

With that done he went to his brother's room taking his pack and shotgun with him. He kicked off his boots and lay down. Almost immediately he was asleep. He dreamed of nothing, his mind totally exhausted.

Joe was startled awake by the sounds of someone knocking over the coke cans in the foyer. He slipped out of bed and picked up his shotgun. He pushed a button on his watch. The luminous light showed him it was 5:40 am. Joe eased around the corner of the hall and kept the shotgun pointed towards the foyer entrance. He stepped into the laundry room and poked the shotgun and part of his face around the frame. It wasn't much cover but it was better than none.

After several minutes he heard one of the cans scrape against the tile floor. Joe could picture someone moving the cans aside with their foot trying to stay very quiet. Then suddenly a dark form fell forward tripped up by his ad hoc trip wire.

Joe charged forward. The man started to push up but Joe slammed his foot between the man's shoulder blades. He leaned over and placed the shotgun next to his head and racked a round into the chamber. "You even move, or look like you are going for that shotgun or anything else I will blow your damn head off. Do you understand?"

Bob Novacheck slowly turned his head towards the voice. The barrel of the shotgun moved to his forehead. "Mister I will do whatever you say. I didn't know you were here. I thought everyone on this block had left."

"So you're here to steal my brother's things, you sorry piece of shit."

Bob tensed as the man pushed the barrel harder against his forehead. "Oh shit!" was all Bob could say.

Chapter 26

Since returning home with the Donovan women, Steve had spent the past few days fortifying his home, and clearing out deadfalls and brush around his home. Though he lived on a back country road sporadic groups of refugees had been traveling the road in front of his house. The numbers had grown in the past two days. Some had stopped and asked for food, and water. Others wanted to know if any refugee centers had been located in Florence. So far none had become hostile.

Steve gave out water freely, while giving food only to those with children. He did not have the supplies to feed every person that walked down the road. Doc kept insisting that he, Amos, and Ben move to his place. Steve said he would after Daphne recovered enough mentally. He felt the she surely didn't need a man she did not know around, especially after what had happened to her. Amos refused outright. The old farmer said he would rather die than move from his farm.

Steve had received a call by CB from Doc this morning. Doc said he needed help chopping and stacking firewood. Steve had agreed to come over later in the morning. He felt uncomfortable though in the presence of Celina. The girl had turned eighteen two days ago. She was strikingly beautiful, and mature for her age. Every time he looked at her and admired her though, a feeling of guilt would wash over him. Diane had only been dead for only two weeks, but it seemed like two years.

Steve decided he would take an old short wave radio he had found in a chest when while straightening up to Doc's. Refugees had told several different stories about what was going on, some where just too hard to believe. They needed to find out what was going on out in the world.

Most of the refugees did talk about more attacks and total chaos outside of government controlled areas.

In the morning after he got up Steve decided he would take a walk. He wanted to head towards Florence and the outlying neighborhoods and get a feel for what was happening in his area.

Steve took another sip out of hi s canteen and went back to work with the sling blade. He had cleared out the brush almost 100 yards from his home. When he finished he decided that some time this week he would build some small log walls. He wanted them to be placed around the back of the property so if someone snuck up on him they would go to the walls to take cover while assaulting his position. The walls would not be sufficient enough to stop the rounds from his rifles though. He wanted to measure the distance from his house to these positions so he could set the dope on his sights to accurately hit the log walls.

Once someone committed to firing from the walls they would most likely feel the walls would protect them. The walls would not be of any advantage to an attacker. After they hunkered down for cover Steve would shoot through the walls and kill the attackers. He also needed to make sure the area around the walls had no adequate cover. An untrained person would assume the wall was the best cover around and not try to make it to something that would actually stop his rounds. Steve's mind continued to picture and devise ideas to make his place safe.

Maude and Daphne stood at the kitchen counter. Before them were different utensils and ingredients were laid out. Maude was explaining the process of making soap again to Daphne.

For the past three days Maude had tried to find different things for Daphne to do. She wanted to occupy her mind to help keep her from thinking about the physical and mental trauma she had been through.

At first she couldn't find a thing to interest young Daphne. Then yesterday afternoon she found Daphne in the bathroom smelling some of her fragranced soap that Maude had purchased on a trip to England. Maude had asked her if she would be interested in making her on fragranced soap. Daphne immediately perked up, her interest sparked. Maude helped her make two bars of soap yesterday. They had stayed up until nearly eleven o'clock finishing the bars of soap up.

Daphne had opened up to Maude. At first the lessons started with Daphne barely speaking a word. By six o'clock the two were laughing and talking as if they had known each other for years. Daphne seemed to enjoy her company. Maude truly enjoyed the time she had spent with the girl. She had always wanted a daughter but was never blessed with one.

Maude was not worried about Celina. The young woman seemed to be years ahead in maturity compared to most eighteen year olds. She didn't laugh much, and rarely smiled. The only time she really smiled was when Steve was around. Maude had thought the girl was going to melt in her chair when Steve gave her a present for her birthday. Steve had carved a small buck deer out of a piece of maple.

Maude knew what would keep Celina's mind occupied. She continually asked about Steve. The girl had a chance to win Steve's heart, and she had started to try at every chance she got. Maude was concerned for Steve though. She would watch his smiles disappear from his face from time to time while talking to Celina. She knew he was thinking of Diane. She hoped Steve would come to grips with her death. Though she loved Diane like a daughter, she knew Steve had to continue on with his life. In times like these she felt one had to find love whenever and however one could. Living a long life was not a sure thing anymore.

Maude jerked as Daphne put her hand on her shoulder. "Did you hear me Mrs. Morrison?"

Maude smiled down at Daphne. "Sorry dear I wasn't paying attention. My mind was elsewhere. What did you say?"

"Go over what I'm going to do one more time."

"Okay. This is what you're going to do. You're going to dissolve the lye in the boiling water. Remember you will use twelve ounces of lye. Once you've done that set it aside to cool. Don't breathe the fumes they can do all sorts of nasty things to you. That's why you going to do that part outside.

In the steel pot you will melt the Crisco, and coconut oil. Remember use thirty-eight ounces of solid Crisco, and twenty-four ounces of coconut oil. When it is melted add twenty-four ounces of olive oil. Then set it aside to cool.

Then you will grease your soap mold with Crisco. Next put the freezer paper on the bottom and both sides of the mold. Be sure not to forget to grease the paper with Crisco.

When both the oils and lye mixture have cooled to about ninety degrees you are ready to blend it. This will take anywhere from ten to forty minutes. Slowly pour the lye/water mixture into the oils. Then stir it real consistently don't beat it like you would eggs when making a cake. If you see bubbles in the mixture you are stirring to fast. Once you start to see traces, pour in eight ounces of oatmeal and begin to mix it in. Then pour four ounces of the perfume I gave you into the mix.

Once everything is mixed up pour it into your mold. Then cover the mold, and then wrap it in towels.

Then we are going to let it sit for eighteen hours. When it's wrapped up the soap's temperature will rise to about 160 degrees. Once it has cooled down we will uncover it. Then we let it sit for twelve hours. After it sits we dump it out and cut it into bars. But then we have to wait three to six weeks to let it cure.

Now have you got all of that or do I need to go over it again?"

"I've got it." Daphne said as she reached for the box of lye.

Maude glanced out the kitchen window to see Steve pulling up in the black truck he and Herb had acquired. "Hey, Steve's here."

Maude pulled off her apron as she walked towards the hallway to go let Steve in. She had to jump back as Celina dashed by her for the front door.

"Sorry Mrs. Morrison!" Celina said as she ran by. Maude just smiled and shook her head.

Steve turned into Doc's drive and shut down the engine. As he got out of the truck the front door jerked open as Celina stepped out on the porch. "Hey Celina, how are you doing this morning?"

"I am doing well." The young woman said as she leaned back against the door frame. Maude stepped around her and came onto the porch.

"Good morning Maude."

"Good morning Steve. Are you here to help Herb with the firewood?"

"Yes mam." Steve pulled his AK-47 out of the truck and walked for the front door.

"Well he's around back stacking some wood now. You two don't be long dinner will be ready in about an hour and a half." Maude turned her attention to Celina. "Celina, would you mind giving me a hand with lunch?"

"Sure I will help Mrs. Morrison." Celina said as she disappointedly turned to walk back inside. Maude stepped aside to let her pass, and then turned to follow as she shut the door behind her.

Steve was both disappointed and glad at the same time that Celina had gone back inside. He had really wanted to talk to her, but felt guilty about it. He walked to the back of the house to help Doc.

Thirty minutes later Doc and Steve had finished stacking wood and had begun to split some more. When Steve remembered that he had forgotten to tell Doc about the short wave radio. "Hey I forgot to tell you I brought a short wave radio over. After we finish up with the wood and lunch do you want to crank up the generator and see if we can find out what's going on?"

Doc rested the ax against a tree stump. "Why didn't you tell me you had a short wave? We could've been listening for important news."

Steve took off his gloves and put them in his back pocket. "Heck Doc, if I had remembered I had it I would've. I found it in a chest in my bedroom when I was straightening up this morning."

Doc started walking by Steve headed for his workshop grabbing Steve's arm as he passed. "Forget the wood, let's go get some wire and make an antenna."

Once in the shop Doc and Steve started looking for old electrical wire, or stereo wire Doc was sure he had. Ten minutes later Doc found it. "Here it is!" He said as he opened an old storage bin under his work bench.

"Steve, open my tool box and get my utility razor." Doc said as he uncoiled the wire.

Steve found the razor and handed it to Doc. Doc began to peel back the plastic wire covering. Five minutes later the forty feet of wire was exposed. "Let's go put this up." The two walked from the shop and towards the house. Steve carried a ladder while Doc carried the wire, and a hammer and some nails.

They placed the wire along the fascia board on the back of the house. When they had that up they ran the rest of it to one of the basement windows. Maude stepped out on the back deck. "What on earth are you two doing?" She asked.

"Maude we have a surprise for yall after dinner." Dock said as he walked to the basement door. Maude just shook her head and tried to imagine what her eccentric husband and his friend had come up with. She went back inside and called over her shoulder. "Dinner will be ready in ten minutes Herb."

While the women cleaned up after lunch Doc headed for the basement and Steve went to the truck to get the radio. Once in the basement Doc cranked up the generator as Steve came down the stairs. "Have you got it Steve?"

"Right here Doc." Steve said as he placed the radio on the bench. He pulled the antenna out to its full length and then wrapped the electrical wire they had stripped around the tip.

They gave the generator ten minutes to warm up and then connected it to the fuse box. Then they plugged up the radio, an old Radio Shack DX-390, into the wall. Steve pushed the power button and began to scan the dial.

Maude and the girls appeared at the bottom of the steps as Steve began to search for an active station. "So Herb, what kind of surprise do you have for us that the power needs to be running?"

Doc cleared his throat and Steve stepped to the side so the women could see the radio. "My dear, Steve has provided us with a short wave radio. Hopefully we can get some news about what is going on." Smiles crossed the faces of the women as the crowded towards the radio. Steve turned and began to search for a station.

After five minutes Steve had come across two German, Spanish, and a possible Scandinavian channel. None in the room spoke the languages so the search continued. No one moved the entire time, transfixed on the little black radio.

Suddenly a voice in English resounded from the speaker.

"...This is Jake Grant signing off. We will bring you more news at 6:00 pm Eastern Standard time." The voice cut off and static replaced his voice. Everyone in the room let out a groan of disappointment. Steve made not of the channel and wrote it down, 5.065. He continued to scan.

Ten minutes later he had gone through the entire dial and only found several other foreign channels. He pushed the power button off. "Well I guess we will wait till six." Another groan came from the women's lips.

Everyone went back up stairs to go about their chores. Steve turned to Celina, "Would you like to do some target practice?"

Celina's face brightened. "Sure!"

"Let me get the pistol out of the truck." Steve headed out the front door, his AK-47 slung over his shoulder.

He opened the passenger door and popped open the glove box retrieving the Ruger MK II. He placed on the seat as he dug in the canvas green bag that sat on the seat looking for a couple of boxes of shells.

"Hello there!" Steve spun as a voice called out behind him, the AK coming off his shoulder and into a ready position in his hands.

"No need for that mister. We're harmless, just trying to find someplace to stay." Said an older man dressed in ragged clothes. He stood on the road in front of a group of about twenty people.

Steve approached the group and stopped when he was about fifteen feet away. "Where are you coming from?" Steve asked.

Most of us came down from Tennessee to the refugee center in Huntsville. The place was overflowing and they had no room for us. They told us there was supposed to be a center in Florence."

Steve continued to scan the group for trouble as he spoke. "I hate to tell you this, but I think most there were rendered homeless or just fled and headed south towards Birmingham." The man shook his head in disgust but his eyes were drawn over Steve's shoulder. Steve turned to see Celina on the front porch holding a Mini-14. Doc was next to her holding a 12 gauge, and Maude was stepping around the corner on the side of the house holding another 12 gauge.

"Listen mister, we really don't mean any trouble. We are just tired thirsty and hungry looking for a place to stay. We won't impose on you and we'll just be heading on now." The presence of the weapons really seemed to make the man and others in the group nervous.

Steve called to Doc over his shoulder. "Hey Doc, can you spare a little bit of food and water for these people?"

Doc looked over to Maude at the side of the house. She gave him a quick nod. "Sure Steve. How do we want to do this?"

Steve looked at the man he had been talking to. "Tell your people to lay down their bags and suitcases and get into a single file line. No one takes any weapons on the property. Then I will pat each one of you down as you come to me one at a time. Then you go and sit under those oaks there in the front of the house. Do all of you understand?"

Everyone in the group nodded their heads. Bags and suitcases dropped to the ground. As they lined up the old man spoke up. "Mister we don't have any weapons. The soldiers in Huntsville Refugee Center took what few pistol, and rifles we had. Hell they even took our pocket knives. Then they told us to head out." Steve just nodded his head and motioned to the man to step forward.

Steve patted the man down. Celina had moved up to cover him, and Doc had moved to cover the group. Maude had stayed where she was. One at a time Steve patted each of them down and then sent to sit under the shade of the oaks.

After everyone had a seat Maude went inside to get Daphne to help with food and water. The group sat in silence while they waited. From the looks on their faces it appeared they felt like they had fallen into some sort of trap. The looks changed though as Maude came outside with Daphne. They each carried a large TV tray with small paper plates on them. On each plate were some chicken meat and three slices of bread.

Maude had stripped several birds earlier in the morning intending to use the meat for some chicken stew for supper. She had also cooked three loaves of bread in a Dutch oven.

Each person was given their food. The two went back inside and brought back tall plastic glasses full of water. The group of refugees made quick work of the meager meal and water. Though the meal wasn't much, smiles adorned their faces.

The leader spoke up again. "Mister we sure do appreciate that. We know how tight things are now."

"Well you seem to be decent folks. I know we can't feed everyone but sometimes you got to help those in need, even if it means you have to tighten your own belt a bit. Can you tell us what's going on out there?" Steve said as he took a knee.

"Most of us like I said came down from Tennessee. It seems that the real small towns we've come through are okay. No power or nothing but as normal as things can be in times like these. Mostly they just escorted us through town and sent us on our way. From what I hear the metropolitan size cities are battle zones. Troops have been fighting it out with gangs and regular folks. It seems the president has decided it would be better for all if everyone were put in central locations. The medium size cities are even worse. With all the troops over seas fighting, or in the big cities the government has left them on their own. I just can't believe in such a short time so much destruction could have taken place." The man paused for a second as he took a gulp of the last of his water in his glass.

"When we left out of Huntsville we headed towards Madison and Athens on our way here. Our group did number about sixty. By the time we reached the center of Athens we had twenty five folks shot. Several women were taken from us at gun point. Well as you can see we are down to eighteen. There are bands of roving gangs everywhere. They aren't like gangs of the big cities, but regular folks who have turned to stealing and killing to get what they need to survive. If you don't mind I guess we will be heading out to see if anything is in Florence." The man and the group began to rise. Steve also stood and took several steps back, just in case.

Doc called to the group from the front porch. "Yall hold up a second. Maude said she had something for you." The group stopped and stared at the front porch was Doc stood.

Shortly Maude and Daphne walked out the front door. Each carried two large pillow cases. Maude held a pillow case up in the air. It was packed tight with what the group could not tell. "We have something here for you. It isn't much." She handed the man the two pillow cases. The old man sat them at his feet.

The old man leaned over and opened the pillow case. Inside were about fourteen cans of food. The other pillow case held the same. Daphne handed her pillow cases to two people in the group. She and Maude had filled up twenty four one liter water bottles that had been sitting empty down in the basement.

A tear rolled down the old man's cheek as he stood upright and hugged Maude. "We thank you. This has been the kindest act that we have received since we began our travel."

After the two parted from their embrace Maude stood back. "God bless each of you and have a safe journey wherever it leads you. You will have to turn back around though and go the way you came, this road dead ends. When you get to the main road head south and it will take you right into Florence."

The old man nodded his head and leaned back down and picked up the two pillow cases. Words of thanks were spoken by all in the group as they each turned and walked back to the road. Once they sorted the small amount of food and water among themselves they picked up their belongings and trudged forward. They waved as they passed by the house. There faces were full of hope that the road ahead would lead to somewhere safe.

When the group passed on out of sight Steve turned to face the Daphne. "Daphne I think it's time for you to learn to shoot."

Daphne had a flustered look on her face as she spoke. "Steve I really don't think that's necessary. Do you?"

"Daphne I don't want to sound crude or cold hearted but I'm going to tell you like it is. This group had no ill will towards us, but the next one might. Doc, Maude and Celina won't be able to hold off a determined group by themselves. I won't be here to help all of the time either. It's going to take us all to make it through these times."

Daphne had never liked guns, they scared her. She had grown up rich and pampered her entire life. Her biggest worry was what she would have to wear for a luncheon at the country club. "Now Steve, things can't be that bad that. I don't need to learn to shoot

Steve quickly repressed the surge of anger that swept over him. Once he calmed himself he spoke. "Daphne, I don't want to sound cold hearted, so when I say this don't get angry or upset." He took a deep breath. "Daphne you are going to learn to shoot because you may have to kill someone to protect yourself or others here that have taken you in. So unless you want to be raped again or see it happen to your sister, you will learn to shoot."

Daphne stepped back as if someone had punched her. Tears welled up in her eyes. She looked to Celina for help, and was met with a blank stare. Daphne looked at the others in the group as tears began to roll down her cheeks. Everyone stood mute, staring at her.

Tears streaked down Daphne's cheeks as she turned and fled back in the house. Maude glared at Steve. "Now Steve, why did you have to go and say it like that?" She turned to follow Daphne in the house.

Steve put a restraining hand on Maude's shoulder. "Maude let me fix it okay?" Maude hesitated for a moment. She stared into Steve's eyes, nodded her head and stepped to the side to let Steve pass.

Steve found Daphne sitting in Doc's leather chair. She had a half finished quilt and a needle and thread in her hand. She made exaggerated punctures, and pulls on the needle and thread as she sewed a new piece of fabric in place, the tears still running down her face.

Steve pulled the leather foot rest in front of the chair and sat facing Daphne. He stared at the young girl in silence for several minutes waiting for her to acknowledge his presence. When none came he reached out and placed a hand on her arm stopping her sewing. Daphne refused to look up at him as the tears fell like droplets of rain off her cheek and onto the quilt.

"Daphne, look at me." Steve said in a soft quiet voice. "Please Daphne." After several seconds Daphne raised her face to look at Steve.

"Daphne, I'm sorry I was so harsh with you out there. I know you have been through a lot, but you have to realize things have changed. I understand what you are going through. It will be a long time before things get back to normal. You are going to have to change to stay alive, and help your sister survive."

Daphne choked back a sob before she spoke. "How can you understand what I have been through? You don't know what its like. I have been raped. My sister has killed people. And the evil bastards killed my dad, and mom!" More sobs racked her as she finished speaking.

"You're right Daphne. I don't know what it's like to be raped. I do know about losing someone you love. I lost my fiancé the day everything came crashing down. Two thugs shot her at Wal-Mart. She died right here in this house. Doc couldn't save her."

Daphne looked back up at Steve as he continued. "Daphne, you're going to have to be strong, not only for yourself, but for your sister. If you want her to live through this, you're going to have to step forward and help defend her. Your sister is willing to stand up and fight to you save and keep you alive. Now you too, are going to have to do the same.

You said your sister has killed people. Well, I have too. I'm sure it tears her up inside like it does me. No matter how bad some people deserve to die every normal person hates to be the one who has to pull the trigger. In times like these if you want live you will have to be that person." Steve stopped talking and took her hands and stood. "Come on Daphne. Come let me teach you to defend yourself and your sister."

Daphne looked up at Steve as he stood holding her hands. Swallowing hard she stood up, the quilt forgotten falling to the floor. "I'm sorry Steve. You are right and I'm wrong." She said as they turned to walk back outside.

"No Daphne, you aren't wrong. There is nothing wrong with wanting to be left alone, and leave others alone to go about their lives." The two walked back outside.

Steve stopped on the porch as Daphne walked down the steps to her sister and Maude. He watched as the three hugged one another. As they pulled back from their embrace he spoke. "He Doc, go grab those two old Single Six's and a bolt action .22 out of your gun safe and let's teach this little lady to shoot."

The next several hours were spent teaching Daphne the fundamentals of shooting. She progressed easily since she didn't have any bad habits to correct. Celina stood off to the side practicing with the Mark II. As the lessons progressed, Daphne learned to shoot Steve's AK, and Doc's Ruger Ranch Mini-14. Steve helped Celina with the stainless Mini-14 he had taken from the men he killed. Then he taught her to shoot a 12 gauge. Daphne did not like the 12 gauge. They decided she would stick with the Mini-14.

Soon Maude came out the back door and called a halt to the lessons, it was time for an early supper. Everyone had almost forgotten about the radio and hurriedly ate after Maude brought it up. Once dinner was eaten, the dishes were cleaned everyone went down stairs to the basement. Steve turned the power on to the radio so they wouldn't miss the broadcast. While they waited Steve and Doc taught the women what everyone hates about shooting, weapons cleaning.

At five minutes till six Steve called a halt to the weapons cleaning. The two revolvers and bolt action .22 were put back on their pegs. Doc handed each of the Donovan women three loaded thirty round magazines for their Mini-14's. He went over gun safety one more time as the two young women put a magazine in their rifles. They all decided to leave the chambers empty so no one would have an accidental discharge. As they stacked their rifles near the steps the radio came to life.

"Good evening America. This is Jake Grant with Radio Free America. It's time for our six o'clock broadcast. First I would like to bring you word about what is happening on the warfront in Asia. The 7th fleet along with the 8th Air Force has started a bombing campaign around our surrounded forces in north of Seoul. The 1st Marine Expeditionary Force has landed on the beaches near the DMZ. The 101st Airborne, and the 82nd Airborne have jumped in behind the forces that are on the DMZ in an attempt to block off any retreat so that the enemy can be crushed between the Marine and Army forces.

Military Intelligence has gathered information that confirms a force of over five hundred thousand Chinese troops are moving south through North Korea to aid North Korean forces. The President has ordered the Air Force to begin bombing runs along their line of advance in hopes of halting their advance. President Engle has stated tactical nukes will be used on the Chinese forces if the advance can not be halted by conventional means.

Now to the news in Europe, Russia advance into the former Soviet Bloc countries continues. The only country that was not once part of the Soviet Bloc left to fall is Germany. German forces continue to hold at their border. Members of the European Union have told Russian officials that nukes will be used to halt their advance. They have also protested the pull out of U.S. troops from the region as they are sent back to the States to help with unrest here at home.

Now for news on the current conditions here in the U.S. Chinese troops, along with several South American Armies are being held from Arizona, north to Central California. Fighting is fierce but the Joint Chiefs have stated they do not know how long they can hold. They have asked for President Engle to cancel his executive order to confiscate firearms from the hands of citizens. They state that every able body man should arm themselves and assist in the fight. They have also asked that troops ordered to maintain relocation centers, and refugee camps be released to help in the fighting. The Chairman states he needs the man power on the front line, not patrolling city streets, and detaining citizens.

The White House has released an estimate of total casualties from the nuked cities, on our coasts and the biological attacks that took place at fifteen relocation centers in the Mid-West. The total killed stands at six million, with another eleven million either wounded or contaminated. Korean sleeper teams continue to raise havoc in every state in the Union. Local law enforcement has been unable to quell the attacks. Many cities police agencies have disbanded or are at only fifteen percent of normal staffing on average.

This will conclude tonight's broadcast. I would like to remind you that if you live near a relocation camp, Presidential Orders are to make your way to them. The government feels that if everyone is in one location the government will be able to assist you better. For those that do not live near relocation camps we ask that you go to the nearest city hall so that your local EMA can begin the construction of new camps. If you have a firearm Executive Orders require that you turn it in to the nearest governmental agency. Also remember that the hording of food can be punishable by death or imprisonment. Anyone caught with more than one week's worth of food can be arrested and placed on trial.

Well folks that's all I have for tonight. Tune in for our next broadcast at twelve o'clock tomorrow afternoon. This is Jake Grant signing off."

Everyone sat in stunned silence. After several seconds Doc spoke. "I believe we need to become as low profile as possible. We need to find a way to block off the road so one else travels our way. We can't chance anyone telling some government official about us. I for one don't intend to be herded into a pen and cared for like some sheep by the government."

"I agree with you Doc. Give Amos a call on the CB and get him over here. We need to make some plans." Doc nodded and headed for the CB. Things were definitely getting worse.

Chapter 27

It was 5:00 am, and Bob Novacheck was in a hurry. He had already lost valuable time. The sun would be up soon, and he considered the darkness a friend when staring out his forays.

Caroline poured Bob a cup of coffee while he loaded his shotgun. "Slow down Bob. It's not like you're going to get fired for starting off late." She handed Bob the cup of coffee as he set his shotgun on the kitchen table.

Bob took a sip of the scalding coffee. "I know Caroline, but I prefer to get to the houses before the sun is up so someone can't set up some kind of ambush. Plus if you are going along I want everything to go smoothly."

"I know, but it's not like this neighborhood was ever filled with your Rambo types. Everyone we've tried to make contact with has hid behind locked doors and refused to band together. What we need to do is get the heck out of here before people start scavenging in our direction. You know eventually that will happen, and I don't know if we're prepared to stay holed up in here for a long period of time"

"Caroline, I have said it before and I will say it again. Just where do you think we should head out to?" Bob let out a yawn and took another sip of his coffee.

"Well Bob, I'll say it again. Let's use our vehicles and go out to the county and find an abandoned farmhouse or something similar. Especially something that has running water, or a well. Your idea about going around and draining water heaters was great, but it won't last forever." She sat down in the chair opposite him, and gave him the look every married man sees from time to time from his wife.

"Caroline I don't want to argue about it right now. Once you go out with me today and see how scary it is going in the houses you may change your mind; especially not knowing if someone is home and is going to blow you away for breaking into their home. Then you think about what going up to some farmhouse, which has an even greater chance of being occupied and those that live there surely armed." Bob rose from his chair and picked up the shotgun. "Come on we're going to hit some of the houses two blocks over. We'll start in the middle. I need to break up my pattern."

Caroline frowned as she stood up. She knew she had to convince her husband that staying here was a losing proposition. "All right let's go."

The two checked to make sure all the doors except the backdoor were secured. Then they met at the back door and went outside. Bob stopped on the deck and pulled out one of his treasured cigarettes. Lighting up he turned to his wife. "You sure you want to come along?"

"Yes Bob I'm sure. Why are you standing here smoking when just five minutes ago you were in a rush to get started?" She said with an irritated look on her face.

"Look this helps me calm my nerves number one." He said holding the cigarette up. "Number two I'm not real thrilled about you coming along. If something happens to you I won't be able to forgive myself. Number three I want to go over what we are going to do one more time."

"Well get on with it Bob. We're standing out here on the back deck with you smoking a cigarette. Every time you take a puff it's like sending off a flare that says here I am. You probably don't realize it but at night when you go outside to smoke and walk back through the trees I can see you all the way up here on the deck."

"Uh, I didn't realize that." Bob tossed the cigarette in his butt can. Glad that the darkness help conceal his embarrassment over something that should have been so evident to him. "Okay, you're right but let's go over this one more time alright?"

"Alright Bob!"

"Now when we get the door open I will go in first. I usually stand near the door and listen for about five minutes and to let my eyes get adjusted, and make sure I don't hear anyone. When I signal for you to come in, you walk with your back to me and watch for anyone sneaking up. If you see someone coming at us and they are not armed tell them who we are and that we will leave, then before we leave ask them if we can meet them later in the day. If we don't encounter anyone you stay at the door of each room I go in and cover the halls. Remember get your body behind the door frame take a knee so you don't silhouette yourself. Have you got it?"

"Yes Bob I've got it. Now let's do this and get back home." She gave Bob a quick peck on the lips, and stood back ready to go.

The two made their way through the backyard to the chain link fence that separated their property from the home behind them. One at a time they crossed over. Bob was not overly concerned that someone was in the house behind his. He had cleared it yesterday. The home had been a virtual treasure trove of camping equipment, fifty rounds for Caroline's pistol, two gallons of gas, one gallon of Coleman camp fuel, and a Cold Steel Recon folding knife, which was now attached to his belt.

They made their way from tree to tree as quickly as possible. Dawn would soon be here and Bob didn't want to be caught out in the open. Even though it was daylight when he made his way home, he still felt it important to start off in the darkness.

Once they made it to the corner of the house Bob studied the street. He saw nothing. He did hear the occasional dog barking but that had seemed the norm on most of his outings. Caroline kneeled behind him with her back to his, pistol in hand looking for anyone who might approach from their rear.

Bob turned and knelt beside his wife. In a hushed voice he placed his lips near hear ear. "Okay. I want you to run across the street first. Since I have the long gun I will cover for you. When you get to the other side I will come over to you while you cover me." Caroline just nodded as she stood and took a quick peek around the corner. Then she bolted across the street.

Bob brought the shotgun to his shoulder, sweeping the barrel from left to right. He stopped the barrel at each window looking for a threat. He saw none, and then Caroline was across the street. He could just barely see her motioning for him to come across. Bob rose up and dashed to his wife.

When he got to the other side Caroline placed her lips next to his ear. She smiled broadly as she spoke. "Man that does get the blood pumping. No wonder you're always out and about looking for things. I feel like a twelve year old kid playing hide and go seek!"

Bob squeezed his wife's arm. "Honey, this is not a game. Stay focused."

The smile did not leave her face. Even though she knew Bob was right, it still felt great, no exhilarating to her. To be out and actually doing something again even if it was life threatening. "Sure Bob, no problem."

"Okay we're going to do the same thing again and again as we get to the house. Then we will try the front door first." The two leap froged like that till they made it to the house Bob had chosen the day before. The garage door had been up and he was almost positive no one was home.

Bob made his way to the front door. He looked over his shoulder to check Caroline. She had her back to him her pistol at the ready. The thought of needing to find Caroline some sort of long gun flashed through his mind. The .380 Sig was no good for what they were doing.

Bob turned back and reached out and took the doorknob in his hand. He twisted slowly until the doorknob stopped. It was locked. He began to search for the key rock everyone in the neighborhood seemed so hell bent on having. He did not find one.

Caroline eased over to him. "What are you looking for?" She whispered.

"Over half the houses I have been into have one of those Rock Keys near the door. I'm just hoping I find one so I don't have to break a window or kick a door in."

Caroline just shook her head and pointed to a small metal box that was attached to one of the pillars. It was a combination lock box just big enough to put a key into. "I knew that. I was just making sure you where paying attention." He whispered with a bit of amusement in his voice. Caroline gave him a quick playful elbow to the ribs.

Bob pulled out his new Cold Steel lock blade, and approached the box. It took him under a minute but he pried it open and out fell a key which he caught in his left hand. He held it up for Caroline to see. "Ah, another family full of geniuses." For the life of him he could not understand why people placed keys to their homes in such obvious places. He turned back to the door after placing he knife on his belt.

Ever so slowly he unlocked the door. He then pocketed the key and eased the door open. "Stay put, watch my back."

Bob stepped into the dark opening. As he stepped into the foyer he felt his feet hit something in the floor. Suddenly the sounds of aluminum cans scattering through the foyer seemed to echo through the house. "Crap! Crap! Crap!" Bob mentally cursed at himself. He looked back at Caroline and placed a finger to her lips. Her only response was her "Look who's talking Bucko!" look on her face. She turned to face the street again.

Bob stood stock still trying to listen for any movement. He didn't feel like he was going to hear a thing. He felt like everyone within a mile could hear his heart pounding in his chest.

Bob started taking deep breaths to calm himself. After several minutes he eased his right foot out. He kept the sole of his boot on the floor in attempt to clear a path towards the carpeted hall before him. He could go either left or right around a four foot wide wall that he was sure lead to some sort of living room.

He stopped as soon as his foot hit one of the cans; he slowly shoved it out of his way. Though not as loud as him knocking over the cans, it still made his heart beat faster. Maybe Caroline was right. They had to get out of the city. He would die of a heart attack he was sure if he kept on making mistakes like the ones he had just made. More than likely he would die from a bullet to his feeble brain.

"Screw this!" Bob thought. If no one had called out or come to investigate the noise he made no one was here. Bob quickly stepped towards the right doorway. Bob felt his ankle hit something and he fell forward. The shotgun fell from his hands as he tried to break his fall. The floor rushed up and his face hit the carpeted floor.

Bob shook his head trying to clear it. As he pushed up from the floor a jarring pain shot between his shoulder blades. He felt cold steel press against the back of his head. Then he heard a sound that almost everyone around the world knew and feared. Who ever it was racked a round into the shotgun pressed against his head. He lay there frozen. He knew he was a dead man.

A deep voice spoke above him. "You even move, or look like you're going for that shotgun, or anything else I'll blow your damn head off. Do you understand?"

Bob slowly turned his head to look over his shoulder. The barrel of the shotgun moved to his forehead. "Mister I will do what ever you say. I didn't know you were here. I thought everyone on this block had left."

"So you're here to steal my brother's things. You sorry fucker"

The barrel pressed harder into Bob's forehead. "Oh shit!" Was all Bob could say.

Caroline's head snapped back towards Bob as the sounds of the aluminum clattered on the tile floor. Bob turned to look at her and raised a finger to her lips. "Bob you clumsy man. You need to be quiet not me." She thought. She turned her attention back to the area around the house.

After several minutes she heard the sounds of a can being scraped across the floor. "Now that was real quiet Bob." She thought.

Within a few seconds she heard something thud to the floor, an also the sound of something metallic hit the floor. Caroline spun around and eased herself into the foyer. She could make out Bob's feet and legs lying in the floor. Her heart shot up to her throat.

Then a dark blur came from the hallway and a foot slammed between Bob's shoulder blades. Then the form of a man leaned forward with a shotgun to Bob's head.

The man spoke, his voice turned even more irate. "So you're here to steal my brother's things, you sorry mother fucker!"

Bob's reply was a meek "Oh shit!"

As she watched the man press the shotgun harder to Bob's forehead she remembered she was Bob's backup. She remembered the gun in her hand.

"Mister if you so much as move I will blow your brains out of the back of your skull like shit through a goose." Caroline's voice was steady and even, the gun unwavering in her hands. Inside she was a quivering mass of jelly.

The man slowly turned his head. "You know if you shoot me your friend is dead don't you." The man stared hard into her eyes.

"That might be so, but I will have the satisfaction of punching your ticket. So drop the shotgun or I might just blow off your jewels and make you suffer a bit before I kill you." Caroline lowered the aim of the pistol to the man's groin area.

Joe's eyes bored into the young woman's. He was in a heck of a predicament, and wasn't sure how he was going to get out of it. He wasn't sure if the man and woman were a couple or just two people who could care less about one another who had banded together in hard times. If it was the later he was dead, well maybe not right off. "Why did women always have to threaten to blow a man's balls off?"

Joe made his decision. "All right I'm going to lay the shotgun down now." Slowly he moved the shotgun towards the woman as if to put it down.

"If that barrel comes one more inch towards me you're dead where you stand! Now go the other way with it!" Caroline's voice assumed that of the business executive she was a voice full of authority, and with no doubt in it.

"Damn!" Joe thought to himself. He carefully turned the other way and laid the shotgun behind him. He put the safety on just in case the man picked it up. It might give him a fraction of a second to grab him or it with out being shot with his own weapon. Then he took a step back his hands raised about shoulder height.

Caroline looked down at her husband. "Bob, are you alright?"

Bob again pushed himself up. This time he wasn't kicked back down to the floor. "Yeah baby, I'm alright. Just feel like I've got whiplash."

As Bob stood both his hands went to his forehead trying to push away the pain his head was feeling. Despite the floor having carpet it felt like someone had sucker punched him. He took a step towards his wife.

"Get your shotgun sweetheart." Caroline said. Bob tuned to the right to retrieve his fallen shotgun.

It was the opening Joe was hoping for. Not only did he now know the two were a couple the man had made a serious tactical error. He had stepped towards the woman blocking her shot. When he turned his hands were still rubbing his face.

Joe took a step forward his knee striking the back of the other man's knee causing it to buckle. His arms stretched out as he attempted to regain his balance. Joe shot his arms under the man's arm pits bringing his hands back behind the man's neck locking the fingers together. The man now effectively blocked the woman's shot. If she made a move to go to the left hand doorway he would push the man forward and get his shotgun and start shooting.

"Let him go! Let him go or I'll shoot you!" Caroline screamed. Her voice was no longer sure. It quivered and had gone up several octaves. Bob struggled but the man's arms were like iron bands he could not break. The man had lifted him up so that he was on his tiptoes and could get no leverage.

"Lady the only thing you have a shot at is sweetheart here. If you don't drop that pistol I will snap his neck." This time Joe's voice was the one full of authority. To prove he meant business he applied an extreme amount of pressure to the man's neck.

Bob let out a gasp. He felt like the man actually had the strength to shove his chin into his chest. His neck muscles felt like they were elastic. Like they were near the point they would snap before his neck would. He struggled to speak. "Caroline, either drop the gun, or go ahead and shoot us both. Then get the hell out of here."

The sun was coming up over the trees behind Caroline. With the morning light she could see the pain Bob was in. The man, who just wore a t-shirt and pants, had huge muscular arms. Indecision ate at her. Maybe he could snap Bob's neck. Bob let out another gasp, and that was all it took. Caroline lowered the gun and put it on the floor. "Please don't kill my husband. We were only looking for food and water. We really didn't know you were here. Everyone on our block has left."

Joe eased some of the pressure to the man's neck. "You live here?"

"Yes. Just two blocks over. We've been getting water out of hot water heaters, and finding what food and other things we could to survive. Mister we're not bad people. Just let us live and we'll go." Caroline pleaded.

Adding pressure to the man's neck with his left hand Joe reached down with his right. When he felt the butt of the revolver on his hip he unsnapped the pistol and drew it. As he drew the pistol he shoved the man into the woman. The two collided, but not hard enough to knock either down. The woman threw her arms around the man's neck.

Joe quickly checked the load and slammed the cylinder closed. "You two back out onto the front walk." As they backed out Joe grabbed the pistol up off the floor and put it in his pocket. When the two reached the front walk he told them to sit. "Sit down with your legs out in front of you and cross them and put your hands on your heads." Joe watched as the two complied.

"Now just how do I know you two aren't some kind of thieves out looting?" Joe said as he gestured at them with the pistol. He pulled one of the front porch chairs over with a foot and took a seat, the pistol never coming off the pair.

"I leave notes." Bob said.

"You leave what?" Joe asked in some confusion.

"When I take something from a home I leave my name, address, and that I will either pay them for the items we took. Or that we will return what items we have not used." Bob hoped the man believed the truth.

"And I suppose you have paper for these notes?" Joe said as a skeptical look crossed his face.

Caroline's face brightened. "As a matter of fact we do." Being the efficient person she was Caroline had pre-written some notes. She felt that the less time they were out the better. That way the only thing they had to fill in was what they took.

The look of skepticism grew deeper. "And where is your paper lady."

Bob hand went for the cargo pocket of his khaki pants. "It's right here!"

Joe's arm shot straight out the hammer being cocked on the pistol as his hand extended. "Slow that hand down mister, or I shoot the woman." A look of horror crossed the man's face. "Yep they cared for one another." The man's hand came out of his pocket in over exaggerated lethargic speed. In his hands were several sheets of folded yellow paper.

"Get up real slow. Walk on your knees over here. Keep both hands on top of your head. When you get to me use one hand and put the paper under my boot. Then back the same way. You move to fast or make a move to grab me your woman dies." Joe watched the man comply with his orders.

When he sat back in place Joe leaned forward and picked up the paper and unfolded it. He quickly read the top paragraph of each page.

Sure enough the man, Bob Novacheck, had his name, address and the other information in place. Just to be sure about the man's identity he asked if he had any identification on him. Joe himself still carried his wallet out of habit. "You got any ID?"

For a second Bob was confused. "Well, yeah I have my wallet."

"Toss it up here. Remember you come out with something beside a wallet she dies."

Slowly Bob retrieved his wallet and tossed it to the man. Joe caught it with his left hand. Flipping it open he looked at the driver's license inside. Sure enough the man was Robert Novacheck and he lived two blocks over on Shadow Wood Dr. Joe tossed the wallet back. "So Mr. Novacheck, who is the lady with you?"

Caroline spoke up before Bob could answer. "I'm sitting right here, and can speak for myself. I am his wife Caroline. May I ask who you are?"

Joe was silent for a few moments while he pondered over the situation. "My name is Joe Donovan. This was my brother's house. I came here looking for them."

"Donovan? Bob that's one of the families that the gangs…" her voice trailed off as she looked back at Joe.

"Yeah, my brother is dead. My sister in law was raped, so was one of my nieces. They got out of here to some friends."

"How do you know that?" Caroline said.

"Note on the kitchen table." Joe said the pistol still pointing at Caroline.

Bob joined in on the conversation. "Sir, while we are getting to know one another can we get up. My ass and back are killing me, and this concrete isn't too comfortable. You can put my gun away too. We aren't going to try anything. Besides you have all the guns."

Joe hesitated for a second then lowered the pistol. He always considered himself a good judge of character. These two seemed on the up and up. "Tell you what. I'm going to go back in here and get my shotgun. If you two want to leave you can. If you don't, once I have my gun I will give you yours back."

Joe stood and started to back away as the two nodded their heads. Once inside Joe dumped the rounds out of the revolver and then emptied the magazine to the Sig, and took the round out of the chamber. He noticed the woman's pistol was loaded with +P+ .380 Hydro Shocks. "Damn that would've hurt." He said to himself. He walked to retrieve his shotgun and the man's. He quickly unloaded Bob's shotgun, and started to head back outside.

Bob stood and helped Caroline to her feet. "Caroline, do you think we should run?"

"Well Bob we could, but then all we would have is the .22's back at the house. I don't think we could hold off a bunch of looters with those. Plus he said his family headed somewhere. Maybe it's on some farm. If it is, this may be our chance to get out of here."

"Okay let's see what happens." Bob said. His stomach was twisted in knots. He almost got killed. Mostly his wife could have been killed. Two minutes later the man named Joe walked back outside with their pistols in his waist band and two shotguns in hand.

Joe leaned Bob's shotgun against the wall and held his a port arms. "Well I guess yall are going to stay, and we're going to get to know each other. Now both of you turn around and get on your knees."

Bob and Caroline stood motionless and mute. Was this man about to execute them? "Go ahead and turn around and get on your knees." Joe said.

Bob and Caroline slowly complied trading a glance at one another. Both were thinking the same thing. They heard Joe walk down the steps and step behind them. "Now don't move I'm going to give you your guns back." The couple both let out an audible breath. Joe leaned forward and placed Caroline's pistol in her holster, then turned and put Bob's pistol in his. "Okay you two get up and come on in and I'll fix some coffee." Joe turned and walked back towards the house. He thumbed the safety off the shotgun as he walked. If he had misjudged the two, at the first sound of a pistol clearing leather he would turn and shoot both.

Once inside the house Joe had set up his little stove and boiled the coffee. Over their cups of coffee the three related the events of the past week each had experienced. Bob and Caroline had been transfixed by Joe's story. It sounded like something out of a dime store action novel. Caroline had explained how she wished to get out of the city and find a farm to wait out the upheaval. Bob chimed in that he felt it was too dangerous to go from farm to farm looking for a vacant one. He cited this morning's event as the main reason. Joe told them of the note and about Doc Morrison's place, and Steve.

Caroline quickly asked if Joe thought that Doc Morrison would mind if they tagged along. Bob apologized for his wife's rudeness, but she quickly silenced him and told him the time for politeness was gone. This was life or death for them. Joe said that the two would most likely be welcome as long as they pulled their fair share. If it didn't work our Doc refused he was sure they could find a place for them, and Doc would probably let them stay till they did find a place.

After coffee the three had decided to head back to the Novacheck's. The next few days the three inventoried everything. They then packed the most essential items into Caroline's Nissan Xterra, and Bob's 1998 Chevrolet 4x4 Z71. They then packed non-essential items, but ones they felt were useful on the trailer Bob had taken from the construction site. Then the three headed out for Doc's. Things were looking up for the three, but life has a way of throwing a few curve balls at you when you think you are on top of things.

Chapter 28

Shortly After the attack on the Florence Utilities Warehouse Sleeper Team 1 made their way to Madison County, just outside of Huntsville, Al. Once they had reached the safe house located several miles south of the city they were joined by Sleeper Team 11.

Team 11 was a twelve man team. Each member was a student at the University of Alabama in Huntsville. The captain in charge of the team was an engineer on Red Stone Arsenal. Their mission had been to attack and destroy important research and development centers on the base.

They had completed their mission with relative ease. Since then they had been attacking utility centers like Team 1 and 4 in Florence had. Team 11 had purposely avoided attacking the refugee center located the western edge of the city limits.

They had however purposely attacked the two other centers located to the north and east of the city. Once the word had spread of the attacks people headed to the western camp, overcrowding the camp beyond capacity.

The National Guard units and FEMA personnel were unable to stem the tide of refugees. Those that could not make it to the camp squatted just outside its perimeter. Team 11 had fought numerous firefights with the Guard inside the city itself. The Guard units had been devastated. They were mostly admin and supply personnel, who had remained while the better equipped infantry and armor units were sent south to Birmingham, Mobile, and Montgomery to stem the riots there.

None of the members except the captain of their unit knew of the reason not to attack the western camp. Tonight however they would be told about the mission they were to undertake that would take America, not to her knees, but hopefully knock her out.

The living room of the safe house was filled with cigarette smoke as eleven of the seventeen Koreans squatted around a large sand map in the center of the room. The other five were positioned outside for security. The captains of each team sat opposite of one another with pointers clasped in their hands.

Dong was the first to speak, a cigarette dangling from his lips. "Tonight is the night that you will take part in a glorious coordinated attack that will hopefully remove America as a superpower. I want each of you to do your jobs to the best of your ability. As you know our homeland has taken numerous nuclear attacks. Millions are dead, and even more are injured or homeless.

Our communist brothers from China have assisted us by nuking several major American ports. Russia has now entered Western Europe. They have pushed through Eastern Germany and are now planning a major push into Western Germany. All of the former Soviet Bloc nations have come back under their sphere of influence. The biggest problem they face now is internal forces within Russia; they may face a civil war. If that war happens our brother's in China will cross into Russia and crush them.

Corporal Wei spoke up. "Captain what has this to do with our attack here in America?"

Dong looked into his corporal's eyes while he took a last long drag off of the cigarette. Dropping it to the hardwood floor he crushed it out as he spoke. "I want to relate these events to you so that you understand if we are successful, western culture will be eradicated from the earth. Asian culture will rise properly to the top of the power chain." Dong paused a moment as he looked around the room at the assembled men. "I will now turn the briefing over to my comrade who will advise you our entire mission. The captain planned this mission and the missions of all other Korean sleeper teams across America, Captain."

The other captain cleared his throat as he began the brief. "All of you from my team have questioned me about why we have not attacked the over crowded western camp. The reason is that I wanted as many people in that location for this attack.

Two weeks ago our team secured a tanker truck filled with Nitrosylchloride. This tanker will be used in our attack. Private," he pointed to one of his men; "You will be driving the tanker."

The soldier's face turned pasty white. "Am I to crash this tanker into a building, sir?"

"No." Obvious relief washed over him knowing he was not to go on a suicide mission.

Private Nah from Team 1 spoke up. "Sir, what is Nitrosylchloride, and how will we use it in the attack if we are not going to crash it into something?"

The captain smiled as he pulled a cigarette from his pack and lit it. He exhaled the blue gray smoke through his nose and then replied. "This truck will be parked one mile from the western camp. We will set several small charges, just enough to puncture the sides in several places. The charges will be set on time delayed fuses of course.

Once the charges blow holes in the sides of the tanker the gas will escape. Nitrosylchloride will hang close to the ground. I have checked with our meteorologists by satellite radio two days ago. Winds are expected to blow from west to east. This gas according to American Emergency Response Training has an evacuation zone of nine to ten kilometers.

When the liquefied gas explodes the gases will be toxic if inhaled, and burns. Since many in the camp will be sleeping the low lying gas will possibly injure or kill hundreds, and incapacitate thousands in the confined camps. Even more will die as they flee from the eastern edge of the camp heading west."

Hengyang raised a hand. The captain nodded to him to ask his question. "Why will the American's be fleeing from the eastern edge of the camp?"

The captain smiled. "Because," he used his pointer identifying two towers in the middle of the camp "we shall have chemical agents located in these two towers. My men have infiltrated the camp several times on dry runs for this operation. The perimeter is very porous. There is one guard per tower, and they will be neutralized.

This time however, they will be carrying eight gallon containers that have a small nozzle, and fan on the top. They will be activated by remote control. The contents of these containers are Lewisite which is an advance form of mustard gas. This gas will cause severe burns and blisters to the skin. Some will be blinded by it. Those that inhale it will have large blisters form on the inside of their lungs causing many to die.

There are approximately thirty-five thousand people in this camp. The northern camp is estimated to have six thousand, and the eastern camp has approximately four thousand inhabitants. We do not know for sure how many people remain in the city. Captain Dong please continues the brief on what your team will do." He nodded to Dong as he finished up the first part of the brief.

"Team 1 and one man from Team 11 will also be armed with similar containers of the mustard agent. Corporal Wei will lead the first element, Mau and Nah, to the northern camp." He pointed to the northern camp on the sand map. "You will place your two devices on this ridge approximately two hundred yards from the western gate. These devices have timers that will activate the fan and disperse the agent. The timers will be set for 1:00 am. You should be out of the area by 12:30 am. You will follow this route," He traced the route with the pointer, "and rendezvous back here at the safe house. A vehicle has been pre-positioned here for you. The keys are under a rock placed by the front right tire. The car is under a camouflaged tarp parked beside a directional sign at the seven mile marker.

My team's timers will be set for 1:00 am, also. We will follow this route back to the safe house. Each of you will be given a map to study before we start the mission. Memorize it because you will not be taking it with you. Do not deviate or take shortcuts back here. You may wind up breathing in something from the tanker truck and will not make back here.

I estimate that there will be one thousand to two thousand dead and injured at both of these camps." He gestured to the other team leader. "Captain."

Pointing to the one who was to drive the tanker truck he began. "You will set the fuses to go off at 1:00 am. Make your way back here immediately and stand watch. You are to remain on watch until other soldiers arrive. The four of you who have been practicing the infiltration runs will of course be making the assault inside the perimeter. You will be wearing your chemical suits this time. You may choose when to don your mask though. I want your tanks in place by 12:30 am. Once you hear the charges on the tanker go off you will remotely turn on your dispersion units. To the east you will hear gunfire and explosions. This will consist of the rest of the team. We too shall have our chemical suits on.

We will make our way to here." He pointed to a row of Lego's that represented a several buildings near the camp. "From this position we will open fire with both RPG's and small arms fire into the perimeter of the camp. This will cause a panic among those on this side of the camp. From our previous experiences attacking the other two camps the people will naturally attempt to escape and flee to the west side of the camp. We will commence firing at 1:10 am.

The wind should be blowing at approximately ten to fifteen miles per hour. This should give the gas enough time to reach the perimeter of the western side of the camp. The people attempting to escape our fire will then be caught up in the mustard agent. The people from the western edge of the camp will flee towards the east to escape the gas from the tanker. They will do this even though they will be running towards gunfire. Of course they will probably never make it to the eastern section. They will run right through the area of dispersion of the mustard agent."

They then went over the finer points of the plan, each team member asking about essential actions pertaining to their portion of the mission. Finally there were no more questions. "Everyone is sure there are no more questions?" Captain Dong asked.

Wei stood and crossed his arms, one hand stroked his chin. "This is a fine plan Captain. I do not like the idea of killing with gas, especially not women and children, but I will do my duty. However, I still don't see how this attack will take America off of the world stage as a superpower."

"I understand your concern for the attack of women and children. This is crucial to the plan though. This will not be the only attack on refugee camps. Every sleeper team that still remains operational shall be attacking one in this manner. If Sleeper Team 4 was still operational they would have taken a chemical truck and set it off in Florence, Team 5 would have hit Athens. Though these cities do not have any camps the attacks would have possibly killed hundreds and injured even more.

Many medium size cities will be hit in such a manner. Even more refugee camps will be hit. What this will do is send Americans fleeing in every direction away from their city centers, and industrial bases. They will no longer believe the government will be able to protect them. Each time American troops or government officials attempt to round them up to help stop lawlessness, or the spread of disease and other contamination they will fight. Word will spread about these attacks and the story and number of dead will grow with each telling. I think there are still a little over one hundred and ten operational teams. The Chinese have their own teams here. I do not know how many, but probably more than we have." He stopped to pull another cigarette from his pack and light it.

As he paused one of his men spoke up. "Sir, you mentioned contamination. What kind of contamination?"

The captain let out a chuckle. "Our Chinese friends are going to deploy Sarin and Ricin in major cities. They also have the plague and new strains of small pox. These attacks will be conducted on the east and west coast in major population centers also. The American government will have to control the people to stop the spread of these diseases. When the stories of dead women and children in the camps cross the country none will trust their children or wives to the government. Our leaders have left Korean teams to deal with the smaller southern and Midwestern cities."

"Well who will be attacking the southwestern states?" Another young private asked.

This caused the captain to chuckle a bit more. "We have convinced the Mexicans that they can have the southwest. They wish to build their Azatlan. Though there are millions of illegal Mexicans in this country their dream will never be realized. Mexico has fallen into chaos along with every South American country. Africa, well no one has heard the fate of Africa. It is once again the Dark Continent, ravaged by tribal warfare.

Once our mission is complete every team, both Korean and Chinese will make its way to a state in the Midwest. I will tell you once we are underway which one. We will combine our forces once there. We shall recruit everyone of Asian descent who wishes to join our forces. Once we have gathered we shall then go about pacifying America's bread basket. We will control the food and therefore the remains of a starving population. When the time comes we shall spread out and conquer as much territory as we can hold. This of course will take years."

"What about those Asians of Japanese descent sir? Are they to join us also?" One private asked.

Another spoke up before the captain could answer. "Captain ,what about reinforcements from home or us going home?

He took a drag off the cigarette and nodded at Dong for him to answer. Dong stood. "Those of Japanese descent will pay for the crimes that their ancestors have perpetrated against Korea for hundreds of years. Especially for their latest transgressions during World War II, We will kill them all.

As for the second question the answer pains me. Our country, though having fought bravely has been crippled by American nuclear attacks. Their forces in our homeland are down to roving bands robbing the innocent to stay alive. China has also been severely crippled. Not so much its vast population but its infrastructures and shipping capabilities. We are on our own, possibly until we are old men. We shall however conquer as much territory as possible so that when the time comes we shall be reunited and take over what remains of America. We will have to find as many Asian women as possible, preferably Korean, to swell our numbers here for the future." The faces of the men around the room varied from outright disbelief that they were on their own to fend for themselves and fight until old age, to obvious rage at the news that their country had been so devastated that no help could come from home. However in each of the men's eyes the captains could see the flame of revenge burning. They would carryout their mission and future missions with the fanaticism of zealots.

⊹⇒⇐⊹

The young private cursed to himself as he started the big diesel up. It was just his luck that he had worked for a year for a local delivery freight company. Now he had thousands of gallons of a deadly chemical six feet behind him. What if one of the locals just decided to take a pot shot at the tanker and it exploded? If he made it to the drop off point he then had to walk the five miles back to the safe house. That in itself was going to be dangerous. Well maybe it wasn't so bad. At least he would not have to infiltrate the camp or be firing on the eastern side of the camp and have to worry about being contaminated by deadly chemicals or gas.

He had seen few people moving the first two miles of his journey. The closer he came to his drop off point the more people he saw milling about. Many stood near small campfires cooking meager meals. Or they just wandered about aimlessly.

When he reached the one mile point he noticed three men standing near a metal building along the highway. A fire, flames dancing out of a fifty five gallon drum, silhouetted them. He could not make out any weapons, but he decided to be safe and drive father down HWY 72.

A quarter of a mile later he stopped the rig in what appeared to be a spot devoid of human activity. Turning out of the rig he grabbed his AK-47 and exited the truck. He took about two minutes setting the timers on the small charges. In his haste to return back to the safe house he forgot to retrieve the keys from the ignition. He racked a round into the chamber of his rifle and walked west.

As he walked he noticed how quiet it was. He could not even hear the sounds of crickets or any other night animal. That was strange. With the collapse of American society the city noises had almost become nonexistent. He slowed, and then stopped. The cool night breeze blowing in his face sent chills down his sweat covered body.

His head cocked to the side as his ears picked up the sound of something metal falling to the ground not far away. His eyes wide with fear he yanked the rifle up to his shoulder, and scanned the darkness around him. His heart pounded in his chest. Though he had done a lot of fighting since the collapse, this was the first time he had been alone on a mission. He worked the rifle back and forth almost pulling the trigger at every form that came into his vision. He knew the darkness was playing tricks on his eyes, but his mind screamed out that there were hundreds of angry American's around him.

A voice with a heavy southern drawl called out from behind him. "What're you hauling in the rig?" The young private spun looking for the threat. His training forgotten he stood in place failing to find cover.

Chapter 29

Amos and Benny arrived at Doc's within thirty minutes of Doc's call over the CB. While they waited Celina had asked Steve to show her how to operate the short wave radio. When Steve went back upstairs Celina remained downstairs with Daphne and began to scan through the frequencies, on short wave, FM, and AM. Benny was tired from working in the field with Amos and had gone to lie down and sleep in Daphne's room.

Amos took another sip of his sweet tea and sat the glass down. "Now tell me again what this radio broadcast said." Doc began to tell the story again when Amos interrupted him. "Not you, you old goat, you have always confused the hell out of me with all those fancy elaborate words when you discuss something. Steve gives it to me like a normal man would."

Doc put on an indignant face as he spouted his response. "Elaborate words! Why you unsophisticated dirt farmer, I aught to....You're just lucky that someone like me who is as supercilious and of an elevated social eminence will extol his presence on you."

"All right, all right you two old farts, enough." Steve said as he tried to keep back the smile on his face. He knew the two old men loved each other like brothers and it tickled him that they acted as though they could not stand one another.

Both men gave Steve a look of exasperation at the old fart comment, but allowed him to give his rendition of the radio broadcast to Amos. "Look Amos it's this simple. The government believes that by controlling all of the people in the metro areas they will have a better chance at rebuilding. By forcing everyone to give over their supplies and weapons the government renders each citizen helpless, and they must depend on the government. I think that once they have stabilized the big cities a large push will go out to pacify and control the medium sized cities. From there they will go to smaller and smaller cities.

Once they have control of the farms they will naturally control most of the food and then everyone will be dependent. I for one think it is a power play by the President, or others within the government to finally take complete control of society and mold it how they want. Before all this happened the government ridiculed independent minded people. If you believed in God, guns, and the Constitution they labeled you a right wing nut. The bureaucrats in Washington don't believe American's are smart enough to take care of them selves. I think we need to organize folks in our area, not only as defense from hostile bands of people, but also for trade. We are pretty well set as are most in this area. Soon however we will run out of essentials. We also need to block the road somehow to discourage travelers."

Amos ran his fingers through his graying hair. "Steve that does not sound like the kind of life I want to live. I don't need a handout from the government. I've done fine for the past few decades on my own.

Now how do you suggest we get organizing folks for one? Do you think anyone would be interested number two? Number three, how do you propose to block off the road to discourage folks, and would it be the right thing to do? We don't own the road."

"I think at least two of us should go out to the surrounding farms and pass the word out about getting organized. I would go and either you or Doc would go with me. Most everyone around here has known you two for a long time."

Doc leaned forward in his chair and placed his arms on the table. "Why does it have to be just either me or Amos? How about just me and Amos and Steve stays behind?"

"Doc, can you or Amos shoot as well me? We might run into some trouble and some firepower may be needed."

"Steve you know that blind fool can't shoot, except for that mouth of his. If a mouth could kill Doc would be deadly." Amos said with a mischievous grin on his face. Doc's response was to give his friend the finger.

Steve let out a laugh. "He is right you know Doc." Doc's face puckered up as if he had just bit into a lemon. "I mean about the shooting part Doc."

"I appreciate the clarification Steve." Doc said with a smirk.

Steve grew serious again. "Amos, how would you love to hear about news from the outside?

"I would love it. I feel like I'm missing something with no news."

"Surely someone in the area has access to more news than we have received. Also just finding out what is going on in our area would be important to people. Also people will have a surplus of some items but will need to replace or pickup other needed items. So I think folks will come just for that alone.

I also feel that we need to do this as soon as possible. The worse things get, the less likely people will come or want to associate with others. Even though it feels like forever since the collapse of everything it still hasn't been so long that folks won't feel skeptical about associating with others."

Maude had walked in as Steve was explaining his theory on organizing people. "Steve's right you know? It has got to be done soon. I would suggest you tell everyone to meet down at St. Florian Rd., and Butler Creek Rd. The gas station and grocery store are there I'm sure they have been looted, but many people in the area frequented those places. It would be a familiar place to them and therefore they would be more inclined to show up." Maude poured a glass of tea and left.

Doc looked over his shoulder and made sure Maude had left the room. "The old battleaxe is right you know. That's exactly where we need to go." He said in a low voice as if he were planning a conspiracy.

"I HEARD THAT HERBERT MORRISON! You will pay for that when our guest leave." Maude's voice came from the other room. Doc winced as if a loud explosion had gone off behind him.

Amos began to snicker; his hand covering his mouth as he laughed. "That's your ass old man. I imagine Maude's going to "extol" her presence on you tonight." Then Amos's laugh suddenly ceased, his eyes going wide as Maude stood in the kitchen door.

"I believe the three of you should quit blabbering away and start to plan. Amos you keep laughing, and cursing in my house and you may be joining Herbert after Steve leaves." She turned and walked from the room. Doc smiled as if he was a five year old who just got in trouble but was pleased to see his friend in the same situation.

"Go on and finish this up Steve, before this antiquated version of Methuselah gets us in anymore trouble."

"As far as your question about the roads Amos, I don't know if it is right. The nearest homes to Doc's are about one quarter of a mile down the road. The nearest home to you is about an eighth of a mile excluding Benny's house.

I think if we fell some trees across the roads at the near the end of yall's property lines it would be ok. We leave enough room to get one vehicle at a time to go around. As things get worse, many will see it as a possible ambush point and turn around. It will however, leave us enough room to drive around if we have to, and anyone else who is so inclined.

It's not going to really stop anyone from getting through but it may discourage folks from traveling this way. Besides we don't have the manpower to set up guards at each end. So in reality even with a roadblock it will be ineffective, but something is better than nothing."

Doc and Amos both shook their heads in agreement. Then Doc spoke up. "I say we get started on blocking the road first thing tomorrow morning."

Amos rubbed his jaw as he thought for a moment then gave his input. "Okay let's do the roadblock in the morning. As far as going out and networking with other folks, I will leave that up to the two of you. I've got some fields that need to be tended. Plus Doc is much better at being diplomatic and convincing folks to do things."

Steve took a drink of his tea and wiped the moisture from his lips. "How long do think it would take to set up the roadblocks Amos?"

"Steve I would say a good six to seven hours. I don't think you would just want trees lying over the road. That won't take but a few hours. I think we need to make one side of each roadblock dang near impassible. So I think we use my backhoe and dig a few trenches and maybe build some type of lookout post at each end. One of these days we may find it necessary and be able to man them.

"That's a great idea Amos. We should probably put the observation post up in the tree line, in an elevated position. Maybe dig out a foxhole or something and camouflage it. Not only would it be out of sight, it would be a great place to fire down on bad guys. They would be forced to go to the passable side into the person's who is manning the post line of fire."

Doc threw his two cents worth in. "Well as long as we are talking about the possibility of one day being able to man the post we should build a second. We can put it on the other side in case they try to flank the passable area and head into the woods on the other side. Then you would have them in a cross fire."

Steve stood and stretched. "Well let's…" Steve was suddenly interrupted by Daphne and Celina running into the room.

Daphne was the first to speak up. "We heard another broadcast from someone different!"

Then Celina jumped in. "Some guy who called his station "American Pirate Radio. He said he was the "Voice of Verisimilitude"."

With a raised eyebrow and a confused look on his face Amos asked the first question. "What in the hail is verisimilitude?"

Doc glanced at his friend. "It means the truth you uncultured inane dolt." He turned back to the girls. "What did he say?"

Daphne took a breath before she spoke. Then she went on to fill the men in on what the man on the radio said. Celina filled in the gaps about things Daphne missed.

⊹⊱⊰⊹

While everyone else was upstairs discussing what to do Celina and Daphne were down in the basement scanning through the frequencies on the short wave radio. Celina manually scanned through the different frequencies while Daphne patiently paced back and forth. Each time a human voice would sound from the speaker the two would huddle close hoping for an English speaking voice. For the past forty minutes there had been nothing but foreign voices.

Daphne leaned against the wall one foot propped against it. "Man I wish I would have paid more attention in Ms. Clark's Spanish class. We've heard so many Spanish voices out of that thing I feel like a burrito."

Celina looked over her shoulder at her sister. "Yeah if you hadn't been drooling over Brad Jenkins during class you might have picked up a few more words other than Uno." Celina smiled as her sister's face turned red.

"That's not true!" Daphne said in a culpable voice. Celina laughed to herself and waved a dismissive hand.

"Well at least I had a thing for someone my own age. Unlike some eighteen year olds I know." Daphne said with a mischievous grin.

Celina didn't turn knowing her face would be beat red. "How did her sister know?" She lowered her head a bit and did her best to sound nonchalant. "What ever do you mean Daphne?"

"Oh like this afternoon when I saw you walking in the backyard. As I recall you were watching Steve stacking wood and you ran into that little apple tree and fell on your butt. Or the day you smacked your head into the cabinet door while your were in the kitchen and were trying to catch a glimpse of Steve while he was talking to Dr. Morrison. I believe you have the hots for an older man."

Celina held her head down in complete embarrassment. Daphne walked up and placed her hand on her sister's shoulder. "Don't worry sis, your secrets safe with me. Just don't crack your head open one day while your staring at him. Besides he does have a cute butt."

Celina let out a laugh. "He does at that!" She stood up and gave her sister a playful punch in the arm. "You take over my back is killing me."

Daphne straddled over the stool and sat. "Do you want me to call Steve down here and get him to give you a back rub?"

Celina rolled her eyes. "Just find a station with someone giving out the news." Daphne giggled and turned to the radio. Celina was glad to see her sister coming out of her depression. It would take a burden off her shoulders worrying about her. Between Daphne's depression and her own grieving over their mother and father it was tough to keep a level head.

Time dragged on but the two were desperate for news. Daphne turned to Celina. "You think I ought to switch over to like one of those AM stations Uncle Joe used to listen to?"

"No sense in not giving it a try." Daphne nodded to her sister and turned back to the radio.

She spun through the channels and about jumped out of her skin when a voice blared out of the radio.

"...serious shit going on folks. Let me tell you what I've seen and you be the judge..."

━┼━═━┼━

Josh Riley leaned out the door of the Winnebago. "Have you gassed that damn generator up yet? Man why do I hang out with you?"

Elroy Perkins screwed the gas cap back on the generator and looked over at his friend. "I guess you hang with me because no one else believes the crap you've been spitting out over pirate radio for years. Just think I'm your only fan."

Elroy laughed as Josh waved him off "Elroy just start the thing." Josh went back into the RV and sat down in front of his radio transmitter.

Josh was a twenty five year old communications graduate from Alabama A&M. He had dark skin and wore his hair in dreadlocks. Despite having the appearance of a dope smoking activist, he was a hard core conservative. He believed the government perpetuated the welfare system and enticed black women to give up stable families to become breeding factories dependent on the government for their every need. By pumping out more government dependent babies the system would not only replenish but grow increasing the power of the government over the people. Those in the welfare system were modern day slaves, the government the slave master. Gone were the days of neighbor helping neighbor or folks down on their luck going to the church for help. The fingers of the government gained a tighter grasp over its citizens with every passing generation.

He didn't think the Republicans were responsible, he felt the Democrats were. Of course just before the collapse he got to the point that he couldn't tell the difference between the two. He felt that now all the man wanted to do was hold a brother down. Not just the brown brother but all of them, red, yellow and white.

He was determined to get out the word. Recent events and what he saw made that belief even stronger. He had seen the camps. It amazed him how fast they were set up around the country.

He had met Elroy at A&M. Elroy had the distinction of being one of the few white people at the university. He was the ultimate geek, pocket pen holder and all. What drew the two together was the love of radio; One spreading the word, the other building them, and maintaining them. After graduating the two had spent the past two years chased by the FCC. They spread the word about government corruption and cover-ups.

Now they were being chased by the military. He reached forward and flipped the toggle switch and the circuits hummed into life. "Hello Alabama and to those that can hear me across America. We don't have much time before we have to shut down. The military is getting closer and closer each day to putting a stop to the truth that I speak.

Since the collapse we have all seen the rise of the power of the Federal government. The old myths about boxcars with shackles, camps that had the appearance of prison camps, black helicopters, and the secret government are no longer myths. They are reality!

'What camps you ask?' I speak of the ones out west. My fellow broadcasters have passed the word across the land, and they are not lying. For those of you who think they are look around you. You may not have actual camps built near you, but they are springing up in the form of tent cities.

'But they are being set up by FEMA.' You reply. Have you not stopped to look at the design of these camps? Barbed wire fences, topped with razor wire, families split up, men on one side women and children on the other. It doesn't matter if you're married. Big Brother doesn't want the family to stand. No father figure for the child means that Big Brother becomes the father.

No food to be brought into the camps. It has to be turned over as you enter. God forbid an American be able to depend on himself. No weapons allowed in the camps. Big Brother will take care of you. Yet the reports I have heard from the camps speak of RAPES! Of THEFT, and MURDER! Not all of it is being done by those in the camps, but by those that keep the citizens locked in. You aren't allowed to leave. If you had a weapon you might try to fight your way out. Big Brother wouldn't like that now would he?

Have you stopped to wonder how these camps were set up so quickly? The collapse was hardly a few days old before they were set up. 'It just goes to show you how hard FEMA has worked,' you say. No it just goes to show you that FEMA is the secret government exposed.

The Bill of Rights has been suspended. FEMA has the power to take your food, clothes, generators, cars, homes, land, money, and medicine with no reimbursement to you. Worst of all they can conscript any they chose to help rebuild. Don't you find it strange how quickly the camps were set up? How fast they tried to move people to them, to "Consolidate and care for the people. To render aid, and rebuild faster." They are pulling people from their homes. They use the local police, the Army, and all the alphabet soup agencies to do it. They have the power to supersede the Constitution. Even elected officials can not stop them.

They have sent the Army to find all that possess radio transmitting gear, to confiscate it, and imprison the operators. The truth does not set you free now. It chains you. They have to control the information flow so that none will know of the atrocities that have been perpetrated against the Republic. My lily white friend and I have been chased day after day as we broadcast the information we receive and see. They fear that the truth will awaken the citizens of this great land. That they will rise up and cast off the yoke that has been placed on them. We, the speakers of truth are now the most hunted. My time is short so I will tell you of events that have transpired in the past twenty four hours.

These are reports that I have received from Alabama, Tennessee, and Mississippi. In Jackson, Corinth, Tupelo, Walls, Iuka, and Ripley Mississippi I have reports of tanker cars from trains, and eighteen wheelers being blown up near the camps, and city centers. These tankers contained some of the deadliest chemicals, and gases in them. Tens of thousands are dead or injured.

Memphis, Nashville, Columbia, Chattanooga, Germantown, and Gatlinburg have had similar attacks as in Mississippi. In a camp in Memphis and one in Columbia eighteen wheelers hauling propane crashed through the camp gates after the government agents that kept the citizens locked in them were killed by machine gun and rocket attack. The tankers were then exploded by unknown means. Nashville camps were attacked three days ago by biological attacks. Cases of small pox are appearing.

In Alabama the attacks were devastating. Huntsville, Decatur, Russellville, Ft. Payne, Birmingham, Montgomery, Homewood, Tuscaloosa, Cullman, Orange Beach, Gulf Shores, Troy, and Dothan have also been the victim of these tanker truck and train chemical attacks. Mustard gas, VX, and Sarin were used in Huntsville, Montgomery, and Tuscaloosa.

These are the only three states, and the cities I have mentioned are the only reports I have heard about. I am sure these attacks are occurring nationwide but I have not been able to get any information.

People stay away from the camps and large city centers, band together in small groups. From what we have been able to ascertain, Korean, and Chinese commando squads roam the nation at will. In the west if you can, get out. Millions of Mexicans and other South and Central Americans have crossed the borders and are killing any American they come in contact with. Fight if you want. I say get out form up in the Mid-West and go charging back in and kick them out. You don't have time to organize a sufficient size force to deal with them. I know that it is your home I speak of. There will be time to take it back later. Don't die with your family at your side. Gather your neighbors together flee and join with others and then come back in force.

In the...." Josh stopped speaking as Elroy came running into the RV. Josh left the radio Mic keyed up. "Josh there here! The choppers are here! They found us man!"

Josh turned back to the Mic. He took a deep breath as he heard the choppers descending towards the RV. "My fellow citizens Big Brother has finally caught up with me. Pass the word, and spread the truth. Take back our country and restore it the way our Founding Fathers intended it to be. My time is over now. God bless each of you and your families. Say a prayer for my soul, and that of my partner Elroy before you sleep tonight. This is the voice of verisimilitude saying goodnight." The thumping sounds of the rotors grew louder as the helicopter outside descended to the grassy field beside the RV. One still hovered overhead shining its spotlight down on the RV.

"Elroy I'm going to go stall them. When I open fire climb out the side window and haul ass." Josh said as he walked over to the small closet by the couch. When he opened the door he pulled out the only thing he loved more than a radio, his M-14.

"I'm going with you Josh." Elroy said as he stepped towards the only true friend he had ever had. Josh had never berated, abused, or made fun of him. The only thing he had ever done was care for him like a brother. He wouldn't let his friend die alone.

Josh turned and grabbed Elroy by the front of the shirt. "Elroy you don't want to die here. You get out that window when I start shooting.

Someone needs to spread the truth, and rebuild the radios. That someone is you." Josh let go of his shirt and with one arm embraced his friend. He let go and stepped back. "Now get ready to get out of here you geek. You know your lily white ass can't shoot worth a crap." He smiled at his friend and began to push by Elroy.

Elroy grabbed his friend by the shoulder. "You always were my only true friend. I'll see you when you finish with these Jack Booted Thugs."

Josh looked at his friend he knew for the last time. A tear ran from underneath Elroy's coke bottle lenses. "Alright, see you when I get back." He stepped for the door.

Stopping at the door Josh racked a round into the chamber of his battle rifle. He peeked through the curtain on the door window. Eight soldiers were exiting the Black Hawk helicopter about sixty feet away. He reached out and flung the door open. As he stepped down to the ground he brought the rifle to his shoulder. As soon as the front sight post rested on the first soldier he squeezed the trigger. The camouflaged figure crumpled to the ground. Josh saw but could not hear, the muzzle flashes winking in front of him. He heard no sound at all. His vision was crystal clear, nothing escaped his vision it was like a vivid dream. He did not even feel the rifle bucking against his shoulder. His scream of rage was mute to his own ears as he fired.

Then he felt something hit his leg. His leg buckled but he felt no pain. More objects struck his arms and chest. He knew what was hitting him now. No pain, but it was quiet evident he had been shot many times. The rifle fell from his grasp as he collapsed, his body coming to rest in the doorway of the RV.

His vision was clouded now. Still the air seemed silent around him. He saw, no he sensed something cross over his body. Then he heard a friendly voice cry out a one of his favorite words. Such a beautiful word to hear he thought as he slipped into the afterlife.

⊰⊱

Elroy stood motionless as he watched his friend go to the door of the RV. Part of him wanted to rush by his friend's side and fight. The other told him to flee. Not in fear like a coward, but to do as his friend asked. Elroy knew Josh was about to die. His mind screamed at him to do something, anything. Instead he stood motionless watching his friend open the door.

Josh flung the door open and pulled up his rifle as he stepped out. A roar of rage left his friends lips; it was almost bestial in nature. As Josh fired Elroy heard the machine guns of the soldiers outside. Bullets thwacked into and through the thin metal skin of the RV. Still he stood and watched.

Then Josh was falling, his rifle seeming to float above him as he fell. He crashed into the pull down steps that led into the RV. Plums of blood shot up like geysers on his body even as he lay there. Rage filled Elroy as he watched the bullets rend into his friends flesh. Then the shooting stopped. A call to move up and clear the RV could be heard outside.

Elroy's brain commanded his body to move, to exact revenge. Stepping over to the couch Elroy reached under the center cushion. He pulled out a nickel plated Ithaca Model 37 twelve gauge, with a black pistol grip and pump. Elroy charged the shotgun and moved for the door.

Elroy propelled himself over Josh's body towards his killers. The night landscape looked like noon from the spotlight of the hovering helicopter above. As he landed on the ground he saw the soldiers come to an abrupt halt as if they were startled that anyone else could have been in the RV.

Elroy raised the shotgun barrel level with his hip. Just before squeezing off his first round he screamed out one word. The word yelled by his favorite actor, in his favorite movie. "FREEDOM!"

Then the hammer fell and the shotgun exploded forth its deadly volley. A soldier dropped to the ground his weapon forgotten as he clutched his face that had been pulverized by the buckshot. Elroy emptied the six rounds in seconds killing two more soldiers before he fell to the ground dead. Elroy had been shot twenty seven times before he died. He died well. He died free.

Josh and Elroy didn't know it, but the radio Mic transmit toggle had been left on. The broadcast was received by a few dozen ham radio operators, several of which had recorded it. The broadcast was transmitted and recorded, passed along through the airwaves across the country.

The two men, standing up for what they believed, freedom, and truth. Those that had been asleep had their eyes opened. They had been awakened. Ignorance was not bliss any longer. They would stand up against the tyranny. Not only against the tyranny of those that attacked from the outside, but against those that attacked the freedom they held precious from the inside.

Chapter 30

Steve woke to the sound of someone knocking on the front door. He tried to will the person to go away but they continued to knock. He bolted upright as he realized what the world was all about now. Reaching for his Glock 17 Steve got up from the couch. His nerves calmed as he heard a familiar voice call out.

"Steve!" Knock! Knock! Knock! "Steve its Amos and Benny, Are you in there?"

Steve peeked out the front window making sure Amos was not being held at gunpoint. Seeing Amos and Benny with no one else around Steve opened the door. "Good morning Amos and Benny. Come on in." The two entered the house and Steve shut the door and threw the deadbolt.

"I told you not to be staying up all night looking for a repeat of that broadcast." Amos said with a smile.

"You were right beside me egging me on. I aught to blame you for being so tired." After the girls told everyone about what they had heard on the radio Steve and the others went down stairs to try to find out more news. Around midnight a Ham radio operator played the recording of Josh and Elroy's last minutes on Earth. The broadcast had stunned them all.

It became evident that they must organize the surrounding area or be picked off one by one and either killed or sent to the "Relocation Camps". First off they decided they would blockade the road the next day.

"Sure blame it on the old man. I can't help I don't need more than four hours sleep to be refreshed. I guess it has something to do with superior genetics." Amos said as he grabbed a seat on the couch.

Steve ignored the good natured jab not wanting to become enthralled in a taunting battle that he would surely lose. "You want some coffee for those superior genes of yours?" Steve walked to the kitchen and began pumping the Coleman stove and fixing up the coffee.

"Love some Steve."

"Hey Benny!" Steve called from the kitchen.

"Yes sir." Benny said from the couch where he sat beside Amos.

"I'm about to turn the generator on to heat the hot water heater so I can grab a quick shower. You want to watch some of those videos?"

Benny sprang from the couch and ran into the kitchen. "You bet Steve. You want me to start the generator for you."

Steve set the coffee pot on the stove. "Nah, I'll get it. Go pick out a movie and I will have the power on in about ten minutes or so." Steve made his way to the generator while Benny sprinted for the entertainment room.

Fifteen minutes later Benny was watching Spy Kids 4 in the back room on video and Steve and Amos were just sitting down with cups of coffee. Amos took a sip of his coffee then crossed his legs sat back and got comfortable. "So do you really think blocking off the roads will do us any good?" He took another drink of coffee waiting for Steve's reply.

Steve thought about it for a moment then answered. "Well like I said before. We don't have the manpower to set guards in place. I do think however, it would be a good idea. It will limit vehicle travel on the road. It will possibly deter those on foot making them think they were entering a trap."

"I don't know Steve. You and Doc both said we would leave one of the shoulders or ditches open so folks could pass. Why waste all that effort if they can still get through."

"Well you said we don't own the road. I just thought it might be a compromise you could live with."

"Steve if we do this I say we block the entire roadway." Amos took another sip of his coffee.

Steve held the warm mug in both hands rotating it in a circle as he thought. Finally he answered. "Amos if we do that, how do we get our vehicles in and out?"

"I've thought about that last night. I say we build some sort of gate that we can open and shut."

The mug had cooled a bit in Steve's hands and he decided it was ready to drink without scalding him. He took a drink emptying half the cup. "That's not a bad idea Amos. Not bad at all."

The two spent another hour and three cups of coffee discussing the design of the road block. Then Steve rose and placed his cup in the sink. "I'm grabbing a quick shower then we'll head over to Doc's and get to work." Amos followed him to the kitchen and placed his cup in the sink and then went in to watch the remainder of the movie Benny was watching.

By eight thirty they were out the door. Steve walked beside Amos and Benny who had ridden Festus and Midget instead of driving. When they reached Doc's place the girls and Maude were out on the side of the house hanging laundry. Doc came out on the front porch to greet them and invited them inside.

⊹⊷⊶⊹

"So what do you intend to use for a road block if you aren't going to lay trees across the roadway?" Doc said as he ran his fingers through his thinning hair.

Amos and Steve looked at one another and then back at Doc. Steve spoke up first. "How do you like the idea of telephone poles?"

"Telephone poles! What if they power was to come back on? We would be without power." Doc said not quiet sure he liked the idea.

Amos shook his head. "How in the hell did you ever make it through medical school? If we don't have power no one else on the road will either. Eventually the Electricity folks would put up new lines. Besides that you have a generator. We will use some trees though to fill the ditches, and make them impassable."

"Well Mister Genius don't you think the law would come out here and arrest us for damaging the lines?"

Steve knew he had to intervene quickly. The two old men would bicker for hours before coming to an agreement. "Doc, the law doesn't come out for people getting murdered. Besides the poles will be easier to work with than the trees."

"Well Super Man are we just going to walk over and pull them up out of the ground and carry them where we want them by hand?"

"Doc have you forgot Amos has a backhoe?"

"Well naturally he forgot to bring it." Doc smiled in triumph since he wasn't the only one to have forgotten something.

"We didn't decide on the backhoe until this morning you old coot." Amos said raising his chin in superiority.

"Yall two mental giants quit the verbal sparing we have to get to work. Amos, ride back to your place and grab the backhoe. Doc I brought my chainsaw, you grab yours. We'll start taking the poles down." Steve went out to the front porch and picked up his chainsaw. Amos got back on Festus and headed for his place, and Doc headed to the shop for his chainsaw.

⊷⊷⊶⊷

The morning was pleasantly cool and Amos enjoyed the fresh air and the songs of the morning birds. He almost could forget what had become of the world. Heck, even Festus was acting like the obedient animal he should be.

As his farm came into sight Amos's daydreaming was interrupted by Festus trotting off the road and towards the tree line. Amos pulled up on the reigns to stop him. "Where the hell do you think you're going?" Festus did not stop until he was in the tree line. Then he stopped facing the farm. His ears stood upright facing the direction of the farm.

"Dagnabbit, what the hell are you doing you stupid jackass! It's not hot out, and you sure as heck don't need to take a break you lazy turd." Festus stood motionless, ignoring Amos as he stared intently ahead.

It took a few seconds for Amos to realize something had caught the attention of the mule between his legs. He quit his bickering and stared at the farm. Then his peripheral vision caught movement and he snapped his eyes towards it.

Two people, a man and a woman came jogging around the side of his home. Amos dismounted and pulled the Remington 2700 from the saddle scabbard. Reaching into the saddle bag Amos pulled out four ten round magazines for the rifle placing them in the large pockets of his overalls.

Amos moved with the surefooted ease of one who knows the ground he is walking. He quietly made his way to the front of the house staying in the tree line. He was probably twenty-five yards away from the house when he spotted three more people, another man and two more women.

The five people grouped up, and Amos could barely hear what they were saying as the wind blew through the trees swaying the limbs, and rustling the leaves. "All the doors are locked, and the windows are boarded up. I don't think anyone is home." One of the women said to the man that had been standing with the two other women.

Amos looked the group over. The two men wore dirty blue jeans and neutral colored long sleeve shirts. They both had OD green backpacks on. The bigger of the two, probably six foot three, had a holster on his right hip. The other man had a long bladed knife hanging from his belt, but appeared to have no other weapons.

The women were similarly dressed except each carried a small day pack. Two of the women also had sheath knives on their belts, the third a small camp axe. The whole group was filthy. Greasy hair, dirty clothes, and dirt smudged on their skin. The two men appeared like they had not shaved in a week or more.

"Any farm animals around?" The big man asked.

The other man motioned with his head back behind him. "Yeah, looks like someone's been feeding them. Saw a few cows out in the side pasture too. They got crops planted, can't tell what though.

The big man wiped some sweat off his brow with his shirt sleeve. "Well they obviously aint home right now. Let's take the door down get what we can. Then we'll take a few chickens with us. At least we will have some eggs every now and then."

The red haired woman spoke up. "We gonna torch this place too?"

"Yeah. No sense in leaving any evidence behind. I know the cops have all but disappeared, but if the military catches you looting they shoot you. Like I said before, we burn the place we don't leave any physical evidence behind."

Anger seethed through Amos. If they had said they would take a chicken because they were hungry and were going to leave everything else alone it might not have angered him so badly. But to just break into someone's home and then burn it for no reason was more than his sense of law and order could take. "The military aint the only ones who will shoot your ass for looting, you damn sons of bitches." Amos whispered to himself as he eased forward towards a large oak.

"Let's do this!" The big man said. The others turned and began to walk towards the house.

Amos raised the rifle to his shoulder and aimed between the two men who walked slightly ahead of the three women. Amos squeezed the trigger. The round kicked up the dirt in front of the two men. All five came to an abrupt halt. The big man eased his hand towards the pistol that road his hip. "You touch that pistol I will put a bullet in your back!" Amos yelled out. "Now all of you get your hands up and go to your knees!"

The smaller man and three women complied, each slowly going to their knees. The big man however turned slowly, his hand just barely above the pistol. "Now mister we don't want any trouble. We're just hungry. Why don't you come on out of those trees and let's talk about this. I'm sure we can work something out."

"Mister you seem to think this is some B movie and I'm going to be stupid and come out from behind cover. Now get your hands in the air, and down on your knees!"

The man let out a chuckle. He truly seemed amused. He didn't give any indication of being concerned in the least bit about being in such a bad situation. "Come on out farmer. You know if you shoot me you would be breaking the law. You don't want to go to prison do you?"

His hand inched closer to the pistol. The man seemed to be staring right at Amos, as if he could see through the underbrush. Amos began to wonder just how good with the pistol this man was to be so confident. "I guess I would be breaking the law like you were just about to do. Don't think I didn't hear what you said. I will be damned if you burn my home down."

The man laughed again. "You must have misunderstood me friend…".

Out of the corner of his eye he saw the smaller man starting to come off his knees. Amos shifted the sights and put a round to the man's left. The smaller man dropped back to his knees.

Amos turned back to face the larger man. His eyes went wide when he saw the man charging his position his pistol coming up. His lips were twisted in a snarl, hate emanated from his dark eyes. The pistol barked twice as he ran, one round snapping past Amos's head, the second spitting the bark near his chest.

Amos worked the trigger as fast as he could, the first and second round missing, going high. Amos fought to bring the rifle back on target as another gunshot from the man's pistol, the bullet catching the cloth of Amos's shirt. Amos's next two rounds kicked up dirt in front of the man's feet since he had over compensated his aim. Amos let the rifle ride up with the recoil and he kept pulling the trigger. The man was no more than ten yards away now.

His next round found its mark in the man's left knee cap. The soft point 30-06 round mushrooming, forcing the bone of the kneecap backwards tearing through the back of the man's leg. His next two rounds struck the man in the stomach as he fell to the moist earth. The mask of rage that he wore now had turn to one of pain. It was a look he would wear to his death as the last round in Amos's rifle tore into the man's throat and out the back of his neck.

The man's body collapsed to the ground his knees bent, feet protruding back towards his buttocks. The man's shoulders inches above the ground stopped by his head which was bent to far back to be natural.

Amos looked to the other four and saw that they had all balled up on the ground seeking refuge from the flying the bullets. Amos's hands shook as he tried desperately to pull out a fresh magazine which seemed to be hung on the inside of his pocket. Finally in frustration he dropped the rifle and pulled the Ruger Red Hawk from the holster on his hip.

His voice quivering a bit he yelled to the four prone people. "Now where are the rest of your friends?" None of them replied. Amos fired a round into the ground near one of the women. "Tell me where they are or the next one goes in your head."

The woman looked up and stared in the general direction of Amos. Tears cut grooves through the dirt on her face. "There isn't anyone else! I swear! Don't kill us. It was all Ernie's idea to burn your place. You saw it. He's the one with the gun, we don't have any guns. We got to do what he says." She sobbed some more as she buried her face into the dirt, her arms covering her head.

Amos took a deep breath trying to calm down. He pressed his right hand against the tree to stop the shaking. "This is what I want yall to do! Real slow each of you; come up on your knees. Then I want you to lose the knives and the hatchet. Throw them out in front of you. Then I want you to take your packs off and dump the contents out in front of you."

The four slowly did as they were told. Once they had dumped the packs Amos gave his next set of instructions. "Now real slow like, one item at a time put the stuff back in. If anything that looks like a gun and I shoot all four of you." The four complied with his orders when they were done Amos had each lift up their shirts and turn in a circle making sure they concealed no other weapons. Finally he was convinced they had no weapons and he stepped out of the trees.

As he did Amos heard the sound of a vehicle coming up the road from Doc's place at a high rate of speed. He turned to see Doc's truck as it slid through the gravel between the trees. Steve jumped out his AK-47 coming up covering the four people. "Amos you okay?" Steve called out.

"Yeah, I'm just shaken a bit Steve." Amos saw Doc and Celina getting out of the driver side of the truck, Doc with an M-1 Garand, Celina with the stainless Mini-14.

"Little slow getting here aint you, you old fart." Amos said trying a little humor in an attempt to help calm his nerves.

"Yeah, but as much shooting as you were doing I thought there would be plenty of bad guys left to shoot. How many rounds did it take for you to plug that fellow, thirty or forty?" Doc joked back, knowing that Amos's humor was an attempt to regain control. He had seen it hundreds of times in Viet Nam, Marines making jokes at the direst of moments trying to stay on this side of sanity during the maelstrom of battle.

Steve advanced on the four, the barrel of his AK switching from one person to the next. "Where are yall coming from?"

In a quivering voice the man answered. "Flor.. Florence."

"What are you doing way out here?"

"We're just trying to find food. We don't want any trouble mister."

The lie angered Amos. He advanced the few feet between himself and the man. Amos drove the toe of his boot into the man's crotch. The man's knees seemed to lift off the ground. His hands groping for his genitals as he fell to his side gasping for breath.

"You damn liar! You said you were going to burn my place down!" Amos pointed the barrel of the big .44 at the man's head while cocking the hammer back. The man never seemed to notice as he began to retch, followed by several dry heaves. The vomit pooled around his cheek and clung to his chin. The three women started to scream in terror.

Steve moved quickly to Amos's side. He knew his friend was about to shoot the man dead. His hand went to Amos's shoulder and he spoke to him in a calm reassuring voice. "He isn't worth murdering Amos. Your house is still here, and so are you. You don't need to kill him."

Amos stood frozen for a moment, his finger tight against the trigger. Finally he lowered the pistol and walked to his front porch and sat on the steps. The pistol hung limply in his right hand. His left hand rubbed the back of his neck.

The crisis halted Steve turned on the four looters. "You four get up off the ground now."

The four slowly stood their, eyes jumping from one face to another. Steve looked at the second woman. With his rifle he gestured to the coil of rope attached to the bottom of her pack. "You and the redhead take that rope and loop it around your friend's body." The two slowly moved towards the man.

They froze when Celina ordered them to. "Just a second Steve."

Celina moved towards the dead man. When she got to him she placed the barrel of her rifle to his head. Her right foot pinned his wrist to the ground. Leaning over she pulled the pistol from his hand. It was a rusted Ruger P-85.

Celina tossed the gun off into the bushes, and backed away. She pointed her rifle back at the women. "Now move."

It took the woman several squeamish minutes to secure the rope around the man's body. The redhead threw up several times when she got blood on her arm. Their task completed they stood.

Steve nudged the man in the back with the barrel of his rifle. "Move over there with them." Once the four stood around their friend they seemed to start to cry and sob in unison. They were certain they would be joining their dead friend.

"Now, all four of you grab some rope. I want you to drag that piece of trash along with you. You carry him all the way back to Florence with you. I'll be trailing you so don't even think about ditching his body. I see you ditch him, I kill you all. Do you understand?"

The only answer he got was four bobbing heads. Taking a good grip on the rope the four began to drag their former leader to the road. Steve followed them out to the road. One of the women looked back at Steve as they began to trudge forward pulling the weight of the dead man behind them. Steve stepped up into the woods and yelled out. "Remember! I'll be following you!"

Steve sat for a time and watched them disappear down the road. Once he was satisfied they were gone he stood and brushed the dirt from the back of his pants and made his way through the woods following the four from a distance. After about a one mile of travel the four dropped their ropes and began walking away. Steve raised his weapon and fired a round in the road ahead of them. The four ran back and grabbed their ropes and continued to pull the dead body. Steve laughed to himself and turned to head back to Amos's

Once Steve returned to Amos's place they gave Amos a chance to lay back and unwind a bit. Doc and Celina had headed back to his place to let Maude know everything was okay. Doc would return shortly with the chainsaws. They decided they would begin working on the barricades near Amos's place first.

Steve sat in Amos's recliner looking at the old man stretched out on the couch. Amos had been dozing for about fifteen minutes. "Amos you okay?"

Amos's eyes fluttered open, his big hand coming up and rubbing his eyes. "Yeah I'm fine. Sucker almost got me though Steve. I'm too old for this crap, my reflexes just aint what they used to be."

"You came out on top and that's what counts Amos."

Amos sat up and swung his legs to the floor as he leaned his back against the pillows. "Yeah I came out on top. But what if all five had had guns? I would probably be dead."

"Amos, don't dwell on the, what could have been. It's not a good thing to do in situations like this. You're alive, and unhurt. That's what counts."

"Yeah I guess you're right Steve." The sound of Doc's truck pulling up into the drive reached his ears. He stood up and stretched. "Let's get outside and get those barricades up. It won't stop the determined but at least it will give us a little peace of mind." The two walked out the front door.

They spent the remainder of the day and the rest of the next building the barricades. Using an auger they dug two postholes on each side of the road. Then they placed telephone poles into them. Each pole stood about four feet high above the ground.

Doc had brought some twenty-four inch bolts back from his shop. They had to take the poles that would cross the road to Amos's barn where they predrilled them with holes. These bolts were used to attach the poles to the upright post. The poles were stacked one on top of another forming two complete walls. There was about a three foot gap between each wall. These gaps were filled with dirt that Amos dug out from the side of the road creating ditches approximately eight feet wide and about four feet deep.

Next they fell several trees on each side of the barricade in front of the ditches. They left the branches in place to hamper someone on foot from easily crossing them. The trees where layered so that the branches covered the exposed trunks of the trees they landed on.

On both barricades they left a ten foot gap on one end of the barricade so a vehicle could drive through. The vehicle would have to drive slowly though because of the obstacles placed in front of the barricades.

The first sets of obstacles were simple tree stumps averaging three foot in diameter and about three feet tall. They were spaced out on the two lane road out over one hundred feet in front of the barricades. These stumps were placed in a zigzag manner. The driver of any vehicle would have to slow and maneuver through the maze of tree stumps.

Then Steve came up with an idea. Using a set of extremely large bolt cutters they began to cut the utility lines in varying lengths. Using hand wenches and eyebolts they attached the utility lines to the trees on the road side. They then ran the lines to the stumps where they were connected to the eyebolts placed on each stump.

Amos used a blow torch to melt the lines together once they were tight enough. This effectively denied the use of the shoulders of the road while driving towards the barricades. Some lines where placed high enough that they would come across the windshield of a car or truck. Others low enough to get caught up under the front bumpers so that it would possibly damage the front end of a fast moving vehicle.

The women and Benny had not been idle in the absence of the men. Using hand saws and axes they cut down small saplings. These saplings were lashed together in pieces of four. They stood about three feet in height. Four ends stuck in the ground while the opposite ends pointed out at forty five degree angles. The ends were sharpened. They also made smaller two foot tall versions.

They placed these improvised pickets along the sides of the ditches. Most of the smaller ones were placed in the ditches themselves. Even though one could easily walk through the pickets under normal conditions to do so under heavy gunfire would most likely cause one to become impaled, or simply shot.

At the end of the second day everyone met back at Doc's place for dinner. After dinner the men had been delegated a turn at washing the dishes. Doc wiped his hands on the pink apron that he wore. Amos had goaded him the entire time swearing it belonged to Doc, and not Maude. "Tomorrow I'm going to lie around on my tail all day long. I am exhausted."

Amos tossed a wet dish towel at his friend hitting him in the face. "Well why your upper crust butt lounges I've got to get up and tend to my fields."

Steve pulled a chair out from the kitchen table and sat leaning the chair back on two legs. "Sorry to inform you Doc, but we have something to do tomorrow."

"What have we got to do tomorrow?" Doc said as he pulled his glasses from his face wiping the lenses on the towel Amos had tossed at him.

"Have you forgotten the radio broadcast? We have to get the word out about what's going on. We also have to tell everyone to meet at Jackson Hwy and Butler Creek Rd. so we can get some sort of trade going."

Doc let out a sigh as he leaned back against the counter top. "Great." He reached over and picked up the oil lamp. "Well let's go hit the sack then."

Doc headed off for bed. Amos and Steve went home. Benny had fallen asleep on the couch and Amos had decided to leave him be.

When Steve got home he cranked up the generator. He wanted to have good lighting while he prepared his gear for the journey ahead of him. Though they would only be gone a few days he wanted to be prepared for anything.

Taking down his Alice Pack of its hanger he began to pack. He stuffed it with eight MREs for his food. Extra socks and underwear were put in a Ziploc bag. Foot powder, first aid kit, two boxes of ammo for his pistol, compass, county map, toilet kit, fire starter, an extra pair of tan BDU pants, and shirt. He had a German water proof sleeping bag cover and poncho liner for a sleeping roll, and he placed a fifty ounce Camelback water bladder in the top of the pouch in the flap of the pack.

Next he field stripped his pistol, and rifle. He cleaned the two weapons and performed a function check once he assembled them. He decided on taking three extra high capacity magazines for the pistol. He would also take six thirty round magazines for his rifle.

Once he finished packing up Steve took a short hot shower. When he finished, he shut down the generator. He fell asleep almost immediately his body sore and tired from the past two days of hard work. He didn't know it, but the next few days would be even harder.

Chapter 31

Despite being exhausted from building the barricades, Steve woke around 5:30 and felt fairly refreshed. There was a slight chill in the room so Steve ambled over to his dresser in the dark room. He pulled out a t-shirt and a pair of jogging pants and slipped them on.

He walked over to his dresser and picked up his pistol and carried it with him downstairs. Once he had a pot of coffee brewing Steve went to the living room, pushing the coffee table aside. Steve began to do some stretches. Once the kinks and tightness had been worked out Steve started doing pushups, crunches, and bends and thrust.

Steve finished up his morning workout in about thirty minutes. His body covered in sweat he made his way to the bathroom. He stripped down and turned on the shower. The water felt ice cold as he went under the shower head. He hated cold showers but decided against using the generator to heat up the water.

Once Steve was out of the shower he dried off and got dressed. He slipped on a pair of olive drab BDU pants, and a gray t-shirt. He went to the closet and pulled out a pair of Matterhorn Gortex lined boots. He loved these boots and had paid a pretty penny for them. The Gortex lining kept the inside of the boots water resistant. They also helped wick the sweat from his feet away keeping them fairly dry in hot weather.

Next he slipped on his gun belt. The gun belt was made of nylon and had a thigh holster attached to it. He also had a magazine pouch that would hold three of his seventeen round magazines. A Marine K-Bar fighting knife was just behind the holster strap.

Once he was dressed he walked into his back room where all of his electronics were located. He connected the jury rigged power cord to the car battery. Doc, Amos, and he had rigged all of their systems the same. The car batteries were trickle charged from wires that connected to a small solar panel outside. Once the CB was powered up he called for Doc. "Steve to Doc do you copy?" He paused for a few seconds and tried again. "Steve to Doc do you copy?"

He was about to cut the CB off when a response came. Though 8:00 am, and 8:00 pm, were the regular check in times for the three sometimes one of the three would be monitoring the CB or scanning the channels listening for life on the outside. "Amos to Steve I copy you."

"Hey Amos everything okay on your end?"

"Yeah. I was just scanning through the channels listening for news while I ate my breakfast."

"Have you heard anything interesting out there in the rest of the world?"

Amos keyed the Mic and Steve good hear him exhale. Probably puffing on his pipe Steve thought. "Did catch some chatter about some fighting down near Russellville. Not sure who was fighting who. They did mention the word "troops". I don't know if they were talking about ours or some of those Koreans, and Chinese."

"Guess its all the more reason we need to get everyone organized around here. Well let me get off of here and head to Doc's. We'll bring Benny by on our way out."

"Okay see you in a bit, Amos out."

Steve turned the power knob to off, and then unhooked the CB from the battery. He was hoping to get hold of Doc and tell him to bring the horses and his equipment over to his place. He forgot last night when he told Doc he would come over in the morning that they would be riding back towards his home. "Oh well. No one ever accused me of being smart."

They had decided when they planned this undertaking to take horses. Though they had plenty of fuel for their vehicles, gas would be a precious commodity soon enough. Horses though slower would allow them the freedom to cut across areas a vehicle could not go. Also if they encountered road blocks they could take to the woods. There would be less of a chance that cars or trucks could follow. The added bonus of the horses would be that they would raise an alarm if they became startled by anyone sneaking up on their campsites.

He picked up his Alice pack and set it beside the front door. He would stop by on the way back out and pick it up. He decided he would take the AK and his LBV with him on the walk over to Doc's. There was no telling what one could walk into now days.

He picked up the vest and put it on. Once he had it zipped up he snapped the attached belt loops around his holster belt. He jumped up and down to test the weight. The vest was a black Tac-3 Vest made by Supreme Protector. The vest had six magazine pouches, each holding a thirty round AK-47 magazine. A large pouch was located on the left and right above the magazine pouches.

He kept a small first aid kit, a small wire saw, two Bic lighters, and a compass in one pouch. The second pouch contained two emergency blankets, Swiss Army knife, fishing hooks and line, and two chocolate power bars. There was a built in fanny pack on the back. In the fanny pack was a military poncho, poncho liner 550 parachute cord, and some small metal tent pegs.

Next he picked up his AK-47, and inserted one of his seventy five round drums. Though the drum made the weapon heavier and a bit unwieldy the added ammunition was a plus. In a firefight having the seventy five round drum would be a God send. He chambered a round and placed the weapon on safe. Opening the door he headed out for Doc's.

Halfway to Doc's he heard the plodding sound of horse hoofs on pavement. He was sure it was Doc but decided not to take any chances. He stepped off the road and into the trees.

As the sound of the horses came closer Steve saw it was Doc riding a Quarter Horse named Brown. Doc held the reigns of a beautiful Paint, named Spot. Both Maude and he had tried to convince Doc to name the horse something that would befit its elegance. Doc had remained steadfast stating that if the name Spot was good enough for a dog it was good enough for a horse.

Steve stepped from the woods. "Morning Doc. I see you realized me walking to your house was a dumb idea."

Doc brought the horses to a stop. "Good morning Steve. Yeah I thought about that this morning when I was loading up. Let's hope this is the dumbest decision we make on our little journey."

Steve mounted up on Spot and the two headed for Steve's to pick up his pack. "What about Benny? I told Amos I we would bring him by on our way out."

"Maude said Celina would follow him over a little later in the morning. I was going to wake him and bring him along, Celina was adamant about doing it according to Maude. Guess she wants the chance to saddle up and ride the area a bit. Get out of the house for awhile for some time alone. It will do her some good."

"I guess we all need a little time to straighten out our minds now days. Of course it's a hell of a lot more dangerous now days. You did tell her to bring her rifle didn't you?"

Doc chuckled. "Heck I don't think she will ever go anywhere without a weapon anymore. She was cleaning the dang thing this morning after breakfast. She cares for that thing like a mother does her baby. God help the fool that messes with her too.

She's been practicing about every day with her shooting. Had to tell her she needed to cut back. She's been shooting a ton of ammo."

Steve looked at his friend a bit concerned about the use of ammo. "Are you running low on .223?"

"Nah I've got enough for everyone to shoot a couple hundred rounds a day for a couple of years. I believe we need to conserve as much as possible though. Ammo in my opinion is going to be worth more than gold in the near future.

I smoothed things over with her though and taught her to reload the ammo she's been shooting. I've got more in reloading supplies than I have in live ammo."

Steve looked back to the road ahead. "Is Daphne doing any practicing?"

"Nothing like Celina, probably about ten to twenty rounds a day. She likes to slow fire. She's not much on that running and jumping and shooting stuff. I thought about giving her one of my deer rifles.

Celina is really good at moving and shooting, but Daphne, with a little work, will be shooting wings off of flies before long."

"Which rifle did you have in mind?"

"I'm going to start her out with my Thompson/Center .22 Classic Benchmark that I bought a couple of years ago. Then I will move her up to that CZ bolt that I bought in .223."

"Sounds good, let's ride up into the woods here and dismount. I want to check the place out before we approach." The two turned the horses down into the ditch and into the woods.

Steve dismounted and Doc stayed in the saddle. "Are you coming Doc?"

"Steve it's only been about thirty minutes since you left. Is this necessary?"

"Remember what you said about stupid decisions? We need to be on our toes all the time now Doc. The more we practice it, the more it becomes natural."

Doc let out a sigh as he pulled his M-1 Garand from the scabbard and dismounted. The two made their way until they could see Steve's place through the trees. "Looks like you've done a lot of work clearing out the under brush."

Steve took a knee and just gave Doc a nod. He pulled out the monocular that was on his web belt and scanned his place. After several minutes he was satisfied. The two went back and got the horses and rode into the yard.

"I'll be right back." Steve trotted up to the front porch and went to the door. Unlocking it he reached in and grabbed his pack. He took a cursory look at his living room and was satisfied everything was as he had left it. Locking the front door he went back to Doc and the horses and they headed to Amos's.

Amos walked Steve and Doc back outside and the three made their goodbyes. "Oh, Amos before I forget. Celina said she was going to help Benny with his shooting before she brought him home if that's okay with you."

"Sure, I don't have a problem with it. Yall be careful out there." Doc and Steve gave him a wave as they turned their horses and headed out to spread the word. Amos knew the trip was necessary, but he didn't like it one bit. A million things could go wrong and one or both of his friends could wind up dead or seriously disabled. He watched them disappear around the bend and then he headed for the barn to continue the days work.

"Amos didn't look to happy about seeing us off Doc."

"I can't say as I blame him much. I'm not too happy about going off. So who do you think we aught to see first?"

"At first I thought we should just ride house to house and tell each person we came too. The more I think about it the more I think we should stop by and see Mr. Flynn first."

"Why should we stop by and see Roy first?"

"Well Doc we are talking about using his parking lot aren't we? I also think he would welcome the idea of getting back to his grocery store. I'm willing to bet he's short on food if he's still alive."

Doc tilted his straw hat back on his head. "Why on earth would you think a man that owns a grocery store would be short on food?"

Steve looked at Doc. "Think about it. If you owned a grocery store would you stock up on food at your home? Heck anything for that matter. Flynn has a pharmacy, sells tools, animal feed, and just about everything else in that store. Heck he even has a gas station. I bet that store is stripped bare."

"I never thought about it that way. I guess we will find out when we get to his place."

Doc and Steve road on in silence, they cut across a field to save some time, cutting about two miles off their journey to Flynn's place. Within thirty minutes they arrived.

Flynn's once manicured lawn was overgrown with weeds and broken limbs. His two trucks were in the driveway and clothes hung out on the clothes line. "It looks like someone is home. So how do you want to do this?"

"Doc I would say I would hide in the woods and cover you as you ride up. We can't do that though. There isn't a thing except open fields around Flynn's place. I guess we ride up and hope for the best." Steve pulled out his AK and rested it across the saddle horn.

"If this works, we're going to have to work out a different approach to homes. Riding up and saying 'How do ya do?' just aint going to cut mustard with me." The two rode forward.

"I don't know Doc. I kind of like the idea about me laying back and covering you. I feel safe when I think about doing it that way." Steve gave Doc a wink and Doc gave back a frown. Then they were at the front drive of Flynn's place.

"Hello in the house!" Doc called out.

The door slowly opened and Flynn's youngest son Charles stepped out. Charles was in his early twenties and carried an old Springfield 1903 A3 in his hands. "Is everything alright Doc? Who's the fella with you?"

Doc and Steve dismounted. "Everything is fine Charles. This is my neighbor Steve Roberts."

Charles shook both men's hands. "Nice meeting you Steve. What's with the visit Doc?" Charles turned to let both men inside.

"Well I need to talk to your dad about some business."

Roy Flynn walked in holstering an S&W 329PD, .44 Magnum. "Hey Herb, wasn't quite sure that was you at first." He reached out and shook Doc's hand. He then turned to Steve. "Roy Flynn."

Steve reached out and took the grocers hand. He was surprised to find it hard, strong and calloused. "Steve Roberts, it's nice to meet you sir."

Roy stepped back and gestured with his hand for the two to have a seat. "Yall sit down what can I do for you. I heard you tell Charles you had some business for me. If its food you want I can't help you there. We're pretty low on it ourselves." He let a chuckle, more in disgust than humor. "Pretty damned amazing a grocer almost out of food don't you think?"

Doc looked at Steve. The boy had been right on the money. "Well Roy I don't need your food. I need your store and property."

"Herb you've always been nuttier than goose ever since grade school but your plum crazy if you think I'm giving up my store."

"Roy have you had a chance to find out what's been going on around the country?"

"Not a thing Herb. I've just been trying to survive. What's that got to do with you wanting my store?"

Doc turned to Steve. "I'll let Steve tell you what's been going on in the rest of the country and then I'll explain how you can get back in business."

"Well Mr. Flynn first off you might want to grab the rest of your family. I'm sure they will want to hear this."

Roy gave Charles a nod and he headed out the door to get the rest of the family. A few minutes later Roy's other son Brent, and Roy's wife Betty walked into the room. Roy introduced Steve to them.

Once introductions were made, Steve described the events that had taken place since the collapse. First he covered what he knew about world events. Then he went on and discussed what was going on in America. He ended with the story of Josh and Elroy.

The family sat back stunned into total silence. Betty was the first to speak. "I knew about the Chinese and Koreans, but what is this garbage about relocation camps. I can't believe the government would imprison a family for storing food. Heck, they would put us under the jail if the store was still open."

Doc leaned forward in his chair. "Betty these reports on the radio have been confirmed by dozens of Ham radio operators across the country. The America we grew up in is gone. I don't know if we will ever have it back. What I do know is that we have to get organized and protect ourselves. That is of course, if you prefer to live in a tent separated from your husband and sons by a barbed wire fence."

"Doc I'm not saying I don't believe you, but what does that have to do with the store?"

Steve spoke before Doc could begin to speak again. "Mr. Flynn what we are doing out here is spreading the word. Not only about what we have heard but also to spread the word about organizing our community. I think your store is an ideal location for folks to meet once a week. They can share news, barter, trade or just plain socialize.

We want your permission to do this. There is an added bonus in this for you that I thought about. You could rent out space in your store for folks with specialties, like doctors, dentist, candle makers, gunsmiths or whatever. You charge a fee of two cans of food for the day. You charge the customers a bullet or something of value as a cover charge to enter. That puts you back in business, and food in your pantry."

Brent spoke before his father. "Dad I think we need to give this a shot. The store has been stripped clean. There is nothing left in there for us. Heck I can sale my homemade beer. I can't think of a man around who wouldn't mind having a swig of beer for a couple of .22 shells."

Charles spoke up next. "Brent's right dad, Steve and Doc have a great idea. Besides the more folks band together the better chance we stand against those little yellow bastards who started all of this. The government too, if what Steve says is true. I'll be damned if I give up my food, guns, or freedom to some stinking Washington bureaucrats."

Roy leaned his head back and closed his eyes. After a few moments of contemplation he opened his eyes and stood up. Reaching out his hand he gave Doc's three quick shakes. "Herb you might be nutty, but that's a fine idea. So when do you want to start this thing up?"

"Well Steve and I will be riding the area the next few days getting the word out. If yall will pass the word along to everyone you can I would say two weeks. That gives us two weeks for the word to spread. Each person we tell will probably tell a couple and they will tell few. So within two weeks we could possibly have several hundred folks at the meet."

"Betty what's today?"

Betty looked back at the calendar on the wall. "Today's the second. So that would put it Wednesday the 16th."

Doc and Steve stood. "Roy we're going to head on now and start telling everyone we can."

Everyone shook hands and said their goodbyes. Steve and Doc mounted up and headed out. By two o'clock they had stopped at ten more homes. So far at each home they had been welcomed in a wary, but friendly manner. It truly helped that Doc knew most everyone in the area. Each family said they would pass on the word.

They didn't need to stop for dinner since many of the family's shared a few bites to eat with the pair. By six o'clock in the evening they had been to four more homes. The sun was setting and it was time to make a camp.

Doc spotted an overgrown field, with a cattle pond in the middle. "How about over there Steve?"

Steve looked the seven acre field over. It was fenced in with barbed wire; the field was devoid of trees except near the pond. Several large oaks were clustered there. "It looks pretty good to me Doc. The fence appears to be in good shape. We can let the horses graze and water and get some sleep. I don't know about you, but my butt is killing me."

Once they had their bedrolls down Steve built a small fire. Doc pulled a large family size can of Chicken Noodle soup out. "You want to share some soup and crackers with me Steve? It'll be a lot better than those nasty MREs you brought along."

Steve quickly agreed before Doc changed his mind. It only took a few minutes to heat the soup. They ate and then cleaned up. The put the fire out just before the sun sank below the horizon. Steve then went and rounded up the horses and tethered them under one of the trees. By eight o'clock both men were sound asleep.

⊹—⊷—⊹

For the next two days the two worked their way south towards Florence. They traveled each county road making their way east and west and then south. The closer they got to Florence the fewer the two knew. They met up with dozens of families each promising to attend. Each was grateful for the news of the outside world, but a dark cloud formed when they learned of the camps and new government mandates.

Doc and Steve had no problems, received no threats. Unless you counted being met with a gun at each home you came to. It wasn't until the middle of the third day that their luck changed.

They had worked their way down to the Petersville area just on the outskirts of Florence. They still didn't meet a lot of people, but the population density had increased compared to the St. Florian area that they had just left.

Steve and Doc halted their horses and dismounted them to give them a break. As they walked along Doc told Steve how he felt about coming this far west. "Steve I think we need to head back home. You and I don't know anyone in the area; we start telling folks we don't know about the meet and we may attract the wrong type of people."

"I think you're right Doc. Let's head over to those trees and eat some lunch, then we'll head back home." Steve pointed to a group of maple trees that stood in front of an exposed basement. The house had either been moved or destroyed. All that remained was the basement.

When they reached the trees Steve was about to take off his pack when a shot rang out and a chunk of the bark was blown off of one of the trees leaving a gaping white scare. Steve snatched up his rifle taking the safety off as he picked it up.

"Doc, take the horses and get in there!" Steve pointed back towards the basement. Doc snatched up the reigns and ran leading the horses around to the back side of the basement. Part of one of the walls had fallen in giving him a crude ramp to lead the horses down into cover. He tied the horses off to a metal pole that stuck up from the foundation then snatched his M-1 from the scabbard.

Taking a quick look at the angle of the bullet hole in the tree Steve set up behind it. Peering over the barrel of his rifle he looked for the hidden shooter. Two more shots rang out and Steve caught the hint of a muzzle blast coming from a darkened broken out window. Steve sent several shots into the open window not knowing the results of his shots. He heard no screams of pain or surprise.

Then three more shots rang out. Bullets slammed into the trees to Steve's left. He threw himself down to the ground to make a smaller target of himself.

Doc ran to the wall and rested his rifle on top of it. The basement walls were only about five feet tall, just high enough for him to get plenty of cover and still be able to shoot from. He saw Steve drop to the ground as gunfire raked the trees around him.

He caught sight of a man holding a rifle running between two houses. Doc led the man about a foot and fired two rounds. He saw his rounds pepper the brick wall of the house that the man was running to. The man dove for cover behind it. "Steve, come on get out of there!" Doc shouted.

Steve rolled right and began to low crawl towards Doc who was firing at something behind him. Dirt kicked up behind him and then in front of him to his left. He crawled faster burying his face against the ground as he scurried to safety.

Doc fired two more rounds at the man he had been shooting at when he appeared at the corner of the house. He didn't hit him, but was successful at driving him back behind the house.

More dirt kicked up around Steve, the sound of the gunfire coming from Steve's left. Doc shifted his fire towards two men who fired as they ran forward. He missed them also, but was successful in shooting out the windows of the car the two men ran towards. "Steve, get up and run before you get a bullet in your ass!"

Steve jumped up from the ground and ran as hard as he could the last fifteen yards. When he neared the basement he dove to the ground as more bullets zipped past him. When he hit the ground he rolled right and then unceremoniously into the basement, landing on his butt.

He hit the quick release straps to his pack and dumped it. He watched the empty clip pop into the air from Doc's rifle. Doc dropped to a knee to reload. "Where are they at Doc?"

"We've got one on the side of the red brick house just across the street. Two more by the blue car on this side of the street, plus the one you shot at in the window. I saw his muzzle flash again." Doc slid another clip into the receiver, and charged the rifle.

"Okay. You fire on the guy by the house. I'll move over hear to the right and take on those guys." Doc gave him a nod, and Steve moved over to the right hand wall.

The two rose at the same time and opened up. As Steve rose up so did one of the men behind the blue car. Steve pulled the trigger first. He pumped out six rounds at the man. Two of the steel core bullets tore into the man's chest. Dirt seemed to puff off of his chest as they hit.

Doc's antagonist had made the fatal mistake of not moving to a new location after firing from the same position several times. Doc took aim on the corner and just as he predicted the man stepped back out to fire at him. He squeezed the trigger. His first round caught the man high in the left shoulder. The man spun and slammed into the wall the rifle falling from his hands. Doc lowered his aim a bit and fired his second round into the man's chest. He watched as the man slowly slid down the wall ending up in the sitting position as if he was just resting.

Doc turned to Steve a smile on his face. "Got mine what about you?" Doc's hands suddenly released his rifle grabbing for his face as two shots rang out from his left. Doc went to the ground holding his face.

Steve ducked and ran to him as bullets tore into the cinder blocks that protruded above the ground; each round sending sharp concrete pieces flying in all directions in puffs of white dust. "Doc, are you alright?" Steve grabbed at Doc's hand to see the damage. He feared the worst.

Doc allowed Steve to move his hands. "I just got hit by some pieces of concrete. I think there are a few more to our left."

Steve felt a great since of relief. "Well you take care of them. I still got a few more to contend with. And Doc remember what we said a couple of days ago about dumb decisions. Next time you want to tell me you shot one at least make a decision to take cover first." Steve turned and headed back for his position.

Doc took Steve's reprove in stride. He was right so what was there to get mad about. He picked up his rifle and moved to the far wall. He caught some movement four houses down and fired a round in the general direction, just to let them know he knew they were there.

The gun battle went on for two more hours. Steve and Doc fired an occasional shot when they caught sight of one of the faceless attackers. The two groups seemed to be at a stalemate. The attackers could not rush the two without getting shot to pieces over the open ground. Steve and Doc could not make a break for the same reason.

Steve had pulled out his poncho and made a small lean-to between three upright metal poles. Doc followed his example on the other side of the basement. The sun had become almost unbearable. The decision to make the lean-to would help stop the possibility of heat exhaustion.

Steve peaked over the wall and saw one of the men running from the front door of one house heading for another. He snapped his rifle to his shoulder and squeezed the trigger.

The round clipped the man in the back of the calf shooting the leg forward causing the man to fall backwards onto his back. Steve was about to finish him off when one of the men who had been behind the car opened up, and so did a second who came out of the house to aid his friend. Steve ducked for cover as the bullets tore divots of sod from the ground in front of him.

Doc rose up and popped off a round to let the men on his side know he was still there. He squatted back down as a round zinged over his head. "Well, did you get him?"

"Just winged the bugger Doc, but it's sure going to hurt like hell in the morning." Steve grinned at Doc.

"Well I hope I'm here to see it in the morning. Steve we have to get the hell out of here. We have plenty of ammo, but water is going to be a problem soon."

"I say as soon as it gets dark we mount up and ride like hell." Steve pulled out a small antenna with a mirror on the end that he had bought at the auto parts store. He scanned the area around him. Seeing nothing he lowered it. "What do you think Doc?"

"Yeah I'm all for it. Hell Maude chewing my butt out beats this. Let's make the break as soon as it is dark. I'm sure they're thinking the same thing though, so who ever acts first wins."

Steve just nodded his head and turned raising the mirror.

Howard glanced at his watch. Five thirty, his watch was about over. Howard's watch was from two in the morning till six. He didn't mind at all, he had always been a night owl. Craig took watch from ten until two. Usually Howard would hit the rack about seven o'clock. He took cat naps through out the day and that was sufficient to keep him going through the day. Occasionally they would skip the watch relying on Meat to let them know if something was wrong.

Howard looked down to the drive at their completed project. They had taken the eighteen-wheeler and transformed it into the ultimate scavenging machine. They first had raided a local body shop taking all the tools and supplies they needed. Their next stop was an iron works where they had taken large metal plates, and pieces of angle iron.

They had fashioned a huge brush guard and attached it to the front. They lucked up on two huge wenches that they had taken off of two crashed SUV's. The wenches were attached on the left and right side of the brush guard. They used some of the metal plating and attached it to the front of the brush guard so that the engine and radiator would be protected from gunfire.

They used more metal plates to cover the doors of the truck. The windows could be rolled down and they could fire pistols, short rifle or shotgun through the ports. The plates that covered the window were hinged to allow them to be turned down if they so desired.

The front window had received the same treatment. The glass had been removed however. The plates were also hinged and ported. So you could drive with the plates down, or up and fire through the port, and the driver could see out of his, which was much longer and wider.

Howard had rounded up some five inch duct work and fixed it into holes that he had cut out of the top of the cab. This was for airflow and ventilation. The faster the rig moved, the faster the air flowed in also helping to cool the interior.

They had also welded metal plates to the roof and sides of the double sleeper cab. Before the roof plates where put on however, Howard had cut out a turret hole. The passenger could pop the hatch and stand up and shoot.

That portion of project had taken two twenty hour days to complete. It almost had cost them their lives. If it had not been for the ever attentive Meat, they would have died. Two men had made it over the wall and others were not far behind as they slapped ladders over the razor wire to the wall.

Craig noted the tone of the dog's barks as being aggressive and had popped out of the hole they had cut in the top of the rig. As Meat took one of the men down, Craig pulled out a Stoeger double barrel coach gun that he was mounting in the cab. He let the second man have both barrels sending him crashing into a holly bush, dead. Howard had been upstairs and grabbed an AR-15 with a one-hundred round C-Mag. From the elevated position of the upstairs room he was able to make quick work of the other four men below.

It was a close call. They thought that the majority of the scum in the area had learned their lesson. Craig and Howard had come into contact with numerous criminal groups who had decided to make the University of North Alabama home.

They had pushed most of the groups back towards the projects on the west side of town.

They had not gone head to head with these groups unless they were attacked back at Craig's place. Craig and Howard had taken to sniping them at night and early morning. Most of the gangs would get high and drunk at night building large fires.

They would dance around to their rap music, screw, and shoot their weapons in the air. They would wait for them to start firing off a few rounds and would snipe members on the outskirts of each group. As the partying died out and the thugs would either go to sleep or pass out, Craig and Howard would move in and kill as many as possible. They always left a few to spread the word.

Pushing the gangs out had an added bonus beside a little more safety. They were able to retrieve hundreds of books from the library. They got everything they thought that could help them, basket weaving, blacksmithing, welding, medical books, dentistry books, chemistry and biology books, and hundreds of other subjects. They also raided the chemistry labs taking chemicals, and lab equipment. Neither had any working knowledge of chemistry, but they were willing to learn if it would make life easier.

They stopped working on the rig for awhile to check the perimeter of the block. They found where the group and come over a pile of rubble that Craig had dozed up to help form their debris barrier. Howard made a toe popper booby trap where the gang had crossed.

Others might have seen them cross here and he needed something to discourage interlopers. Besides using the debris from the burned out homes and cars Craig and Howard had driven to several scrap yards and brought back dump truck load after dump truck load of twisted jagged metal scrap to add to and lengthen the debris wall. The wall was not more than four or five feet high, but it was full of sharp jagged objects that would make crossing it or using it for cover in an attack very unwise.

After setting the booby trap they returned to finishing out the rig which took an additional two days. The most difficult part had been building a frame over the back tires and mounting an old dump truck bed.

They built a frame and attached it to the back of the rig. In the frame they mounted another wench to lift heavy objects into the bed. They also mounted another fifty gallon diesel tank that had been taken off another diesel under, and between the bed and cab. They attached a large fuel line to allow the diesel to flow down towards the driver side tank. This would greatly increase the range of the big rig.

Once the rig was completed the two young men were still not satisfied. Their creation was god awful ugly. Using the salvaged body shop equipment they painted the rig and bed a flat primer black. Across the front plate they painted a mouth with large fangs and eyes on the nose cap. When they were done they toasted each other with lukewarm beers.

Howard was jolted from his memories of the work when his watch alarm sounded. He walked down the hall and beat on Craig's bedroom door. "Get up you lazy good for nothing slouch. It's my turn for a snooze."

Howard made his way down the hall to his room. Once inside he stripped off his LBV, boots, and clothes and crawled in bed for a two hour nap. When he woke he and Craig were going to head north on Wood Ave., cross Cox Creek Pkwy., and travel onto Cloverdale Rd. which would lead them into the Petersville area.

There were not a whole lot of businesses in the Petersville area, mostly residential, and retail. There were however a few auto part, and garages there. They were going to attempt to salvage what they could. They had discussed whether or not what they were doing was stealing, but due to the current conditions in the area, and what they had heard on the short wave they felt it was every man for his self.

While Howard slept Craig made his way down stairs, drank a bottle of Gatorade, and ate a couple of pop tarts. He was going to add a fuel siphon to the bed of the rig. There were several gas stations in the Petersville area on Cloverdale Rd. and they intended to siphon fuel from the tanks.

He made his way to the garage and cut the last of the angle iron and welded up the frame. It wasn't large and he had no problem carrying it to the rig and then welding it into place. He then took the siphon which had an electric motor and bolted it to the frame. It took him another hour to run the wires to the battery and get it working properly.

He had just finished up when Howard walked out the back door. "My, aren't we being industrious this morning. I just knew you were going to lounge around in your underwear all morning and wait for me to help you out with that thing."

"Well since you're just standing there in your underwear running your goober smoocher why don't you toss those drums up here so I can get them strapped in." Craig said as he pointed to four white fifty-five gallon drums.

Howard ambled over to the empty drums and hoisted one up. "You have got to be the laziest man I know. Why on earth I ever teamed up with you I will never know." Howard tossed the drum over the side. The drum bounced end over end as it landed in the bed causing the metal to ring loudly.

Craig bent over and retrieved the drum and began to set it in place. "Way to go there prodigy for mental ineptitude; let's just let every thug in the downtown area know we're out working on the truck again."

Howard gave his friend the finger but handed the last three barrels up. "When do you want to head out?"

Craig climbed down from the bed and stood in front of Howard, his hands on his hips. "I see you've come to your senses and realized my prowess for planning and leadership abilities."

"What prowess?"

"Well, young Howard. First off I like to be referred to as "My Lord." Secondly you're out here standing before all in your serf outfit. Therefore I am the most qualified. Who would take orders from some guy walking around in his drawers? You know I think we should try to find a tanning bed. That sickly pasty white skin of yours looks unhealthy."

"You are one arrogant S.O.B. Go get your equipment I want to be out of here in an hour or so. Craig, one more thing."

"Yeah buddy."

"You are still number one with me." Howard said as he turned to go back inside holding up his middle finger.

Craig laughed as he followed his friend back inside the house. He was joking about everything he said to Howard. He was definitely going to find a tanning bed for his friend.

<hr />

Craig and Howard had made the short trip of three miles with no unexpected surprises. Their first stop was the Winn Dixie shopping center at Cox Creek Pkwy., and Cloverdale Rd. Craig manned the machinegun while Howard went into each store. One of the weapons Howard had packed was a German MG-34. He only had three two hundred round belts for it, but just the sight of it resting on the top of the cab was sufficient enough to scare off most would be attackers.

Inside the pharmacy next to Winn Dixie Howard had managed to find several bottles of aspirin, Advil, some cold and flu medicine, several rolls of Ace bandages, mouthwash, toothpaste, and clothes pins. When most of the stores were looted many everyday items such as these were overlooked for much more valuable merchandise.

The Winn Dixie was about picked clean. Howard did manage to find about a dozen cans of food of unknown contents since the labels had been taken off. In the house ware section he got two buggies full of pots pans, and other eating and cooking utensils. In the dry cleaners he found jeans, leather jackets, and several sets of BDU's that had belonged to local guardsmen. Anything of value that could be traded or used was taken. Of course they had no idea who they could trade with.

At the first gas station they came to they found the tanks still full of fuel. People had not gotten around to tapping into them yet. They filled two drums with diesel fuel, one with gasoline, and the forth they filled with kerosene. Inside the gas station they found several one gallon plastic gasoline cans, electrical tape, battery wires, light bulbs, a few plastic flashlights and two six packs of Pepsi.

When they hit the auto repair shops they were a bit disappointed. They managed to pick up loose wrenches, screwdrivers, sockets, ratchets, hammers, hoses, nut, and bolts. They were not fortunate to run into a fully equipped garage. Most had been looted or the contents removed by the owners.

There were a few restaurants on Cloverdale Rd. These were gone through also, and they came out with a lot of commercial cooking items. No food was found however.

They hit the package store knowing it was going to be bare. They came away with three fifths of liquor, a bottle of wine, and a dented can of Coors Light. Howard also found two packs of cigarettes. These would be great barter items if they had anyone to barter with.

The morning passed relatively quickly and the two parked the rig under a large oak tree to get some shade and lunch. Craig opened one of the cans they had found and was rewarded with tomato soup. He heated it up and began to eat up. "You ready to head back home Howard?"

"I don't know. I thought we would drive up to Underwood Elementary and snag a bunch of school books. I haven't seen many kids but I am sure some parents would be willing to trade something to continue to educate their rug rats."

Craig was about to reply when a gun shot echoed from the distance. Both men rolled for cover grabbing their rifles. They took quick look around and saw no threats. Then two more shots could be heard followed by six quick shots from what could only be an AK-47 or SKS.

Howard crawled over to Craig. "It sounds like there is a gun battle just to the west of us."

"Yeah. What do you want to do?"

"How bout taking a gander and see what's brewing?" Howard said wiggling his eyebrows a couple of times.

"You know curiosity killed the cat?"

"Sure did, but we aint cats."

"I don't know about that Howard. You're the biggest pussy I've ever known." Craig wiggled his eyebrows mocking his friend.

Howard punched Craig in the arm as he got up. "Sorry about that. Let's go." Howard jogged to the rig and opened the door. He pulled out his small day pack and slung it on and grabbed several mags for his FN.

Craig got up and followed Howard shaking out his arm where Howard had froged it. Getting to the rig he pulled out his entry vest and put it on. Then grabbed his Camelback, and his UMP .40 cal. He had to sprint to catch up with Howard who was thirty yards ahead of him.

They made their way through a middle class neighborhood. After traveling two blocks they came to an intersection and crawled under a large Magnolia tree. The large leaves and limbs that hung to the ground provided ample concealment from probing eyes.

Craig pulled out a set of Bushnell 8x40 binoculars and panned the area. "I've got them."

Howard lifted his binoculars to his face. "Where at?"

"Halfway down the block on the right. An old guy and a dude in his twenties in some sort of…I don't know a hole I guess."

"I've got them. Got them a couple of horses tethered too. Wonder if they live there? You notice the two poncho tarps?"

"Yeah I see that. You see the body sticking halfway out from behind that blue car?"

Howard panned towards the car but stopped when he saw a man sitting leaned against a wall. "No. But they got one either sleeping on the job or dead as a doornail by that tan brick house." He then scanned the blue car. "Well it looks like it's two to nothing. The old fart and the young guy are ahead."

Both men were startled as gunfire erupted across the street and up a few houses. They both watched a man kneel beside the corner of the house holding an SAS12 shotgun with a five round magazine. The man fired three more shots then ducked back behind the corner reloading another magazine into the shotgun.

A second man came out the back door of the same house. He carried a semi-auto pistol in his hand. While his friend reloaded he dumped three rounds towards the trapped men. Then he ducked back for cover.

Craig watched as the old man came up from hiding holding an M-1 Garand. The old man popped off three rounds. Each round blew chunks of brick off the corner of the house. "Those two boys are probably going to wind up like their buddies if they keep messing with that old fella. Hey Howard, who do you reckon are the bad guys here?"

"Just from the looks of things I would say the good guys are down in the hole. Let's watch the fun a little longer."

They watched for two more hours. The group on the outside of the hole were definitely lacking in training and tactics. The two men in the hole did not waste a lot of ammunition. They fired only when they had a chance to make a hit.

Then Craig got pissed. He watched as one of the men nearest him rolled up a joint and started toking on it. He passed it to his friend while he fired off a round. Craig hated druggies and thugs with a passion. For the past hour the two had talked about what kind of stuff they were going to take off the bodies of the two trapped men. As they smoked the joint they talked of torture, and how maybe there might be some women back at some camp that the two men had come from. When the talk got to rape Craig stood up under the canopy of the magnolia.

Howard rolled to his side and looked up. "Where the hell do you think you are you going?"

"I'm going to take care of some business." Craig eased through the limbs and sprinted across the street.

—•—◦—•—

"Crap! Steve I have another guy now on my side running across the street towards the other two." Doc raised his rifle and started to lead the running man.

Just as he was about to pull the trigger the man stopped running. He lifted a small carbine of some sort and let off a burst of automatic fire. When he stopped shooting he stepped towards the corner of the house where two of his assailants had been. Then he noticed the lettering on the back of the black vest.

"Hey Steve, I think the Police are here!"

Steve crawled over to Doc then stuck his head up. He just caught a glimpse of a man wearing a black vest stepping behind the corner of a house. "How do you know it was the cops?"

"The back of his vest said Police, and he just smoked those two yahoos." Both men ducked as rounds began to smack against the concrete walls, and the ground outside of the basement.

They both turned to see four men running towards them weapons blazing. Doc and Steve returned fire. It was fruitless there was a lot of lead coming down on them and they were forced to take cover. Then they heard the four loud bangs from a large caliber rifle behind them. Then the shooting stopped.

⊶ ⊷

Howard watched dumbfounded as his friend charged across the street and doused the two men there with automatic gunfire. Both men were totally unaware of their impending death until it was too late. The brick wall were their bodies leaned were now covered in blood, and full of pock marks from the bullets that had passed through their bodies.

Howard turned his attention to the ongoing battle in front of him as he heard gunfire from that direction again. He spotted four men carrying semi-auto rifles laying down a wall of lead at the two trapped men who had been watching Craig charge into the fray. The two men fired a few hopeless shots before being forced to take cover from the onslaught.

"Damn why couldn't this been like Star Trek. Obey the Prime Directive; do not interfere with other lesser life forms." Howard said to himself as he lifted the rifle to his shoulder.

The scope on his FN was set on 5x. He fired four rounds at the four men. He never stopped to see if his rounds hit their mark. He knew they had. After the forth shot he watched the last man drop to his knees, and then fall slowly forward on his face.

He watched the two men peak over the lip of the hole at the four dead men. Then the old man raised his right hand and waved a bit. Then he stood his rifle over his head.

⊶ ⊷

"Doc, get the hell down! You don't know if that's the Police for sure."

"Steve I think this fight is over. If he pops me lie to Maude and tell her I was doing something heroic when I got killed." Doc made his way out of the basement and walked towards the area where he had last seen the police officer.

What a crazy old goat Howard thought. "Stop right there old man!" He shouted. Then he looked for Craig. Where in the hell did he go?

Then the old man called out. "Are you the police?"

He must have seen Craig's entry vest. "No, but my friend is. Tell your buddy to come on out. If I wanted him dead I would have already shot him."

"Come on up Steve. I think it's all right." Doc said to Steve.

Steve had caught the last part of the hidden gunman's statement. He must have a scoped rifle. Well if he wanted me dead I guess he could do it. Steve came out of the basement and walked to Doc's side. "Doc put your hands down." Doc lowered his arms the M-1 still clutched in both hands.

Now what do I do thought Howard. "Drop your weapons." He shouted.

"Are you going to rob us or something?" Steve shouted back.

"NO!" I just want to make sure you don't try anything stupid.

Screw this Steve thought. "Well if you aren't going to kill us and you don't want to harm us then I'm getting on my horse and riding home." Steve turned to walk back to the basement and retrieve his horse. He was tired and was going, if they guy wanted to shoot him so be it.

Howard was dumbfounded. This guy had some balls. He just waved off an unseen gunman and basically told him to go screw himself. He was taking his ball and going home. Well what the hell he thought. Howard got up and walked out from under the magnolia towards the old man.

Steve stopped when Doc called to him. "Steve, the man's coming towards us."

Steve turned to see the young man walking towards them. He carried a scoped FN at port arms. Steve climbed back out of the basement and went to stand by Doc. The man stopped about five feet from Doc and Steve.

"Dr. Herb Morrison is my name. This is my friend Steve Roberts, thank you for saving our butts."

"My Name is Howard. I probably wouldn't have gotten involved if it hadn't been for my partner wherever the hell he is."

Steve was about to say something when he heard the roar of a diesel engine coming down the street. Suddenly around the corner came the biggest ugliest eighteen-wheeler he had ever seen. "What in the hell is that?" He started to raise his rifle.

Howard didn't have to look over his shoulder to know what it was. "That would be my partner." The big rig came to an abrupt halt about five feet behind Howard. All three men jumped as the big rigs air horn blared.

The driver door opened and Craig jumped out. "Damn I love doing that." He walked around to the trio. "High, Craig Wolfe." He held out his hand and shook Steve and Doc's hand as they introduced themselves.

Howard turned and looked at Craig. "Partner I just want to say you are the dumbest fucker I have ever met. Not only about jumping in this gunfight, but blowing that damn horn."

Craig just smiled at his friend and looked at Doc and Steve. "Can't you just feel the love?"

Steve cleared his throat. "Uh…Who the hell are you two?"

"Like I said, I'm Craig Wolfe, formerly FPD SWAT. This is my faithful apprentice Howard Smith, former gun dealer."

"What do you do with that?" Doc asked pointing at the big rig.

"Well Dr. Morrison, Howard and I are in the scavenging business now. Sooner or later folks will need stuff and we will have tons of stuff to trade with."

Steve and Doc looked at one another. Doc gave Steve a nod, both thinking the same thing. "Funny you should bring that up. Doc and I have been out spreading the word about a swap meet in St. Florian Wednesday two weeks from now. We were about to head back after we got done eating when we got ambushed."

"Craig, where do I know you from?" Doc asked trying to place the young man. He had seen him before but couldn't quite place him.

"I took a report from you two years ago when your offices got broke into. It took me a minute to place you when I was looking through the binoculars at you. I'm terrible with names, but never forget a face. About the time I figured it out, the two thugs I shot were talking about capturing you and finding out if you had any women they could go rape. So I decided it was time for a little street justice."

"That's nice to hear Craig. It would help if you advised those that are about to get pulled into a gun battle with you who the good guys are." Howard said with an incredulous look on his face.

"I wasn't concerned one bit buddy. I know you road the short bus to school, but I knew you would figure it out." Craig flashed another mischievous grin at Howard.

"Oh yeah I forgot we shared a seat." Howard said with a disconcerted look on his face.

Steve shook his head and looked towards Heaven. "Dear God I'm in a living hell. I can't believe there are actually two more people on earth who goad one another like Amos and Doc." He thought to himself. He looked back at the two men before him. "Look guys if you would like to do some trading drive up to Jackson Hwy., and Butler Creek Rd. Wednesday the 16th. Mr. Flynn, the owner of the property will be opening his place for people to come and trade. He may charge you something to set up I'm not quite sure.

Howard and Craig shook their heads approvingly. "That sounds great. Craig and I will be there. Can we show up a day or two early?"

"I don't see where that would be a problem. Just let Mr. Flynn or one of his boys know you talked to me and Steve."

"Okay."

Steve stepped forward his hand outstretched to Craig. "Thanks for saving our bacon. Anytime I can return the favor I will. We stay up on County Rd. 306." Craig gave Steve a firm handshake.

Steve turned to Howard. "Thanks. I know you didn't want to become involved, and I don't blame you. You can't tell about anyone now days. Just the same we appreciate it."

"I wouldn't have been so reluctant if my inane dolt of a partner would have told me he knew one of you. I'm looking forward to seeing you the 16th."

Doc shook both men's hands and stepped back. "We're going to be riding off. We need to get back home."

The four said their goodbyes one more time and Doc and Steve headed back for their horses. Craig and Howard got back in their rig and pulled out. Craig tooted the big air horns twice and pulled away.

Steve and Doc took down their poncho liners and packed them up. Once they were packed they mounted up and started to head for home. "Can you believe those two guys Doc?"

"What about them Steve?"

"I don't think their elevators go all the way to the top. They may have actually ridden the short bus to school. They're good with their guns, but man that Craig is one reckless dude."

"I don't know Steve. Put yourself in his shoes. Just a few weeks ago he's a cop on the beat, a member of an outstanding SWAT team, and now what is he? His visions of law and order are gone. He sees two guys being ambushed, realizes who the bad guys are and sees a chance to do what he was trained to do. A bit more violently than what he was trained, I might add, but these are different times.

He probably just saw a chance to right a wrong. Do what he feels he was meant to be, a defender of the Constitution, and peace."

"Yeah I guess I can see that. But the way those two act. You would think they were younger versions of...." Steve stopped himself before he said 'you and Amos.'

"I didn't catch who you said they were like."

"Never mind Doc. Let's just get home." Steve kicked his horse in the flanks and brought him to a quick trot pulling away from Doc.

They spent one more night on the road before reaching home. They managed to tell a few more people along the way about the meet.

They made it home in time for a good home cooked meal that Maude had put out. Now they had to get themselves organized and find out what they could trade, and what they needed.

Chapter 32

Joe lowered the binoculars from his eyes. He sat in the looted out insurance office on Cloverdale Rd. Bob and Caroline's house was two miles to the west of his position. He had come here this morning to check out the flow of traffic along the road.

The three were heading out today and he didn't want any nasty surprises. Just like the one he saw just south of his position at the gas station. He didn't know who the two men in the big black diesel were, but he sure didn't want to tangle with them. He took a special interest in the belt fed MG34 manned in a makeshift turret on the top of the cab.

These guys had taken looting to a new level. The rig was obviously crudely, but strongly built. He noted the wenches in front and one on the back to haul things up into the bed that had to be from a dump truck.

They were using an electric siphon to get at the gas. When he got back to the Novacheck's he would see if Bob had a hand pump siphon and some rubber hose. If he did it would be a boon to their pitiful fuel supplies.

Though they only had to travel about ten miles to get to Doc's there was no telling what could happen. Extra fuel would also help out Doc and Maude with their generator. He decided after he settled in he was going to follow these guys example. He was going into the fuel business. There were hundreds and hundreds of abandoned cars around. Some had run out of fuel, others broke down, and some simply abandoned. He would tap into the gas stations also. Fuel would be liquid gold and help obtain things for his nieces, the Morrison's, and himself.

When the two were finished obtaining fuel he watched the machine gunner detach the MG34, and take it back down into the cab. He heard the metal clank as the gunner closed the hatch. Joe got his first good look at the other man's weapon, a scoped FN. He didn't know if these guys knew how to handle their weapons, but he would sure hate to find out the hard way.

The rig started up and plumes of black smoke belched from the twin pipes. The truck pulled out of the station lot and headed north on Cloverdale Rd. "Damn!"

Joe said beating his fist against the wall. If they were going to head to Doc's, north, then back east would be the quickest way. But after seeing that behemoth he didn't even want to chance meeting that on some back road. He was going to head back to the Novacheck's and see what they thought.

⊹⊱⋯⊰⊹

"It had fangs painted on the front? What the hell has this city turned into, a refuge for Road Warrior wannabe's?" Bob said as he paced back and forth.

"Looks that way Bob."

"Joe surely the chances of running into these guys will be slim to none. I say chance it. My Xterra and Bob's 4x4 pickup can outrun that thing.

"Caroline think about going around a blind curve and that thing sitting there waiting on you. You aren't going to out run a few hundred rounds of 8mm flying at you. I know you are ready to get out of here before things get really bad, but a few more miles won't kill us."

"If that's what you think Joe. What route do you propose that we take?"

Joe sat down on the couch and stretched his legs out. "We turn south at the front of the neighborhood. Head down to Cox Creek Pkwy., turn east drive to Jackson Hwy. Then we can head straight north on Jackson Hwy. It's only like four or five miles up Jackson Hwy till you reach the turn off to go to Doc's, then another two miles. It might even be safer since we won't be hitting so many two lane back roads like we would if we head north then east."

Bob quit pacing and walked over and sat down by Joe. "Joe, what about the traffic, both people, and vehicles?"

"From what I can see there are few people actually out on the roadways. Now there are a lot of cars and trucks that have been abandoned or stalled out. We'll have to thread our way through them. Plus if we have to exit our vehicles because of ambush or vehicle problems the abandoned cars can give us cover."

Caroline crossed her legs, and then her arms as she analyzed what Joe said. "Joe that might be true, except you left out the fact that those same vehicles can be used by someone else for cover, or to set up a trap of some sort."

Joe stood tired of the debate. Daylight was wasting, and he was ready to get out of town. "We'll do whatever yall want to; let's just get out of here. Are we packed and ready to go?"

Caroline looked at Bob to see if he had an opinion. Bob just gave her, his "Whatever you want to do." In the short time she had known Joe, Caroline felt at ease around him, and was growing to respect him. He was very knowledgeable in many things. After a short mental debate with herself she made her decision. "Okay Joe. We do it your way. You're the only one of us who has been outside this neighborhood since this crap happened."

"Good. Now yall do remember the plan right?" Joe said looking at both of them.

"I think its simple enough Joe. You will lead out in my truck. Caroline and I will follow about fifty to sixty yards behind. Never lose sight of each other. We see you making some sort of evasive maneuver we do a U turn and get out of dodge.

"You know where Doc lives now right?"

"Bob has the map you drew out last night. We both have county maps and know the address. I think we'll be fine Joe."

"Remember. If we get in some sort of shootout we need to disengage as quickly as possible. We have enough ammo, but the caliber of our weapons, and type will make them useless unless we are doing some close in fighting.

Caroline, if you don't mind check one more time through the house and see if we forgot to pack anything useful. Bob, let's go out and check the load on the vehicles and trailer."

Bob and Joe headed outside while Caroline rummaged through the house. Caroline did a methodical search of the house. She found plenty of things she wanted to take, but there was no room for them. When she was through searching the house she went into the living room and flopped down on the sofa. She was mentally exhausted. Though it was her idea to leave, the realization of leaving her dream home for the unknown was taking a toll on her.

She and Bob had worked hard starting their business from scratch, never getting a loan from the bank to ease the way. Now, just in their early thirties their hard work had paid off. Their business was profitable, the employees well paid and happy.

They had built their home and paid cash for the elegant home they now lived in. The only thing left to complete their perfect lives was to have children. Now she couldn't even bear the thought of bringing a child into a world gone mad. She surveyed the beautiful room that had taken her four painstaking months to decorate. Tears pooled up in her eyes as the thought of leaving it for some looter, or someone like Bob and herself trying to survive, coming in and defiling her home.

⇥━━⇤

Berry McGee turned and stopped his old Ford pickup at the end of Roy Flynn's driveway. The antenna for his 2 meter radio wiped back and forth like a tree caught in a heavy gale. He blew the horn twice and pulled out his AMT Hardballer .45 ACP and laid it on the dash.

He got out of the truck and held his hands up about shoulder height. He wasn't completely unarmed. He had an S&W 2213 .22 caliber pistol in his back waistband as a hideout gun. He also had a Buck sheath knife hanging from his belt.

Berry cupped his hands around his mouth and called out. "Mr. Flynn! It's Berry McGee. Can I come on up and talk?"

Brent Flynn stepped out onto the front porch. Brent held a Beretta BM59 semi auto rifle in his hands. A smile came to his face when he saw his old friend. Brett and Berry had joined the Marine Corps together on the buddy plan. They had gone to boot camp and infantry school together. They had fought side by side in the Second Gulf War serving in the 3rd LAR.

"Hey Berry! Put your dang hands down and pull the truck on up here."

"Be right there." Berry hopped back into the old Ford, and took his pistol off the dash and placed it back in its holster.

Once inside Berry accepted a glass of water from Mrs. Flynn. "Man I'm glad to see you Berry. I wasn't sure if you were alive or not. What the heck have you been doing, hiding in a hole?"

Berry drained the glass in a couple of gulps and placed it on the coaster that sat on the coffee table in front of him. "No. I've been monitoring my radios is about all. I got in a shootout with some motorcycle guys that came by and tried to steal my goats other than that nothing but surviving."

After the war Berry had gotten a job with TVA as a pipe fitter. His income was almost four times what he made as a Corporal in the Corps. With this influx of cash Berry had begun a hobby piddling with radios. Within a year he was a Ham radio operator.

Roy Flynn spoke up getting Berry's attention. "Have you heard anything about what's going on?"

Berry told them everything he had heard. After about thirty minutes of talking he spoke a little about what he had heard going on in reference to American troops in the states. "Like I said, some troops made it home from Korea. No one is sure whether the commanders ordered them to withdraw, or if they just said screw it and came home on their own. It is the same with the troops in Europe.

On some of the military bands I have heard communications of troops disobeying Presidential, and FEMA orders to round up and detain citizens to be placed in camps to perform reconstruction projects. I had one Ham from out in California who told me he personally witnessed a company of Soldiers attempt to place a Marine squad under arrest for failing to obey the order. Things got a little nasty though."

Brent sat up at the mention of brother Marines in harms way. "Any Devil Dogs get hurt?"

Berry looked down at his feet for a second before continuing. Then he looked back up into his friend's eyes. "Yeah, they're all dead. They got into a hell of a firefight. They killed forty seven soldiers before they last one died. Oh, and the Sergeant leading the squad shot a FEMA

District Coordinator and his three assistants before they killed him." Brent just shook his head in disbelief.

"What is with all the fighting and deserting among our forces? Shouldn't they be fighting the damn Koreans and Chinese over seas, and here at home instead of each other?" Roy Flynn said.

"The problem Mr. Flynn is that the Federal government is confiscating everything usable they can get their hands on. They are forcing folks out of their homes, after they take their food, water, gas, and weapons. Then they send them to a camp to perform whatever work FEMA decides needs to be done.

Some troops are following the government's orders to a T. Others are openly talking about politicians subverting the Constitution, and destroying the Bill of Rights. They're talking about open rebellion if things don't change. So on the one hand you have troops "Just following orders.", and on the other you have troops who say the government has overstepped its bounds and needs to be placed into check."

Roy Flynn stood up from his chair. "It's damn bad enough the government didn't protect the nation like it should have before this crap started. It's even worse now that they're sticking their sticky fingers in everyone's lives. Now our troops are fighting among themselves when they need to be fighting gooks. Mark my words. If the government doesn't change its ways not only will America fall, but so will the rest of the world without us being able to step in and keep things straight, now enough of the news. What brings you by Berry? You need help?"

"In a way yes, Dr. Morrison and his friend came by and told me what yall are planning. Besides fighting the only marketable skill I have is radios. I would like to buy some space inside your store from you to set up my Ham radio."

"What are you going to trade with a radio? How do you intend to power one with no electricity?" Roy asked.

"I figure news is hard to come by, and also folks want to find out what has happened to other family members in different states. So for some food, ammo, or a quart of gas I will send word out through other Hams. If I find out the whereabouts or status of the person they are looking for I will charge them the same thing for a successful contact. I will charge them again if they want the opportunity to talk to them via the radio.

As far as running the radio I have a small generator that is pretty quite that I took off of an old RV. I also have a few solar panels to help trickle charge some batteries that can run the radio. I want to knock a small hole in the wall and build a cage for it. That way I can keep an eye on my generator so no one decides they need it more than me."

"What do you think I should charge you to buy a small piece of my store Berry?"

I've got four hundred rounds of .44 for that hog leg of yours, plus a sealed five hundred round case of .308. I sold my Ruger Red Hawk, so I have no need for the .44 caliber ammo. I have about four thousand rounds of .308 on top of the five hundred I'm willing to trade. So do you want to deal?"

Betty Flynn spoke up for the first time during the conversation. "Roy. Take the deal. Berry won't take up much space. Plus the chance to find love ones will bring more people inside the store, and increase the amount of items we can collect for a cover charge. It's a win, win situation for us and Berry."

Roy thought for a moment, mulling the idea over in his head. Reaching out his hand to Berry the two shook. "You've got a deal Berry."

"I've got one more favor to ask."

"What's that Berry?"

"Can I bring the stuff I'm not going to need at your store here?" I've got some gear, and more importantly three goats, and five laying hens."

"Sure why not." Roy said as he clasped Berry's shoulder and shook his hand one more time.

"Have you been by the store Mr. Flynn?"

"Not since the second day of the collapse. Why do you ask?"

"It's pretty well stripped bare. The only good news is that I checked the gas tanks and they are still pretty much full. No one has gotten around to siphoning it all out."

Roy stepped back from Berry and motioned his two son's over to join them. "This is what we're going to do. We're going to take the tractor and some chainsaws and drive down to the store. We're going to build us a log wall about four and a half feet tall around the place. We'll use an auger to dig the postholes. One person will stand watch on the roof of the grocery store, or gas station, while the other's work. We take two hour shifts on the roof that way each of us can take a break and remain fresh."

Charles didn't look quite satisfied with the plan. "Dad, do you realize how many trees we will have to cut down. That could take months."

"It's not going to take as long as you think. We're going to improvise. There is a log truck on 312. I saw it three days ago. The driver is dead. It looks like he was robbed. We'll take those. Then we're going to go to the old train tracks and start pulling up the railroad ties. The telephone company has a stack of about one hundred poles on 309. When we finish commandeering that stuff then we'll start in on cutting down trees."

The men immediately headed out. They took three trucks, and two thirty foot trailers with them. Betty stayed behind at the house to keep watch, armed with a Remington 870 20 gauge, and a Forehand & Wadsworth .38 revolver given to her by her grandfather in 1960.

Six hours into the first day of work one of the farmers that lived nearby came over and asked Roy what he was up to. When Roy told him he offered his help in exchange for a free spot to sale his crops for two months. The two old friends dickered awhile and a free spot for one month was agreed on. Realizing that the more hands he had the faster and safer the wall could be constructed Roy called Charles over to him.

"Charles, I want you to go to some of our neighbors and offer them the same deal I offered Tony; a free lot for one month in the parking lot."

"How big a spot do they get dad?"

"Tell them two parking spaces."

His instructions received Charles headed out to farmers that his family were friends with. By the second day twelve farmers and some of their family members had shown up to help.

Hank Biggs wiped the sweat from his forehead as he and Roy placed a railroad tie between the wooden posts. "Roy I don't mean to sound nosey or anything but just why are you doing this?"

Roy pressed his hands in the small of his back and leaned back trying to work out some of the pain. "The main reason is I want some kind of barrier in place so undesirables can't just come in here and set up. This wall will give a little bit of cover from anyone shooting from the outside in. Also by having a controlled entrance I make sure I get paid by the folks coming in setting up a stall."

"You always were a smart business man Roy. Even back in grade school when you was always scheming ways to make money."

Roy smiled as some of his childhood memories came to mind. "Yep Hank, I always was a smart business man."

Hank smiled back. "Now don't get all cocky on me Roy. I can still remember hearing you squall like a stuck pig when Principal Mallard caught you selling the answers to Mrs. Pool's geography test." He laughed as he slapped his old friend on the arm.

Roy smiled back as the two walked to the trailer for another tie. "I can't prove it, but I think you were the one who snitched me out. As I recall you wanted to pay five cents instead of the ten cents I was asking."

Hank let out a deep chuckle. "You can't prove anything Roy. I deny everything. Besides if I did rat you out it might have been because I made an F on that test while everyone else made an A. I guess I should have said you've always been a shyster." The two men laughed and joked about old memories as they walked on.

After four days of hard work the barricade was finished. All the families involved in the building held an afternoon picnic. Hank pulled a piece of meat off his chicken leg and slipped it in his mouth. "Roy what are you eyeballing the wall for? You leave something out?"

"I was just thinking. That wall isn't that tall. Someone tries to rush this place they would be able to scale it real easy. I think I need to string some barbed wire across the front."

"Not a bad idea at all. Tell you what. My sons and I will help you out for free if you got the wire."

"I've got several thousand feet back home in my barn. You've done enough Hank, don't worry about it my boys and I will get it strung."

"Roy, you're helping everyone out by setting up like this. Besides I think I still owe you some money for some of that hay I bought last year."

"What? Heck Hank it was only like fifteen dollars out of a two thousand dollar buy. Besides I still owed you for the time you filled my gas tank up when we were in Athens last year."

"We'll be here first thing in the morning."

"Thanks Hank."

"Well what do you think friends are for? Oh I forgot shysters don't have any friends. You know you aught to consider your self lucky to have a friend." Hank said goading his old friend. The picnic wound down after another hour or so and each family said their goodbyes all looking forward to the big meet in ten days.

⊹⊱⊰⊹

"The Novacheck's and Joe stood out in the driveway. After Bob and Joe had come back inside from checking the truck they had debated again on whether or not to head north. Finally they had decided to wait another day and head south. Hopefully the guys with the big truck would be long gone. They didn't get started till almost ten in the morning. "Are yall ready to go?" Joe asked.

"You bet. Let's load up and get the hell gone before something throws a snag our way." Joe turned and got in Bob's 1998 Chevy, Bob and Caroline got in her Xterra. Once loaded up they made their way slowly through the neighborhood.

Joe waited as Bob pulled up beside him. When they were parallel Joe rolled the window down. "I'm going to drive down to Cox Creek and back to you. Keep your speed around thirty."

"We'll probably have to anyway with all these abandoned cars." Joe nodded his head, let off the break and turned onto Cloverdale Rd.

As Bob and Caroline weaved slowly through the abandoned cars Bob looked over at his wife. Caroline stared with vacant eyes ahead. Her right left hand stroked the stock of the semi-auto .22 he had found. "Caroline, is everything okay?"

Caroline turned and looked at him. "I feel kind of selfish Bob. Though everything collapsed around us we stuck it out and did pretty good. I look at all of these empty cars and think about all the people that fled their homes because they couldn't cope, or just had no where else to go but to those camps.

Now we are leaving our home for a place that will increase our chances for survival. I sat on the couch and cried like a baby earlier when I should have been thankful for the opportunity to go to a place that has a garden, a doctor, nurse, and more security. I guess I'm feeling kind of guilty about leaving a good place for a better one."

"Caroline everyone makes their own choices. I made a choice to buy extra food, and supplies. Everyone else got the same information on the news we did. Instead of looking ahead for possible problems they continued on as if they lived down the street from the Beaver.

I'm not saying I don't feel bad that folks are starving and are without medicine and other essentials. I'm definitely not going to feel guilty about surviving and getting a chance to live above what the norm is now."

"I guess you're right. Hey here comes Joe." Both looked ahead and saw Joe coming back towards them.

Joe pulled along side of them. "Besides the cars, it looks clear of people. I didn't see anything suspicious."

Bob nodded his head. "Let's hope it's like that the entire way."

"Let's move. I feel like a sitting duck." Joe accelerated forward and made a U turn and passed the slow moving Xterra, and trailer.

The snaking lines of stalled and abandoned cars grew thicker and longer as they drove closer towards the mall district. They had been unable to turn north at Jackson Hwy. The two lane road was packed full of cars and diesels. A massive pile up with two rigs and several cars had blocked the road. The embankments were to steep for the Xterra to navigate while pulling the trailer. They decided to head farther east and see what kind of route they could take going that direction.

It took them three hours to drive the seven miles to the mall. Once there they had to stop. The intersection of Mall Rd. and Cox Creek Pkwy., was snarled with cars, even the shoulders of the road and the grass area beyond them. Joe got out of the truck and got in the bed of the truck, binoculars in hand. Surveying the area Joe could see nothing but a sea of cars. Part of the mall was burned to the ground. Other retail stores and restaurants had also been burned. Those that weren't had windows smashed. He could make out several decaying bodies that lay in the parking lots, and scattered along the roadway.

He lowered his binoculars as Bob, and Caroline climbed up in the bed. Bob lifted his own binoculars and panned the area. "Holy shit." He said almost in a whisper.

Though she could see the cars and some burned out buildings, Caroline couldn't make out all the details. "What is it? What do you see?"

Joe handed her his binoculars. She put them to her eyes and began to focus them. She jerked her head back as the first thing that came into clear focus entered her vision. She put the binoculars back to her eyes, and stared at what had startled her. The body of a young women laid across the hood of a car. Her clothes ripped from her body. She could just barely make out the gash that ran across the woman's throat even though her body had become bloated and had begun to discolor with decay.

She lowered her binoculars and turned to Joe and Bob. "What do we do now?"

Joe Looked to his left at the where mall road crossed Cox Creek between a bank and discount electronics store. There was room for him to work the truck up to the road that ran behind the shopping centers across the mall. He pointed to the area. "I think I can get the truck through there. I'll run up there on foot and see how that back road looks. If it's not to congested we can use the winch and make our way up to that road. It will lead behind that strip of shopping centers and come out near Wal Mart. We'll hit County Rd. 61, go north to County Rd. 30. From there it will lead us to Jackson Hwy., and Butler Creek Rd."

"Okay we'll keep watch on the trucks while you walk up there." The three hoped down from the truck. Joe reached in and grabbed his shotgun and headed towards the other side of the intersection. Caroline and Bob went to the Xterra.

Caroline opened the passenger side and reached in to pickup the .22 rifle. "Bob, do you think we'll be able to make it through?"

Bob picked up his shotgun and checked the chamber to ensure it was loaded. "I don't know sweetheart. If not, and as much as I hate to, we should drive back to the house and stay the night. Then in the morning take the original route. I'm sure Joe won't like that. Especially after seeing that big truck he was talking about, but I don't see any other way."

The two made their way back to the pickup and hopped up in the bed. Using the binoculars they searched the area for danger. Every time Caroline came across a corpse, despite her revulsion she paused and looked at each one in sickening fascination. Never before had she seen death like this. It chilled her that in a quite place like Florence acts of violence of this magnitude could happen. She shuddered to think what had happened in the bigger cities.

Fifteen minutes later Joe made his way back to the couple. "I think we can do it. Bob I'll need you to put the cars in neutral and steer them if possible while I use the winch to move them. Caroline you keep watch okay?"

"Let's do it!" Bob said as he jumped to the asphalt road.

It had taken them an hour and a half to clear a path large enough for the Xterra and trailer to make it through. Bob and Joe were hooking up the last car to the winch when they heard Caroline call out. "BOB! JOE!"

The two looked up to see Caroline in the truck bed one hand holding the binoculars the other pointing behind her as she called their names. They looked to where she pointed and they made out several figures on motorcycles sitting about four hundred yards away from the Xterra. Both men grabbed up their shotguns and sprinted the fifty yards to Caroline.

Both came to a halt as they reached the Xterra breathing heavily, sucking in all the air they could. "Where the hell did they come from?" He said as he leaned against the truck.

"They came from the back side of the mall."

"Is that all of them, or have you seen any more?"

"Just the six so far, I haven't seen anymore of them."

"Okay Caroline, you jump in the driver seat. Bob and I will sit back on the trailer and keep an eye on our new friends. Bob when we get to the truck we finish clearing the last car. Then you get in with Caroline. I will follow behind and keep them from coming up behind you."

The three hurriedly got into place and Caroline drove as fast as she dared to where the truck and last car were located. She got out with her rifle in hand while Bob and Joe cleared out the last vehicle. "Let's go Caroline!" Bob hollered as he ran to the passenger side of the Xterra. Joe ran to the truck revving up the powerful motor.

As soon as the Xterra turned the corner Joe cut the wheels sharply to the left and spun the truck around to follow. Checking his mirrors he saw three of the motorcycles accelerate forward, the other three turned and headed in the opposite direction. Joe blew the horn twice. When he saw that he had Caroline's attention he pumped his fist three times, letting her know she needed to haul ass.

Caroline couldn't get the heavily laden SUV over forty five miles an hour. She continually checked her mirrors trying to spot the motorcycles she knew would be coming. "Bob what are we going to do?" she said with an edge of panic in her voice.

"Just keep driving. They can't run us off the road if they're riding bikes. Plus it will be hard for them to shoot while riding. Joe and I both have shotguns and can lay down a lot of lead. At this speed they will be easy targets so don't panic." Bob rolled the window down, and then lay his seat all the way back. Then he rolled down the rear window. He turned his body to face backwards ready for any threat.

Joe watched as the three motorcycles quickly gained ground on him. As the three motorcycles drew closer Joe slowed the truck down and began going back and forth trying to block the way. As Joe moved the truck right one of the bikes shot to the left pulling up along side of him. Joe just barely had time to catch a glimpse of a leather clad biker holding a pistol in his left hand.

He ducked his head just as the man fired a shot. Joe jerked the wheel hard left and tried to clip the biker. He missed by inches as the biker shot forward heading for the Xterra. To his dismay the biker he had been trying to block on his right roared by firing two shots that went through the open passenger window and into the front glass.

"Shit!" Joe slammed his foot down hard on the gas pedal. The truck lurched forward in a burst of speed as he sped up to catch the two bikers.

"They got past Joe!" Caroline yelled.

"I see them! Get ready when I tell you too, block the left lane, and force them to come to my side." Bob watched as the two bikers, their long beards flowing behind them, come towards him like rockets. "NOW!" He shouted as the bikers began to move to the left lane.

Caroline jerked the wheel left causing the two bikers to abort their attempt to come up on the driver side. One of the bikers pulled his pistol back out of a holster he had mounted on the gas tank. He fired a round into the back end of the Xterra trying to divert attention to him self as his partner went right.

Bob ignored the rounds as they hit the back of his vehicle. He edged himself forward to the back seat, shotgun pointed towards the open back window. Then the motorcycle came into his line of fire. As soon as the rider's chest was centered on the front sight bead, Bob squeezed the trigger. The blast was deafening inside the interior of the SUV. Caroline let out a yelp in surprise.

Joe watched as the two bikers hit their brakes when Caroline jerked the SUV to the left blocking their path. One rider fired a pistol left handed as the other went right and started coming along the SUV.

He didn't hear the shot but saw the puff of smoke and some flame as Bob fired his shotgun at the rider. The man was blown backwards off the bike, his body still in the riding position as he went backwards towards the pavement.

The bike's front end started to wobble and then went crashing end over end as it left the road way. Joe stared transfixed watching the bike as it crashed. Suddenly he saw the man sprawled out in front of him. He wasn't dead and was trying to get up.

Joe never hit the brakes as the three quarter ton truck's bumper struck the man's head sending a spray of blood and brains into the air. The body twisted and spun, bouncing between the pavement and undercarriage as the truck traveled over the body. Finally it hung up on the rear axel and was drug down the road before finally pulling free and tumbling to a stop in the middle of the road.

Joe watched the body as it skidded to a stop, and barely caught sight of the third biker in his mirror as the bike came along his side of the truck. Again he ducked as the biker fired a couple of rounds at him

Joe reached for his holstered pistol pulling it free. He thumbed off the safety as he jerked the wheel left. The biker had great reflexes and swerved left and accelerated just ahead of Joe.

Joe switched the pistol to his left hand and then rested his arm on the door. He laid the pistol between the door and the side view mirror. Leaning his head down he lined up the sights. As soon as the front sight post was centered on the man's back Joe squeezed off all ten rounds from his Ruger .22 pistol.

The biker dropped the pistol from his hand as he reached around to grab at the pain in his back. The bullets lodging in his back caused him to let off of the accelerator as he almost let go of the grip wanting to reach back and stop the pain with his right hand also.

Joe heard the motor pitch drop as the Harley began to slow. Joe punched the accelerator again steering the big truck for the motorcycle. The truck slammed into the rear wheel causing the front of the cycle to swing left into the path of the truck. As the bike was hit the man was propelled in to the air. The truck bounced into the air as it crushed the bike beneath the tires.

The man's body struck the front edge of the hood. His upper torso raced across the hood his legs flailing out in the air. His body crashed into the windshield almost shattering the glass. His leg bones were snapped in half as they hit the door post causing his body to cartwheel to the side. Part of his left leg went into the open window striking Joe in the cheek.

The pain sent shockwaves into Joe's brain. His vision blacked out momentarily and he slammed on the brakes. The truck fishtailed sideways as smoke billowed from the screaming tires.

His left hand holding his cheek, his eyes still closed Joe reached up and put the truck in park. He sat there for a few seconds waiting for the pain to subside. He gave up willing the pain away and opened his eyes. His vision slightly blurred from his watering eyes Joe reached up and rubbed them to clear his vision.

Almost out of sight Joe saw Bob leaned out of the window firing his shotgun at the last pursing motorcycle. Suddenly the motorcycle locked up its brakes, the back end bouncing back and forth. The rider spun the big Harley around and was head full boar towards Joe.

Joe fumbled for the door and stumbled out on shaky legs. He reached for his holster and found it empty. Looking about he spotted the pistol with the slide locked back laying on the floorboard. His shotgun had slid to the floorboard of the passenger side when he rolled over the motorcycle. The shotgun out of reach he grabbed the pistol, almost blacking out as pain and nausea washed over him.

With trembling hands he fumbled for the magazine release. Finally the magazine dropped to the pavement and he pulled a fresh one from his pouch. He looked up to see the motorcycle had traveled half the distance between his vehicle and Bob's.

The magazine in place he couldn't seem to work the slide release. Suddenly the sound of something thumping into the metal of the front quarter panel startled him. He looked up at the oncoming rider who was now leaned forward over the tank, his left hand extended. A puff of smoke shot from his hand and then washed back over the riders arm as Joe realized the man was shooting.

He strained with his left hand as he tried to pull the slide back to chamber a round. Finally the slide slammed home. Joe raised the pistol up and aimed at the oncoming motor cycle. He could hear the sound of the rider's pistol popping as he charged forward. Joe returned the favor, his own pistol firing as he tracked the rider.

Rounds slammed into the side of the truck as the motorcycle roared by. Joe spun firing his gun as the man passed. As he turned vertigo made his head swim and he collapsed to the ground. He vomited as he lay leaned against the truck. He heard the rider down shift the bike as it slowed to a stop the engine rumbling as it sat idling.

Joe looked back towards the biker to see him stopped sideways eighty yards behind him. He raised the pistol and fired his last two rounds at the man. The man lifted his left foot to the peg and put the bike in gear. He balled the rear tire as he sped away.

The pistol dropped from his weak grip and he closed his eyes. The earth seemed to be rising and falling and spinning at the same time. Then he passed out.

Joe opened his eyes thirty minutes later, he was immediately disoriented. "What, where…"

"Joe it's okay. You're safe now." He heard Caroline's voice to his left. Slowly he let his head roll to see her. She was driving. How did he get in her Xterra?

Caroline saw the confusion on his face. "You've been out of it for about half an hour. We came back for you when we saw you stop. Bob picked you up and put you in here with me. He's driving his truck now."

"Where are we?" Joe tried to rise up and get his bearings but collapsed back onto the reclined seat.

"We'll be coming up to Butler Creek Rd. in a minute. So hang tight. We're almost at Dr. Morrison's, and your nieces will be smothering you with hugs and kisses." Caroline watched Joe slip back into unconsciousness. She reached over and raised his eyelid, then the other. One pupil was severely dilated the other looked like a pin prick. They needed to get to this Dr. Morrison's place quick. Joe had a serious concussion, possibly a fractured skull.

As Bob drove around the bend in the road he slowed then came to a stop. At the fork in the road about a dozen men had stopped working on what appeared to be a wall. Several disappeared and then returned with rifles in their hands. Bob sat there unsure of what to do next.

Then an older man with graying hair and a pistol strapped to his hip came walking forward. The man raised his hand like he was giving his oath in court. He stopped about twenty feet from the truck. Bob scanned the area behind the man. He could see several of the men had scoped rifles.

"Well I guess if they had wanted to kill me they would have already done it." Bob got out of the truck and walked towards the man his hands held out to show they were empty.

"Can I help you young fella?" The older man asked.

"I'm looking for someone." Bob said nervously as he kept looking over the man's shoulder at the rifles pointed towards him.

"And who might that be?"

"My friend, back there has a couple of his nieces staying with a Dr. Morrison.

"Looks like a woman not a man behind that wheel to me." Roy Flynn said as he leaned to take a look into the Xterra.

"Oh, that's my wife Caroline. I'm Bob Novacheck by the way." Bob held out his hand.

The old man took it and shook his hand. "Roy Flynn." He released his firm grip and pointed with his thumb over his shoulder. "That's some of my family and friends helping me out with securing my store. Where is your friend?"

"We got jumped by a few bikers back in Florence. Some how or another he got injured. He wasn't shot and we where so far ahead of him I didn't see how he got hurt. The left side of his face is all swollen though."

Roy eyed the smashed windshield, bullet holes, and blood on the truck. "Yeah I would say it looks like yall been in a scrape. Doc was through here a few days ago. Had a fella named Steve with him. Seems

I remember him saying something about a couple of girls staying with him. What's your friend's name?"

"Joe Donovan."

"Donovan. Yeah that's what he said there last name was." The old man turned. "Charles! Come here. Yall can put the guns away it's alright."

Charles came trotting up to his father. "What'd ya need dad?"

"Get your truck and lead these folks to Doc's place. Slow down when you get near Amos's place though. Doc said they had put up some barricades on the road. Blow your horn a few times and wait for Amos to come out. Just let him know these folks are with you. Otherwise he will probably be putting some double ought buck into these folks."

"Yes sir." Charles turned and ran for his truck.

Charles will get you there. Just stick close to him."

Bob shook hands with Roy again and thanked him for the help. He turned and filled Caroline in on what was going on. Roy went back to his work. Neither man saw the lone leather clad biker in the wood line. Nor did they hear him start the big two wheeled iron horse up and speed back towards Florence.

Celina, Steve, and Doc sat on the front porch talking when Amos's truck came rolling down the road blaring his horn. Doc stood up and walked to the rail. "What the hell is that fool doing? And who the hell has he got with him? Looks like a damn parade."

Steve turned in his seat and looked over his shoulder. "Looks like Charles Flynn's truck. I don't recognize the other two.

The four trucks pulled into the drive. Amos and Charles got out, of their trucks and walked hurriedly towards Doc. A young man exited a shot up truck, and a pretty woman got out of the SUV and walked over and stood beside the man.

"Amos what's going on?" Doc asked.

"Charles can fill you in."

Charles quickly covered what little he knew. At the mention of Joe Donovan's name Celina sprinted towards the couple standing by the truck. "Where is Joe Donovan?"

The man turned and headed for the passenger side of the SUV. "He's over here, and he's hurt." Celina ran with the man to the Xterra. The man opened the back door and Celina looked down at her uncle who was lying with his eyes closed in the reclined front seat. The left side of his face was bruised and swollen.

She took his hand. "What happened?"

"It's kind of a long story, and we're not to sure."

"Let me by young man." Doc eased past Bob and Celina and began to check Joe's vitals. Then very gently he probed Joe's cheek and head. "It doesn't seem to be fractured that I can tell. He definitely has a concussion though. You said you don't know what happened?"

"We were being chased by some bikers. We were way ahead of Joe. Suddenly he stopped and started shooting it out with one of the bikers that was riding towards him. Next thing we see is Joe lying on the ground." Caroline said as she walked up to the group.

"Okay. Let's get him out of here. Steve run down in the basement and get me a back board."

"I'll get it." Maude said. No one had seen her and Daphne walk up.

＋━━＋

An hour later Doc had finished treating and examining Joe. He had pumped him full of pain killers, and antibiotics. Now he sat in the living room with everyone else.

Bob and Caroline told everyone their story about what had happened to them since the collapse. Benny seemed especially enthralled about the motorcycle chase. "Man that sounds like that Mel Gibson movie "Road Warrior."

"And just how do you know about that?" Amos asked.

"My dad had it on DVD. I snuck it out and watched it one day while he and mom went for a walk." He said with an impish grin.

Bob had not broached the subject of staying at Doc's home like they had discussed with Joe. He felt as if he would be intruding on them. Heck he didn't even know them, how could he ask to stay?"

It seemed as if Doc was reading his mind. "So where do you intend to go."

416

Bob looked down embarrassed. "Well Joe had invited us to come along with him. Don't worry though we won't impose on you. We'll find something somewhere."

"Don't be foolish young man." Maude said. "You'll stay here with us. We have plenty of room."

Caroline too, was feeling a bit discomforted. "You really don't have to do that for us. Joe is with his nieces now, and you all. That's what's important. Bob and I have always managed. We'll find something."

Steve held up his hand to stop Maude from saying anything. "Bob and Caroline I'll make a sweetheart deal for you. Doc and I had already discussed me moving in here with him. You two need some time to get to know us. So I'll let you stay at my place and I will move my things here. How does that sound?"

"Steve we couldn't move you out of your home." Bob said feeling more embarrassment and a little bit of shame for having to rely on someone else for shelter for his wife and him. He hadn't thought about this aspect of coming here, and it didn't sit well with him.

"Look I can see you think you're just taking something for nothing. In actuality you would be helping us. The more people we have, the better we can defend ourselves, and survive. If it makes you feel better I'll let you pay me back after all this crap is over and things get back to normal. Now quit arguing and take the deal."

Bob and his wife looked at each other for a moment. Caroline squeezed his hand. Bob looked back to Steve. "Alright Steve you have a deal. Don't think that after this calamity is over that you can refuse me paying you back for letting us stay at your place."

"Good enough for me. Welcome to the neighborhood." Steve leaned forward in his chair and the two men shook hands.

Daphne looked at her sister and wiggled her eyebrows up and down. Celina grinned back ecstatic that Steve would be around her much more now. She grinned that is until she saw Maude giving her a look that said, "I'll have my eye on you."

Chapter 33

Don rolled over and put his pillow over his head. The morning rays of sunlight penetrated through the slit in his curtains. Hey lay there for a few more minutes trying to doze back to sleep, but was unable. Tossing the pillow to the side he sat up and swung his legs off the side of the bed with a sigh.

He leaned forward, his elbows on his knees, and hands rubbing the sleep from his eyes. He walked to the nightstand and picked up the pitcher of water. He poured the water into a large bowl. Taking a washcloth and soap he lathered it up and then scrubbed his face, and hands. He wrung the washcloth out and used it to wipe down his body.

Finishing up he carried the bowl with him to the bathroom and set it down. He relieved himself and took the bowl of now dirty water and used it to flush the toilet. "What to do? What to do?" He said to himself as he walked back to the bedroom and dressed.

Don had a couple of projects he wanted to take care of. He had already started a small garden, and now had to decide what the next most important thing was that he wanted to do. As he finished lacing up his boots he decided on building a small smokehouse. Since he had no refrigeration he needed a way to dry out meat and then jerk it. Food and water were the biggest concerns on his list. Medical and dental were the next. He had plenty of toothpaste and assorted medicines and prescription drugs he had taken from the trailer court, but they would not last forever. He was going to have to find a book on alternative medicines.

As he walked into the hallway he was met by Red. Red appeared to be a Rhodesian Ridge Back, but Don wasn't quite sure. The day after the incident at the trailer court the dog had come wondering up his driveway as if she owned the place. She had a collar that had the name Red engraved on a small brass plate. She was young, maybe about a year old. After tossing her a few treats the dog had surmised that this was her new home. She had walked in the open door and lain down by his fireplace as if it were her own.

"Well at least I'll have someone to talk to." Don had said to himself. After feeding her scraps, and a lot of belly rubs Red became just as attached to Don, as Don had to her, she followed him everywhere he went.

"Good morning girl!" Don said as he reached down and scratched her behind the ears. Red immediately flopped to the ground and rolled over waiting for a belly rub.

Don leaned over farther to rub her stomach, but stopped himself and squatted instead. His ribs still throbbed with pain when he bent over. Digging the trench for his smokehouse was going to be a real pain in the butt.

Don gave her one last rub and slowly stood. "That's it girl. Let's get some breakfast." Red barked twice, her tail wagging as she followed Don to the kitchen.

Once in the kitchen Don fired up the Coleman stove. He put his coffee pot over one of the burners. He had prepared it last night before going to bed. Next he pulled out a bowl and some instant pancake mix. Once all the lumps were gone he poured out four cakes on the pan he had placed on the second burner.

He made twelve cakes, eight for himself, and four for Red. He supplemented her meal with some dog food. He had to go back to the trailer court to pick up several fifty pound bags of dog food that he had seen in one of the trailers. The six bags of dog food wouldn't last forever he was going to have to find a way to feed Red without cutting into his own food supply.

By next spring food would be critical survival issue for Don. He had plenty of canned goods, MREs and dried goods to make till then eating three meals a day. He was going to have to feed the dog which may cause him to go hungry every now and then. He had thought about running Red off. He had decided against that though. He needed the extra eyes and ears. Being alone like he was could detrimental to one's health during the present crisis.

Breakfast finished Don took his dishes to the sink. He placed them in a plastic tub. Before eating he had placed a pot of water on the stove to boil. Taking the boiling water he poured half into the tub and scrubbed the plates clean. Then he rinsed them with the remainder of the boiling water, and placed them on a drying rack.

Keeping his dishes extra clean was something he had to make sure he did. Food poisoning could kill him. Even a bout of diarrhea could incapacitate him enough that he would be unable to get more water from his pump, eventually killing him.

He looked down at Red who had lain by his feet. "Red wouldn't my grave marker be amusing if that happened. Here lays Donald Savage. Survived the collapse of the world, but died on the shitter." Red thumped her tail on the floor in response.

Don smiled down at the dog. "You would like that wouldn't you. Come on let's get outside and get to work." Red scrambled to her feet as Don walked out the kitchen door to the backyard.

First Don dug his fire pit. Next he dug a ten foot long trench. Then he took a ten foot long six inch in diameter stove pipe that had been in the back of the shop for years. He laid this pipe down in the trench, and then covered it with dirt.

That done he took about a dozen bricks that had come from the back of an old fireplace he had found on the back of his property and built a fire box for the inside of his pit. He also made a metal cover that he could adjust to allow air into.

Next he took a fifty five gallon drum and drilled two holes on each side. The holes would hold dowels that would help suspend the meat. He drilled six more holes and bolted hinges in place attached to the lid, and barrel. Next Don drilled holes in the top of the lid. He would use another metal plate that would cover the holes that would act as a damper for the draft. The barrel was then placed over the upturned end of the stove pipe located ten feet from the fire pit.

Don stepped back after four hours of labor to admire his handy work. He took a cigarette out and lit it. Red came over and sat down beside him and admired it with him. Don's left hand gently rubbed

Red's head. "Fine piece of work don't you think girl?" Red looked up at him with a blank stare. "You won't be so blasé about that thing when we have deer meat smoking in there this winter. Come on I'm getting a bath." Don walked out to the shop.

An hour later, Don was bathed and dressed in a set of clean BDU pants, and a t-shirt. He wore a pair of flip flops on his feet. He had just finished cleaning up after a late lunch. Red lay in the kitchen floor watching him clean up. "Red you are one lazy dog." Don said as he stepped over the dog.

Don put the last dish away and had just turned from the sink when Red shot bolt upright and ran towards the living room. The hair along her spine and neck stood up rigid. Don pulled the Kimber .45 from its holster.

Don eased towards the living room the .45 at the ready. "What do you see girl?"

As he entered the living room he saw Red standing at the big bay window staring out. Following her gaze he looked outside. "Who the hell is that?" Four Suburbans, two white, one black, and one blue were stopped just in front of his drive.

A passenger from the second Suburban got out and walked around to the driver side of the first one. Don could tell he was Asian. He felt a knot form in his stomach when he saw the man held an AK-47 and wore magazine pouches across his chest. "OH, shit!" Don ran for the back room to retrieve his LBV, FN-FAL, and his magazines.

‡—‡‡‡‡—‡

The journey from Huntsville had been slow, and full of peril. The two Korean sleeper teams were exhausted. Captain Dong had called a halt for the night. They were just southeast of Athens, Al. The team's road in four Chevrolet Suburbans stuffed with weapons, ammo, food, and water.

Cpl. Wei and Captain Dong were the only two left alive from their team. The other sleeper team had nine members left. They had been ambushed four times while driving from Huntsville to Athens on back county roads. It was going to be a long journey to the Midwest.

Wei had not figured out how to get the information about the rendezvous point. Dong had refused to share the information with Wei, but had advised the sergeant from the other sleeper team. This had angered Wei. How the Captain could not trust his second in command, but give it to someone from another team dumbfounded him.

Maybe Dong suspected that he had killed his two teammates. It did not matter he would obtain the information from the sergeant in due course, Dong did not have long to live. Wei felt antipathy towards the captain every time he bragged about how many civilians they had killed. Once Dong was killed he would be second in command next to the sergeant.

The sergeant did not seem like an unpleasant man. From the conversations he had had with the other NCO, the sergeant had loathed the action taken as much as Wei. He too had lost family in the nuclear fire that the Americans had rained down upon their country. He was more angered at his own leaders for starting the war, than at the Americans who retaliated, and killed his family. He had said that unleashing the chemical and biological attacks against civilians could only bring more nuclear rain down upon North Korea.

"Cpl. Wei." Wei glanced at the setting sun before turning and standing at attention before Captain Dong.

"Yes Comrade Captain." Wei said as his body became rigid in the position of attention.

"I want a sentry on post before the sunsets. Tell the men their schedule. I want you to take the last watch. Wake me at 0500hrs. The rest of the men are to be awakened at 0530hrs."

"Yes sir." Dong turned and strolled away towards his tent. The rest of the men were to sleep under the stars.

Wei went to join the men who had gathered around the campfire where a pot of rice was cooking. He gave the men their times for watch. When the rice had been prepared he did not join the others in their banter. He ate in silence while he plotted the demise of his captain.

Wei went to his sleeping bag after the meal and lay down his decision made. Sleep was a long time in coming as his plan swirled around in his mind. Would he be caught? Or could he do it and get away with it? Finally two hours later he slept.

Wei's eyes snapped open when he felt the squeeze of a hand on his foot. He laid still his hand slipping to the fighting knife he kept sheathed on his side, the rest of his body remained motionless. He focused his eyes towards the foot of his sleeping bag. Then a second squeeze came as his eyes made out the form of the sentry he was to relieve.

He rose up out of the bag, and dismissed the young private with a wave of the hand. He stood on his bag as he moved it to the side and retrieved his clothing that lay between the bag and the ground cloth. He removed the knife from around his waste and dressed.

Picking up his rifle Wei moved to the opposite end of the campsite from Dong's tent. Dongs tent was in the middle of the four Suburbans. Wei silently walked about ten meters outside of the campsite and squatted on his haunches. He closed his eyes and listened to the sounds of the night. Once he felt that he had their rhythm down, he opened his eyes.

He stayed in place though not watching out but watching in. His eyes were glued to the dark form of the young private he relieved. In the moonlight he watched the young man toss and turn for a bit and then finally settle in place.

Wei waited almost an hour, his legs numbing from being motionless for so long. He then stood and felt the legs tingle as the blood flood back into them. He rolled up his sleeves and put on a pair of latex gloves. He slung his rifle across his back as he started to make his way silently around the perimeter of the camp towards Dong's tent.

The short walk of only eighty feet took him close to fifteen minutes. He took his time as he would on a sniper stalk. Stopping and listening to the forest around him and the deep breathing of the sleeping men. Any change at all in their breathing patterns or motion from them and he would wait until another day to kill Dong.

An eternity later he stood crouched before the tent. He reached behind him and took out a knife that he had taken from an American soldier he had killed outside of Huntsville. He had been careful when he took the knife, and he believed no one had seen him take it. The death of Captain Dong would be blamed on an American soldier. He would be sure to bring up the fact that it was most likely one of the American Special Forces. Their soldiers had snuck into enemy camps and killed one or all in all of America's recent wars.

He was in luck when he discovered the tent flap was unzipped. He thought that he would have to cut his way into the tent possibly waking Dong, and that would bring not only Dong's certain death but surely his own.

As he stepped into the tent he stood motionless listening for any change in Dong's breathing. Once he was satisfied the man was asleep Wei kneeled by his head. Placing the knife near the base of his jaw, and one hand poised over Dong's mouth he readied himself. As Dong exhaled he jabbed the knife forward and up, his other hand clamping down over Dong's mouth. The nine inch blade slit through part of Dong's wide pipe, and traveled up into the base of his brain.

Wei stared into the Captain's eyes as they sprang open in pain. Dong's body shuddered and spasm for moment before he died, the zipped sleeping bag keeping him from struggling much. Wei lowered his lips to the Captains ear just before the spark of life left Dong's eyes and he whispered one word, "Murderer."

The captain now dead, Wei stood and removed one of the bloody gloves. He pulled out the sheath for the knife and sheathed the weapon. Next he pulled out a large Ziploc freezer bag and placed the knife inside. Then he took off the second glove and turned it inside out as he pulled it off. Both gloves were then placed in the bag. He placed the items in the bottom of the butt pack, and covered it with his rolled up poncho. He then walked back out and quietly walked to the other side of the camp.

Wei glanced at his watch as he pushed the button to light the luminous dial. Four o'clock. He still had one hour before he was supposed to have awakened Dong. He was sure Dong had probably told the Sergeant what time he would be woken up. At five, Wei would go to the tent, and then sound the alarm that the camp had been infiltrated.

—■—◄■►—

Wei smiled inwardly to himself as he listened to the young private blabbering his apologies, and excuses. "...Surely it did not happen on my watch Corporal. It must have happened around midnight. Every movie I have seen about Americans fighting, they have snuck in at midnight. I went to bed around eleven, and I am sure nothing came into the camp on my watch."

Wei cast a hard glance at the private. "Maybe I should order a tribunal once we get to the rendezvous. It may not go well for those of you who stood watch before me. My record is impeccable, and I am above reproach. How does the other men's and your record compare to mine."

The thought of a tribunal silenced the man. Then Wei continued, "Depending on your performance and that of the other men, maybe I can persuade the Sergeant to just state that the Captain was killed in a firefight. A tribunal could have us all strung up for negligence."

The young private licked his lips, and squeezed the steering wheel. A glimmer of hope could be seen in his eyes. "Yes. You are right as usual Corporal. No sense in having us all hung for the actions of an American Commando."

The young private turned his attention back to the road, his mind in turmoil hoping that nothing would be said when they reached their destination. Wei closed his eyes pleased with himself. He had already spoken with the Sergeant earlier. Both had agreed that if it was known that he Captain was killed in his sleeping bag by an infiltrator, the possibility for a noose awaiting them was high. Command did not tolerate the negligent deaths of their officers.

By the time they reached their destination all the privates would be in line and the same story would be reported, in their debriefing, if their even was a debriefing. There was a high possibility that many officers would be killed, or had already been killed, and no one would even question them.

Wei's plan had worked out quite well. He had entered the tent exactly at five. Then came back outside and fired three shots in the air, and screaming an alarm to the others. It was almost comical when he thought back to the men scrambling around in their underwear waiving rifles in different directions.

Once everything calmed down he briefed the Sergeant on what he had found. Wei then berated, and slapped around the other men who had been on watch. Finally the Sergeant grabbed hold of him and calmed him down. Wei thought he should be awarded one of the American's movie industries Oscar's for his performance.

Wei was brought out of his reverie when the Sergeant's voice came through the earpiece on his headset. "Wei. We're going to stop up ahead. I think we may be getting a flat. My driver said he believes he ran over some debris when we were cutting through Florence."

Wei could hear the irritation in the Sergeant's voice; the Captain dead in camp, a short firefight on the outskirts of Florence, and now a flat. "Roger. Pull over to the shoulder and I will be with you in a moment."

The caravan slowed, and then came to a stop on the shoulder of the road. Wei picked up his AK, and opened the door and trotted up to the lead Suburban, where the Sergeant was located.

Wei approached the driver side of the lead vehicle. The driver had the window rolled down. "I believe the front right tire is going flat Corporal."

Wei flared up in mock anger, as he jerked the door open. "First you let my friend and teammate get killed while you stand watch! Then like an idiot you fail to avoid debris on a paved road! Get out! Get out and change the tire!"

The young private scrambled out of the Suburban raising his arms to deflect the open hand slaps Wei pummeled him with. "Hurry up you fool!"

The young private ran to the back of the Suburban to retrieve the spare. Wei looked inside the vehicle to see if the Sergeant fell for his act of mock anger. He was pleased with the response. "Wei. You must not continue to rebuke the men. We have a long journey ahead of us. This is war, and men, even our friends, will fall. You are a skilled sniper and could have accomplished the same feat. Do you not think the Americans have such men with the same skill?"

"You're right Sergeant." Wei exhaled as if trying to calm himself. "I will apologize to the man and help him change the tire."

"Good. The men respect you, however if you continue with your present attitude that respect will be lost. The cohesion of our unit will diminish, and the men less likely to follow orders as they are trained to do. We have many battles ahead of us, and now is not the time to be raining down your wrath on the men."

Wei nodded his head, placed his rifle in the front seat, and walked around the side of the Suburban. The young private looked fearfully over his shoulder as Wei walked up and stood behind him. "Continue your work private. I will not hit or yell at you anymore. This is war and I know many more of my friends will die. You are a good soldier, as are the others."

The young private immediately looked relieved. He took the last lug nut off of the tire and pulled it off, and rolled it to the side. "Take the tire to the back, we will repair it later. I will put the spare on."

As the young private came erect Wei stepped to the left to get out of his way. Suddenly the private's head exploded and he toppled backwards, his body sliding into the small ditch on the side of the road. Wei dove back towards the rear of the Suburban as rounds began to shred the lead vehicle.

⁘

Don ran to his bedroom and snatched up his LBV and rifle. He quickly put the LBV on and moved to the open window. As he set up the rifle on the window seal he watched the Asian man start to flail away with multiple slaps at the driver of the lead vehicles head.

He popped off the lens cover to his scope and tucked the rifle into his shoulder. He steadied his breathing as he watched the man talk to another Asian in the passenger seat. Then the man walked around the vehicle and stood behind the one he had been slapping.

His breathing now back under control Don rested the crosshairs on the nose of the man. As he was about to pull the trigger he paused. "Something's familiar about him." Don said out loud to himself as he reached up with his left and dialed the scope to fourteen power.

The man's face jumped back into view. Don stared at him trying to place him. Then it hit him like a ton of bricks. It was one of the commando's that had killed his partner Carl Atkins, and Sergeant Ortega. Anger surged through Don. He had only intended on firing if the group turned up his drive.

Now though, there was a chance to take revenge on one of the bastards that killed his friend, and partner Carl. Just as Don squeezed the trigger the man moved left and the one who had been changing the tire stood. Don watched as the man fell backwards. His intended target dove back behind the Suburban.

"Shit! Shit! Shit!" He yelled. "I guess today's a good a day to die as any!" Don squeezed the trigger as fast as he could. First trying for the front passenger who was able to open his door in time and roll out of the line of fire. Don walked the rest of his rounds over the other three

Suburbans, as doors opened and the other men in the group took cover behind the vehicles.

Wei popped up and fired a few ineffective rounds with his Glock 17. Then he ducked back for cover, as he silently cursed himself for leaving his rifle in his vehicle. He needed a rifle; the range to the house was well over one hundred yards.

"Sergeant I need a rifle!" He screamed over the return fire from his men.

The Sergeant tossed Wei his rifle and moved for the open passenger door to grab his driver's rifle. Don caught the movement as the Sergeant reached in to grab the rifle. His shot tore into the man's chest sending him reeling backwards.

Wei looked over at the Sergeant who writhed in pain as more rounds tore into the Suburban. They needed some heavy fire to suppress this sniper. "Damn it, get me some fire on that house!" Wei shouted.

His order was quickly followed as one of the men popped up with an old Russian Degtyarev DP. The gunner let loose the entire forty seven round drum. The steel core 7.62x54R rounds blowing holes in the brick facing of the house.

Don caught movement at the tail end Suburban. He could just make out a man's knee. Placing the cross hairs on the pavement at the side of the Suburban Don fired three rounds. Two of the rounds ricocheted off the pavement at the right angle driving on into the man's knee cap and calf.

As the man fell to the ground Don smiled. "Just like they taught us in the Academy." He pulled the trigger a forth time as the man's chest came into view. The man's movement stopped.

Don didn't have time to savor his kill as rounds began to hit the house. The rounds rocketed through the wall, pictures, and knick knacks disintegrated as the rounds traveled through them, and then through the back wall of the house. Don dove to the floor, his face buried in shag carpet.

Wei crawled over to the Sergeant who was gasping for breath. When he saw the sucking chest wound and felt the exit wound in the Sergeant's back, he knew there was nothing he could do for the man.

"Sergeant, I may not be able to save you. You must tell me were the rendezvous point is."

The Sergeant knew he was dying, and was losing his fight for life. He nodded his head in understanding as he struggled to gain enough breath to speak. Wei leaned his ear close to the man's mouth. "...Iowa..."

Blood gurgled from the Sergeant's mouth as he spoke. Wei could not make out the name of the city, but had caught the name of the state. He leaned up grasping the Sergeant's shoulders.

"I need the name of the city Sergeant!" Wei looked at the Sergeant's now slack face. He released the man's shoulders, he was gone.

Wei snatched up the AKM that the Sergeant's dead hand clasped by the barrel. He leaned to the right and aimed through the two open doors. He let off two six round burst before a round from the hidden sniper slapped into the door by his face. He jerked his head back and moved towards the rear tire as rounds now zinged from underneath the undercarriage.

"Damn these American's. How are their citizens so proficient with weapons?" He thought. The sniper must be military, or police by the way he knew to ricochet the rounds off the pavement.

It was time to end this fight. "I want RPG's now!" Wei screamed.

Don reloaded as he crawled to the hallway so that he could switch rooms. Rounds screamed overhead. His hair white from the white powder dust that floated in the air, which came from sheetrock walls every time a round pierced the house's outer walls.

There was a brief lull in the snipers fire. Wei fired a controlled three round burst into each window of the house. He kneeled to reload and watched as two of his men retrieved RPG's from the back of one of the Suburbans "Hurry up before he fires again!" He shouted.

Don crawled into the next room and peered over the window seal. "Oh shit!" he said as he saw the white smoke trail shoot from one of the men's shoulder launched weapon.

Don ducked back to the floor. Despite covering his ears with his hands the roar of the rocket was tremendous as it entered the front of the house. Then there was an explosion, followed by a secondary one seconds later that lifted him a foot off the floor.

Wei watched as the first rocket flew towards the house. The rocket went through the front bay window. Instead of detonating on the inside of the house though, he rocket smashed through the back glass screen door. It then went through the open garage door on Don's shop then

430

striking the back wall where it detonated. The explosion blew the wall out, the concrete chunks puncturing the plastic fuel tank that rested behind the shop. The shop was engulfed in flames, and the fire ball from the explosion mushroomed one hundred feet in the air. Burning liquid cascaded down into the yard and the roof of the house along with chunks of debris of the shop.

The second rocket that was fired went into the window the sniper had first fired from. This round passed directly through the window and detonated against the back wall. The blast slammed Don against the wall. He had just started to rise up to fire when the second rocket exploded. A chunk of the bed frame in the back room had blown through the wall from the force of the explosion. It was about an inch wide and three inches long. This dagger like projectile sliced through Don's lower torso and lodged into the wall. Don fell semi-conscious to the floor.

Wei emptied his magazine as he fired at the house. "GO! GO! GO!" He screamed.

The surviving members charged forward as Wei reloaded and provided cover fire, along with the soldier who fired the Degtyarev. As his men reached the house Wei ran at full speed across the open field. He felt the shock waves from the hand grenade explosions, and watched as his men threw several more grenades through the big bay window before entering the house.

Wei stood outside as his men cleared the house. Then one of the privates came out of the front door. "We have one man inside Corporal."

Seconds later a two privates carried a limp body between them. When they reached the front porch they tossed the man into the grass of the front yard. The man let out a groan of pain.

Wei walked over to the man. "Where did your friends go?" He demanded.

The man struggled to lift his head, his eyes blinking several times as the man tried to focus. "Alone." He groaned.

Don stared up at the man towering over him. It was the man he had tried to shoot first. "Mu...Mur...Murderer!" he stammered.

Wei was taken aback. How could this man know he took part in the killing of the civilians in Huntsville? "Why do you call me a murderer?"

"You stinking slant eyed cock sucker. You were one of the ones that killed my partner at the dam." Don managed to say.

Wei looked hard at the man's face. He thought back to that first attack, and the fleeting glimpse he caught of the TVA officer's face that he had seen that day. It was the one who had ambushed them. "I remember you. It was not murder. Our countries are at war."

Don wasn't able to reply. His head sagged back on the grass as he threw an arm over his face to shield it from the beating rays of the sun. Don had killed some of this guys unit. He was a goner for sure.

Wei was about to say something else but one of the privates spoke up. "The man's weapons Corporal. We also have found a cache of ammo that was not destroyed by the explosion."

Wei looked at the rifle and pistol in the privates hands. "Take them to the vehicle. Then pull one of the vehicles up here to load the ammo before the house burns to the ground." Wei motioned for the other private to go back inside to help the other team members carry the ammo out.

"What about him?" The private pointed at Don.

Wei kneeled down and pulled up Don's t-shirt. The wound he had was a through and through. It appeared no vital organs were hit. "Leave him. He can suffer a slow death. With no medical attention the wound will fester and eventually infections will kill him." The private nodded and quickly made his way to the vehicles.

Don moved his arm from his face. "Why aren't you going to murder me too? Isn't that what you people do best?"

Wei looked around to make sure he would not be overheard. "I am no murderer. I am a soldier. You have been a worthy adversary. You fight to protect your country, just as I would. I will not shoot you for doing what you must. You are no longer a threat to my team. Who knows you may be able to find help and live."

Wei stood as the men carried out MREs, and ammo cans. The Suburban pulled up and the driver got out and opened the back doors. The men crammed the liberated items into the already over crowded cargo area.

"Load up and let's get going." The men piled into the Suburban. One of the privates held the door for the Corporal. "Get in. I will walk."

The man hopped in and the Suburban pulled away to the end of he long driveway.

Wei turned around and looked at the man lying before him. "What is your name?"

Don stared back for a moment then answered. "Don Savage."

Wei nodded his head his left hand reaching back behind him. "That would be an appropriate name. You have definitely fought savagely." Wei pulled out he baggie that held the large knife he had used to kill Dong with. "You may need this." Wei tossed the baggie to Don's side.

Don stared at the knife for a moment. The man turned and started to walk away then stopped and looked at Don. "Good luck Savage. You'll need it." The man turned and walked on.

"Hey!" Don called out weakly. The man kept walking. "Hey! What's your name?" He called again in a stronger voice.

The man continued walking but looked over his shoulder. "Wei." He turned his head back and threw his hand up in a wave, and walked on.

Don lay in the grass confused by the actions of Wei. He rolled his head over to the right and watched flames rise from the backside of his house. "Great." He closed his eyes again. "Now what?" he thought.

He jerked a bit as he felt something cold touch his cheek. He opened his eyes to see Red standing over him. "Where did you go? Hauled butt when you should have had my back I'll wager." Red licked his face then nudged him on the arm.

"Alright let me compose myself." Don lay in the grass for several more minutes then struggled to his feet. He held out his hands to get his balance as the world spun. His ribs still hurt, and had not healed. Now he had another even more serious wound. Wei was right. He could die of infection if he couldn't get help.

Once the vertigo slipped away he slowly bent down and picked up the plastic baggie. Inside a Gerber BMF knife and two bloody latex gloves. He ripped open the plastic and pulled out the knife. He attached it to his web belt, and slowly stood back up. His face contorted in pain as his wounds screamed at him to quit moving.

Don looked back at his house and then noticed a second larger pillar of smoke behind the house. "Damn! They blew my shop up." Don turned and started walking through the grass towards the road. He shook his head as he looked down at his bare feet. He had no idea where the flip

433

flops he wore went. Of course now his boots were burning embers. "It's going to be a long walk Red." He managed to say.

Two hours later Don had made it to Chisholm Rd., and had walked one mile south towards Florence. The hole in his side had quit bleed about twenty minutes earlier, but every step he took sent shocks of pain through his upper torso. The soles of his feet were becoming raw, as rocks, sticks, and an occasional bottle cap ate away at them. Sweat covered his body, and blurred his vision as he staggered southward to the city. Maybe someone somewhere would help him. He staggered on, willing his feet and legs to keep moving.

Chapter 34

Howard sat on the side steps eating an apple. He took a large bite as Craig came out the door wearing his LBV and carrying his H&K UMP submachine gun. "Where are you going?" He said through a mouth full of apple.

Craig slung his Camelback pack through the driver window and jerked the door to the truck open. "I'm headed up north to scout some things out. Maybe I will be able to find something useful for that big meet coming up. You want to ride?"

"Nah, I think I'm going to lounge around today."

Craig hopped in the truck and cranked the Dodge diesel 4x4 to life. "Well how about getting off your lazy butt and open the gate."

Howard tossed the half eaten apple at Craig through the open window of the truck hitting him in the head. "What was that for?" Craig said as he wiped the juice and pulp of the apple from his face.

"You're just so damn ugly I couldn't resist. How about getting the gate your own damn self?" Howard stood, and gave his friend the finger as he turned to go back inside. "Be careful out there moron."

Craig returned the gesture and pulled the truck up to the front gate. He opened the gate and pulled the truck through. Returning to close the gate Meat walked up. "You want to go for a ride boy?" Meat bound for the open front door of the truck and hopped in.

Craig turned the truck north up Wood Ave. Meat sat panting beside him. Craig looked over at the huge dog, drool and saliva dripped from Meat's mouth. Craig reached over and shoved Meat's head away from him. "Stick that big bucket head of yours out the window."

Meat stood on the bench seat and stuck his head out the window. Craig frowned at the new more disgusting site now a foot away from his face. "Meat, sit down." The dog's only response was to wag his tail. "Great, nothing like a face full of brown eye. Well at least it's better than looking at Howard." He said to himself with a smile.

Craig drove slowly northward until he reached the Seven Points Shopping District. He drove around two corpses that appeared about a day old. His eyes scanned the devastated shopping district looking for any signs of danger. He also watched Meat to see if he sensed any danger. The big dog appeared at ease, his tail wagging, and nose to the wind that blew around him.

Craig turned onto Chisholm Rd. leaving the shopping district behind him as he reached the large residential tracts of older homes that lay past the Seven Points area. Craig pushed the pedal down quickly accelerating and weaving in and out of the stalled and abandoned vehicles. It was beautiful, cool morning and Craig daydreamed of better times. He eventually reached a bare stretch of road were no vehicles were in the way and he increased the speed of the truck, the cool morning air filling the cab of the truck, and the hum of the tires helped lull his senses as he drove on.

Craig gazed out the driver side window at a few of the houses he passed. Some appeared normal, others burned, or damaged. He mentally pictured the area as it had looked not so long ago. Shaking his head he turned to watch the road ahead. As he turned his head a deer scampered across the road just feet in front of him.

Instinctively Craig's body tensed, both feet smashing the brake pedal to the floor. The big all terrain tires shuddered and smoked as they skidded across the pavement. Craig jerked the wheel to the right causing the truck to fishtail, then the passenger side tires left the ground for a heart wrenching second. Meat's body slammed into Craig knocking his hands from the wheel. Finally the truck came to wrest against the street curb, the front bumper inches from a telephone pole.

Craig sat wide eyed staring at the pole for a few breathless moments. He felt Meat move against him and then move to the passenger side of the cab. Craig looked down at his hands and tried to stop them from shaking, but couldn't, the adrenaline still coursed through his body. "Jeez. What the hell was I thinking driving like that?"

Craig took a few minutes to calm down then reached a still shaking hand up and put the truck in reverse. He eased the truck backwards, then put it in drive and began to slowly make his way north again. His near miss set his mind in the right frame of mind. He drove the truck slowly, at about twenty miles per hour, his head continually scanning left and right looking for any threats or danger. The road ahead was not clear, more cars and trucks were scattered before him.

Then Craig spotted an eighteen wheeler ahead that appeared to have jack knifed, blocking the north bound lanes. One of the trailer doors swung back and forth in the morning breeze. He stopped the truck and turned it off. Getting out he slung his sub-gun. "Come on Meat." Meat followed out the driver door obediently.

Craig scanned the area looking for any sign of ambush. Seeing none he looked at Meat. The dogs body was relaxed his tail wagging. Reassured nothing was amiss Craig moved towards the trailer, still at the ready, just in case he and Meat had missed something. The only things he saw with his roving eyes were a few decayed and leathered corpses that sat in some of the vehicles, or lay in the road.

As he approached the trailer the rear door slowly swayed open again. Craig had the UMP shouldered; the tactical light on, just in case the trailer would not be lit by the morning light. The only things he saw were several boxes near the back of the trailer.

Craig let the UMP drop on its sling and climbed into the trailer. He pulled his Marine Corps K-Bar knife from its sheath and walked to the boxes. Craig slit the tape to the top box and then sheathed his knife. Opening the box he was surprised to find a box full of boots, the smell of new shoes reached his nose, and he smiled. Flipping the tongue back it read size six.

Craig pulled out his mini Maglight and shined the beam of light on the other three boxes. Each box was labeled in black with the name of Wolverine Work Boots. Additional writing about each of the boxes content was also labeled. The box he had opened said women's size six, ten pair. The other three were men's, sizes nine, ten and a half, and eleven, also with a ten count of boots in each.

Craig grinned from ear to ear. This find was better than gold, boots would be in high demand if things did not get any better. He wore a size ten and a half and would keep two pair for himself and he and Howard could trade the rest. Howard would be out of luck since he wore a size eleven and a half.

Craig pulled the four boxes to the doors and then took a peak outside. Meat lumbered around the cars lackadaisically marking each individual tire of the surrounding vehicles. If something was near Meat wouldn't have been pissing on tires. He jumped down to the pavement. He then quickly loaded the four boxes in the bed of the truck.

Next Craig went to check the tanks on the big diesel. Checking both tanks, he found that they were about half full. He knew he still had about three quarters of a tank in his truck. He went back to his truck and pulled two full jerry cans from the rack which he and Howard had made to hold four, five gallon jerry cans of fuel. Two were empty and two were full.

He drained the two full ones into the fuel tank. Then he reached into the bed of the truck and pulled out an old shovel handle and put all four cans on the handle. Opening a small box affixed to the side of the rack he pulled out a siphon and pump. He then went back to the rig to fill the jerry cans. Twenty long minutes later all four cans were full of diesel fuel.

As he finished loading the cans onto the rack he looked down at Meat who sat staring patiently at his master. "Well Meat, not a bad haul so far. Think we ought to keep hunting since we are on a lucky streak?" Meat's big tail thumped the pavement, and drool sprayed the side of the truck as he barked his response.

"Keep going huh? My thoughts exactly, and by the way you have got to do something about that drooling of yours. Maybe we can convert it to some sort of new power source. Just think you'll make millions." Craig jumped down beside the dog, and scratched him behind the ears. He opened the door of the truck for Meat. "Now power your big butt in the truck and let's ride." Meat sprung forward and hopped into the truck.

A half hour later Craig had only traveled about two miles, he had left the city limits and was now reaching a sparsely populated area. The houses were few and far between now. So far Craig had not seen anything that interested him. Both the homes and businesses appeared to have been looted, destroyed, or looked a little to inviting. He particularly avoided these fearing some type of ambush.

"Meat let's call it quits and head back to the house." Craig said as he spotted an old white cinder block farm house with a circular drive just ahead of him.

Craig turned the big truck onto the gravel drive. He checked the house visually for any signs of life as he began to drive past it. The windows were all open, and the curtains fluttered in the breeze. Craig slammed on the brakes when a pale hand appeared in the window by the front door. He shut the engine down and pulled out his pistol as he exited the truck. Meat jumped through the passenger window and stopped when he hit the ground. His body was rigid, tail straight out, ears perked. He too had seen the hand.

Craig crouched down, behind the front of the truck. The only thing visible was his head and arms. His pistol was extended out over the hood. "Hello in the house!" He shouted.

Craig listened intently for a response as he checked the surrounding area for any signs of ambush. "Hello in there! I don't mean any harm. I'm looking to trade if you're interested. If not, just tell me to go away and I will leave."

For almost a minute Craig stayed in place, neither seeing nor hearing a response. Then the pale, almost bone like hand appeared again. This time Craig heard a voice. It was almost inaudible, raspy and weak sounding. "Help me." He heard the pleading voice again.

Slowly Craig stood with his pistol still out in front of him ready for action. He made his way to the front porch, his head continually swiveled in every direction looking for danger. The screen door was shut but the door behind it stood open. Craig saw the arm of a couch or chair, with a pair of worn out work boots resting on top of it.

He hated to do it, but he decided he would cross the open door and peer into the window to see who lay on the other side of it. He took a deep breath, exhaled and swiftly crossed the danger area coming to a stop on the other side of the door. He looked into the window and could just barely make out part of a body lying on the couch.

"You okay in there?" He asked.

"Need help...don't think I'm going to last much longer." The voice said.

"Is there anyone else here?"

"No. Ma passed on last week. She..." The man didn't finish the sentence as a fit of coughing cut him off.

Craig reached behind him with his left hand to a pouch that rested on the side of his LBV. He jerked it open and pulled a gas mask from it. He holstered his pistol and donned the mask, then pulled the pistol back out.

He turned from the window and jerked the screen door open and went inside, followed closely by Meat. Craig lowered his pistol when he looked at the disheveled scare crow thin old man on the couch. The old man's right pants leg had been cut off up to the knee. A dirty blood soaked bandage was wrapped around his lower leg. His snow white hair was plastered to his head from the sweat that saturated his entire body.

"What happened mister?" Craig said, his voice muffled from the gas mask.

"Burying my wife..."several coughs stopped the old man from speaking for a few seconds.

When the man caught his breath he began again. "I was burying my wife, and had to cut through a tree root. Axe glanced off the dang thing and caught me in the leg. Ran out of rubbing alcohol and couldn't keep it clean. Now it is infected."

Craig stared down at the old man for a moment. After a second he decided the man probably wasn't carrying anything contagious. He had probably gotten pneumonia, and fever. He pulled the mask off, and put it back in its carrier. "I've got a medical kit in the truck. I'll be right back." Craig turned to retrieve his kit.

"No need in wasting good medicine son. I don't have long before I'm gone. If you could spare some water I would appreciate it. Haven't had any in a couple of days." The old man croaked.

Craig returned a minute later with his first aid kit, his Camelback, and a one liter bottle of water he retrieved from under the front seat. Setting the first aid kit and his Camelback down, he knelt beside the old man and pulled him up, placing a pillow behind his head. Then he opened the bottle of water and brought it to the old man's lips. "It ain't iced down, but I suppose you really don't care do you old timer?" Craig said trying to make the old man smile.

The old man tried to greedily gulp the water down, and Craig had to pull the bottle away to slow him down. "Not so fast mister, just take it easy. There is plenty of more for you."

The old man nodded his head, and Craig put the bottle back to his lips. After several sips Craig pulled the bottle away and set it on the floor. "You can have some more water in a second. What is your name? I'm Craig Wolfe."

"Ollie, Ollie Terrell. I appreciate the water Mr. Wolfe. Sweetest I've ever tasted." The old man's eyes fluttered and closed, then came back open. He gave Craig a weak smile.

"Mr. Terrell I'm going to have to check that injury out. Once I get it cleaned up I know of a doctor that doesn't live far from here, and I will take you there."

Ollie rested his hand on Craig's shoulder and stopped him from reaching for the first aid kit. "There is no need for that Mr. Wolfe. I'm ninety three years old. Been around long enough to know that now is my time. I just want to ask for one more favor from you."

"Sure Mr. Terrell, what is it?"

"Out back is where I buried my Olivia. I've..."Another shuddering cough came from the old man. "I've dug my grave next to hers. When I go would you mind putting me in the ground?"

"Mr. Terrell I'm going to make sure you make it. Quit talking like that okay." Craig began to reach again for the first aid kit again but Ollie stopped him again.

"Mr. Wolfe, do you mind letting me have another sip of that water?"

"Sure Ollie no problem." Craig picked up the bottle of water and Ollie drank deeply this time before Craig pulled the bottle from his lips.

As Craig sat the bottle down Ollie spoke again in a low quite voice. "Thanks Mr. Wolfe, good to see there are still a few good folks around. You can have everything when I go. No sense in all of it going to waste."

"The only place you're going is...Craig stopped speaking as Terrell's eyes closed, and he heard the air exhale from his lungs. Craig stared for a few seconds and did not see the old man's chest rise again. He felt for a pulse and found none.

"Damn!" Craig stood up, and looked down on the old man. "I'll put you out by your wife Mr. Terrell."

Craig made his way through the house checking each room, just to make sure no one else was truly there. He found no one. He stepped out back and saw the mound of dirt. Next to it was an open grave. Stuck in the ground was a piece of wood with the names Ollie and Olivia Terrell chiseled into it.

Craig walked back inside and went to one of the bedrooms and pulled a comforter off the bed. Going back into the living room he spread the comforter at the base of the couch. Very gently he lifted the rail thin old man and laid him on the comforter. Then he rolled Ollie in the comforter and tucked the loose ends in when he finished.

Once he was satisfied Craig lifted Ollie up and carried him to the open grave in the backyard. He laid Ollie beside the hole and climbed in. Once in he reached over and heaved the old man into the grave and gently laid him to rest. He spent the next forty five minutes filling the hole. When he was done he said a few words of prayer over the old man's grave.

Going back inside Craig retrieved his Camelback and took it to the front porch where he sat in an old rocker and drank from his Camelback. Meat lay at his feet dozing. "Well Meat, let's take a look around the place and see what Ollie said we could have." Craig got to his feet and tossed the Camelback through the open passenger side window of his truck.

Craig spent the better half of the hour scouring through the kitchen. He carried several box loads of canned foods, cooking pots, and pans, utensils, flour, and sugar to the truck. He also found several ten pound bags of various dried beans.

After cleaning out the kitchen and pantry Craig moved to the bedrooms, and hall closets. He was able to locate three boxes of batteries and an old Buck sheath knife in the front bedroom. There was nothing of value in the second. In the master bedroom Craig went through the drawers first. He found several pair of wool socks and kept them. Other than that there was nothing of value in the drawers.

In the closet Craig found a Car-hart work jacket. Though it would not fit him, it might fit Howard. As he removed the jacket from the hanger he caught sight of something in the corner of the closet. Reaching back in the back corner he pulled out a Marlin 30-30 lever action rifle.

On the butt stock was a leather ammo holder holding ten rounds. Craig pulled out his flashlight and shined it on the floor of the closet. Also in the corner were four boxes of 30-30 rounds.

"Ollie you sly old dog, I figured you wouldn't have a gun around as old as you were." Craig said to himself with a smile.

Craig's next search began in the small barn behind the house. As he rounded the corner of the house Craig saw Meat stretched out on his belly, tail wagging. "Hey Meat, what do you got boy?"

Meat turned his head to look at Craig and gave a bark. Craig stopped not quite sure what was on his face. Red intermixed with white adorned the dogs muzzle. Then Craig took in the area surrounding the dog. Feathers littered the ground or were tossed in the air by the breeze. The carcasses of several dead chickens littered the surrounding area.

"Meat, what the hell do you think you are doing?" Craig said as he began to walk forward.

Craig stopped beside Meat and looked down at the dog that was now totally ignoring him as he gnawed on the remains of a rooster. "Well so much for the theory that Howard and I could enjoy eggs each morning. Thanks a million there Meat." Craig shook his head and made his way to the barn avoiding the dead chickens and puddles of blood as he went.

The barn was neatly kept and arranged. It was treasure trove of antique farm equipment and tools. Craig immediately began sorting through the items he felt he could take and use. He also mentally logged in his mind the larger farm implements that he could come back for later. Things like the single bladed plow, with harness for a draft animal would be worth ten times its weight when the gas ran out. He did take all of the hand tools he could get his hands on. Things like hand cranked drills, chisels, files, two-man hand saws, hammers, tin snips, hand plainer, nails, screws, and rope, were just some of the items he loaded into the truck.

He also took two fifty pound bags of chicken feed. Even though Meat had crushed his hopes of raising chickens for now, he intended to get some at the big meet in St. Florian. Craig looked around the barn and decided that was all he would take for now. The only thing left was to check the loft. Chances were there would be nothing of value or interest up there but one never knew.

Craig climbed the ladder and pulled out his flashlight when he reached the top. He quickly ran the beam of light over the loft seeing only hay. On the second sweep he stopped when his eye caught sight of an old blanket. Craig walked to the blanket and reached to pull it up to see what was under it.

"Let's see what Ollie has hidden under here." Craig said as he pulled the blanket up.

Beneath the blanket was an old spinning wheel. Craig was excited. He didn't know how to use one, but he was sure someone at the big meet would know how and be willing to trade big time for it. Craig pulled the spinning wheel to the edge of the loft where he tied a rope around it. The rope was affixed to a pulley that had been set up there to haul bails of hay up. He gently lowered the spinning wheel to the floor of the barn. When he finished that he detached the pulley and tossed it to the ground also.

Once Craig loaded the spinning wheel he was ready to go. The bed of the truck was pretty well loaded down. With the spinning wheel and other farm implements Craig felt like he must look like the Clampet's from the Beverly Hill Billy's.

Craig walked back to barn area to get Meat. Meat still lay on his belly crunching on the bones of dead chickens. "You know Meat, that those chicken bones can splitter and kill you?" Meat ignored Craig's advice and kept chewing. "Come on Meat it's time to go."

Meat disappointedly rose to his feet and snatched up a claw to a chicken foot before he turned to go. The two walked back to the front of the house and got into the truck. Craig cranked the truck to life and eased it to the road. He stopped and looked left, then turned to look back to his right when Meat, who was sitting jumped to his feet, the hairs on the back of his neck standing tail. A low growl emitted from deep in his throat.

Craig peered around Meat to see what had gotten the dog's attention, his hand coming to the butt of his pistol. About fifty yards down the road sat a red colored dog. "It's just a dog Meat chill out."

As Craig began to turn his head to movement beside the dog caught his peripheral vision. Craig turned back and tried to focus on what was beside the dog but couldn't quite make it out. He reached into a pocket on the front of his vest and pulled out a monocular. He focused on the eyepiece on the dog and wants it was focused in he panned just to the right of the dog on the shoulder of the road.

What he saw was a pair of legs, and two bloody feet. The left leg bent as if the person was trying to force himself up. Craig put the monocular back in place and turned right towards the downed person, and dog.

He stopped about fifteen yards short of the dog, and what he now saw was a large man, who looked like he had been through hell and back. Meat put a paw on the window and was about to jump out but Craig gave him the command to stay. He picked up his UMP and exited the truck.

Craig looked around but saw no place for anyone to set up and ambush him. There was nothing but untended empty fields around. There was a bend in the road about three hundred yards ahead. The only thing he would have to worry about would be someone with a long gun. But from the look of the man on the ground before him he doubted this was a set up. Not only were his feet bloody and torn, and face cut and swollen, he had a large bloody gash that flies swarmed around on his side.

"Hey Mister, you need some help?" Craig called out.

The man lifted his head and looked at Craig and laid it back on the ground. "What the hell does it look like? You think I'm out here getting a tan?" The man gruffly replied.

<hr/>

Don Savage didn't know how long he had been walking. Every step that he took as time went on became a painful chore. His feet soon became dulled to the pain, though his side still throbbed with each step he took. He knew he had to find help or a place he could hole up and heal. His most immediate need was water. If he didn't get any soon, treating his wounds wouldn't be necessary, he would probably die of a heat stroke.

Soon Don made his way around a bend in the road and stopped to rest for a second in the shade of the trees. He dared not sit, knowing he would never get up. He wiped the sweat from his head and eyes and peered ahead. Through his blurred vision Don made out a small cinderblock house with a black truck parked in the front. It was only a few hundred yards away.

"Come on Red. There may be hope for us yet." Don and Red trudged on.

It seemed to Don that he wasn't making any progress to the house. Each time he looked up to see how far he had made it the house appeared no closer. He would just lower his head and keep shuffling till he got there.

Finally Don's legs seemed to quit on him and collapsed by the roadside. With what little strength he had left he lifted his head to see how far he had to go. "Damn, almost made it Red." His head fell back to the ground. With his hand he tried to push Red away. "Go on girl. No sense for you to hang out and die with me." Red just sat on her haunches staring intently at the house ahead.

Don didn't know how long he lay there but soon he heard the sound of a diesel motor cranking to life. He lifted his head again to see the black truck pulling to the roadway and stop. "I've got to get up, I need some help." Don said struggling to move his legs and get up. It was no use, he was exhausted.

Moments later Don heard the sound of the truck approaching, and stop. The sound of a door opening reached his ears. Then someone called out to him. "Hey mister you need any help?"

Don lifted his head and could barely make out the form of a man holding a compact weapon pointed at him. "Great here I am dieing and now I'm about to get robbed to boot." He thought disgustedly to himself.

"What the hell does it look like? You think I'm out here getting a tan?" Don said not really caring whether the man shot him or not.

"What the hell kind of response is that?" Craig thought. "You know I could just put a bullet in your ass, or leave you for the buzzards?"

"Mister, either lower the gun and get over here and give me a hand or just put a bullet in me. I really don't care which at this point. I got attacked by some dinks, my home blown up, I've got wounds on every part of my body, I'm thirsty, and exhausted. So hurry up and make up your mind, your wasting what little time I probably have left." Don said, meaning every word of it.

Craig stared at the wounded man. After a moment of thought he lowered the UMP and began to move forward. "Alright I'll give you hand. Your dog isn't going to bite me is he?"

"No. Hell she'll probably haul ass. She's the brain of our little team."

Craig stopped just short of the man. The dog looked up at him wagging its tail. Though the man's face was swollen and bruised Craig thought he recognized him. Was he someone he knew from work, a victim he had taken a report from, or someone he had arrested?

"What's your name mister?" Craig asked.

The man took a breath before answering. "The name is Don Savage."

"Holy crap!" Craig thought. He knew this man, had backed him up a few times on calls. Craig eased forward to get a better look at the man's face.

"Are you Don Savage, from TVA Police?"

"Yeah. Who are you? My visions a little blurry right now." Don said as he moved his head to get a better look at the man standing over him.

"I am Craig Wolfe from FPD."

"Well Craig it's good to see you again. Now quit gawking and get me the hell out of here." Don said a broken smile playing across his lips.

Craig ran back to the truck and opened the back door to the crew cab. Meat had jumped out of the truck sometime during his conversation with Don, and now he and Don's dog were getting to know one another a little better the way all dogs do.

Craig took Don's hand and pulled his body forward using the momentum to swing him up into a fireman's carry. Don let out a painful groan as Craig's shoulder dug into his injured side, and cracked ribs. He carried Don to the truck and put him in. He then grabbed another bottle of water and first poured it over Don's head, then handed the half empty container to Don. Don drank slowly from the bottle, savoring the precious liquid.

Next Craig grabbed his first aid kit and cleaned the wounds on his feet and side as best he could. Don let out a gasp of pain when Craig poured rubbing alcohol over his feet and then his side. Then Craig bandaged up the injuries as best he could.

Reaching back into the kit he pulled out a bottle of Lorecet pain pills. "Don, can you take Lorecet?"

"I'll take a bottle of them if you give them to me."

Craig dumped two five hundred milligram tablets into his palm and put the bottle back in the kit. "Here take these." He said handing Don the tablets.

"Got anymore of the good stuff?" Don said holding up the empty bottle of water.

Craig pulled out a second one liter bottle handing it to Don's out stretched hand. "Here you go partner."

Craig turned to look for Meat and spotted him and the other dog lying side by side by a small roadside shrub. "He Don what's your dogs name?"

"Her name is Red."

Craig went around the to the front passenger side door and opened it up. "Meat and Red come on! Let's go for a ride."

The two dogs got up and raced to the truck. Red was first and leaped into the truck, followed closely by Meat. Craig shut the door and got in the truck and cranked it up while the two dogs arranged themselves in the seat.

"Where are we headed?" Don asked from the back seat.

Craig looked down at his watch. It was four thirty. It would take him about two hours of slow cautious driving to reach Doc Morrison's place. By then it would be too dark and unwise to travel back to his place in town. That would leave Howard on his own till the next day.

He made up his mind. "I know a doctor, but if we go to his place it will leave my friend on his own. If you think you can hang on for a day or two to get proper medical treatment we'll head back to my place in town."

Don thought about it for a moment. As long as he kept rested and the wound on his side clean he should not have to worry too much. He felt if he had any internal bleeding he would have bled out and died long before he had reached this point.

"I can make it. Just have to keep these wounds clean and hydrate."

Craig nodded his head and turned the truck around driving as fast as he dared without endangering himself or Don to ambush, or a crash. It would be a long smelly ride. The two big dogs took up a lot of room and

Meat sat with his body pressed next his. The occasional glob of salvia dropping from Meat's mouth onto his arm or leg would be Craig's most obvious discomfort on the way home.

The all terrain tires hummed, and the truck rocked slowly back and forth over the occasional bump, and the pain pills took effect on Don. Soon he was in a deep sleep that his body craved. He wouldn't wake for another fifteen hours.

⊹⊷⊷⊹

Craig's and Don's drive back to Florence was uneventful. The sun was setting as Craig pulled the big Dodge up to the front gate. He blew the horn twice and got out. Howard came down the walk holding his FN.

"I was beginning to wonder if Meat got hungry and made a snack out of you. Where did you pick up the other dog?" Howard said as he unlocked and began to open the gate.

"Remember Don Savage from TVA Police?"

"Yeah I sold him a few nice pieces over the years."

"Found him on the road side all beat to hell and back. He is sleeping in the back seat right now."

"Did he say what happened to him?"

"Said something about some dinks shooting him up and blowing up his house. I'm not quite sure of all the details he was a little out of it." Craig said as he and Howard walked to the cab of the truck and peered in on Don.

"Damn they messed him up pretty bad. Get him on up to the house and I will lock the gate up."

Once both men were at the house Howard ran out to the shop and got an old surplus Army stretcher they had found at the National Guard Armory. They laid it on the floor board and gently as possible placed Don on it. Don's only response was a low grown. They then took him inside and cleaned and properly bandaged his wounds. Don slept through it all. Then they put him in one of the upstairs beds to sleep.

Howard sat down in front of the CB and ran his fingers through his hair. "I'm going to try to raise Doc and see if he can't get over here tomorrow."

Craig just nodded his head and began to strip down. "I'm going to fill the tube up and wash some of this grime away."

"I would prefer you stripped elsewhere. I would hate to have to sit here and see your under developed child like manhood sticking out like a twig."

Craig threw his sweat soaked shirt and hit Howard in the face with it. He turned to go to the bathtub. "Get real Howard. I've seen you peeking when I bathe. You're just jealous at the enormity of the thing." Craig laughed and walked out of the room.

Howard tossed the musty smelling shirt to the floor, and turned to the radio. Several minutes later he finally had Doc on the radio. "Doc this is Howard. Craig has picked up a friend of his that has some pretty bad injuries. I don't think they are life threatening but I think you aught to take a look at him. Should we bring him out to you, or should we wait for you to come here?"

"I've got the map to your place. It would probably be best if I came in to see him. I'll get Steve or Amos to come along with me. I'll radio before we leave. Check your radio every hour from five till about eight. We'll leave sometime in that time frame."

"I copy that Doc. See ya in the morning."

"Alright, Doc out."

Howard got up from the chair and walked to the tub in the other room. He opened the door to find Craig soaking in water that had turned brown. "I got hold of Doc Morrison. He said he would leave between five and eight, and to monitor the radio on the hour and he would contact us when he left."

"Good deal. Now go and fetch me a towel and some clean clothes boy."

Howard rolled his eyes and shut the door. "Why couldn't I have hooked up with someone whose elevator went all the way to the top floor?" Howard said to himself as he went up stairs to set up in the observation post for his watch.

Chapter 35

Doc injected a sedative into Don's arm, turned and placed the syringe in a plastic bottle. He closed his medical kit and left the room. He went downstairs to the kitchen where Steve, Celina, Howard, and Craig were drinking coffee.

"Did you save any for me?" He asked placing his bag on the kitchen counter.

Howard gestured with his coffee cup to an empty mug sitting next to the coffee pot. "Help yourself Doc."

Craig turned in his chair to look at Doc. "How is Don doing Doc?"

"His feet have dozens of superficial cuts. Not dangerous, but he won't be running any marathons any time soon. His side wound isn't life threatening. Well I shouldn't say that in times like these. If you had not contacted me and you had no antibiotics I'm definitely sure infection would have killed him in a few weeks." Doc took a sip from his now full mug and leaned against the kitchen counter.

Craig got up and poured himself a refill of coffee. "Are you ready for the big meet Doc?"

"I can't wait for it. I'm looking forward to seeing folks trading and congregating and acting as normal as one can in times like these. How about you? Do you have anyone in particular you have lost contact with and hope is there?"

"All of the family I have left has moved away. I would like to see some of the guys from the SWAT team though. I hope they have heard about the meet."

"Have you got any way to communicate with them?"

"Nothing besides the CB and they don't have one, no."

Doc looked over at Steve and Celina. "Did you tell our friends here about our new HAM radio operator?"

"Dang! Sorry about that. I totally forgot." Celina said.

"Yeah me too, it should have been one of the first things we told you about." Steve said.

Looking a little confused Howard spoke up. "What about a HAM operator?"

Steve set his coffee cup down and explained to Howard and Craig about what their HAM was doing. "One of the grocery store owner's son's, Brent Flynn, had a buddy come by while we were tossing this idea to Mr. Flynn. The guy is a former Marine, his name is Berry McGee. Anyway he has set up his radios inside the old grocery store. For a fee, he will send out a message via the HAM network and attempt to locate family or friends. Also he gathers news about what is going on in the country and will tell you what he has heard for a bullet."

Craig interrupted Steve. "What do you mean for a bullet?"

"Well the way Berry sees it, no one is making ammo right now so for a bullet, any caliber, he will tell you what he has heard that day. He has a pretty good assortment of ammo. You wouldn't believe how many folks want news about the outside. Berry uses the bullets he gets to stash for his own supply or trade. He is getting more and more business every day."

Howard leaned forward in his seat. "You mean folks are already trading at the grocery store? I didn't think things were supposed to start until the sixteenth."

Doc began to pace and sip his coffee while he answered. "Once news of the upcoming meet got out and spread people started showing up. Some are renting out spaces inside the store and the parking lot in advance. I would say about ten or fifteen vendors have already set up. Mr. Flynn was running low on supplies so he went ahead and started letting folks rent space."

Craig looked across the room at Howard. "I do believe one of us should head to St. Florian and snag us a good spot. Preferably inside the store if you intend to trade some of those weapons, and ammo of yours."

"I'm not going to argue with you on that. I will pack up some stuff later and head out in the morning. The day of the meet you and Don, if he is able can follow on up."

Craig looked at Doc. "Doc you think Don will be well enough to travel there and back in a day. We can't leave the place unprotected overnight."

"Well Craig I don't see why not. His wounds are not that traumatic."

Celina cleared her throat to get the others attention. "I know I'm not Rambo or anything, but it seems to me at least one of you, and maybe one or both dogs should stay back here so no one robs you while all of you are gone. If Don is well enough to travel, he should be well enough to watch the place during the day while you two are gone. Then one of you can come back for the night to relieve him."

"Yeah, that is a great idea." Howard said looking at Craig. "Aren't you the one with all the tactical training? What a shame you let a twenty year old woman who knows nothing about tactics have to plan for you."

Celina lowered her head and tried to hide a proud smile. Steve didn't hide his at all, enjoying Howard's good natured ribbing of his friend. "Hey Howard."

"Yeah Steve?"

"She isn't twenty, she just turned eighteen." Steve said as his smile broadened.

Craig shook his head and grinned. "Okay, enough is enough." He turned and looked at Celina. "Well now that you have shamed me young lady, I guess I will have to defer to you before I make any other decisions from now on."

"Let me help with another tactical decision Craig."

"What's that?" Craig said becoming more serious, thinking he hadn't thought about something that may be important to their survival.

Celina held out her empty coffee mug to him. "Mosey on over here and take this cup and get me a refill."

Craig walked over and took the cup. "What tactical decision are you talking about? Have I forgotten something else?"

Celina smiled. "The tactical decision was about me. I decided I wanted a cup of coffee. I'm comfortable and don't want to get up, and since you have said yourself that you are basically subservient to me I thought you should get used to serving my whims. Also what you forgot is your manners. A good southern gentleman should constantly pamper and serve a southern lady. Now, fetch my coffee boy." The friends broke up in laughter. Especially Howard, who had to listen to Craig the day before try to order him around like a serving boy, now Craig was getting a little taste of his on smart ass attitude.

Craig laughed with everyone else. He had always been able to dish out jokes on people, but he had also always been able to take them too. "Here is your coffee madam." Craig said as he held out Celina's now steaming mug, while he stood in his best butler pose.

Another thirty minutes later the friends were getting up and cleaning up the kitchen. They made their way outside to Steve's truck. Steve opened the door to the truck and turned to Howard and Craig, "We'll let Mr. Flynn know to save you a spot inside before we get home."

Howard reached out his hand to shake Steve's. "We appreciate that and for yall coming over to take a look at Don." He said looking at Doc and Celina.

"Anytime I can be of service..." Doc didn't finish his sentence and stumbled forward as Meat bumped into him as he ran full speed towards the front gate, the cackles on the back of his neck standing straight up.

The others stared at the dog in momentary confusion except for Craig who had drawn his pistol and began to crouch down behind the truck, pistol aimed at the front gate. His eyes bored into the area outside the gate looking for danger.

"Take cover!" Craig shouted to the others.

Just as he shouted his command a volley of gunshots rang out. One round crashing through Steve's back window and buried itself in the dashboard. Howard drew his pistol and began backing towards the house where his FN was located in the front room. Steve, Doc, and Celina grabbed for their rifles that lay inside the truck.

"Get to the house!" Craig screamed at the others. He scanned the area through the gate and fired several ineffective rounds at two passing figures thirty yards away. "Meat, get over here!" he shouted to the dog that was ramming himself against the gate and growling viciously. He obeyed Craig immediately and ran to his master as several rounds hit the wrought iron fence, sending sparks and twisted pieces of shrapnel from disfigured bullets into the air surrounding the fence.

As Meat came abreast of Craig he shouted to the dog. "Go inside boy, go!" the dog obeyed. Craig stood up in a crouch and started to move backwards firing his pistol dry as he made it to the front door. Howard's FN opened up from the second floor. Controlled three and four round burst replied to the steady staccato of gunfire aimed at the house. Rounds peppered the front of the house. Obviously they were not coming from rifles since the rounds merely pocked marked the front of the house, nor were they very well aimed shots.

Craig slammed the door behind him and entered the front parlor. Doc, Celina, and Steve were standing to the sides of different windows looking out, trying to ascertain were the rounds were coming from. Steve turned and looked at Craig. "I can't see much out there, Craig. Did you see anything?"

"You won't be able to see much from here. Yall need to make your way upstairs. Doc, you take the front left bedroom and cover the south side of the house. Howard is in the center room and has the west covered. Steve you take the bedroom on the other side. You should be able to cover most of the north."

Celina turned and looked at Craig. "What about me?"

"Celina there is a door at the end of the hall way by the stairs. Open it and it goes into a round shaped room. Howard and I have really fortified it. It will give you a great field of fire over the east section. Remember don't shoot from the same place more than once, keep moving from firing port to firing port. I'm going to float from room to room. Call me if you need extra ammo or fire power and I will come a running. Now let's move." The four bolted for the stairs

⊹══ ══⊹

Howard bolted for the house before anyone else, and crashed through the front door. He didn't stop running as he snatched up his FN that was leaning against the wall by the door to the hall. Grabbing the rifle he ran upstairs and to the center bedroom that looked out over the front yard.

The center window was open and Howard reached his hand out and pulled the metal bar that held the thick metal plate propped open. The metal plate slammed shut. Howard shouldered the FN and placed the barrel out of the firing port, and began to search for targets. He was quickly rewarded when he saw a figure stand up form one of the distant debris piles and fire.

He let loose a four round burst, three of the rounds stitched their way across the man's upper torso. The man collapsed backwards and out of sight causing a small cloud of dust, and ash to lift into the air above the debris pile. Just as the man collapsed Howard saw two heads peaking not ten feet from where the man fell. He let loose a three, and then a four round burst at the two attackers. Both heads disappeared behind cover as the ill aimed rounds slammed into the debris just in front of them.

A round twanged against the metal shutter, and Howard could hear several more rounds smacking into the wall outside. The rounds were coming from a man by the front gate that had edged out from behind the brick column, and was providing cover fire for another man who was just opening up a set of bolt cutters. Howard shifted his aim and let loose the final nine rounds in his twenty round magazine. Two of the rounds hit the man with the bolt cutters and he collapsed forward into what almost looked like a kneeling fetal position when his body came to rest against the gate. The man who had been providing cover fire was struck in the right leg and he fell backwards onto the pavement.

Howard pushed the magazine release dropping the empty magazine to the hardwood floor. As he reached for a second magazine he kept his eyes on the man at the front gate. In his haste to seat his magazine Howard missed the slot where the magazine fit. The second man drug himself and his shattered bloody leg behind the brick wall. Finally he seated the magazine and cursed at himself for not maintaining his cool. The man was still possibly a threat, and one he could not give his undivided attention to.

<hr/>

Steve entered the bedroom and ran to the window pulling the curtains aside. He definitely liked what he saw. Craig had told him how members of his SWAT team had fortified the house. It was nice to know that he could fire from relative safety through the firing port and stay behind the metal plate that only the highest powered rifles or ones with armor piercing rounds could penetrate.

He began to scan his sector of fire and saw nothing moving. He mostly kept a watch at the small opening that they had drove through earlier when they got there. He knew the ad hoc metal gate would not be able to withstand a vehicle impact or keep people on foot from coming in. He danced back and forth on the balls of his feet as he listened to the others open fire, both anticipating, and dreading the eventuality of engaging in the firefight.

Suddenly a rope with a grapple hook on the end landed on the coiled barbed wire atop the gate. Steve tried to relax his body for what he knew would be a possible rush of men. After a minute or two of jerking and pulling, who ever was on the other side of the debris pile managed to pull the coiled barbed wire from the top of the gate.

Four men dressed in biker leathers, and dirty greased stained jeans jumped the gate. They were armed with pistols and sawed off shotguns. Two other men stepped out behind them and began to fire pistols in his general direction, though none of the rounds impacted near the window in which he had positioned himself.

The men ran in abreast of one another as they charged toward the pungi stake filled ditch, and wall Craig and Howard had built. Steve had no idea how the four intended to cross the ditch then the wall. If they made it to wall they would still have to contend with the razor wire that Howard and Craig placed around it.

Pushing those thoughts from his mind Steve fired two rounds at the leading man. Both rounds tore into the asphalt several feet to the man's left. Steve took a deep breath and made sure he had a good sight picture, he kept telling himself to stay calm, breath and aim. The AK surprised him when it bucked against his shoulder. The man crashed in a heap to the ground.

One of the men changed direction to get farther away from his downed partner bringing himself almost shoulder to shoulder with one of the other men. Steve fired off four quick consecutive rounds downing the two men. Rounds clanged into the metal window cover sending Steve to the floor to take cover. None of the rounds penetrated the metal plates and Steve recovered and manned his position again.

The last man was almost three quarters of the way to the wall when Steve shouldered his rifle. He didn't engage the last running man. Instead he engaged the two men who had fired on him, considering them a greater threat. He fired two rounds at the man on the left missing him but causing him to take cover.

More rounds slammed into the metal shutter as the other returned fire. Steve fired one round striking the man in the stomach as he turned to take cover. The steel core round ripped a ragged grotesque hole across the man's stomach. The man fell to his knees, pistol dropping from his right hand. With his left he reached out trying in vain to shove the long gray coils of his intestines back into the gaping cavity that now adorned his stomach. Steve quickly ended the man's agony with a shot to his chest, dropping the man onto his right side.

Steve lifted his head from the rifle quickly looking for the last running man. The man was sliding to a stop just in front of the pungi staked ditch; his head looking left and right for an alternate way across. Steve didn't give him time to ponder more than a second about turning back or finding another way. Dropping his cheek back to the stock he quickly rested the sights on the man's chest. Steve squeezed the trigger and fired.

The round struck the man dead center in the chest, a red, and pick haze of bone and blood exploded from the man's back. He teetered for a moment then fell forward, his body impaling itself on a piece of rebar that stuck out of the ground three feet high.

The sound of a round striking the brick wall turned Steve's attention to the gunman by the gate. The man kneeled with most of his body concealed by the debris by the gate. Steve fired seven rounds at the man. Each round struck the pile of debris or the ground behind and to the man's left. The man scurried back for cover.

Several long seconds went by and Steve saw no other threats. He rested his sights back on the area of the gate. Steve began to relax a bit while he watched and listened to the others engage in their own little personal firefights. Just as he lifted his head from the stock and took his left hand from fore grip to rub his eyes the man at the gate made his move.

"Crap!" Steve tried regaining a good grip on the rifle and reacquire the man, who was now running away towards the corner of the street. Unable to get the weaving and bobbing man in his sights Steve tried for a lucky shot. He fired over fifteen rounds at the man. Dirt kicked up around his feet, and chunks of bark were blown from the surrounding trees. The man escaped Steve's fusillade of fire as he disappeared around the corner.

No other targets presented themselves in Steve's sector. Soon the firing from his friends slowly died away and then finally stopped. Steve stood back from the window and wiped the sweat from his brow. He then dropped the seventy five round drum from the magazine well. Slinging his rifle, Steve pulled out a loose box of rounds from his a pouch on his belt and began to top off the drum.

⊷⊷

Doc fared a little better than the others as far as not having to engage as many attackers. However, his encounter was much more deadly. As the others began blazing away Doc stood silent watching the empty street before him. Then he saw two figures dashing from behind some bushes towards the debris wall. Lifting the Garand to his shoulder Doc fired two rounds. Both rounds failed to hit the lead man. They did however speed the two men up across the street where they took cover behind one of the ancient oaks that lined Wood Ave.

Doc fired a round into the side of the tree just to let the two men know he knew where they were at, and to keep them in place. Doc blinked his eyes several times to try and clear his vision. A bead of sweat had rolled into his left eye, blurring his vision. It was in these few seconds the two men below decided to return Doc's fire.

Just as his vision cleared both men opened up, the man on the left was firing a Valmet M76. He raked the side of the house with semi-auto gun fire. The man on the right took his time before he fired. He was armed with a Russian Dragonauve SVD.

Just as Doc was about to return fire the second man fired his rifle. The 7.62x54R round peeled through the metal plating Doc was behind like butter. Bits of metal peppered the left side of Doc's face. Doc was able to fire one ill-aimed shot before diving to the ground. Two more rounds punched through the metal plating above Doc's head as he hit the floor.

Doc needed some help, and needed it fast. "Craig! Craig! I need some help in hear!" Doc screamed at the top of his lungs.

Craig was just coming out of his bedroom where he had retrieved his Sig SG 550, assault rifle. He heard Doc's cry for help and went to aid him. As he reached the doorway that led to the room Doc was in he noticed that several bullet holes had torn through the outer wall of the bedroom and passed into the wall across the hall. Someone was firing either an extremely high powered rifle, or rounds with steel cores.

Doc was in the floor when Craig entered. "Doc, are you hit?" Craig shouted as he crouched down making his way to Doc. Another round passed through the steel plating above Doc.

"No, no, I'm fine it just seems the bastard have got me pinned down.

Craig made his way to the window beside the one Doc had been firing from. Standing to the side he tried to peer out of the firing port cut into the metal. "How many are there, and where are they Doc?"

"They were about forty yards from the pile of debris behind an oak tree on the east side of the street."

Craig peered to where Doc had said the men would be. He spotted a man with a scoped semi auto, and a second man had his head sticking out from behind the tree, part of a rifle was visible in his hands. He was attempting to load another magazine into the rifle, but was having difficulty seating it in place.

"Okay Doc this is what we are going to do. I'm going to fire at the man with the scoped rifle and draw his fire if I can't hit him. When he turns to shoot at me I want you to take him out. Then we will work on the second guy together. Got it?"

Doc drew himself to his feet and stood against the wall as another round passed through the metal plating. "I'm ready."

Craig shouldered his rifle and stepped in front of his window. He did not have a good view of the man with the scoped rifle and the man who had been reloading his rifle had disappeared from view. Craig squeezed the trigger several times sending four 5.56mm rounds towards the man who had Doc pinned. The rounds tore chunks of bark from the tree next to the man leaving white scares on the gray colored surface of the tree.

The man never took cover he just calmly pivoted his body and fired a round into the window where Craig stood. It was at this moment the man who had been reloading his rifle appeared from behind the tree charging forward rifle blazing.

The round fired by the man with the Dragonauve tore into the metal plating an inch above Craig's head.

Craig rolled to the right to escape the accurate fire and shouted a warning about the second man to Doc in the same instance. "One of them is charging forward Doc!" Craig stood from the floor about to go back to his firing port and return fire.

"I see him." Doc said in a calm cool voice.

For an instant, time reversed for Doc and he was back on the jungle covered mountains of Viet Nam. Though he never shot anyone that he could think of during his two years in Viet Nam, he had always been calm and cool when carrying out his job as a Combat Medic. His sights rested center mass on the man's chest and Doc calmly squeezed the trigger. The powerful .30-06 caliber round struck the man just below the neck. His legs buckled, and he fell anti-climatically to the ground.

The second man was now just fifteen yards from the debris wall when Doc swung the rifle towards him. He fired striking the man in the left shoulder. The man was spun backwards and landed face first on the street, his rifle flying from his hands. The man tried to rise up but Doc, as calmly as stepping on a bug fired a round between his shoulder blades. As the man's body hit the ground for a second time Doc's eight round clip ejected from the rifle.

Doc slowly lowered the rifle and turned and sat on the edge of the bed. His hands shook a bit as he loaded the rifle. Craig lowered his rifle and looked back, with admiration, to Doc. "Fine shooting Doc. Are you okay?"

"Yes, I'm fine Craig. Just getting a little long in the tooth for this sort of thing."

"You want me to stay with you?"

"No. I'll be fine." Doc said as he stood to man his post again.

Just as Craig was about to tell Doc he would stay a scream from Celina down the hall reached Craig's ears. "I need help! I need help!" She yelled. Craig turned and in seconds was entering the room where Celina was set up.

<hr/>

As Celina entered the room she was assigned she was impressed and felt sure she would be quite safe. The room was circular and jutted out from the house. The ceiling was steeple shaped and rose to a height of fourteen feet. Each of the windows was covered like the rest of the ones in the house with metal plates with firing ports cut in them. This room, unlike the others had been cleared of furniture. The walls had sandbags stacked four feet high around them.

Celina quickly made her way to one of the firing ports and peered out. She looked out over the back yard, and could see the brick wall. The area behind the wall was covered with thick bushes. She quickly spotted the weak point in the defenses. A metal gate with a pad lock sat in the middle of the wall. The area behind the wall was thick with bushes that rose almost fifteen feet.

As soon as she heard the distinctive sound of Steve's AK open up on a threat she saw the bushes moving. Someone, or more than one person, was making their way through the bushes to the hidden gate. Suddenly the bushes stopped moving and Celina spotted a set of bolt cutters stick out from behind the wall. The mouth of the cutters encircled the pad lock.

Celina took careful aim with the stainless Mini-14 and fired. Her round was high, missing the bolt cutters. The mouth closed down on the pad lock cutting the stem in half. The lock fell to the ground. Celina fired two rounds into the dirt just on the other side of the gate to keep those behind the wall at bay.

A hand reached out and shoved the gate open. Celina tried to slow her rapid breathing, knowing what was about to occur. Then two men dashed through the open gate firing at the rear of the house. Celina fired several rounds missing with each shot. The two men made their way to the bull dozer that was parked at the rear of the house and took cover behind it. A third man edged around the corner armed with an SKS and began to fire at Celina's position. Celina could hear the rounds tear through the outer wood of the room she was in, thumping into the sandbags inside. She fired two rounds at the man, missing him as he disappeared back behind the brick wall to safety.

Then the two men at the dozer opened up on her. One armed with an SKS, the other had a handgun. Rounds tore into the room Celina was in. Some bounced off the metal plating, while the more powerful 7.62x39 rounds fired by the SKS ate through the wood wall above, and around Celina.

Celina ducked for cover. She needed some help. She knew she wasn't going to be able to fight off all three by herself. "I need help! I need help!" She yelled as two more rounds tore through the metal plating two windows to her left.

Celina brought the rifle to her shoulder again and fired out the port. All three men were standing now pouring down fire on her position. Celina fired three rounds at the man at the gate missing him, then four more at the two by the dozer, sparks flying from the metal skin of the dozer.

The Celina shifted her fire and fired two more rounds at the man at the gate. Both rounds found their marks. One in the man's left hip, the second piercing his right rib cage shredding the lung. The man fell backwards to the ground. His body spread eagle as if he were making a snow angle in the dirt.

Celina shifted her fire back to the two behind the dozer. As she and the second man with the SKS exchanged shots the man with the pistol made a brake for the house. Celina shifted her fire and after firing three rounds her bolt locked to the rear. She ducked down to reload her weapon as Craig came running into the room.

Celina looked up as she slapped the magazine home. "One of the guys just made a break for the house headed for the back door. I couldn't hit him. I shot one guy and he's down. I only have one man left. Can you take care of the guy downstairs?"

"I'm on it!" Craig said turning on the balls of his feet heading for the stairs. "We've got one in the house downstairs!" He shouted to the others as he slowed down and began to tactically make his way down stairs.

Craig moved his hand forward on the stock of the Sig and turned on the laser sight. He kept to the sides of the stairs to help ensure the old hardwood boards would not creak as he made his way down. The gun fire of the others also helped mask his descent.

Craig stopped at the foot of the stairs, closed his eyes and listened for any movement. Then he heard the hinges on the old door that led to the kitchen begin to slowly creak. It was barely audible because of the gunfire going on in the house. Craig readied himself, pulling the stock of the rifle tighter into his shoulder.

Then there was a break in the gunfire, and Craig heard a board creak, and the soft thump of a heavy boot on the old floors. Craig sprang around the corner bringing his rifle to bear. A tall six foot three man, with long black oily hair wearing biker apparel was moving towards him. A 1911 was grasped in his rising left hand.

Craig fired four rounds from his rifle as he began to dive towards the front parlor. The big man brought the old 1911 in his hand up with obvious experience. He was also as fast as a cottonmouth snake striking its prey. The big bore pistol boomed three times as he rushed forward making for a small alcove that was under the stairs.

Craig came up on a knee spinning around towards the parlor door and sent back two rounds in response. As he ducked back from the return fire he looked left to see Steve coming down the stairs. The two men made eye contact. Craig mimed with his hands where the man was.

Though not very familiar with the house Steve had seen the alcove earlier and felt he understood where the man was. Steve signaled to Craig who had just fired a round at the hidden man. Craig looked to Steve. Steve shouldered his rifle and pointed to himself, then to his rifle and pointing back down at the stairs.

Craig immediately understood what Steve was going to do. He readied himself as Steve opened fire on the stairs below him. He slowly walked the rounds up the stairs towards the area of the alcove beneath him.

As he fired Craig came around the corner his rifle in the ready position. Puffs of exploding plaster came out of the area of the alcove. Then after several rounds the big man couldn't take the intense fire anymore he came barreling out of his hide. Craig was ready. The red dot of his laser played across the big man's chest. Craig put four rounds in the upper torso in seconds.

The big man collapsed lying sideways against the opposite wall. He was still alive, frothy blood came from his lips. His meaty paw fumbled for the pistol that lay in front of him.

Craig had to give the big man credit for not being a quitter. "Don't do it mister! Take your hand away from the gun or I'll put a round in your freaking skull!"

The big man ignored the command. His big hand wrapped around the grip of the pistol. Craig never gave him a chance to lift it up. The red dot of his laser rested on the man's left eye. Craig squeezed the trigger. Bone, blood, and brain matter spattered against the wall were his head rested.

Craig slowly crept forward followed by Steve who was now just behind him. Reaching the body Craig kicked the pistol from the man's hand. Across his left knuckles was tattooed the word HATE. Several tear drops also were tattooed by one of the corners of his eyes. His open leather vest showed a myriad of prison tattoos. On his chest was one that Craig took note of "1%". The man was a hardcore biker.

As Craig finished his inspection of the body the others had come down stairs. "Is everything okay down here Craig?" Howard said as he stepped down to the floor.

"Yeah it's over. What about outside?"

"They're gone. We all saw or heard them run and heard a bunch of motorcycles start up and take off in about every direction. I think its over for now." Howard said as he reached down and picked up the 1911, which turned out to be a 70 series Gold Cup. He unloaded the pistol and handed it to Craig.

"Anyone check on Don?" Craig said tucking the pistol in his back waist band.

Doc was just coming down the steps. "He is fine. I just checked on him, he's still out like a light. Both dogs are in the room with him too."

"Craig we need to help you get this place squared away. I think it is best we get back to our place in case these guys show up in our area. I would love to get there before dark."

Howard leaned over and took the big man in the floor by the boot and started to drag him towards the door. "Well let's get it done."

Steve turned to Celina, "Celina why don't you head back up stairs and kind of keep watch. Move from room to room, we'll collect the bodies."

Though Celina had seen a lot since the attacks, staring at the blood and brain matter kept her from arguing about being able to do her fair share. She nodded her head and headed back up stairs.

The group spent the next few hours collecting the bodies and taking anything of value off of them. Boots, knives, guns, ammo, and other odds and ends that could latter be traded if need be. They found three of the biker's Harley's and brought them back to the house. Doc took several bags of assorted pills that contained everything from pain killers, uppers, downers to aspirin that was found on one of the bikes.

The Craig cleaned the blood soaked hallway up as best as could be done. While he did that Steve radioed Amos, Maude, and Barry McGee by CB to let them know to be on the look out for possible danger. Barry said he would put the word out on the HAM net.

Once everything was cleaned up, weapons, ammo, and equipment divided Doc, Steve, and Celina loaded in their truck to head out. They shook hands all around and said their goodbyes. Howard and Craig went back inside to repair the structural damage to the house and would latter begin to upgrade the weak points that had been discovered in their perimeter defenses.

⊹⊷⊶⊹

Byron Loxley sat at the head of the polished mahogany conference table. He was the director for FEMA's Alabama allocation, and relocation team. He wore an expensive European suit and drummed his manicured fingernails on the table as he listened to a subordinate read off the latest report of confiscated goods.

The door to the conference room opened and a young man in a blue suit and red tie closed the door and stood with a sheet of paper in his hand waiting to be acknowledged. Loxley raised his hand to silence the man reading the report.

"Yes Kyle, what is it?"

The man straightened his shoulders as he cleared his throat trying in vain to hide his apparent fear of the man now addressing him. There were too many rumors floating around about members of FEMA with family members who had angered Loxley or failed him winding up in the camps. He sure as hell didn't want to wind up in that boat. He really enjoyed the perks of this job. Here they were during the collapse of the United States and he was staying in an air conditioned five star hotel.

"Sir, communications has just intercepted more radio transmissions from the Florence area." He paused, waiting for Loxley to give him permission to continue or to leave.

Loxley arrogantly waved for him to continue. "CB transmissions from Florence indicate there was a firefight of some sort between some individuals and a biker gang. The biker gang fled the area after loosing several members. This information was then relayed by a HAM operator located in the St. Florian area. This is the same area where we have been hearing reports of a big swap meet of some sort that is going to take place on the sixteenth of this month."

Loxley waved Kyle from the room as if he was shooing an irritating fly away. His piercing blue eyes turned towards a National Guard Colonel sitting at the center left of the table. "Colonel, why haven't you pacified this area?"

The Colonel, who served in combat twice in Iraq, stared unwaveringly at the arrogant piece of crap who was addressing him. "As I recall Byron," the Colonel never showed Loxley any respect. He was close to having a few trusted men that were assigned to his protection detail dispose of Loxley and then release those in the camps who wish to leave. He knew that Loxley's action would soon turn Alabamians towards rebellion against the government. He had no intention of swinging from a rope that so many of these ivory towered idiots deserved. "You told me to pull all of my troops from North West Alabama and bring them here. So basically, you are the reason the area is not pacified."

Loxley's tanned face turned red, his designer cut, gelled blonde hair quivered, as he fought to maintain control of his temper. If the colonel wasn't so respected by his men, and they didn't have all those guns he would have the bastard shot. Till then he would have to put up with the redneck colonel.

Finally in control, Loxley spoke. "On the sixteenth you will provide me with four helicopters, and troops. I will personally fly to this meet and advise these people to prepare for relocation, and reallocation of their goods. I will give let them have two weeks, but will show up a week early with troops, if necessary my own armed men. Then you will send up a convoy of trucks to start ferrying the people to the camps here. Make up the necessary plans, and arrangements. Do I make myself clear colonel?"

The smile that played across the colonel's lips confused Loxley. The man should be infuriated that he intended to use his precious Guardsmen to corral all of the "useless eaters". Instead he just smiled like he knew something Loxley didn't. Loxley couldn't wait until the government sent him more of his own armed "FEMA Reaction Teams". Though not trained by the military, he would have his own armed men who would not question his orders.

Colonel Haddock smiled even bigger when he saw the confusion on Loxley's face. What the Ivy League turd didn't know is that once he went up north the second time, he probably wouldn't be coming back. Those to weak or dependent on the government had already fled on their own free will and entered the camps. Those that were left were made of the same stuff that their out numbered out gunned, ancestors were. Though Haddock felt the South was wrong on the slave issues during the Civil War, when he read the history of the war, he was always impressed by the rag tag Rebel troops who came out on top again and again until their final defeat. He felt that if the South had been properly supplied they would have smashed the North.

Haddock was from Delaware, and had transferred to the Alabama National Guard ten years ago. He had always been in the forefront of teasing and making fun of people from the south. That is of course until he moved to Alabama, and saw how things really were. Most people in the south were God fearing, honest, polite people who worked hard and had no use for the government intrusion. They just wanted to be left alone to carry on with their lives without interference. Those that he found that had the same attitude of many in the big cities on the east coast weren't originally from the south, or were only one or two generations removed from relatives up north. Yes, Loxley was in for a big surprise.

Chapter 36

The big day had finally arrived. Everyone was up and cleaning up the morning's breakfast dishes. Bob had just called on the CB and advised they were ready and standing by for everyone that was staying at Doc's. Amos had also radioed in and stated he and Benny were standing by.

Steve poured himself and Joe another cup of coffee and the two went out to the back porch for a cigarette, and to enjoy the rising sun. Taking a drag from his cigarette Steve exhaled and turned to Joe. "You sure you're well enough to keep watch Joe?"

"Yeah, I don't get anything but an occasional headache now. I'm just going to have to move slow, and make sure I don't jiggle my melon to much." Joe said as he rubbed his still swollen and bruised face.

Steve nodded his head. "Have you decided which of the guns you took off the bikers that you want me to trade?"

Joe sipped his coffee and took another hit off his smoke as he thought about the question for a moment. He and Bob had split up the guns they had taken from the dead bikers. Joe had come away with an SKS, three S&W .357's, a Rossi .22 revolver, and a Ruger P-95 9mm. "Tell you what. Take the Rossi, the Ruger, and one of the Smith's."

"What exactly do you want me to get for you in trade?" Steve asked as he leaned against the railing of the back porch.

"I would like a good pair of work boots, size 10 ½. Also try to get me as much .357, 7.62x39, 12 gauge, or .38 caliber as you can."

"I'll make you a trade right now if you want. You let me have that stainless Model 65, and I will give you four hundred rounds of 7.62x39.

You add that to the three hundred you got from the bikers that will give you seven hundred rounds."

Joe turned his head and looked at Steve quizzically. "Steve, four hundred rounds for an old .357 is a little much, don't you think?"

"Yeah it is. But besides what I have already stocked away before the collapse I have come up with several thousand more rounds of the stuff. Besides, we're all in this thing together. I need a descent wheel gun for back up. You need a lot more ammo for that SKS. You've done pretty good getting here from Memphis with a Ruger .22, and a sawed off shotgun, but that SKS is going to be a better fighting weapon, and you will need the ammo if a big fight comes our way."

"Well if you want to lose your butt on the ammo, and are serious about it, I'll take that deal." Joe said with a smile.

The two men shook on the deal and went inside to make the trade. While they were in Joe's room getting the pistol Steve went over some of the details of the surrounding terrain, and they went over the emergency procedures one more time. They had decided the night before that Joe would rove between the three properties looking for looters, and other vermin. Amos had volunteered the use of Festus for this purpose.

It was decided Joe would carry a handheld CB, and one person in the group going to the trade would stay with the vehicles and monitor the CB. If anything bad went down on the properties the group would load up and return to help out. Radio checks would be hourly. If anything went down at the trade Joe would set up at the barricade nearest to Amos's property and prepare an ambush if the group came back and was being pursued.

After they had finished trading and discussing the days plans the two men went to the living room where everyone was loading weapons, or packing the last of some of the goods they intended to trade into packs and bags. "Is everyone ready?" Steve said.

He got the affirmative from everyone. They all left the living room for the vehicles outside. Once they were loaded up they headed to Steve's old place and picked up Bob and Caroline. They didn't have a lot to trade, but Bob intended to trade some of the weapons from his share of the biker guns to get a few items he felt they might need. He also had a twenty gallon plastic trash bag full of toilet paper.

Daphne looked at the bag full of the toilet paper. "Bob if you're having some plumbing problems, Dr. Morrison has some medicine that might help solve your problem." She said, an impish grin playing across her face.

Bob stopped unsure of how to respond to the young girl's barb. Caroline bumped him with her hip as she walked by him towards the truck. "Don't sweat it honey. Everyone gets the runs every now and then." She said as she made eye contact with Daphne and the two began to giggle in unison. Bob just rolled his eyes and hopped in the back of Steve's pickup.

The next stop was Amos's place. He helped Joe saddle Festus up, and gave him a few quick pointers about the many quirks Festus had, and how to deal with the animal. Once Joe was mounted up the group headed out for the big swap meet.

⊹══⊹

Dapper Donte woke up earlier than his normal 2:30 pm. He glanced at his Rolex, which he stolen from a man he had killed two days ago, 7:35 am. "Damn it's early." He said as he rose from the bed knocking over and stepping on empty beer cans that littered the floor.

Donte walked to the window and looked out from his second story view. He stared like a hungry lion at a small group of people pushing shopping carts, and pulling wagons heading north. For the past two days a steady stream of people had been heading north. He and his boys hadn't bothered to ask any of their victims why they were going north. Hell, they didn't get a chance to. The West Side Posse shot people from ambush. Occasionally they would let one or two of the women live so they could have entertainment. They were then killed when fresh women were brought in. Donte turned and walked from the window heading downstairs to the front porch.

Donte had to make his way through the trash that littered the floor of the once grand Victorian style home. He and the Posse had been here for two weeks. It was about time to burn this place to the ground and find another fancy house to take over. Once on the front porch he sat down in a rocking chair and lit up a Newport. He slowly rocked back and forth as he smoked and thought of his next step. He decided they would capture a few folks and find out why so many were heading north.

Donte thumped the half smoked cigarette out into the front yard, as the front screen door opened. It was Fat Cat; he wore nothing but a pair of boxer shorts and carried his .357 in his left hand, a cigarette in his right. Donte smiled, he had made a rule that no one was to walk around without a gun. This had saved their butts a few times, his boys were hard core. "What up, fat ass!" Donte said to his friend.

"Bump that shit man. I don't feel like fucking with you right now. That ho gave me problems last night. I finally had to beat her ass to death. She kept on screaming, every time I hit her ass with the hammer, just wouldn't shut up. Now my head is killing me."

"Yo dumb ass deserves a headache. Course she gonna scream you hit'n her ass with da hammer. Lucky she didn't fuck you up like dat one bitch did over in Heathrow."

Fat Cat subconsciously rubbed the fresh scars on his neck, and face. The pistol that had struck him in the face had cut it open pretty good, the wounds had gotten infected, and had healed leaving a hideous looking scar down the center of his face. "Fuck you man. I ever see dat bitch again she gonna git what coming to her."

Donte rocked slowly and let out a laugh. "You betta' keep your ass away from dat bitch. She may chop somting off you like."

Fat Cat gave Donte a fierce look before settling his considerable bulk down on the front steps. "What da hell we goin to do today?"

"Well my fat ass friend, we gonna find out why's all dem people going north. Maybe something we can get into up there. Maybe some new hunting grounds, whatcha tink bout that?"

"Hell yeah. Tings have bout dried up round here, robbing get'n to be too much work."

⊹⊱━⊰⊹

Steve, Celina, Daphne, Bob, Caroline and Amos had all gone their separate ways when they reached the grocery store. Benny stayed behind to man the radio. Doc and Maude went inside to Doc's booth where he traded his, and Maude' medical skills for useful items. The swap had only officially started two hours earlier, and it was already a huge success. Hundreds of people had showed up days before the meet had actually begun, renting out individual parking places, and space inside the store itself.

Mr. Flynn had even converted the four bay car wash stalls into rental space. Two of those stalls had been rented out by a horse fierier, and blacksmith. He had also cleaned out his convenience store and rented space inside of it. Inside the grocery store he had torn out the wall that divided the storage area from the rest of the store, to create more stall space. All in all there were over two hundred individual stalls inside and out, selling everything imaginable. Shoes, guns, ammo, food, canning supplies, tillers, kerosene lamps, seeds, clothes, medical supplies and even a lady selling Tupperware. There were also those who sold their goods out of carts, wagons, and shopping carts, as they walked around hollering to the world what they were selling.

Steve was heading inside the grocery store to find Howard. He remembered Craig had said something about finding some new boots on a truck. Maybe they would have Joe's size. He bumped into Mr. Flynn at the front entrance. "Hey Mr. Flynn, it looks like business is booming."

Flynn had a huge grin on his face from ear to ear. "Great hell, this is stupendous! You would think this was Wal Mart on Christmas Eve. I haven't seen this many people in here since the day before Y2K."

Steve slapped Mr. Flynn on the shoulder as he walked past Flynn on in the store. "Let's hope it's like this every week."

Steve waded through the crowded store till he made it to the back corner of the store where Craig and Howard had set up their booth. Since they had so many items Flynn had let them back their diesel rig up to the loading bay and open the door. Howard had set up dividers he had gotten from a movie theater to guide people into their booth in an orderly manner. He would deal with one customer at a time. People didn't seem to mind since besides having guns and ammo, he had all kinds of items that were needed to survive without electricity.

Steve walked towards the booth and caught Howard's eye. Howard gave him a smile, and pointed to the end of the long line. Steve gave him a friendly frown and walked to the end. "How's it going?" Steve said to the man in front of him.

The man turned and looked Steve over before answering. Then he gave Steve a friendly smile. "Pretty good, but I can't stand waiting in line, but this cat seems to know his business, and have good stuff. I'm hoping to trade some rounds and a few knives for some ammo for my rifle. What do you have for trade?"

Steve appraised the man while he was speaking. He wore German flectar camo pants, a gray t-shirt, and a leather vest that bulged with outer pockets and magazine pouches. Steve recognized it as a leather tactical vest he had seen in a surplus magazine. Strapped to his waist was a web belt with six double magazine pouches containing 1911 mags. He wore a 1911 style pistol on his hip, with a fighting knife resting behind it. At his feet was a large Alice pack that bulged with gear. A scoped Mosin Nagant M-44 was slung over his shoulder. Two bandoleer's full of fifty rounds each of 7.62x54R were across his chest like a Mexican bandito. The sling also had twenty five rounds attached to it.

"I'm trying to find some boots and 12 gauge ammo for a friend. I am also looking for .357 and .38 ammo for the two of us." Steve said.

The two talked for another thirty minutes as they slowly made their way closer to the head of the line. Steve eventually traded four cans of pears for forty three rounds of .38 caliber wad cutters. Steve didn't think it was a bad deal. Wad cutters sucked, but in his opinion so did pears. The other guy had no need for the wad cutters but got overly excited when he found out Steve had canned pears. Apparently he was a fruit fanatic, so both were happy for the trade.

Finally the guy in front of Steve stepped up to area in which Howard did all of his trading. "What can I do for you friend?" Howard said.

The man reached down into a pouch in the front of the Alice pack and pulled out a large doubled plastic freezer bags full of ammo. "This has four hundred and fifty rounds of 5.56 in it. I want to trade it for four hundred and fifty rounds of 7.62x54R."

"Well you know the market is kind of flooded with 5.56 right now. I can go two hundred fifty 5.56 and a box of .45 for your 1911." Howard proposed his counter offer.

"You're right about that. That's because everyone has one of them AR's or Mini's. What that means though is that the demand for the 5.56 will be on the high side. Now looking around here I haven't seen but a few rifles that take the 7.62x54R. That means all those cases you have back there are going to do nothing but collect dust." The haggling went on for another fifteen minutes before the final exchange was made. The man walked away with a smile on his face as he tipped his hat to Steve and told him "Good luck."

Steve stepped up to Howard. "How is it going Howard?"

"I would have told you pretty damn good twenty minutes ago. Now I fell like I've been raped and I paid the guy who did it." Howard replied.

Steve let out a little chuckle. "Yeah it sounded that way. I got to talk to the guy while we were waiting in line. Said he moved to New York thirty years ago after getting his law degree at Bama. Said he closed big international deals or something like that. Came home a few years ago to retire and hunt."

Howard just shook his head and ran his fingers through his hair. "I'll be sure to contact my attorney and have him present before I ever deal with that guy again. Now what can I do for you Steve?"

⊹━━⊹

Donte sat behind the wheel of the Land Rover he had stolen from the Donavan's. He had sent Bright Light and Tater forward to check out the grocery store ahead. Fat Cat, Shady, and High Yella were in the stolen Expedition parked behind the Land Rover. Donte was hoping the old man they had killed a few miles back down the road hadn't lied about all of the people that were going to show up at this big swap meet. He smiled as he saw Tater and Bright Light walk around the curve in the road, smiles on their faces. This was going to be good news, he just knew it.

Donte and the others got out of the vehicles and met the others as they neared the cars. Tater spoke first. "Dat old geezer weren't lying Donte. Man der's folks everywhere. They got all kinds of shit too."

Bright Light edged Tater over and began to give his spill. "Only down side is every mofo in der got's a gun. Won't be no beat downs happening there. We's goin to have to follow the folks afore we waste them."

Donte rubbed his chin for a moment lost in thought before he spoke. "Light, you see any brother's down there, or is they all crackers, and Klan?"

"Nah, I saw some brothers in the mix, few spics here and there too, nobody messing with them. I think we can walk in no problem."

Donte shook his head. "Alright this what we goin to do, We stashing the shotguns in the trucks Shady you going to stay with the rides. We just goin to carry our pistols. We gonna take some of this stuff we got off the old man and walk around and trade. Hell might as well get some more ammo.

The West Side Posse made its way down the road to the grocery store. They paid their way in and wandered about. The talked in low voices and started to choose those they would later rob. They also traded all the goods they had stolen from the old man for about four hundred rounds of .357. Donte had been pleased, that is until the group ran into a couple of pretty white chicks.

⊹⊱──⊰⊹

Celina and Daphne had been having a grand time. They had made some good trades and were looking forward to trying some of them out when they got back home. Celina was laughing at a joke that Daphne had just told and was about to respond when her sister stopped dead in her tracks and reached for the pistol on her side.

Celina put out a restraining hand to her sister's gun hand. "What is it Daphne?"

Daphne never moved her head, her eyes never blinked. "It's them." She almost whispered.

Celina scanned the crowded lot and then she found who had frozen her sister in her tracks. Subconsciously she too reached for the pistol on her hip. The group of black men were talking to a man selling fruit they all their back's turned except two. One she recognized as the leader who had killed her father, the second was the fat fucker who tried to rape her.

Celina released her sister's hand and both young women drew their pistols as they walked with purpose towards the gang. The two men who had not had their backs turned saw the approaching girls but failed to take note of the look of pure hate that was etched onto both of their faces; they also didn't pay attention to the pistols in their hands. Both men turned and stepped to the girls as if they were back on the block going to pick up a few ho's, arms crossed, posing their best gangster stance.

As if it was a choreographed dance, the two girls stepped, and kicked as one as they neared the two gangsters facing them. Both men were struck with such sudden ferocity that they both crumpled to the pavement without so much as a whimper, they rolled and groaned as they held onto their crushed testicles.

Tater turned as Donte went to the ground. "What da hell..." He didn't get to finish his sentence because a bullet tore into his leg.

Daphne kicked the man who had killed her father in the side of the head as he rolled on the pavement. The man he had been standing by turned towards her. Recognition of his face, and voice immediately registered. As he turned Daphne pulled the trigger of the Ruger SP101. The .38 caliber round was fired at a downward angle just above Tater's knee. Tater dropped beside the groaning Donte.

Fat Cat's eyes had grown wide with fear when it finally dawned on him who the brown haired beauty was just a fraction of a second before Celina's boot ruptured his left testicle. Celina was a bit faster than her sister as she turned with her pistol at the two remaining standing thugs.

Both turned in her direction. As her right foot came back down she pivoted towards them and fired three rounds from the hip with her 9mm. Bright Light was struck in the thigh and hip. His body spinning and then collapsing backward into the fruit vendors stand collapsing it. High Yella was struck on the bottom right rib. The round exited through his side causing no more damage as it slammed into a wooden post. Yella however dropped to the ground with his friends.

It all was over in a matter of seconds. Celina and Daphne stood with their guns pointed at the prone groaning thugs. Neither quite capable of just putting a bullet in the back of each ones head.

Celina turned her head and saw dozens of guns pointing at her and Daphne. Then Mr. Flynn stepped forward a pistol in his hand. "Young ladies, I believe you best drop those pistols."

Daphne turned and faced Flynn. "Drop my gun, for what?" She spun back on the thugs. She raised her booted foot and drove the heal of her boot into Donte's outstretched left hand. "This one murdered my father!"

She stepped to Tater her foot whipping out striking him right above the knee where he she had shot him. "This one raped me and my mother!" She stepped to High Yella and Bright Light her boot striking both in the head as she let loose two vicious kicks. "These two raped me and my mother!"

She spun back on Flynn tears running down her cheeks. "So don't tell me to drop my gun. You should be helping me kill them!"

A man in Flectar pants stepped forward. "Young ladies are you sure about the identities of these men? How do you know for sure?"

I stabbed this one with a large needle in his back and face. Then I hit him in the face with a pistol before I got away." She reached down and ripped the back of Fat Cat's t-shirt. Scars that appeared to be puncture marks where on his back shoulders. "Plus I saw them when they stole our SUV's when they were leaving our house."

"What kinds of vehicles were stolen? What were your parent's names?" The man in Flectar asked.

Celina told him about the Land Rover, and Expedition and what her parent's names were. The man just nodded and turned and walked away. Other's stepped forward and took hold of the thugs. They were stripped of their weapons and ammo. A former nurse came forward and treated the gunshot wounds. Flynn told everyone to settle down that they would have to have some type of quick trial.

Amos, Steve, Doc, and Maude came out to the growing crowd and attested to what had happened to the girls. The whole time the thugs screamed and professed their innocents. They begged to be released and sent on their way. Most folks just said shoot them and get it over with. Still a few were not so convinced and demanded the men receive a trial. That is until the man in Flectar pants showed back up.

He had Shady in front of him, his hands tied behind his back. Papers were in his left hand, his rifle in his right. Steve looked at Amos. "That's the lawyer fella that drove Howard nuts haggling."

The crowd parted for the man as he walked forward. He shoved Shady to the ground next to his friends. "I saw these fellows driving around a week ago in a Land Rover, and Expedition. I noticed the Land Rover pull to the side of the road, and then back behind the curve earlier this morning." He pointed behind him in the direction of that he had come from.

In the glove box of the Land Rover, and an Expedition that was parked behind it I found these papers. They state that the vehicles belonged to Nancy and Carl Donovan. I believe that is exactly who the girls said their parents were. I would say these boys had what the girls gave them coming and then some."

Murmurs of agreement rose form the crowed. Then Bob Novacheck stepped out of the crowd and by the tall old man in flectar pants. "I say get a rope and get this over with."

The crowd surged forward and grabbed the injured thugs dragging them to their feet. The thugs screamed and pleaded for a trial by jury, about their rights as citizens. No one listened though. Twenty minutes later Fat Cat was the last to die as his body gave one final struggling twitch. When they were all dead Celina and Daphne turned to go. Steve and Doc stood a respectful distance away. The man with flectar pants was by Doc's side.

When the girls turned to leave the dead the man walked up to them. "Here are the keys to your parent's vehicles. I brought them down and parked them near your friend Steve's truck. There is a lot of gear in the vehicles. The guns and ammo that the men had on them were placed in a cloth bag and are now in the back of the Land Rover. I hope you two have found closure with this, even though it was a bit...shall we say brutal." The man just tipped his hat turned and walked away adjusting his large Alice pack.

Steve walked up with Doc and placed his arm around Celina. "Are yall ready to leave?"

Daphne spoke up first. "No I think Celina and I will sit and talk at the trucks. That will give everyone a little more time to trade, and give little Benny time to run around and find something he likes."

⊬═⊣

Colonel Haddock keyed up the mike. "Byron you will be happy to know that according to radio transmissions six men were just hung at the meet in St. Florian. Sounds like the locals don't need our help. It looks like they are cleaning things up themselves." Haddock wished he was in the back of the Blackhawk Helicopter so he could see Byron Loxley turn purple with rage at that statement.

There was a few seconds of silence before Loxley spoke. "Just get me there Colonel. I don't need any smart ass comments from you."

Forty minutes later the formation of the four Blackhawk helicopters flew over the big meet in St. Florian. Everyone looked up, a few waved, more than a few frowned. Some immediately started packing and heading home.

The four helicopters landed in a large clearing not far from the store. Seventeen soldiers carrying M-16's and one man in an extremely expensive looking suit got out of the helicopters and walked towards the waiting crowd.

Everyone crowded forward as the group neared the wall of the parking lot. Roy Flynn stepped out to meet the man in the suit. "What do you need government man?" he asked. His eyes full of suspicion.

Byron looked at Flynn with contempt. "I need nothing from you old man. Step aside while I address the people." Flynn didn't budge so Byron stepped around him and climbed up onto a cinder block portion of the wall.

"Colonel, hand me the bull horn." Byron didn't look back he held his hand out behind him.

Haddock stepped forward and looked at Flynn. "Sorry for the intrusion sir. Is this your place?" Flynn just nodded. "We need to talk later." Haddock handed the bull horn to Byron.

Byron cleared his throat before beginning. He just barely managed to stifle a gag. The smell of unwashed bodies was pounding his sense of smell; it made him want to vomit. He lifted the bull horn to his lips. "My name is Byron Loxley. I am the regional director for FEMA here in Alabama. I have come here to tell you that you are all to be moved to the relocation camps in Birmingham." Angry defiant voices assailed Byron. He held his ground though. "You will bring all of your belongings and food stuffs here in two weeks. You will then be transported to Birmingham. Again you have two weeks to comply with this order."

Byron turned and jumped from the wall. He handed the bull horn back to Haddock. "These fine people are all yours to deal with now. I'm heading back. You may do your walk through patrol like you requested." With that Byron marched to one of the helicopters and was soon airborne heading back to Birmingham.

When he left Haddock took to the wall as he did angry people threatened him, and yelled insults at him. Haddock lifted the bull horn to his mouth and called for quite. Eventually he got it. "Folks I am Col.

Haddock from the Alabama National Guard. I will tell you this. That man fully intends to come back here and relocate you. Not in two weeks, but next week.

"These sixteen soldiers are all from here in Lauderdale County. They are going to walk through and talk with you and let you know what is going on in these camps. I need to talk to the leaders of this operation, and those who helped set it up."

An hour later Doc, Amos, Steve, Bob, and Howard sat with the Colonel in Mr. Flynn's back office. The Colonel was finishing up with what he had come to tell the residents of this part of Alabama. "So basically next week it won't be National Guard here with Loxley. I just got word that FEMA is finally sending him several hundred armed personnel. They will be here and do exactly what Loxley says."

Steve leaned forward. "Well can't you send some troops to help us?"

Haddock shook his head. "I have some plans of my own that must be implemented when Loxley leaves to come back here. You are on your own. Come up with a good plan and make it work. Otherwise we'll be seeing each other behind the wire. I have to leave now gentlemen, good luck." Haddock shook hands all around and turned to open the door. He stopped and looked over his shoulder at the seated men. "What ever you do, don't let folks know by radio. We've been listening to all of your radio transmissions." With that he turned and left.

Steve stood up. "Well I guess that's it. We either pull everyone together or we're going to be together in some damn camp."

Amos leaned his chair back against the wall. "I believe I got a plan folks." A smile played across his lips.

Flynn leaned back in his leather chair and put his hands behind his head. "Do tell friend Amos. Do tell."

Chapter 37

Joe Donovan walked over the crest of the hill. In his left hand he held the reigns attached to Festus. He stopped and with his right hand he raised the binoculars that hung around his neck and scanned the surrounding area. He lowered the binoculars shaking his head with satisfaction. Nothing moving and everything was quite.

"Well Festus looks like things are nice and quite." Joe rubbed Festus's nose as he walked to the big mule's side. Reaching up he took the canteen that hung from the saddle horn. Opening the cap he took a long pull of water and replaced the cap.

Replacing the canteen Joe mounted the mule. The hand held CB squawked as Steve's familiar voice came from the small speaker. "This is Caravan to Watchdog. Caravan to Watchdog, come in, over."

Joe lifted the CB, "Watchdog to Caravan, go ahead."

"Watchdog we are back en route to your location. ETA is about thirty minutes."

"10-4 is everything Code 1?"

"Roger that. Ran into a bit of trouble, but all of those problems has been hung out to dry so to speak. We will fill you in later."

Joe immediately thought of his two nieces praying neither had been harmed or injured. "Caravan, are the girls okay?"

"They are fine Watchdog. As a matter of fact they both seem to be quite content. Quit worrying they are fine. If you are not already there, meet at Doc's. Maude's going to cook a big meal for everyone. See ya in thirty, Caravan out."

Relief swept over Joe knowing his nieces were fine. "10-4 Caravan, Watchdog out."

Joe put the CB back in its holder and turned Festus's head with the reigns. "Come on Festus let's head to Doc's." Festus turned and headed slowly down the hill heading for Doc's.

Several times on the way back to Doc's Festus would stop and his ears would swivel, and he would neigh nervously. The final time Joe was about fed up. He knew Festus was a peculiar animal according to Amos, but this was getting ridiculous.

"Damn, Festus get a move on would you?" Joe said as he kicked the mule's flanks. Festus just turned and looked at him.

Joe gave Festus an open hand slap on the mule's rump. "Come on you dumb jackass, get moving!" The mule turned and bit him on the thigh, stared at him for a second and moved on.

"Owww!" Joe let out with a yelp. "What the hell did you do that for Festus?" Joe said angrily as the mule stared at him and then turned his head and moved on.

Joe rubbed at the painful bite. "It's a wonder Amos hasn't sent your stubborn butt to the glue factory. You would think you were the one with the brain. You need to learn to do what your told, and go when someone on two legs tells you to go." Festus ignored him and continued walking his ears and eyes turning to the west watching the tree line a hundred yards away.

Fifteen minutes later Joe and Festus reached Doc's place. Joe tethered Festus to a large oak. He went and fetched a five gallon bucket and filled it out with water and placed it next to the tree for Festus. "Drink up you mean useless piece of meat. Next time I'll tell Amos to leave your butt in the stall and I'll ride that little burro." Joe turned and headed back to the house, rubbing the fresh bite, and now bruising flesh on his thigh.

+>==<+

"Big Mike" Somanski watched the man and mule stop for the forth time. The man tried to get the mule going with a slap to the rump. The mule turned and bit him and then continued on his way. The mule's ears standing straight up turned towards his location. Big Mike and his men lay motionless until they passed.

"That was the son of a bitch that killed your brother and the boys! Why we got to wait Mike? Why can't we kill him now?" said the little man to Mike's left.

"Cause I want the woman and the man that was with him, that's why. Now shut the hell up Dweezle, before that fucker hears us." Mike said as he placed his huge meaty hand around the back of the little man's neck and squeezed.

Dweezle's eyes bulged as the man squeezed his neck. "Okay, okay." Dweezle said in a quite whisper.

Big Mike released his grip as he watched the man disappear over the next hill. Once the man was out of sight Big Mike stood and motioned for his men to rise and gave a hand signal for his men to rally around him. The surrounding foliage swayed with motion as twenty men rose almost as one.

The men had long hair, many wore long beards, mustaches, or goatees, and several were shaved bald. They were clad in woodland camouflage pants, and wore camo ponchos, or had camo netting draped over worn black leather jackets or vest. They all carried AK-47's. Their waists were wrapped with web belts, holding a variety of types of pistols, and extra magazines, knives, hatchets, and pouches. They moved to Big Mike, none moving at ease through the briars, branches and underbrush. They were men accustomed to the streets and back alleys of city life.

Big Mike frowned as he watched his men stumble towards him. Wood movements were one thing he never thought he would have had to teach his gang. Big Mike was a former Army Ranger. At one time in his Army career many thought he would one day become a Sergeant Major. He had proven skilled in every task he had encountered as an infantryman, and Ranger.

Big Mike's career had come to an abrupt halt during his second year in Iraq. He had fought bravely during Operation Iraqi Freedom, earning a Bronze Star, and Silver Star for valor. His unit had deployed back home after one year, and Big Mike had volunteered to stay behind and help train the Rangers who had come to relieve his unit.

Towards the end of his second year Big Mike had been caught by his First Sergeant raping a thirteen year old girl while on a patrol on the outskirts of Baghdad.

Big Mike was placed under arrest and sent back to the states. While en route to Ft. Leavenworth to serve out his twenty year sentence Big Mike crippled the two MP's escorting him. He stole their side arms and extra ammunition and fled into America's motorcycle bike gang culture.

Big Mike used his charisma, and natural leadership abilities to raise a small gang of forty die hard bikers. They began to run meth, marijuana, coke, and heroin. He also ran a night club outside of Birmingham through a third party. He ran a very profitable prostitution ring out of this club.

He kept a low profile and had his men do most of the dirty work. He did rob a bank in Florence in 2007 during the Trail of Tears Motor Cycle ride that came through Florence every year with over one hundred thousand motorcyclist participating.

He took his men every month to a small thirty acre farm they had purchased in Colbert County. At this small farm Big Mike had his men construct a shoot house, range, and a dozen small framed houses. Here he taught his men about urban warfare, something he had become quite skilled at during his time in Iraq. He never thought about teaching them wood movements. He regretted that now, but who ever thought civilization would damn near collapse, and his men would have to learn to set up ambushes and sneak up on farms to raid for supplies.

Though the cities provided a lot of loot, food, weapons, ammo, and a supply of women to entertain his men, Big Mike knew the pickings would eventually get slim in the cities as people fled to the country side to escape looters, find food, and safe shelter. After the first couple of weeks he changed his tactics and began plundering in the country. Many farmers and rural people though better armed than their city cousins and putting up stiffer resistance were usually isolated with just a few friends or family members with them. Though the chance of casualties to his men were higher the rewards were usually greater. Food, medical supplies, fuel, and water were almost always present.

Big Mike knew that in time his men would become proficient woodsmen and the scores they made would come more frequently and successfully. He knew the group that he was stalking now was pretty well organized and well armed, but the three he was after had to pay for killing his brother and his friends. Now those three had hooked up with a new bunch that occupied four houses spread out over about three hundred acres of land.

Once this group was overcome he would rest his men and begin training his men intently on woodland operations. According to Leon, his scout observing his intended target, they had just left the big meet. Some niggers got hung because the two girls started shooting them up for something. The group had acquired a Land Rover, and Expedition while there. These two new vehicles, plus the two Dodge trucks, and the two trucks the old men drove would be needed. His gang needed better vehicles to operate in the country.

Leon had advised by radio that the group was on the way. He advised he overheard the group say they were going to the older white man's house for lunch. Once the group got good and settled in and started eating the gang would attack, killing the men and keeping the women for fun.

Big Mike took a knee as his men surrounded him. Four of the men stood behind cover several yards from the circle of men. They faced out with their backs to the gang, their heads constantly moving from left to right looking for any sign of danger. "All right boys. Leon radioed and said the whole group is going to the old white fucker's house for lunch. This is what the plan of attack is…" Big Mike drew a diagram of Doc's farm out in the dirt. His men remained silent and listened to their leaders plan.

<hr />

Steve and the group drove steadily back to Doc's place. Everyone's spirits were high despite the shooting, and hanging two hours earlier. Steve turned to Doc, who sat in the passenger seat of the truck. "Doc what do you think about what happened back there?"

Doc ran his fingers through his thinning gray hair, paused and thought for a moment before responding. "Justice, pure and simple divine justice is all I can say. I know that the brutal murder of the girls' parents and Daphne's rape will always be with them. The death of those that perpetrated those events won't take away what happened, but I think it will let the girls mentally heal. Not only have the ones responsible been made to pay for their crimes, the girls were solely responsible for making those that did it pay, quite viciously to boot.

"I think it will bring closure for them. They also got back two vehicles that belonged to their parents. While not a priceless family heirloom, those vehicles will, in the future, help the girls to survive. Plus they got all kinds of gear, pistols, ammo, cook wear, and food. These items will also help them in the future, whether in defense of their lives or being used to trade for things that will help ensure they can continue in this new world we find ourselves in."

"Well all that is true, but do you think that shooting those guys and watching them hang will affect them mentally? I really mean more so for Daphne than Celina. Celina has already shot a few people and held up well for an eighteen year old. I just wonder how Daphne will do."

Maude spoke up from the back seat of the crew cab. "Steve, don't go worrying about young Daphne or Celina. I think you will see a new Daphne after today. Daphne has avenged herself and personally taken care of her nightmare. She watched it swing from a tree and knows she is in control. If anything I think you will see that both girls will become surer of themselves, and taking control of any environment they find themselves in."

Amos leaned forward a bit as he spoke up. "I think Maude's right, but for the life of me I don't see how Celina can become any stronger than she is. That little gal is one tough cookie."

Steve looked at Amos in the rearview mirror. "Amos that is the understatement of the century."

Doc turned sideways so he could see everyone in the truck. "She's got one hell of ball crushing kick too."

Amos chuckled and looked at Steve. "Yeah, I feel sorry for any old boy that decides to get a little to frisky with her. He might wind up having to walk around all hunched over and in a shuffle for the rest of his life."

Amos and Doc sat sharing a laugh as they stared at Steve. Then Steve caught Maude's hard stare in the mirror. "A man might find my foot up his tail too, if I catch him trying to be frisky with her under my roof." Maude said as her eyes bored into Steve's.

Steve averted meeting eye contact with everyone in the truck as his face blushed red. "What the hell are yall staring at me for?"

"I think you know why. Best thing for you to do is hush up and drive boy." Amos said with a big smile on his face.

That's exactly what Steve did. Twenty minutes later they were pulling up into Doc's driveway. Everyone exited the vehicles and started making their way to the house. Celina walked up and joined Steve as he walked to the house. "It looks like Uncle Joe is here." Celina said.

Steve was about to respond when he got Maude's hard stare. "Uh, I forgot something in the truck." Steve made an abrupt halt and made his way back to the truck for the imagined item. Celina stopped to wait on him.

Maude called to Celina from the porch. "Celina dear, come on in and let's see to dinner."

"Sure Mrs. Morrison." Celina joined Maude and they made their way to the kitchen after putting their guns in the living room gun rack.

Doc and Amos watched Steve from the front porch as they stoked up their pipes. "That boy is gonna have a tough time courting Celina with Maude's mean ass all over him." Amos said between puffs on his pipe, as he fired up the tobacco in the bowl.

Doc let his pipe dangle from his lips as he chuckled. "Damn right Amos, but it sure is hell gonna be fun for us two old farts to watch."

Steve came in the house a few minutes later carrying a canvas bag in one hand, his AK in the other. He found Joe knapping in the front living room. "Hey Joe wake up man. I got some goodies for you."

Joe opened his eyes and swung his socked feet off the foot rest. "What do you have for me?"

"Well I couldn't find anyone to trade for the S&W so you still have it." He pulled it out of the bag and handed it to Joe. "I did trade the Rossi and the Ruger though. I got you for thirty round detachable mags for your SKS, four hundred more rounds of 7.62x39, one hundred rounds of .357, 10 rounds of buckshot, forty rounds of number four buck shot, a LBV that will hold your SKS mags, and these."

Steve dramatically and slowly pulled the last item from the bag. A pair of brown leather work boots came out of the bag in Steve's hand. "Size 10 ½ , insulated, waterproof, Wolverine work boots, with Vibram soles."

Joe smiled and took the boots from Steve's out stretched hands. He quickly put the boots on and laced them up. "Things are brand new where did you snag these things at?"

"I got them from Howard. He said Craig came across a couple of boxes of them one day. How do they fit?"

Joe stood and walked around, then bounced up and down on the balls of his feet. "Feel great! Man I appreciate this. My other boots were about done for." Daphne and Caroline walked into the living room in time to see Joe bouncing up and down. "What do you think about my new boots ladies?"

Daphne frowned. "Uncle Joe, I will definitely say you won't be sporting the cover of GQ magazine wearing those things."

"I don't know Daphne. He might make it on the cover of Grease Monkey Apparel." Caroline said with a smile.

Bob walked in about that time and looked at Joe's new boots. "Hey, nice boots, wish I could have found some like that." Everyone burst out laughing as Bob stood looking confused wondering what was so funny about what he had just said.

About an hour and a half later Maude and the women had a late dinner ready to eat. She had cooked chicken, five full birds, salad, fresh baked bread, mashed potatoes, and black eyed peas. Everyone dug in and enjoyed a rare full meal.

Dinner lasted almost an hour before everyone had pushed back from the table with swollen stomachs, and satisfied looks on every face. Especially Maude, who had always enjoyed cooking for people, and was always satisfied to see clean plates, empty food bowls, and looks of contentment on peoples faces after they at one of her meals.

Joe was the first to stand up from the table. He let out a groan as he slowly stood. "I don't know about the rest of you, but I'm ready for a nap. Maude that was one fine meal." A chorus of agreement, and compliments came from everyone at the table.

The other men began to rise. Bob stretched out his arms and let out a yawn. "I'm with you Joe. I think it's about time for a little siesta."

Maude loudly cleared her throat and gained everyone's attention. "I too, agree that a nap for everyone is a must." The men folk smiled and nodded their heads in agreement. "However, the first ones taking naps will be those of us that prepared this fine meal. While those that lounged around on their backsides while this meal was being prepared can do the dishes. Ladies shall we?"

All the women stood with smiles on their faces, each intent on getting a well deserved nap. The men just stood with blank looks on their faces as they took in the piles of dirty dishes on the table, and those that lined the kitchen counter tops. Caroline picked up a dish towel and threw it at her husband, hitting him in the face. "Boys, you heard the lady." She said.

"Yall keep it down while we're resting. I like it quite while I nap." Daphne said as she and the other ladies left the room laughing.

Each man made his way to the pile of dishes before them. Each had a look somewhat like a small child who has been told to clean his room, on their faces. "They aren't anything but a bunch of cackling old hens." Doc mumbled to himself as he began to boil some water on the stove, the laughter from the women in the other room drifting to his old ears.

—————

The sun was hanging low in the warm afternoon sky as Big Mike and his men moved through the woods towards the old man's house. Big Mike had split his gang up into four teams. Three of the teams had five men each. His team consisted of six men and himself.

The plan was for the men to surround the house on three sides. Three teams would provide fire support, suppression fire, and prevent anyone from escaping from the back and sides of the house. Five members of his team, and Big Mike would make entry through the front door, kill the men, and subdue the women. One member of his team would stay back. He was armed with a scoped Remington Model 03-A3, .30-06. He would take care of any threats coming from the outside while his team was inside the house.

Big Mike froze in place as Dweezle, who was behind him, stumbled and crashed through a small bush letting out curses as he stumbled about. Big Mike turned slowly to face Dweezle, the muzzle of his AK coming up. Dweezle froze when he saw the look on Big Mike's face.

Big Mike placed the muzzle of the AK under Dweezle's chin. The little man stood trembling where he stood. "Sorry, Big Mike, I just aint used to walking in this shit." Dweezle said in a loud voice.

"If you say one more thing or make one more noise I will personally blow your

damn brains out. Now shut your fucking meat cave." Big Mike said in a low whisper. "You fuck this up for me and the rest of the gang you will regret it. Do you understand?"

Dweezle opened his mouth to respond but quickly shut it as Big Mike pressed the barrel of the rifle harder into his chin. Instead he just nodded his head, eyes filled with fear. He let out a sigh of relief as Big Mike lowered the rifle.

"I'm glad we've come to an understanding Dweezle." Big Mike turned and stealthily made his way towards the house. Ten minutes later the gang was in place.

⊹━━⊹

Amos and Doc sat in the living room as they finished cleaning their revolvers. Doc reloaded the pistol placing one round at a time in the cylinder. "Why don't you use one of them speed loaders you got Doc."

"Dang it I left them in the truck." Doc finished loading the revolver and stood up. "I'll be right back."

He stopped by the library and poked his head in. Steve and the girls sat on the floor going through all of the gear, weapons, ammo, and clothing taken out of the back of their parent's vehicle. "I'm headed out to the truck anyone leave anything they need?"

Steve looked up. "Nope I think we've got everything Doc. Thanks though."

Doc gave a little wave and headed outside. He opened the truck door and began to dig out the three speed loaders. He found the speed loaders and a box of .357. He loaded two of the speed loaders from the box and pocketed them. As he began to load the third one Festus caught his attention.

Doc looked over his shoulder at the mule, which was stomping his left hoof on the ground and neighing, shaking his head left and right. "What is it Festus?" Doc said as he finished loading the speed loader and put it in his pocket as well. He drew his pistol slowly walking towards the mule as his eyes searched the wood line. "It's probably a dog or coyote." He said to himself.

Dweezle's fidgeted as he lay watching the old man approach the old man. He continually squeezed the pistol grip of his AK. The old man would be an easy kill. He licked his lips as he pulled the rifle to his shoulder. If he could make this kill surely Big Mike would praise him for such quick thinking to take out the threat before they assaulted the house.

Big Mike watched silently as the old man walk towards the mule. All they had to do was wait till the old man went inside then they would hit the house. He smiled thinking about the easy kills, loot, and pretty women they would take when this was over. Suddenly the quite of the late afternoon was shattered as the sound of an AK rifle opened up. Geysers of dirt kicked up around the old man as he scrambled back towards the truck.

Doc dove behind the truck as rounds thumped into the side of Steve's truck. He pulled himself up to a crouch and fired two rounds toward the blinking orange light that came from the muzzle flash of the hidden shooter. Doc ducked back down under a barrage of fire that came from numerous rifles in the wood line.

"Open fire!" Big Mike screamed. His blood boiled, whoever fired those shots would pay with his life. Big Mike keyed his radio up and ordered the other three teams to open fire. "All teams open fire! All teams open fire!" With that order the other three teams opened up.

Everyone jumped to their feet as multiple gunshots were heard from the front of the house. Everyone reached for their rifles and started for the front door. Suddenly windows shattered, and rounds chewed through the walls. Everyone dove for the cover of the floors.

"Daphne and Celina make your way to the back of the house. Shoot whatever moves!" Steve screamed over the den of gunfire.

Steve grabbed his AK, and loaded the thirty round magazine in the weapon. He reached for his LBV that lay over a chair. Pulling it to him he reached into one of the large pouches he had attached and pulled out a seventy five round drum and inserted it into the rifle. He crawled towards the window, and rose up on his knees as the gunfire from his side of the house started to slow. He caught sight of a muzzle flash in the tree line. Steve raised his rifle and pumped four rounds into the area where the muzzle flash came. He had to duck back down as other hidden gunmen returned his fire.

Amos broke out a window pane with his .44 magnum Ruger revolver. He fired two rounds into the trees hoping to hit one of the unseen gunmen. He saw Doc ducked behind one of the trucks unable to make a break for the house. "Doc's trapped outside by the trucks! I need some help in here!" He said over his shoulder. He fired four more rounds emptying the revolver. He tucked it in his pants and pulled his other .44.

Joe, Bob, and Caroline were in the kitchen firing out open windows at everything that moved when Amos's cry for help was shouted. "Bob you and Caroline hold here. I'm going to help Amos." Both nodded without looking back at Joe, as the two searched for more targets to shoot.

Joe scrambled into the living room SKS in hand. "Where are they Amos?"

Amos had his back to the wall as he reloaded Doc's M-1 Garand. He had retrieved it after firing the second revolver dry. "I would say about forty five yards out just up by that clump of white oaks."

Joe looked towards the area Amos described and spotted several muzzle flashes in the shadows. Joe took careful aim and worked the rifle back and forth. The muzzle flashes stopped as Joe's fire poured down on the shooters hidden there.

Maude had fled to the basement and grabbed her Browning semi-auto shotgun that she used to hunt turkey with. She also grabbed three bandoliers that contained thirty rounds apiece of buckshot, slugs, and number two shot. She wrapped one around her waist and two across her chest like a Mexican bandito. Then she loaded the shotgun with seven rounds of low recoil Federal slugs. Once loaded up she ran upstairs to aid Amos.

Maude ran into the living room just as Joe emptied the last rounds from the thirty round magazine. She moved up to his position as he rolled to the side of the window to reload the rifle. She brought the shotgun to her shoulder. "Where are they Joe, where are they at?"

"They are by the cluster of oaks on the hillside!" Joe said as he worked the new magazine into the magazine well of the rifle.

Maude fired one round after another into the cluster of trees. Amos joined her sending out a steady stream of .30-06 rounds zipping down range. Their rate of fire was much slower than Joe's and one by one the gang members began to return fire.

Steve caught sight of two men making for one of the small out buildings. Ignoring the incoming rounds Steve led the first running man by about a foot. He adjusted to about a foot and a half lead because of the speed the man was running at. He slowly squeezed the trigger and was rewarded for his calmness under fire as he watched the man stumble and then fall, dead, to the ground.

The second man tripped over the first man as he collapsed to the ground. The second man fell forward and then rolled head over tail and came to a halt on his back. He scrambled to all fours frantically looking for his rifle that he had dropped.

Steve swung the rifle to the second man, but instead of a single round Steve unleashed a barrage of copper jacketed, steel core rounds into the man's body. Geysers of blood exploded from the man's back, legs and head as the rounds ripped through his body. Steve dove for cover as the other gang members zeroed in on his position trying to exact revenge on the man that had just killed their friends.

Daphne and Celina ripped the drapes down from the two windows in the room they occupied. The two girls had armed themselves, with their rifles. Celina had her stainless Mini-14, and Daphne had a scoped CZ bolt action rifle chambered in .223.

The two girls scanned for their assailants but only caught fleeting glimpses of them in the wooded area behind the house. Celina caught sight of one of the men sprinting for the barn. She fired round after round at the running man but missed every shot, each round kicking up dirt a few feet behind the man. The man dove the final few feet to the barn, and disappeared from view.

"Damn, damn, damn!" Celina said to herself. Then it dawned on her that Steve had told her always to lead a person or animal when it was running.

Rounds started impacting in the room the girls were in and both were forced to take cover. Celina came up on one knee and fired several rounds and dove back for cover. Suddenly rounds started impacting on the floor. Celina frantically looked for where the fire was coming from. Her eyes stopped on the loft door of the barn. The man that she had missed was firing down into the room. There was nowhere for Celina to go. She rolled from side to side trying to avoid from being hit.

Daphne had rolled up beside the wall under the window seal. Seeing her sister's predicament and realizing she was being fired on from above Daphne made her move. She rolled out from under the window stopping on her back. The rifle came to her shoulder and the crosshairs of the scope came into view. She found the chest of the man in her sights and squeezed the trigger. She watched the man fold at the waste and fall to the ground below.

Daphne smiled at her sister. "That takes care of that little problem."

"Thanks sis!" Celina slapped a fresh magazine in her rifle and came back up on her knees.

Celina spotted two men running to the barn. This time she remembered lesson Steve had taught her. She unleashed six rounds from the rifle. The first two rounds struck the first man in the right side. The third round kicked up dirt between the two men. The last three rounds struck the second man in the right leg and left hip shattering the hip bone. Celina ducked back down as rounds impacted the window, and wall in front of her.

Daphne came up on one knee. She took in the two men out in front of her. One was apparently dead. The second flailed back and forth on the ground screaming in pain. She brought the rifle up and centered the cross hairs on the man's bobbing head. As the man's head moved in front of the cross hairs Daphne squeezed the trigger. The man's head exploded like a ripe melon. More rounds poured into the room.

"Get down Daphne!" Celina screamed at her sister.

Daphne reacted too late and a stray round struck her on the right arm. Her rifle tumbled to the floor with Daphne right behind it. "No!" Celina screamed and stood her rifle at her hip. She sprayed the remaining rounds in the direction of the attackers. When her rifle ran dry she dropped it and ran to sister.

"Daphne, are you okay?" Celina said in a panicked voice. She pulled her sister's hand from the wound on her arm.

"It hurts Celina, it hurts." Daphne cried as her sister jerked a pillow case from a pillow and attempted to staunch the flow of blood.

"It'll be okay. Doc will get you fixed up." Celina took her sister's hand. "Keep pressure on it. I've got to keep these bastards off of us." Celina retrieved her rifle and reloaded, then began to fire at the hidden attackers.

Bob and Caroline squatted behind the island bar in the center of the kitchen as the two reloaded their pistols. Caroline looked at Bob trying to stay calm. "Bob this sucks."

"Well you ain't going to hear any arguing from me, beautiful." Bob closed the cylinder on the revolver.

Just as he rose up the kitchen door came crashing in. A large burley man with long hair and shaggy beard came into the doorway an AK in his hands. The man sprayed the interior of the kitchen with gunfire. Bob dove to the left as Caroline stuck her pistol over the top of the counter top firing off six rounds to no avail.

The big man raised his rifle and was about to fire through the island and into Caroline. Bob pushed himself across the floor and around the left side of the island. He raised his pistol and fired four rounds into the man's chest. The big man was cut down, and fell face forward and to the floor.

Bob scuttled forward and grabbed the AK from the dying man's hands. He stepped out the kitchen door and leveled the rifle on a startled biker who came to an abrupt halt. Bob pumped the trigger and watched the man's body shudder with every round that hit him. Bob had to dive back into the kitchen as the other bikers began to fire at him.

⊶⊷

Bullets tore into the brush around Big Mike and his team, and they all dove to the ground. Some hid behind downed trees others pressed there faces into the dirt. Then the heavy fire ended and was replaced by what sounded like a shotgun and a big bore rifle. The men rose back up and started to return fire.

Big Mike turned to tell Motor Oil to use the 03 and kill the old man. "Motor Oil, I want you to take out the old…." Big Mike's order was halted as he recoiled in shock as the side of Motor Oil's head burst open. Blood, brain matter, and shards of skull splattered across Big Mike's face.

Big Mike wiped the gore away with a free hand. "If I find out who fucked this raid up I'm going to kill him with my bare hands." Big Mike growled.

Ten yards away, Dweezle, who was curled up behind a large oak heard Big Mike. Knowing Big Mike wasn't bluffing, he knew he had to do something to make up for his screw up. Reaching in his front pocket Dweezle pulled out a small glass vial that contained cocaine. Dweezle opened the cap to the vial and placed the vial next to his nose. Closing off one nostril with a finger, Dweezle snorted up the contents of the vial.

He felt the rush of the cocaine spread through his body. He suddenly felt invincible, powerful. He would take care of the old man and those inside on his own. Snatching up his rifle, Dweezle leapt to his feet and charged forward.

Rounds zipped passed Dweezle as, Amos, Joe, and Maude tried to shoot him. The three had no luck hitting the running man, and were forced to take cover as Big Mike and his team laid down covering fire for Dweezle.

Doc was nestled behind one of the big front tires of Steve's truck. The incoming fire had been so intense he had not had a chance to shoot back, or make a break for the house, since the first shots were fired.

Peeking over the window seal Amos saw the man charging out of the wood line towards Doc. Amos tried to bring his rifle to bare but was forced back to cover as rounds began to pepper around him. He had to warn Doc.

"Doc! Doc! You got one charging right toward you!" Amos shouted at the top of his lungs.

Doc barely heard Amos's warning. Peeking around the tire Doc saw the running feet of the man charging towards him. Doc adjusted his grip on his pistol and surged to his feet. The man was now only fifteen yards away and closing fast. Doc raised his pistol, and the man began firing his AK from the hip. Rounds slammed into the truck, and zipped past his head as he started squeezing the trigger.

Dweezle ran harder than he had ever run in his life. He could hear the bullets zip past him. He felt no fear, the cocaine giving him the resolve he needed to kill the old man and those in the house. Suddenly the old man stood up from behind the truck a pistol in his hands. As

Dweezle started shooting from the hip, he saw flames shoot out from the end of the barrel of the pistol.

Dweezle felt the rounds slam into his chest. He felt no pain, and knew he could not die. He smiled in glee knowing he was the meanest, toughest biker around. He saw the old man collapse and as he disappeared from view. As he came around the front of the truck to deliver the final killing shot and was disappointed to hear the hammer fall on an empty chamber.

As he came to a stop and looked down at the now empty rifle, he saw the bloody, torn, mess that had been his chest. Realization came to his drug filled mind that he would not live. Dweezle dropped the rifle and collapsed to the ground on his butt. He suddenly found it hard to breath and began to gasp for breath.

———

Maude ducked down to reload the shotgun with slugs when she heard Amos scream out the warning to her husband. Maude looked out the window to see a small man, with unkempt hair, and black leather jacket charging forward firing from the hip. Doc was standing shooting at the man. Doc's rounds were shredding the man's chest apart but he kept charging forward, a smile on his face. Then Doc collapsed backwards and hitting the ground, arms, and legs spread out.

Maude's blood boiled with rage as she saw her husband fall to the ground, possibly dead. Ignoring the rounds that ripped the walls of her house and buzzed through the living room like angry bees Maude made for the front door. The scum would pay for shooting her man. Maude was mad. Jerking the door open she purposely strode forward to Doc.

She stopped and looked down at the little greasy man, who sat gasping for breath. "You worthless piece of trash, you're going to pay." Maude said, her eyes filled with hate as she glared down at the man. She placed the barrel to the man's head and squeezed the trigger.

Maude turned as she heard yells coming from the woods. Out of the woods came several men firing at her as they ran. Like an angry mother grizzly protecting her wounded cub, Maude stepped in front of Doc's body protecting him from the charging men.

Joe and Amos saw the charging men and ran out to help Maude, and Doc. Maude didn't need any help though. Raising her shotgun she placed the bead sight of the shotgun on each man and squeezed the trigger. Each round she fired was center mass the 12 gauge slugs dropping each man into a crumpled heap.

The last man she shot was a huge man. He dropped to the ground but struggled to get back up. Maude walked up to the man as she slowly reloaded the shotgun one round at a time. She stopped just a few feet from the man who was on his hands and knees now. Lashing out with her foot, she kicked the man in the face flipping him backwards onto his back.

Maude stepped over the prostrate man and looked down on him. "No one messes with my man." She snarled. Maude pulled the trigger over and over emptying the twelve gauge into the man's chest at point blank range.

The threats terminated Maude turned back to Doc. Amos had Doc's head cradled in his lap, tears rolling down his cheeks. Fear, and dread gripped Maude's heart, surely her husband wasn't dead. Amos looked up at her grief on his face. Maude dropped to her knees beside her husband, tears now falling like rain down her cheeks.

Chapter 38

The gunfire slowly subsided from the woods and inside the house. Amos wiped the tears from his eyes, so he could clear his vision. Looking off to the right Amos caught a glimpse of two of the attackers fleeing deeper into the woods. Hearing foot steps behind him Amos turned his head to see who was approaching.

Bob, Joe, and Steve came running as fast as their legs would carry them to Doc's side. Joe was the first to kneel down beside Amos and Maude. "How bad is he?"

Maude lifted her hand from the right side of Doc's chest. Blood dripped from her hand has she lifted it for all to see. Steve looked down on the gruesome sight below him. "Get him inside. Daphne is hit too."

Amos stayed on his knees as the others lifted Doc's limp body from his lap. Amos watched as the other's carried Doc inside. Doc's head hung back, his face ashen, and pale from the loss of blood. As Amos stood he heard limbs, and sticks breaking in the woods in the direction almost behind the house. Three more of the attackers fled off deeper into the woods. Rage filled Amos's body. He walked slowly inside the house and headed for the basement where everyone else was.

Walking into the basement Amos took in the scene. Caroline and Celina were cleaning Daphne's wounded arm. Daphne lay on a couch with her head propped up by a pillow. Her face glistened with sweat, her eyes glazed over as the shock of her predicament settled in her mind. Little Benny sat in the corner crying.

The rest hovered over Doc. His shirt ripped open, chest covered in blood. Everyone's voice seemed distant to Amos. Barely audible as if he was hearing everyone talk and he was underwater. Their voices came to him in muted, and staccato tones, "I can't find a pulse!", "Is he still breathing?", "I think we should start CPR!".

None seemed to notice as Amos walked over to where he had earlier left his semi-auto Remington 2700. He picked it up, along with a medium sized OD green canvas bag that contained eleven ten round magazines for the rifle. He also picked up a box of .44 magnum shells and took his things upstairs and out to the front porch.

Once on the front porch, Amos put one of the ten round magazines in his rifle. He then loaded the .44 Magnum Ruger Red Hawks. He placed the extra bullets in the front pocket of his overalls. Slinging the pouch holding the magazines over his left shoulder, Amos picked up his rifle and walked out to Festus who was still tethered, amazingly unscathed, to the tree out front.

Putting his foot in the stirrup Amos swung himself into the saddle. "Let's go do some killing boy." He said as he twisted Festus's reigns in the direction the attackers had fled.

Amos who had hunted and tracked for years had no problem picking up the trail of the city bred villains. Three men had left at a dead run from the side of the house that Steve had been defending. He followed the trail for another one hundred yards until it appeared the men had stopped. Foot prints covered the area as if the men had been pacing.

Dismounting he circled the area. Then he discovered more tracks that had come from a different direction. After studying the prints for awhile he determined the new tracks consisted of six to seven more men. Circling farther out Amos found the foot prints had combined and headed north, deeper into the woods.

Taking Festus's reigns he followed them. The group was walking two to three abreast in a column. He found droplets of blood among some of the bushes. One or more of the men had been wounded. Following further along he noticed that one set of prints stand out from the rest. They were a little farther to the left than the rest, and one leg seemed to be dragging.

More blood on an old log confirmed Amos's suspicions that the wounded man was lagging behind. He found where the man had stopped to rest. From the looks of the way he was dragging his leg, Amos felt this would be the first man he found. Amos quickened his pace in anticipation of exacting a little revenge. Festus walked obediently behind his master.

✦—✦—✦

Farley watched the big woman walk up to Dweezle and blow his brains out. He attempted to get a shot off at her, but the gunman on his side of the house was laying down hellish return fire and he had to take cover. When he rose back up he witnessed the big woman single-handedly take out Big Mike and his team. That made up his mind for him.

Taking out his hand held radio he called out the retreat for the other teams. "Let's get the hell out of here guys. Big Mike and his boys are down. Meet at the bikes!" Like the coward he truly was deep down, Farley turned tale and ran, not waiting for what was left of his team who were still firing their weapons into the house.

Tuck and Scoot ceased firing when they realized Farley had already boogied. Tuck rolled to look at Scoot. "You think it's safe to get the hell out of here?"

Scoot looked at the woman and black man who knelt over the bloody old man. "Let's wait and see if the rest come out to help the old fuck basket. Then we move."

The two didn't have long to wait as other people came pouring out of the front of the house. Tuck started to rise, patting Scoot on the shoulder as he stood. "Let's roll motherfucker!" Scoot was seconds behind him as the two crashed through thick underbrush.

A few minutes later the two caught up with Farley who was leaned up against a tree heaving for air. Tuck came to a halt and caught his breath. "Farley, where the hell is everyone at?"

Farley coughed and hawked up a wad of snot and spat it out. After a few more coughs he reached in his pocket and pulled out a smoke and lit it while he talked. "They're coming. I just talked to Duck, he and his team hooked up with Smokey and his boys."

Scoot dropped to the ground on his butt, and pulled out a cigarette of his own. "They need to hurry the hell up before those people decide to come after us. I especially don't want to cross that big bitch with the shotgun. That cold hearted whore just walked up and blew Dweezle's brains out."

503

Tuck paced back and forth and started gesticulating madly as he talked. "Dweezle better be glad that big bitch killed him. Ass wipe really screwed up, and ruined a damn sweet deal for us. Did you see that broad that drove that Nissan. I was looking forward to a piece of that. If she hadn't of killed him, after this was over I planed on feeding the shit licker his balls to him one at a time."

A few minutes later the other six men came crashing through the brush into the clearing. All were sweating profusely, and heaving for air. Duck limped forward ahead of the others, blood dripping from a whole in his right thigh. "Where are Gizzard and Hank?"

Scoot exhaled and blew a large cloud of smoke from his lips. "They got smoked man."

Smokey walked into the clearing with the others. "Man that means they killed twelve of us."

Tuck picked up his rifle. "I'm glad you can figure out the math, now let's get the hell out of here."

Duck hobbled forward. "What about my leg. Yall got to help me out."

Farley, who had always disliked Duck spoke up. "Duck you always talked about what a bad motherfucker you are. Why don't you prove it? You just keep up with the rest of us. I don't intend to get my ass shot off helping your lame ass."

With that Farley turned and headed for the bikes. The others followed with out a word. Duck stood motionless for a moment, and then started following the rest of the group. "When we get out of here Farley, I'm going to kick your ass." He shouted.

Farley looked back over his shoulder as he walked on. "Duck, your ass will be the first one killed, if those bastards come after us. I really don't think I got much to worry about. Besides as slow as you're walking we're going to be long gone before you get back to the bikes." Farley snorted out a laugh and walked on.

After a short while Duck had fallen far behind. He had to stop to rest or he knew he would never make it to the bikes. Sitting on an old log, Duck pulled out a flask of whiskey. Pouring some on his wound, and the rest down his throat he gave a small shudder. The liquor coursing through his veins gave him renewed confidence that he could make it. He stood and walked on dragging his wounded leg behind him.

Ten minutes, and two steep hills later Duck could barely walk. Collapsing to the ground he pulled himself over to a large rock and rested his back against it. Reaching in a small pocket in his leather vest, Duck pulled out his kit. Opening the small tin, he pulled out a couple of pain pills and swallowed them dry.

Next he pulled out his rolling paper and marijuana. Quickly and expertly Duck had a joint rolled. He fired up the joint inhaling deeply. Holding the smoke as long as he could he finally coughed and exhaled. In the distance he could hear the rest of the gang plow on through the woods without him.

"Fuck you assholes!" He said to his departed gang. "I'll make it, then I'm gonna kill all you sluts."

Closing his eyes he took another hit off the joint. He felt the THC course through his veins, and he began to relax. His high was disturbed though as he sensed someone over him. Opening his eyes he wasn't happy about what stood before him.

"Hey man chill out. I ain't with those guys."

⊹⊶⊷⊹

Farther along the rest of the gang moved out. They pulled farther and farther away from Duck. None were too concerned about his fate. They knew no real concept of friendship, or loyalty. When someone was down and about out, the only thing they knew to do was leave them, or kill them.

Fifteen minutes later one of the gang called out to Farley. "Hey man! Aint we close to where we are supposed to be yet?" A few others grumbled also.

"Hey Pumpkin, shut the fuck up. It's getting dark and we still got a couple of miles to go. We may have to sit out the night or we might wind up getting lost out here. If we stay we will make for the bikes in the morning." Farley turned back and walked on.

As the group walked up another hill they all froze in their tracks as the sound of a gunshot echoed through the woods and hills. All heads turned to their rear. One of the bikers started to shuffle his feet in agitation. "Farley, those fuckers are after us."

Farley looked at what was left of the gang. They all seemed scared shitless. Of course he was too, but he couldn't show it if he wanted to take over the gang. He had to show guts. "Tootsie Roll shut the hell up, those folks aint chasing us. I guarantee you Duck just sucked on the end of his pistol. Now let's get moving, I think we're going to have to make camp."

The gang looked around and felt none to comfortable about sleeping out in the woods. They knew Farley was right though, it was getting dark, and none of them knew enough about the woods to make it back to the bikes in the dark. The trudged on in silence.

⊹⊷⊶⊹

Amos decided he needed to catch the obvious straggler of the bunch. He mounted up and set Festus to a steady gallop. After crossing a couple of hills Amos came to a third hill and as he neared the crest he smelled something similar to burning hemp rope. Then as he came to the top he saw one of the bikers resting against a rock, a cigarette in his mouth.

Amos dismounted and walked slowly towards him, rifle at the ready. Amos stopped a few feet from the sitting man, and flicked the safety off of his rifle. The man slowly opened his eyes. They went wide when the man saw Amos standing in front of him.

"Hey man chill out I aint with those guys." The marijuana cigarette fell from Duck's lips, his hands coming up, and palms facing outwards towards Amos.

Amos stood silently for a moment. "Where are the rest of your friends?"

"I told you man, I aint with them." Ducks voice began to quiver a bit as he spoke.

Amos stepped forward. He took his right foot and pressed the heavy size thirteen boot against the man's wounded thigh. The man let out a scream, and then Amos removed his boot. "I'll ask you one more time. Where are your friends?"

"Th…Th…They is headed for the bikes dude. Don't hurt me. I didn't shoot any of your friends I swear." Tears spilled down Ducks cheeks as he spoke.

"Take the gun belt off and toss it at my feet." Amos motioned towards the man's gun belt with his rifle as he spoke.

With shaking hands Duck fumbled at the catch of the web belt at his waist. "It's cool man. It's cool. You can have my gun." Duck finally managed to release the clasp and pulled the belt loose tossing it at the big black man's feet.

Amos knelt and re-secured the clasp, the barrel of his rifle never leaving the wounded biker. Backing a few steps he looped the web belt, which contained a Walther P-99, and four magazines around the saddle horn. That done he spoke again. "Son, where are your friends headed to?"

"They're headed for the bikes. We parked them inside this old barn a few miles off. You aren't going to kill me are you man?" Duck said, his eyes pleading for mercy.

Amos grabbed the saddle horn with his free hand and pulled himself up into the saddle. He turned Amos to the left a bit, the barrel of the rifle resting across the saddle, pointing at the man's chest. He smiled down at the man. "What do you think?"

Duck smiled in relief, and closed his eyes, surely the man wouldn't kill him, and he had smiled at him. Opening his eyes he was about to tell the man thank you when he saw the look on the man's face had changed from a smile to a scowl. He reached out to plead once again for his life his arms outstretched. He never got a chance to say a word as the old black man pulled the trigger. The hollow point .30-06 round tore into his chest exploding his heart, the fragments of bone, and metal shredding his lungs. Duck never saw the smile return to the old black man's face as he turned and rode away.

Amos rode on; his thirst for revenge had not yet been quenched. He was sure that the man was talking about John Taylor's big barn just north of his property. The trail the bikers were leaving was headed in that general direction. He would scout ahead for a bit. He was sure the group would have to stop for the night. By the looks of the trail they were leaving these boys had no skill in the woods, and would have to stop when night fall came or become lost.

As the last of the day's sun faded from the sky Amos stopped Festus and looked across the woods several hills over. A large fire flared into life. Amos was sure it was the bikers. Even though the trail they left veered east from Taylor's barn, he was sure the group was becoming lost.

Amos dismounted and led Festus back the way they had come on the back side of the hill. He unsaddled Festus and tethered the mule. Out of his saddle bag he took some jerky and a canteen of water. He also took his bedroll and spread it on the ground.

He ate the jerky and drank his water. When he finished he lay back and closed his eyes. He would wake in a few hours and go pay the bikers a visit.

—•——•——•—

Around three the next morning Amos opened his eyes. He threw the blanket from his body and felt the chill of the night air wash over him. Ignoring the chill Amos stood and walked to his nearby saddle. He placed his rifle in the scabbard. Reaching next to the saddle bag he pulled a long machete from its sheath.

Machete in hand Amos made his way through the darkness to the biker camp. He could smell the smoke from the wood fire floating in the air. As he neared he could see the fire still burned bright.

At the edge of the campsite just at the limit of the light the fire threw off Amos crouched. All of the bikers slept except one. He stood over the fire, rifle slung, and a whiskey bottle in his right hand. Amos backed a little father into the darkness. Feeling around on the ground he picked up a stick, and with one hand snapped it in to.

The biker, who was short and squat with a head shaved bald save for a pony tail sticking out of the back of his skull, spun around at the sound. The man peered into the darkness that surrounded the camp. He slowly lowered the whiskey bottle to the ground and then stood drawing his pistol. On drunken legs, he wobbled a bit, but made his way into the darkness.

Amos had pressed himself against a large hickory tree and watched as the man passed. When the man had gone by a few feet from him Amos lashed out with his left hand grabbing the ponytail pulling the man to him. With his right hand he simultaneously thrust the machete forward into the back of the neck of the sentry. The razor sharp blade sliced through the man's neck and came out the front of the man's throat. Blood gushed through the gaping wound as Amos silently lowered the man's body to the ground.

As he slowly laid the man on the ground he removed the machete. With his free hand Amos lifted the man's head up, and with a powerful swing severed the man's head from his body. Blood slowly pumped out of the stump as the man's heart slowed to a stop.

Taking the severed head with him, Amos quietly made his way to the center of the camp. He laid the head beside the fire and just as quietly made his way back out of the camp site. The sleeping bikers, most all of them drunk or stoned slept oblivious to the events that had just transpired.

Amos made his way back to his campsite. Once there he saddled up Festus, and then made up his bedroll. When he was finished he took a drink from the canteen and replaced it in the saddle bag. Quietly he led Festus through the night to Taylor's barn.

An hour later Amos had reached the barn. A dim light burned inside the barn. Amos quietly dismounted Festus and tethered him to a low branch. He made his way through the false dawn to the barn. The barn door was slightly open by about a foot. Amos pulled out one of his .44's and made his way to the door.

Stealing a peek around the door Amos saw all of the motorcycles of the gang parked inside. The only sound came from a lone man dressed in a black leather jacket that lay snoring in a pile of hay. An AK-47 rifle lay next to the man's left hand. A half empty fifth of vodka lay by his right.

Amos pulled the door open another few inches and squeezed himself into the barn. His feet made no sound on the dirt floor of the barn as he walked up the sleeping biker. Amos didn't say a word as he walked up to the biker. Leaning over a bit he placed the barrel of his pistol against the man's chest. He squeezed the trigger sending a round through the man's heart and out of his back.

Amos took another quick look around the barn for any others. He knew he should have done that first but revenge, not tactics, is all he could really think about at this point. Once he was sure no one else was in the barn he gathered the materials he would need to lay his trap.

The bikers rose almost as one as the morning sun peeked over the tree tops. They were all stiff, and cotton mouthed from the liquor and drugs they had the night before. Scoot lay on the ground for another minute while the others started to rise around him. He slowly opened his eyes blinking them to help adjust to the brightness of the morning sun. When his eyes focused, they focused on the head of his friend Croaks. He stammered a bit and then let out a blood curdling scream, as he scrambled away from the severed head.

"OH SHIT! OH SHIT! The mother fuckers killed Croaks!" He screamed.

The others gathered around the head taking a few seconds to register that someone had killed Croaks and left his head in the middle of their camp. They started pulling pistols and knives and facing out towards the woods. Their eyes searched the trees for any sign of danger. Fear gripped the band of cold hearts.

Farley was the first to regain his composure. "Put your shit away guys. If the fuckers were still out there we would all be dead. Pack up your crap and let's get to the bikes."

The gang slowly responded to Farley's orders. Despite his reassurances of no one being around them they all kept a close eye on the surrounding woods. Once everyone had gathered their belongings they moved out for the motorcycles.

Amos sat patiently hiding in the woods around Taylor's barn. He daydreamed of all the good times that he and Doc had, had over the years. Now he didn't know if his best friend was alive or dead. Either way this trash would pay for what they had done. The morning hours ticked by, Amos oblivious to the passing time, like a big cat he waited patiently for his quarry.

As noon drew nearer Amos finally heard the group of bikers approaching the barn. The men came into the clearing. Their clothing was dirty and torn, their long hair pasted tight against their skulls with sweat. They stumbled as they walked towards the barn, most looked near exhaustion. One by one they staggered into the barn.

Amos stood and casually walked to the barn. Around the back of the barn Amos pulled out one of the road flares he had found in the barn. He lit the flare and tossed the flare on the large pile of hay bales he had tossed from the loft earlier. The flames from the flare quickly caught the dry hay on fire, and the smoke and flames grew larger by the minute.

As he rounded the front corner of the barn Amos reached down and picked up a large glass bottle filled with gasoline. A rag stuck out of the top. As he lit the rag he could hear the voices inside the barn, "Hey does anyone smell smoke?"

"Shut the hell up and give me some of that whiskey."

Amos pulled open the barn door and stepped in. Heads turned, and mouths hung open as Amos smiled at them. "Boys time for you to head for hell. Let me give you a little taste."

Amos threw the gas bomb straight at a motorcycle that four of the men were standing near. The glass bottle shattered, and the flames and gas mixing causing a huge fireball to engulf four of the men. Their clothing, saturated with gas burned like a lanterns wick.

Amos stepped back out of the door and shut it. He quickly turned to the other corner where he had placed a five gallon bucket full of gasoline. Picking up the bucket he quickly returned to the door of the barn. Amos poured the contents against the door, and then dumped the bucket over sending the remaining three gallons under the door of the barn to the hay strewn floor inside. Taking his last flare, Amos lit it and tossed it on the ground by the door. Flames engulfed the door, and shot up from the floor inside the barn. Amos turned and walked back to get Festus.

Once he mounted up Amos, and Festus trotted back to the barn. The entire back of the barn was engulfed in flames. The front too, was burning nicely also. From inside he could still hear some of the screams of pain, and cries for help from the few living bikers inside.

"Looks like things have just heated up for those boys Festus. To bad it's going to get a lot hotter for them when they die. Let's go." Amos turned Festus around and headed for Doc's. A happy smile was on his face. A tower of black smoke and hot orange flames shot to the sky behind him as he rode away.

Chapter 39

Byron Loxley sat behind the huge polished mahogany desk, the receiver of a telephone pressed to his ear. "Yes Mr. Benson, I understand completely. Northwestern Alabama will be secured in a matter of days." He said nodding his head.

Mr. Benson Director for the Southern Region of FEMA spoke again. "Byron we have sent you one thousand of our new security force troops. They were very successful in the Northeast, and parts of the south.

The security force Benson referred to had been secretly organized during the 1990's. It actually consisted of ten thousand men and women who were trained in civil unrest and police action. They had never been used till now. They had been used very successfully all over the United States since the collapse, especially in the north. Millions of people without power, food, or water packed FEMA camps. Those that didn't comply were handled by the military. That is until the military got tired of shooting it out with American citizens who wished to be left alone. What American troops were in the States had been relegated to border security, and patrolling of the empty streets of many American cities fighting roving gangs.

FEMA and the UN had been extremely surprised at how easy they had pulled millions of Americans into relocation camps. They used chemical attacks on large populations that refused to comply with their orders. These attacks were blamed on the Chinese, and Koreans who had been reeking havoc across the land, and conducting some chemical attacks of their own. Now all that was left were small isolated communities, usually located on the outskirts of medium and small cities. Soon Americans would be located in concentrated population centers, leaving vast portions of America empty. Those that did not comply would be dealt with, accordingly. The Nazi's had, had a brilliant plan for disposing of undesirables, of course more efficient methods had been developed, and with little or no press around it would go on undetected.

They had been used with great effectiveness backed by UN troops, mostly consisting Europeans. The UN troops had been sent by sea and unloaded at cities that had useable docks. They dressed in American BDU's. Many that witnessed the unloading of these troops thought they were American troops that had been recalled from foreign lands to help at home. Now more and more UN troops had been deployed and took care of serious incidents which the FEMA security forces were unable to handle.

Unknown to all but a few, the new President, John Engle had been imprisoned, his Secret Service detail killed. Engle was now being forced to rescind the order for American troops to come home. He refused at first. They killed his wife in front of his eyes. When told to cooperate again he still refused. They then raped his fourteen year old daughter in front of him. When that didn't work they killed her. When they told him the same would happen to his nine year old son Engle, now mentally broken and shattered relented, and complied. Soon America and her vast resources would be tapped into by the rest of the world, at least those that were represented by the Group.

Benson continued. "Well Byron, what are your plans to deal with Northwestern Alabama?"

"I recently returned from there Mr. Benson. We estimate there are approximately six-eight thousand people left in Lauderdale and Colbert Counties."

Benson interrupted his underling. "What was the total population before the collapse?"

Byron's face turned red, with anger when his boss interrupted him. The man was nothing more than a simpleton. He was holding a position above what his station in life should have been.

Byron calmed himself before speaking. "Total population for those two counties was approximately 140,000. Most of the population fled east to the Huntsville relocation camp, or to Birmingham here in central Alabama. Most of the remnants of the population are in the city of Florence or just on the outskirts."

"You said you had recently been in the area. What was the situation up there?"

"Well sir, we have been monitoring numerous radio transmissions from the area. They have a HAM radio operator set up. We have jammed his signal to help prevent him from gaining any information about the rest of the country. We have been unable to jam localized radio traffic in some instances.

When I surveyed the area we discovered a large ad hoc market set up. There were well over one thousand people in attendance. From radio intercepts, and intelligence reports this was the first of what is to be a weekly event. I advised them to pass the word to meet in two weeks where they will be gathered and relocated here."

Benson interrupted again. "Now Byron, that wasn't very smart. Now they will scatter to the four winds or not show up in two weeks."

Anger and contempt flooded through Byron again. After a short pause to control his voice he spoke. "Well sir that is not my intention. I feel the word will spread and more people will come to the next meeting to find out more information. I will be there with my security force to take this rabble into custody. Once this occurs I will unleash UN forces to round up the rest or dispose of them as necessary. I have devised a battle plan and it is being sent to you and a copy to the Group"

"Well done Byron. Why I doubted you could handle this I will never know. I want a report when your mission is completed. Don't fail Byron you know the Group will be watching." Benson hung up before Byron could respond.

Byron threw the receiver of the phone against his desk, sending papers and pens in all directions. "Fool! Of course I know they will be watching. When my time comes and I am placed in a station worthy enough for me you will be history."

Byron stood and stormed around his desk to stand before a full length mirror that was ever present in every office he had ever occupied. He fixed his hair, and then took in the sight that reflected back at him from the mirror. He looked dashing in his new uniform. He wore spit shined jump boots, and a crisp gray uniform of the FEMA security force. He had obtained four stars for each of the shoulder boards. Around his waist was a black leather belt supporting a holster which contained a Browning Hi Power.

Byron was impressed at how well he looked in the uniform. "Today I command Alabama, tomorrow America." He said to himself. Visions of the secret members of the Group appointing him to his proper station filled his mind.

Smartly spinning away from the mirror he pulled out his cell phone and pushed the autodial. "Thomas. Have the security force assembled. I want to address my force." Byron was pleased that he would not have to rely on National Guard troops now that he had his own to command.

"Yes sir." Thomas replied.

Byron hung up the phone and placed it back in his pocket. From the hat rack he pulled down a gray field cap adorned with four stars. He glanced back at the mirror one more time and smiled at himself. He then briskly made his way to the assembly area.

Colonel Haddock leaned back in the leather chair he occupied and snuffed out the cigarette he was smoking. "Sergeant, give me the recording of that conversation. Forget what you heard do you understand?"

The comm. Sergeant handed the Colonel the tape. "Yes sir."

"Call this satellite phone. Read the message once you get a response and cease communications. Be sure to remind the guys in signal to resume jamming the airwaves as soon as you are done. We don't need FEMA knowing what we are up to." Haddock stood and stretched. Pocketing the tape he left the communications room and headed for his office.

Once in his office Haddock unlocked the titanium suitcase which held his secure telephone. He pushed one button and awaited a response. The phone was answered on the second ring. "Hunter here, go ahead."

"This is Haddock. Our golden boy is set to go for Saturday. I have notified my field agent, and he will pass the word on to those in charge in the Florence area. I offered the golden boy a battle plan, and he snatched it up. He is advising his superiors it is his plan. That should help in concealing our involvement until the plan is in motion."

"Very well, let the idiot do his thing and then drop the hammer on them."

"Yes sir, Haddock out." Haddock hung up the phone and re-secured the suitcase. He then sat back and smiled, Loxley was going to get his, and then things would begin to change. With his old friend Dixon in place in Florence he knew he could trust him to organize the citizens there and from there everything would fall into place. FEMA and the UN would suffer and it would all start at his command in Florence. He had contacted Dixon after his visit to Florence and filled him in on where to place the civilian fighters for maximum effect.

Johan Dixon sat quietly in his small cabin reminiscing about the past, he absent mindedly wiped down his Colt 1911 with an oil rag. He was brought out of his revelry when his sat phone began to chirp. Laying the pistol down, he picked up the phone. "This is Shyster."

"The Eagle says the party is on for Saturday."

The phone went dead and Dixon tossed it on the bed. Dixon sat beside the phone and pulled up both pants legs of his flectar pants. He bent down and put on his boots and tied them up. He leaned forward and picked up the pistol off the nightstand and holstered it. He was going to do his boss's bidding as he had always done.

Johan Dixon had been an Army Ranger for ten years before leaving the Army for college and then on to law school, and finally an attorney in New York. He had served with Dixon in Desert Storm, and in operation Iraqi Freedom. He didn't spend much time practicing law. His old boss Colonel Haddock had offered him dozens of clandestine operations to make fast easy money.

Despite only reaching the rank of Colonel, Haddock was very powerful and well connected. He was placed in the National Guard as a cover. If anything was ever discovered, who would ever believe a National Guard Colonel would have the power to do the things he was in actuality in charge of. Even the liberal press wouldn't believe any reports of his involvement in clandestine operations. He was the man the Joint Chiefs came too when dirty work needed to be done and regular Special Ops units were not to be used. Johan Dixon was Haddock's favorite pick for these excursions. Dixon had only recently put all that behind him just before the collapse. When the collapse had occurred Haddock had contacted Dixon and advised him he may be needed.

Dixon strapped the bandoleer containing his extra rounds across his chest. He then picked up his beloved M-44 and headed out the door to spread the word. He would make his way to St. Florian, and then go and talk to Dr. Morrison, and his group. The Doctor seemed to know everyone in the area. He would be vital in getting people moving and defenses set up. They only had a few days to get it all done.

Little Benny sat on the front porch of Amos's house playing with some toys when he suddenly felt he was being watched. He stifled a scream when he saw the man standing not ten feet in front of the house. He calmed himself when he realized it was the man that had brought Celina, and Daphne's things to them at the big swap meet.

"Can I help you mister?"

"I understand Dr. Morrison lives in the area. I would like to speak to him."

"Hold on a second." Benny jumped up and ran inside.

A few moments later Amos stepped out on the front porch. He held a .44 revolver in his hand. "Howdy there mister, what can I do for you?"

"There is no need for that sir." Johan motioned at the pistol. "We met at the swap meet."

Amos looked at the man in silence for a few seconds and placed the revolver in his waistband, his arms crossed, right hand close to the butt of the pistol. "Never can tell now days, I understand you want to see Doc."

"I have some important information that I have received and need to pass along to Dr. Morrison."

"Why don't you pass it along to me and I will get it to him."

"I don't have a problem with that. You need to hear this too."

"Come on in." Amos stepped to the side and motioned for the door. Johan came up the steps and walked inside.

The two men sat opposite each other in the living room. Amos crossed his leg and lit his pipe. "Let's hear what you got to say fella."

"First off my name is not fella. I am Johan Dixon, and I understand your name is Amos Brown."

Amos nodded his head. "Sorry about my manners Johan. I've just gotten real wary of people lately. Please continue with what you were going to tell me."

Johan smiled at the man across from him. "Well I was out hunting this morning and got the scare of my life when I was surrounded by four men dressed in Army fatigues. They said they were a recon team sent up from Birmingham by that Colonel that was at the swap with that FEMA guy. They passed on some info on what kind of troops are coming up and how they are armed and where they will deploy when they get to the swap meet Saturday."

Amos pulled his pipe from his lips. "Well we already know them troops are coming. Is that all they told you?"

"Well they said it would not be military troops. It seems FEMA has some armed security forces of its own now. They also told me how they are going to deploy the security force when they get to St. Florian. We need to get people there now and set up proper defenses." Dixon went on to explain the plan FEMA had in place and how the recon team said things should be set up. He also told Amos that the citizens could expect some air support from the National Guard.

"Well I guess we can definitely alter the plan we came up with. Hell now we can really tear them a new one. Let's head over to Doc's." On the way over to Doc's Amos filled Johan in on the biker attack, and the tragedy that had befallen Doc.

Amos, Benny, and Johan pulled up in front of Doc's house. Bob and Joe sat on the front porch drinking glasses of water. There rifles rested within easy reach. Johan took in the bullet pocked walls of the dwelling. "You weren't exaggerating when you said there was a hell of a shoot out."

Amos introduced Bob, and Joe as the three men exchanged greetings. The five went inside where the others were waiting. Johan took the group in. He had talked with most at the swap meet, but didn't know their names except for Celina, Daphne, and Steve.

Steve offered Johan a seat. "Mr. Dixon, go ahead and fill us in."

Johan cleared his throat and began to tell his tale once again. Everyone grew excited when he mentioned air support from the National Guard. Steve quieted everyone down. "Johan you seem familiar with military jargon, from the way you described how the recon team told you to set up the defenses, it sounds like you have some military training. I thought you were an attorney."

"I did four years in the Army Reserve to help pay my way through college. I was in an infantry company in Huntsville."

"Well I suggest we get some gear and food loaded up. We have about seven hours of daylight left. We got to get this thing rolling or we will be caught with our pants down." Steve said as he stood.

"I will go ahead and start back that way. I will pass along the information to any I come across. Mr. Flynn and his son's have already started passing the word. I think we will have a good turn out for our surprise party." Johan smiled. He then turned towards Maude. He extended his hand and she took it. "I pray your husband recovers from his wounds Ms. Morrison. Give him my best." Johan said his goodbyes to everyone and headed back for St. Florian.

Chapter 40

Craig panned the darkness of the early morning hours with his thermal imager. The thermal imager was a hand held tool, similar to the FLIR system most people associate with police helicopters. Though the Florence Police did not have helicopters they did have several of the hand held thermal imagers. Craig had taken one as part of his share of the departments equipment when he and his fellow officers called it quits. It had come in handy several times, and saved him and Howard's bacon.

He lowered the imager and looked at his watch, 3:00 am. He put the imager back to his eye. He was trying to locate the sound of the voices he had heard for the third morning in a row. He couldn't make out what was being said. The voices had echoed through the empty streets and buildings of the college one hundred yards away. He and Howard had decided to check it out if it continued. They had to know if the people would become friend or foe.

"No luck." Craig turned off the imager to conserve power. Picking up his rifle Craig made his way to Howard's room. He tapped on the closed bedroom door. "Yo! Howard, get up."

A few seconds later a groggy Howard opened the door, a Glock 36 in his hands. "What, are ya scared again and want me to sit up and hold your hand?" Even half asleep Howard never missed a chance to throw a quick verbal jab at his friend.

"No, I've always known you were the ugliest fucker I ever met. I just had to be reassured about my judgment." Craig was just as quick to insult his friend at any given chance.

"Cut the bullshit. What have you got?" Howard said rubbing the sleep from his eyes.

"They're out..." Craig stopped speaking as the door behind him opened and he and Howard turned to look.

Don Savage stood with a small candle in his hand. His face still swollen, he looked like hell. "Look. I know you two are like sweethearts or something, but let's keep the pillow talk in the bedrooms." A smile cracked Don's battered face.

Craig turned and faced Don. "Sorry Don. Didn't mean to wake you."

"It's okay. I wasn't sleeping anyway. What's up?"

"There are people over near the campus again. I was going to get Howard up and go check them out. Are you up to going out with us?"

"Not this morning. I'm not one hundred percent yet. I may slow yall down. I'll go if you absolutely need me though."

Craig ran his fingers through his hair. "No. We're just going to check them out and then head back here."

"Yeah we're just going for a quick recon. You could however provide us with some cover fire if need be. I'll give you my FN with the night sight attachment."

"I can handle that." Don said as he absent mindedly reached down and scratched Red behind the ears with his free hand.

"Great. Just don't get any ideas about taking us out and taking this palace over for your own." Craig said with a friendly smile.

"You can never know what might go through a man's mind." Don said with a mischievous grin on his face as he turned back to his room to get dressed.

"Don't forget that Craig. Don and I have discussed what a pain in the ass you are. Place sure would be nice with just the two of us hanging out. There would be a lot of piece and quiet without you blabbering and drooling everywhere." Howard turned back to his room to get dressed himself.

Craig just shook his head. "See what happens when you give a couple of ingrates a place to live." He said to Howard's disappearing back. Craig went to his own room and began to don his gear.

The three met back in the hallway. Craig had replaced his rifle with his H&K UMP. He was wearing his police entry vest minus the Police emblems. Howard was armed as always with his FN, and was wearing an LBV. He handed the FN equipped with the night scope to Don.

"Well are we ready to do this? I'm ready to find out who those people are." Craig asked.

"I'm ready. I want to find out too. Let's hope they aren't a group of thugs. I really don't feel like getting shot at again for awhile." Howard answered.

"Will you two quit yakking and get the hell going before the sun comes up and you loose the darkness. You two are worse than a bunch of old women at the hair dressers."

Howard hefted his rifle on his shoulder. "I don't know if you can say that about me. Now this old hag is a different story." Howard patted Craig on the shoulder and walked downstairs, for the back door.

Craig and Howard moved swiftly and quietly through the debris field, and wall they had created. At the edge of the wall the two took a knee. Craig lifted the thermal imager to his eyes. He scanned the darkened campus looking for any signs of a threat. Then approximately eighty yards away he spotted two men moving across the campus towards one of the buildings. Both men were armed with long guns, though Craig couldn't quite make out what type of rifles they were. The two men disappeared into one of the buildings.

Craig scanned the tops of the buildings and windows for more threats. He found none, and lowered the imager. "We've got two armed men that just entered Rice Hall. I didn't see anything else."

"It looks like they've got an oil lamp or candles burning. How many do you think we are dealing with?" Howard asked.

"Shit, do I look like I have ESP or something? Let's go." Craig rose up and moved forward with Howard not far behind.

The two men moved in tandem stopping every ten yards or so when they could find cover and concealment. Craig would pan the area with the thermal imager looking for danger. The move to Rice Hall was met with no surprises.

Craig, and Howard moved slowly around the corner of the building, and then edged their way along the wall to the entrance way. Craig peered around the wall to the recessed glass doors and windows. Howard had been right. A lantern was sitting on the front desk. A man dressed in dark clothing sat with his feet on the desk and was smoking. The smell of marijuana hit Craig's nostrils. The man pinched out the joint and swung his feet to the floor. Then the pleas and sobs of a female's voice reached their ears.

Craig watched as the man at the desk stood, and reached down coming up with a sawed off shotgun. He walked around the desk and made his way to a doorway to the right. The man called out to someone deeper in the building.

"Yo man! Quit fucking with those bitches. You know the boss said not to touch them till after he had them." The man disappeared from view.

Howard edged around Craig. "Let's check it out man."

Craig grabbed his friends shoulder. "Just a recon man, we don't know what we're up against here." He said in a hushed voice.

"There is only one way to find out man." Howard pressed on past his friend bringing his rifle to his shoulder. Howard made his way to the open foyer doors, his rifle swinging back and forth looking for a target.

"Shit man, get back here." Craig said in a loud whisper. Howard continued to move forward. "Crap!" Craig moved to back his friend's movement.

Howard moved towards the open double doors that the guard had gone through. He slowly cut the pie and peered down the hall. The guard was approximately fifty feet down the hall. There were several lanterns that lit the way. The guard stood at another doorway talking to others. He couldn't make out what was being said.

Craig moved towards the doorway on the left. As he neared the other doors Craig heard footsteps coming from the hallway beyond. Craig stepped back against the wall and stood behind a large indoor plant to take cover. Before he could warn Howard of the coming threat the oncoming man stepped into the foyer. A pistol in his hand pointed at Howard's back.

"Hey! Who the hell are you?" The man said.

As Howard spun towards the new threat behind him he saw he would not be able to bring his gun to bear in time. "Damn. This was a stupid idea." He thought as he moved in an attempt to save his life. Suddenly two shots rang out, and Howard watched the man's head explode. As he turned fully around he saw Craig to his left, against the wall, his UMP at his shoulder.

"Thanks for the warning Craig."

"Let's get out of here before we get our asses shot up."

Howard was about to reply when he was cut short by the sound of a shotgun blast coming from the right hallway. Howard winced as he felt one of the 00 buck balls graze his right arm. The other deadly balls tore into the desk, doors, and walls. The distance had been too far for a total hit on Howard by the shotgun toting thug he had been watching.

Howard spun out of the kill zone, and planted himself against the wall. "Hell we're here Craig, we might as well go check out who they are holding." With that he spun back around the corner, his H&K 91 on full-auto. He fired an eight round burst down the hall at his would be killer. The man's body bucked as four of the .308 rounds tore into his upper torso. A second man stepped from the doorway that the downed thug had been standing at and fired an M-1 carbine at Howard. Howard dodged back around the corner to take cover.

Craig immediately moved to Howard's position. As soon as the man down the hall fired his last round, he stepped to the open doors exposing only a portion of his head, left shoulder, and arms. He had transitioned the UMP to fire left handed. He fired a two round burst catching the man with one round that hit his right hip. The man stumbled out further into the hall and exposed himself to the two friends. Craig charged forward, and in quick succession fired three rounds into the man's chest. The thug collapsed beside his dead partner.

Craig moved forward at a brisk pace along the right side of the hallway. "Cover my six Howard!"

"I got it! Howard shouted back over his shoulder, as he began walking backwards scanning for threats to their rear.

As Craig approached the open door, movement caught his attention. A man had just run across the room and pressed himself against the interior wall. Craig moved to the door, and stopped just at the threshold pressing his own body against the wall. Suddenly, an arm came through the door a pistol in its hand. The man inside the room had just made his last mistake, he telegraphed his movement.

Craig grabbed the man's wrist, jerking him forward into the open. As the man appeared Craig depressed the trigger on his sub-gun. Five rounds peeled through the man's clothing and flesh mincing the man's internal organs. Craig never stopped as the man collapsed forward onto his friend's dead body. Craig stepped over the bodies and entered the room.

The room was lit by several lamps; the only living things in the room were two nineteen or twenty year old women. They huddled arm in arm crying, and shaking with fear. Both women wore dirty jeans and t-shirts. Their faces and exposed arms covered with dirt, scratches, and bruises.

"If you two want to live, get off your asses and come on!" Craig shouted.

It only took a few seconds for the two women to realize this was their one chance to live. They scrambled to their feet and ran to Craig who was now waiting at the doorway. "Howard! I'm coming out with two women, is it clear?"

He was answered by the report of Howard firing four rounds from his H&K. Taking a quick peek around the wall Craig could see that Howard was on the opposite side of the hall one room down firing from the doorframe. Several shots came from down the hall and Craig could just barely make out the figures of several men.

Howard emptied his magazine. While he reloaded Craig put a steady stream of fire down to cover his friend. Once Howard reloaded he swung back into action and called out to Craig.

"Get them the hell out of here! Take the fire exit at the end of the hall!" He shouted as he began to fire again.

Craig looked back at the two women who now stood just feet from him, fear written all over their faces. "When I start to fire run for the fire exit do you understand?"

Both girls nodded, and Craig turned and placed his body just enough past the door frame to fire his weapon. As Craig pulled the trigger, he saw one of the men at the end of the hall go down from Howard's fire. The two women rushed past him.

Howard looked back to see the two women run for the exit. He yelled to Craig. "GO! GO! I'll cover." He turned to fire at the on coming men who had made it up to the front desk. Howard laid his sights on the lantern that sat on the desk. He ignored the rounds that smacked into the wall near his head, and zipped past his him.

Howard squeezed the trigger just as two men stood to fire. The .308 round struck the oil reservoir of the lamp. The round ripped the cheap metal reservoir to pieces. The lamp was flipped into the air, oil spraying out. As the lamp crashed down on the desk the glass globe shattered. The flame inside ignited the flammable liquid, causing a flashing fireball.

One of the two men was able to dive away from the flash, and saved himself from serious burns. His friend however was not so lucky. Oil had splashed on his face and chest. His head and chest were suddenly engulfed in flames. Howard didn't bother putting the man out of his misery as he thrashed on the ground. Maybe his cries of pain would make his friends falter. Howard searched out his friend with fire from his rifle. The big rounds blowing large chunks out of the sheetrock as Howard fired through the wall searching for the target.

Craig looked back as he ran down the hall to witness the man being engulfed in flames. He was spurred on though as rounds from the other men down the hall fired through the flames. He turned to see the two girls smash their way through the emergency exit door to the outside. He wasn't far behind.

As he crashed through the doors he almost ran over the two women. "Get against the wall!" The two women quickly complied.

Craig propped open the door with his leg and began to fire down the hall. The middle of the hall was on fire. Either Howard or the other group had shot the two lanterns on the wall. Flames and black smoke billowed to towards the ceiling and curled back down towards the floor.

Craig paused his firing to call to Howard. "Come on Howard! Move that skinny ass!" He fired another round dropping one of the men who was rushing down the hall past the flames. Howard fired off a six round burst then turned and ran for the door. Rounds snapped past his head as he ran. Some were Craig's the others were from the other group of men down the hall.

As Howard dove through the door past Craig a group of seven or eight men started to rush past the burning front desk. Craig depressed the trigger of his weapon emptying the last twelve rounds from the magazine out. Two of the men crumpled to the floor. The other men rushed past them some firing as they ran.

Craig jerked back as rounds slammed into the metal door. "Let's go!" Craig said as he grabbed one of the girls by the arm to pull her with them.

Howard pushed up from the ground. He turned and fired half of his remaining rounds in the magazine through the door in hopes of slowing the men down. He then turned to follow Craig and the two women.

The four had made it about thirty yards when they heard the heavy metal door slam open against the brick wall. With in seconds rounds flew by them and kicked up dirt around their feet as they ran. Howard and Craig zigzagged as they ran. The two girls had put themselves a few yards ahead of the heavily laden men.

Don perked up as he heard the first muffled shots being to echo through the empty night. He began to search the darkness for targets. He had familiarized Craig's and Howard's forms through the night vision scope as they left. He began to search for figures that didn't match their forms.

More shots rang out and Don began to shift nervously back and forth searching for any approaching danger. "Come on you guys, get your asses back here."

Then Don caught sight of two figures running toward him. They appeared to be female. He tightened the stock of the rifle to his shoulder. He slowed his breathing down, and put gentle pressure on the trigger ready to pull it at anytime.

Don released the pressure when he caught sight of what looked like Craig and Howard running behind the two females. The one he assumed was Craig stopped and turned. A flare of green light shot out of the muzzle of Craig's weapon. Don could also make out the rounds from their pursuers zipping through the air, looking like tiny green missiles through the scope.

Don lost sight of the four running figures as they disappeared behind the debris wall. Then not far behind he caught sight of several figures running and firing weapons.

Don rested the reticule of the sight on the closest figure. As he squeezed the trigger a green flash filled the scope. When the scope cleared the figure was down. Don began to methodically shoot one after another. After the fourth man dropped, the others turned tail and ran back in the direction they had come.

Don watched through the scope as Craig, Howard, and the two unidentified females made their way to the house. He then returned his attention to the surrounding area just to make sure no one else was near. When he heard the four make it to the front of the house he turned off the scope, and headed downstairs to the others.

Don made his way to the front living room. Howard was lighting a lamp, Craig paced back and forth. One attractive, and one unattractive plump woman stood in the center of the living room, both shaking with fear and adrenaline.

"That was the dumbest fucking thing I think I have ever seen you do Howard!" Craig said flailing his arms up and down.

"Don't sweat it Craig. I know you were scared and shit, but you made it out with my help. Plus you got to save two damsels in distress." Howard said waving a hand at the two women.

Craig plopped down in one of the plush Victorian chairs. "I didn't intend to leave them. I sure as hell would have preferred to come up with a plan to get them out instead of walking in like Wyatt Earp. Dumbest damned thing I have ever seen."

The pretty brunette walked up to him and leaned over and gave Craig a kiss on the cheek. "Not to dumb if you ask me. Thanks

Chapter 41

Steve turned from the fighting position that he was digging when he heard the footsteps approach behind him. "Hey Craig, and Howard, are yall coming to help dig in?"

Howard reached a hand out to help Steve out of the fighting position. "Not right now. I just brought by my MG-34 by for one of the machine gun pits. Craig and I have to head back to Florence and pick up more equipment."

Craig pulled a twig from between his lips before speaking. "Yeah numbnutz and I rescued a couple of college girls near the house. We've got to figure out where we stand with them, and what to do with them while we are here for the fight."

"Is Don here?" Steve asked

"No he stayed behind with the girls. He still isn't one hundred percent. He wants to be here for the ambush, but I don't think that will happen. He may have to wind up watching the house and girls."

Steve wiggled his eyebrows. "Damn all sick and pitiful and having to watch a couple of college co-eds. I think I would be saying I wasn't one hundred percent either." He said with a broad smile across his face.

"How is Doc?" Howard asked changing the subject from the girls.

"Maude has got him doped up pretty good. She said he will pull through in time." Steve replied

Craig shook his head. "I was hoping he would be in a lot better shape. I think when this thing kicks off we're going to need every person we can get with medical skills."

Howard duplicated Craig's thoughts. "These boys we may be going up against may be para-military police types, but they will be a lot better trained than about anyone we have."

"That's true, but we have the advantage of surprise." A voice came from behind the three men. They all turned to see the man in flectar camo pants, with the M-44.

"Oh shit, the man who tore me a new one on the trade." Howard said in a low voice.

"Tore you a new one my ass. That thing of yours has been torn by many a man on more than one occasion." Craig said punching his friend on the arm.

Steve stepped forward and shook the man's hand. "Craig, Howard, I would like you to meet our Ace in the hole. This is Johan Dixon." Craig and Howard shook the man's hand.

"Well as long as he negotiates and the other sides surrender I know we will come out on top." Howard said with a grin, as he thought back to how the man had negotiated him out of ammo at the big meet.

"Well Johan tell me why you are our Ace in the hole." Craig said.

"Let us walk while I show you what we've done, and I will tell you." The four men began to tour the ambush site.

"As you can see I have had the people set up numerous spider holes, and bunkers." He said as he walked sweeping his right hand out.

"How do you know this will be the best place for an ambush?" Craig asked.

"As I told Steve and the others I am former Army and have personal contact with Col. Haddock, the National Guard Commander for the remaining troops in Alabama. He has given Mr. Loxley, the FEMA Director for Alabama, and a battle plan. Loxley has accepted it and is forming his attack from those plans."

Howard interrupted Johan. "Well that is all well and good, but though we will have surprise, how will we be able to fight against so many well armed troops?"

Johan turned and smiled at Howard, then looked at Steve. "Is he one that can be trusted Steve?"

"Both of them can be trusted Johan. They will not tell everyone of the big surprise."

Johan nodded his head. "Very well, you see once the attack commences and Loxley has committed his forces Col. Haddock will enter the fight. He will start off his attack from the rear, destroying command and control of FEMA. He will use what is left of the Guards Apache-64's. The Apaches will then move forward and take on the actual ground forces. These strafing runs will be followed by a flight of Black Hawks that will deploy approximately five hundred infantry units. These units will push the FEMA units toward you civilians, basically a hammer and anvil tactic."

Craig let out a whistle. "That sounds pretty good. What happens after the battle? What happens with the state? Will the feds come in and mop the Guard units up? Surely they will not stand by and let that happen."

"I shouldn't be telling you this, but if I am killed the word must be spread after the battle. The remaining Guard and military units in the United States are planning to take control of the government, and return it to the proper civilian control. The recruitment of foreign troops, and un-Constitutional laws passed has been the last straws that have caused the military to take action."

"I don't know if I like the sound of that Johan." Craig said.

"What would you be saying if the military was just standing aside and letting this continue. I would imagine you would be mad as hell that the military wasn't casting off the yoke of these oppressors."

Craig thought for a second before replying. "Yeah I guess you're right, I would be."

Johan nodded with a smile. "That is what I thought. Let me show you where I would like you to set up that MG-34. We will be glad to have it. The Colonel was able to sneak us five of the old M-60D machine guns. Your MG-34 will be an added bonus for the killing field I have chosen." The men walked on amazed at the flurry of activity, and set up of the ambush site.

"Johan since you have communications with the Army do you know how the rest of the country and world are?" Howard asked.

Johan stopped and leaned against an old oak tree. "I have received several reports from the Colonel. Most of our troops fighting in Korea have been killed or captured. Apparently the Koreans had a few tactical nukes. They used these to destroy most of our men who had stopped the advance of the North Koreans into the south.

The Chinese are effectively out of the fight. Their population has been cut down to approximately one billion. The government ordered a complete nuclear attack against the Chinese. They hit every major city and military installation in the country. The attacks were carried out by our submarines.

The Mid-East is in complete turmoil. The Israelis got pushed into a corner by the Arabs. They had more nukes than we knew about. Most of Iran, Syria, Egypt, and Jordan are glass parking lots. We won't be getting any oil from there for a hundred years or more. The Israelis however have managed to stabilize the immediate region of Israel. Our troops stationed in Iraq and Saudi Arabia have moved to Israel."

"What about Europe?" Craig interrupted.

"Well the Europeans have turned on themselves. Russia is trying to take back all of the old Soviet bloc countries. Nukes have been used very conservatively by all who possess them. England is holding strong, but the French were able to nuke London. Paris was nuked in return by the English. They have entered a cease fire.

The German's are trying to redo what Hitler did during WWII. They pretty much have accomplished most of it too. Now the Russians and Germans are starting to butt heads.

The Australians and Japanese are starting to bump heads. The Nips have done the same thing the Germans have. They are conquering all the small islands and countries they did during WWII.

Central and South America is almost an unknown, many radio intercepts reports a blood bath going on in every country. Everyone is trying to snatch power. Mostly it is turning into little fiefdoms run by warlords."

"What about the Koreans and Chinese located here in the states?" Craig asked.

"Apparently all the units left have banded together and met up in the mid-west. They killed anyone they came across. They offered any Asian an opportunity to join them or die. Naturally most Asians they have run across have joined them. Their estimated strength has swelled to about eight thousand actual Korean and Chinese troops, and about twelve thousand people that have joined them. They have been armed with captured weapons from civilians and overrun Guard and other military units."

"Has the Colonel said what they intend to do about them?" Steve asked.

"Right now parts of Missouri, Nebraska, and Kansas have been written off for the time being. Apparently the Chinese, and Koreans had some biological, and nerve agents left, and used them on dozens of medium size cities, and relocation centers when they entered the area to reduce the population near their new area of operation. Those states will be cleared when most of the south and eastern seaboard are repatriated under Constitutional law.

The southwest is a major battle ground between Mexicans and other Hispanics flooding those states. The area is in total chaos. The military is still operating in small bands, but most of the fight is being carried on by the citizens of those states. They are not fairing well at this time. The western portion of the United States will be the last to be repatriated.

Alaska has been invaded by the Russians and no one has heard much from the state since the invasion. The Japanese have invaded and taken Hawaii. One sub was deployed to take care of Japan. Tokyo and Hiroshima were nuked by the sub. However the sub was sunk by the Japanese navy. The Pacific Fleet, or what is left of it is headed for Hawaii but it is unknown if they will be able to take the island back, all U.S. forces on the island have been killed or captured."

"Damn! It sounds like we have our work cut out for us." Craig said.

Johan nodded in agreement then continued to give a little more information. "Once the eastern seaboard and the south are secured the military is going to help train volunteer citizen militia units to help stabilize the rest of the country. The central northern states will be next on the list to re-patriot."

Steve asked the next question. "Well how are they fairing?"

"Well Steve they are in pretty much the same boat as Alabama. There are hundreds of relocation centers, many of the larger cities were hit with biological and nerve agents. There is a lot more chaos and mayhem going on than here in the south. Special Forces troops have been dropped in to help start a functional fighting force to help return those states to some semblance of order. It is going to be a long tough road."

"Damned woman, Quit treating me like a three year old. I can get up and go to the bathroom on my own. I don't need to piss in a bottle." Doc said in a weak, but defiant voice.

Maude gently pushed her husband back down, with little effort. She then yanked his pajama bottoms down and held up the bedpan. "Herbert Morrison, I will personally stick a catheter in that little friend of yours if you don't quit trying to get out of bed. Now do your business in this bedpan or things will not go well for you."

The look in Maude's eye told Doc he had better back down, or things that didn't need to have objects stuck in it would have something there in seconds. "Alright, alright, just get the hell out of here so I can piss in peace."

"Herbert, you had better watch your filthy mouth. There are two girls in this house that don't need to hear such language. On top of that you are a doctor, so use the proper terminology. The word is urinating." Maude turned to leave the room and give her husband some privacy.

"I sure will watch my mouth. I will do that while I piss in this pan. Damn old bitty." Doc said in a low hushed voice.

The door cracked back open just as Doc began to relieve himself. He about peed on his legs and the bed when Maude's voice reached his ears. "I heard that Herbert. Remember what I said." Maude closed the door.

"Shit! Can't even talk in my own house."

"I heard that too!" Maude's muffled voice came from down the hall.

"Damn woman must have bat ears." Doc said in an even lower voice.

Maude made her way downstairs to the basement where Daphne and Celina were organizing Doc's examination room. "Girls have you got all the medical supplies organized and set up."

Celina looked up from the pile of blankets she had just stacked. "Yes, Mrs. Morrison. We are about ready to take up the stuff to the make shift ambulance Amos is rigging up."

Maude began to look over the items that had been set up. She was pleased with how well the two girls had followed her instructions. "To bad things have gone to pot, you girls would make wonderful RN's." Both girls beamed with pride.

Then the three started picking up items to take up stairs to Amos and the make shift Ambulance that he and the machinist John Anderson had constructed out of one of the pickups.

Amos tested the last rack by laying down on it to see if it would hold his weight. "It looks like it's going to hold John." He said as he got up and hopped down.

"Good deal. I wasn't sure about your idea but it looks like it will work." The big burley bearded man said.

He and Amos had taken one of the trucks that had a ladder rack on it. They welded make shift gurney's attached to the rack, two on the outside of the rack on each side. They also put one on each side of the inner portion of the rack. The idea was not comfort, but to be able to transport as many of the wounded one the truck as possible.

The group had decided they would transport the wounded from the ambush site to Doc's because of the medical supplies and Doc's examination room would serve well as a mini ER. Though it would be a mile and a half drive no one wanted the FEMA troops to be able to fire on a front line field hospital. Being able to work without coming under fire would allow Maude and her chosen retired RN's the ability to work without the worry of death or injury.

Amos turned to see the girls and Maude coming from the house with an armful each of medical supplies. "Yall need some help?" He called.

"It's not going to get in the truck by itself." Celina said playfully.

"No rest for the weary." John said walking to the house to help out.

⊹╞══╡⊹

Byron Loxley looked up as he heard the rap on his office door. "Enter!" He ordered.

A FEMA Security Force Trooper entered wearing a starched urban camouflaged uniform; an MP-5 was strapped across his back. "Sir, we have contact with our operative in the Florence area. He is standing by for you now."

Byron spun the large leather chair around to face the credenza behind him. "Leave." He said harshly.

With a one finger salute to his commander's back the trooper turned to leave closing the door behind him. Byron pushed the hidden release button under the lip of the top of the credenza opening a hidden compartment that contained an encrypted radio. "This is Loxley. What do you have to report?" He said into the Mic.

"Sir, I have located where the insurgents have a field hospital. Here are the coordinates." The man on the other end rattled off the GPS coordinates of Doc's home.

Loxley wrote the coordinates down. "Do they intend to fight or give up?" He asked.

"It only appears twenty to thirty will fight. No fortifications have been set up; they intend to fight from the grocery store where people will be gathering to trade. It is their belief your troops will not fire into the unarmed crowd." The voice said.

"Well they are in for a surprise. Have you identified the leaders yet?"

"Yes sir. I will terminate them as your troops arrive."

"Very well carry on with your mission, and let know of anything suspicious. I want these people placed in the camps, and the resistors crushed."

"Yes sir." The man signed off.

Loxley replaced the radio and smiled. According to his agent little or no resistance would be put up. It would be a triumph for him to report to his leader about crushing the fighters and capturing hundreds of refugees, and placing them in camps. He would of course inflate the number of insurgents killed. It would be wonderful if he took no casualties and reported his men, under his leadership of course, were able to kill several hundred insurgents. He would have to get up with his public relations people. He would have them move the bodies into different spots to look like there were more killed than actually were. The pictures would be quiet impressive in his power point briefing to them.

Two hundred miles away in St. Florian, Johan turned the radio off. He hated to have given the coordinates for the doctor's residence, but he had to give the man something or he would become suspicious of the small amount of information he had given him already. "Well, sacrifices must be made." He said to himself.

Chapter 42

Byron Loxley opened his sleep filled eyes and blinked them trying to block out the bright sunlight that came through his window. Rolling away from the morning light Loxley rubbed the sleep from his eyes. "Who in the hell opened those curtains" he thought to himself sourly.

His mood immediately brightened though when he realized today was the day. He would lead his troops into battle and crush the resistance in North West Alabama. Rolling onto his back he stretched his arms and legs enjoying the feel of the satin sheets and soft bed. As he tucked his hands behind his head to think about the glory he would win this day a small arm and leg came across his chest and waist.

Momentarily he was surprised until he looked down at the sleeping form of the young girl he had, had brought to him from the relocation camp. His mood shifted again at being snuggled by the harlot. Using his left arm and leg he gave a heft shove to the sleeping young girl.

"Get out of my bed slut!" The girl, no more than one hundred pounds, and five feet tall was shoved from the bed and onto the hard marble floor.

Her nude body made an audible slapping sound as she hit the floor as she let out a yelp of surprise. Sitting up and rubbing her head where it had hit the floor she looked up at him. "What the hell did you do that for?" She said with a look of fear and confusion on her face.

"Get up and get the hell out of here." He fired back at her.

The girl slowly stood and made her way towards the bed to retrieve her clothes that lay scattered on the bed. "Just let me get my clothes and I'll leave."

Loxley sat up quickly, his hand lashing out like a coiled snake as he snatched her wrist and squeezed hard against the fragile girl. "If I wanted you to have your clothes I would have ordered you to get them. I however told you to GET THE HELL OUT!"

He slung the girls arm away from him. He relished his power over people, especially the defenseless ones like this girl. The tears that rolled down her cheek only strengthened his belief that he was one of the people at the top of the food chain. He had the right and privilege to control those of lesser mentality, and ability like the useless eater before him.

The girl clutched her now bruised wrist to her breast and turned and fled from the room. Loxley reached behind him and fluffed the satin pillows behind him. Resting back he took a calming breath, satisfied with the way he had handled the young slut. To think she wanted to snuggle up against the most powerful man in Alabama. She was nothing more than something for his amusement. He would have one of his aids send her back to the camps.

Once Loxley got comfortable he picked up the small hand held radio that lay by his bedside. "Harvey. I'm ready for my breakfast. Also bring me my battle uniform, laptop and papers." He said in a condescending, and arrogant manner to his servant.

"Yes sir. I will be in immediately." The voice of his personal attendant crackled back through the small speaker.

Within a few minutes Harvey entered the bedroom. His right hand supported a silver dinner tray, and a silver covered dish. His uniform, a white jacket, black pants, and white gloves were impeccably pressed, and groomed. Harvey walked with a certain grace while carrying the tray. He had worked for years in some of the finest hotels as a waiter, and knew how to put on a show for arrogant and wealthy customers. Harvey was an educated black man but for the sake of the upper crust he had always poured on the southern black accent. It had always seemed to get him bigger tips.

"Your breakfast is served sir." Harvey said as he expertly brought the tray down and rested it across Loxley's lap. As the tray came to a rest he simultaneously used his left hand to lift the silver dish cover revealing Loxley's breakfast. He then poured Loxley a cup of coffee from a small silver pot that was also on the tray.

"Will there be anything else sir?"

Loxley looked at Harvey with disdain, and loathing. "Didn't I tell you to bring in my battle uniform, computer, and papers you fucking idiot." Loxley said in a low voice.

"Yes sir you did. I will retrieve those items immediately." Harvey gave polite bow and turned and walked from the room his face still a calm blank mask. "What did the son of a bitch want me to do balance the computer on my head, shove papers in my mouth, and drape the uniform over my other arm? Hope the son of a bitch takes a bullet in the head from one of them deer hunting bubba's up in Florence today." Harvey thought to himself.

Loxley began to eat his breakfast his mind churning over his victory speech that he would give to his superiors. After several sips of coffee, and several bites from his eggs, and caviar Harvey returned to the room Loxley's computer and papers under one arm, his uniform hanging from a hanger in his other hand.

Harvey laid the uniform at the foot of the bed. He then walked to the opposite side of the bed from Loxley and placed the laptop and his papers next to him. "Will there be anything else sir?"

Loxley looked Harvey in the eyes and then back down at his half empty coffee cup. "Do you think it will fill itself?" "Damn what a worthless black piece of trash." Loxley thought.

"Please forgive me for my inattention sir." Harvey said in his best southern drawl as he circled the bed to fill the coffee cup.

Loxley held up the morning reports with one hand and began to read them Harvey already out of his thoughts. As he read and Harvey poured his coffee he reached down for his cup of coffee. Instead of grabbing the cup his hand went directly into the scalding liquid that poured from the spout of the coffee pot.

His hand jerked away, and his body involuntarily jerked at the pain that emitted from his now burned hand. The food tray was knocked to the marble floor with a resounding crash, food and coffee scattered across the floor. "You stupid NIGGER, look what you did!" Loxley screamed his hand clutched to his chest, much the same way the young girl had done just minutes before.

Harvey knew he was in big trouble. He didn't dare say what he felt. The enraged man before him could send him back to the camps.

"My apologies sir, it was my fault. Please forgive me." Harvey said his southern drawl disappearing into his normal speech as fear coursed through him.

"Get your black ass out of here before I have you shot for assault on a government official."

"Yes sir!" Harvey said as he spun around and almost ran from the room.

"Shit! What the hell else can go wrong today?" He said as he rolled off the opposite side of the bed.

Loxley changed the channel on his hand held radio as he walked towards the bathroom to run cold water over his injury. He keyed the radio as he entered the bathroom. "Stefan! Stefan! Get your ass in here now!" Loxley ordered and then tossed the radio on the vanity.

Minutes later Stefan came into the bathroom breathing heavily, since he had ran up two flights of stairs to Loxley's penthouse suite. "Sir what happened?"

Loxley looked up in the mirror at Stefan as he held his hand under the cold water spewing from the faucet. "That stupid black bastard you recommended to be my servant poured coffee all over my hand."

"I'm so sorry sir. That is not like Harvey at all. He was the head waiter at one of the hotels I used to eat at and had always been very competent. I will reprimand him immediately, and get someone in here to clean this mess up." Stefan said.

Loxley let his hand run under the cold water a bit longer, letting his underling sweat bullets as he waited for his reply. He then took a cold wet washcloth and wrapped the hand. As he finished wrapping it he turned to face Stefan.

"You won't reprimand that worthless piece of filth; you will haul his ass back to the camps. I want his ass on a truck for the shittiest work detail you can find. I then want you to find that little slut you sent up here and send her with him. Make sure it is a very dangerous work party. You will then find me a descent servant befitting someone of my station in life. He had better be top notch and here in the morning or you may find yourself on that truck with Hardy." Loxley's speech was slow, methodical, and laced with venom.

"Yes sir and the man's name is Harvey." Stefan sputtered.

"I could give two hoots in hell what his name is. Get rid of him and get me some descent help. Now get the hell out of here while I bath."

Stefan, unlike Harvey, didn't try to maintain his composure he ran from the room. He knew if he didn't find someone as competent as Harvey he would be on that same truck.

Loxley strode purposefully towards the podium. His grey battle dress uniform was starched and pressed. The creases appeared like knife blades. His Cochran Jump Boots were spit shined. The only thing out of place on the impeccable FEMA Director was his hand which was bandaged in gauze. Despite this minor flaw in what he considered one of his finest moments he was pleased at how dashing he knew he appeared to the men before him.

The men before him numbered one thousand. They were lined up in blocks of forty, ten men per row, four deep. Behind them the Black Hawk helicopters that would fly them to the Florence area sat menacingly. A brief flash of an old movie came to mind. He almost felt like Darth Vader looking over his storm troopers in one of the Star Wars Movies. He had always wanted the Empire to win when he watched it. In the movie the Empire was all powerful, just as the group of men he represented would soon be. Unlike the movie however, the rebels would loose in the real world. How could they even think of standing up against a force like the one he commanded? He was disappointed that there were not more men here to hear his speech, but due to logistics the trucks that would carry the survivors back from Florence to the Birmingham camps had to leave the day before with reinforcements.

After what Loxley felt was a sufficient enough pause he began his speech. He gave a stirring speech if you were into listening to what a great leader he was. Loxley went on for over an hour until one of his aids stepped forward and whispered in his ear about the time table. Loxley ended his speech and told the men he would personally lead them into battle. The men gave the expected cheer, and were then ordered to their waiting helicopters.

Loxley had to control his excitement and walk calmly to his helicopter. He had to give the appearance that this was nothing new to him. He had watched numerous videos of different military leaders and tried to imitate their posture and how they carried themselves when in front of their troops.

Once in the chopper Loxley buckled and signaled to the pilot to take off. The bird lifted into the air and began to circle the field below. Loxley looked on with excitement as the helicopters in his contingent lifted threateningly into the sky. A smile was pasted across Loxley's face. His bleached teeth shone in the midday sun. This was going to be the finest day of his life. The day where he knew after it was complete, he would be offered a position within the inner circle.

Chapter 43

Craig finished buckling his gun belt on. Reaching over to the night stand he picked up the Glock 22C and press checked the weapon to insure a bullet was in the chamber. Seeing the silver glint of the shell casing he released the slide, and dropped the magazine to ensure he had fifteen rounds in the magazine. He slapped the magazine back into the magazine well, and holstered the pistol.

Today he and Howard were going to take the girls out and give them some more shooting lessons. Don was still out of action and could just barely get around the house and yard. The two college girls, Ann Harvey, the pretty brunette, and Shelly Polk, her chunky friend, were not going to participate in tomorrow's ambush of the FEMA troops. The three men had decided the two girls needed all the training they could get when it came to self defense, and scavenging. The girls had nowhere else to go and it was voted they would stay. The operation would grow and so would their ability to gather more goods for trade.

Both girls turned out to be pretty good shots with both pistols and rifles. Ann carried a Browning Hi-Power, and an AR-15 shorty. Shelly was armed with a Glock 26 and a full size AR-15. The past few days had been spent showing the girls how to properly clear a structure, shoot, combat reloading, and various other practical shooting exercises. Today he and Howard were going to practice with them on urban movements, and go over the hand signals the girls had been learning at night.

Craig made his way downstairs followed by Meat. The aroma of cooking eggs, and bacon reached his nose as he walked downstairs.

Meat also smelled the food and almost knocked Craig over as he quickly passed him heading for the kitchen.

Entering the kitchen he saw that everyone was already eating. Shelly stood over the Coleman camp stove whipping up another batch of scrambled eggs. Red sat on her haunches, pleadingly staring at the woman in hopes of some scraps. Meat had stationed himself between Howard and Ann. Meats head turned looking from one to the other in hopes of a few morsels of food.

"Bought time you got your lazy carcass out of bed." Howard said as he chewed his food.

Craig took the plate that was piled high with bacon, eggs, and toast from Shelly and turned to sit at the table. "Well if I didn't have to carry your load of work most of the time I wouldn't be so damn tired."

Don took a sip of his coffee and put the mug back on the table. "Can you two go just one day without talking crap to one another?"

Ann smiled lovingly at Craig. "I think it is cute, and Craig is such a hard worker."

Craig smiled at Ann then looked at Howard and stuck out his tongue. "See now we know who does most of the work around here. Don acts like he is disabled so he can be waited on by our two pretty new friends. Howard, I never understood how someone who was mentally challenged was allowed to run a half ass gun store operation."

Soon everyone was good naturedly ribbing one another. The meal ended and everyone stood to help clean up. All the while they talked and joked. Soon the kitchen was clean and the dogs lay happily in the floor their bellies full of the scraps given to them by everyone.

Don started limping his way out of the kitchen. "Okay, fun time is over kids. Let's get to the living room and discuss today's training for the girls."

Once Don and the girls were seated in the living room he began to go over the hand signals. Both girls advised what sign they saw and what action should be taken. Meanwhile Craig and Howard unrolled a large tube of paper. They had salvaged the paper from the local high schools art department. Craig and Howard had spent hours diagramming every building and stalled car in the surrounding area. They intended to mark out a path the girls were to take.

Craig and Howard rolled out the map. They went over the route with the girls and told them that even though this was an exercise they were to keep vigilant for actual threats. Craig and Howard would be observing their movement and provide over watch against any threats while they graded how the girls did.

"Have ya'll got it?" Howard asked.

Shelly nodded her head, and looked at Ann, who nodded. "We got it sugar britches." She said with her light brown pony tail bouncing up and down as she shook her head in understanding.

Ann looked up from the map at the three men in the room. "Guys we really appreciate you teaching us how to survive. I guess things won't be the same again for a long time. Hell if it ever is, it will be amazing."

"Not a problem Ann. Now Red and I will go upstairs to the lookout and watch your back from there." Don hobbled from the room, cinching up his gun belt as he left the room.

"Okay let's do this thing lady." Craig said putting his hand out for Ann to take as she stood.

The advance team for the FEMA convoy consisted of eight Hummers. One was a command vehicle that sprouted numerous antennas. One had MK19 automatic grenade launcher mounted up on the top. The others had FN 240 7.62 machine guns mounted on top. The commander of the scout party scanned the O'Neal Bridge below and ahead of his team. The man took the Kevlar helmet from his head and ran his fingers through his dirty hair, and let out an exhale of breath. The trip up from Birmingham hadn't been too bad. They had only hit a few pockets of resistance along the way.

The Cullman exit on Interstate 65 had been a tickler though. The folks had set up a hasty ambush that almost worked, if it had not been for an observant machine gunner things would have taken a turn for the worse. He was still pissed that Loxley had not allowed any helicopters to follow the convoy. An eye and gun in the sky would have changed the whole trip. The ambushers were well armed but their hastily built bunkers could not withstand the 40mm grenades fired by the MK19. Once their backs had been broken he sent the team forward like a pack of rabid wolves, and finished off everyone still breathing.

He felt bad about killing the wounded and those that tried to surrender. But on the other hand Loxley had made sense when they were told those that still held out were worse than the people who had brought on the destruction of his country. They refused to comply with the orders of the government and turn themselves, food, water, and valuables in for the greater good of the country. Who did these people think they were? They were offered food, shelter and health care. Instead they wanted to horde their property and keep the government from helping those less fortunate. No, the more he thought about it the better he felt about what he had done and ordered done.

Now he had to make a choice. Backtrack to 2nd Street and head for the Patton Island Bridge, or Wilson Dam Bridge that would lead directly towards the area of this so called meet. He felt it would be necessary though to cross the O'Neal Bridge that led into downtown Florence. If there were any stragglers or members of the resistance in the downtown area he would be in deep trouble if he had not cleared anything to the convoy's rear.

The young man in the driver's seat looked over at the commander. "So what it is going to be Sir?"

The commander rubbed his eyes and looked wearily at the young man. "Take us in over the O'Neal."

The driver started forward, and the commander reached for the radio. "Team One, we will clear the area of downtown Florence." He paused for a second as took a quick glance at his map. "Just do a cursory search of the area and remain mounted. We will converge at Wood Ave., and Tennessee St. Wood Ave. eventually hits Cox Creek Pkwy. This will allow us to travel to Alabama 17, or Chisholm Rd. This will lead us to the St. Florian area. Command out."

All the team members acknowledged the order. Men straightened out their LBV and checked their weapons to ensure they were loaded. The scout party slowly crossed the bridge scanning for danger. After a slow tedious drive avoiding decaying bodies and abandoned cars the scout party entered Florence. As they reached the city proper the vehicles split up in different directions and began to search the dead city. The only living things they saw were a few packs of roving dogs, birds of various species that still fed on the carcasses of the former residents who once occupied the once prosperous city.

"Damn sir! This place has been torn to peaces. I was here a couple of years ago and this place was a really clean city."

"Obviously it wasn't as clean and wholesome as you thought. That is why we are here now to clean out the rats that remain here. Now shut up and quit sight seeing. Look for rebels." The commander said with a look of disgust that the peon next to him would bother him with such trivial crap.

"Rover Two to Command, I've got movement at..." There was a pause as the trooper oriented himself. "It will be near Tuscaloosa St. and Wood Ave."

Craig and Howard lay on their bellies watching the two women through binoculars. Craig lowered his and looked over at Howard. "So what's up Sugar Britches?"

Howard never lowered the binoculars. "Shut the hell up you jealous pig. In a matter of a few weeks they will both be mere putty in my hands. You know women have never been able to resist me." Howard lips turned into a grin beneath the binoculars.

Craig snickered as he lifted the binoculars back to his eyes. "The only reason women have ever been putty in your hands is because your ass stinks so bad they collapse. Then you have your way with them after they are unconscious."

They gazed through the glasses and watched the two girls move, using hand signals to communicate. The girls were catching on pretty good. A few more weeks of training and they would be a worthy adversary for the average thug around these parts.

Shelly eased forward and looked around the corner of the pile of rubber they were taking cover behind using a small dental mirror Howard had given her. Things looked clear she turned to give Ann the all clear sign and stopped when she heard the sounds of a diesel engine.

She rose up a bit to peer over the pile of rubble. Ann's hand shot out and grabbed Shelly by the leg. She too had heard the rumble of a diesel motor. In a hushed voice Ann called out to Shelly. "Get down! You heard what Craig said. There are still thugs out here. Get your radio and call them and see what they want us to do."

Shelly jerked her leg free. I've got to see what it is before I go telling them we stumbled on to something." Shelly made her way up the rock pile a little higher.

She peered over the top of the pile to see a gray colored Hummer. A man wearing grey battle uniform and Kevlar helmet sat behind a machine gun mounted on top of the vehicle. "Soldiers!" Shelly said back to Ann. "We can go to one of the camps and be taken care of without having to learn all this stuff."

Ann scrambled to try to pull Shelly back down as her friend scrambled to the top of the pile. The FRS on Shelly's hip fell at Ann's knees. Ann's shaking hands fumbled for the radio to call Craig or Howard.

Shelly reached the top of the pile. She raised her arms above her head and waved them back and forth. She had totally forgotten about having the AR-15 that she clasped in her right hand. "Over here! Over here!" She shouted at the top of her lungs, and bounced up and down on the balls of her feet.

Howard rose to one knee trying to get a better look at what Shelly was doing. Craig panned the surrounding area seeing nothing but burned out buildings and piles of debris. "What the hell is she doing Howard?"

"Hell I don't know I can't see over the rock pile she is standing on." Howard said in a frustrated voice.

Then Ann's voice, filled with fear crackled over the radio's on their LBV's. "Shelly said there are soldiers out there. She is trying to get their attention. I told her to get down but she won't listen. What do I do? What do I do?" she cried.

Craig got on the radio first. "Stay crouched down and get the hell out of there."

"This is Rover Two to command, over."

"Go ahead Rover Two, over."

"I have one female on a rock pile, obviously a rebel or sympathizer. She is armed with M-16. What are your instructions? Over."

"Two, take her out! All other units converge on his location now." The commander put the mike back in its holder and turned to the driver. "Move your ass boy! You heard the order!" The commander was pushed back into the hard seat as the driver pushed the pedal to the floor.

As Ann rose from the ground into a crouch she looked one last time at Shelly before running with all her might. She was spurred on by the image of her best friend being torn to pieces as large caliber bullets ripped through her flesh. For an instant of a second time stopped and Ann saw a fine pink mist floating around Shelly's head as it exploded from one of the bullets that had been fired at her. She forgot all about crouching and stood running full speed towards the house.

Howard dropped the binoculars to the ground as he fumbled for his FN. "Holly shit they killed her." He began to run forward but Craig stopped him.

Craig stood unlimbering his UMP .40. "Stay smart friend they have us out gunned we need to come in behind them. They are going for Ann."

Howard turned to see Ann running back towards the house at full speed. Dirt shot up like geysers around her feet. Chunks of concrete debris turned into white chalky clouds as the bullets whipped past her.

Craig and Howard ran at an angle away from the direction Ann was running. They took cover behind a torn down cinder block wall. The big grey hummer came plowing around the rock pile Shelly's blood and body now covered. Craig raised the UMP to take out the gunner whose back was now to them.

Howard pushed Craig's barrel down with his left hand as his right brought the FN to his shoulder. "Mine." He said in an icy tone. Once his left hand gripped the fore end of the rifle Howard pulled the trigger, the FN was switched to full auto. Howard road out the big bore bucking rifle as he emptied the twenty round magazine into the exposed gunner. The man collapsed forward over the machine gun.

Craig raised his radio to his lips. "Don you there?"

Craig was answered by report of a large boom that came from the direction of his house. Don had gotten the Rhino .50 caliber out and fired at the on coming Hummer. The hummer's hood exploded open as the thumb sized HE round slammed through it and into the engine. The hummer came to a stop, steam pouring from the engine compartment.

The back doors to the hummer opened and two grey clad FEMA troopers came jumping out with pistols in hand. Craig took his time and deliberately placed the site picture on each man's head as he pulled the trigger. Both men collapsed to the ground one on top of the other. The driver stepped out rifle in hand feverishly trying to work the bolt to chamber a round. Howard had reloaded by this time and smoothly took the young trooper out. The passenger in the front seat leaned out of the window, a Berretta 92 in his hands, flames shooting forth from the muzzle. Howard put a three round burst into the man's chest.

As the two men surged forward the roar of more diesel engines came to them from the distance. "We got to beat feet Howard!" Craig said as he ran.

"What the hell does it look like I'm doing?" Howard said as his long legs carried him ahead of Craig of the debris filled yards and streets.

The two made it to the gate where Ann was frantically trying to open the gate and get inside. Tears rolled down her dirt smudge cheeks as she sobbed. Howard unceremoniously bumped her out of the way and opened the gate. He turned and grabbed Ann by the hand. "Let's go Ann!" The three made their way into the house.

The recon commander pulled up next to the large debris pile and got out as the other hummers pulled up. One of the troopers ran up to him, his rifle at the ready. "What are your orders sir?" The young man said eagerly wanting to prove himself in his first firefight.

The commander pointed to the debris pile. "Get up there and see what is going on."

The young trooper scrambled up the debris mound. As he neared the top the commander shouted out a warning to him. "Keep your damn head down man!" Just as his words left his mouth the young troopers head exploded. The report of what the commander knew was a fifty caliber reached his ears a second later.

Craig ran towards the stairs as he heard Don shoot. Climbing the stairs two and three at a time he made it to the improvised watch tower. "What have you got Don!" He shouted noticing the ear muffs on Don's head.

Don turned his head and as he pulled one of the muffs from his left ear. "Got at least six hummers out there. I disabled one, and shot one trooper."

"Damn! That isn't good news." Craig said as he tried to calculate how many they would have to fight. It would be tough to fight a highly mobile heavily armed group of men.

"Well friend it just gets worse. All of them but one has a machine gun mounted up top. That isn't what worries me though. It's the one with the MK19 that gives me the willies."

"Can you see them?" Craig asked as he took a knee beside Don.

"No. They're behind that pile where Shelly bought it." He placed his cheek back on the stock of the rifle. "Hold on got something." He said as he adjusted his position a bit and brought the muff down over the exposed left ear. Craig plugged his ears with his fingers waiting for the explosion of the rifle going off and the concussion that would follow if Don fired again.

The commander ordered the hummer with the MK19 forward. "See where they went and blow them to hell."

The hummer eased around the pile slowly. The grenade gunner swiveled the big grenade launcher back and forth searching for a target to destroy.

Don let the hummer come fully around the pile before getting ready to shoot. As the gunner turned the barrel of the MK19 away from their position Don fired. He had centered the crosshairs on the receiver of the big gun firing an HE round. The round struck the receiver with tremendous force. The impact destroyed most of the inner workings of the big gun. When it did the detent pins that hold the back plate on were destroyed. The recoil springs shout out the back taking the back plate, and handles with it. These pieces slammed into the gunner crushing his ribs and puncturing one of his lungs.

The man gasped for breath as he screamed in pain. Don ignored him and lowered the crosshairs on the driver's face. He squeezed the trigger. Except for the thumb size hole in the windshield it remained intact. Through his scope Don could see the windshield had been splashed with blood, from the man's headless body as the heart still pumped blood up in geysers. It was a ghastly sight but it did not phase Don one bit as he panned to the right as the passenger exited the vehicle. The man's gray uniform and exposed skin were covered in blood and gore from his dead comrade. He fired blindly in Don's direction as he stumbled backwards over rubbish that littered the ground. Don did not hesitate to take in the scene. As soon as he had control of his breathing he pulled the trigger.

Don had messed up when he loaded the rifle. He was supposed to have all HE, but the last round he fired was a tracer round. Like a lighting bolt Don followed the trajectory of the round as it hit the man squarely in the chest. The impact blew the man backwards in a reverse summersault. Blood, bone, and a few shredded vital organs came out of the gaping hole in his back just before he hit the ground.

The commander had gone to the opposite side of the pile and watched as his men where completely wrecked. The gunner still screamed as the commander watched the tracer round take out the last man from that vehicle. He backed slowly out of sight on his belly then looked over his shoulder. "I found them, five hundred yards north of here. Red brick house tile roof, with a brick and iron fence around it. The outer perimeter is surrounded by debris. Destroy those sons of bitches now.

The remaining hummers, except the command vehicle swelled forward in a cloud of dirt and diesel smoke. The commander resumed his position and began to observe the charge. A smile crept across his face. He knew he might lose a few more men, but those shits would all die.

"Shit here they come!" Don screamed.

Craig peered through the shooting port as Don tried to reload the big fifty. He slung the UMP across his back; the thing would be useless in this fight. Leaning against the wall he picked up an AK47 with a seventy five round drum.

He made his way one room over and began to methodically pump rounds into the oncoming vehicles. From the looks of things he wasn't doing that great of a job. He kept waiting to hear the big bang of the fifty in the room next door. It never came.

Ann and Howard came running up the stairs. AP rounds sliced through the brick house like a knife through paper. Furniture shattered and lamps were busted as hundreds of rounds struck the house as the FEMA gunners cut loose with their FN 240's.

Ann and Howard came into the room where Craig was firing and took up positions at the other windows. The hummers were closing the distance now. The gunners and faces of the passengers becoming more clear. Craig inserted another drum into the magazine well of the rifle and looked at Ann. She had snapped out of her shock and was trying her damn best to exact revenge on those that had killed her best friend. As her rifle went dry she crouched down and dropped the now empty magazine from the rifle.

"Ann!" Craig shouted. The girl turned to look at him. "Find out why Don isn't shooting and help him if he needs it."

Ann just nodded her head and stood up and made for the door. Rounds slicing through the wall came precariously close to the young woman but she never faltered or flinched. Ann went across the hall and stepped into the watch tower, as the men called it. Lying in the floor she saw Don.

She knelt by his sides oblivious to the bullets that whipped past her head like angry hornets. Don lay shattered. A dozen bullet wounds pock marked his chest like craters on the moon. The only difference was that blood oozed from these craters. Ann knelt in shock oblivious to the armor piercing rounds that tore through walls. She couldn't understand how men would just wantonly kill her best friend who only wanted help and a safe place to stay. Then on top of that they kill a man like Don. Don had treated both Shelly and her like daughters the short time they had been here at the house. He had been patient, and caring while he helped teach them to survive in this strange new world.

She was jerked back to reality when a round struck Don's lifeless form with a meaty thwack. She pulled herself to her feet and ran back across the hall. She dove to the floor as more rounds raked the room she entered. Craig and Howard lay propped up against the wall, both reloading their weapons. "Don is dead!" She said.

A quick expression of grief came across both of their faces, but quickly disappeared and a look of resolve was expressed on both men's faces and in their eyes. By this time most of the hummers had cleared the debris wall and one had just rammed through the front gate. The gunner began laying it on hot and heavy while the other three men dismounted, and charged towards the house.

Chambering a round Craig rolled up and fired down at the three men. Two were minced up like meat through a grinder as the bullets from Craig's AK tore into them. The third man scrambled back for the cover of the hummer.

Craig rolled back down into a sitting position and looked over at Howard. Howard had just killed the gunner in the lead hummer when he was forced back down by a torrent of bullets. Howard met Craig's gaze. "You got a plan dip shit?"

Craig balled up as more rounds tore through the wall around him. "Yeah, I think I am going to sit here and make a puddle of piss and cry like a baby. Hell no I don't have a plan."

Howard smiled at his long time friend. "You get up! Take Ann grab the packs and beat feet out the back gate. I will cover you from here."

"I'm not leaving you here to screw up my escape. We stick together."

The fire from outside slowed to a trickle as the machine gunners reloaded and changed barrels. A few troopers popped off a round here and there just to keep heads down inside the house. "Don't think I'm staying and going to martyr myself for your ugly ass. I will be right behind you, now go."

Craig looked at Ann who was still just standing in the door way, miraculously unharmed. He looked back at Howard and nodded. "See you on the other side brother." Craig said as he stood and clasped hands with his friends.

"Yeah, on the other side, now get the girl out of here and head for St. Florian."

Craig ran from the room grabbing Ann by the hand as he passed her. Stopping at his room he grabbed his pack and one that he had just recently packed for Ann. Off the dresser he grabbed five more magazines for Ann's rifle. He also picked up three more loaded drums. He shoved the items into his pack. "Let's go Ann." He said holding out his hand. She took his hand and they sprinted for the back stair case.

When Howard heard the two going down the back stair case he rose up on one knee. Below him in the front yard fourteen troopers slowly made their way to the house, their rifles at the ready. The machine gunners played their guns back and forth waiting and searching for something to destroy.

Howard knew he couldn't take all of the machine gunners out so he chose to open fire on the grey clad troopers that had begun to knot up as they approached the front of the house. Pulling the stock tight in his shoulder Howard took aim. "This is for Don and Shelly you cock suckers." He whispered to himself as he squeezed the trigger.

The big FN was set on full auto. In seconds twenty rounds screamed out of the barrel searching for something to kill. Three men dropped in the barrage of automatic gunfire. Troopers scrambled backwards for the cover of the hummers now on the front lawn.

Howard jerked back from the shooting port as rounds pierced the metal shutters. Dropping the empty magazine to the floor he inserted a fresh magazine, and chambered a round. He scrambled through the torrent of incoming rounds to the third window. He fired a burst through the port taking out one of the machine gunners and was lining up the sights on a second when his right leg collapsed out from under him.

His rifle fell from his hands as his brain instinctively told him to hold onto his hip which was now sending shockwaves of pain through his nervous system. Howard tossed and rolled in pure agony as blood soaked under and over his hands. A round had punctured through the metal wall covering and had struck him on the hip shattering it. Howard had broken a few bones in his time but the pain had never been this intense.

The fire silenced from the house, the troopers charged forward with new courage as the machine gunners made Swiss cheese of the house. They stacked on the front door. A trooper reached out and found it unlocked and shoved the door open and stepped back. Another trooper threw in a fragmentation grenade. When the grenade exploded the men surged into the house and began to clear it room by room.

As they made their way upstairs they could hear the moans of pain that escaped through Howard's lips. The other rooms cleared, four troopers stacked on the door to the room where Howard lay wounded. One of the troopers threw in a flash bang. A second and a half later the charge exploded. The four men charged in. They found Howard semi conscious lying in a puddle of blood.

The team leader slapped one of the men on the arm. "Flex cuff his ass, and take him outside for the commander."

"Yes sir." The man went forward while his companions covered the wounded figure that lay in the floor. After a short struggle they subdued the man and took him outside.

Craig and Ann had made it to the back door when they heard Howard open up with the FN. Red and Meat were cowering under the kitchen table, and scrambled to their feet as the pair went out the back door followed closely by the dogs. They had made it out the hidden back gate when they heard the sound of a grenade go off. In his mind Craig knew they had just breached the house. Howard would have to get out now if he was going to.

He didn't slow or look back however. He understood what Howard had just done. Howard had told him to keep the girl safe, and he would do that for his friend. The sound of a second grenade reached his ears as he ran. Craig fought back tears of rage and sadness as he ran. He knew Howard had not made it now. Visions of what he would do to the FEMA troopers when they came to St. Florian started to fill his mind.

He had to clear those thoughts now. First thing first, he had to get Ann safely out of the city and make his way to St. Florian. This wasn't the time to envision the deaths he would inflict on the troopers. He had to stay focused on surviving and evading any possible search for Ann and him.

———

Howard laid face down, his hands flex cuffed behind his back, in the front yard. He slipped in and out of consciousness as he listened to the troopers around him smoke and joke and take pride in their victory. He smiled, or tried to through cracked lips, at the surprise these troopers would shortly run into once they made it to St. Florian.

Then a new voice reached his ears. This one carried authority. "Put those damn cigarettes out. The mission isn't over yet. Is this the only survivor?"

"Yes Commander." A voice answered

"Roll his ass over Jamison."

"You got it boss."

Rough hands grabbed him by the hair. The hands jerked and twisted him onto his back. Howard let out a groan of pain as he was rolled over, his wounded hip digging into the ground as he rolled. He was too weak to do anything about it though, and would have to endure it.

The commander looked down at the tall lanky man. The man's face was pale from blood loss, and shock. "How many more of you are there freak?"

Howard shook his head back and forth. Trying to say none but the words wouldn't come out. The Commander put his left foot on Howard's gunshot wound and applied pressure. "You're lying to me boy!"

Howard's eyes bulged out and he screamed. Then the pressure abated. "No more. No more. They are all dead or gone." He managed to get out in hoarse raspy voice.

"You better not be lying to me boy, or it will go bad for you. Bandage this rebel piece of trash up. I am sure Mr. Loxley would love to have one of his men interrogate this maggot."

Howard just laid there shaking his head no. "Like I said; for your own sake I hope you aren't lying to me." The commander gave a swift, powerful kick to Howard's shattered hip. "Fix him up, strip our dead of weapons and gear and let's mount up."

Chapter 44

The house had been abandoned, probably since the collapse. It had obviously been looted. Trash, clothing, rat droppings, and animal feces littered almost every room. Craig had cleared out a spot in front of the fireplace for him and Ann. The red coals from a small fire he had built earlier left the room with a faint orange glow. Though having a fire could have possibly attracted unwanted guest Craig felt that a fire would help sooth Ann. There was always something about having a fire when alone, lost or tired that helped sooth the human soul.

After escaping from the attacking FEMA troopers he and Ann had ran several blocks. They had cut through several back alleys, followed a ditch for about two hundred yards and came upon one of the old Victorian homes on Oak St. Craig had correctly assumed that the troopers would not finish what they had started. He felt they were a scouting unit for the main element of FEMA troops coming. He felt safe enough taking refuge in the old house, and had decided to lay low till the following morning.

Though the night temperature was not cold, he had wrapped Ann in his poncho liner and let her lie down and sleep off the days events. He would periodically get up and check outside for any possible threats and return and keep vigil over Ann's sleeping form. Staring into the dying fire Craig played the events of the firefight over and over again in his mind. There wasn't much else that could have been different, except maybe for all of them to run like hell. But he kept telling himself there should have been something he could have done different to save the lives of Don, and Howard. There was no way he could have saved Shelly.

Looking down at Ann's face, he could still see the paths her tears had cut through the grime on her face. He tried not to be angry at Shelly for what she had done, but he almost couldn't help himself. Not only had she gotten herself killed, but she had gotten two of his close friends killed as well. The prospect of his salvage business had probably gone up in smoke. He didn't know if the FEMA troopers had burned his house to the ground, or stole all his vital supplies. If they hadn't done either there were probably a hundred other scavengers crawling through his supplies right now. The big rig would surely be gone.

Craig jumped in surprise as Ann spoke up to him. "What are you thinking about Craig?"

Craig looked down at her, a sad smile played across his face. "Just thinking what a crappy day this has turned out to be. We both lost great friends. I have probably lost my home and all of my supplies that would have made our lives easier in this new world we have found ourselves in."

Ann propped herself up on an elbow, here chin resting in her palm. "What are we going to do?"

Craig looked into her eyes for a few moments before answering. "Well for one thing we can't sit around here and have a pity party." He paused for a moment and collected his thoughts before speaking again. "I think the troopers have probably left and are headed towards St. Florian. I think we should go back to my place before first light and scout it out. If the way looks clear and the house is still standing we are going to see what is left of our supplies. Then we are going to give Don and Howard a proper burial. Then we will head to St Florian. If the radio is still working we will call Steve, and let him know a scout team is probably observing them. If they have reached St. Florian the whole ambush we have planned will turn into a charnel house for us."

Ann sat upright. "You will take me with you won't you?" A bit of fear had crept into her eyes.

"I won't leave you Ann."

The fear disappeared from her eyes and was replaced with fire and resolve. "Thank you Craig. I want my chance to kill a few of those sons of bitches that killed Shelly!" Her voice had slowly risen in volume as she spoke.

Craig smiled and placed a calloused hand on her shoulder. "Calm down there Ann. I want you to lay back down and rest. You will have your chance, we both will. I will wake you in a couple hours."

Ann nodded at Craig. Her features had softened somewhat and a look of admiration showed on her face. "Thank you." She said softly and lay back down and was almost immediately asleep.

An hour later Craig stood to make his rounds around the house. Both Meat and Red woke up, and clambered to their feet. "Come on Meat. Red, lie down and stay with Ann." He said placing his palm down motioning for the dog to lie. Red hesitated for a moment then lay down.

"Let's go Meat." Craig said as he turned to leave the room. Meat's nails clicked as he walked across the hardwood floors.

Once outside Craig flipped the safety off of his AK. He crouched down into a kneeling position and closed his eyes. He listened for several minutes to the night sounds. When he felt comfortable no one was moving about he opened his eyes, stood and began circling the house.

On his second round Meat froze in place ahead of him. Craig eased forward and knelt beside the huge dog, placing a hand on the dog's shoulders just below the neck. He could feel the muscles tensed, and his cackles rose. "What is it boy?" He whispered to the dog.

Then Craig heard a voice. "I'm telling you I saw them running towards this house earlier man."

"I think you're full of shit. There ain't no hot looking chick and some dude running around town. And if you think I am going to go to that big house on Wood Ave. With you dumb pricks you are crazy. You know them crazy white folks got all kind of guns and shit."

Craig watched the two shadows come closer. Once they started talking again he felt sure they were alone. Craig made his move. Pulling out the Marine K-Bar fighting knife out with one hand, he slapped Meat on his hind end with the other. "Get them boy!"

Meat sprang forward, his muscles shooting him forward like coils relived of a heavy load. Meat crashed into the man on the left, bowling the man down. His cavernous jaws opening wide and slamming shut around the man's throat. The man never even got a chance to scream before his throat was ripped out.

Craig shot forward right behind Meat. The man on the right fumbled for something in his waist band. The blade of Craig's knife rested against his forearm, the pommel facing forward, as he closed the distance Craig shot his arm out as if he was throwing a round house punch. The blade of the knife coming out to the side like a wing, the razor sharp blade sliced through the man's throat like a red hot blade threw butter.

The man's hands went to the gaping wound that now appeared on his throat looking like a toothless smile. Dark blood poured threw his hands. He tried to cry out in pain, but only a gurgling, and the choking sounds of him drowning in his own blood came out. Craig finished the man off by driving the seven and a half inch blade down into his heart. As the man's knees buckled Craig kicked him away.

He looked down at Meat who know sat on his hind quarters panting. Craig couldn't see the blood that surely covered his face. Reaching down he scratched him behind the ears. "Good boy Meat."

Craig wiped the blood off of the knife on one of the dead man's pants. He sheathed the knife and dragged the bodies behind an old tool shed. He didn't need Ann seeing this in the morning. He looked around and realized that dawn was coming. The morning sky had already begun to lighten, the sun just below the horizon.

"Well let's wake Ann, and go check the house out." He said to Meat as he turned and walked towards the old house.

Once in the house Craig picked up an old shirt from the floor and turned towards Meat. "Sit boy." Meat obeyed, and Craig began cleaning off as much of the blood as he could. Red had walked up and stood close and began to busily smell both Meat and Craig.

Once he finished cleaning up Meat he walked to the living room where Ann slept. Kneeling down beside he gently shook her awake. Ann's eyes jerked open in fear for a few seconds until she focused on Craig's face. "Is it time already?"

"Yeah we need to get going" Craig said as he picked up Ann's LBV.

Ann stood and stretched then rolled up the poncho liner, and handed it to Craig and took her LBV with the other hand. She then picked up her AR and pulled the bolt back about a quarter of an inch to insure a round was in the chamber.

"You learn quickly, for a college girl." Craig said smiling.

"I had a good professor." She replied beaming with pride that Craig had noticed she had ensured her weapon was loaded.

An hour later Craig and Ann had scouted the house, surprised it was still standing. Once sure no one was about they entered the house. Both dogs seemed to be relaxed and had not sensed any danger so Craig was pretty sure the house was clear. Craig's vehicles, including the big rig were intact and undamaged also.

The interior of the house was riddled with hundreds of bullet holes. Furniture, lamps, pictures, and dishes were smashed. Stepping over the debris Craig and Ann made their way upstairs. They found Don's body where he had died. The big fifty caliber rifle lay near his outstretched hand. Turning from the room the two went across the hall.

"Where is he?" Ann asked confused. "Surely he couldn't have lived through all that shooting."

Craig stepped farther into the room and discovered a congealing pool of blood in the floor. It was then he noticed the trail of dried blood that led to the door. Someone had drug Howard from the room. Craig stepped to the window and searched the front lawn. He saw nothing.

"He isn't dead. They have him." He said with some conviction. He wasn't one hundred percent sure of analysis of the situation, but his cops instincts told him he was right.

"Craig. What do we do now?"

"First we try to contact Steve. Then we are going to wrap Don up. We will come back and bury him after the fight. I don't think we have time to bury him now. Then we load up the rig and head for St. Florian." Craig said as he marched from the room and went to retrieve Don's body.

Once Don's body had been wrapped in a poncho and Ann began to load the rig with weapons and supplies Craig got in the rig and started it up. He powered the CB up and took down the mike. "Scavenger One to Market."

The commander in charge of the scout party rolled out of the bed. His mouth was dry and his vision blurry. Shortly after the firefight, he and his men had come across a group of rebels. They shot the two men on the spot and captured four women. Delving into some of the liquor he and his men had picked up on the way to Florence, the commander ordered a little victory celebration. He hadn't intended it to last all day and half the night but what the hell. He and his men had fun with their new found girlfriends.

He wasn't too worried about getting in trouble with Loxley. The man would never know he hadn't gone straight to St. Florian. They still had plenty of time to get there, observe the rabble and report in. After all Loxley was the one who said they would face little or no resistance from the trash that refused to obey federal laws.

"Henson!" He shouted and quickly regretted it as his brain suddenly felt like hot daggers stabbed into his brain.

A few moments later Henson staggered in. "Yes sir!"

The commander eyed the trooper for a moment and hoped he didn't look as trashed as Henson did. "Dispose of the women, and round up the men. We've got to get a move on."

"Yes sir." Henson said, his voice sounding like gravel was grating against his vocal chords.

A minute or two later while the commander laced his boots four quick gunshots could be heard. The sound of each shot pounded into the commander's brain like a sledge hammer. His boots laced he slowly stood and made his way outside.

Looking to his left he saw the four women sprawled on the ground. The four all had hideous gunshot wounds to their heads. "Did you have to do that?" He said looking at Henson.

Fear crept across Henson's face. "You said dispose of them sir." He stammered.

"I meant did you have to shoot them. I have a hell of a hang over, and you blasting the four bitches didn't help any."

A wave of relief flowed over Henson, and a bit of color returned to his face. "Sorry sir. I should have used my knife. I wasn't thinking."

"Well next time use the knife. Let's load up. It is already after ten. The air assault will be here in a couple of hours so we need to get on sight and make some kind of report."

The FEMA troopers loaded up their Hummers and pulled out for St. Florian.

Bob and Caroline sat sipping their morning coffee, and talked about the up coming battle while the two monitored the CB's and Ham radio that had been set up inside the St. Florian Market. Both were startled and jumped when the CB speaker squawked to life, Bob nearly spilling his coffee in his lap.

"Scavenger One to Market. Scavenger One to Market do you copy?"

Bob fumbled for the mike. "Market to Scavenger One, go ahead."

"Be advised the mansion has been penetrated. You may have eyes watching. We will be en route to your location, ETA thirty minutes, Scavenger one out."

Bob replaced the mike to its rest, and turned to Caroline. "Go tell Steve to have everyone stop what they are doing and look helpless. The ambush may be blown."

Caroline bolted from her chair, and ran for the front doors of the grocery store. She had to stop several folks as she searched for Steve. In the process she passed along the information, and word began to quickly spread. Finally she located Steve just outside the perimeter of the defense wall.

"Steve! Steve!" Caroline yelled when she saw Steve and Celina talking near a hidden firing point.

"Hey Caroline what's up?" Steve asked.

"We just got a call from Craig. His place has been hit, and he says we may be being watched."

"Did he say who attacked them? Is everyone all right?"

"He didn't say. He just said that they were en route."

Steve ran his fingers through his hair as he thought for a moment. "The Colonel said FEMA was coming by air. It was possibly a scouting party, unless they changed plans. I doubt that though. I think the Colonel would have told us about it."

"That's if he could." Celina interjected.

"I know Celina, but I think he would have found a way. He seems to be a pretty resourceful fella. Tell you what. You and Caroline go pass the word for everyone to take up positions just in case. We may be sitting here twittling our thumbs for awhile, but that will be better than a scouting party observing us making preparations. The attack isn't supposed to occur for another four hours so let's hop to it."

Caroline and Celina took off to spread the word. Steve headed to the market to talk to Bob. As Steve walked through the outer parking lot he could see people already had started to conceal weapons, and began to walk around as if shopping for goods. Some groups stood around and talked just as they would have in normal times. Before entering the market store he looked out across to the tree line and couldn't even make out the hidden bunkers even though he knew where they where. If it had not been for people moving around in the wooded area he would have thought it was deserted.

He turned and entered the store. Inside the store was a flurry of activity. People loaded spare magazines, made improvised explosives, and prepared medical bags. He greeted folks as he made his way to the back where Bob was monitoring the radios.

"Hey Bob." Steve said as he walked up behind Bob.

Bob turned to look at Steve and removed the headset that covered his ears. "Hey Steve, how are things going on the outside?"

"Caroline told me about Craig's call. I have her and Celina getting everyone into position. Have you heard from Craig again?" Steve asked as he sat down on the edge of the table.

"Nothing at all from Craig, Howard, or Don as of yet, I have tried to raise them several times. Craig and Howard may be maintaining radio silence, but I can't understand why Don won't respond. I didn't think he was coming for the big show down. Howard had said he was still down and out."

"Well I hope nothing has happened to any of them. Not only are they good guys, their help will be invaluable."

"Maybe they will get here in time for the big show. I just got off the HAM with a guy who is an old retired police chief living outside of Birmingham. He said his people have told him FEMA is preparing to load the helicopters with gear and equipment. The troops will be ready soon. He also said a convoy of FEMA trucks left out yesterday real early. I suppose they intend to use those to transport us back to the relocation camps."

"Won't they be in for a surprise?" Steve said slapping Bob on the shoulder as he stood to leave and go to his position. "I'm out of here, and you and Caroline need to get to your positions too."

"As soon as old Mr. Clark get's here to relieve me I will be on the way."

"Be safe Bob." Steve said as he left the radio room.

"You be safe too Steve." Bob said replacing the headset back on his head.

⊹⊱━⊰⊹

Ann's knuckles were white as she held the big steering wheel of the big diesel. Ann's cousin was a long haul driver and had taught her how to drive big rigs when she was sixteen. She had not driven a rig in about two years and she was extremely nervous, especially with Craig continually urging her to go faster.

Craig stood in the copula manning the machine gun. Craig pulled his goggles down over his eyes as the speed of the rig increased and the flow of the wind watered his eyes. He wanted two things. He wanted to get to St. Florian as soon as possible, but what he really wanted was to find the FEMA troopers that had killed Don, and captured Howard. He absently caressed the machine gun and tracked it back and forth hoping and praying for a chance at revenge.

The FEMA commander groggily got into the hummer. His driver had his throbbing head resting on the steering wheel. "Wake up man. We need to get on the road." The commander said.

The driver slowly raised his head and looked over at the commander with bloodshot eyes. "I think I'm going to be sick sir."

The driver fumbled for the for the door latch as the alcohol from the night before made it's way from his stomach up his throat, just as he opened the door and began to step out he wretched. Vomit sprayed over his hands and legs as he tried to get out of the hummer. The commander turned his head and covered his nose hoping not to view or smell the other man's vomit, fearing he would do the same. The whole team was still half drunk from the night's festivities.

The gunner in the rear hummer was leaning against his machine gun rubbing the sleep from his eyes. "That's the last time I drink rum." He said to himself as he tried massaging the throbbing in his temples. Then a noise caught his attention. It sounded like a diesel motor coming from behind. He couldn't quite tell because of the diesel motors of the hummers running. He turned to look behind him.

As he turned he saw a huge black diesel with steel plating all over it. "What the hell....?" He said in confusion.

As Ann crested the hill she saw the hummers ahead. Her foot let off the gas pedal. "Craig, Craig, it's them."

Craig saw them too. "Don't slow down! Drive right down the middle of them, and don't stop for nothing!" Craig yelled.

"I'll crash into them Craig." Ann said. The seven hummers were parked along the road alternately facing left and right. The big rig would slam into the rear of each one, if she continued down the road.

Craig stuck his head down into the compartment. "Ann, drive right down the middle. You will probably hit every one of them. If we have enough speed there is enough room between the vehicles that we can force our way through. Now do it."

Ann just nodded her head and gripped the wheel tighter as her foot pushed the accelerator to the floor. Craig stood back up in the copula and racked a round in the chamber of the machine gun. When they were two hundred yards away he opened up on the right side of the column. His first burst tore into the tail hummer and Craig worked the rounds into the gunner. His body twitching as his torso was stitched with bullets. The distance was quickly closing and Craig switched his firing to the left side of the column. He hit another gunner, and managed to wing one FEMA soldier in the shoulder as he ran for the cover of one of the hummers. A smile played across Craig's face as he wreaked havoc on the unsuspecting troopers.

The rig was now almost on top of the column and Craig braced himself for impact. The big diesel smashed into the first two hummers sending them careening off the roadway. One, losing a front tire from the force of the impact. In seconds the big rig had plowed through the column. They had managed to hit and wreck all but two of the hummers.

Craig screamed down to Ann. "Turn around and stop about fifty yards from the column." He then rotated the machine gun to the rear. And began firing at any moving thing. Not much was moving. As Ann slowly turned the rig Craig kept the gun trained on the FEMA troopers. Hot brass fell like rain drops from the breech of the machine gun as Craig kept pouring out fire. He took out all of the gunners first, most seemed to be already dead, or unconscious, from the impact of the big rig. Craig took no chances and ventilated their bodies with multiple rounds.

He then began working on the drivers of each vehicle. As the gun ran dry Craig reached over and pulled another belt out and slapped it into the feed trey. As he chambered another round he saw several of the troopers stagger from their wrecked vehicles. Some were armed, some weren't. It didn't matter to Craig; they were all going to die. He squeezed the trigger at the first group of men to exit the vehicles. The men were sliced down like grass under a lawn mower blade.

A round ricocheted off the top of the cab. Craig panned to the left just as a trooper let off another three round burst at him. Craig replied with a six round burst of his own. The rounds slapping into the man's chest flipping him on his back.

Ann began to cry as bullets twanged against the metal shutters that had been placed over the front windows. It wasn't fear that caused her to cry. It was anger and joy. She was angry at these men who had killed her friends, and joyful that she was taking part in exacting revenge for her friends.

She had finally got the rig turned around and had put the pedal to the floor. She quickly went to through the gears as she gained speed. Then to her delight several troopers stepped into the roadway. Craig was gunning down some men to her right. She smiled as the big rig bore down on the men who desperately tried in vain to shoot through the vision ports of the driver windows. Then she was on them, literally. The big rig didn't even shudder as it plowed through the men. Some crushed under the tires, others thrown like dolls as the rig crushed over them.

When Ann made it through column a second time she slowed to turn the rig around again. Craig came down from the copula. "Once you get the rig turned around I want you on the gun. I am going to check and see if anyone is left."

Once the rig was turned around, Craig took his AK47 and hopped out of the rig. Ann climbed over into the passenger seat and then stood in the copula. She had only fired the weapon twice but felt she could handle...she hoped.

Craig walked slowly towards the carnage before him, the rifle in his hands sweeping left and right. As he drew closer Craig brought the rifle to his shoulder. Each trooper he saw, he put a round into his head.

He wasn't going to take chances. One by one he checked each hummer. He found two troopers still alive in one hummer. He never said a word to them, he just pulled the trigger. The rest of the troopers he found had either been killed by the rig hitting the hummers, were run down by Ann or he had shot them. Those that had been unconscious never woke up; they each received a sleeping pill in the form of a 7.62x39 round.

Craig approached the last hummer. This one had been knocked into the ditch. It was a command model with the command compartment on the rear. Craig checked the driver first. His head lay on the back side of his right shoulder. His neck had clearly been broken; his eyes were lifeless and vacant. Craig shot him anyway. The passenger lay slumped against the door. The man was moaning in pain. His femur bone protruded out of his leg.

The man's eyes fluttered open, and focused on Craig. "Need help. Get radio and call for help."

Craig smiled at the man. "Sure I would be glad to help." The man smiled back at him relieved that help would soon be there. The smile quickly changed as Craig raised his rifle and shot him dead. "Glad to have been of help asshole." Craig said as he lowered the rifle.

Craig made his way to the back of the hummer. He slung the AK and pulled out his Glock. With his left hand he jerked the door open and peered inside. Lying in a heap against the back wall lay Howard. Craig leaped into the back of the hummer holstering his pistol as he made his way to Howard.

He knelt beside his friend and felt for a pulse. He found one but it was weak. "Howard can you hear me man."

Howard's eyes slowly opened. "Craig?"

"Hey buddy. You ready to go see a doctor?"

In a weak voice Howard replied. "Craig, how the hell did you find me?"

"Man I was the best damn cop in Florence. There isn't anyone I can't find, especially your goofy ass."

"Well quit bragging and get my ass out of here."

Craig flipped out his knife and cut the flex cuffs from Howard's wrist. "It's hard not to brag when you're the best, and beautiful." Craig said as he lifted his friend from the floor.

Chapter 45

Loxley stood on the platform and watched his small army load up in the waiting Black Hawk helicopters. A smile played across his lips as he soaked up the view before him. The feeling of power surged through his veins. "

"This is how Caesar must have felt when viewing his legions before battle." He thought to himself.

The helicopters were painted a flat gray. The word FEMA in large black letters was painted on the tail booms of each helicopter. It had taken a lot of ass kissing to take the helicopters from the Army, but he had gotten it done. The pilots had to be coerced with the threat of their families being placed in the camps to get them to cooperate and realize they were now part of FEMA.

His men were dressed in grey BDU's, with black LBV's carrying their gear. Each had been armed with M4 Carbines. The carbines had been taken from the Army just like the helicopters. They carried two hundred rounds of ammunition apiece, two hand grenades, and a Glock 17 9mm pistol with two extra magazines. Also each had non-lethal gear such as pepper spray, tasers, and ASP batons. Each trooper also carried ten flex cuffs to detain any surviving insurgents.

Once the last helicopter had been loaded, Loxley stepped from the platform and made his way to his helicopter. He ducked his head and put a hand on his cap as he neared the chopper and boarded the bird. Sitting in the jump seat in the rear of the helicopter he placed the comm. headset over his head.

He moved the comm. Mic. near his lips. "All right pilot, let's go take care of the resistance."

The pilot rolled his eyes. This guy was so full of shit. He hadn't seen anyone so arrogant since his first tour in Iraq. He had a 2nd Lt. Who was a West Pointer and thought he was Patton. Of course the man didn't last long, crashing his helicopter in Mosul after pulling a few stupid stunts that had been unnecessary. Unfortunately he also got his crew killed. Maybe these so-called insurgents would clean this guy's clock. One thing was for sure. He was glad that he wouldn't be participating in the fighting against fellow citizens. It was bad enough he was taking these jack booted thugs to do the deed.

"Yes sir!" He said was false enthusiasm.

Loxley's stomach lurched into his throat as the helicopter lifted from the ground and soared into the sky. He wished that he could have flown in a corporate helicopter, but he couldn't locate any. This military helicopter was filthy, loud, and the military trash flew with the side doors open. Of course he knew it was necessary so that the gunners could fire their weapons. But just like the military they had not figured out how to come up with some way for the gunners to fire and have the doors closed. The military was filled with nothing but fools and idiots. It was a good thing he commanded his own men. He would show the Group that his troops under a Harvard educated, politically astute civilian leader were far superior to the baboons of the military and the way of the future.

❖

Steve ran his forearm across his brow, wiping the sweat away. The heat in the bunker was stifling, even being situated under the surrounding oaks. Celina dozed quietly in the corner, a soft snore coming from her throat. They had been in the bunker now for two and a half hours. Not quite sure when the FEMA troopers would show. Steve silently prayed that the information that Colonel Haddock relayed to them was accurate. Maybe he should go talk to Johan, and see if he had heard anything else.

As if to answer his thoughts Johan slid down into the bunker. "Hello Steve, how is everything going on your end Steve?"

"I am hotter than two rats fucking in a wool sock, Johan. I told Celina to get a little shut eye because we may not get a chance to sleep again for awhile if the Colonel is correct about the FEMA troops."

Johan gently caressed the M44 Mosin Nagant that he cradled in his arms. "Steve I can tell you this. The Colonel is never wrong. Those stupid FEMA boys will land those choppers right out there in the middle of that field. When the choppers take off the troops will assemble in an orderly fashion face the grocery store area and we will hit them from the sides and rear. They will do that because the Colonel, always a persuasive man, convinced that idiot Loxley that it would be so awe inspiring to you humble little country folk."

"That is all well and good Johan, but I still think we should shoot the helicopters out of the sky before they land."

"That would only make matters worse. The plan is for the choppers to quickly drop the troops and return to Birmingham. If you start shooting at them they will make numerous strafing passes with the machine guns mounted in the doors. Then they will go to an alternate landing zone drop the troops and come in on the group. Then we will most likely be overrun. We keep to the plan and we will destroy them."

Steve shook his head. "Johan, we aren't an army. We are a bunch of average men and women trying to make a go at it. To tell you the truth, I am worried about how well we are going to do here. I feel responsible for getting these people organized and willing to fight what is left of the government. I just feel it would be safer if we shot as many out of the sky before they land. I think we would stand a better chance that way."

"Steve." Celina's voice came from behind him.

Steve turned to look at Celina where she still sat leaned against the wall. "Yes Celina."

Celina stood up and placed her hand on Steve's shoulder. "You are right Steve. We are just a bunch of ordinary folks. We aren't an army, but like you said a dozen times convincing these people to stand up for ourselves. We are Americans. The government has no business taking our things, moving us from our homes, and putting us in camps.

Johan is a military man. If he and the Colonel think that the best way for us to beat these thugs is to let them land and then kill them, then so be it. Believe in yourself Steve, and believe that these people believe in what you told them, they will fight and fight well."

Steve looked at Celina for a few seconds and then nodded his head. "You're right Celina." He turned to Johan. "Sorry Johan, I shouldn't have any misgivings about what you and the Colonel said."

Johan clapped Steve on the shoulder. "Don't sweat it kid. Sometimes all we need is a good woman to talk some sense into us." He gave Celina a mock salute and turned and made his way from the bunker. "Watch your six Steve and Celina." With that said Johan disappeared into the woods to check the other bunkers.

Steve leaned against the bunker wall and looked out across the open field before him, he absent mindedly lay several magazines on the lip of the bunker so that he could easily reload in the battle. "Do you think we can do it Celina?"

Celina moved to stand beside him. "Steve, those sorry bastards aren't going to stand a chance. From what Johan said about the FEMA Director for the state. He is an arrogant piece of crap. Remember how he stood there looking down on all of us that day? Just like we were dirt that needed to be swept up and put in the dust bin. He'll listen to the Colonel and do just what the Colonel convinced him to do.

All we are going to have to do is stand our ground and let them have it." Celina had a fierce determined look on her face as she spoke.

Steve chuckled and bumped her hip with his. "You've got to be the meanest, most determined girl I have ever met. I sure would hate to piss you off and meet you in a dark alley."

Celina smiled and gave him a playful push. "I'll take that as a compliment. Speaking of being determined I am tired of playing around with you. I expect a dinner and movie after this is over. As soon as this is over you better start thinking about what kind of date you are going to take me on or I just might get pissed and you will meet me in a dark alley" With that said she spun away and exited the bunker to cool off in the shade.

Steve stood stuttering unable to respond. "Bu...Bu...But...where are you going?" He said to her back as she left the bunker.

Without turning she replied as she climbed out of the bunker. "To cool off, and give you a little time to figure out what we are going to do for our date after this crap is over."

Steve turned and sat down leaning against the wall. He ran his fingers through his hair and let out a breath. "Playing around? I didn't realize I was playing around." A million thoughts ran through his mind. Standing up he turned around and looked out at the field again. "Now where the hell am I going to take her to a dinner and movie at?" He said to himself.

He sat there thinking over this new, but welcome problem for several minutes. His thoughts quickly changed gears however as the sound of beating rotor blades reached his ears. He picked his VEPR back up and tucked it into his shoulder. He was so intent on scanning the skies for the approaching helicopters he didn't even realize Celina had hopped back down into the bunker and was at his side, the stainless Mini-14 coming to her shoulder.

"So what movie are you going to take me too?" Celina said calmly, her eyes straight ahead. A hint of a mischievous grin played across her lips.

Steve looked at her wide eyed. "Hell I don't know."

"Well I expect an answer after we're done here. So quit looking at me all goofy like and let's take care of these suckers. I for one am looking forward to our date."

Steve shook his head. He would never understand women. How could she think about a date at a time like this? The thoughts melted from his mind as he spotted the first helicopters on the horizon. "There they are Celina."

Celina tucked the rifle in tighter to her shoulder. "Let them come." She said in a soft voice.

◆━━◆

Colonel Haddock looked up from paper work he was going over when he heard the light knock at his office door. "Enter." He said.

A young PFC stuck his head in the door. "Sir, the FEMA troopers have just lifted off."

Haddock thought for a moment. Then the young PFC spoke again. "Sir, are there any orders you would like me to forward?"

Haddock nodded his head. "Dell, have the Apaches, Blackhawk's and troops on standby. Advise my pilot that I will be there shortly. That will be all."

As soon as the PFC closed the door Haddock flipped a switch under his desk. This switch turned on a mechanism that disrupted sound vibrations. This device would ensure anyone who had managed to bug his room or was listening with a sound dish would get nothing but garbled noise. He then picked up the attaché case that sat by his desk.

Placing it on the desk he dialed the combination, which in turn disarmed the explosive booby trap inside. Inside the attaché case sat a secure satellite phone. He picked it up and pushed the button that would connect him with the Joint Chiefs of Staff.

A gruff voice came through the earpiece of the phone. "What is your situation Haddock?"

"Good afternoon sir. At this time Loxley has lifted off and is headed to the Florence area. I have ordered my birds to be on standby. We will be pursuing them shortly."

"Very well, good luck Haddock."

"Thank you sir, may I ask the status of the other ongoing operations sir."

"Everything is going according to plan. The FEMA districts out west are under our control. We have placed a total communication black out from that area. The civilian authorities and other FEMA directors, and UN still have no clue as to what is going on. So I am fairly certain that members of the Group are unaware that their plans are being spoiled.

I am sorry you didn't get to have first crack Haddock. I know this is your battle plan, but things started to unravel out west and we had to secure it as quickly as possible.

By this time tomorrow the southeast should be in our total control. Your strike today will be the first one in the region. The northeast and mid-west will be ours within two days. Haddock I am going to say this again. Your evaluation of the situation was right on. The FEMA boys went absolutely bonkers with power and turned it over to the UN. Because of your planning we will put an end to them. Then power can be placed where it properly belongs. Good luck Haddock."

"Thank you sir." Haddock hung the phone up and then re-secured the attaché case.

He stood up leaving the attaché case on the desk. Walking across the room he unlocked a large military wall locker. Opening it he took his web belt down and secured it around his waist. He then took a Colt 1911 from the shelf. He inserted a magazine and charged it, then holstered the weapon. He closed the wall locker and headed for the door. He whistled a happy tune all the way to the airfield where his personal Black Hawk helicopter awaited him.

Sitting in the back jump seat of the helicopter he keyed up the radio. "John, get this bird in the air, and let's go kick some ass."

The pilot stared the engine. "I'm all for that sir!"

Chapter 46

Craig down shifted, and then accelerated as he pushed the big rig past eighty miles per hour on the straight away. "Ann, are you sure you want to be involved in this fight? I can understand if you want to sit it out."

Ann pushed a long strand of hair from her face. "Craig you've told me what the government is planning on doing with everyone. I for one am not living in some concentration camp. Plus you said the people you will be fighting are part of the ones that killed my best friend and Don I am going to be there."

Craig took his eyes off the road for a moment and looked at her. Just by the look on her face Craig could see the look of resolve on her face. Win, lose, live or die this girl was going to be in it till the end.

Craig then called back to Howard in the sleeping compartment. "Howard, how are you doing back there?"

Howard turned his head towards Craig, his face pasty white, covered in sweat, his hair plastered to his head. Even in pain he was coherent enough to answer Craig's question with one he felt it deserved. "How the hell do you think I am doing dip shit? I got a bullet stuck in my hip; I am bleeding like a stuck pig. You continue to drive like a bat out of hell hitting every bump in the road."

Craig smiled as he looked straight ahead. If Howard could give him an answer like that he was going to live. Since he was going to live he deserved no pity. "Quit your damn belly aching Howard. Ann and I go through all the trouble of saving your skinny ass and all you can do is bitch. Now quit your crying and be quiet. We will have you at Doc's place and patched up in no time." Smiling he turned and looked at Ann. "Do you see what I have to put up with? He has been like this since grade school."

Ann shook her head in mock disgust. "Craig I really like you both, but you two are so full of macho manly penis envy syndrome it is unbelievable." Ann laughed at the expression on Craig's face.

"You hear that Howard? Ann says you have penis envy." Craig said.

"Craig, just get me to the freaking doctor and shut the hell up." Howard said. He let out groan as the rig hit another bump in the road.

Craig looked back concerned hearing his friend groan in pain. "Hang on buddy; we will be at the doctor's in just a few minutes. Howard just closed his eyes and nodded as another wave of nausea swept over him.

Five minutes later Craig slowed the big rig as he approached the intersection were the grocery store was located. He scanned the area. To his front he could see forty to fifty older men and women filling sand bags, loading weapons and trying disguising some of the firing positions. They seemed to be doing a pretty good job. To his right he could make out movement in the tree where men and women moved about most likely finishing up the preparations of their fighting positions. Craig brought the rig to a stop as Mr. Flynn stepped out on the shoulder of the road and waved him to a stop.

Once the rig was stopped Mr. Flynn stepped up on the side board of the big rig. "Are you back to help Officer Wolfe?"

"Yes Sir Mr. Flynn. I have got to get Howard over to Doc's place; he has been shot but should make it. Once I drop him off Ann and I should be back."

Flynn leaned over and took a look at Howard in the sleeping compartment. "Didn't mean to hold you up Officer Wolfe, we will see you back soon then." Flynn said as he shook Craig's hand and jumped down to let Craig continue on to Doc's place.

Craig put the big rig in gear and made the left turn heading north on Butler Creek Rd. The road leading north was full of twists and turns and Craig had to keep the rig at less than forty miles per hour. Another ten minutes later and he reached the turn off road that led to Doc's place.

As Craig made his way down the road he noticed all of the Barricades and obstacles that lay on the side of the road. Steve had told him it had taken a better part of a day to clear the road so the medivac vehicles would be able to make it to Doc's quickly with any of the injured. Shortly he arrived at Doc's pulling the rig to the side of the house. Before opening the door Craig pulled the chain that activated the air horn. He let out three honks from the horn to announce his arrival.

Looking back at Howard, Craig laid a reassuring hand on his friends shoulder. "Hang tight for just a few more minutes Howard. We will have you fixed up in no time."

Howard gave Craig a feeble smile. "As long is your dumb ass isn't going to be the one doing the operating." He said in a hoarse voice.

"I know you really don't mean that, and I would love to stick a scalpel in you, but I have bad guys to kill." Squeezing his shoulder Craig turned and exited the rig.

Ann had already exited the rig and had gone to meet Maude and Daphne who had brought out a stretcher. The three were running to the rig. Craig went to the side of the sleeping compartment and opened it up.

The three women waited patiently as Craig reached under Howard's arms and began to pull him from the rig as gently as possible. Howard let out a bawl of pain when his body was halfway out of the rig and his tail sank towards the ground. "Jiminy Fucking Cricket Craig, are you trying to kill me!" Howard yelled.

"Shut up ya damn baby, I have to get your butt out of here some how don't I." Craig snapped at Howard, frustrated with his self for hurting Howard, and a little peeved at Howard for being angry. He was doing his best not to hurt him.

"It's going to be all right Howard. We are going to take care of you" Maude said as she reached under him to straighten his bent frame back level which caused Howard to moan and pass out from the pain. Daphne and Ann stood holding the stretcher as Maude and Craig placed him on it.

Maude strapped Howard onto the stretcher, and turned to head for the house. "Let's get him inside people."

The four raced for the house. They made their way around back to enter the lower back door thus avoiding having to manipulate Howard through the hallways and down the stairs.

Once inside Doc's office they placed Howard on the table. Maude began to give orders. "I've got to start an IV and get some fluids in him, Daphne you will find some bags in that cabinet over there, get me one.

Craig, strip Howard down now. Ann I want you to get in that cabinet over there and get me some Betasept skin cleanser, and sterile gauzes." Maude began to peel back the field dressing from Howard's wound she was stopped as a set of hands reached down and took over.

"Step aside Maude, I will take over." Doc said.

"Herbert, get back upstairs you still are not fully recovered." Maude ordered.

"Maude enough people have died in my home since this has started. I am well enough to do my job and I will. Now step aside, shut up and do what you do best and that is being my nurse." Doc said with an unusual steel edged tone in his voice he rarely used with Maude.

Though Maude ruled the house, her husband had always been in charge in the doctor's office. She knew Doc was one of the best doctors in the south and when it came time for medical action she was his obedient servant. Maude quickly stepped away and headed to retrieve other items Doc would need to repair the damage done to Howard.

As Craig finished pulling Howard's pants off of him he looked at Doc who was probing Howard's wound. "What do you need me to do now Doc?"

With out stopping what he was doing Doc spoke. "You aren't needed here Craig. Get back in that rig and go kill some of those imperious government troops."

"Yes sir." Craig said stepping back and heading for the back door. "Ann, are you coming or staying here to help with the wounded?"

Ann looked at Maude. "Do you need me here mam?"

Maude looked at the girl and could tell she wanted to get out of the basement and leave with Craig. "We will be fine now that Herbert is up and working. You go with Craig and be safe dear."

Ann bolted for the door hard on Craig's heels as the two made a dash for the rig. It had been almost forty minutes since they had left the grocery store. Craig was sure things may have already started to go down while they were away. As they reached the rig Craig stopped Ann from getting in the passenger side. "I want you to drive Ann. Things may have already started at the ambush. I will man the machine gun okay?"

Without warning Ann grabbed Craig by the cheeks and kissed him full on the lips. When she stepped back she smiled at Craig's stunned expression. "Just in case things don't turn out well I just wanted to let you know how thankful I am for what you have done." She said then smiled. "Plus you're kind of cute." Ann turned and ran around to the other side of the rig and hopped in the driver's seat.

Craig got in the passenger side and into the sleeping compartment. He then stood and brought the machinegun up and mounted it to the roof. He wore a grin on his face the entire time. As he loaded the machinegun Ann called up to him. "Are we ready?"

As Craig was about to respond the grin washed from his face as he looked up to see an Apache 64 hovering a quarter mile off in the distance. He saw a flash from underneath the right weapons pod and watched as a missile headed straight for Doc's home. "Ann, go! GO! GO! There is an attack helicopter!"

Ann couldn't see the threat but from the urgency in Craig's voice she knew bad things were about to happen. Slamming the rig into gear, her foot hammered the gas pedal. The tires dug deep furrows in the soft soil as she sped for the road way. Her hands tight on the wheel gripped even harder as Craig opened up with the machinegun.

Craig pressed the butt stock hard into his shoulder. Taking aim as best as he could at the helicopter, Craig's target lurching in and out of view of his sights as the big rig bounced and slid for the road, Craig squeezed the trigger as the front sight post rested on the lethal bird that hovered overhead.

Suddenly the flash of the missile streaked down into the house. The shockwave of the blast shoved Craig's body sideways in the cupola. The rig fish tailed on the dirt road as Ann fought to regain control of the vehicle.

Straightening himself back up Craig looked back at the house. The house seemed to have collapsed in the center. Flames licked the surrounding trees as they danced high in the air, and smoke bellowed towards the sky. Craig tore his eyes from the house back to the helicopter.

Obviously some of his rounds had struck home, the helicopter had turned towards him and was pressing forward towards the rig. "Die you sorry mother fuckers." Craig said as he brought the machine gun back to his shoulder. "Ann drive like a bat out of hell the helicopter is coming for us!" Craig yelled down to Ann. Then taking aim he let loose with a torrent of machine gun fire.

Tracer rounds rocketed towards the helicopter some striking their target with little results, the bird of prey still came on. As Craig fired he could make out the muzzle flash as the Apache opened up with its chin gun. Geysers of dirt danced on the roadway beside and ahead of the rig as the rounds came streaming down. Some of the rounds striking trees on the side of the road ahead of the fast moving rig, the trees shattering like match sticks broken by a child.

Craig kept firing all fear of dying forgotten. He was out for revenge, all of his wrath was pouring out of the barrel of the heavy machine gun towards the Apache that just killed some of his new friends and his best friend.

Ann's eyes were wide with fear as she saw the huge rounds strike the ground ahead of her. Several trees shattering in half as the bullets shredded them apart. Though scared out of her mind Ann maintained control of the big rig driving with all the skills she possessed as she tried to escape.

Then the Apache finally struck its target. The first rounds the gunner had fired had been fired in haste as they took fire from the semi truck below. Now the gunner and pilot had both calmed and they were going to end this little game of cat and mouse. The gunner received a lock tone as he centered the target acquisition sight on the rig. First he fired a burst from the chin gun. Watching the gun camera he could see rounds tear into the back end of the rig the back right tires being blown off. As the rig began to loose control he fired one of the smaller rockets from the rocket pod, he had to save the Hell Fire missiles for more threatening and hardened targets.

He watched as the rocket struck the rear of the truck. After a momentary flash and explosion he and the pilot watched the big rig flip once end over end, a body flying from the whole cut in the sleeping compartment. Then the rig rolled twice and came to rest on its side.

Smoke and flames billowed up from the engine compartment and two of the back tires that had caught on fire.

The gunner smiled and lifted his visor. "Damn good shooting Randy." He heard the pilot's voice in his ear piece. "Thanks Carl. How are we doing as far as damage?"

"We appear to be loosing hydraulic fluids, and one of the rounds punctured the armor and has blown out my instrument panel. I think we can still accomplish our support role on the main attack though."

The co-pilot looked back over his shoulder checking the bird for damage. Just as he looked over his left shoulder he saw flames shoot from the left engine. "Carl I think you better find a place to land…" He never finished the sentence. The explosion sent metal fragments into the rotor shattering two of the blades. The helicopter spun out of control the pilot screaming "mayday" into the radio as he fought for control. In seconds the helicopter nose dived into the ground. The fuel bladder exploding as flames washed over the ruptured tank. The fireball and then the fireballs from the secondary explosions from the ordinance cooking off went hundreds of feet into the air.

Chapter 47

Amos and Mr. Flynn lifted the last railroad cross tie and put it in place on the wall they had now completed. Part of the defensive plan for their defense of the market was to build earthen ramparts and walls built out of railroad ties taken from a near by train track. Though the railroad ties were at least a foot thick a heavy caliber rifle round such as one fired from an M-60, AK-47, or even a .30-06 deer rifle could penetrate the thick wood. So once the ties were stacked and placed others would come in and fill dirt and creek gravel taken from a nearby stream and build an earthen rampart to help deflect or stop incoming rounds.

Reaching up with a calloused hand Amos took the straw hat from his head and wiped the sweat from his forehead with the back of his arm. "Roy, I think I am way too old to be playing soldier. What I would give for a tall glass of iced sweet tea and a tall shade tree."

"Of course you're to damn old to be playing soldier. That's why your old butt is over here with the rest of us old farts while the young guys play ambush over there." Roy said with a chuckle as he wiped the sweat from his own brow.

"I hope all this goes as planned Roy. If it doesn't a lot of good people will die." Amos said as the two turned and started walking towards the grocery store entrance.

"Amos, the sad thing is that a lot of good people may die even if we win this thing. Hopefully that Colonel Haddock fella has given us good information, and everything will go down as planned. I just hope that the loss of life is going to be worth our freedom."

Amos reached up and rested his hand on Roy's shoulder as they walked. "Roy, I would rather die a free man than live a life of servitude under the iron grasp of a government who is willing to make me live as their slave. I think most everyone here thinks the same thing, otherwise they wouldn't be here."

"I feel the same way Amos, but what if the government people keep coming? Can we as a community continue to hold out against the government if they keep coming? If we do and the world and this nation get back on its feet and things get back to normal, will we be outlaws?"

"Roy, I think that we as a community can stand against this tide of oppression. If it comes down to things getting back to normal I would rather be considered a criminal and be hunted than live in some government camp being told when to eat, sleep, and shit." As Amos talked he caught sight of Benny walking threw the hectic crowd of defenders. "Roy, I will talk to you later I just saw Benny." Amos turned away to catch up with Benny.

"Benny! Benny get over here!" Amos hollered towards the disappearing boy. Amos saw Benny stop and turn, his shoulders slumped head bowed down. He was wearing his .22 pistol in a holster on his belt.

Benny shuffled towards the looming Amos. He walked up to Amos his head still lowered. "Yes sir."

Amos stood looking down at Benny for a moment trying to control his anger. "Benny why weren't you on the truck that left with the rest of the kids?"

Benny shuffled his feet a bit more then looked up at Amos. "I couldn't leave with the other kids Amos. It wouldn't be right leaving all of yall behind. You said these guys coming here to get us were bad guys and bad guys are the ones that killed my mom and dad. I want to fight the bad guys too." Benny's voice rose in confidence as he spoke, his chin proudly lifting up.

Amos took a knee to look the boy in the eyes. "Benny that is very admirable, but I am responsible for your well being. I can not put you in harms way. Now we are going to go into the grocery store and you will stay put until I come and get you. Do you understand?"

Benny nodded his head and followed Amos as he stood and turned towards the market doors. Amos didn't know whether to be angry at or proud of the boy. It took a lot of guts for a ten year old kid to want to stay and fight, but of course Benny was too young to understand that death was final and this wouldn't be a TV show or movie. The picture of young Benny staring in on his dead mom and dad came into his mind. "Maybe he does understand." Amos muttered to himself as he pushed the door open to the market.

Betty Flynn was behind one of the counters with Elbert Little's and David Miller's wives. The women were loading their scoped rifles and discussing the possible outcomes of the event that was about to unfold. Betty looked up as Amos and Benny came in the store. "Amos what is Benny still doing here? I can't believe you let him stay!"

Benny spoke before Amos could reply. "I hid behind the store while the other kids were loaded up Mrs. Flynn. Amos thought I was getting on the truck, he didn't know I promise."

Amos took a deep breath before speaking. "Betty is there some place in the store he can stay?"

Betty walked from behind the counter and reached out and took Benny's hand. Turning she began to lead Benny to the back of the store. "Michael Marks is in the back manning the radios. Benny can stay with him, of course I don't know how safe it will be if bullets start flying."

Amos followed the two to the back of the store. Amos looked around the office when they entered. During the past few weeks the group in charge of the radios had really outdone themselves. Beside the HAM radio, he could see they had added 2 meter, and ten meter radios, several CB's, and about four different scanners. The chatter from the radios and scanners seemed a bit overwhelming to Amos and for the life of him he could not see how one person could monitor everything coming across the speakers.

Michael turned in his chair as the three entered. "Hey folks what can I do for you?" He said as he cast a confused glance over at Benny.

Betty put her hands on Benny's shoulders and gently pushed him forward. "Well Michael it seems little Benny here took it upon himself to hide out when all the kids were being loaded up and taken to the Bracken farm. Amos and I were wondering if you could keep an eye on him while things are taken care of outside."

Michael's lips puckered a bit and he rubbed his chin as he thought about it for a moment before answering. "Benny do you reckon you could keep quiet and out of the way?"

"Yes sir, I won't say anything, or touch anything, I promise." Benny said.

Michael looked at Benny for a moment as if he were judging he could trust the boy not to mess up any of the equipment, or talk so much that he could not monitor the radios. "Okay I will do it. Benny you can sit over there." He said pointing to an old recliner in the corner of the office.

Benny walked over and dropped in the chair. His expression looked like a dog that had just been chastised. Amos smiled at the boy. "It will be all right Benny, this is for the best." He turned back to Michael. "Michael I will be..."

Michael held up his hand cutting Amos off in mid sentence as he spun in his chair back to the radios behind him. He picked up his head set and put them on his head. After a moment he pushed the transmit key on the Mic. "This is the Market, go ahead Rover 2, over." There was another moment of silence as Michael listened to the information being radioed in by one of the lookouts a few miles away. "Rover 2 I copy that they are inbound. Market out."

Michael tossed the head phones back on the cluttered desk scattering several empty Styrofoam cups, and he spun back to face Betty and Amos. "That was Rover 2. He said a large flight of Blackhawk helicopters just passed over his position. Go tell everyone they are almost here, I will call the ambush site and let them know."

Betty turned and hurried out the door. Amos took several steps over to Benny and kneeled down. "Benny, I want you to stay put. I will be back for you when this is over do you understand?"

"Yes sir, I understand." Benny said meekly.

Amos placed his large calloused hand on Benny's knee giving him a reassuring squeeze before he stood and quickly left the office. Amos broke into a trot as he zigzagged his way through the aisles back to the front door. Out of the corner of his eye he saw Betty, Mrs. Little, and Mrs. Miller heading up the stairs that led to the rough top, their rifles clutched in their hands.

Amos pushed the door open and stepped out into the bright sunlight, blinking his eyes as they adjusted to the glare of the midday sun. He stopped and raised his eyes towards the sky scanning to the south to see if he could make out any helicopters. Nothing, he looked back at the people around him who were still building up their defenses. Amos moved to center of the parking lot and stepped up on a large box. "Let me have your attention folks, your attention please!" He bellowed.

The crowd of people stopped what they were doing and turned to give Amos their complete attention. "One of the scouts just called in and reported that there are a large flight of Blackhawk helicopters coming our way. Yall know what to do. Hide your weapons mill about and act like this is any other day of trading. Once they land, and start to assemble and the helicopters are gone from the area get your guns, man your positions and wait till I give the order to fire." Amos stepped down from the box as people hurriedly stashed rifles, ammunition and other items they felt they would need.

As Amos began walking to his position the sound of rotor blades reverberated through the air. Everyone stopped and turned to the south heads tilted back eyes searching, and then straining to make out the growing black silhouettes in the sky as they drew closer.

As Amos came to a stop near his position on the wall Roy Flynn spoke to him. "My God Amos, there are so many of them."

The two men turned to look at each other. "Yeah there are a lot of them Roy, but there are a lot of us too. They think they are going to come in here and we are going to roll over on our backs and piss on our bellies like dogs. Well I don't think that is going to happen." Amos turned and scanned the people that still gazed up into the sky. "I know I have pretty much already said this to you, but maybe I need to say it again to give you and maybe myself a little hope everyone here is a hard working, freedom loving American. I don't think one of them will give up without a fight. None here would want to live as a slave in some camp."

Roy let out a chuckle. "Amos you should have been a football coach." Roy turned back to see the first few helicopters land one hundred and fifty yards away. Others landed farther away.

The smile faded from Amos's face as he turned to watch the helicopters start landing. They disgorged squads of men who fanned out setting up a perimeter. These first landings were followed by three more waves of helicopters. Soon the field was swarming with troopers; they formed up in platoons and began to make their way towards the waiting men and women.

Amos could sense those around him shifting back and forth waiting almost impatiently to launch their surprise attack. In a voice just loud enough to carry to those around the market he tried to calm them, hoping no one would grab a weapon and open fire too early. "Steady people. Wait until I raise my rifle and fire."

The seconds seemed to tic slowly by as the troopers advanced. To Amos it seemed as if they would never get to the road, as if the were moving in slow motion. Their forms seemed to flutter in and out of focus as the heat mirage from the roadway blurred their forms.

Finally the first group of troopers reached the road way fifty yards from the market. Amos no longer felt the blazing sun beating down on him. He was oblivious to the sweat that dripped into his eyes. The only sound Amos heard as he raised his rifle to his shoulder was the loud throbbing of his heart as it beat in his chest. Amos lined the sights up on a trooper. The sights were clear the trooper behind the sights a blurry image as Amos squeezed the trigger and screamed "FIRE!"

⊹╾╼⊹

Chapter 48

Byron Loxley looked out the side door of the Blackhawk out into the clear blue sky. His gaze took in the flight of helicopters that filled the air around his own helicopter. They looked like a flight of deadly steel locust. His heart pulsated harder as thought of all the deadly power now in his control. This was his small army and he was about to use it to hammer a group of rebellious civilians who thought that they had a right to stand in the way of the new world order that the government had deemed righteous. The will of the government was ultimately the will of the Council, a council he knew he was destined to lead. By leading that council he would not only be secretly leading the American government but governments all over the world.

He had all the power he needed to do the job at hand; it was aggravating that the incompetent Colonel Haddock could not acquire the Apache gun ships he requested. Even after he had contacted the council and requested them they were unable to provide any. The military had dedicated them to other uses. For a change his boss, Mr. Benson, was correct when he said that it would be unwise to reveal some of the power and influence the Council had by forcing Apaches to be placed under his command. The military needed to be kept in the dark about who was really in charge for as long as possible. It really grated his nerves to have to agree with the imbecile Benson, but one day he would have Benson taken care of.

Loxley looked at the troopers in the helicopter with him. These men were the cream of the crop. All had at one time been in Special Forces, and had been recruited and groomed to serve the final goal of the Council, just as he had been recruited, groomed and placed in the position at FEMA. They were hard corps killers who would do anything he asked.

Loxley closed his eyes day dreaming of his upcoming engagement and triumphant victory. His mind filled with visions of him leading his troops forward into battle, stepping over the mangled corpses of the vanquished. Then being brought before the Council in Geneva and elevated to a post worthy of his stature.

"Mr. Loxley, Mr. Loxley!" Byron was brought out of his reverie by one of the troopers calling his name and shaking his shoulder.

His eyes snapped open. "What is it?" He shouted in order to be heard over the beating of the helicopters rotor blades.

The trooper extended a headset to Byron. "There is a secure call coming in for you from Mr. Benson, sir."

Loxley took the headset and donned them. "Mr. Benson this is Loxley."

A female voice replied to his call. "Mr. Loxley, please hold for Mr. Benson."

Loxley's blood boiled. Here he was on the eve of battle and the fool Benson has his secretary call him and place him on hold as if this was some type of business call. Loxley's mind was flooded with visions of various forms of torture and death he would love to bestow on the insolent piece of trash. His visualizations of Benson's future were interrupted by Benson's voice coming through the headphones.

"Byron, are you there?" The older man's voice came through the small speakers.

"Yes Mr. Benson, I am here. What do you need?" Loxley said trying his best to hide the revulsion he had for Benson in his voice."

"I just received word from your headquarters that you are presently inbound to the northwest sector to take into custody a renegade group of civilians who refuse to comply with directives to turn themselves in to the nearest relocation camp. I need to know about the other on going operations in northern Alabama. Would you tell me the status of those please so that I can make a full report to the Council?"

Loxley took a deep breath. He had already made a written report of the recent operations, but apparently Benson didn't have time to read about his stellar successes. "As you are aware sir, Everything north of

Birmingham, and east of interstate 65 has been pacified. The relocation center in Huntsville was overcrowded but the attack by the Korean terrorist thinned the crowed so to speak.

Guntersville was completely pacified after the city council, chief of police, and other city leaders were tried for treason and executed. My troopers had a brief fight with forces made up of citizens organized and led by the local police. This was pretty much the same scenario that occurred in Fort Payne, Albertville, Gadsden, and Oneonta.

West of interstate 65 consist mostly of rural areas. It took a little bit of effort but the groups we encountered in Lawrence, Franklin, Colbert, and Limestone County were much smaller and easily overcome. I had some of my elite troopers release toxins from several tanker train cars in Athens to push the civilians toward Huntsville. Approximately four thousand were killed by the chemical cloud but this was a necessary evil to thwart any recurrences that occurred farther east in Fort Payne, and Gadsden. The remaining population was sent to Huntsville and Madison relocation camps. So that sums up the ongoing operations to date. Do you have any more questions sir?"

Benson cleared his throat and spoke. "Well it does sound if you are doing a fine job Loxley. It is unfortunate that you had to have your people sabotage the chemical tankers to get these people to comply. There deaths are regrettable, but hopefully it will be a lesson learned for the other civilians and they will obey when given orders that are for their benefit.

Can you tell me why you have decided to lead this particular operation in the Florence area? I hate to see you put yourself at risk. Are your troops not performing well enough under current leadership?"

Loxley's tempered flared again. In his mind the old bastard was saying that he had not wielded enough influence, and lacked the leadership to train his men to conduct the operation without him present. "As you know sir, the northwest sector, and Florence in particular has the largest most organized group of hold outs. I felt it was imperative that I lead this mission from the front. My troops and their leaders are above reproach and the best in the country; so no I don't need to be here, but want to be here to lead them in this final battle to pacify Alabama.

Naturally this will not mean that everyone in the state has been rounded up and placed in the relocation centers. It will however crush any future organized resistance movement. Once the Council brings the entire plan into operation and people and resources are placed where they belong, we can begin rounding up those that we missed. That is all I have to report at this time Mr. Benson. I will inform you when victory has been achieved and file a complete report of actions taken. Now if you do not mind I have a job to get to."

Benson chortled a bit, seeming amused. "Well Byron I am glad to see you have fire burning through your veins. Do keep us informed."

Static filled Loxley's earphones when Benson cut the connection. Loxley threw the headset to the deck. "The bastard was laughing at him. He would see who has the last laugh. After this operation was completed and successful he would personally fly to see the Council and give them the report in person."

The Captain of his team leaned forward and placed his mouth close to Loxley's ear. "Sir, we have arrived at the LZ. Do you want to be the first in?"

Loxley's heart fluttered in fear and he swallowed the bile that had suddenly come up into his mouth. No first in, first to die. It was best to circle and see what would happen to the men that landed first. Placing fierce look upon his face, that did not conceal to the battle hardened Captain the terror that could be seen in Loxley's eyes, he gave the Captain his orders. "I want the pilot to climb and orbit the LZ. If the men are attacked I want to be able to see the entire battlefield and organize the counter attack."

The Captain nodded his head and retrieved the headset off of the flight deck and placed them on his head. "Pilot, Loxley wants us to climb and orbit the LZ so he can observe. I will advise when to put us down." If he doesn't piss his pants and have us run, the Captain didn't add.

Loxley's stomach leapt into his throat as the helicopter suddenly nosed up and began to climb to a higher altitude. Then the helicopter banked hard right as it began its orbit. Loxley gripped the jump seat, his knuckles turning white from the pressure he was exerting. After several seconds Loxley realized he would not fall from the helicopter and his grip loosened somewhat.

He watched below as the first wave of helicopters landed, and the men dispersed and formed the perimeters around the helicopters. As the first set of helicopters landed he watched as the process was continued with the final three waves of helicopters.

The men below began to form up as planned. It was apparent nothing had happened, no shots were fired. In the market below he could see several hundred people milling about most though were transfixed on the armada of helicopters and men that had landed. Few had weapons that he could see. His courage restored now Loxley gave the order to land. "Captain put us down in the middle of the formation." This is where Loxley wanted to be. If the shooting started he would have his platoon around him and the platoon surrounded on all sides by the rest of his men.

The helicopter came to a rest in the center of the field. Loxley's men jumped out of the doors and set up their perimeter. Loxley was the last to step off the bird. He held his hat to his head as the rotor wash beat down on him. He stood in place until the Blackhawk lifted into the sky and headed back south.

Loxley surveyed the area around him. The platoons were formed up; well all the platoons except his own who all seemed to be in the prone position facing in all directions. "Captain Harris!" Loxley shouted out.

Harris ran to Loxley in a low crouch then took a knee near Loxley. "Sir you need to get down we are way too exposed out here in the middle of this field."

"Harris I want the men in formation. I am ready to move out." Loxley snapped.

"Sir I know I have already told you this but I am going to say it one more time. Despite the fact these are a bunch of civilian riffraff we need to treat this as a military action until everyone is secure. All the platoons should be spread out not in formation; we need to take that tree line to make sure there isn't a possible ambush. The troops that clear the tree line then need to set up where they can provide cover fire for those that are moving in on the market. Sir if those civilians open fire on us and we are all formed up it will be a slaughter."

"Captain, get up off your knees and get my platoons formed up, and prepare to move forward. This plan is fool proof. I have a man on the ground here and have all the information I need, which you don't. As a matter of fact Colonel Haddock reviewed my assault plan and was very pleased with what I came up with." He lowered his voice and spat out the rest of his reply like venom. "Now tell me Captain. Why should I listen to a pathetic little Captain when a full Colonel was utterly impressed with my grasp of military planning and tactics? I will tell you. There is no reason to listen to you, you pathetic coward. NOW GET UP!"

Because the Colonel hates your guts and wants you dead, and now I do the Captain didn't say. Instead he rose to his feet. "You heard the commander men. On your feet and form up." The platoon rose to their feet and formed up as ordered.

Loxley drew his pistol from the holster, sweeping it from left to right then pointing it straight ahead he shouted "Forward Men! Loxley's radio operator passed on the word to the other platoons.

A breeze blew across Loxley's face as he moved forward. He scanned left and right taking in how formidable his force looked. "I bet they are pissing there pants about now." He thought to himself. He was a bit thirsty and wanted to quench his thirst but had forgotten to bring any water. He noticed the canteen on the trooper's belt ahead of him. "Trooper, I need some water."

The trooper knelt down and took out his canteen. He handed it back to Loxley as he continued to search the area ahead looking for any sign of danger from the civilians ahead. His sixth sense was telling him that something was about to go down and the idiot commander was standing there drinking water as if he was on a Sunday afternoon hike. He was about to tell the commander to take a knee when a single rifle shot echoed across the field. One of the lead troopers collapsed to the road pavement one hundred yards ahead. Then hundreds of rounds poured into the advancing troops from the market area.

The trooper raised his rifle and fired a short burst from his rifle. Looking back he saw the commander was still standing dumbfounded as rounds whipped through the air like angry hornets. "Get down Commander! Get down!"

Loxley almost choked on the water he was gulping down when the first shot was fired. As more rounds whipped by and more troopers fell to the ground with bullets shredding into them

Loxley dropped the canteen from his hands. "What was happening? What was going on? Where did they get all those weapons?" He was asking himself these questions when he heard the trooper in front of him scream at him to get down. Loxley looked down at the trooper who was looking back at him shouting for him to get down just in time to see his forehead explode outward as the round that struck him in the back of his head exited his face.

Loxley's eyes grew wide as the man teetered then fall backwards at his feet, blood, bits of skull and brain matter slop out of the gaping wound and onto his highly polished jump boots. "My God, that bullet could have struck me! What am I going to do?" He thought as his mind raced through the options. Suddenly he was tackled from behind, a shoulder slamming into his back pinning him to the ground. He felt the weight of the person's body roll off of him. Out of breath he rolled over to see who had tackled him.

One of his sergeants crawled up beside him. "Sir, I know you like to lead from the front but I can't let you stand out in the open and be exposed."

Finally catching his breath Loxley spoke. "What is going on sergeant? These people weren't supposed to be heavily armed."

The sergeant fired a long burst from his rifle emptying it. He rolled on to his side to retrieve a magazine from his magazine pouch while he answered. "Well sir, someone gave you some bogus intelligence. We need to move forward to the market."

"Forward, into people shooting at us?" Loxley said utterly confused now.

"Sir when you are caught in an ambush you charge into the face of it, and while doing so fire an overwhelming volley of fire. Once you are into the ambushers' position you can make mince meat out of them." The sergeant said as he slammed home another magazine.

Loxley suddenly remembered reading that in one of his military manuals that you were supposed to charge into an ambush. His mind cleared as he began to regain his composure. "Doxie bring me the radio!" He shouted to his radio operator as a plan of action formed in his mind.

Doxie low crawled towards Loxley as rounds struck all around him. "Here you are sir." He said handing the handset to Loxley.

"This is Phoenix to all units. Deploy the rockets. I say again deploy the rockets. All even numbered platoons are to advance forward, odd numbered lay down covering fire..." Loxley cut short his orders as a fusillade of machinegun and rifle fire exploded from the tree line to the north.

Spinning on his stomach Loxley made out the winking orange flames coming from the muzzle flashes of hidden rifles and machine guns. Captain Harris crawled up beside him. The man had a hate filled grimace on his face.

"I told you, you stupid son of bitch. I told you to send troops to clear the tree line. Now what the hell do you plan on doing "Little Hitler"? Harris spit the words out his disgust and hate for Loxley very evident.

Loxley scanned those around him. Everyone seemed to be engaged firing at the market or the new threat in the tree line. "Well I am waiting for your orders you dim-witted cum bucket." Harris shouted at him.

Rage filled Loxley as the inferior excuse for a soldier shouted at him. "Yes Captain, I have a plan." Loxley's hand shot out like a snake his pistol in hand. He squeezed the trigger twice silencing the man forever. It was really better this way. Not only had the Captain paid for his insolence, but he would be unable to file a report that would reflect negatively on Loxley.

As Loxley holstered the pistol he looked up and saw the radio operator had stopped firing and was looking at him. "Do you have anything to say Doxie?"

Doxie thought about his reply for only a second. "Sure was sad to see the Captain get hit by a sniper round sir." Doxie turned back towards the tree line and began firing.

Good answer thought Loxley, but he would have to take care of Doxie later. He didn't need any loose ends lying about. He put the handset back to his ear and mouth. "Platoons one through five, lay down covering fire on the market, use your rockets. Platoons six through ten, advance on the market. Platoons eleven through fifteen cover fire; and use your rockets, platoons sixteen through twenty one advance on the tree line." Loxley handed the handset back to Doxie.

The sergeant crawled over to him. "Sir, which way do you want us to go?"

Loxley looked at the market then scanned the tree line. Tracer rounds came from several heavy machine guns tearing into the exposed troopers. The volume of fire was tremendous compared to what he observed coming from the market. "We will assault the market." Loxley was tempted to order that they stay put and lay down covering fire. However even in the prone position they would be sitting ducks. Ever one for self preservation Loxley realized that he would have to charge forward with his men to the market.

Even though the defenders outnumbered his men almost five to one he had superior fire power. Loxley lay prone until he saw the first AT-4 rockets being fired. He couldn't get the Apaches from Haddock, but once he saw that the military units had the AT-4's he demanded and got the disposable rockets. The rockets slammed into the earthen works that the civilians had built. Loxley saw bodies fly like rag dolls into the air.

"Move forward!" He screamed at the top of his lungs.

Loxley began sprinting forward with his men. The market was a little over three hundred yards from his position. Some of the platoons were a little less than fifty yards from the market. Hopefully those men would take the brunt of the fire coming from the market and then once over the walls be able to disrupt the defenders so that he could make it to the wall unscathed.

The field was filled with death, fear, and rage. Troopers either charged towards the tree line or the market, or they laid down a salvo after salvo of machine gun or rocket fire. The troopers only had thirty AT-4s but they were using them with great efficiency.

More rockets were fired at the tree line where the heavy machine gun fire came from. The few that were used against the Market were none less effective. The left side of the market had been destroyed, the car wash that had been converted into a blacksmith shop was totally destroyed from two simultaneous rocket hits, and four of the reinforced firing positions had been utterly destroyed.

Loxley's legs burned as he crossed the roadway. Two more troopers in front of him crumpled to the ground, one from multiple rifle rounds that tore into his chest, the other fell screaming blood spewing from his severed arm where a 12 gauge shotgun slug ripped off his arm above his elbow. None of that mattered to Loxley his only goal was to make it alive into the market compound, form his men around him and bequeath the death that these inconsequential people so richly deserved.

Finally Loxley reached the wall. Several men in his platoon leaped forward onto the wall. Some were cut down immediately others making it into the interior of the protective walls. Still other men in his platoon stayed on the outside of the four and a half foot tall walls and threw hand grenades or poured machine gun fire into the throng of people behind the walls.

As more troopers arrived at the wall the volume of fire going out towards the oncoming troopers died down, now most of the firing was inside the compound. Still standing Loxley observed the carnage within. Fear once again awakened inside him. A round struck just in front of him sending up debris into his face. Loxley reacted swiftly and took cover behind the wall. "I will just wait here a bit till most of the shooting dies down, he told himself."

The minutes passed like hours behind the wall. Loxley saw his men across the road fighting and making their way to the tree line. Well over two hundred and fifty of his men littered the field. Many were dead the rest wounded he could see that some screamed out in pain, though he could not hear their cries over the den of battle. Loxley pulled his knees tighter to his chest, his pistol hanging limply in his hand.

Abruptly a man in civilian clothes leaped over the wall landing on his feet. He held some type of assault rifle in his hands. The man's back was to Loxley, as he raised the rifle to his shoulder. The man started to shooting at several troopers that lay wounded and unable to defend themselves a few feet in front of him. Loxley watched the man in an almost immortal fear doing nothing to save his men as the civilian shot each trooper one by one. "How could he shoot the man in the back? To shoot may draw unwanted attention to him." Loxley justified to himself.

As the man exterminated the last of the wounded troopers he turned towards Loxley. Their eyes met. Loxley read his death in those eyes. The man ejected the spent magazine from his rifle reaching for a full magazine, his eyes never leaving Loxley's. Loxley's will for self preservation overcame his cowardice. He raised the pistol in his hand and pointed it at the man's chest. Loxley saw fear register in the man's eyes as he fumbled for the fresh magazine which he seemed to be having problems with pulling it out of the pouch where it rested.

Loxley pulled the trigger, and kept pulling it. Shooting the man and seeing the fear, then the understanding of his impending death register in the man's eyes and facial features. He kept pulling the trigger as the man fell to the ground, not because the man was still alive and a threat, but because Loxley seemed to feed off of the powerless feeling the man had, unable to stop his own death, yet seeing it happen at the same time. It was the greatest sense of arousal Loxley had ever felt.

The man's body finally crushed to the ground in a mutilated bundle of blood and broken bones. The slide of the pistol locked to the rear, the pistol now empty. A feeling of power washed over Loxley as he stared into the man's now vacant eyes. He pushed the magazine release on the side of the pistol and reached for a fresh magazine and inserted it into the magazine well.

Loxley felt like a new man, a warrior! He had come face to face with the enemy and defeated him. Loxley now stood and turned to the wall and leapt over it and into the compound. Men and even some women fought hand to hand with his troopers. The air was filled with smoke from burning timbers, and even a few bodies. Loxley walked calmly among the clashing foes as if nothing could touch him.

As Loxley walked he would occasionally raise his pistol and shoot one of the civilians. Most that he shot were locked in hand to hand combat with one of his troopers, others were still firing their weapons, all however dropped dead when he pointed his pistol at them and pulled the trigger.

Loxley caught site of three of his men drop dead to the ground and two others spin away wounded by gunfire. His gaze followed in the direction that the shots would have come from. Making his way through the fighting he saw a tall black man in overalls, wearing a straw hat. The man held two large revolvers in both hands. Loxley turned and made his way towards the man who now had his back against the market wall. He watched as one of his troopers charged the man, his empty assault rifle raised over his head in an attempt to bludgeon the big black man. The black man in an almost casual manner lifted the revolver in his left hand and shot the trooper almost point blank in the head.

"This is a man I must kill." Loxley thought to himself. Raising his pistol he fired. His round struck the man in the left thigh. The big man collapsed as his leg gave out from underneath him. Loxley walked almost casually towards the man. Seeing that the man had dropped both pistols and was clutching his hands around his wounded leg sent a thrill through Loxley.

He would enjoy this kill just as he had with the man outside the compound wall. Loxley no longer heard the den of battle around him; he ignored everything as he walked up to his prey. When he was just a few feet from him he stopped and raised his pistol. "Look into my eyes while I kill you." He said.

Amos raised his head up and looked into the man's eyes. "Do you want to beg for your life old man?" The man pointing the gun at him said.

"All I'm gonna beg for is a chance to kick your ass boy." Amos said as he looked hard into the other man's eyes. Just for good measure Amos spat up at the man, the gob of spit splashing across the man's face.

"Why you arrogant nigger, you will definitely die now." Loxley's finger tightened on the trigger.

"NO! Don't do it mister."

Loxley eased the trigger forward and turned to see a small boy standing just a few feet from him. "Why what do I have here? Young man I am going to kill this nigger and then for good measure I am going to kill you for interrupting my fun." Loxley said to the boy as he gave him an evil stare. His expression went from evil to slightly confused as he looked at the boy. There was no fear in his eyes, the boys expression was one of pure hate.

"I don't think so mister." The small boy said. His arm rose from his side. Loxley's eyes bulged in fear as he saw that the boy held a pistol in his hand. With cat like reflexes Loxley turned his own body bringing his pistol to bear on the boy his finger tightened on the trigger as the front sight post rested on the boy's chest.

Chapter-49

Bob and Caroline both leaned against the wall of the fighting position they had dug out. The top of the fighting position had a layer of twenty four inch in diameter logs placed on top. Several of the men had gone around cutting down trees to help bolster the defenses of each fighting position. It had been hard work but hopefully the added defenses would save their lives.

The two now shared water from a canteen searching the sky for the incoming helicopters that would soon be there. "Do you remember what Howard showed you about loading and firing the AK?" Bob asked his wife as he passed the canteen to her.

Caroline took the canteen and took a long pull of water from it. Despite having their fighting position twenty feet back of the clearing under several trees it was still stifling hot where they were at. Caroline wore a pair of woodland camouflage pants, brown leather hiking boots. Her BDU top was tied around her waist and she only wore a black tank top covering her upper torso. Rivulets of sweat poured down her chest and arms cutting small trails through the dirt and grim that coated her skin.

"Yes, I remember my lesson. Do you remember yours?" She smirked and then playfully spit a stream of water at him.

Bob tried to dodge the water but it hit him squarely in the face. The two laughed for a moment glad to have even the littlest act of mischief to break some of the tension they both felt. "Okay, okay. Enough, I give up." Bob said holding his hands up in mock surrender.

"I just want to make sure we both have our brains working when this thing kicks off. We didn't get a lot of time to practice with these things." Bob said reaching over picking up the AK 47 that Steve had let him use. "I still have a little problem working the damn magazines in." Bob removed the thirty round magazine and inserted it and took it out several times with difficulty still trying to master the loading of the weapon. He just didn't seem to have the knack for it.

Caroline picked her AK 47 up and duplicated Bob's action but had little problem feeding the magazine into the magazine well. "Boy genius, you've got to remember to tilt the bottom forward and catch the indentation on the front of the magazine right here." She said as she showed Bob how she was completing the action.

"Oh yeah, I keep forgetting that little important matter." Bob said as the magazine clicked into place.

"Well now that you've got it don't forget it." Caroline said turning to lay her rifle back on the lip of the birm.

As Caroline laid the rifle down she froze. She wasn't sure if she had just heard thunder or not. She closed her eyes and tilted her head and concentrated on the sound.

"What is it?" Bob said bringing the AK to port arms scanning the area to the south.

"Hush." Caroline commanded lifting her hand palm out towards him in a gesture to stop. Then she heard the sound it was a continuous beating sound as if horses galloped across the sky. The helicopters they were coming. She opened her eyes and lifted her rifle to her shoulder and propped herself against the birm. "They are coming Bob."

Bob's hearing wasn't the greatest, and he still had not heard the sound of the helicopters. He followed suit with Caroline and began to scan the sky. Several seconds later he spotted the first silhouettes on the horizon just above the trees. "There coming!" Bob shouted to those positioned around him.

The sound of men and women scuttling to their positions, and the sounds of rounds being racked into the chambers of rifles as bolts slammed home echoed through the woods. Soon everyone was motionless, the sounds of the birds and insects had ceased as if the wildlife knew of the death and destruction that was soon to plague the woods and grassy field beyond.

The helicopters drew closer, and soon each person could make out the details of each individual helicopter as they descended upon the field. "Bob, I know you can't load that rifle worth a crap, but I sure hope you can still remember how to shoot it as well as you did when we were practicing." Caroline said not taking her eyes off of the helicopters.

"I may not be able to load but I can sure as hell shoot it." Bob said tucking the rifle tighter into his shoulder, as he tracked the lead helicopter as it prepared to land.

With in seconds the thundering sound of the helicopters' rotating blades made conversation impossible. Knuckles turned white as the men and women of the ambush gripped their rifles and shotguns in anticipation of unleashing a deadly blow to the incoming troopers.

"Hold your fire until the helicopters have left and the people at the market open fire." Bob nearly jumped out of his skin as someone spoke behind him. He turned looking over his shoulder and saw Johan; well at least he thought it was Johan, leaving his fighting position to spread the word. Johan was dressed in his German Flectar camo, and had a ghillie suit on. His Mosin Nagant M44 now sported what appeared to be a four power scope.

Bob let out a deep breathe out and turned back into position. "Damn, he scared the shit out of me." He said to himself as the second wave of helicopters came into the clearing. The first wave of troopers had spread out in a circular perimeter just as the Colonel had said they would. The second then third wave touched down and discharged their troopers. With in minutes the troopers had organized and themselves into platoon formations and began to move towards the market.

It was so tempting just to pull the trigger but they had to hold fire until the people at the market opened fire and the troopers were fully engaged in fighting the threat to their front. Bob nervously shifted back and forth on his feet; Caroline showed her nervousness by clenching and unclenching her grip on the fore stock of the AK.

After what seemed hours the troopers started moving forward. Bob watched the troopers march by not more than seventy five yards away. Dust started to rise and fill the air as the heavy black boots of the troopers crushed the grass and stirred the dirt up as they moved.

Caroline was scanning the front of the enemy line as it moved towards the market. The troopers drew closer and closer to the road that separated the field and the market. "What are they waiting for? Shoot damn it, shoot." She said in a muted voice that even Bob could hardly hear.

Finally the crack of a rifle filled the air and one of the front troopers collapsed backwards. Caroline and many others almost squeezed off rounds in a sympathetic reaction to the gun shot. Everyone held their fire though. With in seconds the din of battle had risen to fervor as the two opposing forces clashed in battle.

Those in the ambush position waited for the order to fire as troopers continued to move past their position. Then they heard it. Johan's voice carried out in the air over the gunfire, "FIRE!"

Bob and Caroline simultaneously began to fire. Bob worked from left to right, Caroline from right to left. At a little less than seventy five yards, those troopers near the wood line were cut down like a scythe through wheat. Being in tight platoon formation the large caliber rounds fired by those with assault rifles, and deer rifles sometimes would not only cut down one trooper but keep on going and strike two, sometimes three troopers.

For the first few minutes of the battle both Bob and Caroline were almost relieved at how well the ambush was going. At the current rate of troopers being killed the battle would soon be over. What Bob and Caroline both didn't understand about battles is that they often had unexpected twist just when someone thought they were going to win.

That is just what happened, suddenly troopers fanned out and turned towards the ambushers. The attackers became the attacked, as machine gun fire poured into the woods. Despite the onslaught of fire now being returned in their direction the ambushers continued to lay it on. Then the rockets and grenades began to explode around them. The troopers with AT4 rockets were able to make out the muzzle flashes coming from the darkened bunkers and let loose well aimed volleys of rockets.

The bunkers that contained several of the ambushers belt fed machineguns were the first to be destroyed in a ball of fire. The heavy machineguns destroyed the troopers were now able to advance. Canisters of smoke were deployed by the troopers obscuring the vision of the ambushers; more grenades were thrown as the troopers advanced.

Bob ducked down behind his defensive wall as his AK ran dry. Reaching into a pouch that hung on his side he grabbed one of the fourteen magazines inside of it. He kept his breathing calm, trying not to let the rush of battle overcome him while with his hands shaking from the rush of adrenaline he inserted the fresh magazine. Just as he was about to rise up the supersonic crack of several rounds snapped over his head slamming into the timbers on the back wall.

Caroline dropped down beside Bob ejecting her spent magazine. Her arms and hand too quivered, not from fear, but from the rush of battle. She smoothly inserted a new magazine and charged a fresh round into the chamber. "Bob this sucks. Who was it that said this was going to be a piece of cake?"

"I think that would have been old Johan blowing smoke up our asses." Bob said spinning up from his crouched position back to his firing position. He searched through the clouds of smoke looking for a target.

Abruptly several dark figures materialized in the white haze. Bob lined up his sights on the first figure and pumped the trigger rapidly. Three rounds smashed into the chest of the first shadowy figure dropping him to the ground. As he panned his rifle over to the next trooper he saw the troopers arm rare back and then rotate forward lofting a small object right towards their fighting position.

"Grenade!" Bob screamed. He spun towards Caroline; she was in a half crouch coming up from the squatted position when Bob tackled her back down to the ground. Bob grab laid his upper torso over Caroline's to protect her from the blast.

The grenade landed on the roof of the bunker, bouncing twice before coming to a rest directly in the center. A heart beat later it exploded. The explosion tore through the timbered and dirt covered roof. Pieces of timber soared into the air. Other pieces were split and shattered and thrust into the bunker itself.

Bob felt the huge concussion of the grenade surge over his body. Milliseconds later Bob felt dozens of wood splinters pierce his body. Luckily for Bob the splinters neither pierced deeply or any vital organs damaged. His back arched, and legs stiffening straight as if he had been electrocuted as the pain exploded through his body. Bob groaned as he rolled off of Caroline, using his legs he pushed himself up against the back wall and sat up.

Caroline felt Bob stiffen as the explosion cracked overhead. She scrambled to her knees slightly disoriented. She shook her head to clear her mind and compose herself. Caroline turned her head to Bob. He lay against the back wall of the fighting pit his head rolled back eyes closed. Panic coursed through her veins.

"Bob!" Caroline scrambled to Bob on her hands and knees. Then the sound of men shouting just outside the bunker caught her attention. Caroline looked back towards the front of the bunker. To her amazement she peered out at a gaping hole where timbers and dirt had once shielded them. Suddenly the figure of a man with a rifle jumped down into the fighting position. He was hard to make out due to the fact that smoke from the smoke grenades and some of the destroyed timbers burned sending up clouds of smoke. Caroline reacted with lightening reflexes. She snatched the SIG230 .380 from her holster She fired two quick shots striking the trooper in the head with both shots. The man dropped to his knees, and then he fell backwards against the front wall.

A second trooper appeared in the opening. Caroline didn't hesitate, and she pulled the trigger again, and again, the first round striking the trooper in the shoulder. The second round struck him in the throat, his left hand reaching up to close the gaping wound that now pumped his own blood down his esophagus. He fell just outside the fighting position slowly dieing.

Caroline kept her pistol trained on the opening waiting for more troopers. The only thing she saw was the convulsing body of the second trooper she shot as his body fought to live. Then his body stopped moving. Caroline was satisfied no more troopers would come in she turned back to Bob. "Bob are you okay?" Caroline's hand reached down and touched Bob's right ankle. "Bob. Bob talk to me." Caroline started to lean towards Bob, her hand reaching towards his neck to check his pulse.

Bob opened his eyes the third time he heard Caroline call his name. It was almost impossible to hear her over the explosions, and gunfire that reverberated over the battlefield. "I am okay." He said licking his parched lips.

Caroline leaned farther over reaching for Bob's shoulders so that she could check the wounds she knew she would find on his back and legs. Just as her finger tips brushed his shoulders Bob's leg curled up and then shot forward. Caroline was lifted up and over the left side of the fighting position. Caroline gasped for air as the wind was knocked out of her.

Just over Caroline's shoulder Bob saw another trooper jumping down into their position. Bob still held his AK by the pistol grip; he swung the rifle up pulling the trigger as soon as he had his arm extended. The rifle bucked in his hand as he pulled the trigger. Multiple steel core bullets perforated the trooper's body. He did a dance of death as his body was forced backward over the wall.

Another trooper just outside hole reached around the side of the broken logs exposing only his arm and rifle. The trooper had his rifle on full auto as he squeezed the trigger, swinging the rifle back and forth in an attempt to kill the unseen defenders inside.

Bob squeezed his own trigger as fast as he could in an attempt to shoot through the logs or hit the concealed troopers exposed arm. The rounds from both rifles passed in the air, each seeking to strike a target. Neither Bob nor the trooper hit one another.

Some how with fifty seven rounds fired between the two they both came out of the exchange of gunfire unscathed. Bob dropped the rifle and struggled to get his pistol out of the holster. The trooper stepped into the opening. His rifle pointing down at Bob as he stepped down into the bunker pushing the magazine release dropping his empty mag. His left hand pulled out a fresh magazine and he moved to insert it into the rifle. He seemed calm almost assured that the wounded man on the ground before him wouldn't be able to clear leather and shoot him.

Bob panicked as he saw the trooper insert the magazine and release the bolt forward. Bob's pistol belt had twisted causing his holster to move behind his back. In the confined space of the bunker Bob couldn't get his pistol out. Bob looked up one last time to see the trooper raise the rifle to his shoulder, a smirk on his face. Bob's body sagged in defeat it was over for him and he knew it.

Elbert Little and David Miller side by side in the fox hole. Both men armed with M16 A1's just like they had used in the Panama Invasion. The only difference was that this time both men had 100 round Beta dual drum magazines attached to their rifles. The two mowed down everything in front of them as both of them expertly fired their rifles on full auto.

For a brief moment there were no troopers left in front of their position. "Loading." Elbert called out.

"Covering." David replied, as his rifle swept the area before them. "You know Elbert after we pulled that cop out of the river you said things were going to go in the shitter. Man was you ever right."

Elbert stood back up his rifle reloaded. "I'm hot, go ahead and reload."

David dropped down to reload as Elbert covered the area. "Have I ever been wrong before about bad shit going down?"

David stood back up rifle at the ready. "Nope, not since Panama, here comes some more lets take them."

Many of the troopers had stopped their advance on the market and turned towards the ambushers. Now rockets and machine gunfire filled the air around the two life long buddies. The two never flinched or cringed as their position became the focus of a counter attack.

As Elbert was dropping down to a knee to reload again a round struck him in the chest. The blow felt like sledge hammer crushing into him. He was sent reeling to the bottom of the foxhole. "David I'm freaking hit!"

David dropped to a knee to reload his own weapon. "Can you fight or do I need to get you the hell out of here!" he said as he started to reload his rifle.

Elbert drew his 1911 Kimber Eclipse from his shoulder holster. "Hell boy you know I can always fight." He replied just as two troopers loomed over the top of the foxhole. Elbert double tapped both troopers killing them instantly as the .45 slugs ripped into them.

"Nice shooting." David said as he came back up firing his rifle killing three more troopers that attempted to overrun the two men. Out of the corner of his eye he saw two more troopers. Before he could turn to engage them Elbert dropped both, emptying his pistol into them.

Then a round struck David in the hip. The hip bone shattered sending David spilling to the ground. A scream of pain came from his lips as he hit the ground. Elbert slapped a fresh magazine home and charged his pistol. With great effort he leaned forward and pulled his friend to him. "Can you fight, or do I need to get you the hell out of here."

David laughed through his pain. "Hell boy, you know I can always fight." David drew his own 1911.

"David I don't think we are going to make it out of this one."

"Well like I said, you've always been right about when the shit is going to hit the fan. I'll see you on the other side."

Elbert clasped his friend's hand. "Alright brother, I'll see ya there." Then troopers swarmed over the lip of the foxhole firing down at the two wounded me. David and Elbert replied in kind, their .45's blazing. Four more troopers died before the two former Rangers gave up living on this side of life and headed to the halls of Valhalla. Their lives ended like it started, the two side by side.

Joe Donovan lay behind a fallen log. He searched the swarm of troopers for those that appeared to be officers and NCOs. He located finally located a young trooper who was apparently an officer. He couldn't hear what he was saying but from the way he was gesturing with his arms he knew the man was giving orders. Joe rested the cross hairs of the scope on the man's chest and waited for the order to fire.

The order from Johan finally came and Joe exhaled stopping when most of the air had left his lungs. He gently squeezed the trigger on the Remington 700 loaned to him by Craig. Craig had also armed Joe with two Glock 17 9mm pistols. Joe hoped he would never have to use the pistols. If he had to go for them then it meant the whole shooting match was screwed and so was he.

Joe took his time at first rhythmically selecting targets, squeezing the trigger, working the bolt and locating a new target. He was able to take down four officers and five NCOs until the troopers regrouped and launched a counter attack. Then he took every target of opportunity that presented itself.

Joe lined up the crosshairs on the forehead of a trooper who was swinging what looked like a rocket launcher of some sort into action that had been strapped to his back. Joe squeezed the trigger. He didn't see the round disintegrate the man's head but he watched the trooper fold up and fall down into the tall grass as he rode the recoil and re-acquired his target as the rifle came back to rest.

Then the rockets and machinegun fire began to slam into the defenders in front of him. The rockets reeking havoc on the bunkers thirty yards in front of him. Tracer rounds struck clumps of dry brush and leaves setting them ablaze. The troopers then set off smoke grenades, finding targets was starting to become a problem in the fog of battle.

Joe gazed through the scope moving the rifle back and forth attempting to identify a target. The smoke was so thick now it was almost impossible to make out the bad guys from the good that were now coming up out of their foxholes to engage the enemy at close quarters.

"Damn it! Give me something!" He said to himself trying in vain to find someone to kill. He couldn't just blindly start shooting at the shadowy figures the clashed before him.

Then the bunker directly to his front exploded as a rocket screeched out of the smoke, flames trailing behind it. Dirt and timbers burst into the air along with three bodies belonging to the men who had defended that position. Troopers rushed forward to take the position. Bam! Bam! Bam! Bam! Bam! Joe fired and worked the bolt like a machine dropping five troopers in quick succession.

Joe rolled to his side and extracted five more rounds from his pouch. He slid a round into the rifle. Looking up to check his surroundings for any threats Joe was taken aback as troopers rushed into the lines in front of him. A guttural yell came from his left.

Joe turned to see a trooper, the barrel of his rifle in his hands, the rifle over his head like a club. The man charged towards Joe, he was only a few feet away. Joe rolled right as the trooper brought the rifle down in an attempt to crush his skull. With both hands Joe raised his own rifle up to block the blow.

The trooper's rifle crashed into his shattering his scope. Shockwaves went up Joe's arms causing him to drop his rifle. The trooper recovered, raising his rifle for a second blow. Joe rolled left this time as the butt of the rifle descended into the soft earth where his head had been.

Joe, now on his back again, reached for the Glock that rested in his shoulder holster. The trooper tossed the rifle aside and drew a knife. Joe watched the big twelve inch blade rise above the trooper's head as he stepped forward to drive it down into Joe's heart.

Joe's pistol cleared leather and Joe squeezed off three rounds in seconds. The man must have worn a bullet resistant vest because the first two 9mm rounds seemed to have little effect on the man. The third round struck the trooper just under the bridge of his nose. His head whipped back, blood and brain matter exploded out of the back of his skull.

The momentum of the trooper wasn't slowed as he fell forward, dead. The man's chest fell across Joe's feet. The trooper's outstretched hand came crashing down like a guillotine. The blade stabbed into the earth to the hilt less than an inch from Joe's face.

"Shit, that was close." Joe said as he scrambled backwards kicking the man's body off of him.

Joe rolled up to one knee drawing his second pistol in his left hand. Joe surveyed the battlefield. Bodies lay scattered everywhere. There were still hundreds of troopers out in the open field firing into the woods, and dozens with in the defensive line.

Looking to his left Joe spotted a half a dozen troopers methodically going from foxhole to foxhole and shooting the defenders. Even the wounded were not safe. As they passed wounded defenders they would fire a round into their brain.

"Damn. Well Joe it looks like the shooting match is screwed and so are you." He said to himself. Joe now totally exposed felt he had no other options left. The troopers had their backs to him. Joe stood up and charged both pistols blazing as he rushed the group of troopers. Two of the troopers went down, dead. A third wounded managed turn and open fire on Joe. Then the rest of the group turned raising their own rifles.

Bullets flogged the air around him as he ran forward. Joe fired a return volley too and was rewarded as another trooper dropped to his knee as one of his rounds struck him in the thigh. Just as Joe jumped a fallen tree he saw the grenade land ten feet in front of him. He dug his feet into the soft earth in an attempt to stop and dive for cover. One thought ran through his mind, "Damn this is going to hurt."

Steve and Celina watched as the third wave of helicopters touched down. The troopers in front of them organized into platoons, as if they were going on parade not about to conduct a combat operation. Even to Steve's and Celina's untrained eye they both knew who ever was in charge of this operation needed to be shot by his men.

As the troopers moved forward they both felt the anticipation growing inside them, waiting for the order to fire. Then the group at the market opened fire. The battle was on. Celina looked over at Steve. "Steve, I want you to remember one thing."

"What's that Celina?" Steve said never taking his eyes off of the troopers in front of him.

"I want that dinner and movie after this is over." Celina turned back to face the enemy and shouldered her rifle.

Steve turned and looked at her, a look of utter confusion on his face. "How in the hell can you think about that at a time like this? I don't understand you women at all."

"After this is over maybe you will have plenty of time to figure it out." She said. This time she was the one who didn't take her eyes off the enemy.

"Fire!" The command reached their ears. Celina opened fire immediately. Steve on the other hand fumbled with his rifle as he tried to switch gears trying to understand how a woman could think about a dinner and a date right now, to fighting and killing. In seconds though Steve was back in the game, a long continuous tongue of flame shooting forth from the end of his rifle as he pulled the trigger as rapidly as possible.

At first, just like everyone else, they had the feeling this was going to be a cake walk. The couple dropped trooper after trooper, without a round being fired in their direction. That all changed in a matter of minutes. Soon the rockets, grenades, and machinegun fire began to pour into the area around them.

Steve and Celina both dropped down behind the wall of the foxhole at the same time. Steve had fired his first seventy five round drum dry and was switching to a second one. Celina was on her third magazine. During her last magazine change a bullet struck the ground just in front of her as she was looking down to change magazines. She now wisely opted to reload from cover.

Steve was about to rise up when two troopers leaped over the fighting hole to the back side of it. Steve twisted his body as he stood and leveled the VEPR at the backs of the two troopers who were now firing down into a position just behind and to the left of his foxhole. Steve bump fired the rifle causing it to fire full auto. Multiple rounds tore into the backs of the two troopers killing both instantly as they fell into a heap on the ground.

Just as Steve turned back to engage any threat to the front of his position, Celina stepped in front of him as she came up from cover. She fired from the hip as she did. Steve watched as her rounds tore into another trooper that had just run up on their foxhole.

"Nice shooting little lady." He said as he side stepped her bringing his rifle to his shoulder and shooting two more troopers that were charging forward.

As Steve glanced right he saw a grenade land just feet from their foxhole. Reaching out he grabbed Celina by the belt and drug the two of them to the ground. The grenade exploded sending shockwaves through them. Steve's left hand shot up to his ear as his ear drum exploded.

Hearing Steve scream she spun around. "Where are you hit?" she screamed to be heard over the shooting.

Steve held up his hand. "I am fine, but my eardrum is busted." Steve stood back up looking for more targets.

Celina squeezed his shoulder and stood with him. The two worked well together; each covering a selected field of fire, killing or wounding anything that came within that field. Their rhythm was interrupted as the troopers fired AT4 rockets into their lines. Several rockets passed mere feet over their heads causing the two to duck for cover.

As Steve came back up from cover he saw a trooper aiming a rocket launcher at his position. Reacting rapidly Steve fired three rounds into the trooper just as he triggered the rocket. As the trooper fell backwards the rocket bounded from the launch tube.

The rocket shot skyward, its flight stopped as it slammed into the upper trunk of a large oak tree. The explosion sent Steve back down to the bottom of the foxhole diving for cover. Celina and Steve looked skyward frozen, unable to move as the upper portion of the tree, now in flames came hurdling towards the earth below and them.

The tree slammed into the ground sending flaming broken branches and cinders flying in every direction. Steve sucked in a breath of air; he had held his breath as the tree came falling towards them. "Damn that was close."

"Close only counts in horseshoes and hand grenades, and that wasn't a horseshoe." Celina said trying to joke away the fear of impending death she had just felt.

"Well don't forget there are still plenty of hand grenades out there." Steve said as the two stood up.

The flames grew higher as dead branches on the tree caught fire. The heat was becoming almost unbearable. "Celina, we've got to get out of this hole and quick before we fry."

Celina didn't need to be told twice. She rolled over the front lip of the foxhole and came up on a knee. Spotting a trooper through the smoke she fired two quick shots dropping the man.

Steve was seconds behind her and tapped her on the shoulder to follow him. Steve and Celina worked their way through the smoke filled woods engaging targets as they appeared.

As Celina stepped around a tree that had been blown in half by a rocket she was struck in the cheek by the butt of a rifle. She cried out in pain as she was knocked to the ground, her head reeling, stars dancing before her eyes.

Steve heard Celina cry out. He spun around to see a trooper raring back to bayonet Celina who was obviously disoriented on the ground. Steve charged forward lowering his shoulder and bowling into the man, who was at least, six foot four and two hundred thirty pounds of lean muscle. The two men went sprawling to the ground, their rifles knocked from their hands.

Steve came up with his Marine K-Bar in his hand. The big trooper was just as fast and was already on his feet. "That the way you want it boy?" The trooper said as he pulled out his own knife.

Steve's mind raced, he was no knife fighter and from the way this guy was handling his knife he was a pro. Only one thing to do, Steve lashed out with his knife, trying to cut across the man's throat. The big man was lighting fast, with his left hand balled into a fist he smashed down on Steve's forearm as he slashed at the man.

Steve's hand went numb, his knife falling from his fingers. The trooper followed up with an upward slash in an attempt to gut Steve from the waist up. Steve managed to stagger backward and avoided being gutted; he did receive a four inch gash across the left side of his chest. He winced in pain and back peddled away from the man.

"Where the hell do you think you are going? I ain't done with you yet." The man was over confident now that Steve was unarmed, he over extended himself and slashed at Steve's face.

Steve ducked below the attack. His legs now coiled beneath him he sprang forward driving his shoulder into the troopers gut. The two men sailed backwards, the trooper landing on his back, Steve on top of him. As they hit the ground Steve used his momentum and shoulder rolled over the big man. He came up on one knee.

Steve spotted his knife just in front of him. He reached out and snatched the knife up and spun away at the same time giving himself some distance from his opponent. As Steve came to a stop the trooper was already on his feet and coming for him. Steve knew he couldn't keep this up, the man was too good. He was going to end this fight right then. His hand snapped back, the blade of the knife clasped in his fingers. Steve threw the knife as hard as he could. He sent the knife spinning end over end at the trooper.

The trooper staggered backwards letting out a howl of rage and pain as the big knife sank into the outside of his thigh. "Oh shit." Steve thought when he saw the big man reach down and jerk the knife from his leg. "I am definitely fucked now."

The trooper gulped in several large breaths of air, then the pain seemed to wash from his face as he got it compartmentalized and put it to the side so he could continue the fight. "Let me show you how to throw a knife dick weed."

Before Steve could react the trooper snapped the knife from his hand in an underhanded throw. Steve saw the knife coming for his head but couldn't seem to get out of the way. Luck was with Steve again, Steve was hit in the forehead with the knife. Not by the blade but the pommel.

Steve's head snapped backwards and he saw stars, his vision went blurry. The trooper seeing his attack had failed to kill Steve charged forward. Just as Steve's vision cleared he saw the trooper's size thirteen boot slam into his chest. Steve felt the air being knocked out of him as he was lifted up and backwards by the blow. He landed on his back stunned, trying to breathe.

The trooper stepped forward and came down hard on Steve's chest with his knee. "Looks like you're out of luck motherfucker. It's time for "Big Sam" to skin your dead ass." An evil smile played across Big Sam's lips as he picked up the knife and raised it up over his head.

Steve's entire body was numb as he fought for breath. He started seeing small dots dance in front of his eyes when the trooper came crushing down on his chest with his knees. He couldn't hear what the trooper was saying. The only thing he could hear was his gasping for air and the pounding of his heart. The big trooper raised the knife over his head. Steve watched almost fascinated with the blade as it came hurtling towards his throat.

Chapter 50

Colonel Haddock ran forward in a crouched posture as made his way through the rotor wash beating down on him from the whirling blades of the Blackhawk helicopter. Reaching up he opened the co-pilot door and jumped in. Strapping himself in, he looked over to the pilot. "Let's get her in the air Bill." He said gesturing upward with his thumb. The pilot pulled back on the collective and the helicopter eased forward and up in a gentle climb.

Haddock scanned the air around him to see the flight that surrounded his bird. Dozens of helicopters flew in formation around him. Most were Blackhawks carrying his assault force. There were also a dozen Apache attack helicopters that would provide air support for the assault. "Control, this is Spear Leader come in over."

"Spear Leader this is Control, go ahead." The voice came over Haddock's headset.

"Control, are all my birds in the air? Over."

"Spear Leader you have three birds that had to abort for mechanical reasons. One Apache and two Blackhawks are still on the field, over."

"Roger that Control, Spear Leader out." Haddock wasn't surprised that a few of the birds were down due to mechanical reasons. They had spent a lot of time flying missions cleaning out the remnants of other areas. This last mission up in Florence would put an end to the high tempo of operations his units had conducted. Loxley would be taken out and then the state would be solidified and out of FEMA control.

Haddock's adjutant leaned forward into the cockpit area and tapped Haddock on the shoulder. Haddock turned to see his aide handing him the headset to the secure comm. Unit that went everywhere he did. "Thanks David." He said taking the headset and placing it over his head.

"This is Haddock."

"Haddock this is Solar. I just got done examining your preliminary report on the on going ops in your theater. Am I correct that all FEMA relocation centers and the troopers operating them have been neutralized?"

"Yes sir that is correct. I am heading north to Florence to take care of the last operational contingent at this time. Once this group is taken care of the rest of the FEMA troopers will most likely fall right into place or suffer the same fate as the unit in Red Bay." Haddock said to Solar.

"Haddock I know you are a hands on type of commander but is there any particular reason you are leading this op? You haven't been on any of the others according to your report."

"Well like the op plan I sent you advised, Loxley is leading his FEMA boys in this push up north. I just want to personally make sure he is finished off, and if he isn't I want to personally be the one that puts a bullet in that pretty little face of his. Don't worry though sir everything is going according to plan. I have Sergeant Major Dixon organizing things in Florence."

"I thought Johan had retired." Solar said.

"He did general, but Johan does a little free lance work on the side for me from time to time. He retired to a farm just outside of Florence before the collapse. He has done a thorough job organizing the civilians up there and once we come in on the attack Johan will have the civilians organized and ready for the second phase of my plan."

"Very well Haddock, I just got a little worried when I found out you were leading the attack. I thought something might be going awry and I needed to get to the bottom of it. Just to fill you in on the status of things, all members but two of the Council have been eliminated. Delta is also in the process of taking out all their lieutenants and associate members at this time. They should be finished within the week. If you and Johan had not had them infiltrated I don't know if we could have pulled off this little palace coup of ours, soon though things will be as they should. Good luck Haddock, Solar out." The transmission ended.

Haddock took the headset off, and handed it back to his aide. Haddock placed the other headset back on his head. "Bill have we had any contact from the column moving north?"

"Negative sir, there has been no contact since their last check in time an hour ago. I would say that they should have their first objective complete by now and on the way to the final checkpoint to wait on us. Would you like me to switch to their frequency so you can contact them?"

"Yeah Bill go ahead and switch over to their freq. "Haddock said as he adjusted the headset to fit better on his head.

The pilot reached over to the frequency dials and after a few seconds found the one he was looking for. "You're ready to roll Colonel."

"Spear Tip, Spear Tip this is Spear Leader, do you copy, over?"

"Spear Leader this is Spear Tip go ahead, over."

"What is your status Spear tip, over?"

"We ran into a little trouble as we crossed O'Neal Bridge. Apparently a couple of dozen gang members decided they wanted to make it a toll bridge, and thought that some cars blocking the bridge, and a few Saturday night specials would be a match for a dozen Bradley's. No survivors among the tangos, no friendly casualties.

We have arrived at the final check point and taken the objective. We have twelve FEMA troopers KIA, fifteen WIA, and fifty three unharmed. Total captured is sixty eight troopers. What are your instructions on the captured, over?"

Haddock paused for a moment in thought. "Spear Tip, dispose of the captured troopers; Collect their weapons and gear and turn them into supply upon your return. Are the five ton trucks still operational, over?"

"Roger Spear Leader, copy dispose of the captured troopers and collect the gear. Twelve of the five tons were destroyed when we took the objective. There are forty eight operational; we also captured three fuel trucks, over."

"Roger Spear Tip. I want you to leave a squad to guard the trucks when you move out for the final objective. I will coordinate with you when we reach the jump off point. Stand by one." Haddock released the Mic key and switched over to the cockpit com. "Bill, give me an ETA to the jump off point."

The pilot checked his GPS coordinates for their location and the FDP (Final Departure Point), then his air speed. "At our current speed we will be on site in thirty two minutes Colonel."

Haddock nodded his head, and then switched off the cockpit com and got back in touch with his ground force. "Spear Tip, this is Spear Leader, do you copy over?"

"Spear Leader this is Spear Tip, clear copy, over."

Haddock looked down at his watch we will be crossing the Final Departure Point in thirty one mikes, over."

"Roger Spear Leader, I copy thirty one mikes. We will be ready, Spear Tip out."

"Spear Leader out." Haddock pushed the Mic away from his mouth. Reaching down he pulled out his canteen. He took a long mouthful of water and swished it around his mouth before swallowing it and placing the canteen back in its holder.

Fifteen minutes later Haddock checked his watch; it was time for another phase of his plan. Haddock reached over and changed the frequency of the radio to contact his headquarter. "Control, this is Spear Leader do you copy, over?"

"Spear Leader this is Control, go ahead, over."

"Control, Spear Leader, Tea Party, I say again Tea Party."

"I copy Tea Party, Control out."

"Spear Leader out." Haddock changed the frequency again for the next stage of his plan then sat back in his seat.

Haddock had just set in motion the next step in his plan. At this very moment members of the 1st Battalion 61st Infantry from Ft. Polk, Louisiana were systematically taking down FEMA troopers in the camps in and surrounding Birmingham. They would take control of camps and confine the surviving FEMA troopers in with the civilians that had been relocated. Haddock doubted they would live very long. That wasn't his concern however. The more FEMA troopers' dead the less likely any type of insurgency would crop up.

The 3rd Brigade of the 3rd Infantry Division was assisting National Guard units in Montgomery doing the same thing. The 1st Battalion 30th Infantry Regiment was assisting in Tuscaloosa. All other FEMA camps were being handled by Alabama National Guard units. His plan he was sure would come off with few problems. Though the FEMA troopers were well trained and well armed with light machineguns and grenades they would be no match for combat blooded soldiers.

Haddock was brought out of his daydreaming. "Colonel we are two minutes out."

Haddock just nodded his head and turned and looked down at the ground below. They were just passing over the convoy of five tons that his troops had taken over. Black columns of smoke rose up from the twelve destroyed five tons below. Haddock could also make out a few scattered bodies of FEMA troopers killed in the initial attack. Just off to the shoulder of the road was a steep ravine a pile of bodies in FEMA battle dress uniforms were piled at the bottom. One of the soldiers left behind to guard the trucks appeared to be dousing the bodies with fuel. Just before the bodies were out of sight Haddock saw the trooper toss a flare on the bodies. There was an orange flash and flames and black smoke from the diesel fuel rose into the air.

Just as they passed the convoy sight the helicopter dived down towards the trees. The other helicopters followed suit. They were now flying at approximately two hundred feet off the deck at one hundred and fifty knots. Glancing at the trees below Haddock felt like he could almost reach out and touch them.

"Fifteen seconds out." The pilot said as he maneuvered the helicopter into a steep climb. The Blackhawk leveled out at two thousand feet and began to orbit the site of the battle below.

As his chopper banked Haddock observed the Apaches in his formation. They had popped up above the trees roughly at five hundred feet and came to a hover. Half had opened up with their 30mm chin guns. Tracer rounds shot out like fingers of death destroying everything they came into contact with. The other half of the Apaches had split into two groups and come up on both flanks of the open field below. They unleashed a barrage of the 2.75 inch 70mm Folding Fin Ariel Rockets. Their altitude was to low for them to accurately unleash their Hellfire missiles.

"Spear Tip, this is Spear Leader, do you copy, over?"

"Spear Leader this is Spear Tip I have a clear copy. We are standing by for your command, over."

"Spear Tip, begin your attack ten seconds from my mark.....mark." Haddock could see the Bradley fighting vehicles in lager in a depression a quarter mile away from the battle that was raging below. After ten seconds the Bradley Fighting Vehicles powered up and out of the depression and in a matter of twenty seconds had cleared the lightly wooded area where they had been concealed at.

Once they had a clear line of sight the Bradley's opened fire with their 25mm chain guns. Haddock smiled at the sight of the light armored vehicles and the fire power they produced. Many said the Bradley was a rolling coffin and wasn't heavily armored enough. What the nay sayers failed to remember was that the Bradley was designed as a troop carrier and scout vehicle not a main battle tank. The Bradley's main armament is the M242 25mm "Bushmaster" Chain Gun, manufactured by McDonnell Douglas. The M242 has a single barrel with an integrated dual-feed mechanism and remote ammunition selection. Either armor piercing (AP) or high explosive (HE) ammunition may be selected with the flick of a switch. The Gunner may select from single or multiple shot modes. The standard rate of fire is 200 rounds per minute, and has a range of 2,000 meters (depending on the ammunition used). A wide range of ammunition has been developed for this weapon, making it capable of defeating the majority of armored vehicles it is likely to encounter, up to and including some main battle tanks. The M240C machine gun, mounted to right of the Bushmaster, fires 7.62mm rounds.

As the Apaches peeled away the Bradley's opened the back hatches deploying the troops inside. The Bradley normally carries six soldiers and three crew members. Haddock had his commanders stuff them with eight soldiers instead of the regular compliment of six.

Once the soldiers had deployed the Bradley's moved forward again at a crawl the soldiers following behind as they moved towards the battle. The Blackhawks then filled the air and two companies of soldiers fast roped down behind the Bradley's and joined the soldiers already on the ground. While the soldiers fast roped down the door gunners fired 7.62mm mini-guns raining .30 caliber rounds down into the FEMA troopers still in the open field. Once the drop was completed the Blackhawks peeled away.

Haddock looked down at the battle below. "Damn would you look at the mess down there Bill? I bet there won't be many FEMA boys left after this one is over."

"Mess is an understatement sir. I bet there won't be many civilians left either the way those Bradley's are laying down fire." The pilot said.

"War is hell Bill; if the civilians listened to the Sergeant Major they will have taken cover. We will soon see though."

"I don't think so mister." Benny looked down the barrel of his pistol, the front sight resting on the head of the man holding Amos at gunpoint. The man spun swinging his own pistol back at Benny. Benny saw the movement and started to squeeze the trigger as the man turned fully to face him. The pistol fired sending the hollow point round into the right eye of the man. The bullet penetrated the eye and the eye socket, traveled through his brain and hit the inside of his skull. The bullet had been slowed and had mushroomed once it traveled through the brain it shattered into a dozen pieces; each piece ricocheted back into his brain scrambling it like an egg.

The pistol the man was holding slipped out of his hand and clattered on the pavement at his feet. Then the man followed suit collapsing to his knees, and then falling on his face. Benny didn't know it but he saved Colonel Haddock the time and a bullet by killing Loxley.

"Help me up Benny." Amos said as he watched the man fall to the ground.

Benny holstered his pistol and ran to Amos and grabbed his out stretched hand. Amos pushed up with his right leg, keeping his back against the wall to help guide him up. Once he was standing he pointed to his pistols. "Get my pistols Benny."

The boy quickly bent down and picked up the two Rugers. Turning he handed them butt first to Amos. Amos holstered one of the pistols and reached out to Benny with his free hand. "Help me out Benny and lets get inside, I've got to see how bad I am hit."

Benny did his best to support the big man as they made their way to the front doors of the market. "Are you going to be okay Amos?" He said as he struggled to keep Amos upright.

"Don't you worry about me, I will be fine. Let's just get inside." Amos kept the pistol in his right hand extended out searching for any threats in the throng of people and troopers fighting that whirled all around them. Just as they reached the front doors a FEMA trooper came at him raising his rifle. Amos snapped off two shots with the big .44, both rounds hitting him squarely in the chest and dropping him immediately.

Amos shoved the door open and the two made their way inside. Both almost tripped over the bodies of two FEMA troopers that lay in a pool of blood on the floor. Amos and Benny shuffled to a stop as the distinct sounds of two shotguns being racked echoed in the building.

Barry McGee, one of the radio operators stood up from behind an overturned display. He and another operator had been stationed inside the store to protect the three women on the roof with scoped rifles so no one would come up from behind them. "Holy crap Amos, are you okay?"

Amos and Benny moved to one of the check out counters and Amos sat down on the floor behind it. "Yeah I think I will be alright. I took one in the leg." He moved his hands so Barry could take a look at the wound.

Barry opened up the first aid kit he had brought over and began to administer to Amos' wound. The other radio operator, Al Shoemaker, remained in his concealed position monitoring the front door covering it with his shotgun.

"Okay Amos I got you patched up as good as I can for right now. Let's get you tucked away in the back in case some more of those troopers make it in here." Barry was strong as an ox and pulled Amos to his feet, and then picked him up over his shoulder in a fireman's carry. He swiftly had Amos tucked away in one of the back storage rooms where the radio operators had been sleeping. "I'll be back to check on you when this is over."

"Go on and get back to your post. Benny and I should be alright back here. It sounds like things are picking up out there."

"Damn it sure does, let me get going." Barry hopped up, and made his way back to his position.

Caroline pulled herself up to her hands and knees, she gasped for air, still confused as to why Bob would kick her in the stomach when she was only trying to help. She began to try to breathe deeply, she couldn't hear anything due to the ringing of her ears, Bob had fired so many rounds just seconds ago it had overwhelmed her hearing in the confines of the bunker.

Caroline looked over to where she last saw Bob. Bob was tossing his rifle to the floor; he scrambled to reach for his pistol that lay underneath him. Fear was all over his face. Caroline looked back over shoulder to see what the source of his fear was. Coming down into the bunker was a trooper. He released his magazine from the rifle and was reaching for another.

Caroline's hand swept back and forth searching for her pistol that had fallen to the ground when she hit the wall. Her head snapped back and forth from the trooper and the floor of the bunker. Then the glint of the stainless pistol caught her eye, her pistol lay there half covered by dirt. She snatched up her pistol and spun on her knees back to the trooper, raising her pistol towards the man.

The trooper had just inserted a fresh magazine and was raising the barrel of the rifle up towards Bob. Everything seemed to go into slow motion for her. She took in his soot and sweat covered face, his knuckles bloodied and scuffed. She heard nothing, not even the ringing of her ears. It was as if the entire world had slowed and a calm stillness had overcome everything.

Caroline squeezed the trigger as rapidly as she could. The crack of the pistol as it fired barely registering in her ears. She saw each round as it impacted on the tactical vest of the trooper, tufts of dirt blossomed as the rounds hit. The trooper staggered backwards but did not fall. Then the .380 pistol ran dry, the slide locking to the rear. Suddenly the world around her came back to life. It was as if someone had flipped a switch on and the world sped up, her hearing returned and the orchestra of the battle that raged around her flooded her ears. Then the man regained his footing and spun towards her raising his rifle.

"You fucking bitch!" The trooper screamed. All of the rounds Caroline had fired had struck him in his level IIIA ballistic vest. The only damage done to him was severe bruising. He was still fully functional, and ready to kill. He raised his rifle.

Unexpectedly the trooper's body seemed to dance as if a jolt of electricity had shot through his body, and his face exploded outward. His rifle dropped and then he fell to his knees. Bob and Caroline both stared in wide eyed disbelief as a shadowy form stepped through the smoke filled opening raised his foot and kicked the body of the trooper forcing him to fall face first to the floor.

Then the man who had killed the trooper stepped all the way into the bunker, a Stoner rifle in his hands. "Everyone all right in here?" said the grizzled old man of about sixty five.

Bob and Caroline both clambered to their feet, both reaching out for one another. Bob kissed Caroline on the forehead and then broke away adjusting his pistol belt then stepping forward his hand squeezing the man's shoulder. "Thanks a million mister we were both gonna be toast if it wasn't for you."

"Not a problem, I am sure you would have done the same for me." He said as Caroline reloaded her pistol and went for her rifle. Bob to had turned and picked up his rifle and reloaded it.

The three moved towards the shooting ports searching for more targets. "I am Bob Novacheck, and this is my wife Caroline. We owe you our lives." Bob said as he scanned for a clear target through the smoke. "What's your name mister?"

"I'm just an old Nam vet. The names not important, you don't owe me nothing." Then a breeze seemed to clear away some of the thick smoke from the air. "Oh hell looks like the calvary is here! We better get down." He said ducking down.

Bob and Caroline stayed up just long enough to see several Apache helicopters open up with machineguns, then noticed a few to the left firing down clusters of small rockets down towards the field in front of them. Bob and Caroline ducked down a smile on their faces.

Bob turned to Caroline as they squatted down. "Looks like Johan wasn't blowing smoke up our butts. I do believe the tide of the battle is about to turn."

Caroline gave him a quick peck on the lips. "We might make it after all."

Bullets flogged the air around him as he ran forward. Joe fired a return volley and was rewarded as another trooper dropped to his knee as one of his rounds struck him in the thigh. Just as Joe jumped a fallen tree he saw the grenade land ten feet in front of him. He dug his feet into the soft earth in an attempt to stop and dive for cover. One thought ran through his mind, "Damn this is going to hurt."

As Joe's forward momentum came to an abrupt stop Joe threw himself to the right, hoping to make it over and behind a fallen tree just a few feet from him. As he pushed off the ground with his powerful legs he sailed into the air. As his body lost momentum Joe realized he wasn't going to make it over the log in time. Hell, he wasn't even going to make it over the log, his body was coming down and it looked like he would land right on top of it.

The sound of the grenade going off reached Joe a split second before the shockwave and shrapnel. The loud hollow crumpling sound and the shock wave reverberated through Joe's body. Tiny pieces of shrapnel peppered the backs of his legs and arms before his body was sent over the log. Joe lost consciousness as his body dug in and slid on the soft forest floor.

For a second he came to lying on his side. His head was turned to the side looking skyward. Through the smoke he could see blue sky and trees. Sunlight came down in beautiful beams as it pierced the smoke. There was no sound, just the vision above him.

Joe blinked several times but felt the blackness creeping up on him. He felt nothing. White noise filled his ears, a sound almost like the wind blowing through the trees. "It didn't hurt much at all." Joe said as his eyes closed and blackness engulfed him.

Steve's head snapped backwards and he saw stars, his vision went blurry. The trooper seeing his attack had failed to kill Steve charged forward. Just as Steve's vision cleared he saw the trooper's size thirteen boot slam into his chest. Steve felt the air being knocked out of him as he was lifted up and backwards by the blow. He landed on his back stunned, trying to breathe.

The trooper stepped forward and came down hard on Steve's chest with his knees. "Looks like you're out of luck motherfucker. It's time for "Big Sam" to skin your dead ass." An evil smile played across Big Sam's lips as he raised his knife.

Steve's entire body was numb as he fought for breath. He started seeing small dots dance in front of his eyes when the trooper came crushing down on his chest with his knees. He couldn't hear what the trooper was saying. The only thing he could hear was his gasping for air and the pounding of his heart. The big trooper raised the knife over his head. Steve watched almost fascinated with the blade as it came hurtling towards his throat.

Without warning what seemed to be a red laser struck the big trooper just below the right arm pit. His upper torso seemed to explode, and rip apart as the red light passed through him. Blood, chunks of flesh and bone coated Steve's face and body. The weight of the big man lifted from

Steve as his upper torso, what was left of it, fell to the right his lower body falling to the left.

Steve lay there for a few seconds struggling to get air back into his lungs. Finally after several deep breaths he managed to start breathing again, although raggedly. Wiping his hands across his face, Steve smeared away the blood and guts from his face. He rolled over to his stomach and took in his surroundings.

The sounds of helicopters, missiles, and heavy machine guns filled the air. The sounds were not the only things that filled air around Steve. What appeared to be a red laser striking the trooper was in fact a swarm of tracer rounds coming from Apache 64 helicopters Steve could make out on the horizon. Not only were the Apaches raining down death on the FEMA troopers still out in the open field but they were raining death down on troopers and his fellow ambushers alike in the forest.

"So this is what real war is all about." Steve thought as he scrambled on his belly towards Celina who was sitting with her back up against a tree. Steve could see she was alive her eyes were blinking, but the blow she took to the head had literally knocked her senseless.

Steve came to a stop as he scooted up next her. "Get down Celina!" He said as he forcefully jerked her to the ground.

Celina's eyelids were slits but not quiet closed. Steve pried both sets of eyelids open checking her pupils. She didn't seem to have a concussion. Steve rolled her body over his, hooking his right arm under her armpit, and reaching around griping her right bicep. He low crawled with her on his back towards a fighting hole. He had to get to cover before they were both killed by troopers or the friendly fire of helicopters, or the Bradley fighting vehicles that Johan had told them would be their shortly after the air assault.

His arms quivered from near exhaustion as he finally made it to a nearby fighting hole. He slid in and lay Celina on her side. After insuring Celina was alright he lay back against the wall. He pulled out his Glock in case any FEMA trooper decided to have the same idea about taking cover in the fighting hole.

Steve flinched as he suddenly realized they were not alone in the fighting hole. Across from him lay the riddled bodies of David and Elbert, the two fishermen who had saved Don Savage. Three other bodies, FEMA troopers, lay across their legs and chests. Steve also noticed the leg of another trooper hanging over the lip of the fighting position, and the arm of yet another on the other side.

"Well at least you took a few with you." Steve said to the two dead friends.

Steve crawled over to the five bodies. He rolled one of the trooper's body over and pried an M4 carbine from the trooper's hands. Then searching his magazine pouches he pulled out five fully loaded magazines and shoved them into his pockets. One he kept out and he reloaded the M4.

A new sound reached his ears as he crawled back to Celina. He took a chance and peeked out over the lip of the hole. It appeared all of the troopers had moved back to the edge of the forest and were firing at a new threat. The Bradley's were moving up now, and he could make out soldiers walking behind the armored vehicles.

Steve was tempted to start shooting the troopers from the rear. He remembered what Johan had told him though. "When the soldiers attacked from the rear take cover. Don't be caught out in the open or chances were you will get killed. After the troopers are defeated stay put. Wait for a soldier to come and get you. Leave your weapon behind so some trigger happy soldier doesn't mistake a movement for an aggressive move." He had also gone on to tell the defenders that the military planned on getting the citizens modern main battle rifles, and gear. Once outfitted those that chose to could be trained for a resistance movement to fight a federal government that had gone crazy with power.

Steve laid Celina's head in his lap, keeping watch for any troopers. Thoughts of a different, truly free America filled his mind. Then Celina groggily opened her eyes and shook her head. She raised her hand to the huge knot that was forming on her forehead.

She winced as she touched it. "Owe!" she piped out. She moved her hand and focused on Steve. "What happened?"

Steve looked down at her. "You got to meet the butt of a rifle. I don't think you have a concussion. I am sure you are going to have one hell of a headache in the morning though"

"What's going on?" She said.

"The military has arrived. The FEMA guys have pulled back out of our position. They are about fifty yards back towards the field. They have their hands full. Now all we have to do is wait and hope the troopers decide to surrender instead of retreat back this way."

That is exactly what seemed to happen. Slowly the shooting died down, as FEMA troopers threw down their weapons. Many were confused by the attack by the military. They just about all thought the same thing. The army seeing the battle below must have thought they were a bunch of civilians fighting and came to crush both sides. Most were not concerned at all feeling that once it was discovered who they were the military would finish up and mop up what was left of the resistance.

The fighting finally came to an end. FEMA troopers left alive in the filed raising their hands over their heads. Those in the forest made their way into the open hands on their heads, both groups fully expecting to be released as soon as the mix up became apparent. Of course they all hoped the command element of the military would be arrested and charged for this friendly fire incident.

The citizens that were left alive peered through the smoke filled haze at the scene before them. Out in the field FEMA troopers were being flexed cuffed and stripped of any weapons or gear. Finally after some time hundreds of troopers had been cuffed and placed on their knees.

Haddock viewed the battlefield below. Haddock had been monitoring the radio traffic from the battle below. They had lost fifteen soldiers KIA, and twenty two with minor wounds, thirty with serious injuries. The wounded had already been medivac back to Birmingham. Soldiers on the ground had just finished securing all of the FEMA troopers. Only three hundred and eighty were left alive out of nine hundred and sixty that made the assault. At this point he had not received a tally on the dead and wounded among the civilians. Looking at the bodies scattered around the market it was going to be a hefty toll. There were not many left standing in that area.

"Bill, go ahead and put us down. Let's see what's left."

"Yes sir." The pilot made a gentle decent to the now bloody field.

The helicopter touched down gently. "Bill I want you to stand by one. I am going to have some men load up to head back and get the five tons to bring them back here. Get in touch with our pilots that landed the FEMA troops and have them stand by to load up prisoners."

"Yes sir, I will get right on it Colonel."

Haddock exited the helicopter and made his way to the where the Bradley's were now parked. Haddock was passed by two squads of soldiers who were heading for his helicopter. Two soldiers approached Haddock and met him halfway to his destination. The two men came to a stop three feet from him, neither saluted since they were on the battlefield.

"Well major, you did a fine job. Have you started rounding up the civilians yet?"

"No sir. We are waiting for Sergeant Major Dixon to make the contact. We have not entered the woods yet and don't know what we will find. Once Dixon comes out and gives us the okay we will go in and see what is left of the civilians."

Haddock nodded his head. He turned his attention to the second man who just stood to the left and behind of the major. "First Sergeant Hammond, go ahead and see if you can raise Dixon. I am ready to get this show on the road."

The First Sergeant jogged back to one of the Bradley's that had numerous communication antennas arrayed on it. The major and Haddock walked and discussed the particulars of the battle.

Johan put his radio back in the pouch on his vest; he shrugged off his ghillie suit coat and stood up from his position of concealment. He drew his 1911 pistol and began walking to the tree line near the field. He passed a wounded FEMA trooper moaning on the ground, he had been shot in both legs. "Help me." He said as he raised up a bloody hand seeking help and mercy. Without hesitation Johan fired one round into the man's skull snapping his head back like a whip.

"Alright people, listen up!" He bellowed out in his best drill field voice. "Everyone lay down your weapons like I told you before we let the soldiers come to you. They will pat you down and lead you to the market where they will verify your identity to make sure no one is on the FEMA agent list. Just cooperate and the injured will be taken care of, then you will be fed and get new gear."

Johan continued to give out his instructions as he walked to the field. Along the way he shot thirteen more wounded FEMA troopers. As he finally reached the tree line he dropped his second spent magazine to the forest floor, reloaded and holstered his pistol. A squad of soldiers met him as he stepped out from the shadows of the forest and into the bright afternoon sun.

"They should be ready for you to process Sergeant. Go ahead and get started."

"Yes Sergeant Major." The sergeant said, and he led his squad into the forest. Johan walked towards the waiting Bradley's.

Haddock walked out to his old friend and Sergeant Major. The two clasped hands then embraced in a bear hug. "Johan you old son of a bitch, I knew you could pull this off for me." Haddock pulled two cigars from his front pocket. He handed one to Johan and placed the other in his mouth. From his other pocket he pulled out a Zippo lighter. He lit Johan's and then his cigar.

Johan inhaled deeply on the Cuban cigar, and exhaled a cloud of blue smoke. "Damn that's good Colonel. The world is in the shitter and you still have the no how to get the best, that's why I have always loved being your go to guy."

Haddock slapped Johan on the shoulder and turned back towards the Bradley's. "How many casualties do you think the civilians took?"

Johan fell in beside Haddock. "I would say roughly forty percent killed and another twenty five percent wounded from the ambush group. I haven't had a chance to find out what happened over at the market."

"Well from the air it looked like the group at the market had it even worse. Damn bodies everywhere, hardly anyone moving. We will send the boys over when we gather everyone from the forest. Oh, sorry about having to give AT4's to Loxley. The Joint Chiefs said I had to go with the request. I hope I gave you enough warning."

"Yeah I'm sorry too. I about shit my pants when the first few came in and I knew they were coming. The civilians did pretty damn good up to that point. They were smoking the hell out of those FEMA boys. If you hadn't come in when you did I don't believe we could have held them. I was about ready to beat feet, hell I haven't done that since the operation in Bogotá."

"Damn Johan, why did you have to bring that one up? We barely got out of there with our skin." The two men laughed at the memory and walked on.

"You in the foxhole raise your hands above your head and stand up. This is the U.S. Army. Comply with my orders or I will have to shoot."

Steve laid his rifle down and un-holstered his Glock laying it down beside it. This was the part of the plan he hated. He understood however that according to the Colonel there may be a few FEMA collaborators who had been in the group of survivors. "I am going to stand up. There is a woman in here with me. She is injured and I am going to have to help her up. Is that okay?"

Two soldiers appeared at the lip of the foxhole as Steve stood up. "Go ahead and help her up, but do it slow do you understand?"

"Yes I understand." Steve reached down in a slow exaggerated motion and helped Celina to her feet.

Once Steve and Celina were out of the foxhole Steve saw that several hundred soldiers were moving about in the woods. He and Celina were both checked for weapons. One soldier had to hold Celina up to keep her steady while a second searched her.

"They're clean." The soldier said as he stepped back from Celina, his hands holding her by the shoulders. "Take her and move out to the clearing you will be directed where to go from there." He said to Steve.

Steve took Celina by the waist as the soldier draped her arm around his shoulders. The two slowly made their way to the clearing. "I can't believe we made it through Steve." She said trying to keep her head up and concentrating on her placing one foot in front of the other as she walked.

"I can't believe it either." Steve looked around the forest floor as they continued to walk. Bodies lay strewn about, small fires burned broken trees and under brush, even a few bodies were on fire or smoldering with smoke rising up from their burned clothes or flesh. "Jesus, how many died?" He said in a whisper.

There were others walking out of the forest with them. Once in the clearing Steve and Celina were directed by a soldier to walk to the parked Bradley vehicles. Celina blinked her eyes against the bright sunlight. Her head was throbbing, and felt as if someone was stabbing an ice pick between in her skull. She stumbled as she tripped over something on the ground. Steve caught her and prevented her from falling.

Celina looked down to see what she had stepped on. She almost threw up when she looked down to see the body of a trooper with his intestines hanging out and spilling out onto the blood soaked ground. She quickly averted her eyes.

"Come on Celina just look straight ahead." Steve said guiding her around the rest of the gore that swathed the ground.

It took almost ten minutes to walk to the gathering group of their fellow fighters. Besides Steve having to support most of Celina's weight he had to guide the two of them threw the bodies, body parts, and blood that seemed to carpet the field. Finally they arrived, a soldier advised Steve and Celina to sit down with the others. He handed both a large bottle of water.

Steve and Celina took a seat in the grass among the others. Everyone was still, and quite, some dozing, others chain smoking, and a few sleeping. This was the first taste of killing and fighting most had ever experienced they all seemed to be lost in their own thoughts, trying to come to terms with some of the things they did and saw.

Celina laid her head on Steve's shoulder and fell asleep. Steve looked around trying to get a head count. After several minutes he came up with four hundred and thirteen. There were still more walking out of the woods. Steve closed his eyes and shook his head. There were over three thousand people that had come to St. Florian to stand up against being relocated to the camps. He hoped that many had just fled deeper into the woods once the missiles started flying.

He hadn't heard about the status of those at the market. There were only four hundred or so that had defended that area. "God, I hope Amos and the others are okay." Steve said to himself. Steve looked to his left and saw the soldiers leading several hundred cuffed FEMA troopers towards his group. When they were about fifteen yards away they were stopped and ordered to sit on the ground.

"What the hell are they bringing those guys over here for?" The man next to Steve said.

"I don't know but I guess we are about to find out. Here comes Colonel Haddock." Steve said pointing to Haddock as he climbed up on one of the Bradley's.

"Alright everyone give me your attention." Haddock said into a small bullhorn. People stirred and got more comfortable waiting to hear what the Colonel had to say.

Once the crowd gave Haddock their full attention he began. "I know many of you are wondering what is going to happen next. First off I would like to say to you that you fought one hell of a battle. I haven't seen this kind of fighting in some time.

Now I know you FEMA troopers are expecting me to release you. Sorry boys that aint going to happen. Just to let you know you and your friends have been relieved of your duties by the US Army. Sorry there won't be any severance checks for you. You will be detained in the camps that you once guarded." Haddock was interrupted by the loud cheer that came from the group that had defended themselves from the attack.

Haddock raised his hands up to quiet the crowd. "Now you people calm down. There are new rules that must be obeyed. Now that the military is in charge you don't say shit unless you are told to or there could be dire consequences, if you will observe."

Haddock motioned to one of the soldiers who walked up to one of the FEMA soldiers and dragged him off of the ground. Once the trooper was standing the soldier pulled out a Berretta 9mm pistol and shot him once in the forehead. The trooper fell down were he stood. The soldier stepped back to his position.

A gasp came from the crowd of citizens. Some started stand. Soldiers leveled their rifles at the crowd. Haddock raised his bull horn. "Now sit down and shut up people. I am going to explain some things. Before the collapse this country was already headed down the shitter. Well we in the military have put a stop to that. We are going to bring America back to its former glory. Of course to do that drastic measures must be taken. All of you will be sent to the reeducation camps. You will follow orders, you will conform. Once the military has decided that the citizens of this country have learned the essentials of an orderly, lawful society we will hand the reigns of government back over to civilian control.

That is all you need to know for right now. Some of you will be transported by truck, others by helicopter to camps located in Birmingham. Don't ask questions just keep your mouth shut and listen, learn and conform."

The man beside Steve jumped to his feet. "This is bullshit! You can't do this to us we are Americans!"

Johan stepped forward and in one fluid motion drew his 1911 and fired one round. The big forty five slug made a thwackingsound as it smacked through his forehead, blood and brains deluged the crowd behind him. Johan waived his pistol back and forth pointing it at the crowd. "Now does anyone else need an object lesson?"

"Oh shit Steve. What are we going to do?" Celina whispered into Steve's ear as she moved her body closer to his.

"I think right now we better learn from the object lesson." Steve wrapped his arm around her shoulders. "Give me some time Celina we will get out of this some way, and kill those two mother fuckers if it's the last thing we do." He whispered back to her, his eyes never leaving Johan and Haddock.

Chapter 51

Amos rolled over and sat up, he had to clench his teeth to keep from gasping in pain as he put to much pressure on his wounded leg. "Benny, pass me the first aid kit." He said as he pulled away the blood soaked gauze he had put on when he first entered the room.

The wound did not look to bad, though it did hurt like the devil. He was going to have to get Doc to fix him up right. The wound did not appear life threatening and he didn't think any major blood vessels or arteries had been hit. The round had hit him in the meaty portion of the thigh. Even though there were no major vessels or arteries near the wound one could never be quite sure if the bullet had not made its way to a vital organ or vessel as it careened and tumbled through the body.

Benny knelt beside him and placed the big industrial first aid kit they had found in the office between his legs. "What do you need Amos?" He asked as he opened the lid to the big box.

Amos wadded up the bloody bandages and laid them in the floor beside him. He knew he should have left the old gauze on and placed another on top of it to help with the clotting. He had not cleaned the wound to his satisfaction when he first treated himself. He was dirty and he was more concerned with infection setting in than he was with the bleeding, which so far had been minimal.

"Hand me the bottle of hydrogen peroxide first." He said as Benny lifted the jumbo size bottle up and handed it to him.

Amos cringed as he spread open the wound with his free hand. Fresh blood oozed from the small hole. He poured the hydrogen peroxide into the wound and watched as it fizzed and bubbled as it made contact. He flushed the wound out two more times this way. When the wound quit bubbling he put the cap back on the bottle and handed it to Benny. "Give me the bottle of rubbing alcohol now."

"Okay. Are you sure you want to do that? It sure is going to hurt." He said as he reluctantly handed it over shaking his small head all the while. Memories of cuts and abrasions being cleaned with alcohol by his mother flashed through his mind.

Amos spread the wound open again and poured the alcohol into the hole. Most of the alcohol splashed around the wound and on to his leg. Enough made it into the small opening and followed the channel the bullet had made. Pain flooded his senses as the alcohol began to make contact with the inside of the wound channel.

Amos sucked air deep into his lungs sounding almost as if he was hissing. "Damn, damn, DAMN! That stuff hurts!"

Benny stared at Amos for a moment dumbfounded why an adult would subjugate himself to such pain. He shook his head and took the alcohol from Amos and replaced the lid. He cleared a spot in the first aid kit and replaced the bottle to its original position.

"Quit shaking your damn head like I was some kind of bleeding idiot. Now give me some more gauze so I can stop this bleeding." Amos said in a mock tone of anger.

Benny tried his best to keep from laughing but failed miserably. He let out a big snort as he tried to keep the laugh in. "What are you laughing at little man?" Amos said as he began wrapping the wound.

"I didn't call you an idiot. You are the one who wanted the alcohol and knew it was gonna burn like the devil when you poured it on the hole. Plus you are bleeding and instead of alcohol you could have used some of this antibacterial stuff that doesn't burn." He said holding up a bottle of cleaning solution. "When you said bleeding idiot I couldn't keep from laughing cause that's probably what Doc is going to call you when he finds out what you just did." Benny's laughing slowed then ended in a big smile as he put the antibacterial bottle back in the kit.

"If Doc finds out from you what I did you'll be cleaning up Festus's dung for the next two weeks. Where ever that old dumb jack ass goes you'll be right behind him with a pooper scooper in hand." Amos smiled and ruffled Benny's hair.

"Don't worry Amos your secret is safe with me." Benny smiled, and then tilted his head. "Amos I don't hear anymore shooting. Do you think it is over?"

Amos tilted his own head and closed his eyes in a straining to hear any sound of battle. He heard nothing. "I don't hear anything either. Can you do something for me?"

"Sure. What is it that you want me to do?" Benny replied.

"I want you to head out to the main part of the store and take a peak out the front doors. See if Barry and Al are still around. If they aren't head upstairs and see if Mrs. Flynn and the other two ladies are there. If they have left, or something bad has happened to them take a peak and see what the situation is. What ever you do, do not go outside, and if you are on the roof, do not stand up. Just take a peak over the wall. Do you understand?"

"Yes sir." Benny said as he stood to carry out Amos's request.

"Be safe Benny." Amos said his voice full of concern.

Benny turned to walk out of the room. As he reached the door he pulled the .22 pistol from his holster. His heart was hammering in his chest. He was terrified but he was going to be brave for Amos. He knew Amos needed to know the situation outside.

He hesitated as he reached the open door. He tried his best to calm his breathing. The sounds of gunfire from inside the store several minutes before were definitely still fresh in his mind. Benny stepped slowly through the door not knowing what he was going to find or see. Would the two men who had guarded the front door be alive or dead? Would he find FEMA troopers and be arrested and taken away like the man had said they would? He wouldn't know until he went out there and found out.

Benny slowly made his way through the back storage area of the market. He paused at the big metal swinging double doors. He slowly reached out to push the doors open then stopped. He had to do this smart. Walking over to a desk he holstered his pistol and picked up a small stool and took it back to the doors.

Standing on the stool Benny peered out into the store through the small plexi-glass window in the center of the door. Smoke hung like a cloud in the interior of the store. After several minutes of listening and looking, Benny was satisfied it was safe to proceed farther into the store.

Benny made his way towards the front being careful to avoid stepping on any of the debris that littered the floor. Many of the shelves were bullet riddled, and many of the few canned goods had been destroyed by gunfire. Their contents spilled out, and many of the cans scattered across the floor.

He walked in crouch as he prowled his way forward. As he came to the end of the aisle he took a knee, and slowly drew his .22 pistol. Gathering his courage he slowly peaked around the corner of the shelf beside him. What he saw chilled him to the bone. Barry McGee and Al Shoemaker both lay dead behind the barricades they had set up. Both bodies had blood pooled around them. Just in front of the barricades were seven bodies of FEMA Troopers that were strewn about. A chill ran up his spine at the sight of all the dead.

Cautiously he moved forward, out of the corner of his eye he spotted the body of another trooper who lay spread eagle just past the registers. Benny couldn't make himself move any farther forward towards the shattered front glass doors of the store. He really couldn't make anything out on the outside. Grayish, black smoke billowed inside the doors from the fires outside.

Benny, too scared to go any closer to the doors decided he would make his way to the roof top where Mrs. Flynn and the other two ladies were stationed. He sat motionless for a few moments listening for signs of people fighting, and gun fire. The only sound that reached his ears was the crackling of the fires outside and the tortuous moans of the wounded and dying outside. Satisfied that he heard no one else inside the store he moved forward.

As he reached the empty frozen food section he stopped, and once again took a knee. Cautiously he peered around the corner to where the stairs were located. The first thing he noticed was a large swathe of blood seeping down the wall from the stairs pooling in a small puddle on the floor. A scoped rifle lay beside it the scope shattered.

With his eyes he followed the blood back up the wall and then noticed a hand sticking out, the body it was connected to was obscured from his view. Benny's body began to shake as the image of his mother's lifeless hand stretched out over the edge of her bed filled his mind. His vision blurred as he fought back the tears. He tried as hard as he could to fight away the vision of his mother that was his constant companion when he closed his eyes at night. After several sobs he wiped the tears away and told himself it was okay because the hand was not his mothers.

Standing up on trembling knees he rounded the corner to the stairs. He stopped in his tracks and raised his pistol as the bodies of two troopers lying at the foot of the stairs came into view. He stood there for what seemed like an eternity to see if they breathed. Neither of the two unmoving bodies gave any sign of life. Benny proceeded forward.

Very carefully he tiptoed around the bodies and turned up the stairs. The bodies of two more troopers were on the stairs. One lay with his feet pointing to the top of the stairs, a bullet hole between the eyes, rivulets of blood had cascaded down the stairs from the gaping exit wound in the back of his skull. The other trooper's body was slumped against the wall, a stroke of blood smeared above his head were he had slid against the wall after he was shot.

By force of sheer will the young boy made his way past the two bodies, terrified that at any second the corpses would rise up and drag him to his death. Benny stopped and knelt by the third body on the stairs. It was Mrs. Flynn. Benny's bottom lip trembled. He bit it to make it stop. With his left hand he slowly reached out to touch Mrs. Flynn and see if she was alive.

He took her by the shoulder and gently shook her. "Mrs. Flynn, are you okay?" He said in a quivering voice. Benny knew she was dead but just couldn't bring himself to believe the nice old lady had met a fate such as this. He kept his eyes averted from the cream colored shirt which was saturated in blood. Mrs. Flynn had been shot under the left arm pit. The bullet had went straight through her, tearing threw her heart and lungs and then exploding out of her right side. She had died instantly.

Mrs. Flynn lay with her eyes wide open, and expression of shock on her face. Benny finally tore his own eyes away from the once piercing blue eyes of Mrs. Flynn. He quickly stood and forced himself to move on up the stairs. The door to the rooftop was open. Several bullets holes and perforated through the thin metal.

Benny stopped at the door frame and lay on his belly, and peered around the corner, his face inches from the floor. He scanned the rooftops looking for any type of movement. The only thing he saw was the columns of smoke rising in the air from the front of the store. Slowly he stood to a half crouched stance and quietly made his way onto the roof top.

As Benny made his way around the huge air conditioner he saw the body of Mrs. Little. Her body limply hanging over the roof wall, hands, and head over the side, feet barely touching the ground. Benny made out three bullet holes in her back. His grip tightened on the pistol in his hand as moved closer, his eyes darting back and forth searching for her killer.

Around the second air conditioner he came upon the bodies of two more troopers, one lay face down on the hot tar roof, and a pool of blood encircling his body. The second lay in a fetal position, his dead eyes and mouth gaping open. Ten yards away lay Mrs. Miller. She lay sprawled on her back arms and legs splayed out.

Benny warily made his way past the two dead troopers and then he sprinted the last few feet to Mrs. Miller. Benny dropped to his knees beside her. Frothy blood red bubbles, bubbled up out of her mouth. She lay gasping for air. Her lips moved and Benny could not make out what she said. He leaned forward resting his ear next to her mouth.

"Benny everyone is killed or captured. The army is taking everyone away. Get out of here, go out..." She didn't finish the sentence. She exhaled her last breath and died.

Benny slowly stood up refusing to look at Mrs. Miller's face. He slowly turned and made his way to the rooftop wall. Peaking over the wall with just the top of his head and eyes visible he looked out onto the battlefield.

It was like nothing the young boy had ever seen except maybe in the movies. The smoke had cleared somewhat as the wind blowing from the north increased in speed. Out in the field Benny saw FEMA troopers and people from his own group being tied up and sat in orderly rows. He watched horrified as a soldier shot a bound FEMA trooper in the head. His fear intensified as a few moments later a person who looked a lot like Mr. Johan shot one of the citizens who had leaped to his face and was yelling.

Down below him in the parking lot his eyes took in the enormous amount of carnage. Bodies were scattered everywhere. It didn't seem as if anyone left alive down there wasn't suffering from at least one type of wound or another. Many of the barricades were shattered; the logs that had been placed to form the barricades were splintered and burning. More than a few of the bodies of the people who had manned the barricades burned along with the logs.

Benny caught sight of a group of soldiers making their way from the field to the market, and then the wind shifted blowing smoke and the smell of battle full into Benny's nostrils. He doubled over to his left behind the wall as the sweet sickening smell of burning flesh, and the smell of human excrement assaulted his sense of smell. The young boy gagged as he vomited. Soon the contents of his stomach gone he was left dry heaving.

Benny fought to control himself. He had to tell Amos what was going on. If he couldn't do that he was sure he and Amos would suffer the same fate as the two men he saw shot. Everything that had happened that day was beginning to overwhelm the young boy. Finally the memory of waking up in Amos's house with a the Silver Star belonging to Amos's son pinned on his chest made the young boy realize he was given that because Amos thought he was a brave boy.

Gathering back up his courage Benny told himself he was going to prove he was brave enough to wear the medal pinned on his chest by the man he now loved like his own father. He crawled the half dozen feet to the second air conditioner to remain out of sight. Then on wobbly knees he staggered into a run for the door to the stairwell.

Benny made it to the door without being spotted by anyone below. He caught his breath inside the stairwell and with his arm wiped the vomit from his lips and chin. Benny didn't want to have to go past the bodies again, so instead of going down the stairs he climbed over the rail and hung by the bottom rail by his hands. He let go dropping the ten feet to the floor.

Pain flared from the soles of his feet as they slammed into the tile floor. Benny rolled and regained his feet. Throwing caution to the wind he ran as fast as his skinny legs would carry him for the storeroom doors. As he threaded his way through the pallets in the back he slid to a stop as he rushed into the room he and Amos had been in. His eyes bulged wide as he looked down the barrel of a gun.

Amos's own eyes bulged as he jerked the pistol in the air, his finger quickly releasing the tension he had placed on the trigger. "What the hell you trying to do boy, give an old man a heart attack?"

"I'm, I'm sorry Amos." He stammered. Then everything he saw poured out of him in spastic incoherent sentences.

Amos holstered the pistol and put both his hands on Benny's shoulders. "Slow down boy. What did you see?"

Benny took several deep breaths and started over. "Everyone in the store is dead. Mrs. Miller was still alive when I got to the roof, and she told me the army tricked us, and then she died."

"What do you mean the army tricked us?" Amos said somewhat confused.

"I looked over the wall and the army had a bunch of FEMA guys tied up. They also had a bunch of our people tied up too. I saw Steve, and Celina, and Mrs. Novacheck. Then this soldier stood a FEMA guy up and shot him. Then one of the people I don't remember his name, stood up yelling. He had his hands tied behind his back, and I think a guy dressed like Mr. Johan walked up and shot him. Almost no one is left alive out in front of the store. It's terrible Amos, there was dead people every where and a bunch in the store too."

Amos pulled the boy to him and hugged him as he began to cry. "Benny, I am sorry I made you go out there and see all that, but I couldn't have done it with my leg like this. Is there anything else you can tell me?"

Benny jerked back from Amos's grip as if he had been electrocuted he looked up at Amos wide eyed. "I almost forgot there are soldiers coming this way towards the market!"

"Shit!" Amos hissed as he looked around the room trying to think of where they could hide. He knew he couldn't run, and he didn't want Benny taking off on his own. His eyes rested on an empty refrigerator box. He made his way to the box. It was empty.

Amos laid the box on its side and folded the bottom tabs inside. He then lifted it up. "Come over here Benny and sit down.

Benny sat down and pulled his knees to his chest. Amos sat down beside him and pulled the big box over the two of them. Fate was with them once again, and Amos said a silent prayer as voices from the front of the store reached his ears. The two listened silently as the soldiers cleared the front of the store.

Finally they made their way to the back storage areas of the market. Amos and Benny could hear the soldiers calling out to one another, "Clear left! Clear Right! Clear center!" They called out as each room was cleared of any possible threat. Then the inevitable occurred. The soldiers burst into the storage room where Benny and Amos hid. "Clear left! Clear right! Clear center!" The soldiers in the room bellowed.

Amos held his breath and gripped the pistols in his hand waiting for one of the soldiers to check the box they hid under. "All clear, building secured. Regroup." Amos heard as one of the soldier's radio crackled with the order.

"Let's go guys there isn't anyone left alive in here." One of the soldiers said.

Amos and Benny stayed in place for another hour. "Okay Benny, lets go see if we can get the hell out of here." Amos pulled the box over their heads and tossed it to the side. Amos tried to stand, but both his legs had fallen asleep, and the muscles around the wound in his leg had tightened and were seized up.

Benny stood and looked down at Amos. "Arc you okay Amos." He said with great concern.

"I am fine Benny. Its just these old legs of mine seem to have fallen asleep. Kneel down here and help me rub the feeling back in them would you?" Amos began painfully kneed the muscles around his wound. Benny worked on the other leg.

After a few minutes Amos could stand and walk. The two made their way to the front of the store. Amos checked out the bodies of Al and Barry. The two were definitely dead. Both men had multiple gun shot wounds about their heads and chests. Barry had a .44 Smith and Wesson on his hip holster. Amos un-holstered the pistol and dumped the six rounds into his hand and placed them in his pocket. He found a box of rounds for the pistol in Barry's left cargo pocket. He pocketed these rounds also. He laid the gun on Barry's chest; he was already armed with two Ruger .44's and didn't see the need of carrying a third.

"Rest in peace my friend." He said has he stood and made his way over to one of the downed FEMA troopers.

Amos pried the Bushmaster M4 from the dead man's fingers. He then took the troopers gas mask holder from his hip. He dumped the mask and slung the carrier over his shoulder. Searching the troopers magazine pouches he found three fully loaded magazines. He dumped them in the gas mask carrier. He methodically searched all the troopers and came up with fifteen more fully loaded magazines. Off the last trooper he took another M4 and slung it across his back. "You never knew when you might need another rifle." He thought to himself.

"Let's go Benny." He said taking Benny's hand. In his right hand he carried the first M4.

"Where are we headed Amos?" He said looking up to him.

"I think we will make our way to Doc's house. I have got to get him to look at this leg." The two walked through the shattered front doors and into the carnage scattered around the market.

The two slowly walked down the road towards Doc's. They both tried to avert their eyes from the grassy field where bodies lay scattered like broken sticks after a winter storm. As they walked down the road they came to the forest. Both welcomed the shade of the trees, which blocked the hot afternoon sun.

The two walked in silence, both lost in their own thoughts, both trying to come to terms with the events of the day. "Mind if I hitch a ride fellas?" A voice said coming from the shadows of the forest.

Amos staggered back almost falling as he put to much weight on his wounded leg. With his left hand he shoved Benny behind him with his right he began to bring up the rifle to his shoulder. Once he had stabilized himself he swept the rifle from left to right looking for the person behind the voice.

"You better step on out before I blast the living hell out of you." He said in his most intimidating voice, hoping who ever it was would fall for his bluff and step out where he could see him.

"Well Amos, if you want to blast me I guess you better point that gun in the right direction." The voice said and then the man appeared from the trees to Amos's left.

"Well I'll be damned. I figured you were dead or captured like everyone else."

Joe slowly opened his eyes he tried to focus but everything was black, and it was hard to breath. As his mind cleared he realized he was laying face down in the dirt. With immense effort he rolled over to his back. Pain seared through his body as the dozens of small shrapnel wounds came in contact with the ground. Joe moaned as he rolled to his side.

"You've got to take stock Joe." He said to himself. Joe remembered charging the group of troopers with his pistols blazing. "Dumbest damned thing you ever did Joe." He said to himself again. "Now what the hell happened to my back, and why in blazes can't I hear a damn thing except for the ringing of my ears?" After a few moments of thought the memory came back to him. "The grenade, oh shit did I loose my legs?"

Joe rolled his head to the side and glanced down at his legs. Thank God they were still there. He assessed his body as he probed himself with his hands. Nothing seemed to be missing. Not a lot of blood either. I must have got hit with shrapnel in the back and back of my legs.

Once he was satisfied that he wasn't going to immediately die Joe rolled back to his stomach and made his way to the downed tree he had jumped over to escape the grenade. He realized that there was no more gunfire or explosions. Joe crawled closer to the tree and made his way to a portion of the tree that was slightly off the ground due to the branches suspending it a few feet off the ground.

He scrutinized the area around him. There were dozens of fires burning, bodies of troopers and his fellow ambushers lay tossed about the forest floor. The only thing that moved were the trees as the wind danced through their branches. He didn't see any wounded or people walking around for that matter. "How long had he been out?"

Joe slowly stood up. Even standing he saw nothing but the death around him. Joe staggered back over to where he had fallen and located both of his Glock pistols. The slides were locked backed on both, he had fired them dry. Joe pulled out two fresh magazines and reloaded both weapons and holstered them. He put the spent magazines in his cargo pocket.

Joe walked the forest floor looking among the dead for anyone living. He found no one, friend or enemy. "I need to get a rifle; a pistol just isn't going to cut it if I come across more of those troopers." Joe began to look around for a suitable rifle. He really didn't like the M16 or its smaller M4 cousin.

Finally he found what he was looking for laying a few feet from one of the dead ambushers. Joe picked up the AK47 pulled the mag out and verified that it was almost full. He jacked a fresh round in the chamber. He walked back over to the body of the ambusher. On the man's belt were two large pouches, one on the left the other on the right. Joe checked each pouch and found that each contained four fully loaded magazines for the AK. Joe released the clips on the back of the pouches and then affixed them to his own belt.

Joe then turned the man over. He was wearing one of the larger Camelback hydration packs. Joe removed the pack from the man then quickly sorted through the contents. The 100 oz. water bladder was almost full. In the front pouch he found a pretty descent first aid kit. Opening the kit he found a prescription bottle that was labeled Darvocet. Joe pondered the ups and downs of taking one of the pain pills.

Finally he decided he would take one of the tablets. He was really starting to feel the pain from the small shrapnel wounds in his back. He wasn't sure if he had a lot of ground to cover but he knew he would need to take the pill to take the edge of the pain away so he could concentrate on what was going on around him. He popped the pill in his mouth and took the drinking stem from the pack and took four large mouthfuls of water. "Damn, I didn't realize I was that thirsty."

Further inspection of the pack revealed a dozen energy bars, extra socks, foot powder, four more magazines for the rifle, two Zippo lighters, a poncho, a set of 10x30 binoculars, and some leather gloves. It wasn't much but it was a hell of a lot better than nothing. Joe stood and decided to make his way to the field where the FEMA troops had landed. The smoke was much thicker as he neared the field obscuring it from his view.

After carefully navigating his way through the trees he reached a destroyed bunker just near the edge of the tree line. He jumped down in the hole and almost landed on two dead men. A trooper and one of the ambushers lay intertwined in a frozen dance of death, both men had knives protruding from their chest.

Joe moved to the other side of the bunker and threw the pack up on the lip of the position. He fished out the binoculars and put them to his eyes. He scanned the area before him. He wasn't seeing a whole hell of a lot due to the smoke. Finally a strong breeze settled in from the south and he was able to make out the battlefield before him.

"Holy shit!" He said to himself as he focused in on the image before him. "It couldn't be." He thought as he pulled the binoculars from his face. Rubbed his eyes with his free hand not sure he had just seen what he saw. Then he brought the binos back up to his eyes and refocused them.

Several hundred yards away dozens of five ton army trucks were lined up in the field; their rear gates down and an armed soldier in the back of each. Another soldier stood at the rear of the trucks helping people with their hands tied behind their backs to board the trucks.

He finally rested the binos on one of the trucks in an attempt to see if he could make out anyone he knew from the citizens involved in the fighting. "Ah, shit, say it aint so." He said. He brought the binos into better focus. "Hells bells!" he grumbled. He saw the Novacheck's, Steve, and Celina in the back of the truck.

Joe slowly and patiently scanned the crowd of people on each of the trucks looking for Amos, Craig or Howard. For over thirty minutes he searched while the people and even FEMA troopers were being loaded up. His search came to no avail as he watched the last of the people load up. Then the trucks started up and blue smoke bellowed from the exhaust pipes above the cabs and they began to pull out in an orderly fashion heading south.

Joe watched in disbelief. What the hell was going on? Then the sound of a helicopter reached his ears as the last of the trucks made it to the road way. The helicopter came gently to a rest twenty yards or so away from several Bradley fighting vehicles which were beginning to pull out. From behind one of the stationary Bradley's Joe's astonishment doubled when he saw Colonel Haddock, and Johan walking towards the waiting helicopter with cigars hanging from their lips.

The two men tossed their cigars and boarded the helicopter and it lifted off and headed south. Everything became clear to Joe then. The military had not only double crossed the citizens that had gathered here to fight, but had double crossed FEMA, which could only mean they had circumvented civilian authority. Joe shoved the binos back into the pack. "You dirty rotten mother fuckers." He said as he jerked the zipper closed on the pack.

"I've got to get to Doc's and let him know what has happened." He thought as he picked up his rifle and pack and headed back into the forest. He decided he would follow the road by walking along the tree line to keep out of sight. There was no telling what kind of surprises that dirty son of a bitch Haddock had left around.

After walking slowly for an hour Joe took a knee and brought the drinking tube from the Camelback to his lips. He filled his mouth with water and sloshed it around and spit it out. He then sucked down another couple of mouthfuls of water before replacing the drinking tube to the clip on the pack strap. He took one more look around making sure he didn't spot anything suspicious when a man and a boy came into view. "Well I will be dipped in shit." He said as Amos and Benny walked around the bend in the road. Amos limped and had one of his thighs bandaged.

Joe remained still not wanting to spook Amos. He didn't know how well Amos knew how to use the M4 he was carrying and he didn't want to find out the hard way. As the pair drew closer Joe called out. "Mind if I hitch a ride fella?"

Amos's reaction was comical as he almost fell over while pushing Benny behind him. Amos panned the tree line with the rifle and finally stopped pointing the barrel off to Joe's right.

"You better step on out before I blast the living hell out of you." Amos shouted.

"Well Amos, if you want to blast me I guess you better point the gun in the right direction." Joe said as he stood up and stepped out of the trees.

"Well I'll be damned. I figured you were dead or captured like everyone else." Amos said as he lowered the rifle.

"Well I haven't been captured but I feel like I have died and been crapped out of a cat." Joe laughed and turned so Amos could see his back.

"Damn Joe what the hell did they shoot you with?"

"I caught some shrapnel from a grenade. I don't think it is to bad mostly superficial wounds. Where are we headed?"

"Benny and I are going to stop at my place get the truck and drive over to Doc's before I pass out. It looks like you will be joining us."

The trio began to walk. "Yeah I am going to need Doc or Maude to spend a little time picking metal out of my butt. Amos did you see what happened with the Army?"

"Yeah I know they double crossed us. Benny and I hid in the back of the market till they left. Have you seen anyone else?"

"They got Celina, Steve, and the Novacheck's. They loaded them up on trucks and headed south." Joe swallowed hard trying to control his emotions as he thought of what might await his favorite niece.

Amos saw the concern on Joe's face and knew he was thinking about Celina. "Don't worry Joe well hook up with everyone else and go get our friends. We are just going to have to tough it out and heal up before we go." The three walked the rest of the way to Amos's in silence.

Once they reached Amos's place Amos turned to Benny. Benny, run inside and get the keys to the Bronco. Then come straight back out here."

Joe turned to Amos. "Do you want to rest a little before we go?"

"No. I figure we better get in the truck and go while we are still able. If I lay down I aint getting back up until I sleep a day or two."

Benny ran back outside and handed the keys to Amos. "Alright let's load up." The three hopped into the big 4x4 and headed for Doc's.

They had just passed Steve's place and were coming out of the curve when Amos slammed on the breaks. "Joe does that rig belong to who I think it does?"

Joe opened the door and stepped out. "I think so Amos. Benny you better stay put." The two men slowly walked towards the destroyed eighteen wheeler. Not only due to caution but both were starting to feel the effects of their wounds.

"The cabs empty Amos." Joe said after he climbed down off the running board.

"Over here Joe." Amos called from the other side of the rig.

Joe ran to the opposite side of the rig and immediately saw Amos kneeling down beside Craig and Ann. Both were leaned against a large oak. Craig's face looked like someone had done a number on it. His face had several large bruises on it and his left eye was swollen shut. Ann didn't look to bad; she had a bruise across her forehead.

Joe ran back to the truck and got his pack, and ran back to Craig, Ann and Amos. He came to a stop and went to his knees. He pulled the drinking tube out and gave it to Ann. She drank greedily from it. When she was finished she placed it between Craig's lips. "Drink this Craig." Craig sucked down the water more feverishly than Ann had.

"What happened to you two?" Amos asked.

Ann spoke up first. "Howard got shot before we made it to the market by a FEMA scout party. We loaded him up and brought him to Doc. When we were leaving Craig spotted this helicopter in the sky. It started shooting at the house and then fired a missile at Doc's house. I don't know if it hit the house or not because then it turned on us."

Craig cleared his throat before he began to speak. "I don't know if anyone is alive back at the house or not. I am sorry we didn't head back but we were trying to save our own skins at the time."

Joe leaned close in to Craig. "What about Daphne?"

Ann rested her hand on Joe's shoulder. "Daphne was downstairs with everyone else fixing Howard up. I'm sorry Joe. Have you seen or heard from any of the others?"

"It's a little hard to explain and believe but the army double crossed everyone, including the FEMA boys. I saw the Novacheck's, Steve and Celina being loaded into a truck and they headed south. We've got to get yall loaded up. Then we need to head back to Doc's and check for any survivors."

Once everyone was loaded up Amos drove the short distance to Doc's. He and Joe stared in disbelief at what was once Doc's home. "Ann were they upstairs or down?" Amos asked.

"Everyone was downstairs when we left." She said.

Amos pulled around to the back of the house. He, Joe, and Ann had exited the truck. Craig had been given two of the Darvocet pills, and had immediately fell asleep, Benny stayed in the truck watching over Craig.

The three entered the back door of the basement and stepped inside. Most of the floor had collapsed, wires, and light fixtures hung from the ceiling. As Joe turned to look right relief swept over his body like a wave. There in the corner sat Daphne with Howard's head in her lap. "Daphne!" he shouted as he ran to her.

A smile full of joy swept across Daphne's face as her eyes locked with her Joe's. "Uncle Joe you have to help me Howard is hurt bad."

Ann and Amos came and stood beside Joe. "Daphne, are you okay?"

"Yes sir, I just wasn't strong enough to pull Howard outside. I knew someone would eventually come to help so I just stayed here with Howard."

Amos stepped forward and knelt beside her. "Daphne, have you seen Doc and Maude?"

Daphne bit her bottom lip, afraid that if she spoke she would burst out crying again. She only pointed to the rubble that covered the stairs. Then looked away not wanting to think about what happened to Doc and Maude.

Amos and Ann began clearing away some of he debris when Amos found Doc's arm sticking out from beneath a large timber that once helped support the roof. He leaned over and felt for a pulse. There was nothing. Try as he might he couldn't dislodge any more of the debris. On the other side of the stairs Ann found Maude's body crushed by more debris. Even with Amos and Joe trying to help her remove the debris they couldn't get to Maude's body either.

Joe stepped back and mopped the sweat from his brow. "Amos there is nothing else we can do. We need to get Howard back and tend to his wounds and ours. I can barely move."

"Alright Joe lets get out of here." Amos and Joe turned to go get Howard and leave.

"Wait a minute!" Ann shouted at them. "You can't just leave them here. They're our friends!"

Amos walked back and took Ann's hand. "Ann there is nothing we can do for them. Joe and I have been wounded, Howard, Craig, and even you. We have to go back to my place, get rested up and there will be time for Doc and Maude then."

Ann distressingly nodded her head and went to help the others load the unconscious Howard into the truck. Once they had Howard loaded up Joe and Amos each took one of the five gallon fuel cans from the back of the truck. They walked to the first level of Doc's house and doused as much wood and roofing material as possible. Joe lit a match and touched off the gasoline. The house began to burn again. Joe and Amos stood and stared at the flames both saying a prayer for their now dead friends. For the first time in a long time Amos cried.

Chapter 52

Steve, Celina, Bob, and Caroline were loaded onto the same truck by the soldiers. Most of the FEMA troopers had been flown out by helicopter for the camps in Birmingham. Steve dreaded what was to come, but with the hot sun beating down on them, a trip to Birmingham by helicopter would have been much more favorable than the long drive south. They had been told that any talking among the prisoners would bring down severe punishment. No one knew for sure if that meant some type of physical punishment administered by one or both of their guards on the truck, or a bullet to the head like in the fashion that had been administered to the poor guy who had opened his mouth when they were first told of their fate.

The convoy moved along Jackson Hwy. at a fairly good clip and traveled the few miles to Florence in quick order. When they reached Hwy. 133, also known as Cox Creek Parkway, the first thing they saw was that the clothing store that occupied the corner was burnt to the ground. If one looked closely enough you could make out the dried up husks of human remains that littered the department store. Dozens were scattered about and had most likely had been killed during the early rioting right after the collapse of American society.

The convoy made a left turn and formed up in the center turn lane of the broad five lane road. As far as the eye could see the parkway looked like a parking lot filled from shoulder to shoulder with stalled and wrecked vehicles. The turn lane had apparently been cleared by the soldiers when they convoyed north from Birmingham. Steve was stunned at how many dead people he saw. Many were nothing more than mere skeletons their flesh and organs picked clean by the weather and scavenging animals.

Soon they made their way into Florence's retail district. The area was densely packed, and full of clothing stores, restaurants, and a variety of other specialty stores found in almost any city in America. The majority of the businesses still stood, but had shattered windows, and doors. Still others had been burnt to the ground by roving bands of rioters, and looters.

The most shocking to Steve was the mall. Portions of the huge structure had been burned while other parts remained intact. That wasn't the shocking part. What was shocking to Steve was the number of bodies that littered the parking lot. Like the rest of the corpses they had seen these had decomposed and the flesh stripped clean after months of laying exposed to the elements.

Steve thought back to the early pandemonium when the lights first went out when he and Diane had been in the local Wal-Mart. Though he knew things had fallen into total anarchy he wasn't really prepared to believe that so many people would turn on one another and that so many would have died. If Florence a city of roughly fifty thousand people appeared to be in this condition what did the rest of America look like, especially the big cities? "Well I guess I will get to see that first hand when I reach Birmingham." He thought to himself.

He could tell by the looks on his friends faces that they too were just as shocked as he was. Despite all of the adversity his group of friends had been through it appeared as if they had, had a cake walk compared to those that had not prepared for possible disaster. Steve didn't feel he was as prepared as he should have been, but he pondered what it must have been like for all of those that relied on the government to make sure their every need would be taken care of.

Steve thought back to the time before the collapse. He thought of how the government was always telling the American people how they had everything under control during every emergency, which in most cases they did. He also thought of how the government labeled those that prepared for any disaster, man made, or natural, as kooks and paranoid. Before Y2K the government played down the possible dangers the public faced and told them to remain calm. While they were telling the public this the government, both federal, state, and to some extent local, spent billions in preparations erecting bunkers, and stock piles of food, medicine, and weapons. Not for the public at large but for the officials that led the country. Y2K turned out to be a nonevent, but it was a nonevent by the skin of the country's teeth. The government had spent billions to head off the collapse that was coming and had pulled it off.

After the September 11th attacks by terrorist the government had actually told people to keep seventy two hours worth of supplies on hand in case of a possible terror event. This amounted to the government doing little to prepare the citizens to be ready in case of a major event. The government spent billions on the military, on new surveillance systems, and taking away more freedoms from the American people. They spent almost nothing on civil defense, on educating the public about how to prepare, because the reality was that in a major event the government wouldn't be able to care for everyone. It would be the responsibility of each family to take care of itself until things were restored to normal. The government moved one hundred eighty degrees in the opposite direction though, passing laws forbidding the hoarding of food. What actually was the hoarding of food if you purchased supplies in times of plenty? Everyone had the same opportunity to plan and prepare during the times of plenty.

As Steve viewed the devastation around him he realized there was only one entity to blame for the collapse of the world that had been, the government. A government that frowned on individualism, on self reliance, it was a government that wanted to know everything you did, and wanted you to rely on it for everything you needed. It would have been so simple for the government to push the idea that everyone should have a three month supply of food and necessities not three days worth in the event of a major terror attack on the nation. It would have been so easy for the vast majority of Americans to go to a bulk discount store such as Sam's or Costco and purchased several cases of soups, stews, rice, beans, powdered milk, medicines and toiletries. Then when the bio and nuclear attacks had occurred instead of people rioting and running to the camps they would have been safe at home giving the government an opportunity to take a step back and use resources where they were best needed instead of having to declare martial law, patrol city streets, and fight rioters. Sure there would have been looting and rioting but not to the scale that the nation had seen after the most recent attacks.

Steve's thoughts were interrupted as the convoy slowed. He leaned back to see what the hold up was. The convoy had reached Wilson Dam and they were about to cross the Tennessee River. Both ends of the dam had an M1 Abrams tank and a group of about ten soldiers. The huge concrete walls of the power house by the dam were blackened and charred by fire. Steve could see groups of army engineers rebuilding the roof, and others were replacing the destroyed power lines and transformers. It appeared the army had made a small outpost by the dam and were busy getting its hydroelectric capabilities up and running. Who was the power for if everyone was being sent to re-education camps?

The convoy passed through parts of the city of Muscle Shoals. Florence's sister city though smaller looked to have suffered the same fate as Florence herself. Steve could only surmise what Sheffield and Tuscumbia was like. Most likely the four cities in the Shoals were nothing more than empty devastated husks of their former selves, populated by nothing but the dead.

Once the convoy cleared Muscle Shoals it headed down Hwy. 157 towards Interstate 65. The small towns of Moulton and Cullman didn't appear to be in as bad of shape as the Shoals but they were empty and desolate none the less. Once in Cullman they turned onto I65. The convoy drove south in the north bound lanes. Apparently the military had only cleared one section of the interstate; the southbound lane was filled with cars.

After more than an hour of riding Steve grew weary of staring out into the endless sea of cars, and the areas off of the off ramps were gas stations and restaurants had once stood. One only wanted to see so much of death and devastation. Steve closed his eyes and slept.

Steve was jerked awake as the truck came to an abrupt halt. It took him a few seconds to adjust his eyes to the bright glare of the sun. Like all the others on board Steve shifted in his position on the hard wooden bench to get a better view of what was coming up. The truck edged forward and then began to slowly drive forward at around ten miles per hour. The truck began to drive in a serpentine pattern as it drove through a maze of concrete obstacles.

"One more check point till we dump off this lot, and then it is Miller time!" the guard in the front of the truck said to the other.

"Don't get your hopes up this lot is going to the stadium for processing. Don't be surprised if the Lt. doesn't make us baby sit this trash all the way through the processing station."

"Naw, I don't think so. The Lt. is still higher than bat shit that he got to see some combat and kill some folks. I foresee wine and women in the forecast. I am sure the Lt. will find plenty of available women who are willing to get out of the compounds for some fun and relaxation."

Steve listened to the two guards banter back and forth. To him it sounded as if the army had its own little kingdom set up. They had all the guns therefore all the nicer things in life. The comment about the women being willing to do anything to get out of the compounds told Steve that the compounds had to be miserable places indeed.

As they passed through the check point gate Steve saw one hundred and fifty to one hundred and sixty men and women with shaved heads wearing drab grey jumpsuits, pouring concrete and into what looked like fortification walls going across all six lanes of traffic. Steve did a quick look behind him and realized there were no cars blocking the interstate behind them. He would have to find out later from Celina just what all he missed when he fell asleep. Evidently the army was building some type of fortified position just outside of Birmingham, and was using prisoners for the construction. Steve wondered what crime they had committed to be forced to work at hard labor.

They passed through the budding fortress within five minutes and were on there way to Birmingham itself. If Steve and the others had been shocked at the scenes of devastation in Florence and other smaller towns their shock was tripled when they arrived in Birmingham. Large skyscrapers like the Bell South building were burned out skeletons. Entire neighborhoods that could be seen from the interstate were all burned to the ground. Unlike Florence though it appeared the army had cleared most of the obstructions from major throughways and intersections. Nor did they see any decaying bodies on the roads below the interstate.

One thing they did see plenty of was armored Humvees sporting machineguns mounted in the open turrets guarding dozens of grey clad prisoners clearing debris and wreckage. Steve was positive the prisoners he viewed numbered in the thousands. He wasn't sure what crime they committed but he supposed the army had arrested thousands of looters and rioters and put them to work cleaning up the mess they had made.

"Alright folks we are almost there. Once we get to Legion Field you will be off loaded and lined up in an orderly fashion. You will not speak; you will keep your eyes on the floor. Anyone caught eye fucking the area, or talking will be dealt with severely. Once you are processed you will be assigned a sleeping shelter and cot. A crew boss will be waiting on you in your shelter. He is a prisoner that has shown above average conformity and loyalty and will give out your orders and dispense punishment.

At no time will you ask questions on your own accord. The only time you will ask a question is if you are asked to do so. Any attempt to flee from the re-education centers or a work detail will end with you being shot on the spot. No jury, no trial, nothing but a bullet. Oh and before I forget, any of you lovely ladies who are interested in entertaining a man in uniform can ask any soldier if he has needs of your services and it will get you a days pass on work details or extra rations. Alright we are here, remember what I said." The soldier finished his speech as the convoy pulled into the huge parking lot that surrounded Legion Field.

As Steve and the others stood he could see other convoys unloading people at different gates of the stadium. "Get your head down scum!" Steve heard the soldier behind him say just before he felt the butt of his rifle hit him between the shoulder blades. The blow knocked him to his knees. Before he fell forward he felt the soldier grab him by the hair and start to pull him to his feet. "Get your ass up and move boy!"

Steve groggily made his way to the end of the truck and jumped to the ground almost loosing his balance and falling face first on the pavement. Steve kept his head down and tried to catch glimpses of what was going on finally his group entered the stadium. Despite the numbers of prisoners and soldiers there was little commotion or speaking, just the occasional bark of an order from a guard or the groan of pain when a citizen was rebuked for some mistake.

Once inside they were formed into a single file line. As the passed guards station their flex cuffs were cut off. The line slowly shuffled forward and would stop. "Next twenty, move forward!" A guard shouted as he shoved Steve forward through a door that at one time had been a concession stand. "Sit!" another guard ordered. Steve made his way to a chair and noticed the mounds of human hair in that covered the floor. As he sat he heard the buzz of hair clippers come on.

The man cutting Steve's hair ordered him to look straight ahead. Steve lifted his chin and saw that there both men and women seated in the chairs to have their hair shaved off. One woman on the row ahead of him pulled away from the barber screaming "No! Not my hair!" The barber's hand lashed out like a cobra striking its prey and jerked her back in her seat, at the same instant a guard stepped forward with a long cattle prod and struck the end right between her breasts. The woman howled in pain and then slumped in the chair when the guard released her from the electrical shock. It was everything Steve could do not to jump up and try to kill the man. He knew though that once he did that he was dead. He had to bide his time and wait for the right moment.

The barber turned his head to the left and it allowed Steve to look at Celina. She had her face facing him; tears flowed down her cheeks as the barber shaved her beautiful long hair from her head. Finally the barbers were done. "Stand up and look at the floor! Face left and file out now." One of the guards ordered. The filed there way up to the next level of the stadium.

Steve's group entered an area that had apparently been recently constructed. From his memory of the stadium lay out this should have been a seating area. Apparently the army had built some type of platform and placed a concrete room in place of the seats. To his left Steve could make out a enormous pile of clothing. One of the guards stepped forward. "Everyone eyes forward and on me!" The guard paused for the group to comply with his orders. Once he was satisfied he continued. "At this time you will be showered and deloused. Now everyone will strip. You will keep your shoes though. Now do it!"

Steve began to take off his shirt and noticed that Celina had not moved. Their eyes met. All Steve could do was to nod his head to try to get her to comply. Celina didn't move.

Steve stripped finished stripping and held his boots in his hands. "What the fuck is your problem missy?" A guard shouted. "Strip you freaking little whore and do it now."

Celina stood her ground. "Screw you pervert." She said and spit in his face.

The guard didn't say another word. He struck Celina in the stomach with the cattle prod dropping her to her knees screaming. "You stinking son of a bitch!" Steve roared swinging his heavy boots up catching the guard in the chin sending him flailing backwards. Steve halted his assault and turned to reach for Celina.

Before their hands could touch Steve felt an electrical charge surge through his body dropping him to the floor. As he rolled to his back he raised his arms over his face as he saw the heal of a combat boot come crashing down towards his face. Steve writhed in pain as several soldiers kicked, stomped and electrocuted him.

Celina got up and reached out to help Steve but received rifle butt to her stomach doubling her over. She tried to get back up but Bob and Caroline rushed forward, both fully nude. Caroline whispered as loud as she dared into Celina's ear as she held her back. "Just do what they say Celina. We'll get our chance at payback, now is not the time to stand up to them. Follow their orders and stay out of sight out of mind, we'll all get a chance at our revenge."

Celina's head dropped to her chest and she began to strip. The guards jerked Steve's bruised and battered body to his feet. "Next time you touch a guard you'll be dead you son of a bitch." One of the guards said and finished the sentence with an open hand slap to the back of Steve's neck that rocked him where he stood.

Steve didn't raise his head to look in the eyes of the guards, but he remembered their faces for future reference. He might have been beaten down but he was far from being beaten into submission. A fire for revenge burned deep in his chest, and he would have it sooner or later.

Celina finished stripping and turned back into line her head hung low. Her heart was heavy with guilt for getting Steve beaten for trying to protect her. "Now isn't that better?" The guard said patting her on her bare butt. "Pretty nice, you come see me later and we'll see about keeping you off the work crews. Now get moving." He finished with a shove between the shoulder blades.

The group made their way into the small fifteen by fifteen room. Over their heads were a dozen shower nozzles. The group was packed into the room like sardines in a tin with almost no room to move. Then ice cold water cascaded down from the nozzles everyone gasped as the air felt like as if it was being sucked from their lungs. The group endured the deluge of water for five minutes then the water stopped and the door on the opposite end of the shower room opened.

"Alright let's go people! Get your shriveled up asses out here." Another guard shouted.

They were herded along another corridor until they came to another large newly built room. They shuffled into the room. There was a large thirty foot long counter top and a three foot space for the group to move along the front of it. Stationed behind it were other prisoners. The guard called out the next order. "File all the way down and line up in front of one of the people behind the counter. Let's move I haven't got all damn day maggots."

Steve stepped forward to the man in front of him. "What size pants and shirt do you wear?" he asked in a monotone robotic voice.

"My waist size is thirty, thirty two length, chest size is forty eight." Steve replied.

The man turned to a bin behind him and came back with grey colored pants and shirt, and a pair of heavy socks. "Dress and move along." The man said his eyes looking lifeless, his voice deadpan.

Steve quickly pulled the socks on his feet then the pants, they were about two inches to long but fit okay in the waist. His shirt was way too big in the chest. Finally he put on his water soaked boots. "Let's move maggots!" The guard said shoving the prisoner closest to the exit against the door frame for moving to slow.

"Well I guess I figured out what crime those prisoners committed on all those work parties, they were Americans." Steve thought to himself as he moved out of the room. "How in the hell had America come to this sorry state of affairs?"

The next station they were processed at they were all given shots for various viruses, and were hurried to the next station located on the third level. The room they were herded into next was huge. It was filled with chairs, the guards ordered the prisoners to sit. The room filled up and held over two hundred prisoners. A small man in army BDU's wearing the rank of major stepped to a small podium equipped with a microphone.

"Welcome citizens!" He said in a cheerful voice. "I am Major Danner, I will be conducting your introduction briefing today. This briefing will fill you in on your duties and function here at re-education camp 457. I will also inform you about the status of the United States and the rest of the world. I am sure most of you have had little or no communication with the outside world, obviously because you have taken so long to choose to come here and help build a better America. Now let's get started shall we?" The Major took a sip of water from a glass under the podium, and cleared his throat.

"Now as I am sure you are all aware we were attacked by the Chinese and Koreans and a limited nuclear war followed. What many of you don't know is that a second major biological attack occurred several months after the limited nuclear exchange. This biological attack wiped out over eighty percent of the population. Most of the deaths occurred in the metropolitan cities." The major paused again to let the news take its effect as it had with so many rural people that had been isolated and knew nothing of the second attack. In many cases this news alone was enough for people to believe they had to buckle under to the army so order could be restored.

"As far as the rest of the world is concerned, well Europe, Asia, Australia, and South America were also plagued by this biological attack. From intercepted radio reports it is believed that the population of the earth is now only two billion people. For those of you that don't remember the population of the world was six and a half billion. So in a nut shell it's every country for themselves. There are no relief efforts or monetary aid everyone is scrambling to secure their own countries.

Now, to the current situation here in the states, as many of you are aware the federal government through FEMA went power crazy. They took your food, supplies, and forced many Americans into re-location camps. The military decided that the government had exceeded its authority and stepped in to take control. We will reestablish a Constitutional government. To do this we need every citizen to comply with our orders and do as we say.

I know many of you may be confused since some of you were a bit reluctant to join us and were forced to come. You are confused about the position you are now in. All you have to know though is that obedience and conformity is the only path to a renewed America. Follow the rules of the camps. Lift your chin proudly as you help clear the debris from our cities, and rebuild them. One day, maybe not in your lifetime, but in your children's lifetimes America will be reborn.

After you leave here you will be assigned to a work battalion, your DNA, and fingerprints will be taken, and then you will be given your identifier. From there you will be led down to the field for your temporary housing. After several days you will be moved through the west gate. The parking area and the old housing tracts have been converted into living areas. Your battalion will be assigned a barracks. The barracks compound is surrounded by razor wire and guard towers for your protection.

There is a chow hall for every four barracks. Your crew boss will show you which chow hall is yours. Toilet and shower facilities are communal and each barracks has its own. For your protection on work detail a detachment of soldiers will accompany you. Any attempt to run away from a detail is considered treason against the United States and violators will be either shot or captured and returned for corporal punishment.

One of the most important things to remember is that obedience and conformity is the one path to a renewed America. I am sure I have covered everything with you now if..." The major's speech was interrupted when one of the men on the front row stood up and shouted him down.

"Obedience and conformity for a renewed America my ass! You sons of bitches are creating a dictatorship. I've kept my mouth shut as long as I could stand; you people are the traitors to America! You people..." The man never finished his sentence. Four of the eight guards in the room rushed forward. He was struck almost simultaneously by four cattle prods.

The man went down to the ground screaming and withering in pain. He tried to stand back up and fight but was met with boot heels, fist, and cattle prods each time. "That's enough!" The major shouted.

The four soldiers stood back but were ready to pounce the instant the man made any type of offensive move. "I guess I did forget to tell you people something." The major said, with a tone of irritation and anger in his voice. "What this man just did is treason. Speaking out against the government in any fashion is treason and punishable by death." He said walking up to the man who still lay on the floor. "Pick him up." He ordered the soldiers. "Now since you are new here I will not charge you with the maximum penalty."

The major reached in his back pocket and came out with a slap jack. "But I will not tolerate any one of you ungrateful pieces of trash raising your voice to me." Then with a lightening quick motion of the arm the major began to bludgeon the man across the face and head. The slap jack tore open the man's freshly shaved head in four different places and blood covered his face and head and puddle up on the floor as he once again went down.

The major finally stopped and took a deep breath replacing the slap jack in his rear pocket. "When he is finished processing take him to the hole. Put him in for a week, bread and water only once a day. Maybe he will figure out his place in that time." He said to the nearest soldier. Now the rest of you get up and get the hell out of my classroom."

Everyone stood and made their way for the door. On the next level they were brought to another large room. Inside they found fifty women sitting behind small desks with an empty chair in front of it. On each desk there was something that appeared to be some type of electric pin. Steve, Bob, Caroline, and Celina were in the first group of fifty to enter the room. They were ordered to take a seat at one of the small tables.

Steve sat and looked at the woman in front of him. "Give me your right arm palm down." She said in an expressionless voice which seemed characteristic of all the prisoners here.

Steve laid his arm on the desk. The woman rolled his sleeve up and then picked up what Steve finally recognized as a tattoo pen. The woman turned it on and began to put a tattoo on Steve's forearm. "Don't move if you screw up your identifier you will most definitely regret it."

Steve kept his arm steady as he watched the woman work. Beads of sweat formed on his forehead and the muscles in his arm twitched as she worked. When she was done she wiped the blood away with alcohol soaked gauze. Steve stood and made his way for the door with the others. Before rolling his sleeve down he looked at the tattoo. "What the hell did all the numbers mean? C457Z12:14A.

The group was then taken to another room were they were told to show their identifiers, give their names, and date of birth. A cue tip swab was taken and rubbed on the inside of their mouths for DNA, and their finger print and hand prints taken. The group was then led down to the bottom of the stadium near the entrance to the field.

The doors opened and the soldiers pushed them out into the opening. Steve looked up to see the night sky but the field below was well lit from the stadium lights. The interior of the stadium looked nothing like he remembered from watching Alabama, Auburn games in the past. There were no more seats in the stands. Hell there wasn't any more stands. The army had torn them out and enclosed the seating area turning it into their processing center which Steve and the others had traveled through.

"Alright I want everyone to line up in rows of tens. Each of you look at the tattoo on your arm. The last three numbers are you. I want numbers one through ten A to line up in the first row. Eleven through twenty A on the second. I think you can figure out the rest." A big muscle bound man towering over six and a half feet tall dressed in prison garb said. "My name is Schumer, and I am your work boss. You are work battalion Zulu 12. You will follow my orders or you will regret you ever met me. You will also follow the orders of any other work boss. You can identify us by the red stripe on our pants." He pointed down to the blood red stripe on his right leg.

"For the next couple of days you will sleep here inside the stadium until your barracks is ready. Enjoy the next couple of days because after you leave here you are going to get to work. Right now there are one hundred of you in Zulu 12 I expect in the next few months there might be thirty or less of you. You better look out for one another because there are never any replacements for a work battalion. Once your all dead a new Zulu 12 will be formed the only difference is that the sucker that gets your number will have a B after it and next a C and on down the line.

Now keep your mouths shut and follow me." Steve followed Bob who was just in front of him. Schumer took them to the field which was covered with cots. The only things to protect them from the elements were large plastic tarps that were held up in the air by eight foot tall tent poles.

Schumer walked under the tarps and led them to an empty section of one hundred cots. Each cot had a wool blanket folded on top of it. "This is where you will sleep. If you have to piss or shit there are Porto johns on the south side of the field. You will not get a shower for the next couple of days until you get to your barracks. Morning chow will be at

0700, dinner at 1200, and supper at 1800. It will be served at the north end of the field. You will be given a paper plate, plastic fork and spoon, and a cup of water. Keep your plastic cup; you can get water to drink on the east end of the field. The army has a couple of water buffalos set up." With out another word Schumer left them.

Steve, Celina, Bob, and Caroline all took cots next to each other. Steve and Bob each chose to sleep on either side of the women so they could offer some type of protection. They were not really concerned about anyone from their work battalion since it was made up of people they had fought with. They had not seen many people yet from Florence since entering the re-education camp.

Steve and Celina sat on a cot beside one another Bob and Caroline on the one across from them. Steve wrapped his arm around Celina who laid her head on his shoulder. "How many people do you think we saw getting processed in today Bob?"

"Hell I don't know Steve. There had to be at least a few thousand. I know I at least saw a couple hundred of those five tons filled with people when we got here. The thing I want to know is how many camps are there?"

Caroline rolled up her sleeve and looked at the tattoo that was beginning to scab. "Well I image the C is for camp, and the major did say welcome to camp 457. So I would assume there are at least 457 camps at a minimum."

Celina piped in with her thoughts on the subject. "Well are there 457 camps in Alabama or what is left of America? I mean how many people can they actually hold? Damn, how many people are really left alive. I can't believe we were hit with another biological attack."

The two couples talked for a little while longer before Steve called a halt to the discussion. "I don't know about yall, but I think we better get some sleep. I know I can use the rest, my body feels like it was run over by a train." Steve said good night and the others followed suit. He groaned as he lay down on his cot and covered himself with the blanket. He closed his eyes to sleep.

"Steve. I am sorry I got you beat up today." Celina said as she rolled over to face him.

Steve turned his head to look at her. "Celina don't blame yourself. At least you had the guts to stand up to the bastards. Although it was probably the wrong time to do it, you still had the guts to do it. Now quit worrying about it and get to sleep." Steve rolled back over and fell into a deep sleep.

—•——•—

Two days later Schumer came to their shelter. "All right lets fall out and I want yall to fall out like you were lined up the other day by the numerical order of your identifier."

Steve rolled over and set up on his cot and leaned over and shook Celina's shoulder. "Get up Celina we're moving."

Celina sat up and rubbed her eyes. "Well it's about time. I'm ready to get a real roof over my head and get a shower. What has it been two days since we bathed?" Celina rubbed her now stubble covered head as she stood.

They made their way to the others and took their place beside bob and Caroline. Schumer stood before the group like a drill sergeant. "I am going to call roll. I will call out the last digits of your identifier. You will respond by saying here boss. Roll call will conducted first thing each morning, lunch, and at the end of the work day." Schumer cleared his throat and began roll call.

"21A!" He called. The man identified as 21A responded with a "Here boss." The man was on the forth row. Schumer paused and looked up from his check list. "21A, front and center." Apparently the man had some former military training as he moved to face Schumer with military precision. As he came to a stop in front of Schumer he came to the position of attention.

Without warning Schumer landed a meaty fist to the man's solar plexus instantly dropping him to his knees. Schumer followed up with a knee strike to the man's face crushing his nose, blood exploded down the man's face and onto his chest, as he fell toward the ground. Schumer stopped his collapsing form by grabbing him by the throat, his iron like grip squeezing like a vice almost collapsing the man's esophagus.

"Tell me 21A, what part of numerical order do you not understand?" Schumer lifted his gaze to those who remained in formation. "When I give an order I expect it to be followed. What you see before you is a man who obviously defied my authority."

His grip tightened and the man struggled in vain as he tried to pull Schumer's hand from his throat. The man gasped and gagged for air, his eyes bulging lips turning blue as he struggled to breath. Then in one swift motion Schumer switched his grip to the man's chin his other hand coming behind the back of his skull, he made a twisting motion. There was an audible snap as he broke the man's neck. Schumer let him drop and didn't bother to look at the man's twitching body.

He bent over and picked up his clip board. "Now that, that little spectacle is over, let's get back to business." Schumer began to call out the roll again as if nothing had taken place.

Once the roll was called Schumer led them out of the stadium to the barracks area. The barracks area was a buzz of activity. Prisoners marched in silent formation, some with picks, shovels, axes, and other outdoor working tools. Others marched with empty hands their function unknown. As they passed between barracks Steve was able to see the perimeter. The perimeter was surrounded by twenty foot high chain link fence, barded wire laced through it and razor wire on the top and on the ground on both sides. Steve also made out electrical insulators on the fence.

Schumer led them into one of the barracks. The building was approximately seventy five feet long and thirty feet wide. Along each wall were twenty five bunk beds. There was a small office that had a full size bed and desk. Over the door were the words "Work Battalion Boss". There were no windows and the interior was lit by weak naked bulbs every ten feet down the center of the large open area. Showers and toilets were located in another room by the Boss office.

"Alright folks, the beds are numbered. Go to your bed, turn down the mattress, and lay your blanket over the mattress. Then form back up we have a work detail slated. Let's move!" He said barking out the last of his order.

The work battalion scrambled to find their numbered bunk. Within moments the bunks had the mattresses turned down and wool blankets laid over them. All of them that is except for the bunk marked 21A. As they filed back out the doors Schumer handed out brown leather work gloves. "Hurry up and form up." He said as each took a pair of gloves from the box.

Work Battalion Zulu 12 was informed that they had cadaver cleanup. No one really knew what this was going to entail, but were not that eager to find out. In short order five ton army trucks pulled up in front of the barracks. They were flanked by four Humvees sporting M249 machineguns, and crewed by four soldiers each.

"Alright in groups of fifteen I want you to load each truck. Just to let you know if you try to escape you will be shot. Women who try to escape may be captured alive, depending on how good they look of course, and be put on moral lifting details for the troops. Be advised that unmanned observation drones are circling overhead. They have FLIR, infa-red and are armed with 2.75 inch Zuni rockets. So why you are going through these homes looking for bodies don't even think of running." Groans from more than one person could be heard from Zulu 12 at the prospect of moving corpses. "One more thing, if any of you find a weapon and plan on using it or concealing it for later use, beside your self, five other prisoners will be executed. If you kill a soldier one quarter of the battalion will be executed. Now with that in mind load up."

The trucks drove through debris littered streets, some with work battalions working to clear the roads. Steve and the others were astounded that the wreckage was even worse than what he had glimpsed from the interstate on the trip into Birmingham. Soon the trucks slowed then stopped in a residential area in the western part of the city. They were herded off the trucks and put into groups of ten.

The groups were then placed in groups of five in front of each house on one side of the house. The Hummers were stationed to be able to watch the front and rear of the homes. The soldiers that had ridden in the hummers had exited and took advantageous positions to monitor the prisoners. Then the groups were ordered to enter the homes. Some came up with nothing, while others found the decomposing remains of the former residents.

Steve, Celina, Bob, and Caroline were in a group and were joined by another woman named Fran. Bob entered the master bedroom of the house. "Uh, guys I think we have some work to do." Bob called out to the other four. In the bed lay two decomposed bodies, a man and a woman. The two bodies intertwined in an embrace of death. On the night stand sat two glasses and an empty pill bottle.

The other four came into the room. "Good find Bob! Glad you are so eager to find this shit." Fran said with her hands on her hips.

Caroline turned to Fran. "Why don't you zip it Fran. None of us want to be here and sure as hell don't want to be picking up dead bodies. So suck it up and let's get these people out into the street before we wind up like 21A."

"Like hell I will pick up that!" She said in disgust her finger pointing at the two dead bodies.

"Fran obviously you forgot what Schumer did to that guy this morning. He killed that guy and no one said crap about it. What do you think he is going to do to you if you don't work?" Celina said, trying to persuade the woman that to defy the orders meant death.

"Screw you guys! I am out of here." With that said Fran headed out the room and then out the back door.

The four friends took the sheets and folded them in and carried the two bodies out in the wrapped sheets. They carried the bodies to the center of the street as they were ordered, and saw two soldiers dragging Fran out from behind a nearby house.

"Let me go you freaking bastards!" She said as she screamed and kicked trying to get away.

One of the soldiers reared a balled fist back and cold cocked her. Her body slumped as she slipped into unconsciousness. "Hey Daryl" The soldier called to one of the soldiers by the truck. "Looks like we have entertainment for the night." The two soldiers and the third by the truck all laughed.

Fran was literally tossed up into the back of the five ton like a sack of potatoes. The third soldier had climbed in the back of the truck and drug her by her hair to the back. He then hogtied her, then sat down on the bench seat and rested his feet on her back while he lit a cigarette.

"If any of you other ladies wish to entertain tonight please feel free to make a run for it." He yelled to some of the female prisoners as he exhaled the smoke from his lungs.

Celina and Caroline quickly averted their eyes so as not to egg the soldier on. "Come on lets hit the next house before they decide to tie up a few more of us." Celina said keeping her head bowed submissively.

They entered the next house on their gruesome scavenger hunt. Caroline walked into the first bedroom which was decorated as a nursery. Hesitantly she approached the crib that sat against the wall. In the crib was a bundle of blankets. She slowly inched her hand forward and reluctantly pulled the blankets back. What she saw made her gasp and cry out in shock.

Bob was just walking by the room when Caroline cried out. He rushed into the room to see what had frightened his wife so. "What is it Caroline? What's wrong?" He said as he walked up behind her putting his arms around her pulling her to him.

Caroline said nothing and just pointed to the crib. Bob moved Caroline behind him and approached the crib. He knew what he was going to find even before he stepped up to the rail. The sight shocked him just as it had Caroline, but at least he had mentally prepared himself for what he was going to see.

In the crib a baby, the body swaddled in blankets the head visible where Caroline had pulled back the blankets. The skin looked like dry leather, the cheeks sunken in, the eye sockets staring blankly into eternity, a tuff of blond hair sprouting from the little skull like spring grass blooming for the first time.

He turned back to Caroline. Steve and Celina had entered the room and stood by her side. "I'll take care of this. Are there any others?"

"No, the rest of the place is empty. Come on Caroline, you come with Celina and me." Steve said taking her by the elbow.

As the other three left the room Bob covered the infant's face and cradled it into his arms. The small bundle weighed nothing. He felt as if he was just carrying the blankets and nothing else as he walked out to the street. He gently lay the baby down beside a stack of twenty corpses in varying stages of decay.

The four then went on about the business of the cadaver patrol as Steve had come to think of it. As they finished clearing all of the houses on the street several of the men were given cans of diesel and flares and ordered to torch the bodies. They moved on to the next street, and the next. It seemed to last forever. A never ending horror show of the dead. "Damn, did everyone in Birmingham die?" Steve thought to himself at the end of the day as they headed back for the camp.

No one said anything the entire ride back to camp. They were off loaded in front of their barracks. Schumer stood before them. "Okay its chow time in forty minutes. If you prefer you may shower before coming to chow. There will be no formation march for chow. Chow is served from six pm till seven thirty. I would suggest you go get in line now. You share this chow hall with three other barracks. "With that Schumer dismissed them and headed inside to his personal room, and shower.

The four friends made there way to the chow hall. A long line had already formed. They fell in behind an older man in his mid fifties. The man turned to Steve. "Yall with the new bunch that came in a few days ago?"

"Yeah we got here three days ago." Steve replied.

The man turned away from them and angled his body towards the wall. "Listen, they really don't like you talking in the chow line, or in the chow hall. After chow you can go to the exercise yard and talk all you want there. You've got to be back in the barracks by ten thirty though, otherwise you get shot." The old man faced back to the front of the line.

"Thanks." Steve said.

The four finally made it inside and got their chow thirty minutes later. They were given a metal plate and a glop of something was slapped on the plate. They were given a hunk of bread and a glass of water. The food was hot and appeared to be some type of stew with little meat. They mimicked the other prisoners around them and wolfed the food down. They silently stood and dropped their dishes off and headed for the barracks.

They arrived back at the barracks along with the majority of their battalion. Every one sat on the bunks and began to talk about the order in which people should shower. After ten minutes of discussion Steve had had enough. He stood. "Hey folks lets make this real simple. Let the ladies go first. When they are done the men get in. I don't know how much hot water there is so let's make sure everyone just bathes quickly and then get out."

Everyone nodded in agreement. One of the women stood. "Does anyone know if we get towels?"

"I guess we can ask Schumer." One man said as he rose and walked over to Schumer's door, and knocked.

"Come in." Schumer barked.

The man came sailing back out of the office blood pouring through his fingers from a broken nose, where Schumer had punched him.

Schumer stepped out of the door. "I don't know if you fuckers think this is the Hilton. Get in there and wash your nasty bodies and leave me the hell alone. By the way you're picking up the dead again tomorrow so if any of you ladies wish to get out of that detail you can come in and entertain me and I will put you on kitchen detail." He stood there for a moment with his hands on his hips. "No takers huh? Well some of you will change your mind soon enough." With that he turned and slammed his door shut.

Steve and Bob went over and helped the injured man to his feet and sat him on a nearby bunk. The women filed into the shower area and began to bathe. "Lean forward and squeeze your nose." Bob said to the man.

The man leaned forward holding his nose dripping blood on the floor. "I'm going to kill that son of a bitch first chance I get." He said in a nasal tone.

"I'm not sure if you want to do that. They find out you did it your as good as dead." Steve said.

The man sat up and looked Steve in the eye. "I think I prefer death over living like a slave."

"No one said we had to live like slaves forever. One day when the opportunity comes up I am going to kill as many of these bastards as I can, then get the hell gone. I'm not wasting my life by just killing some over sized bully like Schumer."

The man stood and began to walk back to his bunk. "You kill the ones you want, I am killing that fucker. Thanks for the help." The man walked back to his own bunk.

Bob looked over to Steve. "Well Steve when do we make our break?"

Steve leaned forward resting his elbows on his knees while he rubbed his temples. "Bob I am not sure when we can make a break for it. As far as I can tell when we are out today, the soldiers keep a pretty good eye out on us. I didn't see any sign of the drones they are supposed to be flying overhead, but do we chance a break with those things flying overhead?"

"Well maybe we should wait awhile and see how things go. I just hope we can live long enough to make that break. As far as getting a shot at Johan, and Haddock, I would love to kill both for their treachery but I don't know how feasible an attempt would be, even if we could find out where they are now."

"Alright I guess we keep our eyes open, and our mouths shut. I don't think we should ask too many questions about how the soldiers and the camps are run. I am sure there are plenty of informers. After we get done with the showers I say we head over to the exercise yard and see what we can find out."

"Sounds good to me. Looks like the ladies are through showering let's get in and get out and head to the exercise yard.

Chapter 53

Steve slowly opened his sleep filled eyes, his mind still troubled by all of the faces he kept seeing in his dreams. Faces of lost family, friends, and even those of the enemies he had killed. He eased the wool blanket off of his prostrate stiff aching body. He stifled a groan as he swung his bare feet to the cold wood floor. Looking around he saw the others still slept, most balled up in the fetal position under their wool blankets.

Taking a deep breath he exhaled blowing a plume of condensation from his mouth. "Damn, its probably thirty degrees in here." He thought to himself as he walked to the end of his bed.

Kneeling down he unlocked the small wooden chest that he had been allowed to keep. The rules had been relaxed somewhat as time went on and members of the work battalions were allowed to keep some items they had scavenged. Opening the chest he reached in and moved a wool sweater he had been issued. Underneath lay half a case of king size Snicker bars. He and Bob had found a dozen cases in an old convenience store just before his battalion was to head back to camp after a day of scavenging. They had distributed the bars and were able to smuggle them back to camp. Steve, Bob, Celina, and Caroline saved theirs for when they felt the most drained and weak. Others had just gobbled them down with in a day or two. Now the four friends had to sneak theirs and keep them locked up to keep the others from getting a hold of the treasured candy bars.

He slipped the bar into the pocket of his well worn pants. He pulled out the sweater and a towel and locked the chest back up. Picking up a five gallon bucket at the end of the bed he made his way to the showers. The shower room was pitch black but he confidently walked past the toilets and sinks like he had a few hundred times before. He found the door which led to the shower room and opened it.

Two small windows filtered light into the room. Steve had to blink his eyes several times to get them adjusted to the light. Even the overcast light of false dawn was harsh on his eyes. He sat the bucket on the floor and pulled a large plastic tote tray out, and sat it on the floor. He folded and placed the sweater in the tote, then began to shuffle his feet back and forth on the cold concrete floor of the shower room as he undressed.

Placing his clothes in the tote Steve made his way to one of the knobs and turned on the water. Cold water showered his body making him lose his breath. He forced himself to stand under the blast of cold water. Every second invigorating his body waking him, slowly the water warmed then turned scalding hot, just like he liked it. Finally warmed and awake he reached out with his foot and pulled the bucket to him. Flipping it over, he sat down and let the steaming hot water cascade over his body. This was the one luxury the camp offered. The government had brought in some engineers during the summer and actually built a steam plant to help power the camp and surrounding area, and also providing the camp with hot water.

The hot water was the only humanity left to many in the camp. Steve often woke early in the morning before dawn just to sit under the spray of hot water. On cold mornings like this it helped soothe his sore muscles and joints. He slowly massaged his calf muscles as his mind wandered.

The days had turned into weeks, the weeks into months; the months had slowly turned into a year or more. Steve wasn't quite sure; he had lost track of time some where along the way. The days and many nights were filled with back breaking labor, fights, some to the death, even over little things like the two cans of peaches he found in an almost empty warehouse. A man from a different work battalion, Kilo 7, had attempted to steal the cans from Steve. The two began to fight, and then the fight turned to a death match when the man had pulled out a shank. Steve had thrown the bigger man over a banister and he fell down three floors to the hard concrete floor below. His head exploding in a spray of blood as it impacted the floor. The two soldiers who had witnessed the fight barely batted an eye when they saw the man fall. Steve could still see the look of horror on the man's face as he fell screaming to his death.

The opportunity to escape had never seemed to come. Slowly though over the past few months the guards had become more lax, well they had with work battalion Zulu12, and other battalions that were down to nothing. Those that still had a large contingent of workers were still ruled with an iron fist. Work battalions thinned out due to death, or some members were deemed recoverable. In other words they had the right temperament to be ruled. These people had been moved out of the camps and into homes that had been cleaned up for their occupation. They still were told exactly what to do and what jobs they could have. Farmers for example worked in collectives modeled after the old Soviet style. People like Steve and those of his battalion who had fought occupation and government rule were relegated to a life in the camps. So far it appeared to Steve the only escape was death.

Steve's work battalion only had ten members left. The other ninety had perished, either from murder, sickness, escape attempts, work accidents or suicide. He and those that were left had been discussing escape the past few weeks. They had to make their move soon or they would be too weak not only to fight if necessary, but run. They were now down to having only three guards accompany them on work parties. Because there were so few of them they mostly did scavenging work, because they could be controlled easier than a large work battalion.

Their means of escape they hoped would be during inclement weather. The men who guarded them had become very lax and anytime it stormed they would find a suitable structure, and let them all wait out the weather. Number one because they didn't want to get wet. Number two usually the members of Zulu 12 chose to sleep, or a couple was allowed to head to a back room with no exits to become intimate. This made guarding them so much easier. Usually one or two of the guards would nap during these times. The third reason and their possible avenue to escape was Sally.

Sally was a reformed prostitute, and had changed her life before the collapse and had chosen to make something of her self. She had fought along side other members of the battalion during the battle at St. Florian. Since their capture she earned a reputation as a hard, honest worker willing to help any in need. The last attribute came to the forefront once she learned the others were discussing escape.

She discussed her idea with the group. Caroline, Celina and Mary were adamant that in no way should she subjugate herself to doing the things she talked about. "Listen up!" She had said. "I was a prostitute for five years before I changed my life. Sleeping with these three guards in no way is going to traumatize me. Beside that if it is going to free us then it is a sacrifice I am willing to make. That is unless one of you girls wants to take my place." The other three women were brave, but not that brave.

So the plan had come about that the next time they were holed up in some building during a storm Sally would offer her services. Once one or two of the guards were distracted they would make their move and kill their guards, and escape and hopefully make their way back to Florence. So far though, the weather had not cooperated. There had been nothing but clear skies for the past month.

Steve cracked an eye open when he heard the door squeal on rusty hinges as it was opened. Celina walked in carrying her own bucket, and towel. "Good morning gorgeous. What are you doing up so early?"

"I've got to wash my hair before we get started today. You know how I like to have my hair looking its best when we go out." She smiled playfully as she ran her hand over her shaved head. She quickly stripped and placed her own clothes in a tote and pulled her bucket under the shower head next to Steve.

Steve had thoughtfully turned on her shower and the water had quickly heated up by the time she was undressed. There was little modesty between the two; they had become intimate almost a year ago. "You want a bite?"

Steve opened his eyes again to see Celina holding up one of her Snicker bars. "I've got my own good looking." Steve said as he leaned his bucket back and reached underneath and pulled out his own. "I am so damn tired I think I am going to eat the entire thing. I need the calories bad."

They both agreed they needed the calories and without another word the two gobbled down the candy. Celina walked over to her tote and pulled out a bar of soap. Celina began to lather up with the bar of soap she had found several days ago. Keeping clean wasn't just a matter of smelling good any more; it was a matter of life and death, any type of infection could kill you. She began to bathe as they talked. "Steve I think we need to chance an escape whether it is storming or not."

"Celina we have been over this a hundred times. Our best chance is during a storm. The army can't fly the Predator drones during storms. If we smoke those bastards and haul ass and they don't report in they will have a drone up in a heart beat. Then we are done for. Don't you remember those four guys from Beta 11 that killed a couple of the guards and hauled ass in the Hummer? They already had a drone up and an Apache toasted them before they were an eighth of a mile away."Steve took the bar of soap Celina offered as she began to rinse.

"I know Steve, but I can't stand this any more. The longer we wait the weaker we get, and the greater the chance that one of us may die. I want to spend the rest of my life with you Steve, but not here."

Steve handed her back the soap stood and rinsed the soap from his body. Celina stood and joined him under his shower head. The two embraced. "I promise Celina, I will get us out of here."

Celina looked up and gave him a quick peck on the lips. "I know, but make it soon. Now lets get dressed the others will be getting up and wanting to take their own showers.

Craig slowly brought the binoculars back up to his eyes. He adjusted the focus so that he could clearly see the five men roughly three hundred yards away. The men all wore sullied clothing. Their pants were covered in stains and dirt, their matching black leather jackets all bore the same club moniker, Satan's Son's, with the face of Lucifer surrounded in flames. Craig placed the binos back on the assault pack next to his rifle, and picked up a small FRS radio.

"Hey Joe, you copy?" He whispered into the radio.

"Roll with what you got Craig." Joe said, his voice coming in loud and clear through Craig's ear piece.

"I found the bastards, well at least five of them. I have been watching them for about twenty minutes. There is no sign of the rest of the gang. They have just been basically smoking and joking. Doesn't seem like they have a care in the world." Craig said leaning his head forward and peering into the Leopold ten power scope affixed on top of his Blaser LRS2 sniper rifle. Craig had found the weapon among the dead after the battle in St. Florian, and it had become his constant companion.

"Do you think they are waiting on the others or do you think they have split from the main gang?" Joe said his speech coming in huffs as he worked his way through the forest towards Craig's position.

"It's hard to say with a bunch like this Joe. They could be scouting for the main group for easier prey, or they could have split for a separate area of operation. I think you ought to make your way to the ridge to my east and set up. We should probably go ahead and take these monkeys out. If we wait for them to hook up with the main body it will turn out to be a hell of a fight, and I don't feel like running these hills and hollers for days trying to escape."

"Alright give me a few minutes and I will be in place."

"I'll be waiting with bells on." Craig said with a snicker.

Craig placed the radio back in the carrying pouch on his load bearing vest. Then pulled the rifle butt snug into his shoulder and began to pan the group of bikers below. They were bunched up around a campfire and once Joe was in position the two of them should be able to take them out in short order that was if no one came up on them and took them out. This reminded him he needed to check with Howard.

Craig pulled the radio back out. "Hey there you gimp bastard are you asleep our are you still watching my ass?"

"I'm here you arrogant shit. You better watch how you talk to me or I just might put a round in that over sized melon of yours. Also you fail to remember I am now handicap and it isn't politically correct to verbally harass me." Howard replied.

"Yeah, yeah, I hear you crip, keep your eyes pealed, out." Craig placed the radio back in the pouch again.

They had been hunting the elusive bikers for five days. This was the first time they had crossed paths with any of them. They had found a few camp sites they had used, and several burnt out farm houses. There were not many people left in Lauderdale County since the round up. They had met a few people while traveling the county and had found out that on the same day as the battle at St. Florian, other National Guard units had swept through the rest of the county.

They had also learned about the other attacks by foreign powers on the United States. He could not believe the magnitude of death which was inflicted on his country or the rest of the world for that matter. He now often wondered what kind of world the kids he hoped to have one day would grow up in.

He was looking forward to actually offing the trash down below him. Maybe it would elevate his mood to remove some of the trash in the world. He had been in a real funk for the past four months since his return from his second trip to Birmingham. He and Joe had spent two weeks snaking their way through the ruined city and it's out skirts looking for Steve, Celina, Bob, and Caroline. There had really been no way for the two of them to distinguish their four friends from any of the other thousands of shaved headed drab clothed people they had seen.

He knew Joe had been particularly disturbed by what they had seen. He could see the frustration of not finding Celina and fear for the life of his niece on his face. He damn near had to drag Joe home when their supplies ran short. The longer they waited to return and attempt a rescue the greater chance that they would all die, and the more entrenched the government troops would become.

Their trip home had been uneventful. Everything had been uneventful since the big battle. That was until five days ago. They had been attacked by about fifty of the Son's of Satan early in the morning. Since they had the road blocked the Sons' had been forced to dismount and attack on foot. Thankfully they had continued the habit of posting a guard.

Benny had woken them all when he heard the rumbling sound of their big Harley's. They had killed six right off the bat. The following gun battle lasted for two hours until the Sons retreated. After the shootout they found five more bodies. Craig estimated there had been approximately 35-40 of the bikers. He, Joe, and Howard immediately began attempting to locate the bikers for a little preventive maintenance on the area and clean it up and attempt to kill all the bikers. The only sign of them they had found were campsites filled with empty liquor bottles, drug paraphernalia, and an occasional mutilated body.

Joe's voice brought him back from his thoughts. "Craig I am in place. Do you copy?"

"I copy Joe. How do you want to do this?

"I'll work from my right to the center, and you work from your right to center. I think we can drop two or three before the last ones have time to react and attempt to take cover. Looks like the nearest cover, except the big log by the fire is about fifty feet in any direction. I think we can get them all before they get to any. I am already on target and will wait for your shot, out."

Craig keyed up one last time. "I copy that, stand by."

Craig placed the radio down and brought the rifle back tight into his shoulder. He rested the cross hairs of the scope on the back of a red headed biker. Slowly he released his breath then held it after letting half of the air out of his lungs. The cross hairs now steady he gently squeezed the trigger.

Craig didn't bother to check to see if his shot had hit, he knew it had. The biker sitting beside his target was facing Craig. He was stunned into inaction as blood and brain matter from his friend splashed across his face. The look of shock and disgust on his face didn't last long as Craig obliterated it with his second shot.

As soon as the crack of Craig's rifle reached Joe's ears he pulled the trigger. He didn't go for a head shot, but the chest instead. Joe was a fine shot, but when it came to combat he preferred to put his rounds center mass. His round struck the bicker dead center of the man's chest. The heavy .308 round sliced through skin, bone, and muscle before exiting in a mushroom of blood out of his back.

As the rifle came back down to rest on the log after he fired Joe aligned the cross hairs of the scope on his second target. The biker, a beefy red head stood quickly his right hand slipping under his jacket, and coming back out with a stainless revolver. His mistake was not attempting to take cover or run. Joe exhaled slowly and squeezed the trigger. The round impacted just under the man's right arm pit as he raised his pistol at his unseen attackers. The full metal jacket round easily penetrated the tissue it bored through, exploding the man's heart as the bullet came to a rest. He stood there for a second then collapsed face first into the camp fire. Sparks danced up around his face and shoulders like fire flies.

The fifth and final biker was a bit luckier and smarter than his companions. As soon as the first round was fired he was up and running. He zig zagged through the trees and underbrush putting as much distance between him and the frenzy of death behind him. Both Joe and Craig tried several shots apiece at the fleeting figure, both missing each time.

Smokey finally slowed to a walk after running almost a hundred yards into the forest and up the hill. His chest heaved as he tried to regain his breath. Smokey knew he had to go into stealth mode if he was going to escape the hidden snipers; it would be his only chance at survival.

He walked several more yards then stopped to catch his breath placing both of his hands on a nearby tree and resting his head on them as he tried to breathe. "Damn I've got to quit fucking smoking." He gasped.

"Yep, you should quit smoking, it will kill you." The voice behind him said.

Smokey slowly lowered his arms and turned. He didn't want to make any sudden moves till he evaluated the situation, and threat the voice posed. He turned slowly to see a tall skinny, black haired man with a shotgun pointed at his chest. "I've got to play this cool." He thought to himself.

"Damn right smoking will kill you. Matter of fact I think I will quit right now, and throw the damn things away." He put on his best smile and slowly reached towards a pocket as if he were going to pull out some cigarettes.

"Yeah they will kill you, but not as fast as this thing." Howard pulled the trigger on the twelve gauge. Nine .32 caliber pellets from the 00 buck round shredded Smokey's chest into a bloody side of beef, dropping him to the forest floor in a heap.

"Joe, Craig, you non- shooting turds can rest easy I just plugged number five." Howard said into the radio as he cautiously approached the downed biker. Howard was pretty sure he was dead from the looks of the biker's minced chest, but you could never be to sure.

"Well glad to hear you finally did something beside run your suck for a change. Are you gonna come down here to us or do we have to come up and carry your crippled ass back down the hill side?" Craig replied.

"Be down in a few." Howard said as he kicked the biker in the head to see if he was playing opossum. The man didn't flinch as the heavy boot struck him in the head. Howard bent over to check the body for valuables, and weapons.

Opening the bloody leather vest Howard pulled a Browning Hi Power from a shoulder holster the man wore. "I figured you were reaching for a gun." Howard said to the corpse. His quick search turned up four thirteen round magazines for the pistol, and a bag of marijuana. Dumping the dope, he placed the pistol and magazines in his back pack then headed down the hill an obvious limp in his stride as he walked to his friends. His wound had healed well over the past year, but he would have a limp for the rest of his life.

Craig turned as Howard raucously made his way through the brush and into the clearing where he and Joe waited for him. "I don't know how the hell you are going to make it in this post apocalyptic world gimp. You sounded like a heard of buffalo coming through the woods."

"If I hadn't capped that guy up the hill he probably would have doubled backed and taken you two sorry excuses for gunslingers down if it hadn't been for my prowess." Howard said with a grin. "You guys find any good weapons off these four? I picked up a nice Browning Hi-Power."

Craig pointed to four rifles that had been bundled together with some twine. "Nothing fancy, two SKSs an AK, and a Winchester 30-30. Let's get these rifles and head back to the truck." Craig bent over and picked up the bundle of captured rifles. Though they had plenty of weapons among the group, they kept any weapon they found.

The trio made their way slowly through the woods to their hidden truck. The going was fairly slow, since Joe, and Craig had to maintain a slower pace because of Howard's bad leg. The two mile walk took a little over an hour but they finally reached the truck. Craig and Joe pulled the camouflage netting from the truck, as Howard sat on a nearby stump, rubbing his bad hip and leg.

Craig tossed the now folded bundle of netting in the bed of the truck; he then turned his attention back to Howard. "Howard, you are about as weak as a three year old kid. Look at you sitting there all pasty white like a virgin at a Hell's Angels convention."

Howard rolled his eyes. "You know…"

"Quiet!" Joe commanded in a harsh tone. Both men turned to stare at Joe, confused looks on their faces. "Listen. I thought I heard a motorcycle."

The three men sat in silence, Craig closing his eyes in concentration. Then almost simultaneously the three friends heard the throaty rumble of several motorcycles. The engines' RPMs lowered as the motorcycles slowed, and then the engines shut down.

Joe reached back into the truck and pulled out Steve's VEPR he had been carrying since he found it after the battle. He had vowed to himself he would return the weapon one day to its proper owner. The rifle was loaded with a seventy five round drum. Once he checked to insure the weapon had a round in the chamber he reached back in the cab and pulled out a large canvass OD green pouch that contained four more of the seventy five round drums. "Let's go find out if our biker friends have set up over the hill." He said as he turned to walk to the hillcrest.

Craig slung his Blaser rifle and pulled another battle pack of .308 caliber rounds out of the cab. "Let's do it. Howard are you coming or staying?" Craig said as he followed Joe who was already on the move.

"Let me drop this, and get my rifle." Howard said as he placed the shotgun back in the truck and grabbed his scoped FN-FAL. Weapon in hand he quickly hobbled after his two friends.

As the three men drew near the military crest of the hill the crouched and entered a nearby thicket. Then they lay down on their stomachs and inched forward so that they could observe those below. Craig and Howard both placed their scopes on the maximum settings, Joe pulled out a pair of binoculars.

Joe lowered his binoculars. "It looks like they have a few prisoners." He said referring to the group of people tied to several trees in the area below.

Howard took his eye from the scope and looked over towards Joe and Craig. "Well the question we've got is do we start smoking these fuckers now, or just sit back and observe?"

Craig never took his eye from the scope. "Well I guess it's decided then." He squeezed the trigger on the Blaser. The 150 grain Sierra Match King round screamed out of the end of the rifle at over 2800 fps. In a blink of an eye one grease and dirt stained biker's head exploded into a pink mist just as he raised the butt of his rifle to strike a bound female captive.

Chapter 54

Zulu12 dismounted from the back of the five ton. The morning air was damp, the sky overcast. The mood of Zulu12 cheerful, the overcast skies were a promise of rain. Zulu12's task for the day like most now was to scavenge for any useful items. They were on Green Springs Ave. just south of George Ward Park.

Each battalion member carried a large canvas sack to put the scavenged items.

"Okay folks, we are going to start out in that store over there. Remember my rules. You make a break for it you die. I doubt yall will be that stupid, you've made it this far. Today for my personal needs, I need some smokes, and hard liquor. PFC James, is wanting beer, and chewing tobacco. PFC Donaldson wants coffee, and some batteries for his stereo. You find those items let us know. The rest of the shit will go in the back of the truck understand?" Sergeant Copeland's question was answered by ten yes sirs from the ten members of Zulu 12. "Well move you emaciated asses and get to work." He shouted.

Zulu 12 moved out. "Donaldson, you head back to the hummer and man the machine gun. James you stand watch on the back of the store. I am going to check out that house over there and see if I can't come up with any jewelry or coins for us." Copeland didn't wait on a reply from the two PFCs. There was no way the two would bitch about a thing. Guard duty on scavenging detail was a prime position everyone tried to get on. The opportunity to find gold, guns, drugs, and anything else that could be sold on the black market was too great to get kicked off for bitching about what post one was assigned while one's sergeant went looking for loot, sleep or just take one of the female prisoners off into a back room to take care of business.

The group of ten shuffled off to the store. Once inside Steve turned to the others. "Listen up gang. It looks like the weather is about to turn pretty crappy. If it starts raining and the guards decide to hole up in a house I suggest we try to take them out and escape whether or not we locate any weapons or not. Anybody disagree?"

Steve's question was answered by excited replies of agreement. Sally took a quick look around at the store. It appeared to be a odds and ends store, carrying a variety of items. "I say the first thing we do is all try to locate us some weapons. Maybe we can find some steak knives or something."

"What are we standing around talking about it for? Lets get to it." Caroline said.

The group scoured the store searching for weapons. As they did so they absent mindedly grabbed items and stuffed them in their carry sacks to maintain the appearance of doing what they came in the store to do. Everyone froze in there tracks then turned to head towards Celina when she let out a hoot of excitement.

"I found some! I found some!" Celina called out.

Steve was the first to reach her. "What have you got for us?"

Celina turned to face Steve and the others as they reached her. "I present to you the latest in culinary tools. These fine knives can be yours for only $10.99." She said holding a case of knives up in a manner of the models that once appeared on TV game shows.

Everyone was elated at the find. Mary stepped forward with a huge grin on her gaunt face. "Honey I don't seem to have any cash on me. Would you mind putting one of those things on my tab?"

"Why certainly mam, we aim to please here at Dandy's Discount." Celina said getting into the act. She removed an eight inch steak knife and handed it to Mary.

Mary's eyes gleamed as she eyed the knife in her hand. "It aint much against a machinegun, but I'm sure as hell tired of living as a slave." She stepped back from Celina as the others crowded forward to get a knife.

"Come on everybody let's get back to work before Copeland comes strolling in here." Steve said. Everyone concealed their weapon and got back to work.

The group returned to work with a renewed vigor. Each hoping the darkening clouds would bring enough of a storm to cause the guards to call a halt to the work. Each of the group also knew their chances of survival in an escape attempt was slim to none, but were willing to risk their lives for a chance at freedom.

An hour later the group emerged from the store, their sacks full as they made their way to the five ton to off load their haul. As they unloaded their sacks into the truck rain began to pour down. Copeland emerged from a near by house, a large bottle of whiskey in his beefy left hand. "James! Donaldson! Get those sorry excuses for human beings over here and lets sit this out."

The two soldiers nudge a couple of the group with the barrels of their rifles. "Lets get moving shit bags."

Copeland went back inside and took a seat in a large leather chair. The group came in behind them and sat in the floor. All attempted to act as if nothing was going to happen, none wanting to give up any advantage of surprise they would have. The other two soldiers entered the spacious living room; one sat on a couch the other a nearby love seat. They lit up cigarettes and began to pass the bottle of whiskey back and forth, engaging in small talk.

It was time to set the plan into action. Steve cleared his throat and raised his hands like a child in school. "What is it Roberts?" Copeland said as he glared at him.

"May Celina and I have a little time together in the back room?" He said his head down, submissive.

Copeland stared at the group sitting against the wall for a few seconds before answering. "Sure. Any one else got the need to take care of business?"

Bob and Caroline both raised their hands. "Fine get to it, and remember if you make a break for it the rest of the gang here gets a bullet in the head." Copeland said as he pulled out his service pistol and pointing it at the rest of the group.

As the four got up and headed to the back of the house PFC Donaldson spoke. "Any of you ladies willing to get out of work for a day or two?"

Sally stood up. "I am willing to do all three of you if I can have the rest of the week off." She posed herself as seductively as a woman could dressed in coveralls, with her head shaved. Sally did a damn good job despite being half starved and bald she was still strikingly beautiful.

"Sally I am sure its going to be good, but you get two days and that's it." Copeland said.

Sally made a show of disgust and acted as if she was about to argue but then succumbed. "Yes sergeant. Would you like me to start with a strip tease?" She said pointing to PFC James's small boom box.

"Hell yeah, that's a damn good idea!" James said leaning over and picking up his boom box and selecting a song from the MP3 list on the stereo.

The music throbbed and almost seemed to be in sync with the booming thunderstorm outside. Sally began to sway her shapely body hypnotically, the three soldiers attention glued to her rhythmic gyrations. Sally took her time using every trick in the book she had ever learned from her more sultry days hoping to give the four in the back room time to make their way around to the adjoining room and a chance to charge out to overtake and kill three soldiers.

Bob slipped back up the hallway and peeked around the corner to ensure the three soldiers were totally occupied with Sally. He got a glimpse of a now bare breasted Sally and the three soldiers behind her, looks of lust adorning their faces. "Yep, she definitely has their attention." He whispered to himself as he slipped back to the bedroom.

Bob came into the master bedroom to find the other three scouring through drawers, and two closets for a gun. "Damn! There's not a freaking thing here." Steve said in disgust as he finished searching the last drawer.

"You can lay all that disgust to rest sweetheart." Celina said holding a now raised mattress.

Caroline reached down and came up with what appeared to be a stainless steal .357 magnum. She popped the cylinder open and smiled. She looked up at Bob and Steve as they walked up. "Its loaded and ready to go." She turned the butt of the pistol towards Steve. "You're the best shot so you should take it."

Steve took the pistol and checked to ensure it was really loaded. "Lets get on with this before we lose the chance.

The other three pulled out their hidden knives, and they all made their way through the hall to a room that adjoined the living room. Looking in the living room they could see Sally was completely nude and finishing up her dance as the music wound down. "I am going to shoot Donaldson first, he has the SAW." Steve said cocking the hammer back on the pistol.

They all prepared to follow Steve in the room and pounce as Steve stepped in and opened fire. Things seemed to go into slow motion for Steve as he stepped into the room. His senses going to hyper alert, his vision seemed to tunnel as he focused on Donaldson who now was turning his head to Steve. In his peripheral vision he could make out Sally's nude form diving for the floor, PFC James, and Sergeant Copeland turning towards him. The soldiers' shouts and curses sounding like someone screaming underwater.

Donaldson's SAW machinegun lay across his lap. Steve was surprised with the speed that the once lounging soldier was already halfway up from his once seated position. The sights of the pistol came into his vision; Donaldson's battle dress uniform was a fuzzy background behind them. He squeezed the trigger on the hand cannon, and flames and smoke billowed from the pistol obscuring Steve's vision for a split second.

As Steve shifted the pistol towards Copeland he was aware of Donaldson falling backwards, his SAW booming in a staccato of full automatic fire. Copeland was out of his chair swinging his pistol towards Steve, pulling the trigger on the semi-auto as he brought it to bare on Steve. Steve squeezed the trigger two times as Copeland's body filled his sight picture. Steve's body now in full combat mode, all of the gun shots sounded as distant pops, not the booming thunderous roar that actually filled the room.

As Steve fired his first round Celina, Bob, and Caroline descended on PFC James with their steak knives. The three charged forward, James started swinging his rifle up pulling the trigger as it swung towards the trio just as Copeland was doing almost simultaneously. He was able to get off two last rounds in their direction, the rounds narrowly missing the three charging friends. Then his screams began as three large steak knives perforated his chest, and throat. Blood spouted from several cut arteries and veins.

It was over in seconds that seemed to last an eternity. "Is everyone okay?" Steve shouted as he began switching the pistol's point of aim from soldier to soldier in anticipation that any of the three were playing dead. That wasn't likely; all three men lay in huge pools of their own blood.

"Oh God, oh God!" Sally said as she scrambled and crawled over to the others in the group who had remained in the living room.

Celina, Bob, and Caroline ran over to where Sally had joined the other members of the group. They all lay in a bloody heap except Mary who sat on her butt on the floor, her eyes glazed over in shock. Apparently as the four had attacked and the shooting started, the soldiers' fire, and especially that of PFC Donaldson had shredded five of the six that had remained in the room. Mary the only one to survive was untouched.

Bob checked the last body and looked up. "They're all dead."

Steve went over to Donaldson's body and retrieved his SAW, and some extra ammunition. "Let's go guys. We can mourn our friends later. We have to get out of here before the weather clears, and the drones are back up in the air."

Sally, still nude, scrambled over and picked up Copeland's 9mm pistol. She dropped the now empty magazine and retrieved the three that were in a magazine pouch on his belt. She inserted one and charged the pistol. Then she went over and picked up her clothes and began to dress.

Celina went over to Steve and took the revolver from him. She gave him a quick kiss on the cheek. "I'm ready." She said as Steve gave her a quick reassuring hug.

Bob stood and grabbed PFC James's M4 rifle, and all the extra magazines. "Caroline and Sally get Mary and let's go."

The six prisoners scrambled out the front door into the down pour of rain, and towards the Hummer. Steve got in the driver side and started the vehicle up. "Hold on for a second." Bob said running back towards the five ton truck that was parked behind them.

Bob grabbed a case of MREs and tossed them over towards the Hummer. Next he located six more M4 magazines, and a box of 9mm shells. He threw the ammo into an empty gas mask carrier and ran to the back of the Hummer. Once there he smashed a white disc shaped object located on the hard shell top of the hummer.

He opened the front passenger door and hopped in. "What were you hitting back there?" Steve asked as he pushed the gas pedal to the floor.

"I found out about a month ago that they have installed GPS locaters on all the vehicles. Hopefully by breaking it, we will buy ourselves some more time." Bob said.

The group traveled for three days, in a relatively and surprisingly uneventful trip. They had managed to successfully hide and avoid several helicopters, and one military patrol. Finally they reached the Natchez Trace Bridge that crossed the Tennessee River from Colbert County into Lauderdale. Bob and Steve lay in the tree line using a set of binoculars they had found in the Hummer. They scanned the Lauderdale side of the river looking for any possible military presence, or danger.

Steve lowered the binoculars and looked over at Bob. "Looks clear to me. I say we go for it. This may be our only chance. What do you think?"

Bob stood brushing the dirt from his coveralls. "Let's get the girls, and get home."

The six clambered back into the Hummer, Bob in the driver seat. Steve took the SAW and climbed up into the turret hatch, affixing the saw to the mount there. Caroline sat up front with Bob, the M4 in her hands pointing it out the window. Celina sat behind Bob with revolver in hand. Sally by the other door with her 9mm, Mary crammed in beside her.

They drove slowly across the bridge, bodies tense in anticipation of an encounter on the other side. Their arrival on the other side was anti climatic to say the least. They all breathed a sigh of relief as they leveled out on the roadway and headed east towards home.

Bob took a little used county road that would take them to Butler Creek Road and lead them home. As they turned on to Butler Creek Road several shots rang out, the rounds striking the armored quarter panel of the Hummer sending out a shower of sparks. In the turret Steve caught the muzzle flashes in the tree line. He spun in that direction and laid down several burst from the SAW, as Bob gunned the engine to get out of the ambush. Rounds whipped through the air after them, several thudding ineffectually against the back of the Hummer.

Steve continued to track the wooded area as they sped past. Out of the trees several dozen motorcycles came flooding out. They were followed by several vehicles, two were pickups laden with armed men clad in leather coats and vest. For several seconds Steve looked on, transfixed by the site. The group giving chase to them looked like something out of the old 1980's movie "Road Warrior".

Steve snapped out of his trance and laid the machine gun into his shoulder. He fired quick short burst at the pursuing pack of killers. Several riders and motorcycles went crashing to the ground as others roared past them. They came on with increasing speed. Men in the back of the trucks laid their rifles over the cabs of the truck and fired a fusillade of gun fire in their direction. Rounds began to strike the Hummer.

"Keep shooting Steve! You have to keep them off of us." Bob screamed from below.

Steve was doing his best but was trying to conserve the amount of ammo he fired; they only had a finite amount of ammo for the machinegun. The bikers soon caught up with and began to surround the Hummer. The problem for the bikers was that none of the six were going to be intimidated into giving up so easily.

Celina emptied her three rounds from the .357 into two bikers that had pulled along side of them, one pulling a pistol out of his waist band with his left hand. On the other side of the Hummer, Caroline, and Sally fired into several bikers, dropping five riders. Their bikes and bodies crashing and tumbling into a ball of dust, debris, and blood.

The other bikers backed off but not before Bob threw a monkey wrench into their midst. Slamming the brakes on and cutting the wheels Bob managed to cause four bikers to slam into the rear of the Hummer, and hit three others as they swerved to avoid the big rig. The seven bikes caused three other bikes to wreck as they attempted to avoid the wreckage in front of them. In a matter of minutes seventeen riders were out of the picture.

The bikers parted as they let the two big trucks come forward into the fray. Steve brought the SAW back into action. He unleashed a torrent of fire at the lead truck, a large Ford F-350 Crew Cab 4x4 dually. As the 5.56mm rounds raked over the hood, small craters appeared as the rounds were walked into the windshield. The two front passengers attempted to duck under the dash but both were to late. Rounds punched through the windshield, making it look like a series of spider webs as the window cracked from the onslaught of rounds. The inside of the cab was splashed in a spray of blood as both men died almost instantly.

Then the unthinkable happened, the SAW jammed. Steve worked frantically to clear the weapon. "It's jammed, you need to shoot!" He screamed down to those below. Caroline leaned out of the window and did her best to hold off the on coming truck. When her weapon ran dry she sat back inside to reload, and Sally leaned out and fired her pistol. One of her rounds caught a biker just behind the second truck sending him tumbling from his ride, and then her slide locked to the rear, the pistol empty.

The suppression fire abated and the driver saw Steve frantically fumbling with his weapon. The big truck surged forward as the biker pushed the gas pedal to the floor. Just as the Hummer steered into a curve in the road the dually slammed into the right rear corner of the Hummer. Bob frantically tried to maintain control, but to no avail as it left the road way into an open field. The big knobby tires dug huge ruts in the soft earth as the Hummer did several three sixties. Just as it came out of its last spin it reared up on two wheels, then slowly as if in slow motion the Hummer rose on two wheels for several seconds and then fell over on its side.

The six friends were tossed around like rag dolls inside the Hummer. Steve lost his footing and fell into the inside of the Hummer just before it rolled to it's side. Sally and Celina had been knocked unconscious; the rest of the crew was dazed. Just as Steve cleared his head he was tossed again along with everyone else as something jarred the Hummer knocking it over on it's top.

The bikers had swarmed around the Hummer as it rolled onto it's side. The second truck, another large Ford dually, pulled forward and rammed into the undercarriage of the Hummer flipping it over. Once the Hummer came to a final rest the bikers, two dozen in all, surged forward jerking open the doors and grabbing hold of those inside before they could come to their senses and open fire.

Steve felt something touching his hand. It was the 9mm pistol. He grabbed hold of the pistol and just as he began to raise it and look up all he saw was the butt of a rifle. Steve felt a sharp pain then everything went black.

"I don't think so motherfucker." The shaggy, bearded biker said as he butt stroked Steve in the jaw, laying the skin open.

All six were dragged from the overturned Hummer with little fight. There really was no reason to fight when there were twenty four or so gunmen pointing rifles, pistols, and shotguns at you. All were bound and gagged, even Sally and Mary as they lay unconscious on the ground.

A particularly large man walked up to were group was gathered. "You folks earned yourself a lot of pain shooting my boys up like that. You're all gonna die hard." He punched Bob between the eyes with a meaty fist dropping him to the ground. "You bitches are gonna have a little fun though before we off you." His hand shot out and grabbed Caroline by the breast.

Caroline let out a startled yelp as the man squeezed down hard on her breast. Then she tried to lash out by kicking at the man. "Bastard!" She screamed.

The big biker stepped back avoiding the kick and laughed. Then like a rattler his fist struck out catching her in the jaw. Caroline went sprawling backwards over Bob who was just managing to try to get to his feet. They both feel in a pile. "You got spirit bitch. I like that in a woman. You're gonna get to be first in line tonight."

He turned back to the gang. "All right Sons of Satan, let's load these bald headed pieces of shit up and head back to camp for some sex and torture." A chorus of cheers, and a few gun shots in the air were the gangs response as the friends were manhandled into the back of one of the trucks.

As Steve came to his head throbbed with each heartbeat. He shook his head to help clear his vision and took a look around him. He tried to lift his hands to rub his eyes. His hands didn't budge an inch they were tied behind his back. Then the images of what had taken place flooded into his mind.

He took in the scene around him. The bikers were all around him several had started a large bonfire. It seemed as if everyone of them were either drinking liquor or smoking a joint. There were about a dozen rough looking women walking around the camp also. He looked to his left and right to see his friends either tied to wooden stakes or trees. "We are in deep shit." He said to no one in particular. His jaw sent shock waves of pain through his body as he spoke.

Sally was just to his right and he turned to look at her when she spoke. "Well that's a no shitter Steve. Look at the bright side though, the big guy said me and the other girls get to have some fun." She said in a sarcastic tone.

Steve looked at the huge knot on the side of her head. "They butt stroke you too? Are you okay?"

"I'm fine. I didn't get hit by any of them, I banged my head and got knocked out when we wrecked. Mary is still out." She said motioning her head to her right.

Steve leaned forward to peer around Sally and saw Mary upright, tied to a tree, her chin resting on her chest. "What about Celina?" He said with a bit of panic rising in his voice.

"Calm down Steve we're all here." Steve turned to his left to look at Bob, and Caroline. Leaning a little farther forward he could see Celina. She smiled a bit then turned her attention back to the bikers who kept walking up to her and groping her.

Then the large biker walked up to Caroline. "Well bitch it looks like its time for you to have some fun with Sultan. Don't look so glum baby look what you get to play with." The man reached down and unzipped his pants and pulled out his penis. "What ya think now?" He said as a chorus of praises, and catcalls for his manhood sounded from some of the women and men in the gang.

The man was definitely hung, but Caroline saw no sense in boosting his ego. "I don't know if I am supposed to be impressed or not, but I've seen bigger dicks in a room full of kindergarten boys. It looks to me like you didn't get out of pre-school."

Sultan's face turned red, the veins in his neck and his temples bulged out. "You are so going to pay for that remark. You'll be begging for me to kill you before I get done with you."

His hands shook with rage as he struggled to put his business back in his pants. As soon as he did he reached for the rifle that was slung to his back. Sultan pulled the sling over his shoulder, and raised the rifle over his head getting ready to bring it down in a brutal butt stroke. "Let me see that smart ass smile one more time, cause I am about to knock those pretty teeth down your throat whore."

Just as the rifle came swinging down, his head vaporized. The explosion of Sultan's head was followed by the sound of a sonic crack from a rifle. That single round was followed by a hail of gunfire coming from the hillside above the camp. Gang members scrambled to either find their weapons or drew the ones they had. They fired in every direction not knowing exactly where the attackers were shooting from.

Steve and the others struggled with their bonds trying to get loose. "Damn! We've got to get loose before someone decides to shoot our ass." Steve yelled over the din of gunfire. He didn't get a response from the others, he didn't need one. He knew they were trying to get loose; he was really talking to himself and he knew it.

<hr />

As soon as Craig fired his shot Joe pulled the VEPR into his shoulder and quickly acquired a target, several in fact. Six bikers had hunkered down beside several metal fifty five gallon drums and were pulling out their weapons. They never got a shot off. Joe hammered them with a fusillade of thirty rounds. The men danced a macabre dance of bloody death.

Howard's first shot took down two bikers. One was kneeling down behind a downed tree. The second man was standing directly behind him. Howard fired the FN as soon as the crosshairs were aligned on the bridge of the man's nose. Once he fired, the round rocketed through the first biker's skull and struck the second man behind him in the chest. "Damn I'm good." Howard said with a smile as he transitioned the aim of his rifle searching for more targets.

Two of the bikers near one of the trucks had located their firing position and laid down an imposing volley of return fire with their M-16's. Joe was the first to react. Turning his attention to the duo behind the truck Joe hammered rounds right back at them. Rounds shattered the trucks windows, pierced the radiator, and perforated through the trucks quarter panels forcing the two men to seek cover.

The two bikers had also drawn Craig's attention. By the time he had a clear view of where the two were they had ducked down behind the truck for cover. One of them hadn't concealed himself well enough. His left knee stuck out from behind the bumper. Craig laid the cross hairs squarely over the man's kneecap and squeezed the trigger.

The man's kneecap exploded sending blood, and bone fragments flying. The biker fell forward in front of the truck. His screaming could be heard above the concerto of gunfire. Craig was about to put a round in his chest when the man's partner reached out to pull him back to cover. Craig shifted the crosshairs to the now visible arm. He fired striking the man in the elbow, the heavy .308 round nearly severing the arm in half.

The man fell forward screaming in a duet with his friend. Quickly Craig followed up with a second round into the man's skull silencing him. As he shifted to the first man he had shot he saw blood and dust plume up from his chest as several rounds smacked with brutal force into his chest. He lay still, his screams now silent, his mouth gaping open in a silent scream. He was dead.

"Damn Craig! You need to quit playing games with these boys and kill them. Either that or you've suddenly turned into the shitty shot I always knew you were." Howard said as he lay on his back inserting a fresh magazine into his rifle.

Craig rolled to his side so that he could reload his own rifle as he responded. "Hell Howard, I was just slowing them down to give you a chance to shoot someone." He gave his friend the one finger salute and rolled back into a firing position and commenced to killing those below.

Joe stopped firing and began to insert his third seventy five round drum. "You two dumb shits pick the worst moments to talk smack to one another."

"Hell Joe, if you can't enjoy your work while you do it you might as well find a new job." Craig said, and gave Joe his best million dollar smile before returning to the job at hand.

Steve had given up on getting free, and seriously commenced praying that he and the others would live through this firestorm of death and destruction. Several gas cans, and gas tanks on motorcycles had been punctured by the bullets that shrieked through the biker's camp. Sparks caused by rounds slamming into metal had finally ignited several fires, and two gas cans had exploded in colossal fireballs.

Gas wasn't the only thing burning. Several bikers had been caught up in the two blasts killing them. Their bodies now nothing more than black charred husk that lay smoking on the ground. Some of the tires of the motorcycles were on fire sent an oily black smoke throughout the camp obscuring everyone's vision. Chaos now reigned in the biker's camp.

Five minutes after the initial onslaught from the hillside the firing from both sides slowed and then stopped. The only sounds that could be heard were the moan of the wounded and the crackle of the fires that still burned. The friends still tied up and somehow alive, were in disbelief that they had made it through alive. Now the only thing left to do was wait to see what fate would bring when those on the hill side came down to check their handy work.

Minutes later two figures, faces smeared with camo paint, and dressed in camouflage, could be seen walking down the hill side and making their way to the camp. "Here they come." Steve said.

"Who are they? I can't see a thing because of the smoke." Celina said at the other end.

Caroline squinted her eyes against the smoke that blew in her direction as she tried to see who was coming. "I don't know. I can only see two of them, and they look heavily armed and obviously aren't taking any crap." She said as she let out cough as more greasy black smoke enveloped her.

As the two men approached they began to check the bodies of the bikers around the camp. Slowly making their way towards the captive friends, one of the two would occasionally pull out a pistol and shoot a wounded biker. Someone still up on the hillside would also put a round into the prostrate form of a biker he believed to be alive.

"I hope shooting hostages aren't on the agenda. " Bob said as he watched the two methodically go about their bloody business.

Finally the two men apparently felt comfortable that there were no more threats left alive in the camp. One pulled out a hand held radio. "We're checking the prisoners now. Keep an eye out in case we missed anyone playing possum." He said into the mike. "Roger." A response crackled from the radio.

Joe walked up to a male who had a gash alongside his left jaw. Blood had caked around the wound, and several flies buzzed about it. "Damn this poor boy has been through the ringer." Joe thought. "Why are you being held prisoner." Joe said to the man, poking him with the barrel of his rifle.

Something was familiar about this man's voice and face but with the camo face paint, and his ears still ringing from the gun fight Steve could not place it. "We were trying to make it home, but we crashed and they captured us."

"Make it home from where, son?" Joe asked. He two was beginning to feel an inkling in the back of his mind that this man was familiar to him.

"We were captured after the battle in St. Florian, and taken to Birmingham…" Steve didn't get a chance to finish his story as the man in front of him dropped his rifle and grabbed him by the shoulders.

"Steve! Steve Roberts! My God son I can't believe you are alive! It's me Joe." Joe turned and looked at the others as he drew a knife from his belt. His eyes met Bob and Caroline's, and then to the end of the line he saw Celina. Tears started pouring down his cheeks as he cut the bonds that held Steve.

Quickly he cut Bob, Caroline, Mary, and Sally loose as he made his way to Celina. "Craig, call Howard and tell him to get down here with the truck and first aid kit."

Craig, who was kneeling beside a still unconscious Mary quickly, complied. "Howard, get the truck and get down here now."

"What have we got?" Howard answered back.

"Damn it Howard, not now. Just get down here okay." Steve said with excitement and urgency in his voice.

Bob, Caroline and Sally knelt by Craig as they all took a look at Mary. Bob reached out and shook Craig's hand. Caroline leaned over and gave him a quick hug and kiss on the cheek. Sally said a quick thank you as they all turned there attention back to Mary who apparently had a concussion but appeared to be fine otherwise.

Craig poured water from his canteen onto a handkerchief and wiped some caked blood from Mary's face. "She'll be okay. Howard will be here in a minute with the truck, and we will get her over to Amos's place." He said standing up.

Caroline looked up at Craig. "What about Doc and Maude's place? Wouldn't that be better?"

Craig paused before answering and rested his hand on her shoulder. "Doc and Maude didn't make it. Their place was destroyed by a helicopter attack. I'm sorry."

Caroline bowed her head and began to sob. Bob scooted around towards his wife and placed his arm around her, and tried his best to consul her. "It will be alright sweetheart. We can morn later, but right now we have to put our pain aside till we get home."

Caroline let out a few more sobs then took a deep breath and wiped her eyes. "I'll be alright Bob. I knew not everyone would make it, but I just can't believe such good people didn't make it." She and Bob stood.

Joe cut loose Celina's ropes and she immediately spun on him wrapping her thin arms around his neck. Sobs racked her body, tears flowed down her cheeks. "Oh, Uncle Joe, I didn't ever think I would see you again."

Unashamedly Joe let his own tears flow down his cheeks. "Me either baby. We went down to Birmingham twice looking for you. We could never pick you out among all those prisoners." Joe pushed his niece back just a bit and kissed her on her cheeks.

Howard came roaring up in the truck, and jumped out of the truck as soon as it slid to a stop. "What we have?"

"It's Bob, Caroline, Celina, Steve and a couple of their friends." Craig shouted to him.

Howard ran up to the now gathered group shaking hands with Steve, and Bob, hugging Celina and Caroline. "High I'm Howard." He said to Sally sticking out his hand to shake hers.

"I'm Sally. That's Mary." She said indicating with her head to Mary down on the ground, now covered by a blanket.

"Let's get her loaded in the truck and get you guys back home." He said.

Joe looked over to Craig. "Craig see if you can't get one of those trucks started and let's load every one up and get them out of here. Howard get on the CB and call Amos and let them know to have some food on the table, our friends are home and that we have two injured coming in with us."

Craig ran and got one of the Fords cranked with no problem and pulled it up to the group. "Let's get Mary in the back seat." Joe, Bob, and Steve lifted the unconscious woman and gently slid her into the back of the crew cab truck.

Howard turned on the CB, and picked up the Mic. "Amos, this is Howard come in."

He was answered almost immediately, not by Amos but Benny. "Howard this is Benny. Go ahead."

"Benny tell Amos, Ann, and Daphne that we have found our friends and a couple more folks. Two are injured, but not seriously. Joe wants some food cooked up and we will be there in about thirty minutes."

Benny started asking dozens of questions as soon as Howard finished. "Benny, you'll find out everything in short order. Now just get busy do you understand."

"Sure thing Howard, I'm on it." Benny said into the Mic and ran to tell everyone in the house that their friends were alive.

Amos paced back and forth across the front porch, the weathered wood planks creaking with each of his steps. Benny sat in a rocker nearby. Amos had already had gotten out and prepped the first aid kit. Ann and Daphne were already in the middle of cooking lunch when Benny came with word that Howard had said they had found their friends. No details were given, but he really didn't give a damn, they were coming home.

Amos pulled his old pocket watch out of the front of his overalls. "Where are they at? It's been thirty five minutes." He said to Benny as much as himself.

Benny jumped up from the rocker. "I hear them!" He jerked open the front door and screamed inside to the girls. "I hear them coming! Come on out!" He slammed the door and ran towards the road.

Amos's old ears finally picked up the sound of diesel engines. He reached back and picked up his double barrel, and shouted to Benny who was now racing towards the end of the driveway. "Benny, get back over here. We got to make sure it's them before we go gallivanting around the road."

Benny shuffled back, towards the house shoulders slumped. The front door opened. "Are they here?" Daphne said as she and Ann came out onto the front porch.

"See for yourself." Amos said as the two trucks pulled up into the drive and stopped. Each person stood like a statue in anticipation.

Craig, Howard, and Joe were the first to exit the trucks. Then the other doors open and out stepped five people. They were almost unrecognizable to those on the porch. All dressed in stained coveralls, heads shaven, faces smeared with grime and soot. Except for their facial features and build around the shoulders one almost couldn't tell who was man or woman. They all walked forward slowly, looks of relief on their faces. Howard and Craig pulled another woman from the back. She was awake but had trouble walking, even with her arms around each of the men.

Then the two groups came together. Friends and family now reunited after eighteen long months of separation. They all entered the house towards the dining room. Craig and Howard took Mary to one of the spare bedrooms where Amos gave here water and some pain pills. Mary quickly fell asleep. Amos then treated and cleaned Steve's wound while the others cleaned up and set the table.

Amos put the last stitch in Steve's wound. "You took one nasty hit there boy."

"Well I will have to say it was one hell of a welcome home greeting party." Steve said as the two rose and walked to the dining room.

The table was packed with food. They all crammed around the table shoulder to shoulder, the table to small to seat them all but none of them cared. They each told a piece of their story that had happened over the past year and a half.

Soon they had finished their lunch, their stomachs tight, filled with food. Amos stood. "Okay folks we have got to get yall cleaned up and down for some rest. Sally you and Mary will stay here with us. Howard and Daphne can take Steve, Celina, Bob, and Caroline over to Steve's cabin. We've added two more rooms over there, just as we have here to. There is also an extra shower over at your place now Steve.

We'll have to do some rearranging of living quarters, but that can wait. Hell we'll have to probably build a couple of more cabins. Let's get cracking folks."

One hour later Steve stepped from his own shower. Howard and Daphne had brought the four of them to his cabin. Bob and Caroline had showered and were now sleeping in one of the new bedrooms. Celina had taken her own shower and was now upstairs in his bed. He dried his body and then wrapped the towel around his waist. Reaching forward he wiped the steamed mirror clean. He stared at the fresh stitches on his face then looked over the rest of his face.

"That's gonna be one nasty scar. It makes a once beautiful face one ugly mug." He said with a laugh as he rubbed his chin and then his stubble covered head.

Steve walked out of the bathroom and into the small kitchen. He searched a couple of cabinets and then found what he was looking for. He pulled down a bottle of whiskey and poured himself a large glass full. On the counter lay a pack of cigarettes. They must have been Joe's. He had been staying with Daphne and Howard here in his cabin while he was away.

Steve hadn't had a cigarette in almost two years. He didn't know where Joe had got them but he really didn't care. He took the cigarettes and his whiskey out to the front porch. He sat down on the front swing, still wearing his towel. The cool autumn afternoon breeze felt wonderful on his freshly scrubbed body. He took out a cigarette and lit it. He took a deep draw off of the smoke and exhaled, expelling a cloud of blue smoke towards the sky. He followed up with a long pull from the glass of whiskey. He let out a satisfied sigh. "Ah, whiskey neat and straight just like it should be." He said to himself. Shortly the effects of the whiskey coursed through his body. He felt his tense muscles relax as he continued to smoke and drink a feeling of warm contentment coursed through him.

Howard walked out on the front porch, a glass of tea in his hand. "Well Steve, were damn glad to have yall home."

Steve stood and walked over and leaned against one of the porches columns, cigarette hanging from his lips, drink in hand. The lost feeling he had felt for the past two years now almost washed away by the good meal, shower, and liquor. "Damn right Howard, it's good to be home." He said. A smile appeared on Steve's face as he watched a crimson sun set behind the forest covered hills to the west.

"Well, as much as you guys went through I am sure you are looking forward to some time to just sit back and do nothing. Heck you should have nothing else to worry about, I mean what else could happen?" Howard said.

The cigarette dropped from Steve's fingers. He slowly raised his hand pointing to the sky. "That."

Howard looked off into the distance where Steve pointed. Hovering about a mile away was a Blackhawk helicopter. Howard's moth dropped open. "Well, so much for rest and relaxation."

About the Author

Jeff Stanfield is a former Marine. He has served as a police officer for sixteen years. He spent several years working in North Carolina, and now works in North West Alabama as a police officer. He has worked in Patrol, Vice, Criminal Investigations, SWAT as an entry team member, and sniper. This story is his first story.